THE KAISHO

THE KAISHO

A Nicholas Linnear Novel

ERIC LUSTBADER

HarperCollins*Publishers*

HarperCollins*Publishers*
77–85 Fulham Palace Road,
Hammersmith, London W6 8JB

Published by HarperCollins*Publishers* 1993

1 3 5 7 9 8 6 4 2

A catalogue record for this book is
available from the British Library

ISBN 0 00 224194 3
ISBN 0 00 224330 X (Pbk)

Grateful acknowledgment is made to the following:
Kodansha for permission to reprint the haiku of Matsuo Basho from *Matsuo
Basho* by Makoto Ueda. Copyright © 1982 by Kodansha International Ltd.
Reprinted by permission.
Doubleday for permission to reprint the haiku of Masaoka Shiki from *An
Introduction to Haiku* by Harold G. Henderson. Copyright © 1958 by
Harold G. Henderson. Used by permission of Doubleday, a division of
Bantam Doubleday Dell Publishing Group, Inc.
The Hokuseido Press for permission to reprint the haiku of Issa from
Haiku, Volume 2, Spring by R. H. Blyth. Copyright © The Hokuseido Press
1950, 1981. Reprinted by permission.

Set in Linotron Ehrhardt by
Rowland Phototypesetting Ltd
Bury St Edmunds, Suffolk

Printed and bound in Great Britain by
Butler & Tanner Ltd, Frome and London

Acknowledgments

Thanks to all at the Hotel Montalembert, Paris and the Gritti Palace, Venice for all their assistance.

Thanks to Rosalind Andrews for her insight into the workings of WITSEC.

Nicholas Linnear's air transportation is scheduled exclusively by: Bob Kunikoff, Mark Allen Travel, NYC.

Most of all, to Victoria, for her sage advice and skillful editing.

For Mike
My brother-in-law, my friend,
who died too soon.
He is remembered here, and always.

*A false enchantment
can all too easily
last a lifetime.*

W. H. Auden

*I don't mind living in a
man's world as long as I can
be a woman in it.*

Marilyn Monroe

THE PERSISTENCE OF MEMORY

You can't say that civilization
don't advance, for in every
war they kill you a new way.

Will Rogers

Hollywood/New York

AUTUMN

His name was Do Duc Fujiru, but everyone who knew him in Hollywood, Florida called him Donald Truc because all the forged papers he was using identified him by this name. Do Duc, a physically intimidating man, claimed that while his muscles came from his father, a Vietnamese martial arts expert, his inner spirit came from his mother. Not that anyone in Hollywood was that interested in his inner spirit or anyone else's for that matter. At least, no one at the auto mechanic shop where he worked. In fact, Do Duc's father was not Vietnamese at all.

At thirty-eight, he was the oldest mechanic there. While the younger mechanics all surfed in their spare time, Do Duc worked out at a gym and a martial arts *dojo* that, by his standards, was woefully inadequate, but better than nothing at all.

He was an exceedingly handsome man in a dark, exotic manner, charismatic to women, frightening to other men. He had thick blue-black hair and bold, explorer's eyes. The sharp planes of his face gave him an aura he could intensify from deep inside himself when he deemed it necessary. What he was doing wasting his time in an auto shop was anyone's guess, save for the fact that he quite obviously had an extraordinary affinity for vehicular devices. He could remake engines of any kind so that they far outperformed their factory specs.

In fact, Do Duc had chosen Hollywood because he could blend into the ethnic stew, could most easily remain anonymous within the grid of the bleak post-modern metroscape of endless strip malls, nearly identical housing developments and shoreline freeways.

He had been married for the past two years to a beautiful all-American woman named Hope. She was a tall, lithe, blue-eyed blonde, who had been born and raised in Fort Lauderdale. Besides adoring Do Duc, she was deeply in love with fast cars, fast food, and a life without responsibilities.

To Do Duc, who had been raised to treat the myriad responsibilities of

3

adulthood with care and respect, she was like some gorgeous alien creature, unfathomable, a curiosity from a zoo whom he took to bed as often as he liked. In those moments, when her screams of ecstasy echoed in his ears, when her strong, firm body arched up uncontrollably beneath him, Do Duc came closest to finding life in America bearable.

But, in truth, those moments were fleeting.

He was in the bedroom of his ranch house, pulling on his oil- and grease-smeared overalls, when the front doorbell rang. It was a clear, hot late October morning, the sunlight already so strong it would have made a northerner's eye sockets ache with the glare. He looked first at his wife, lying asleep on her stomach amid the rumpled bedclothes. He was abruptly overcome by a sense of distaste, all eroticism drained from the sight of her naked buttocks.

This feeling was not new to him. It was more like a toothache – if not constant, then recurring when one bit down on a roll. The sound of the doorbell came again, more insistent this time, but the woman did not stir.

Making a hissing sound in the back of his throat, Do Duc padded in his bare feet down the hall, through the kitchen and the living-room to open the front door.

There, a young Federal Express agent bade him sign his name on a clipboard, then handed him a small package. As the agent did so, he caught a glimpse of the image tattooed on the inside of Do Duc's left wrist. It was a human face. The left side was skin-colored, its eye open; the right side was blue with dye, and where the eye should have been was a vertical crescent.

The agent gave an involuntary start, then recovered himself, and hurried off. Do Duc turned the package over. He saw that it had come from a store in London called Avalon Ltd. He offered a strange smile to the already insubstantial house around him.

With the door closed behind him, he unwrapped the package. Inside was a dark-blue matte box within which he found a pair of socks swaddled in hunter-green tissue paper. The socks, green and white striped, had what seemed to be a pattern running down their outsides. Do Duc stepped into the kitchen where the sunlight slanted in through the large eastern-facing window.

It was then that he saw the words emerging from the pattern. They were in a vertical strip down the outside of each sock. **PRIMO ZANNI**, they said.

The packaging dropped from Do Duc's hand, and he felt the slow thud of his heartbeat. He sat on an aluminum and plastic chair while he donned the green and white socks. Then he walked through the house,

4

looking around each room as he passed through it, fixing them all in his mind.

At length, he returned to the bedroom. He went to his closet, pulled down his dusty overnight bag, thrust into it what he needed from the closet and his dresser drawers. He found it wasn't much. In the bathroom, he did the same.

Back in the bedroom, he gave one swift glance toward his still sleeping wife before moving his dresser to one side. He took out a folding pocket knife, inserted the blade beneath the exposed edge of the carpet, pried it up.

He removed two lengths of floorboard he had sawn through when he had first moved into the house, before he had met Hope, and removed the old olive-metal ammo box. He opened this, pushed aside the cushioning wads of unmarked bills, plucked out a mask. It was a remarkable item. It appeared old and was hand-painted in rich, burnished black, with accents of green and gold on the cheeks, over the eyeholes and the lips. It was constructed of papier mâché, and depicted a man with a rather large nose, prominent brows and cheekbones, and a crowned forehead in the shape of a V. The mask ended just above where a person's mouth would be. Do Duc held the mask as tenderly as he would the body of an infant.

'What's that?'

He started, looking around to find Hope sitting naked on the corner of the bed.

'What are you doing?'

She ran a hand through her long blonde hair, stretching in that sinuous manner she had.

'It's nothing,' he said, hurriedly thrusting the mask back into its incongruous container.

'It's not nothing, Donald,' Hope said, standing up. 'Don't tell me that. You know I hate secrets.' She came across to where he was still crouched.

He saw her with the morning sun firing the tiny pale hairs along the curve of her arm, and the air around her exploded in a rainbow hue of arcs. The aura emanated from her, seemed to pulsate with the beat of her heart or the firing of the nerve synapses in her brain. Do Duc's lips opened just a bit, as if he wanted to taste this aura with his tongue.

A sly smile spread across Hope's face. 'We're supposed to tell each other everything. Didn't we promise –'

Do Duc drove the blade of the pocket knife into Hope's lower belly and, using the strength coming up through the soles of his feet, ripped the knife upward through her flesh and muscle, and reached her heart.

He watched with a trembling of intensity as surprise, disbelief,

5

confusion and terror chased each other across her face. It was a veritable smorgasbord of delicious emotions which he sopped up with his soul.

He stepped quickly back from the bright fountain of blood that erupted. A foul stench filled the bedroom.

Silence. Not even a scream. He had been trained to kill in this manner.

Do Duc looked down, staring at his wife's viscera which gleamed dully in the morning light. Steam came off them. The iridescent coils seemed to him beautiful in both pattern and texture, speaking to him in a language that had no rules, no name.

The sight and the smell, familiar as old companions, reminded him of where, soon, he would be headed.

On the plane ride up to New York, Do Duc had time to think. He drew out the strip of color head-shots of himself he had taken in an automated booth in a mall where he had stopped on his way to the airport in Lauderdale. Then he put it away, along with his ticket stub, which was made out in the name of Robert Ashuko, and opened a copy of *Forbes*. While he stared at the text, he pulled out of memory the information he had memorized just after he had moved to Hollywood. It had been sent to him in a book of John Singer Sargent's paintings, remarkable for the extraordinary sensuality of their women, the lushness of their landscapes.

The information was contained on a page on which was printed a full-length photo of Sargent's magnificent painting *Madame X*, which seemed to Do Duc to secure the imperious eroticism that smoldered in these female creatures of another age.

He had decoded the information, memorized it, then had burned it, flushing what ashes remained down the toilet. The book he had kept to gaze at again and again. It was the one item he regretted leaving behind, but it was far too large and cumbersome to take with him on this particular journey.

Deplaning at Kennedy Airport, Do Duc went immediately to the wall of lockers in the main terminal. There he produced a key with a number stamped into it. He inserted it into the appropriate lock and removed the contents of the locker, which consisted of what appeared to be a physician's black bag.

Do Duc rented a car. He used a false driver's license and a protected credit card, one that could not be traced to him, and would not show up on a hot sheet. He had spent some time in New York, and so had no trouble finding the Belt Parkway even through the tricky maze of the airport grounds. Some miles east, in Nassau County, the highway became the Southern State Parkway.

It was heading toward evening, and traffic was barely moving. A Mack truck loaded with gravel heading west had jumped the divider, and plowed head-on into, first, a VW bug, then a Toyota MR2, and finally a Chevy Citation. Do Duc didn't mind the slow going; he had time to kill and, besides, the vectors of the disaster interested him. By the degree of the carnage he began calculating the speeds of the respective vehicles. Then he began to imagine what it must have been like inside them.

Death, whether quick or drawn-out, was his meat, and he was never sated.

He could hear a howling filling his ears, flooding his mind until his fingers resonated to its frequency. Feral lights danced before his eyes like forest sprites, and every manifestation of civilization dropped away. Time, thus naked, turned primeval, and Do Duc, a beast in the forest, was fearless, omnipotent. He thought briefly of Hope, not of her life, but of her death, and he feasted on it all over again.

Do Duc took the Wantaugh State Parkway exit, and headed north for two exits. He was now on Old Country Road. By this time, the world had reverted to normal, except for the slight aura visible to him around each person he passed.

Old Country Road took him into Hicksville, where he came upon the sprawling Lilco building on his right. At first glance, it could have passed for a school: a two-story red-brick structure. He pulled over, unfolded a hand-drawn map of the building's interior. Everything he needed to know was clearly marked. He memorized the map, put a lit match to one corner, watched it burn into his fingertips. He mashed what ashes remained into the car's ashtray, then got out and went quickly across Old Country Road.

He was in and out within seven minutes, having retrieved boots, over-alls, shirt, webbed utility belt and, most important, an official laminated clip-on ID. The photo of the man, Roger Burke, looked nothing like Do Duc, but it made no difference.

Three miles from the building, Do Duc stopped the car and changed into the Lilco uniform. Working with an artist's knife, provided for him in the capacious doctor's satchel, he pried up the outer layer of lamination. He cut one of his photos from the strip he had taken outside Lauderdale, glued it over Burke's black countenance, replaced the lamination. The result would fool no one for long, but Do Duc didn't need long.

He looked at his watch: just after seven. Dinner time. He found a Chinese take-out restaurant, ordered, brought the loaded plastic bag back to the car. He broke open several cardboard containers, extended the first and second fingers of his right hand. With this utensil, he shoveled into

7

his mouth cold rice lacquered with a glutinous fish sauce. He washed this down with draughts of strong black tea. Refreshed, he was ready to go.

He made his way back to the packed northbound Wantaugh Parkway, which soon turned into the Northern State Parkway heading west. The first exit was Post Avenue, and he took this north. Just after he crossed Jericho Turnpike he found himself in the tony suburb of Old Westbury. He went under the Long Island Expressway, made a left onto the north service road. Just past the Old Westbury Police Station, he made a right onto Wheatley Road. Here, in stark contrast with the industrial clutter of Hicksville, he cruised slowly past large old-money estates, complete with white-brick walls, stately oaks, winding driveways and massive brick or fieldstone houses with whitewashed porticos or columned porte-cochères.

The house he was looking for stood well back from the road, behind a ten-foot-high serpentine red-brick wall. It had a black wrought-iron gate and an electronic security squawk-box. Do Duc pulled up to it.

'Roger Burke, Lilco,' he said into the grill set into the metal box, in response to a thin, electronicized voice. He had to put his head and shoulders out the window of his car to do it, and this afforded him an excellent view between the posts of the gate, along the wide crushed-clam-shell drive that swept up to the white and dark-green house. He noted a large black-and-tan Rottweiler bounding through the thick privet hedges. Dangerous beasts, they had originally been Roman cattle dogs centuries ago. Nowadays, they were most popular as police and guard dogs because of their ferociousness and their strength.

He gave Burke's Lilco ID number and a line about having to check the feeder cables because of a dangerous outage in the area. The simplest lies were the most believable, he had been taught, and the risk of raw electricity made even the most stout-hearted people nervous. A moment later, he heard electronic servos start up, and the gates began to swing slowly inward.

Do Duc pulled on padded gloves with a black rubberized exterior, put the car in gear, went slowly up the driveway. He drove with his left hand only. His right hand was buried in the open jaws of the black physician's bag.

He saw the armed guard coming toward him across the wide sloping lawn and he stopped obediently. Not far away the Rottweiler, unleashed, was urinating nervously in some sheared boxwood as he eyed Do Duc with a half-open mouth.

The guard came up, made eye contact, and asked for Do Duc's ID. He was clad in sneakers, jeans, a chambray workshirt and a corduroy jacket beneath which his piece bulged from its shoulder holster. Mafia button-man or ex-cop, Do Duc mused; these days it was difficult to say.

8

In either case, he was not a stupid man, and Do Duc had made his move before the guard could get suspicious about the hand in the bag. With his left hand, Do Duc grabbed a fistful of chambray, jerked the man toward him. The guard's hand was on his way to the butt of his gun when Do Duc's right hand, wrapped around a slender steel blade, flashed upward.

There was a certain amount of galvanic reaction when the blade buried itself in the soft flesh of the guard's throat. Do Duc was ready for it, but even so the guard, who was very strong, almost jerked out of Do Duc's grip. Do Duc rose up off his seat, slamming the blade through the roof of the guard's mouth into the base of his brain.

The body in his hands trembled. There was the quick offensive stench as the guard's bowels gave way. The Rottweiler was downwind, and it began to whine, then growl as its nostrils filled with the scent of death.

'Couldn't be helped,' Do Duc said as if to an invisible companion as he heard the dog coming fast at him. He let go of the corpse and opened the car door in almost the same motion.

The Rottweiler, ears flat back, teeth bared, was already upon him. The frightening, stubby muzzle was white with saliva. Do Duc led with his left hand, catching it between the dog's snapping jaws as it leapt, flinging him back against the car roof.

The long teeth penetrated into the rubberized glove, and while the animal was thus occupied, Do Duc took the bloody blade and inserted it into the Rottweiler's left ear, punching it right through to the other side.

The teeth almost came through the padding then, as the dog bit down in reflex. Do Duc stepped away from the fountain of blood, holding the twitching beast at arm's length, grunting at its weight, but happy at the resistance in his biceps and deltoid muscles.

In the end, he was obliged to slip off the glove because, even in death, the Rottweiler would not relinquish its hold. Do Duc bent, extracting the blade from the dog. He wiped it on the leg of the guard's jeans, then climbed back into the car, resuming his journey up the driveway to the massive porte-cochère.

The mock Doric columns rose above him as he pulled in, turned off the ignition. He took the physician's bag from the seat beside him, went up the brick steps to the front door.

'Mr Goldoni?'

The well-dressed man standing in the doorway shook his head. 'Dominic Goldoni is, ah, away.'

Do Duc frowned, consulting papers on a steel clipboard; papers that were meaningless to the situation. 'This the Goldoni residence?'

'Yes, it is,' the well-dressed man said. He was handsome in a

9

large-featured Mediterranean manner. His brown eyes were hooded, liquid. He was pushing fifty, and seemed foreign, almost courtly in his rich Brioni suit, Roman silk shirt and thousand-dollar loafers. 'Are you the Lilco man?'

'Right,' Do Duc said, flashing his ID briefly as he stepped across the threshold.

The man's eyes tracked the plastic badge. 'I'm Tony DeCamillo, Mr Goldoni's brother-in-law.'

'Yeah, I know,' Do Duc said, burying his fist in DeCamillo's solar plexus. He held the man up almost gently as DeCamillo retched and gasped for air. Then he brought a knee up into DeCamillo's chin, snapping his head back.

Do Duc let DeCamillo's unconscious form slide to the floor. While so bent over, he took the time to inventory the man's gold jewelry – rings, watch, cufflinks, tie pin. Then he took DeCamillo under the arms and dragged him into the coat closet in the huge marble-floored foyer. Do Duc used flex he produced from his bag to tie DeCamillo's wrists and ankles. He took a scarf from a shelf, balled it up and stuffed it in DeCamillo's mouth, then secured it with more flex.

There was no cook; Margarite DeCamillo prided herself on being a first-class chef. But there was a live-in cleaning woman. Do Duc found her in the kitchen pantry, preparing her own dinner. He came up silently behind her, looped a piece of flex around her neck and exerted pressure. She gasped, tried to cry out. Her nails flailed the air, scratched him down one burly forearm before her breath gave out and she pitched forward into the cans of Redpack tomatoes. He left her there, hunched over, cooling quickly. He crossed to the phone on the wall next to the enormous built-in refrigerator, cautiously picked up the receiver. It was not in use, and he dialed a local number, listened while the electronic clicks and relays sent it carooming on its way out of State. He counted off the requisite five rings before the call was answered, then said into the silence, 'I'm in.'

Back in the foyer Do Duc mounted the wide mahogany staircase. The wood was polished to such a high gloss he could see himself reflected in it. His shoes made no sound on the Persian runner.

Margarite DeCamillo was luxuriating in a steamy bath in the master bedroom wing. Her head was back against a rubber pad, her eyes half closed as she felt the heat seep through her muscles into her bones. This was her favorite time of the day, when she could shut the world away, relax and let her thoughts drift free. The added responsibilities her husband had taken on recently had changed him irrevocably. She knew he was worried, definitely over his head, and probably in trouble.

10

She knew she was the only person in the world who could help him, but he was Sicilian, and she knew she would have to tread a careful path. It would do no good reminding him of the roster of show business personalities who had become his clients because of her contacts.

Serenissima, her highly successful boutique cosmetics company, catered to many of the biggest stars of Hollywood and New York, and because she was the creator of all the products they wanted to meet her. Because she was such a shrewd judge of character, it wasn't difficult to pass some of them on to Tony.

As her mind drifted, her fingertips almost unconsciously explored her body, pressing those spots that hurt, the bruises that recurred. The heat of the bath drew the pain out, like the tendrils of some sea creature, and she relaxed.

Eventually, as they inevitably did, her thoughts turned to Francine. At fifteen, her daughter was at a difficult age, too old to be considered a child, too young for the responsibilities of adulthood. The fact that she already had the body of a woman only compounded the problem. Several times, before her brother Dominic had entered the WITSEC program, Margarite had been forced to go to him and ask for his help in extricating Francie from difficulties at school or with a boyfriend too old for her.

Margarite sighed. She loved Francie more than anything in life – and perhaps the resonances of that love were overwhelming to her. She had been torn between following a career and raising Francie virtually alone. She was all too aware that she had never spent enough time with her daughter. But what was she to do? She would shrivel and die if she were chained to the house. Tony had no time or patience for a female child – she believed he continued to resent her for not giving him the male heir he so desperately wanted. But now Margarite could no longer bring a baby to term, and there would only be Francie. No wonder Tony was angry all the time.

The outsized tub was carved from a monstrous piece of black-and-brown onyx, an oval bowl filled now with hot water, aromatic salts and Margarite DeCamillo's voluptuous form. The water spigot was gold, carved in the shape of a swan's head and artfully curved neck, the taps, also gold, its wings. The niche into which the steeping tub had been set was clad with floor-to-ceiling mirrors, which now reflected the image of Do Duc as he entered the humid room.

Margarite DeCamillo started, simultaneously sitting up straight and clasping her hands over her naked breasts. Her amber eyes opened wide, her ample lips forming an O.

'Who are you? What do you mean by coming –'

11

'I'm here to make you an offer.' Do Duc's deep voice was soft. Nevertheless, Margarite was compelled to silence.

She stared at this interloper and, somewhat to Do Duc's surprise, had the presence of mind to say, 'What have you done to my husband?'

'He's not dead,' Do Duc said, 'if that's what you're thinking.' He approached her slowly across the steam-sheened tiles. Her eyes watched him as a mongoose will scrutinize a cobra, with equal degrees of fascination and dread. 'He's not even badly injured. Just – sleeping.'

Do Duc now stood at the edge of the tub, looking down at Margarite. She was an exceedingly handsome woman in her mid-thirties, with high cheekbones, wide-set, direct eyes, prominent nose and a thick head of curling dark hair, wet now at the ends so strands stuck to the pearlized flesh of her shoulders and neck. It was an altogether aggressive face, yet he could see that she had learned to guard her private thoughts well. She had that canny, intelligent look that he had seen in many a successful gambler. The initial fright was over, and color returned to her cheeks as she recovered her composure. Do Duc gauged that she was not as frightened of him as she ought to be.

'You said something about an offer.'

Do Duc nodded, noting the choice of her response as well as the coolness of her voice. 'That's right. We both have something the other wants.' He allowed a smile to spread over his face. 'For instance, I want to know where Dominic Goldoni is.'

A look of relief came over Margarite, and she laughed. 'Then you've come to the wrong person. Ask the Feds. I have no idea where my brother is.' Then she snorted derisively. 'Now get the hell out of here, you cheap hustler.'

Do Duc ignored her. He said, 'Don't you want to know what I have that you want?'

She smiled sweetly. 'What could you possibly –?'

Do Duc had already stepped into the tub, the water slopping noisily over the side. He put one hand over her face, the other on her chest, and pressed her violently down until her head disappeared beneath the hot water.

He sidestepped her thrashing legs and dug his fingers into her thick hair, pulling her sputtering and coughing from the water. Her eyes were tearing, her heavy breasts heaving. He saw that, at last, he had gotten her attention.

'Now,' he said, 'can we agree that we have something to talk about?'

'Bastard,' she moaned. 'Bastard to do this to me.'

You haven't seen anything yet, Do Duc thought with a measure of satisfaction.

12

'I've got nothing to say to you.' Margarite pulled her hair off her face. She sat on the edge of the tub, seemingly oblivious now to her nudity. 'My own life means nothing to me. I'd never betray my brother, even if I knew where they've put him.'

Do Duc drew an oversized bath towel from a rack above his head, threw it at her. 'Dry yourself off,' he said, stepping out of the tub. 'I've got something to show you.'

He herded Margarite out of the bathroom. She had wrapped the towel around her so that it covered her from just above her breasts to just above her knees.

'How stupid are you? Don't you understand it doesn't matter what you do to me? I don't know anything. The Feds made sure of that.'

He took her through the vast master bedroom with its canopied, four-poster bed and sunken sitting area, complete with curved velvet loveseat and ornate marble fireplace, its mantel held aloft by carved cherubim. A hideous ormolu clock ticked sonorously in the center of the mantel.

Halfway down the hall, Margarite felt her throat catch. She knew where they were headed. 'No,' she said in a very small voice. 'Oh, please, God, no!'

He allowed her to break away from him, and she ran the rest of the way through a half-open door into another bedroom suite. Do Duc followed after her, stopped at the threshold, stooping to retrieve the bath towel that had come undone. He put it over his left arm as he entered a room painted pale pink. Ruffled curtains covered the windows and a number of large stuffed animals sat or stood on the bed.

'Francie!'

Do Duc watched the scene: the naked mother, distraught, teary, hands clasped to her face, staring in horror at her fifteen-year-old daughter strung up by her ankles to the central light fixture.

'Oh, my God, Francie!'

The teenager's oval face, flushed with blood, was wholly inexpressive. Her eyes were closed, her lips half open.

'She isn't dead,' Do Duc said. 'But she will be if you don't do as I say.'

Margarite whirled. 'Yes, yes. Anything. But take her down!'

'When you've done as I ask.' Do Duc's voice was gentle. 'I've no wish to hurt her, you see. But know that her life is in your hands.' He came across the room, handed Margarite the towel. 'Do we understand one another now?'

Margarite again gave him that look he had seen so often in canny gamblers, and he knew that she was thinking of slipping a letter opener

13

between his ribs. He wondered whether she had it in her to actually commit such an act of finality, to be party to an act that would forever alter the core of her. Contemplating her, this was the question that intrigued him the most, because now that he had come in contact with her, he recognized something in her and was drawn to it.

'What is it you want from me?' she asked.

Downstairs in the library, he poured them both brandies. He had allowed her to dress, but only while he watched. She had put on a short black pleated skirt, a cream-colored blouse and suede slipper-shoes worked with gold thread. He was impressed that she dressed with an economy of movement and a dignity to try to protect herself from his presence.

At first, she refused his offer.

'Drink,' he insisted. 'The brandy will calm your nerves.' He eyed her. 'It will be to your benefit.'

She accepted the glass balloon from him, sipped slowly, evenly.

Do Duc took his drink, sat down on the plush sofa beside her. 'All right,' he said. 'This is what I require. When your brother calls you, you will contrive a way to get him to tell you where he is.'

Margarite put her balloon onto the glass and brass coffee table. 'You're crazy. It'll never happen. For one thing, calling me – or anyone else in his family for that matter – is strictly against the rules.'

'Nevertheless,' Do Duc said, 'he'll call.'

Margarite studied him for a moment, before leaning forward to extract a cigarette from a silver filigree box. As she did so, her breasts strained against the blouse. It was the first provocative gesture she had made, and Do Duc knew she had begun to think the situation through. That was good for both of them. Better the demon you knew . . .

'You stupid beast. My brother Dominic was put into the Federal Witness Security Program almost a year ago. He was allowed to take his wife and children with him. Since then, I have not heard from him. Neither has his mother. He was told in no uncertain terms what the rules were – no contact with family or friends, otherwise the Feds could no longer guarantee his safety.'

She watched him as he picked up the tooled silver lighter, lit the flame for her. She hesitated only fractionally before leaning forward to light the end of her cigarette. She inhaled deeply, blew out a stream of smoke in such a way that he could mark her agitation.

'Are you aware that in the entire history of WITSEC not one inductee who has stuck to the rules has been gotten to?' She continued to watch him as she smoked. 'The WITSEC Deputy Marshal at the Office of Enforcement Operations told us that, and after what Dominic had done, I

14

know he took it to heart. He's got no death wish, just the opposite. He's got everything to live for.'

Suddenly she stopped speaking, and Do Duc knew that she desperately wanted a response from him. This had been her first shot at trying to gain the upper hand, and for this he awarded her more points. He said nothing.

Margarite continued to smoke until the cigarette was finished. Then she stubbed it out in a Steuben ashtray. Do Duc expected her to reach for another but, again, she surprised him with her willpower. She sat with her hands in her lap.

'Let my daughter go,' she said softly.

'We were speaking about your brother Dominic.' Do Duc watched with interest the single line of perspiration make its way from her hairline down her temple onto her cheek. He was aware of the tension in the same way he often saw the auras around people. There was a tangible humming in the air.

He could see the tiny tremble of her lips before she put her head down. 'Okay, say Dominic *does* call,' she said in capitulation. 'Then what?'

'Set up an immediate meeting – without his WITSEC handler.'

'He won't do that.'

He took another cigarette out of the silver box, lit it and handed it to her. 'But he will, Margarite,' he said. 'I know that he's phoned you several times before. The last time, let's see, wasn't it because he found out what Tony D. does to you behind closed doors?'

Margarite gave a tiny cry. She drew her knees up just as if his words had assaulted her physically. Her face was white and she was breathing hard through her half-open mouth.

'This time, information will come to Dominic that your husband has beaten Francie.' He seemed as calm as if he were reading a number from the phone book, and this matter-of-fact delivery was the most horrifying element. 'He'll call you, Margarite, won't he? And when he does you're going to act the part. You'll be properly hysterical, and if Dominic doesn't suggest it, you'll insist on a meeting.'

'Ah, you bastard.' She closed her eyes. *He's ruined everything*, she thought.

She felt her control slip away, salty tears sliding down her cheeks, panic turning her mind to jelly. She fought to put one coherent thought in front of another. 'You know what you're asking me to do,' she whispered.

Do Duc abruptly slammed his hands together. Her brandy balloon was between them and it shattered with a loud crackle, making Margarite jump. He liked what that did to her eyes, and he was poignantly reminded of the Sargent painting of Madame X.

15

He said, 'I have killed your bodyguard, your Rottweiler and your maid. Don't think for a moment that I will hesitate to take your daughter's life.' His glittery eyes would not let hers go. 'As I have pointed out, Francine's life is quite literally in your hands.'

Margarite stubbed out her cigarette. 'Christ, how do you manage to sleep at night?'

Do Duc stood up. 'An interesting question coming from Dominic Goldoni's sister. Don't you use your maiden name – *his* name – in your own business? Of course you do.' Giving her a small, convincing smile, he said, 'I wonder how Tony D. feels about you being known as Margarite Goldoni? Is that part of the rage he feels for you?'

She watched him with a kind of fascinated awe that walked the razor's edge of revulsion. He went around behind the sofa, stood looking at a large painting by Henri Martin of a wheatfield fecund with color and texture.

'Margarite, you're intelligent enough to know we all have our ways of rationalizing what we do; that's hardly the sole province of the fanatical and the righteous.'

He waited, losing part of himself in the Provençal landscape Martin had conjured with the arcane power of a sorcerer. Do Duc thought that he would gladly give up everything, even the constant proximity to death that kept him focused and stable, to be able to paint just one canvas like this one. He had no children – at least none that he knew of – but this masterpiece was better than a child because it sprang godlike from your head and stayed exactly as you had envisioned it. He could imagine no greater reward in life.

'How interesting, a beast who appreciates fine art,' Margarite said at his elbow.

He had heard her coming or – more precisely – had felt it, and he recalled his own question of whether she would have the guts to wield the letter opener. He did not turn his head away from the Martin, but said, 'Dominic will call within the next two hours. Are you ready to keep your side of the bargain?'

'Give me a moment,' she said. 'I've never made a deal with the devil before.'

'Perhaps not,' he said as he swung toward her, 'but I'll bet your brother has – more times than he can count.'

You know nothing about my brother, she wanted to shout at him, but she was terribly afraid that he would prove to her in quite precise terms just how wrong she was.

Their eyes locked, and Do Duc recognized the ambivalence lurking behind the overt animosity she projected. He doubted whether she was yet

16

aware of how attracted she was to him. He was certain that she had no knowledge of his use of the classic interrogator's tactic of personalizing, then making intimate what was in all respects a cut-and-dried relationship. But she could recognize the other side of what he was doing. It was not so much that women wanted to be dominated, he had concluded some years ago, but that they appreciated more than men what such domination could produce in others.

Margarite's tongue came out, moistening her lips. 'Do you have a name?'

'A few,' Do Duc said. 'You can call me Robert.'

'Robert.' She took a step toward him so that she was very close. She studied his face. 'Curious. That's not an Oriental name, and you're so obviously Oriental.' She cocked her head at an angle. 'Or are you? What other race ... Let me see ... Polynesian?' She smiled. 'I'm Venetian, myself, so I know what it's like.'

'What what's like?'

'To be an outsider.' Margarite walked away from him, back to the sofa. 'I live among Sicilians. No one trusts you, not really.' She sat down, crossed her legs. 'You're always being put in the position of having to prove your loyalty, even to Family.'

Do Duc smiled to himself. He liked this part of her, the schemer. He stared at the long expanse of her legs with desire – which was hardly difficult – in order to encourage her. Just because his desire was deliberate didn't mean she had to know that. He wanted – no, to be truthful, he *needed* – to know how far she would go, what she might be capable of under the most extreme conditions. Now he knew one thing: she was going to allow him to find out.

'Do you have family?'

The question knifed through him, so he smiled at her, charming her with one of his many masks. 'That was a long time ago.' But his voice sounded hollow even to his own ears, and Margarite was clever enough to pick up on this.

'Were you an orphan?'

'The seeds of my destruction were sown when I was very young.'

Margarite held his gaze. 'What an extraordinary thing to say. Is it true? You have no family?'

It was, so he shrugged in order that she should discount it. He was appalled at what had come out of his own mouth. Was he mad?

He broke the connection with her that was beginning to disturb him as profoundly as it did her.

'What do you want with Dominic?' Margarite asked to his back.

17

'Information,' Do Duc said, 'that only he can provide.'

'That simplifies things,' she said. 'I can get it for you when he calls.'

Do Duc smiled coldly so that she knew in her heart he was nothing more than a weapon. 'Margarite, I will tell you now that if you deviate at all from our prepared scenario, Francine will die and you will witness it.'

'All right!' She shuddered and put her face in her hands. 'Just – don't say it again. I don't want you even thinking it.'

She looked up at him, her eyes searching his face through her tears. 'You know, despite what Dominic did, he's still got a number of friends he saved from the Feds and they're very powerful.'

'Yes, I know just how powerful,' Do Duc said. 'Who do you think sent me?'

It was a calculated risk, but a necessary one to help him maintain his control over her.

'Christ, you can't mean it,' Margarite said in alarm. 'That would kill him.'

Do Duc shrugged as he came and sat down beside her. 'Life is full of surprises – even for me.'

'No, no, no,' she said in a breathless voice, 'you're lying to me.' She shuddered. 'I know Dominic's friends. They're utterly loyal. If you harm him they'll come after you. Doesn't that worry you?'

'On the contrary. I welcome it.'

He watched the emotions flurry across her face.

'My God, who are you?' she whispered. 'What sins have I committed that would bring you here?'

'Tell me, are you as innocent as your brother is guilty?'

She ignored the tears as they rolled slowly down her cheeks. 'No one is wholly innocent, but I – this is like Judgment Day. No matter what I do I will have blood on my hands.'

'In the end, we're all animals,' he said. 'We've got to get dirty sometime. This is your time.'

She pulled out another cigarette. 'Become like you, you mean? No, never!'

'I wish you wouldn't,' Do Duc said.

Margarite put her hand around the lighter, then apparently thought better of it. She returned the unlit cigarette to the filigreed box.

'It frightens me that you know Dominic is going to call.'

'Yes. I know.'

'His friends . . .'

'He has no more friends.'

He dipped his fingertip into the sticky residue of the spilled brandy, brought up on it not only the sweet liquor but a tiny shard of glass. She watched as he pressed the glass until it pierced his skin and drew blood. By this gesture of *machismo* she reckoned that pain in one form or another was a significant component of his personality. She filed this inference away, not yet able to deduce its usefulness.

She wondered why he hadn't assaulted her. He had had every opportunity to take advantage of an entire array of provocative situations: while she was naked in the bath, while she was dressing as he watched, any time while they had been here in the library. Certainly, after she had recovered from the initial shock of his presence, she had given him every opportunity, knowing that he would not be thinking clearly trapped between her thighs with his blood filled with testosterone.

She had to try something to extricate herself from this nightmare. She shifted on the sofa, in the process hiking up her skirt to the tops of her thighs. She saw his gaze shift from the blood on his fingertip to her flesh. His gaze had weight as it rested on her, and heat. She could feel her cheeks beginning to burn.

'What is it about you?' She did not recognize her own voice.

Do Duc looked at her. His fingertip traced a red crescent on the trembling flesh of her inner thigh. He stroked higher, into the spot where she was warm, even now. She felt a kind of connection, and she did what she could to draw him on, to make the heat rise in his blood.

The harsh jangle of the phone made her start. She stared at it as if it were a deadly adder. He took his hand away, and her one chance was gone.

'Answer it,' Do Duc ordered, staring into her terrified eyes.

Margarite hesitated, trembling. It didn't have to be Dominic; it could be anyone, she told herself. Please let it be anyone but him.

She snatched up the receiver with a convulsive gesture. She swallowed, then said hopefully, 'Hello?'

'Margarite, *bellissima*!' Dominic's voice said in her ear, and she slowly closed her eyes.

BOOK 1: OLD FRIENDS

Year after year
On the monkey's face,
A monkey's mask.

Matsuo Basho

ONE

Tokyo/Marine on St Croix/New York

So early in the morning Tokyo smelled like fish. Perhaps it was the Sumida River, still home to hundreds of fishermen plying their ancient trade. Or, thought Nicholas Linnear, perhaps it was the steel-hued haze that squatted like a gluttonous guest over the sprawling metropolis.

Somewhere in the countryside far away the sun was struggling up over the mountaintops, but here in the heart of the city it was still dark. Just a hint of predawn light turned the shadows nacreous.

As Nicholas ascended the Shinjuku Suiryu Building in the non-stop chairman's elevator he considered the formidable array of decisions awaiting him at Sato International, the vast *keiretsu*, industrial conglomerate, he ran jointly with Tanzan Nangi.

Nangi was the canny Japanese, a former vice-minister of MITI, Japan's all-powerful Ministry of International Trade and Industry, with whom Nicholas had decided to join forces, merging his own company, Tomkin Industries, with Nangi's Sato International.

It was interesting that both men had inherited the top position in their respective conglomerates: Nangi from his best friend's dead brother; Nicholas from his late father-in-law. For this, and many other reasons, there was a unique bond between the two men which could never be severed.

Nicholas stepped off the elevator at the fifty-second floor, walked past the deserted teak and chrome reception lobby, past silent offices and work stations, into his own office which, together with Nangi's, comprised the entire western-facing end of the floor.

He crossed to a low couch in the welled seating area alongside a huge window, and sat staring out at the city. The haze, pale as green tea, was a filthy nimbus, occluding his coveted view of Mt Fuji.

He knew that very soon he needed to return to America, not only to sit down face to face with Harley Gaunt, but also to lobby in person in Washington against the rising tide of animosity toward the admittedly arrogant Japanese. Gaunt had hired a man named Terrence McNaughton, a professional lobbyist, to work on their behalf, but Nicholas was beginning

23

to believe that in these retrogressive times persuasion by proxy was not enough. Nicholas had thought of flying to Washington many times during the last several years, but always Nangi convinced him of the need to stay here, to lobby their pro-international stance with the Japanese themselves.

Nicholas, Nangi had argued with unassailable logic, was uniquely qualified to do this since the Japanese did not view him as an *iteki*, a barbarian outsider. Nicholas's father, the Englishman Colonel Denis Linnear, held a special place in the hearts of the older generation of Japanese, for he had been seconded to General Douglas MacArthur's SCAP headquarters just after the end of World War II. It was he who had liaised so successfully with the upper-echelon officials when MacArthur had given the defeated Japanese a new democratic Constitution which had survived into the present. When Colonel Linnear died, his funeral was as widely attended and reported as that of any Japanese emperor.

Nicholas became aware of Tanzan Nangi emerging onto the floor before he actually saw him. Nangi was now well past middle age. His face was striking, but not in any normal way. His right eye was an unseeing milky-white orb set behind a damaged lid forever frozen half-shut. Otherwise his face might have been that of a top-flight diplomat who knew the exigencies of his world and how to maneuver among them.

Nangi tapped on the half-open door to Nicholas's suite with the end of his walking stick which was capped by a carving of a dragon. Depending on the time of day, his state of health and the weather, he moved more or less stiffly on legs that had been damaged during the war in the Pacific.

The two men greeted each other with warmth and the minimum of formality. It would have been far different had anyone else been in the room with them.

They savored their green *macha* tea in the silence of close companionship, then commenced their morning business – the strategic planning for Sato which they liked to have set before the rest of the staff arrived.

'The news is very bad,' Nangi began. 'I have been unable to come up with the capital you feel we so desperately need to expand into Vietnam.'

Nicholas sighed. 'Ironic since business is so good. Look at the last quarter's figures. Demand for the Sphynx T-PRAM is far exceeding our current production capabilities.' The T-PRAM was Sato International's proprietary computer chip – the first and only programmable random access memory chip on the market. 'That's why we need to expand into Vietnam as quickly as possible. Ramping up new manufacturing facilities which meet our standards and which also hold down production costs is an exhausting marathon.'

Nangi sipped his tea. 'Unfortunately, Sphynx is only one *kobun* in the

24

keiretsu's vast network of businesses. Not all of them are doing so well.'
Kobun was a divisional company within the *keiretsu*, the conglomerate.

Nicholas understood the reference. Unlike Tomkin Industries before the merger, Sato International had always had ready access to capital until now, when the ground rules in Japan had suddenly changed. The most radical difference between American and Japanese corporations had in recent years turned from being a valuable asset to a dangerous liability. All major *keiretsu* in Japan were either owned by or folded into a commercial bank. In Sato's case, it was the Daimyo Development Bank. This cozy relationship within the *keiretsu* allowed it to borrow money for expansion or research and development at low rates and with exceedingly generous terms.

Now, however, Japan was in the grip of an economic crunch of a size and gravity unknown since the horrors of the immediate postwar period. It had begun in 1988 with the Government's misguided efforts to prop up an economy already suffering the first effects of a far too strong yen by artificially creating a land boom. Investing within their own country, these ministers reasoned, would mitigate, at least to some extent, the value of the yen. And the theory worked – up to a point. Then values began to stretch the bounds of reality. And still Japanese businessmen – cash-rich and arrogant in their seemingly unflagging success – poured money into real estate. Inevitably, the bubble burst. Over-leveraged on property they could no longer unload even at steep discounts, many businessmen went under, losing vast fortunes virtually overnight.

The carnage grew, widening like ripples in a pond. Money-center banks which had blithely extended credit for what had appeared to be gilt-edged real estate were left with foreclosed properties that could not resupply them with sufficient capital. They were forced to draw down assets to pay the huge loan losses, and within the space of a year their balance sheets were stained with the red that is the only blood a banker recognizes.

Daimyo Development Bank was no exception. Though hit less hard than some that were now out of business, the bank was weathering an exceptionally rocky period, and its losses had recently become a significant drag on Sato International's bottom line. As recently as six months ago Nangi had had to replace Daimyo's chairman, and still the mess was far from being under control. It was a source of particular humiliation to him since he had once been the bank's director.

The new watchword in Japan was *risutora*, something heretofore unheard of: industrial contraction. Japan Inc. was coming to terms with restructuring – a painful reduction in factories, consumer goods, and Japan's most precious resource, superbly trained and loyal personnel. In a country

25

where the expansionist 'bigger and better' had been the key economic phrase for over four decades, *risutora* was a bitter reverse course indeed. Thankfully, Nangi and Nicholas had never allowed their *keiretsu* to become bloated and inefficient. And Nicholas's role within the conglomerate was increasing exponentially, since he had more experience with significant economic downturns than any Japanese. Nevertheless, the crunch in their operating capital was real enough.

'Still, one way or another, we've got to come up with the capital,' Nicholas urged. 'If we don't get involved there in a major way – and quickly – we're going to find ourselves run over by all the other major *keiretsu*.'

'I need to give the situation some more time,' Nangi cautioned, not for the first time. 'Vietnam is still newly opened, and I don't fully trust the Government.'

'What you mean is you don't trust the Vietnamese at all.'

Nangi swirled the dregs of his tea around in his cup. He disliked this tension between them. Ever since Nicholas had first gone to Saigon several years ago to recruit this man Vincent Tinh as their director in Vietnam, Nangi had been worried. Tinh was a Vietnamese, and he supposed Nicholas was right, he did not trust them. So much money already committed to this strange, newly capitalist Vietnam, and Nicholas had been pushing him to commit so much more. What if the Communists returned and nationalized all private business? He and Nicholas would lose everything.

'These people are opaque to me,' Nangi said, raising his eyes from the shifting runes of the tea leaves.

'They're just different.'

Nangi shook his head. 'The Hong Kong Chinese are different and I deal with them all the time. They're devious but I must admit I enjoy their intrigues. I have no feel for the Vietnamese.'

'Which is why I'm handling them,' Nicholas said. 'But just look at the bottom line. Profits from the small amount of goods we now manufacture out of Saigon under Vinnie's direction are astronomical. Think what these lower manufacturing costs would do for the *kobun* whose profits are currently in a downward spiral.'

Of course, Nicholas was right, Nangi thought. He most often was in these matters. Also, he could not minimize Nicholas's success in predicting trends in business.

He nodded. 'All right. I'll do what I can to squeeze the capital we need out of some rock somewhere.'

'Excellent,' Nicholas said, pouring them both more tea. 'You won't regret your decision.'

'I hope not,' Nangi said. 'I am going to have to call on some of my Yakuza contacts.'

'If only you knew the Kaisho,' Nicholas said with no little sarcasm.

'I know you have no respect for the Yakuza,' Nangi said. 'But then again you've never made any effort to understand them. I find that particularly curious considering the pains you've taken in assimilating virtually every other aspect of Japanese life.'

'The Yakuza are gangsters,' Nicholas said flatly. 'Of what use would understanding them be to me?'

'I cannot answer that,' Nangi said. 'No one can, save yourself.'

'What I *can't* fathom is your connection with them. Leave them to their own dirty business.'

'That is like saying "Please don't inhale nitrogen with your oxygen." It's just not possible.'

'You mean it's not practical.'

Nangi sighed, knowing he was not going to win this argument with his friend; he never did.

'Go see your Kaisho, then,' Nicholas said, 'or whoever he is.'

Nangi shook his head. 'The Kaisho is purported to be the *oyabun* of all *oyabun*. The boss of all the Yakuza family bosses. But let me assure you he does not exist. It is a term some clever Yakuza concocted to keep the police in their place.' Kaisho meant the mysterious commander. 'As long as there is a sense among us outsiders that there is a quasi-mythical boss of all the *oyabun*, there's a level of the Yakuza hierarchy no one can penetrate. It aids their mystique, enhances their face whenever the cops stage a gambling-parlor raid or two for the media.' He shifted in his seat. 'All of my Yakuza contacts deny any knowledge of a Kaisho.'

Their conversation eventually turned to the Hive computer, Nicholas's pet project, which was now on hold because Hyrotech-inc, the American firm designated by the US Government to design the computer for all its branches, had inexplicably reneged on the deal Nicholas had negotiated to manufacture it.

'The most worrisome aspect of this is that no one at Hyrotech will return Harley Gaunt's calls,' Nicholas said. 'I've told him to go ahead and institute a lawsuit claiming breach of contract. In addition, I instructed him to name the US Government as co-defendant.'

'The Government?' Nangi said, concerned.

'Yes. I think they're behind the whole thing. Stonewalling is their forte, not Hyrotech's.'

He brought Nangi up to date on the company's progress on the Chi Project. Nicholas had chosen the name – Chi – which meant wisdom. It had been his idea to turn one entire *kobun* – division – of the company over to the Chi Project. The Chi was a new kind of computer that required no software: it was literally as flexible as its user. It needed no software because it was a neural-net machine. The Chi prototype contained over a thousand minuscule 'cubes' – as opposed to chips – composed of sixty-four electronic neurons whose design was based on those in the human brain. This machine operated by example. A 'correct' decision as determined by its user produced one kind of current through the neural net, a 'wrong' decision another kind of current. In this way the computer actually learned the functions required of it and how to best perform them without having to be configured for different software interfaces.

'Though it looks as if Ricoh will be the first to market with a neural-net computer,' Nicholas said, 'I'm convinced Chi will be far more advanced and will gain us market share very quickly after its introduction.'

The early-morning meeting ended. Nangi rose, took up his walking stick and went down the hall to his office.

Nicholas spent the next hour and forty-five minutes calling his manufacturing managers in Bangkok, Singapore, Saigon, Kuala Lumpur, Indonesia and Guangzhou, in southeastern China. It should have taken less than half the time, but the phone systems in such places were maddeningly inefficient, and he had to accustom himself to busy signals, being cut off in mid-sentence and dialing one number and reaching an altogether different one. But these calls to what had once been remote, unvisited backwashes were becoming increasingly important.

At last the arduous task of dealing with third-world telephone communication was done. He glanced at the time, then set about making a pot of green tea.

He had just taken up the whisk when his private line rang. He put the heavy iron kettle down, stared at the phone. Too early in the morning for this line to be ringing, he thought. He picked up the receiver with a distinct sense of foreboding.

'*Moshi-moshi.*'

'Mr Linnear? Nicholas Linnear?' said an unfamiliar voice in his ear.

'Who is calling?'

'I represent Mikio Okami. Does the name mean anything to you?'

Nicholas could feel his heartbeat, strong and heavy, in his throat. He fought to control his breathing. 'How did you get this number?'

'Mikio Okami extends his personal greetings,' the voice said. 'Okami-san takes care of everything.' There was a brief pause, during which Nicholas was certain he could hear the other person breathing softly. 'Okami-san wishes to –'

28

Nicholas said, 'Here is a phone number.' He reeled off eight digits. 'Use it in ten minutes.'

He took the first sixty seconds after replacing the phone to regain complete control of his breathing. Then he did five minutes of *zazen*. But even the meditation could not stop his mind from racing backward in time.

Before Nicholas's father had died he told him that Mikio Okami was a friend of his – a very special friend. The Colonel had told Nicholas that he owed Okami his life, that if Okami should contact Nicholas the situation would be such that Okami had no other recourse but to ask for Nicholas's help.

Now, after all these years, the call had come.

Nicholas went out of his office, down the still-deserted corridor to the bank of elevators. The chairman's elevator was waiting for him, patient as a loyal servant, but he wondered, as he pressed the button for the mezzanine level, where it was taking him this time.

Nicholas and Nangi had decided to buy the mezzanine space in the Shinjuku Suiryu Building late last year, after an unconscionably overpriced French restaurant went bust. Since then, they had gutted the vast three-story space, installed their own interior walls, and begun work on an opulent nightclub called Indigo.

The smells of lathe and plaster, varnish, paint and heated flex greeted Nicholas as he stepped off the elevator. The foreman recognized him at once, bowed and handed him a hardhat, which Nicholas wordlessly put on. He went straight to a wall phone. He had only thirty seconds to wait before it rang.

'Yes?'

'Mr Linnear.'

'Speaking.'

'Ah.' There was a great deal of emotion in that one brief exclamation. 'I understand it is safe now to speak. I am gratified that we have connected so quickly.'

Nicholas was gazing into a space composed of a series of curled-edged platforms large enough to hold three or four small tables, each with a semi-circular banquette which the architect had designed to appear as if they were floating like magic carpets above a cuneiform dancefloor, laser-etched to resemble a Persian rug.

'Who is this?' Nicholas asked. 'You obviously know me, but –'

'I am employed by Mikio Okami. My name is therefore of no matter.' The voice waited a beat. 'Do you remember your promise?'

'Yes, of course,' Nicholas said.

'Okami-san is in need of your most immediate help.'

29

'I understand.'

'He requires you to go to Venice, Italy. A first-class ticket in your name is waiting for you at the Air France counter at Narita. Please be prompt and pick it up at least two hours before flight time, 9.40 p.m.'

'*This* evening? I can't just drop every –' Nicholas stopped, realizing he was speaking to dead air; the voice had already hung up.

Nicholas replaced the receiver. Plaster dust hung in the air, made sharp and glittery by the many workers' tungsten clamp-lights which were strong enough to define every edge and sweeping curve, reveal even the most minute flaw in the skin of sand-dusted stucco being applied to the major vertical surfaces.

He thought about what little his father had told him about the mysterious Mikio Okami. *There are times, Nicholas, when one exhausts every ordinary means of accomplishing one's goal*, Denis Linnear had told him when Nicholas was no more than thirteen. *Still, that goal* must *be achieved – at any cost. You are young now, but believe it or not there* are *such times when the end is so vital that the means to that end must be overlooked. It may be unfortunate, but one cannot live one's life as a saint; one must oftentimes make compromises, painful and questionable though they may be. So there are times when one is grateful one knows a man such as Mikio Okami.*

Suddenly, in the wake of the call, the Colonel's words had taken on a very sinister cast indeed. Nicholas had surmised even then, so long ago, that Mikio Okami had to be Yakuza. In fact, given the difficult and demanding nature of his father's work in the muddy postwar flux of Japanese political circles, it seemed natural that he would have come into contact with this potent and rather ubiquitous element of Japanese society. Nicholas remembered hearing persistent rumors of factions of Yakuza being hired by the American Occupation Hierarchy to quell certain labor strikes in 1947–8, said to be coordinated and funded by the Communists. The fierce and intimidating Yakuza were the logical foot soldiers in such an internecine war, since they were the quintessential capitalist-loyalists, ready and willing to die for the freedom of their country, virulently opposed to any leftist tilt.

But if Mikio Okami had been a Yakuza *oyabun*, family boss, just after the war, and assuming – generously, Nicholas thought – that he was thirty at the time, he would be in his late seventies now – possibly over eighty. Too old to continue the neverending orchestration required to maintain the Yakuza's unique symbiosis with the police, government and bureaucracies? Or old enough to be in need of reinforcements against the encroachment of the other Yakuza families on the rise in power and influence? Either way, he did not like the possibilities.

Back in his office, Nicholas hastily dictated two memos to Seiko Ito, his assistant: the first, to tell her of his trip and to confirm his reservations; the second regarding the eight most vital matters that required follow-ups, letters, calls, faxes. He faxed Vinnie Tinh in the Saigon office that he would be postponing his planned trip for at least a week, then made a raft of calls which he was planning to put off until after the Saigon trip.

That done, he thought about Justine. She would be livid, of course. Bad enough he had refused to take her back to the States; now he was leaving her alone in Japan. How was it, he thought, that she had come to despise this place? Was it her refusal to learn Japanese, her eternal homesickness, or just her intolerance of the Japanese themselves? Perhaps it was a combination of all three. Other than her friendship with Nangi, she had made precious few connections in Tokyo, and thus found herself isolated, enisled on an Elba of her own making. Or was it of her own making? Nicholas wondered if he was being unfair to her – or whether he was simply fed up with her complaining.

Of course, there were pressures peculiar to their circumstance. Justine had been pregnant twice. The first time, she had given birth to a girl who had quickly died. The second time, less than a year ago, she had miscarried in her sixth month. Now there seemed to be no solace for her agony.

Nicholas put his head in his hands, his mind haunted still by the face of his three-week-old daughter, her blue-white face distorted by the oxygen tent. His dreams echoed with the feeble sound of her small cries like the febrile panting of a wolf snapping at his heels.

He heard sounds from the corridors as the offices began to fill up. He had no interest in facing anyone at the moment, so he slipped out the side door to his office, took the spiral staircase down one flight to the fully equipped gymnasium. There, stripped to shorts, t-shirt and sneakers, he spent the next three hours working first on aerobics, then abdominals, weight-circuit training and, finally, his beloved martial arts: aikido, kendo, as well as the various sub-disciplines of Akshara that were so ancient that they had no names in the Japanese language. In this manner he cleansed first his body, then his mind and, finally, his spirit of the various negative toxins that the post-modern world invariably built up.

Nicholas was long-muscled and wide-shouldered. It was obvious that he was an athlete of some kind, but it was his presence, what the Japanese called *hara*, that made him such an extraordinarily intimidating figure. He moved from the waist down as if his feet were a part of the floor or the earth he walked upon. Seeing him for the first time, one had the distinct feeling that he could not be moved from the spot on which he stood even with extreme measures. He had the unusually upswept eyes that were a legacy of his mother, along with the angular, rugged cheeks, nose and chin of his father. He was handsome in a charismatic rather than a poster-boy manner, with dark, curling hair flecked here and there with silver.

He himself did not see it, but those old enough to have known Colonel Denis Linnear saw the striking resemblance between father and son in the overall shape of Nicholas's face, the line of his nose, lips and jaw. The father, who counted among his ancestors calculating Romans and wild Celts, rather than barbarous Saxons, had that extraordinary gift of being both warrior and statesman. It was said by those who knew them both that the son possessed the same quality.

Nicholas's mother, Cheong, was Oriental, and it was only recently that he had been able to unravel the puzzle of her origins. She had been secretly tanjian, like Nicholas's Chinese grandfather, So-Peng, who had adopted her. So was Nicholas.

Trained in the arcane mysteries of Tau-tau, the tanjian, whose origins harked back to myth-shrouded ancient China, were ancient mage-warriors, who wielded a knowledge so potent, so elemental, that most humans had been cut off from it for centuries.

The basis of Tau-tau was *kokoro*, the heart of the cosmos. *Kokoro* was the membrane of life. Just as in physics the excitation of the atom caused the most extraordinary reactions of energy – light, heat and percussion – so, too, did the excitation of the cosmic membrane manifest its own ethereal energy.

Akshara and Kshira, the Way of Light and the Path of Darkness, were the two main branches of Tau-tau. Nicholas, who had been only recently trained in the basics of Akshara, had nevertheless some experience as well battling those versed in the deadly path of shadows. He was perhaps the only man on earth who had faced and defeated two Kshira adepts. This he had done partly by utilizing the gift So-Peng had passed down to him, the mystic emeralds of the tanjian. They had become a kind of psychic weapon which had penetrated even Kansatsu's Kshira and, at Nicholas's bidding, had destroyed him.

Kansatsu had instructed Nicholas in Akshara, but all the while he was also secretly an adept in Kshira, and it was Kshira which had almost destroyed Nicholas. In a very real way, it was Kshira which had destroyed Kansatsu. He had believed himself capable of containing the two separate disciplines inside himself; he had believed himself powerful enough to keep Kshira harnessed, using it only when required, but he was wrong. Its pollutant had seeped out, and so slowly that he had not been able to recognize it; it had poisoned him, turning him from good to evil.

The more Nicholas studied Akshara, the more he understood Kansatsu's temptation, for it was becoming clear to him that the Way of Light

32

was in some aspects an incomplete discipline. No records existed that far back in time, but he suspected that in the first days of Tau-tau the two disciplines were part of one whole. At what point they were riven in two – or why – he could not say. Perhaps at some date now long forgotten the mind of man – even a tanjian mind – could no longer be trusted to use the knowledge of Kshira in a prudent fashion; perhaps the lure of massive power became too great even for these ancient mages of the mind.

In any event, what was once one was now forever separated by such a profound philosophical abyss that proponents of Akshara were forbidden to plunge into the dark mysteries of Kshira.

Once, Kansatsu had spoken of *koryoku* – the Illuminating Power – with the kind of reverence he reserved only for gods. If there had ever been a focal point – real or imagined – between Akshara and Kshira, Kansatsu had been convinced *koryoku* was it. His anguish that for all his expertise in Tau-tau he could not achieve the Illuminating Power must have been a crushing blow to him – one so deeply felt that he had not allowed anyone to suspect.

In his studies after Kansatsu's death Nicholas had come to believe that *koryoku* might be the Path, the needle-like fulcrum from which the whole would open up like a flower.

He had named this whole *Shuken* – the Dominion: where one mind could contain Akshara and Kshira, both hemispheres of Tau-tau, without being destroyed by the dark side.

But *koryoku* was not like other states of deep meditation. Though little was known about it, it seemed clear that one needed to be born with a kind of psychic trigger that would access the doorway. Without that trigger no amount of study, concentration or incantation at *kokoro* would prove useful.

Nicholas had never encountered anyone with *koryoku* and so had never been able to test his theories. He did not even know whether he himself possessed the trigger that would access the doorway. Only another so gifted could tell him.

Sometimes, lying in the shallows of night, Nicholas started awake to discover that he had been dreaming. In his dream-world, he existed in *Shuken*, as he believed his forebears had once done, open to the full limits of Tau-tau – the full sphere of Akshara and Kshira at his command. And he knew with the certainty that comes in dreams that *koryoku* was the sole path to *Shuken*.

As he rose out of theta, parted from his dream, he could almost reach out and touch *koryoku*, the doorway, just another second and . . .

But when he became fully awake, the knowledge was lost to him, and

33

he could not help but feel an acute sense of loss which brought tears to his eyes.

Still, he knew he had an entire new world to explore. This reason perhaps more than any other had compelled him to remain in Japan, even though this was a source of increasing friction between him and his wife, Justine, who longed to return to America.

The thought of Justine's unhappiness was as painful as the sight of a stunned sparrow. He put his hand across his eyes as he closed them. Even this far from her he could feel her distress like a child's cry in the night. And yet there was a kind of abyss between them, dark and unfathomable. How long had it been there? Nicholas, beginning to slide into Tau-tau, tasted it, found it as familiar as an old jacket. With a start, he realized that it had begun to form at the time he had discovered he was tanjian. Was he slipping further away from the world most people knew? Were his explorations of the Tau-tau universe giving rise to a form of anomie from which he could not extricate himself? He did not think so, and yet there was that abyss yawning between him and Justine.

Sometimes, his anger at Justine was palpable. She had been in Japan for years now, yet she had failed to make the requisite effort in joining in. She had no Japanese friends of her own – save Nangi, and that was at his instigation and continuing effort. She still exhibited the Westerner's typical bewilderment at the complex net of customs, courtesies and expressions of respect that defined Japanese society. And, worst of all, she was beginning to exhibit that kind of blind impatience and outright resentment toward the Japanese Nicholas had witnessed in a number of American business contacts.

As Kansatsu had taught him, he began the journey inward, until he reached *kokoro*, the heart of all things. Then he selected the proper rhythm, began to beat at the membrane of *kokoro*, creating the psychic resonance that would transform thought into deed.

Sinking deeper into Akshara, the reverberations of *kokoro* filling the space around him, Nicholas's consciousness expanded until it filled the entire gym, then burst beyond the confining walls. In his mind he saw the city stretched out before him, and then, as if he were gathering enormous speed, the image of its bustling sprawl blurred. That familiar sensation of confinement fell away as, with a burst of psychic energy, he broke through the womb of Time.

Outside in the spangled darkness past, present and future existed only as meaningless definitions of concepts that did not exist. He did not yet know his way through this space or how to most effectively utilize its infinite horizons. That would take many years of trial and error. Instruction would have been preferable, of course, but the only other tanjian who had been qualified to teach him was now dead at his own hands and the inexorable forces of Tau-tau.

How long Nicholas spent in exploration of his new world it was difficult to say, because time as humans knew it did not correspond in that state. They had a taste of what it was like to be Outside in the midst of dreams when hours, even days, could seemingly be compressed into the space of micro-seconds.

When he again opened his eyes he felt refreshed and invigorated; the ghost of Justine's unhappiness was a scent in the air soon dissipated.

During his workout, the cordless phone at one end of the gym rang several times and, even though he knew the calls must be for him, he ignored them. His staff was used to his eccentric schedules, and they understood that if he did not answer he should only be disturbed in case of a full-scale emergency.

He stood beneath a cold shower, took a steam, then showered again, and dressed in new clothes. Even the terrible image of his infant daughter as she took her last gasping breath had been expunged for a time.

Seiko was waiting for him outside the gymnasium. True to her work ethic, she had taken several folders of paperwork, and while she sat on a low rung of the spiral stairs, she industriously made notes, corrections and scheduling rearrangements for her boss.

'Seiko,' Nicholas said.

She jumped up, slammed her folders shut and bowed deeply, then pulled her gleaming hair back from her cheek. Her beauty, seeming so fragile because of her translucent skin, actually appeared to have deepened during the time she had worked as his assistant.

'Linnear-san,' she said, 'I have received faxes of the litigation our New York lawyers have prepared against Hyrotech-inc. I think you should review them before you leave.'

'Have you looked at them?' Nicholas asked as they mounted the stairs toward his offices.

'Yes, sir. I have questions on clauses 6a and 13c.'

'Seiko, I don't know how long I'm going to be away,' he said as they reached the landing. 'You've got to get used to relying on your own good judgement. Just remember I trust you.' He smiled at her as he led the way to his office. 'Now tell me your concerns on how the lawsuit is worded.'

She answered him in clear, concise phrases, and he saw immediately that she had a facility for cutting through the mind-numbing legalese.

'I agree,' he told her when she had finished. 'Let me see how you would solve the problems in a revised draft before I leave the office this afternoon. If I agree with you, we'll run it by the legal department in New York.' Before she left, he added, 'And tell Nangi-san that I need to see him as soon as possible.'

Here I am in a sleazy motel off Highway 95, Margarite Goldoni thought. *What am I doing here? I must have lost my mind. No, not your mind*, she reminded herself. *Your freedom.*

They were ten miles from Marine on St Croix, Minnesota. This small town was where WITSEC, in their infinite wisdom, had chosen to transport Dominic Goldoni. They had given him new identity documents, a house, two cars, a consultancy job that fit in with his background as a construction engineer, the whole nine yards.

Robert had insisted she bring Francine with them, which had quite naturally terrified her, but she could see his point. Holding her and Francine hostage would keep Tony quiet.

Of course Dominic's first reaction was to kill Tony. *Slowly*, he had said to her. *I'll kill the sonuvabitch so slowly his eyeballs will pop out with pain.* A very Venetian response. But then she had said, *We both need Tony, Dom*, and he had gone quiet, ruminating, she was quite certain, on hatred and ambition. And when she had suggested they meet alone, he had agreed. Under the circumstances, it made sense, and he knew it.

All the way out to Minnesota she had begged Robert to let Francine go. Robert had merely turned to her, smiling into her face as if he were her lover instead of her captor.

If it had been just the two of them they could have taken a plane, she supposed, but there was Francine to think of – so he had her drive them in her BMW. Besides, she came to see that any other means of transportation would have left a more distinct trail. In the car, Robert could see a tail and take evasive measures. On the other hand, he had had her write out a message to her husband. In it, she had written that if her captor even suspected that Tony had posted surveillance, he would kill Francine. She thought that was a directive Tony the Sicilian could take to heart.

To be truthful, she didn't really mind the driving; the endless miles of the interstates lulled her into a false sense of security. Here on the American roads they seemed unbound by time, lost in a wilderness of strip malls, convenience stores and used car lots, and it seemed to her that she almost forgot that they had a destination, could push it into the furthest reaches of her mind as if it only existed in some nightmare realm that had lost the immediacy of reality. Besides, there was a relief, vivid as hunger pangs, at being away from Tony.

Then they entered Minnesota and the future became inescapable. She wept bitter tears in the mean motel by the side of the highway. The inconstant hum of the passing cars took the place of the drone of insects. It no longer mattered whether she was in the city or the country because she existed in a twilight world, a fly trapped in amber, consumed by what was about to take place.

Francine, who was drugged throughout the entire trip, lay on the cot provided by the motel owner. Robert sat on his side of the bed reading an issue of *Forbes* magazine just as if he was her husband, Tony. He appeared unmoved by her tears, but as she dragged herself beneath the sheets he had put away the magazine and said, 'Tomorrow we'll see your brother and it will all be over.'

Margarite, shivering so much that she drew the covers up to her chin, said, 'What will happen?'

For a long time Robert did not answer. She could feel him, his heat, hear his slow tidal breathing, smell his peculiar though not unpleasant scent, but she could not look at him. To give him such reality, she knew, would be too much for her to bear.

'Go to sleep.' His voice was soft, almost gentle, so that in the end she felt compelled to turn her head, look at him.

His face was handsome in the light endemic to motels at night – a pallid violet-blue from the neons and bug-zappers that seeped through the flyblown curtains like ash. In another, all too imaginable reality he might have been her lover, tenderly turning to her as she extinguished the lights.

She closed her eyes, trying in vain to imagine such a reality, as if by that mental effort she might be able to conjure it up and escape the terrible trap that had been laid for her.

On that last night of their journey to the nexus point that would forever alter her, she thought again about the vicissitudes of escape. Of course, Dom had insisted that Francine come to see him, but now Margarite saw what Robert had known all along: that escape with a drugged girl was impossible.

He knew what she was thinking.

Margarite was left with this one unalterable fact: In order to escape, she would have to kill him.

She did not know whether she had it in her – not whether she had the courage to put a bullet into his brain or a knife into his heart, but whether she was smart enough to get the opportunity to do it.

He carried with him an old-fashioned straight razor. She had caught a glimpse of him their first night on the road, shaving his arms while she was tied to the bed, twisting on one side so that part of the mirror over the sink in the bathroom brought her his reflection. He had very little hair on his body, but apparently he was happier with none.

The bathroom was the only place he allowed her to be alone, but she could not lock the door, could not even close it all the way. And, squatting on the seat, she was always aware of his breathing, his bulk just out of her sight.

Also, she worried about Francine, who was sleeping in the grip of the liquid he would force down her throat each morning. He had a bag of phials and small canisters tucked away in the kit bag in which resided, like a death's-head, her savior the razor. Every night, he would spend an hour or so grinding what looked to her to be roots and herbs and unidentifiable dried things in a stone mortar, adding at times liquids from his phials. What was he doing? These alchemical constructs which, by degrees, perfumed the close air of their mean motel rooms seemed the most menacing part of him. She was certain she could feel an almost primitive heat emanating from them, a kind of power which frightened her.

She was not, by nature, a superstitious person, but his almost cabalistic absorption in these ceremonies in the dark unnerved her. It was as if he possessed a power to make real the stuff of nightmare. She could imagine him extending himself into a dark corner, wrenching out a shadow and, turning it inside out, making it real.

'Lights out,' he had said to her, stretching toward the bedside lamp.

'Wait,' she had whispered. 'I have to use the bathroom.'

Her face taut with fear, she had crossed the room, shut the bathroom door just enough to block him out. As she lifted her nightgown, she could hear him getting out of bed, padding after her to stand, breathing shallowly, behind the door. Hearing him without seeing him was in some ways worse because her imagination, working overtime, conjured up his presence, ghostly and evil, as if he had the power to drift through solid objects to reach her.

She peed noisily, wiped herself, then flushed the toilet. Under that meager cover, she twisted toward the sink, turned on the tap with her left hand. With her right, she picked out the straight razor from his open kit bag.

She experienced an instant of panic then, because she had not thought it through. Where was she going to secrete the thing so that he would not see it? She could only imagine one place, and she quickly bent her knees and spread her legs, inserting it into her warmth. It was not easy, but the pain served as a tangible confirmation of her will to do this terrible thing.

With a trembling hand she turned off the tap, went out to where he waited for her in the semi-dark.

38

'Finished?'

She nodded at him, too terrified to speak. In bed, she pulled the covers over her, turned away from him. He extinguished the light. She felt him – she imagined that she would always feel him: that curious sense of menace and arousal which confused and appalled her.

She put her hand on the thatch of hair between her thighs, moving her forefinger over the end of the razor. She forced herself not to shudder. She closed her eyes, trying to still the hammering of her heart, but surely it was only her imagination that warned her this might betray her.

All the same, she started when she felt the press of his hand on her shoulder.

'You're vibrating.'

She had given a little moan.

He knew what she was thinking.

'What do you mean?'

'I can see the energy boiling off you like smoke.'

She turned around in the dark to face him. 'You can see what?'

'I can see auras,' he said. 'There's a way. I've been trained.'

'Okay. So you can see I'm frightened. What did you expect? I'm all alone here with my little girl.' Had her voice cracked? She bit her lip, determined to keep better control over herself. But she could feel the rivulets of sweat under her arms, in the small of her back, at the idea that he had the ability to see inside her, to know her very thoughts.

He said, 'We're all alone, in the end, with our sins.'

She shuddered. 'I was never alone. Ever since I can remember I've been in the company of men: my father, my uncle, then boyfriends, lovers, a husband. What must it be like to be alone? The freedom it must –'

'I've always been alone,' he said thoughtfully. 'Even in the most crowded city street I am isolated.'

'Don't you have *any* family . . . friends?'

'Who can I really count on,' he said, 'but myself?'

For the first time she thought she could see behind the dangerous shell of him, and she thought, *He's been damaged.*

'What family I had is dead. Dangerous.'

Margarite turned toward him, clearly fascinated. 'Dangerous?'

He continued to stare at the ceiling, striped by pale, phosphorescent light. 'Family,' he said, after a time. 'Family is dangerous.'

'No, no. You're wrong. Family is the only solace in times of tragedy.'

'Not if the tragedy destroys what family you had,' he said.

'All the love you missed.'

Damaged.

39

'We rise at dawn. Go to sleep,' he said.

She watched him, afraid now to turn away. 'How in Christ do you expect me to sleep?'

What would it be like to see mother and father, sister destroyed in front of one's eyes? she asked herself. The very idea was impossible to imagine. If she were an actress, perhaps, weeping bitter tears she contrived to well up out of her, the bodies strewn in front of her, blood that would never coagulate or turn brown smeared over them, weeping, until the director yelled 'Cut!' and the cameras stopped rolling. Only then. But in real life? No, never.

'Come here,' he said, in a voice that floated over her like a buzzard crossing a ravine.

It took her a moment to realize that he was holding his arms out to her.

She wanted to laugh, to spit in his face, but she also felt the razor, warm inside her – and there was something else, a mysterious emotion, elusive as mist, which locked her lips together.

In retrospect, it still surprised her that she crawled into his embrace, as meekly as a child; stunned her that in the grip of that embrace she felt more protected than she had ever felt before.

What was happening to her? She had no answer. Had he somehow managed to enchant her with one of his magic potions? She thought back to when she had eaten or taken something to drink. Had he secreted something at those times? Terrified, she could not say.

'How like his signature these bruises are.'

With his fingertips on her purple flesh she could not speak; her mind was blank save for the warmth she felt flowing from him, entering her where she hurt the most.

His head bent and his mouth opened against those bruises, and she felt his tongue, a pressure, and then nothing, as if even the memories that had lingered in those painful places had been exorcised.

She shivered when she felt his lips on her neck, at the tender place where her carotid artery softly pulsed. He did something then with his tongue that sent ripples of desire through her. She felt her nipples stiffen, and she grew damp between her thighs. It was then that she reached down. The razor thus lubricated came out without the difficulty she had had in sliding it in. It lay in the palm of her hand, gravid with its promise of death, warm as a living thing.

Margarite closed her slender fingers around it, and her lips opened to expel a soft groan. She used her forefinger to swing open the blade, and now she was ready.

40

His tongue slipped into the hollow between her breasts, a place that had always been a spot of intense arousal for her. *He knows*, she thought.

The blade moved as if of its own volition, a beast hungry to taste blood, to slice through flesh and sinew.

Kill him now, said a voice in her mind. *It's what you want. It will get you out of the trap.*

She squeezed her eyes shut and, grunting with the effort, swung her arm across the space between them. The edge of the blade struck him dead on but, instead of cutting him, the steel slid harmlessly along the skin of his lower belly.

She could see him grinning, his teeth large and white in the dimness as he held up her hand with one of his, clasped the opened razor blade with his other one.

Margarite gasped as he opened his fingers. They were uncut.

'Touch it,' he said. 'The blade is unsharpened. The one I use is locked away.' His grin broadened. 'I could feel you watching me, your eyes following the track of the blade as it scraped away my hair. I know greed, Margarite, and I could feel your greed. You wanted my razor ... and I gave it to you.'

'No,' she said faintly, dropping it on the sheets between them. 'You gave me nothing.' The acrid taste of bile was in her mouth. She thought she might be sick.

'On the contrary,' he said, taking her in his arms again. 'I have given you what is most important: a taste of your revenge.' His tongue touched her skin again. 'I wonder, Margarite, was it as sweet as you had imagined it to be?'

She had refused to answer him, instead swallowing heavily to try to rid her mouth of the awful taste. And again she thought, *He knows*.

'Answer me!' His voice so sudden, so harsh that she started.

And said, 'Yes.'

'I suspected as much,' he said with a curious satisfaction which caught her. 'You would have killed me; you have it in you.'

She could smell his breath, a scent of cloves, hear his heartbeat. 'I don't have to listen to this.'

'And what else have I given you, Margarite? Do I need to tell you? Now you know you have the strength of purpose ... to do *anything*.' He touched her nipples, setting them on fire. 'Now you see that I know you better than you know yourself.'

Lying there, quiescent, the impotent razor digging into one buttock, she tried to summon up her revulsion of him and, shockingly, could not.

41

She was dizzy with a longing she could not name, with a desire she could not acknowledge.

Slowly, as if her body weighed a thousand pounds, she turned over, away from him, into the darkness.

Outside the window, cars passed, whirring like insects.

Home. Once it was all the comfort he required. Nicholas's house was located on the outskirts of Tokyo. It had been a strictly Japanese structure inside and out when he had first bought it from the estate of his late aunt, Itami, but gradually Justine had transformed the inside, ordering tiles, wall coverings, fixtures and furniture from the States, Italy and France, until he no longer recognized the place with which he had originally fallen in love.

The camphor-wood beam exterior and the surrounding landscape had so far been spared her hand, but lately she had been making noises about wanting to turn the expanse of painstakingly manicured rare miniature parviflora and cryptomeria into a traditional English perennial garden. Denying her what she really wanted – to return to her home in America – Nicholas had been loath to deny her these smaller concessions which would surely make her feel more at home here.

Not only had these transformations failed to assuage her essential unease but, he realized now as he spun around the dangerous hairpin turn near the house, they had made him uncomfortable in the one place he had once felt most at ease. Even the construction going on two lots further down the road hadn't dampened his love for the place, but he took the last half-mile at a slower than normal speed. It was a good thing he did because just before the driveway to the house he came upon one of the gigantic earth-movers being used to excavate the new house's foundation, and he was obliged to pull into a neighbor's driveway so that the monstrous vehicle could safely pass.

Justine was waiting for him. He saw her as he went up the rough-hewn stone path from the gravel parking area. Her hazel eyes were the green they turned when she was upset or under stress, and the red motes danced in her left eye.

'Seiko called,' she said even before he had a chance to kiss her hello. 'Were you too busy to phone me yourself?'

She turned on her heel, went inside, where he followed her into the kitchen.

'The truth was I was too upset,' he said. 'I had to work out to calm myself down.' He went past her, began the preparations for brewing green tea.

42

'God, you've become just like all your Japanese friends. When only talk will do you go ahead and brew your foul-tasting green tea.'

'I'm happy to talk to you,' he said as he measured out the finely cut leaf, took up the reed whisk.

'Why did you ask Seiko to call me?'

'I didn't,' he said. 'She saw it as her duty.'

'Well, she was wrong.'

The water was boiling in the ceramic pot. He took it up, poured it carefully into the cup. 'Why can't you understand? Here, efficiency is the most prized –'

'Dammit!' Justine's outflung hand slapped the cup across the counter. It skidded into the wall, smashed to pieces. 'I'm tired of hearing about what's important to the Japanese!' She ignored the reddening mark on her wrist where the boiling water had scalded her. 'What about what's important to this *American*! Why is it always a matter of *my* having to adapt to *their* way of doing things?'

'You're in their country, and you –'

'But I don't want to be here!' Tears were coursing down her cheeks. 'I can't stand it any more, being the outsider, feeling no emotion from them but this subtle hostility. It's freezing my bones, Nick! I can't memorize one more minuscule custom, ritual, protocol, formality or courtesy. I'm fed up with being shoved out of the way on the streets, pushed aside when I'm trying to use a public washroom, elbowed on a subway platform. How a people who are so insufferably polite in their own homes can be so rude in public is beyond me.'

'I've told you, Justine, if a space doesn't belong to any individual – like a public space – the Japanese feel there's no need for politeness.'

Justine was trembling and weeping all at once. 'These people are nuts, Nick!' She turned on him. 'If I'm going to be left alone with these madmen at least I should have heard it from you.'

'I'm sorry.' She said nothing. 'Justine, Seiko was only doing her job.'

'Then she's too efficient by half.'

'How can you be angry with her for being efficient?' He looked at her carefully, and was struck by how strange this house had become. It was like a suit you had liked in the store but didn't in the clear light of day. 'This isn't about Seiko calling you, is it?'

She turned away, her palms flat against the counter, her arms like rigid poles. Her long dark hair was disheveled, her body almost painfully thin. 'No,' she said in a strangled voice, 'but it *is* about Seiko.'

He saw the extreme tension in the hunch of her shoulders, the way she stood spread-legged. She had unconsciously assumed the stance of a street fighter spoiling for a confrontation.

Nicholas was about to say something, then thought better of it, intuiting that she would use anything he said now as further provocation.

Justine turned, her face dark with anger that had been pent-up too long. 'Are you having an affair with Seiko?'

'What are you talking about?'

'Tell me the truth, dammit! Anything will be better than this hell of suspicion.'

He took a step toward her. 'Justine, Seiko is my assistant, period.'

'Is that the whole truth? You'd better search your soul before you answer.'

'Why would you doubt me?' Her stricken face hung before him and his heart broke. 'Justine . . .'

'You've spent so much time with her.'

'It was necessary.'

Her shoulders shook. 'Taking her to Saigon –'

'She knows Vietnam far better than either Nangi or I. I couldn't have completed my business in Saigon without her.' He went to her, took her in his arms.

'Oh, Christ, Nick, I'm sorry. I don't know . . .'

At his touch all the tension went out of her, and a heat flowed through her to him. His lips came down over hers and her mouth was already open, her tongue hungrily entwined with his. Her heat suffused him, warming a body whose bones, it seemed, had indeed grown cold in the bitterness of her accusations.

It had been unfair of her to suspect him, he knew, even as he was uncomfortably aware that it was unfair of him to continue to imprison her here in a land she despised and could never understand.

He opened her shirt, held her breasts in his hands as the nipples grew taut and hot. Her mouth would not relinquish its hold on him, and he thrust his hands down further, unfastening the Western belt, dragging her jeans off her thighs.

He was so hard he pushed up against her urgently, but she shoved him back with surprising strength, slipping to her knees before him. She undressed him with sure knowledge.

'Justine –'

Her hand encircled the base of him while her hot mouth slipped over the tip. He tried to pull her up and away but she resisted him. He did not want this now, to see her submissive, so terrified of losing him that she would do anything to keep him hers. He wanted only to lose himself inside

44

her, to block out all else, in their intimate twining to remove her doubt about him and their life together. But, in the end, her busy tongue and lips obliterated his resolve and he dug his fingers into her thick hair, feeling her head move back and forth.

At last, he found the strength to drag her away from him. He picked her up as if she were a child and her thighs came around him. He could taste the sex in her mouth as it came down over his. He found her open and waiting, and with a deep groan, she impaled herself on him to the hilt. She was so wild that he had no choice but to cede control of their movements to her. It was all he could do to keep up with her. He felt her belly ripple as her nipples whipped back and forth across his chest. He felt the tremoring of the muscles on the insides of her thighs, and the vibrations of her hard, breathless grunts into his mouth.

There was no rhythm, just a clawing, animalistic response of pleasure and, surely, of pain as she bit him deep enough to draw blood. With that, her ecstatic spasms began in her groin, spiralling outward until she shook and trembled as if in the grip of a terrible illness. She cried out, and tears flew from the corners of her tightly closed eyes. The dense cloud of her wet hair engulfed him as he felt her working her sex against him in stages, as she rose higher and higher in a series of orgasms that brought him over the edge. He felt her fingers on his scrotum, clutching urgently while she whispered incoherently into his ear, and he collapsed to the floor with her still clasped tightly in his arms.

She was weeping uncontrollably, and he kissed her lips, her cheeks, eyes, forehead and temples.

'Justine, Justine, as soon as I get back from Venice, I promise we'll go to New York.'

For a long time she said nothing, her face buried in his shoulder, her mouth half open as she tasted his sweat and blood. When, at length, she looked up into his face he was sick to recognize the despair there. 'Please don't go, Nick.'

'I – Justine, I have no choice.'

'I'm begging you, just stay with me a few days. Take time off from work, from . . . everything. We'll go away, into the countryside – to Nara, the *ryokan* you like so much.'

'That sounds wonderful, but this trip is not of my making. I can't –'

'Just tell me what's so important in Venice and I swear I'll try to understand.'

'An old friend of my father needs my help.'

'Who is he?'

45

'I'm not sure.'

'You mean you don't know him?'

'Justine, I gave my word to my father just before he died. I have a duty.'

She shook her head, tears rolling down her cheeks again. 'Ah, now we come to it. Your duty. Don't you have a duty to me?'

'Please try to understand.'

'God knows I've tried, but this Japanese concept of *giri*, of a debt of duty, I most certainly do *not* understand. And, d'you know what? I realize now I don't want to try any more.' She rose unsteadily, stared down at him. 'First it was your business, then your friendship with Nangi, then your trips to Saigon with Seiko. Now this – a duty to a father who's been dead for years to help someone *you've never even met*. Christ, you're as crazy as all the rest of them!'

'Justine –'

He reached out for her but she had already spun away from him, was fleeing down the hall. In a moment, he heard a door slam, but he made no move to go after her. What would be the point?

Sadly, he got up, slowly dressed himself with wooden fingers. He went silently out the back door, through the whispering cryptomeria. The sky was misted gray, a soup thickened by swirling clouds that hung low like the robes of ghostly *daimyo* from ages past. He made his way through the garden, and before he knew it, found himself ascending the slope filled with a copse of carefully planted ginkgo, ancient of ancients, their white trunks like sentinels, the vestiges of their copper bi-lobed leaves trembling like the fingers of an oracle.

He had no conscious idea of where he was headed until he topped the rise and, below him, saw the lake. The water was invisible beneath the curling layer of nacreous mist.

Father, Nicholas thought.

He crouched on the boggy bank of the lake, looking into the mist as if it were an alchemist's mirror that could break the barrier of time. In that mirror, he saw the Colonel and himself, younger and innocent, as the elder Linnear gave him the present of Iss-hogai, the dai-katana, the long samurai sword that, many years later, Nicholas had hurled into this lake.

He could feel Iss-hogai now, just as he could see it as it struck the water so many years ago, plunging vertically to the bottom. And now, as past and present began to collide, it seemed so close to him that he could reach out and touch it.

He had thought he was quits with it then, that he had no more need of its power to inflict death, but like his own past with his father, like

46

his present with Justine, there was an essential element, unknown, as yet unwritten, that remained unresolved.

The Colonel, whom Nicholas loved and revered, had nevertheless had a secret life wholly apart from Nicholas and Cheong. Nicholas had discovered years after the Colonel's death that he had murdered a dangerous political radical named Satsugai. He was the husband of Nicholas's aunt, Itami, and though she despised him still she was his wife. The Colonel's action had had the profoundest effect on Nicholas's life when Satsugai's son, Saigo, had sought to murder Nicholas in revenge.

The phone call from Mikio Okami had stirred waters that, for a long time, had remained unruffled.

The Colonel's secret life. What had he been up to with Mikio Okami? Why had he made friends with a Yakuza *oyabun*? Nicholas had no answers to these questions. He only knew that, in seeking them, he was being drawn once again toward his father – and toward the unknown past.

At last, he rose, went as silently as he had come, returning through forest and glade, past dreaming gardens, along stone paths laid centuries ago, to the kitchen of his house.

For the longest time he stood looking out the window at the cryptomeria and the cut-leaf maples whose boughs were dancing in the wind he had only moments before felt against his flesh.

At last, he turned to the counter, reached for a cup, measuring out the *macha*, the finely cut green tea leaf.

He took up the reed whisk, waiting for the water to boil.

Harley Gaunt was in the middle of a crisis of Brobdingnagian proportions. Bad enough that Tomkin-Sato Industries was losing accounts, pressured no doubt by retrocessive Democrats espousing pernicious isolationist economics with the feverish zeal of born-again Christians, but now the corporate headquarters here in Manhattan was literally under siege by consumers incensed by what placards on the street below misidentified as 'consorting with the enemy'.

All chickens eventually come home to roost, Gaunt thought as he stared gloomily out his office window at the gathering demonstration. As he watched like a hawk in its eyrie, he saw a CNN remote TV truck pull up. Within minutes, the local TV stations were represented, then the networks, as usual dead last.

Christ, he thought. I need Nicholas over here. We've ridden the economic rollercoaster of our merger with Sato International all the way up to the top of the loop, and from where I'm sitting the ride down is going to be scary as hell.

His intercom buzzed, and he answered curtly, 'Suzie, is that Mr Linnear on the line?'

'I'm afraid not, Mr Gaunt,' his secretary's voice spoke out of thin air, 'but your ten o'clock appointment is here.'

'What ten o'clock appointment?'

'You remember, he called late yesterday. I told you I put it on your calendar just before I left for the day.'

'I don't . . .' But Gaunt was already turning from the stomach-churning scene out his window, his eye catching the hastily scribbled notation on the calendar section of his computer terminal.

'Who the hell is Edward Minton?'

'He's from Washington,' Suzie said, as if that solved the riddle. 'He flew in first thing this morning on the shuttle to see you.'

Gaunt's stomach knotted. He didn't like the sound of that. Those Democrats on the Hill were positively incendiary on the subject of the Japanese. According to them, an economic war was brewing, and all Americans required the benevolent protection of the Democratic Party in order to avoid the economic humiliations plotted for us in some moldy sub-basement of the Imperial Palace in Tokyo.

Tojo Lives! might well be their battle cry, though he had begun to notice springing up like noxious mushrooms in a humid climate posters of the Imperial rising sun of Japan encircled with a red line, another red line running diagonally through it.

These were to him nothing more than a symbol of the moral bankruptcy of his own country – an advertiser's dream, where even the most complex issues could be reduced to simplistic decals.

Gaunt closed his eyes for a moment. He was a massive man, with as much fat as muscle, a three-letter man in college athletics who, typical of his kind, assumed that heavy physical exercise once accomplished need not be continued to maintain form. He had been a wide receiver of no little renown, and on the mound of a baseball diamond had once possessed a slider that justifiably intimidated the opposition. Only being hit in the shoulder by a wicked line drive had kept him out of professional sports.

Lucky for him, no doubt, since even if his bank account would have swollen, his mind would have atrophied. The fact was that Gaunt was possessed of an intelligence rare in his chosen field of administration. He could summon up that astonishing leap of insight usually the purview of programming geniuses and maverick entrepreneurs. This was how he had come to the attention of Nicholas Linnear, and why Nicholas had promoted him to Managing Director, North America of Tomkin-Sato Industries.

Now that intuition told him that his ten o'clock was poison. He put his fingers to his forehead, closed his eyes for a moment as if with force of will alone he could cause Edward Minton to disappear.

'Mr Gaunt?'

'Yes, Suzie.'

'It's ten fifteen.'

Gaunt sighed. 'In that case send Mr Minton in.'

If Gaunt's body had lost the hard athlete's edge it had possessed in college, his face had not. It was still firm-jawed, and there was no wattle under his chin as, astonished, he had noted in many of his classmates at their last reunion. His hair, still thick, was flecked with gray, but this matched the sprays of that color in his brown eyes. What lines appeared in his face were like those etched by a fine sculptor – they seemed to belong there, to, moreover, have always been there, part of his craggy strength, his canny insight.

Edward Minton was, on the other hand, a whole different story. Tall and thin, he had that stoop-shouldered mien of those made self-conscious at an early age of their ungainly height. He had skin the color of wax paper, by which hue Gaunt's worst fears were realized: he was government-issue, and right now that was as ill an omen as a crow in a cornfield.

Minton wore a three-piece suit, shiny at the elbows, rumpled at crotch and sleeves, of an indeterminate color and material. No doubt it was fire-retardant. He wore steel-rimmed spectacles above a straight nose, thin lips. Behind them were the clear blue eyes of the raptor. Gaunt was unsurprised to see a gold Phi Beta Kappa chain strung from the watch pocket of his vest. Politicians were like dogs, Gaunt observed silently. They liked best to lie down with their own breed.

'Mr Minton,' he said now, wrapping a smile around his lips, 'won't you sit down? What can I do for you?'

Minton, who had brought with him his own gust of ill-scented air, settled himself in a leather and chromium chair on the other side of Gaunt's old, scarred mahogany desk.

'Quite a crowd you've collected downstairs,' he said with the brittle tone of a scolding mother.

'These things have a way of blowing over,' Gaunt countered. 'By tomorrow afternoon the war in Yugoslavia will be back on the front page.'

'Perhaps not this time,' Minton said. As he spoke he fondled his Phi Beta Kappa in that conspicuous way certain men will a magnificent woman whose services they have bought for the evening. 'These are hard times in America and the populace is aroused.' His lenses flashed with light as he turned his head slightly. By the practiced way he did it, Gaunt could tell he was well schooled in the tactics of intimidation. 'I believe that we are

49

seeing a locomotive of incalculable energy stoking up steam.' Fondle, fondle, Phi Beta Kappa. Gaunt was willing to bet this bastard knew he had never even finished college. 'When it gets under way, Mr Gaunt, I pity the person – or company – that stands astride its tracks.'

Gaunt cleared his throat but said nothing. He felt a bit like Marie Antoinette. It was always like this, he thought, when you waited for the guillotine to fall.

'We on Capitol Hill have taken the pulse of the growing unrest in America and we're determined to respond with alacrity and force to what the people want.'

'What *you* want, more like it,' Gaunt said under his breath.

'What?' Minton leaned forward, suddenly alert as a terrier scenting its prey. 'What did you say?'

'I merely cleared my throat.'

A certain rigidity had come into Minton's spine. 'What the people of the United States want is for Japan Inc. to get out of their face. And that, Mr Gaunt, is precisely what the Congress of the United States proposes to give them.'

He slapped a folded sheet of paper onto the desk. 'I am a prosecutor in the US Attorney General's office on assignment to the Senate. I am here to inform you that you, Harley Gaunt, as Managing Director of Tomkin-Sato Industries, and one Nicholas Linnear, Chairman and Chief Operating Officer of Tomkin-Sato Industries, are hereby subpoenaed by the Senate of the United States of America. I am also to inform you that you are the subject of an investigation of the Senate Strategic Economic Oversight Committee, by order of Senator Rance Bane. You are hereby ordered to appear before the Committee one week from this Thursday promptly at ten o'clock in the morning.'

Senator Rance Bane, Gaunt repeated to himself. Somehow, after that name had been uttered, he had ceased to listen to the remainder of Minton's governmentese spiel.

Bane was a Democrat from Texas who had his sights trained firmly on the White House, where it seemed – whether Democrat or Republican sat in the Hot Seat – the mountain of debt incurred for decades wasn't getting any smaller.

Rance Bane was an opportunist. He had come out of the heartland of America's southwest, from a state perhaps battered by economic woes, but still fabled as the birthplace of America's movers and shakers, from cowboys to Texas Rangers to gung-ho senators. Which was surely what Rance Bane was: the President's fiercest foe, purporting to be the staunchest ally of America and Americans 'First, Foremost and Only', as he would say. But in the end Bane was a telegenic good old boy who understood modern-day power politics, and who knew how to best utilize its acolytes: advertising and the media. His state, among others in the south and the rust belt, had become staunchly protectionist. Losing jobs to the Japanese was no fun and Bane, ever the canny psychologist, had picked up on this economic fear, and had fanned it into a bonfire of paranoia. The most alarming thing was he wasn't alone.

Bane's uncommon brain trust drew from such divergent American loci as Hollywood, Detroit and New York. Not surprisingly, the men Bane chose to present him to the public all melded into a synergistic whole. Gaunt was certain this was because they had one thing in common: they lived and died in the marketplace. They knew how to sell, whether it be on the silver screen, on the roads of America or on Wall Street and Madison Avenue.

And sell him they did. Until he became what he was today: politics' great, shining hope for resurgence after years of declining interest and then outright animosity on the part of the American populace.

Flash of a magnetic face seen almost daily on TV and in the papers: curling reddish hair, wide forehead, quick eyes, ready smile, hearty handshake. A raw-boned, rangy man not unlike a youngish LBJ but without the blubbery lips. A man associated not only with oil but with cattle as well, the farmers and oilmen combined into a formidable special-interest base that drew not only from a traditional Democratic sector but poached on Republican territory as well.

And a new brand of McCarthyism – this time safeguarding the country against the infiltration of the Japanese – was raising its head, this time in the guise of liberalism and a return to good old-fashioned American values.

'What the hell is the Strategic Economic Oversight Committee, anyway?' Gaunt asked, although he suspected he already knew.

'The Committee is the brainchild of Senator Bane,' Minton said, toady-like. His blatantly righteous admiration for Bane was nauseating. 'It has been convened to review all companies whose business with the Japanese consists of more than fifty per cent of their gross annual earnings, or who have entered into partnerships of any kind with Japanese-owned corporations.'

'Why?' It was perhaps an unnecessary question, except that Gaunt wanted this paranoia spelled out for him from beginning to end.

'Certain information has come into Senator Bane's possession that some of these transactions may involve transgressions of national security.'

'National security?' Gaunt almost laughed in Minton's face. 'You've got to be kidding.' But he could see by the attorney's expression that neither he nor his newly anointed champion, Rance Bane, were kidding. 'What information?'

'At this time I'm not at liberty to say.' Minton rose abruptly, as if he were concerned that a prolonged stay here would expose him to some form of insidious contamination.

'You have been served, Mr Gaunt.' Minton continued to fondle his Phi Beta Kappa, flaunt and taunt to the end. 'The Committee expects to see you at the appointed time.'

'What about Nicholas Linnear? He's currently out of the country.'

'A formal request for his appearance has been duly filed with your Tokyo office.' Minton showed the yellowed teeth of a hound. 'We got you; we'll get him.'

With a curt nod, Edward Minton was gone, taking with him the faintly rank smell, an unappetizing confluence of Egg McMuffins and week-old socks, but leaving behind a residue like rime: the ramifications of inexorable power.

Wallowing in the wake of this rather godlike visitation, Gaunt had not the slightest interest in laughing in anyone's face. Rather, he was experiencing the queasy sensation of being caught in the jaws of a gargantuan machine that had no other interest than to chew him up and spit him out. Or an even worse nightmare, engulfing and devouring him, so that months from now he might become the first of the American *disappeared*, a direct translation from Argentine Spanish, a New World fascist fad, spreading like an unwitting virus northward along the continental drift.

Seiko met Nicholas at Narita. He saw her walking serenely through the chattering throngs which filled the airport terminal. She smiled, bowing as she came up. She handed him a slim briefcase. He had been standing at the Air France First Class check-in desk, and he moved them away from the line.

'I brought some documents for you to look at on the flight over,' she said. 'Included in there is a coded fax from Vincent Tinh.'

Saigon again, Nicholas thought. Tinh, Sato's director in Vietnam, had big plans for the company there, but he sometimes had a tendency to get ahead of himself and the physical resources allotted him. It was he who had been urging Nicholas to allocate more capital to their start-up operations there. 'Thank you, Seiko-san.'

She recognized the sorrow in his eyes, but true to her nature she made no overt comment on it. Instead, she said, 'Did you remember your passport?'

'*Hai.*' Yes.

'There is some time before your flight,' she said.

Nicholas knew a cue when he heard one. 'Why don't we go into that shop and have some tea.'

Seiko nodded her head, and they made their way across the crowded concourse, to stand at a curving counter while green tea was served them in paper cups.

The smell of fish was very strong and, looking down into his tea, Nicholas was reminded of Justine's disgust for the national drink which, she said, tasted of fish.

'This trip,' Seiko began in a halting fashion, 'it is very important to you.'

'Yes.'

'To honor your father in such a fashion is very . . . Japanese.'

'Thank you.' Usually serene even in a crisis, Seiko seemed filled with a curious energy. 'Seiko-san, what is it?'

'I had –' She paused to lick her lips. 'I had a premonition. It was – do you remember I knew everything about Vincent Tinh? That was partly a premonition, as well. We met him and he was everything I told you he'd be – and more, given the cost figures beginning to come out of Saigon.'

Her small hand clasped the paper cup so tightly, the green tea slopped over the side. 'I was right then and I – this trip will be very dangerous. I beg you to be careful.' She was speaking very quickly now, the words tumbling one over the other as if she knew she must spill out her secret knowledge before she had a chance to bite it back. 'I may never see you again. I have this feeling that even if I do everything will be changed. I will not be the same and certainly you will be different – so different that no one will recognize you.'

Despite his Western impulse to laugh at her melodramatic words, Nicholas felt an unpleasant chill race down his spine as he recalled his own sense of foreboding earlier when the call summoning him to Mikio Okami's side had come in.

'Even if what you say is true I must go. There is an old debt which my father incurred that I must pay.'

Seiko took a quick gulp of her tea, almost choked on it.

Nicholas placed his hand on the center of her back, massaging the spasmed muscles as she coughed. She turned to stare at him, her face reddened not only by the paroxysm, but by something else.

It was not proper for him to be touching her in public, even in such an innocent manner. 'Pardon me,' he said, as he hastily took his hand away.

Her head swung back to her contemplation of her tea. Nicholas became aware of the intense anxiety radiating from her.

'Seiko-san, what is it?'

Her hands were clasped tightly together on the countertop, as if she were terrified she could no longer keep them under control. 'I am an evil, selfish woman.'

'Seiko-san –'

'Let me finish. Please.' She took a breath. 'Ever since Nangi-san assigned me to work for you I have known that I have a – special feeling toward you.'

Nicholas's mind was now caught in a minefield that was part electrifying present, part recent past, in which he heard over and over again Justine's accusations.

She looked at him, finally, with a directness he could not dismiss. 'I fell in love with you against my will. I knew you were married; knew that I could never have you. But none of that mattered. In affairs of the heart, I am afraid logic and common sense have no place.'

There was a silence between them. Now that the appalling truth was out, Seiko slumped over as if exhausted. 'I never would have told you – never, never, never. But then this premonition – if it were true that I would never see you again, I knew I could not keep this secret inside me. I am not strong enough, you see.' She bit her lip. 'I apologize, though any apology I make is inadequate. I am weak and self-indulgent. My love should have remained my own private anguish.' She put her head down. 'You see how kindness is repaid. But I am helpless. I love you, Nicholas.'

Nothing she had said before could have prepared him for the effect of her use of his first name. He felt as if he had abruptly walked off solid land into a patch of quicksand from which he could not recover.

My God, he thought, Justine must have known – must have seen this awful secret in Seiko's face. No wonder she had confronted him. Part of him wanted to rush home to Justine's arms, to tell her that he loved her, that he would never leave her again. But here he sat rooted to the spot, in a neon-lit tea shop in a crowded concourse of Narita airport with a beautiful young woman who said she loved him. And for the first time, he acknowledged what he had unconsciously known from the moment he heard Mikio Okami's name invoked: that he was on a collision course with a future from which he would not emerge unscathed.

You will be different – so different that no one will recognize you, she had told him, and he shivered now because he began to suspect the truth of those words even while he had no idea what they could mean.

'Please don't say anything,' Seiko murmured. 'It doesn't matter if you don't love me as I love you. What good would it do anyway? You are married and in love with your wife. I have been betrayed by my heart, and now I do not expect you to keep me on as your assistant.'

54

'If you suppose I'll send you away like a disobedient child, you're wrong,' Nicholas said. He hardly knew how to respond to everything she said, but he did know that he did not want to lose the best assistant who had ever worked for him. 'Whatever you're feeling toward me is irrelevant. You are so quick to learn, so good at everything I've given you to do that I expect you'll outgrow your job within a year. At that point, we'll have to talk about a promotion and a raise.' He shook his head. 'Whether or not you can recognize it, Seiko, you're on a fast track at Sato International. You're far too valuable to me to risk losing you now. You work for me and that's the way it's going to be, period.'

Seiko gave a little bow. 'I thank you again for your unending kindness, Linnear-san. I cannot imagine what my life would be like without you.' She glanced at her watch, slipped off her stool. 'It is time for you to go through immigration control. Your plane will be boarding in five minutes.'

She walked him as far as she could. She looked quite composed, even calm, now that the emotional storm had passed.

'Do you have a contact number for me while you are in Venice?'

Nicholas opened the thick buff-colored folder that had been waiting for him at the First Class Air France check-in counter. 'I'm staying at a hotel called Il Palazzo di Maschere Veneziane.' He showed her both the phone and fax numbers printed on the hotel's reservation confirmation slip. Seiko jotted them down in the tiny leather notebook that Nicholas had given her as a present her first day on the job.

'I think that's it, then,' he said as they reached the end of the line waiting to go through immigration and security. He watched her as she stood apart, looking very beautiful and very alone. She seemed so full of pain his heart went out to her. He was about to say something but she put her forefinger to her lips.

'No goodbyes,' Seiko said. 'We will see each other again.'

On the far side of the barriers, Nicholas took the few minutes as his plane began boarding to call Justine. He let the phone ring nine times but there was no answer. He wished now that he had his last hours with her to do all over again. It was only now that the reality of the physical leaving swept over him. He longed to talk with her, at least, to tell her how sorry he was. But, as he walked toward the departure gate, he consoled himself by thinking apologies were better delivered in person. There would be plenty of time for that when he returned.

Tanzan Nangi was dictating letters to Umi, his assistant, when Seiko walked in. He broke off, looked up at her for a moment, silent. Then he said, 'What is your news?'

'It is not good,' she said. She opened a file, handed over several type-written sheets. 'We have just received a formal request from the United States Senate. Linnear-san is required to appear before the Strategic Economic Oversight Committee to answer questions regarding the merging of Tomkin Industries with Sato International.'

'Good Lord, this has the smell of an American witch-hunt,' Nangi said. He scanned the documents. 'I've read the stories on this Senator Bane. The international news has been filled with him lately. I saw him interviewed on CNN. And there was a feature about him in last week's edition of *Time*.' He pointed. 'Did this request come in the mail?'

'No, sir,' Seiko said, obviously uncomfortable. 'It was delivered by someone from the American embassy. They told me it arrived this morning via diplomatic pouch.'

Nangi carefully folded the sheets, handed them back to Seiko. 'Well, if we don't know where Nicholas is we can't very well serve him with these papers. Seiko, draft a reply to the Committee outlining the bare bones of the current situation. You know the drill, Linnear-san's urgent business, somewhere in Europe, currently out of touch with the office, et cetera.'

'Yes, sir.'

But after she left he did not immediately go back to his dictating. His mind was on Senator Bane and his Committee. He had been dreading something like this as Bane's status and prestige escalated exponentially. Someone was going to become the touchstone for the Senator's righteous anger and Tomkin-Sato was a logical choice.

The fact was that Nicholas was vulnerable. He had been an outsider brought in to run the company by decree of his father-in-law's will after Tomkin's untimely death. Nangi supposed that it might not be too difficult for Bane to make a case for Nicholas, a neophyte in the ranks of corporate businessmen, relying rather too heavily on the Japanese side of the merger. Hell, Nangi thought, *he* could make the same accusation and make it stick. Look where Nicholas had chosen to live for the past eight years – Tokyo, not New York.

Now Nangi was overcome with guilt. He began to second-guess himself for talking Nicholas out of returning to the States to lobby on the conglomerate's behalf. The fact was Nangi had been selfish – not only in the area of business, where Nicholas's presence caused the most astonishing results both in research and restructuring, but also because he was Nangi's best friend.

What have I done? Nangi asked himself as he sat, silent in his office. *By keeping Nicholas at my side I may have condemned him – and us – to oblivion.*

56

TWO

Marco Island/Venice/Tokyo/Marine on St Croix

Lew Croaker squinted through the glare of the tropical sun and uttered a hearty curse under his breath. The Coast Guard cutter had just appeared through the heat haze, heading straight for him.

He was aboard his sleek boat, *Captain Sumo*, which he hired out for exorbitant fees for the best sport fishing on Florida's West Coast. A mile and a half out of Marco Island, Croaker was not currently chartered. In fact, he had left port not only to try and outrun recent memories, but for some peace and quiet. The last thing he needed, he reflected sourly as he cut the engines and came about, was another semi-official visit from the CG.

Croaker was an ex-detective from the NYPD. He had retired down here with Alix Logan, a former model who, much to his surprise and delight, had fallen in love with him. Now she was gone, back to the glittery high life she missed more than she loved him. She was in New York – or was it Paris? He couldn't keep track any more. And even though she called him regularly, he had no illusions that her fidelity to him would last. The lure of her previous life – and all the perks that went with it – was far too strong. How had he ever thought that she would be content with him, a wide-shouldered man of forty-five with the slightly pushed-in, weather-beaten face of a cowboy? He couldn't call himself handsome, and though his hair was still dark and thick, it wasn't styled and slicked back like that of her once and future model buddies. *You remind me of Robert Mitchum,* Alix had told him early in their relationship. *So much character, so much history in your face.*

The evening she had left, he sat behind the wheel of the vintage 1969 flamingo-and-white Thunderbird he had completely and lovingly restored, and watched her plane cleave the last of the long, languorous sunset. Despair washed over him, and his first thought was to call his friend Nicholas Linnear, with whom he had shared so much danger. But it was not Croaker's way to cry into his beer, even with a close friend like Nicholas. Brought up in the vicious Hell's Kitchen area of Manhattan's west side,

57

Croaker had seen his policeman father gunned down in an alley, seen his mother's spirit broken. He had learned how to be tough the hard way, and for him there was no going back.

The Coast Guard cutter had throttled down, and he threw his engines into neutral, then cut them entirely. He let go the electronic windlass and heard the anchor hit the water.

As he made preparations to be boarded, he considered what streak of altruism had made him accept the CG's offer to help them from time to time in controlling the drug trade that was endemic to Florida's seemingly endless miles of coastline. Perhaps he was not as truly quit with police work as he had convinced himself he would be when he had moved down here.

The cutter was now fully powered down, bobbing in the swell. Croaker made fast the lines thrown up to him by the small boat launched from the cutter. He peered down at the three men as they began to climb up the vertical ladder he had let down.

He had expected to see his friend, Lt Mark McDonald, who had become his liaison with the CG. Instead, he counted two young ensigns with service revolvers on their hips. These serious-looking sailors were flanking a man Croaker had never seen before. He was tall and as thin as a whippet, with dark brows and ruddy cheeks. As he came on board, Croaker was struck by the intensity of his clear blue eyes. He had a distinctly boyish look even though Croaker judged him to be somewhere in the vicinity of fifty. He was carrying a briefcase made of what looked to be a kind of dull gray polycarbonate.

The two ensigns were very formal. They saluted Croaker, then stood at military ease on their side of the ladder entry.

'Mr Croaker,' the man said, extending his hand. 'Good to meet you. My name's Will Lillehammer.' His eyes crinkled but his mouth refused to smile. 'Kind of you to let us board.' Those blue eyes were like an X-ray machine, measuring everything. 'I'm on special assignment for the President of the United States.' He did not say with whom, and Croaker did not think it was the Coast Guard, even though Lillehammer was wearing a CG lieutenant's uniform. He had a faint but discernible British accent. 'Is there somewhere we can speak in private?'

Croaker looked around. Besides the cutter close to, there was a fishing boat, a brace of sailboats tacking into the wind, and a sleek cigarette booming its way back to shore. All were quite a distance away. He spread his arms.

Now Lillehammer smiled, and it wasn't a pleasant sight. It brought into view a spiderweb of pale scars at the corners of his mouth. 'You'd be astounded at the advances in electronic surveillance since you left the Force,' he said.

So he's been briefed on my history, Croaker thought as he led Lillehammer into the cabin. He broke out iced beers, and they sat on a vinyl-covered bench. Lillehammer lifted his bottle, said, 'Cheers,' and took a grateful swallow. Then he drew the briefcase up onto the bench, unlocked it, and opened it. Inside, Croaker saw an array of what might have been the guts of a computer, except there was no keyboard. Lillehammer inserted an odd-looking key, turned it left, then right.

Croaker made a face.

'Getting a slight headache, are you?' Lillehammer said. He extended a hand. 'Here, swallow this.'

Croaker took the tiny white pill, gulped it down with a swig of beer. In a moment, his head cleared. 'What the hell was that?' he asked.

'Electronic surveillance has become so sophisticated so quickly we've been forced to bring into the field countermeasures not always one hundred per cent refined.' He indicated the workings of the briefcase. 'This baby will do the job, but it's still a bit hard on the brain. Something to do with the pitch of the vibrations it sends out.' He looked down at it rather fondly. 'Seems I've gotten used to the bastard. Doesn't say much for my ears, I suppose.'

He finished his beer, smacked his lips. 'Regards from Lieutenant McDonald, by the way. I'm certain he's sorry I pitched him out of his own wicket.'

'Another beer?'

'Only ever have one during the day,' Lillehammer said. 'Thanks just the same.'

'Just how British are you?' Croaker said, opening another bottle for himself.

Lillehammer laughed. 'Very, actually. But where I come from I've gotten so used to American idioms I sometimes find myself worrying that the English part of me has gotten snowed under. Out of the office, I'm afraid I have an alarming tendency to become a flaming Brit. It's what comes from being afflicted with an English mother and an American father.'

'And just where is your office?'

'I don't have one.'

'You don't?'

Lillehammer lifted a forefinger. 'If you have an office eventually everyone knows what it is you do. It took the CIA decades to work that one out.'

Croaker saw those X-ray eyes fixed on his left hand. He uncurled the

59

titanium and polycarbonate fingers. 'I imagine you're curious about this. Everyone is.'

Lillehammer nodded deferentially. 'If you wouldn't mind.'

'I've long ago gotten over being sensitive about it.' He laid open the artificial hand which a team of bio-mechanics and surgeons in Tokyo had grafted to what had been the stump of his left wrist.

It looked, more than anything, like a work of art: four finger-like appendages and an opposable thumb, articulated where human joints – or knuckles – would be. They had underpinnings of titanium and boron, were sheathed in matt-black polycarbonate, and were affixed to a stainless-steel and blued titanium hand: palm, back and wrist.

'I don't fully understand how it works,' Croaker said, 'but the main servos are somehow connected to my own nerves. The hand is also powered by a pair of special lithium batteries.'

Lillehammer bent over, examining the hand like an archeologist poring over an historic find. He said, 'Do you mind telling me what happened?'

Croaker suspected that he already knew, but said, 'I was in a pitched battle with one very smart bastard. He was a champion sumo and very strong. He was also an expert in kendo – do you know what that is? Japanese swordsmanship.'

Lillehammer nodded. 'I've been lucky enough to examine a number of *katana* close up.'

'Then you know just how sharp those swordblades can be. In the best of them, the very edge of the blade is so finely ground it virtually disappears. The sumo severed my hand with one of those.'

'And how well does this work?' Lillehammer said, tapping one of the long, articulated fingers.

Croaker made a fist, very slowly, then released the fingers back again, revealing the iridescent blue titanium palm. 'This is the second model – new and improved. The prototype was amazing enough, but this . . .'

He rose, went over to pick up one of the empty beer bottles. He held it in his right hand, pressed the tip of one articulated finger against the glass. There was a strange sound, like the tearing of thin fabric. The razor-sharp tip traced its way down the bottle, across the bottom, up the opposite side. A moment later, the bottle fell open in two equal halves.

'Remarkable combination of strength and delicacy,' Lillehammer observed.

Croaker came back, sat down. He pointed to the briefcase Lillehammer had brought aboard. 'What's that made of?'

'Dunno, really. Some space-age plastic tougher and lighter than steel.

But I can tell you it's bloody well indestructible. Couldn't get a bullet to dent it in the lab. Couldn't blow a hole in it with plastique, either.'

Croaker held up his hand for Lillehammer's inspection, carefully retracted the long fingers until they were only the equivalent of one knuckle in length. Then he leaned over, took one corner of the top of the case between his left thumb and attenuated forefinger in a pincer motion. He pressed inward.

Foomp!

His fingers clicked together through the small hole they had pierced in the material.

Lillehammer sat staring at what Croaker had done to his previously indestructible briefcase. 'I think I'll have that second beer now, thank you very much,' he said softly.

Lillehammer sat nursing his beer for the longest time. Croaker was aware of the sun moving across the cabin's cowling, the light changing as the wind shifted. Storm coming, he thought, scenting the phosphorous in the air. But we still have time. For what? He waited patiently for Lillehammer to tell him why he had come.

The chop had picked up, and the boat was bobbing quite a bit on its tether. Croaker felt distinctly unwell, and he got up abruptly, went out of the cabin. He bent over the rail on the opposite side of the boat where the young ensigns still stood watch, and vomited over the side.

'Sorry about that,' Lillehammer said when he returned. 'I'm afraid those pills haven't quite been perfected yet, either.'

'Do me a favor and next time keep that shit to yourself,' Croaker said, and rinsed his mouth out with beer. 'I'd rather deal with the slight headache.'

'I quite understand. My apologies.'

'*De nada,*' Croaker said.

Lillehammer put down his beer, came close to him and said quietly, 'Does the name Dominic Goldoni mean anything to you?'

'Sure. Mob boss, sang his brains out so that the Feds took out two of his leading rivals, lock, stock and barrel. For that, they didn't fry him. They put him into WITSEC. From which sanctuary, so I have heard, he's been running his entire East Coast machine through his brother-in-law, the respected attorney Anthony DeCamillo, also known as Tony D., among his friends. I also hear that Goldoni's remaining chief rival, the Clam Man –'

'You mean Caesare Leonforte.'

'That's right. Bad Clams, they call him. Anyway, I understand that the Clam Man is thinking of taking fate by the throat, making the move he's been itching to make on Goldoni's territory.'

Lillehammer nodded. 'Commendable. You have details not known to the general public. However, the connection between Goldoni and Anthony DeCamillo, a well-renowned legit lawyer, cannot in any way be proved. I know. WITSEC has tried.' He squinted at Croaker, the effect of which was to further intensify the focus of his extraordinary eyes. 'I see you have kept up your contacts.'

'Some of them,' Croaker said. 'Others, I can no longer afford.'

Lillehammer made that awful smile again. 'I fancy your humor, Mr Croaker. Dry and distinct, like a fine wine.'

'But not half as complex,' Croaker said, giving in to the man's nuttiness.

Lillehammer's smile broadened, and now Croaker could see the tiny crosshatch lines of the stitching on the pale scars. It had been a hurried job, perhaps in a red zone somewhere far away from the high-tech civilization that had provided Croaker with his remarkable prosthesis. But the fact that the scars were on *both* sides of Lillehammer's mouth ruled out an accident or a wound taken in the pursuit of a clandestine enemy. Rather, they seemed the deliberate hallmark of the torturer – there was a sadism implicit in what the incisions had tried to do as well as explicit in the scars themselves.

'I wouldn't talk, so they tried to make my silence permanent,' Lillehammer said as if reading Croaker's mind. Of course, that wasn't true; he had merely seen the direction of Croaker's scrutiny. 'I suppose they could have slit my throat and been done with it but that was not their way. I had frustrated them, and they wanted me to live with what they would do to me. They tried to sever the muscles that worked my lips. As it happened, they failed. I count myself fortunate.'

Croaker was about to ask him who *they* were, when he realized it really didn't matter. And perhaps in his day he had encountered as many of *them* as had Lillehammer. It appeared as if he and this Brit might have a great deal in common.

Lillehammer fingered his upper lip. 'Pity I can't grow a mustache. Whatever they did to me killed the hair follicles here.'

He shrugged. 'Well.' He rubbed his hands together briskly. 'We'd better get down to it. The wind's swung round and is picking up. As it is we'll have a bumpy ride home.' He peered through one of the cabin windows, where the brace of sailboats had turned and were running for the shelter of Marco Island. No other boats seemed to be around. 'Back to Dominic Goldoni. Your intelligence is spot on, as far as it goes. Fact is, yesterday, Goldoni inexplicably and overtly broke his covenant with the Federal Government of the United States.'

'What did he do?'

'He got himself killed, is what he did,' Lillehammer said.

'Dominic Goldoni dead,' Croaker mused almost to himself. 'Seems impossible.'

'Not only got himself killed,' Lillehammer continued, 'but did so in a manner that has got the best people at WITSEC totally freaked out.'

'Can you tell me why?'

'Well, now, that depends,' Lillehammer said, 'on whether you agree to work with me on this.'

Croaker thought a moment. 'Why the hell would you want me? You're obviously a Fed very high up in the bureaucratic organization. You've got zillions of candidates to choose from who are younger, trained in the latest techniques.' He swept his right hand toward the anti-surveillance case. 'I mean, I had no idea that kind of hardware existed.'

Lillehammer shook his head. 'Don't give me the old warhorse routine, it won't hold with me. I found your name in our computers. You worked with Nicholas Linnear some years ago when he was recruited by C. Gordon Minck, who was then head of Red Station, our Soviet Affairs bureau. You and Linnear ferreted out a very nasty mole in Minck's henhouse.' He frowned. 'The truth is I can't trust anyone back home, not until I've discovered how someone got to Dominic Goldoni, a man supposedly tucked away from all harm.

'Frankly, I need help,' Lillehammer said. 'Goldoni had strict orders not to call anyone from his house where the line could be tapped at the other end, and never to meet with someone without his WITSEC handler's knowledge. So how did this happen? WITSEC's record of protecting its inductees who obeyed the rules was, until this incident, absolute.'

'So somebody got to him some way.'

Lillehammer looked away for a long moment. Then his head came back and his piercing blue eyes fixed on Croaker's face. 'The way I see it, someone inside, someone he trusted, betrayed him. I'm telling you his security was one hundred per cent as long as he didn't break the WITSEC rules.'

Croaker turned the problem around in his mind a while before he said, 'It's clear you need help, but I doubt it's from me. I'm a maverick. I never was much good at memorizing the rule book. I go my own way.'

Lillehammer looked him square in the face. 'Just answer this question: are you intrigued enough to be my field man – or would you rather continue your quiet existence chauffeuring beer-guzzling businessmen around this pond?'

Croaker laughed. 'You *do* have a way with words, Mr Lillehammer.'

'Call me Will.'

Croaker looked down at the extended right hand before taking it in his and squeezing it. 'Why do I feel like Ishmael about to sign on the *Pequod?*'

Lillehammer let out a heartfelt belly-laugh, and this time his grotesque scars disappeared in the folds of his tanned face. 'I'm going to enjoy our association, Lew. May I call you Lew? It will be for the last time, because our operation names have been set for all non-secure communication – which, under the circumstances, means *everything*. Ishmael, meet Ahab. We're going to make one crackerjack team!'

But when the Coast Guard cutter had taken the mysterious Ahab away, Croaker remained at sea, waiting for the sun to go down and wondering what the hell he was doing getting involved with the Feds again. He had a week's charter beginning tomorrow morning with Maracay, the Venezuelan magnate who Croaker entertained three or four times a year. Maracay had made his enormous fortune from the land, dragging iron and diamonds from it in profusion. He was a gregarious man of immense appetites, an excellent fisherman, a big spender, and a generous tipper. Not to mention the harem of eager young women he brought with him that he was more than willing to share.

Croaker felt the sun on his back as he bent over the side of *Captain Sumo*. He spotted some flotsam riding at the waterline and, fetching a boat-hook, pulled it away from the hull. Maybe the boat needed a good scraping.

Right, he told himself. *Think about everything but Alix.* Maybe Lillehammer's offer had been the catalyst but he felt a sick, hollow sensation inside him as keenly as if he had not eaten in days. The truth was he missed Alix. And he resented her leaving him here, marooned on a diet of seawater and booze while she jetted off to her glamorous former life in the glittering capitals of the Western world. What other choice had he had? But now . . .

He could see her face, burnished by the flamboyant Florida sunset as they stood just outside the Miami International airport terminal. Neither of them had wanted to say goodbye.

What exactly do you think you're doing here? she had said softly. *You don't even like this life any more.*

He had vehemently denied it, but she was right, of course. Thinking now about Maracay and his floating whorehouse, Croaker understood what she had been trying to tell him. He had come here because he had seen one too many corpses, had ventured down one too many mean streets. He had smelled the stink of corruption, power, inhumanity all around him and he had been sick unto death. So he had dropped out, migrated south . . . only to find another kind of death.

He loved Alix but what could he do, marry her and take her away from

64

the life she loved, or marry her and endure the long separations her work would demand of them? Neither was a tolerable solution so he had let her go and had remained here among the sea grape and the decaying palms.

He turned the boat-hook, watched the flotsam disentangle itself, purl away, a dark stain upon the sunlit water. *If I stay here a day longer*, he thought, *I'll feel as useless as that piece of flotsam.*

He put the boat-hook away, climbed into the cabin and pulled up anchor. Then he throttled up and, turning about, headed back to Marco Island. His blood had begun to sing. It felt good to have a purpose again, to be caught up in mystery and intrigue, to have a murder to solve.

To hell with babysitting the rich and spoiled, he thought. *Time to get back into life.*

Beneath the bloated red sun of a late autumn afternoon, Venice lay domed and crowned in a shimmering pool of green and gold.

Nicholas had never been to Venice before, and he was unsure what to expect. It was a rotting city, sinking like Atlantis into the lagoons that surrounded it like the sheltering arms of the ancient earth mother. The putrefaction of centuries clung to the stuccoed walls of its *palazzi*, perfumed the air, and within the dense, dank maze of the city one lost all sense of direction.

These dark and disturbing reflections Nicholas had heard from people who had come, seen, and departed unmoved and vowing in the unrelenting crowds and the stifling heat of summer never to return.

How unfortunate these people were. This was his first thought, instinctive and unbidden, as he rode a spotless *motoscafo* across the lagoon toward a city that seemed to rest not on bedrock and silt but on nothing less ephemeral than dreams.

He rode up top with the captain, and he was obliged to draw closed his padded whiskey-colored suede jacket against the stiff, chilly breeze. As the launch plied its way at high speed across the gunmetal water, the city appeared to create itself out of seawater and cloud, rising from a low, nacreous mist which swam in amorphous schools across the water.

Above, the vast bowl of the sky, a breathtaking blue so lucid it seemed infinite, reflected at its lowest reaches the splendid golden domes and umber towers that seemed to have been magically preserved from the time of the Arabian Nights.

The vibration of the *motoscafo*'s powerful engine changed, deepening to a liquid gurgle as the craft hit the outer limits of the inner lagoon and, taking a long, sweeping curve along the high wooden poles that served as channel markers as they had for centuries, commenced a slow, almost ritualistic final approach through the belly of the city into the Grand Canal.

Now, they swung round the point of the San Georgio Maggiore and dead ahead he was greeted by the sight of the Basilica Santa Maria della Salute, pale and magnificent, over which the oblate sun, ruddy as dried blood, was slowly settling like a great winged steed whose day of racing was done.

Nicholas felt the small hairs at the back of his neck stir, and he was electrified by an image of himself, striding across a cobblestone piazzetta. He was dressed in high black leather boots, long black cloak and a kind of mask which covered his face from his nose to his hairline. On his head he wore a stiff felt tricornered hat. Far above him, flags he could not recognize cracked and fluttered, and he knew without understanding that it was a time of war. He had the distinct sensation that he was coming home.

He blinked, as if having been blinded by the huge autumn sun. The *motoscafo* had turned again, and he was now face to face with the Piazzetta di San Marco, with the Doge's Palace on the right. To his left rose the statues of the magisterial Venetian winged lion and of Saint Theodore, the patron saint of Venice. His sensation of déjà vu was so strong that for a moment he staggered, and he grabbed the cowling of the mahogany and brass hatch cover in order to keep himself from stumbling down the companionway. This was the piazzetta in his vision, and though he knew that it had been of a time long gone, still the unmistakable scent of war was in the air.

Il Palazzo di Maschere Veneziane was approximately midway between the Punta della Dogana, where the Basilica Santa Maria della Salute rose in burnished splendor, and the Campo della Carità, where sat the Galleria dell'Accademia at the far end of the fairy-tale confection of its wooden bridge.

Once, the hotel had been an ornate summer palazzo for the ruling Doge. Its spot overlooking the Grand Canal was impeccable: on the Rio di San Maurizio, a *canale* itself, of course, but as Nicholas was to learn in Venice only the Grand Canal bore that designation. Also, the grand structures commonly called *palazzi* were, in fact, *case*. During the age of the Serene Republic only the Ducal residence could technically be called a palazzo.

The hotel had its own private dock, and its green-and-gold-uniformed porters were on hand to greet him, take his bags and lead him past the tables of the hotel's open-air restaurant being set for dinner.

Inside, the public rooms were sumptuously decorated in the florid style of old Venice with arching, beamed ceilings, sconced walls covered with opulent moire silks, and lush color everywhere – the wholly Venetian shades of blue, green, yellow and burnt orange. And always rococo gilt edging on furniture, picture frames, massive clocks, Murano candelabra and chandeliers weeping pear-shaped tears of blown glass.

Nicholas was checked in with great formality, almost as if he were an old guest returning for a special occasion. An enormous mask hung above the burnished burlwood counter. It was painted a glossy white, with a protruding nose and a wide, aggressive upper lip. Nicholas, curious, asked the concierge the nature of the mask.

'Ah, *signore*, Venice is a city of masks – or at least it once was in centuries past. The name of this hotel – Il Palazzo di Maschere Veneziane – means the Palace of the Venetian Mask. The particular Doge who built this palazzo and summered here was a rather mischievous fellow, prone to donning his Bauta to go among the common folk and perpetrate – well, all manner of, er, indelicate activity.' The concierge stroked his upper lip. 'In this disguise I believe the Doge fathered any number of illegitimate children, and consummated many a nefarious political arrangement.' He pointed upward to the oversized mask. 'This is the Bauta – the mask known as the great leveler because it was used by many a powerful Doge, judge or prince to conceal his identity. As The Common Man he roamed the *calli* and *rii* of the city in perfect secrecy.'

'And no one ever knew who he really was?'

'No one, *signore*,' the concierge assured him. 'Venezia keeps its secrets.'

Nicholas's second-floor room was huge. The porter put down his bags and, crossing the Persian carpet, flung open the twelve-foot wooden shutters to let in the sounds, smells and, most significant of all, the light from the Grand Canal.

Bathed in the aqueous illumination of this city, marooned for all time in the geographical twilight between the shore and the sea, the ornately furnished room appeared just as it might have three hundred years ago when the Doges ruled and the songs of the East perfumed their *campi* and gardens with enchantment.

Left alone, Nicholas went into the marbled bathroom to shower away the dry grit of travel. He shaved before a gilt mirror, watching the subtle transformation of his face as the stubble came off, and he was reminded again of Seiko's words, *You will be different – so different that no one will recognize you.*

He splashed cold water on his face and, with a towel in his hands, returned to the room. He stood at the open window, watching night stretch its long fingers across the Grand Canal. To his left, the Santa Maria della Salute was powder-white in the tungsten lights and, below and to his right, across the water further down, four gondolas, painted blue, green, black and red, bobbed at a deserted *imbarcadero*. Their high, arching prows, six-pronged to represent the city's *Sestieri*, its districts, seemed to Nicholas in that velvet light to be musical instruments that gave off melody and harmonies as beautiful as they were ancient.

Wiping his face dry, he turned away from the scene to find a large cardboard box on the king-sized bed. He went to it, certain that it hadn't been there when the porter had shown him in. He called down to the front desk, was assured that no package for him had been delivered to the hotel.

He opened the box and, peering into it, stood as still as a statue. He felt, again, the small hairs stirring at the base of his neck and a thin line of sweat snaked its way along his spine.

Reaching into the box, he drew out the long black cloak of his vision. Beneath it was a mask, hand-made of papier-mâché. Like the Bauta over the concierge's desk downstairs, it was painted a glossy white, had a prominent nose and even more aggressive upper lip line which defined its lower edge, so that there was something vaguely apelike about its overall appearance. It was the mask that secured the identity of the high-born.

At the bottom of the box was a sea-green envelope bordered in gilt. He opened this, slid out a single sheet of stiff paper. On it was beautifully written one sentence in large, back-sloping script:

'Your presence is requested, cloaked and masked, at thirty minutes past ten o'clock p.m. at Campiello di San Belisario.'

Nicholas looked at his watch. It was fifteen minutes to seven, not yet time for dinner. He dropped his bizarre costume, dressed and opened up the briefcase Seiko had handed him at the airport. He had deliberately ignored it during his flight; he had not been in any mood then to look at work.

He settled himself into an overstuffed chair and, with the hydrous light from outside mixing with the room's lamplight, began to read the latest coded report from Vinnie Tinh. Tinh had been born and raised in Vietnam, though he had emigrated to Australia for his college and post-graduate years. He was an expert in international business law, and had even spent a year in the trading pits of Wall Street, researching his thesis.

Nicholas had spent a good deal of time with Tinh, both in Tokyo and Saigon, and had found him to be bright and clever, two assets not often found in the same person. There was also a devious streak to him. Though Nicholas had come to understand that this somewhat dubious talent was necessary in order to be successful in Southeast Asia, he was nevertheless convinced that Tinh bore watching. In fact, this was one of his reasons for scheduling the now postponed trip to Saigon.

Nicholas skimmed over the summary of Sato International's projected grosses and nets for the coming quarter, the rising success rate of the on-going training program for potential employees, and the continuing problems in getting enough petroleum products at a reasonable cost. The Japanese were buying almost ninety per cent of Vietnam's crude oil, so it seemed ludicrous that it should be so difficult to obtain petroleum products within the country. He scrutinized Tinh's assessment of the political regime and the current business climate. Most importantly, he read Tinh's updates on his political and business contacts. Among the wealth of fascinating information, one bit of unfocused data stood out. According to Tinh, there was a spate of recent rumors – none of which he could confirm – of the establishment of a kind of shadow government, wholly independent from the Vietnamese Government. What this shadow network meant or what it proposed to do Tinh could not say, only that it was said that its power and influence was growing every day. Tinh proposed finding out more about it before any of their competition could possibly exploit it.

He made a mental note to fax Tinh not to waste his time. It was preposterous, he thought. Saigon was filled to overflowing with rumors of this sort. Anyway, who would support such a regime? How could it come into being and how could it possibly be maintained? If it was becoming more and more powerful, who was funding it?

These were questions that would have troubled Nicholas had he believed in Tinh's smoke. If Vietnam were to abruptly destabilize again, the hundreds of millions of dollars that Sato International had invested in the country would be in dire jeopardy. In any event, it appeared as if Tinh had been out on the edge of the jungle too long and was in urgent need of direction from civilization. Making notes in the margins of the report, Nicholas resolved to get to Saigon as soon as he was able.

By the time he went down to the hotel restaurant for dinner he was hungry. He sat inside the deep blue room, staring out the windows at the *vaporetti* putt-putting past, their running lights winking and darting like fantastic fireflies. Gondolas glided by, carrying Japanese and German tourists festooned with cameras and colored souvenirs from Murano.

He dined on *spaghetti con vongole*, a magnificent pasta dish with tiny, delicate clams whose briny essence exploded in his mouth like caviar, and *seppia in teca*, squid steamed in its own ink. He let the captain suggest the wine, a Prosecca, but was loath to drink more than a glass and a half. He declined the dessert tray, settling for a double espresso instead. By the time he signed the check it was almost ten and, remembering the address on the note, he asked the concierge for directions to his rendezvous.

He was given a small, folding map of the city on which the concierge circled with a pen the location of the hotel and traced several alternative routes to the Campiello di San Belisario.

'The best way is, of course, to walk,' the concierge said in the best Venetian tradition. 'It is not the quickest way but certainly the most beautiful. Have you the time for a twenty-minute stroll?'

Nicholas said he thought he did, an answer that pleased the concierge. '*Bene*. Each hour of the day or night brings its own particular eminence to La Serenissima, *signore*,' he said with a wide smile.

Upstairs in his room, Nicholas tried calling Justine again, but there was no answer. Where could she be? It was two in the morning in Tokyo. He cradled the receiver, pulled on a thick sweater, then, feeling vaguely foolish, wrapped the long, dark cloak across his shoulders. The mask he took up in his hands and, tucking it beneath one arm, went out the door.

The unique intonation of the city swept over him, a kind of language composed of small sounds – really a peculiar combination of noise and echoes thrown back by the narrow streets and the houses built up against the *rii*. The sounds of footsteps, for instance, took on otherworldly tones; the vigorous slap-slap of leather striking stone and paving hovered in the cool night air like ghosts.

He would pass a late-night bar and hear a quick burst of laughter, a snatch of conversation that would follow him down an alley or across one of the innumerable tiny bridges. And always there arose like a dream the faint susurrus of the water lapping against the wooden pilings of a *traghetto*, where, invariably, a gondola was moored; or against the moss-covered stone foundations of the houses themselves.

Once, he turned a corner and came upon a *rio* filled with gondolas. An old man in a black suit, who stood at the rear of one of the fleet, had commenced a song, his pure tenor voice ringing off the stones' façades as his gondola passed beneath the bridge where Nicholas stood, entranced.

He passed a small palazzo within which was a postage-stamp-sized *corte* where bougainvillea bloomed in long, opulent crescents and a fig tree rose, gnarled and twisted, the last of its lush foliage bronzed by the street and *rio* lights. He could see a wrought-iron bench, patinaed with age, and could imagine Casanova on one knee, seducing the young woman who sat upon it, staring up at the night sky.

Nicholas, trained to *sink in*, to feel the cross-currents of places and of people, was beginning to find his way toward the metaphysical enigma of Venice as he made his way to his rendezvous with Mikio Okami. This, then, was the secret of Venice: its unique locus in the world, situated neither on land nor on the sea, had imbued it not only with otherworldly sounds and light, but with the ability to immunize itself against the ravages of time.

70

No cars, buses, trains or subways had insinuated themselves into this magical place. People traveled within its breast now as they had done for centuries. Buildings were restored in the traditional Venetian style using the same techniques craftsmen had employed for centuries. Nicholas walked down *calli*, *callesse*, over *ponti* of stone, black metal and wood, along *fondamenta* that fronted *rii* that had remained constant for hundreds of years. If he had been alive in the 1600s, his views would have been fundamentally the same.

And as he walked, Venice took him up in its arms, enfolded him lovingly, bound him to it as it had done to so many travelers in their time. He lost himself not so much in its maze of streets, *rii*, bridges and quays, but in its sorcerous heart, feeling time slip away like an old, withered skin, experiencing the bracing and ultimately exhilarating gift that the city brings to those willing to accept it: a renewal to the bone-weary, a reaffirmation of life to the sick at heart.

And so his frustration and anxiety over his relationship with Justine dissipated; he saw his displaced anger at her for losing two of their children for what it was; he forgot about his last vertiginous encounter with Seiko. Miraculously, he even found himself calmer about his imminent meeting with Mikio Okami.

This enchanted mood stayed with him as he entered the Campiello di San Belisario. It was a small square, cobbled and clean, but with no adornments whatsoever: no trees, fountains, benches or the like. Just as in most Venetian campiellos, the earth-colored buildings stood on three sides and, on the fourth, rose the imposing white façade of a church. This one, Nicholas saw as he approached it, bore the same name as that of the small square. He had never heard of Saint Belisario but, it seemed, the Italians and, especially, the Venetians venerated a plethora of otherwise unknown holy men and women.

The campiello was deserted. He strained his ears and heard the echoes of footfalls, fading. Pigeons rattled briefly in the eaves of a building, settling themselves for the night and, far away, he heard the drone of a *motoscafo* plying the water of some unseen but not unheard *rio*. Mist crept along the cobbles, hanging at the foundations of buildings like a mendicant.

Nicholas waited, the Venetian night, unlike all others, settling upon him like a second cloak. All at once he remembered the Bauta and, taking it from beneath his arm where he had rather self-consciously kept it during his walk, he slipped it over his head so that it settled upon his face. The sensation was at once singular and oddly familiar, and he recalled his vision as he had passed the Piazzetta di San Marco earlier that evening. Again, he was aware of an acute sense of déjà vu. *Who was I*, he wondered, *to have called this home?*

'Bauta!'

He swung round to see a figure in priestly attire holding open a small door to one side of the Chiesa San Belisario's main bronze-doored entrance.

'Bauta!' the priest called in an odd, throaty voice. 'You are late for Mass!' He gestured urgently. 'Come! Come!'

Nicholas mounted the worn stone stairs, past the cloaked and hooded priest, into the dank interior of the church. He heard the sharp clang of the door as the priest shut it behind him.

The atmosphere of the interior was infused with a plethora of scents: incense, candle wax, mildew, stone and marble dust, and age.

The priest scurried past Nicholas. 'This way!' he said under his breath. 'Follow me!'

The church was dimly lit. Only flickering flames from a profusion of thick, pale-yellow candles intermittently illuminated vaulted ceilings, frescoed walls, magnificent tiled floors in the intricate Byzantine style, gold-encrusted religious icons. The interior was a treasure trove of historical relics and religious art. A ceiling of blackened wooden beams gave way to an elegant, high ogival arcade encrusted with mosaic scenes from the Bible. But there was an almost Eastern undertone, too, which permeated the dense atmosphere with the pungency of star anise.

Somewhere Nicholas heard the murmur of voices, the call and response of the solemn liturgical rite. Improbable as it seemed, Mass was being performed this late at night.

'This is a very old church,' the priest whispered as they hurried down stone passageways. The odd, parchment-dry voice carried no intimation of age or, even, of gender. It was, rather, a voice wholly of intent, stripped of any ornamentation or color. 'Some say it is the oldest religious structure in Venice. Certainly there is evidence in the foundation and elsewhere that it was once a Greek temple.' The voices of the Mass were fading, only echoes of echoes now. 'But before the Greeks, who knows? The Scythians, yes, and perhaps the Cycladeans, giants who roamed the earth at the time of the Phoenicians and, before them, gods now long forgotten by even the oldest living Venetians.'

Nicholas was surprised. This did not sound like the philosophy dispensed by any priest he had ever encountered or read about. He was about to ask the man about his peculiar theories when they stopped at the arched entrance to a small but impressive space.

'The *schola cantorum*,' the priest whispered, as if this explained everything. A moment later, he had scurried away into the bending and twisting shadows dancing at the edge of the candlelight. That uncertain illumination made elemental cave paintings along the curving stone walls.

Nicholas walked into the room, which was all of stone. He went over, ran his hands over the rough-hewn surface. He was certain that this stone predated that of the exterior of the church – or even of that part of the interior lavished with the labors of Byzantine craftsmen. Could this be part of the original Greek temple? The age of this spot! He looked upward, saw that the ceiling was groined in a pair of unusual arches set at right angles to one another.

'This is where the sacred choir sang,' a melodious voice said. 'So many centuries ago.'

Nicholas turned to see a tall woman in a black mask that shone like a dark sun. She was dressed in the cloak of a priest or perhaps a monk; in any case, an ecclesiastical habit that hid her clothing as well as her body.

'The *schola cantorum*,' she said. 'This room was constructed to maximize the beauty of the human voice. It was, in those days long ago, the center of the nave . . . the very heart of the church.'

'And now it is relegated to the back,' Nicholas said. 'Tucked far away from the everyday liturgies of the modern church.'

'But no less awesome for that,' she said. Then a smile broke over her generous mouth. Her deep-set eyes flashed, and it seemed as if the entire interior, ancient and esoteric, was held in their depths. 'Forgive me, my name is Celeste.'

'And you know mine,' Nicholas said, 'that is, if you can be certain of who I am behind the Bauta.'

Celeste laughed, the sound picked up by the extraordinary acoustics of the ceiling, thrown back at them in segments like a Gregorian chant. 'Yes, I know who you are.'

'Where is –' But he stopped at Celeste's signal, a long, delicate forefinger pressed against her lips.

'Please – do not mention his name even here in the sanctity of the *schola cantorum*.' She came toward him, the rustling of her ecclesiastical cloak amplified until it sounded like the murmur of a field of insects on a hot summer's night. As she crossed a patch of candlelight he saw that she wore a silk turban on her head. It was the color of the Venetian sky in the moment after sunset, and was draped with crescents of white and black pearls. Pale green stones hung from its perimeter, and an intricately worked gold medallion was affixed to the front, from which a long black ostrich feather rose.

'So you know of the mask I chose for you to wear?'

73

'The Bauta. Yes, a little.'

'I am wearing the Domino,' she said softly. 'Actually, the name is taken from the Latin *benedicamus Domino*, Bless the Lord, a priestly banality.'

'You were the priest who led me here,' Nicholas said with sudden insight.

'I was,' Celeste said. 'I needed to be certain that you were not followed here.'

'Who would follow me?'

Celeste did not answer him directly. Instead, she said, 'Do you know what tonight is?'

'The end of October, the beginning of November. With the time change I can no longer remember if we have moved from one to the other.'

'It is All Hallows Eve,' Celeste whispered. 'The one night, other than during Carnival, when masks once again become the norm. It was important we meet this night. The masks protect us, as they once did our ancestors.'

'Yours, perhaps,' Nicholas said. 'I don't think any of mine came from Venice.'

Celeste's lips produced a peculiar smile. 'Welcome to Serenissima,' she said in her husky whisper. 'The Serene Republic.'

Where have I seen that smile before? Nicholas asked himself. 'Isn't it time we were leaving?' he said. 'My summons here seemed quite urgent.'

'It was,' Celeste said, 'and the reasons for the urgency are ever more apparent. But, even so, caution has dictated our itinerary for the evening.' She slid her arm through his, and he caught a whiff of a scent, both musky and spicy, wholly unfamiliar to him. 'I trust you won't find my company entirely disagreeable.'

She took him out of the church through a back entrance that let them out beneath the arch of a stone bridge. It was very dark, the somber water lapping gently against stone, green and crusty with algae and barnacles. Only the reflection of lights came to them where Nicholas stood in a semi-crouch while Celeste locked the ancient wood and iron door behind them.

'This is a wondrous spot,' Celeste said, turning to him. 'In the year 535, the Byzantine Emperor Justinian sent his armies across the sea to Italy to retake what had once been part of his empire before Theodoric wrested it from Byzantium's control. At the head of this host was the brilliant general, Belisarius.' Nicholas could just make out the ghost of a smile curling her lips. 'It seems ironic now that this ancient church should be dedicated to someone named Saint Belisario.'

'Surely you're not saying that the two are the same?' Nicholas said.

'It's impossible that a Byzantine army general could become a Christian saint.'

'This is Venezia,' Celeste told him. 'If you read its history you know that here nothing is impossible.' She took his hand, led him out from beneath the bridge. On a small, private *traghetto*, a deep green and gold gondola awaited them like a steed. Celeste bade Nicholas climb in and, when he was settled, came aboard. She cast off, then took up the long pole, began to steer them out into the *rio*. Hooded and cloaked, she seemed an illustration out of some historical account of Venice.

'Venice was created as a kind of Shangri-La, a haven from the waves of barbarians – Goths, Huns and the like – who periodically ravaged Italy,' Celeste said. 'However, as Homer reminds us, Venice was not founded by those folk indigenous to Western Europe, but rather by the peoples of the far eastern Mediterranean. Whether these were the remnants of those who fell at the sack of Troy, as Homer apparently believed, or whether they were of an even more ancient sea-going people, the Phoenicians, the fact remains that Venice was established because of its natural defenses of malarial salt marshes, quicksand banks and treacherous shoals whose contours were constantly recreated by the tides.'

Her voice drifted over the *rio* like the wispy fog that lay in strands across the water. Nicholas absorbed this fascinating history as he took in the passage of houses with ornate wrought-iron balconies, tiny, romantic gardens with surprising bursts of color, and deep, curving Oriental arches and windows that forever spoke of the manner in which the city's ancestors had chosen to remember their own origins.

'Whatever the case,' Celeste went on, 'the founders of Serenissima were intellectuals on the run from war, rape, pestilence – from annihilation itself. And here they plied their chimerical arts – and their labyrinthine forms of intrigue. Here, the golden politics practiced by the Greeks became collusive, then quickly gave way to bitter internecine vendettas.'

'Which is where the masks came in,' Nicholas said.

'Yes.' Celeste poled them into a *traghetto*, waited patiently while a late-night *motoscafo* purred its way past them. 'The masks were pure illusion for purpose. What purposes? Well, in politics they were used by those who came before the State Inquisitors to confess confidences. In the personal lives of those ancient Venetians, they allowed anyone and everyone, from high-born prince to lowly fishmonger, the freedom to pursue their amorous heart's desire.' Celeste leaned on her pole. 'These are historical perspectives, but what was the reality? Considering human nature, the masks fostered corruption at every level of Venetian society.'

The launch had disappeared into the low-lying mist, and she pushed

75

them away from the tiny landing.

'These masks, the Bauta, the Domino, the Gagna, the Primo Zanni, the Plague Doctor, are not figures from the Commedia dell'arte, as is often thought. They are characters of a wholly Venetian construct and they all have their origins in political paradigm rather than in the Commedia's theatrical stereotypes.'

They passed a gondola, with purple velvet seats and gold-painted hand-rails. A man wrapped in a mohair blanket slept with his head in the lap of his daughter, a dark-haired girl of no more than ten, who smiled at them as her hand stroked the crown of his head.

When they were alone again on the *rio*, Celeste continued. 'The masks became the symbol of all things Venetian – the profound mysteries hidden behind the fabulous fairy-tale façades clustered in profusion throughout the city. Think of Venice as a magnificent shellfish that contains within its shell a prize of inestimable worth.'

'Have you lived here all your life?'

'Sometimes it seems so,' Celeste said somewhat enigmatically. 'In any event, I was born here, which is all that matters.'

They had turned onto the Grand Canal, and ahead of them on the right Nicholas could see the imposing structure of the Accademia. Celeste steered the gondola to the right, gliding silently over the glittering water. There were only the tiniest sounds: lappings and creakings and, even, the soft puffs of her breath as she rhythmically worked the pole into the thick muck of the *rio* bottom. Out of all of this arose a kind of melody, ethereal and enthralling, played on an instrument of the imagination.

At length, they glided into a rather ornate *traghetto* where two other gondola were tied up. Nicholas felt a start of recognition go through him; these were the gondolas he had seen from his hotel window! Tonight, he had made a long circuit to end up almost back where he had started from.

The gondola bumped gently against the ancient wooden poles. These were striped gold and green. Nicholas jumped out of the gondola, caught the ropes as Celeste threw them, tied up the slender boat.

The palazzo they entered was painted in the Venetian style, sea-green and an earthy ocher-yellow. Oriental filigree edged the double-curved arches toward which they strode. Past the forbidding sea-gates, Nicholas found himself in a courtyard garden much as the one he had glimpsed on his walk to the campiello. Bougainvillea and climbing roses perfumed the air even this late in the year, and a massive pear tree overhung the stucco walls in almost every direction.

Inside, Nicholas saw a gleaming teak and stainless-steel *motoscafo* set on a low scaffold of raw two-by-fours. Typical of such *palazzi*, the floor was a worn and cracked checkerboard of red Cattraran marble and white Istrian stone, used because water intensified their colors. They went up a wide set of stone stairs onto what Europeans called the first floor, the *piano nobile*. The downstairs was deliberately unreconstructed, Celeste explained, because high tides often caused flooding, and the *rio*-level floors were useful now only as garages for private motor launches.

Upstairs, the rooms were sumptuous, sensual. The ceilings were composed of Indonesian teak, stained dark by centuries of smoke; the walls were painted the original Venetian ultramarine, highly costly because the pigment was composed of ground lapis lazuli or inlaid with Byzantine mosaics of dusty colors and swirling patterns. The floors were covered with worn Persian carpets of fine wool and silk, and statuary of carved porphyry and veined Oriental marble, plundered perhaps from ancient Constantinople, were placed in prominent positions.

Oversized pillows in jewel-toned raw silk were strewn in areas where normally chairs and sofas would have been placed. At the far end of the living-room was a short flight of marble steps up to a sitting area filled with more sumptuous pillows against a wall filled with double-arched windows overlooking the *rio*. Fairy lights winked and bobbed through the glass, entering the room along with the amorphous reflections from the sheened water.

Everything, down to the silver matchbox on the marble table, the flowers in the gem-like Murano glass bowls, seemed to have its precise place and relation to everything else, as if the person who inhabited this domain had a highly developed mathematical mind.

As they entered, Nicholas made out a dim figure sitting on the window ledge up in the sitting area.

'Mikio Okami,' Celeste whispered before she slipped from his side, disappearing behind an incised teak door.

'Celeste, wait –!'

'So you have come.'

Nicholas turned at the sound of the voice. For all his age, Mikio Okami still had the power of command. Taking off his mask, Nicholas crossed the room, went up the marble stairs.

Before him stood Mikio Okami, Colonel Denis Linnear's old and valued friend and compatriot. Or had he merely been such out of expediency? In the aftermath of the war, the Occupation created its own turbulence. Those had been extraordinary times, and now and again, extraordinary measures were required to deal with them. Nicholas found himself staring into the face of one of those extraordinary measures.

'You look so much like your father!'

Okami, a bald, bullet-headed man, had the round, jovial face of a benevolent dictator. He had eyes too close together, a rather severe nose and a mouth always on the verge of a smile. His ears were tiny, close to his head, and there was a dark mole on one side of his chin. He was of medium height, but seemed somehow shrunken within the Savile Row suit he wore. He was old, yes, but in the way of the Oriental: his skin had yellowed, like the patina on parchment, and seemed to have grown thin, so translucent that the blue veins in his temples showed clearly.

'In a strange way, it is like meeting him again.'

He extended a hand in a Western greeting and Nicholas shook it.

'It is good of you to come, Linnear-san,' he said in Japanese. 'I imagine my summons came as something of a shock to you. I trust it has not proved overly intrusive.'

'Not at all,' Nicholas said. 'I was in need of a vacation, in any case.'

Okami's lips held that strange demi-smile. He ducked his head once, his only passing reference to traditional Japanese custom. 'And have you enjoyed cloaking yourself as the magistrates and princelings of old Venezia used to do?'

'I had no trouble imagining myself as Casanova.'

Okami gave him a cool, appraising look, then said abruptly, 'May I offer you a drink to warm you? Sambucca? Napoleon brandy? Or perhaps an espresso.'

'An espresso would be perfect.'

'Excellent. I believe I'll join you.'

Okami went to a sideboard where bottles of liquors and aperitifs surrounded a gleaming stainless-steel espresso machine. He seemed to take great pleasure in making the coffee himself. His small, bony hands worked deftly at their tasks and, though he must have been over eighty, Nicholas could detect no unsteadiness in those fingers.

Okami brought over two tiny cups, complete with a small twist of lemon rind floating in the dark depths. They sat on the cushions, while diamond-shaped sprays of reflected light from the canal played over their faces.

'I do so enjoy my espresso,' Okami said after he had taken a first sip. Then, abruptly, he laughed. 'I suppose you were expecting green tea and *tatami* mats.'

'As a matter of fact I make it a habit never to expect anything,' Nicholas said. 'It makes for clear thought and pure reaction.'

'Instinct, eh?' Okami nodded. 'It may be that everything I've heard about you is true.'

Nicholas said nothing, sat cross-legged sipping the excellent Italian coffee that this Yakuza had learned to make. From outside came the chug of a delivery boat, perhaps even putting in perishables for the larder of his own hotel's kitchens, somewhere close across the *rio*.

'I imagine you're wondering what I am doing in Venice?'

Nicholas studied the old but still powerful face.

'It's an odd story, certainly.' Okami finished his espresso, put the cup aside. 'First, you must understand something of the changing nature of the world I have inhabited for all of my life. For many years, the Yakuza were interested only in what went on within the borders of Japan. I was one of the first to understand the myopic aspect of this policy.' He cocked his head to one side. 'The simple fact is, in matters of business we're not so different from anyone else. There came a time when it became increasingly difficult to make money in Japan.' He lifted a hand, let it fall to his thigh. 'Well, that's not, strictly speaking, true. What I mean is that there came a time when it became difficult for us to make *enough* money in Japan. That was when I called a meeting of the *oyabun* and said to them a phrase which your father had taught me and I, in turn, taught to them. It was simply this: *The world is our oyster.*'

Okami sat back, clapping his hands over his small, round belly. 'Of course, they did not understand me – not immediately, anyway. I had to provide a demonstration, and for that I had to leave the country. Since that time, perhaps twenty years ago, I have been back only rarely. Too much here overseas required my direct attention to make certain everything was done correctly the first time.' He nodded his head again. 'While it's true that we have a kind of' – and here he used a Japanese word that had no literal translation, but might best be described as the phrase 'tacit understanding' – 'with the police, the politicians and the bureaucracy, the other *kobun* of Japan, it is never as cordial as we would like it to be. The truth is, these modern-day samurai cannot forget our humble beginnings. Since the Yakuza traditionally came from the lower classes, these high-bred ministers can do nothing but look down upon us. They may fear us, yes; they may even, now and again, do our bidding because we, in turn, make ourselves of use to them. But in their hearts I have no doubt that they despise us, and if the opportunity arose where they could be fully protected they would do everything in their power to see us annihilated.' That demi-smile again. 'So I set up my base here in Venice.'

Nicholas recalled Celeste's brief but vivid history lesson on the origins of Venice and saw now that this was no idle chatter on her part.

'It was the historically correct thing to do,' Okami went on. 'And from a business point of view this city has its unique uses, not that much has changed since the time of the Medicis. Although we are nominally in Italy, Venice is still its own city-state. And it is wise to remember that when you are here you are in Venice, not Italy or, for that matter, Europe.' He shifted restlessly on the pillows. 'But now I am beginning to wonder whether I haven't made a political blunder.'

'Something has happened,' Nicholas said.

'Yes.' Okami's eyes went abruptly opaque, and he rose with their empty cups in his hands to pour more espresso. He did not return immediately but, rather, stood contemplatively by the sideboard, staring out at the lights of Venice.

All at once, as if making a difficult and agonizing decision, he came back, handing Nicholas his cup. He stood, looking down at Nicholas. 'The simple fact is that within the next two weeks someone will try to murder me.'

A mournful horn hooted and a brief shout sounded as a boat pulled into a nearby *traghetto*. Okami broke his brief stasis, went quickly to the window, looked out. The expression on his face betrayed his nervousness.

'Someone wants me to retire. But I have no intention of doing that.'

'Okami-san,' Nicholas said, 'you must be able to mobilize every man in your clan to protect you.'

Okami turned away from the window, and looked at Nicholas with some surprise, as if he had just appeared out of thin air. 'Oh, more than that,' he said absently. 'Far more than just one clan's worth. But this man who is coming . . .'

He came back to where Nicholas was sitting, squatting very close to him. Even his beloved espresso was ignored now. Nicholas recognized the strain of anxiety on his face.

'This is not the real issue, for me,' he said. 'One of my *oyabun* has turned against me. Knowing this, I can afford to trust no one. I trust Celeste, of course. And, telling you all this, putting myself in your hands, I am trusting you. But no one else!' For the first time, he had raised his voice. 'No one,' he repeated, more softly.

'I am calling upon you, upon the debt your father owed me,' Okami said. 'I need your skills and your – arts – to protect me so that I may finish what I have started. And to discover the traitor among my most trusted *oyabun*.'

Nicholas sat very still, absorbing what Mikio Okami was telling him. It washed over him like a tide, chilling him. At last, when he had regained control of his breathing, he said, 'You have made reference twice to *your oyabun*.'

'Yes.' Okami raised his eyebrows. 'Didn't you know? This is how the debt came into being. I am what your father helped me become and, from my position of power, I accomplished many, many difficult things for him.' The demi-smile. 'You see, Linnear-san, here is the truth behind the myth: I am Kaisho, *oyabun* of all Yakuza *oyabun.*'

Justine sat in a room at the Tokyo Hilton, the most American of the major mega-hotels in the city. With the heavy curtains closed against the blaze of the Tokyo night she could be anywhere in the States – New York or Chicago; even, if she were to imagine it, London's Hyde Park or the Serengeti's veldt could be just outside her double-glazed windows.

She sat, hunched over, her clasped hands tight between her knees, staring at the wall-to-wall carpet. She seemed incapable of movement, of even thinking in any coherent manner. Her mind was a sea of emotion, a cauldron too long on a burner that was now overflowing, inundating her like the sorcerer's apprentice in massive overload. She felt gripped by a kind of desperation such as she had not felt in many years. In fact, after she had met Nicholas, she had felt certain that she would never feel this way again.

Then, he had been her savior, her protector from the kind of debilitating desperation that had threatened to disintegrate her. Now, much to her horror, Nicholas himself seemed to be the cause of this feeling. She felt as if she were imprisoned, marooned on the shore of an alien land with no hope of reprieve. Nicholas had done this to her with his inexplicable love of Japan and its arcane concepts of *giri* and honor and its 10,000 meaningless rituals that served only to distance people – even family members – from each other.

This last thought, perhaps more than any other, had begun to haunt her from the moment she had become pregnant for the first time. She had visions – nightmares, really – of Nicholas wanting their child sent off to a Zen Buddhist monastery or a martial arts *dojo*, there to be immersed in the alien precepts of Eastern religion and philosophy – away from her. This thought – perhaps farfetched and even a bit paranoid – haunted her with a tenacity that was inescapable. Its horror wore away her resolve to be a mother, eroded her self-esteem, poisoned the one thing in all the world she had believed to be unassailable: her love for Nicholas.

She became, in the end, frightened of him. As strong and invincible as he had once been as her protector, now he had become by some alchemical process unknown to her a being possessed of a monstrous power. His tanjian origins terrified her, and the deeper he delved into the dark mysteries of Tau-tau the less tangible his humanity seemed to her.

And now that she had dared touch her anger and her fear, had seen it dragged into the light, she recognized that from the moment her daughter had died she had become a different person. She was forever restless, in sleep as well as during the day, as if she were fated to continue searching for that one special connection her daughter in her brief life had brought to her. She knew she might never find it again, true, but she was utterly certain that she had no hope of finding it here in Japan with Nicholas.

She sobbed now, alone in her anonymous hotel room which, for all its American blandness, was calming after the interior of her own house, which seemed to resonate with a black magic that threatened to suffocate all who were not initiated into its secrets.

When was it that she had realized she had nowhere to go? Had it been when Nicholas had left despite her entreaties? Or when they had had sex that last time and she had felt inexplicably abased? Or had it been far earlier, when she had lost the second baby and, secretly, had thanked God?

How she had suffered for that thought! *I am wicked and selfish*, part of her admonished, even while another part felt a profound relief. How to describe the panic that had overwhelmed her when she had gotten pregnant for the second time? Just the thought of bringing another life into the world, of having once again that special connection, and then having Nicholas intervene with his Tau-tau and his martial obsessions, made her stomach cramp with dread. *I am dying inside*, she mourned. *Soon there will be nothing left to salvage.*

She had hit the breaking point minutes after Nicholas's car had pulled out of the driveway, and with a kind of violence that precluded thought she had packed a weekend suitcase and had driven into the city. That had been an ordeal in itself, driving on the wrong side of the road in a right-wheel car – something she had never been able to get used to – on roads without signs in English. She had to rely entirely on memory which, in her heightened emotional state, had been somewhat less than trustworthy.

She had made it at last into the labyrinth of Tokyo, and by instinct alone had headed directly for the Hilton. It was where her American friends stayed during their infrequent visits, her house being too far out of the city to be convenient.

She had been sitting in the same position for hours, changing it only to make a single phone call forty minutes ago – that to Tanzan Nangi, Nicholas's friend and hers. Every so often she shivered as if she were suffering with a disease – which, in point of fact, she was: it was called despair.

Nangi had been unavailable, but his secretary, Umi, recognizing Justine's voice even before she introduced herself, had promised to give her boss the message that Justine was waiting for him in her room at the Hilton. Putting down the receiver, she had no idea what she would say to him when he arrived – really she had no idea why she had phoned him, except that some core of self-preservation deep inside her recognized that she had become a mote in a black void, spinning out of control, that she desperately needed a reference point from which to return to the process of logical decision-making.

A soft knock on the door dispersed her inertia just enough for her to rise, move across the room on leaden feet and open the door. She had been ready to greet Nangi, but her heart froze in her chest.

Standing in the hall outside her door was a handsome American with long dark hair, light eyes and a smiling mouth. He was less tanned than she remembered him in Maui, but somehow more fit, admirably filling out his dark-blue suit.

He gave her a quick grin as he strode across the threshold to her room, then took her in his arms and gave her a long kiss.

'God, it's great to see you again,' Rick Millar said, his arms still encircling her.

Justine, the taste of him still in her mouth, remembered how he had followed her all the way from New York to Maui after he had promoted her to vice-president of his advertising firm, Millar, Soames & Robberts. She had walked out on him when she had discovered that he had fired her friend in order to make room for her. In Maui, she had almost had an affair with him. Almost. Now, seeing him while in this terribly vulnerable state, her throat locked up and her heart ached. She was so close to weeping she could feel the tears burning beneath her eyelids, and she thought, *Oh, Christ! It won't take much more to rip me into pieces.*

'Rick, what are you doing here?' When she found her voice it was high and breathless.

'I was with Mr Nangi when his secretary phoned about your call. He was going to come here but I persuaded him that seeing a friendly face from home would be the best tonic for you.' His face creased in genuine concern. 'He'd been telling me a bit about your problems adjusting to the lifestyle here. He's very worried about you but at a loss as to how to help.'

Justine shook her head, still confused. 'But how is it you're *here*, in Japan?'

He would not let her go, looking deep into her pain-racked eyes, and she felt herself trembling beneath his touch. 'I could lie to you, Justine, and tell you that I'm out here making Far East contacts or that I'm on vacation, but I'm not. The truth is I came here to find you and somehow

83

– I admit I don't yet know how – to convince you to come back to New York and rejoin the firm on a permanent basis.'

Justine thought she would faint. How many times as a little girl had she dreamt her dreams and wondered what would happen if they came true?

'You can't be serious.'

'Justine, listen to me, we're about to expand. After going through a bad patch during the recession, business has never been better. The problem is, I'm doing everything myself. Try as I may, I haven't been able to replace you. Would you believe I've gone through four VPs since you left? I can't put in any more seventy-two-hour weeks.' He squeezed her. 'I need you. I'm not making it a secret. If you come back, you can do so on your own terms. I mean it. I'm prepared to give you a piece of the business. A quarter of it, if that's what it takes.' He squeezed her again, his obvious enthusiasm running like a fever from his veins to hers. 'Just say yes.'

Justine closed her eyes. She knew what she would say before she heard the word on her lips, and a curious sensation of warmth washed over her, of some hard carapace breaking open, shattering irrevocably.

'Yes.'

'What in the name of God d'you make of that?'

Croaker looked up at the waxy-skinned corpse hanging by its heels from the ceiling fixture in the kitchen. Outside the window filthy gray clouds streaked with purple pressed down on the inchoate clutter of a rumbling Interstate – a landscape so familiar it was frightening.

Though the blistered vista was cloned virtually everywhere throughout America, this particular portion was just outside Marine on St Croix, Minnesota.

Croaker stared at the blood which still filled the stainless steel sink, turning it brilliant carmine in the center, rich maroon where it had begun to cake at the sides. It was preferable to looking at the corpse, although no matter what he did he could feel the psychic weight of it like a painful prickling beneath his skin.

As a former detective-lieutenant in the NYPD, Lew Croaker had seen many a grisly sight strewn about the garbage-laden streets of New York. But nothing like this.

Every bone in the late don's limbs had been broken. That kind of torture was not new to Croaker, but the rest was. With the precision of a surgeon, his heart had been cut out of the cavity of his chest, neatly, cleanly, and lay nestled like a shiny nascent being on the don's navel. Croaker moved closer now, and he saw a peculiar thing.

84

'The heart,' he said, 'has been stitched to Goldoni's navel.' His gaze moved lower. 'And all the digits seem to have been broken in order to turn them 180 degrees around.'

'Most curious, isn't it? Smacks of some kind of ritual.'

Christ, what I wouldn't give to have Nick here, Croaker thought. Arcane rituals were his métier. He thought about calling him, then rejected the idea. At one time, he wouldn't have had a second thought, but these days Nick had a huge corporation to run, a wife, and still trying for a family. His priorities had changed. He had no time any more for jetting across the Pacific to solve bizarre mysteries. Croaker felt a deep pang of regret. He had never been one to long for the good old days, primarily because they'd never been all that good, but now he found himself wishing that time could be folded back upon itself and in a blink of an eye he'd find himself and Nick as they had once been. A team on the run, heading full tilt into dangerous waters.

He blinked, just to be sure, but the only live person in the room with him remained Will Lillehammer.

Lillehammer's extreme thinness seemed cadaverous in this grisly setting. He apparently flew around the country – perhaps the world, for all Croaker knew – in a US Air Force plane. The vehicle had been waiting for them, fueled and spotless, in an 'AUTHORIZED PERSONNEL ONLY' section of the Naples airport. The military flight crew deferred to Lillehammer in a way they normally would not with a lowly civilian.

A shadow moved across Croaker's field of vision and he noted it. He marveled at Lillehammer's power. It was clear that neither the FBI nor the State Troopers who monitored this stretch of the Interstate nor the local hound dogs from Marine on St Croix had been in here; yet the place was cordoned off by enough cops to handle a small-scale riot. It took a great deal of influence to keep this kind of murder scene pristine, he reflected.

During the flight here Croaker had read the Fed sheet on the Goldonis. It was unusual and oddly incomplete. Dominic was born in 1947 to a woman named Faith Mattaccino, who, seventeen years later, would become the second Mrs Goldoni. Nothing, apparently, was known about Dominic's father – or even if she had been married to him.

According to government files, there was little known about Faith Goldoni herself save that she was an American of Italian ancestry born in 1923. A year after she married Enrico Goldoni she convinced him to adopt her son, Dominic. He had two daughters from his first wife, one of whom – Margarite – lived in New York and was married to the attorney Tony 'D.' DeCamillo. Faith died in 1974, in a boating accident off the Lido, the beachfront resort of Venice.

As for Enrico Goldoni, by the time of his marriage to Faith, he was already firmly entrenched in the nether world of the Mafia. How a Venetian came to power in the essentially Sicilian criminal organization was not known, except that it seemed clear that through Enrico's company, which manufactured and traded in fine silks and handmade brocades, other less savory articles were easily transshipped worldwide.

On 11 December of last year, the authorities pulled Enrico's corpse out of the Grand Canal, where it had been hooked around a wooden pole like a sack of debris. Who had killed him or why remained unanswered.

The Goldonis were, apparently, a family of death and secrets, but nothing in the file could have prepared Croaker for Dominic's eerie and disturbing end.

Lillehammer came round from behind the corpse, his mouth quivering. 'Do you ever get used to the stink?'

Croaker smiled, took a pair of baffled plugs out of his nostrils, replaced them almost immediately. 'I wonder what happened to the head?'

'Perhaps he buried it.'

'Why would he do that?'

Lillehammer shrugged. 'Why would he do any of this? The person's deranged.'

'You think so?'

'What other conclusion could one make?'

'I don't know. But my experience is there's a wide range of possibilities.'

They moved out of the kitchen, down the hall. Through a dirt-smudged window Croaker could see the clouds lowering. He felt the pressure drop, but some of his discomfiture surely came from the defilement in the kitchen. Inch by mental inch he turned his mind away from the images firing behind his eyes. He thought they had been lucky to land before the storm hit.

'This the house WITSEC bought for Dominic?'

'Lord no,' Lillehammer said. 'This is where he was brought . . . to die.' He flipped open a black alligator-skin notebook. 'This place's for sale . . . been so for eight months now. No one has been in here since the bank took it over.'

'Except Dominic and his murderer.'

He flipped on a mini-flashlight, playing it over all surfaces. The white walls and ceiling glared back at them as if with evil intent.

'What's this?'

Croaker had stopped. The circle of light hovered on one spot on the wall, darker than the surrounding area. The two men peered at it.

'It looks like –'

'Yeah,' Croaker finished for Lillehammer, 'sweat.'

And he had smelled it then, his fear, and Lillehammer's as well, he supposed, like an animal whose fetid breath spoke of spilled blood and kills without number.

That psychic pressure again, like an ache in his soul, more insistent now, even though they were further from the kitchen, from the site of the defilement.

'Something happened here,' he said. 'Something . . . evil.'

'Evil?' Lillehammer looked at him quizzically. 'What d'you mean, man? What could be worse than what's hanging back there in the kitchen?'

'I don't know . . . yet.'

Croaker played the beam of light over the entire area. The stain, ovoid and almost perfectly symmetrical, stood out like a stele in the Southeast Asian jungle, marking the passage of an ancient, enigmatic people.

He played the light along the baseboard of the wall, then down along the floor. Almost directly at his feet was another stain, this one smaller but thick, viscid.

'That almost certainly is semen,' Lillehammer said from over his shoulder. 'Perhaps the murderer raped Goldoni before he strung him up and decapitated him.'

'No,' Croaker said. 'As you pointed out, there was some kind of ritual performed on Goldoni – like a sacrifice.' He glanced up at Lillehammer. 'No violation of the sacrificial victim would be permitted.'

'How the hell do you know that for certain?'

'I don't,' he said. 'It's just a . . . feeling.'

'Yes. I've been in the jungle,' Lillehammer said, 'where feeling is everything. Brush of a ghost's breath can save your skin . . . or lead you astray.'

Lillehammer smiled his ghastly smile, the tiny crosshatched scars standing out white and livid in the intense beam of the flashlight. 'I want this bastard, you see. Need to run him down, actually.'

'Need? Maybe you picked the right name for yourself, Ahab.'

Lillehammer gave a harsh, metallic laugh, and his rather large teeth clacked together like the jaws of a crocodile.

'Sure,' he said, employing one of his few Americanisms. 'I'll tell you all about it sometime.'

That'll be the day, Croaker thought. He watched as Lillehammer knelt, opened his small black case, drew on a pair of surgical rubber gloves, went about preserving the semen. 'I'll have it tested. Probably a dead end, but with the level of DNA mapping available these days maybe we'll get lucky

– such as finding he has some odd genetic disease that will help us track him down.'

Lillehammer was a total enigma, and that, Croaker thought now, was why he was drawn to him. The simple fact was Croaker loved mysteries. His father's murder had led him to become a cop, but his own innate curiosity about the far side of human existence had caused him to become a homicide detective.

'Still,' Lillehammer continued, as he packed up his gear, 'we have no idea what happened here.'

'Not quite,' Croaker said. 'The murderer was involved in a sexual act, most likely just after he killed Goldoni. It's clear that Goldoni was killed in the kitchen – exsanguinated there.'

'All right. Perhaps he got off on the killing so much he masturbated to ejaculation. That would be consistent with a good many homicidal psychotics. They're normally impotent, but the intense rage that causes them to kill – the very act of bringing death – releases their sexual restraint.'

Pressure on his psyche, a shadow on his soul.

'Possibly,' he said. 'But in this case, I don't think so. Look at what we found in the kitchen. There was no sense of rage at work there, only a meticulous precision. And the sacrificial aspect? Only magicians, shamans perform these complex rituals – power after power. I don't see impotence in this particular psychic equation.'

Lillehammer seemed willing to accept that. He took another look around them. 'If he didn't have sex with Goldoni and he wasn't masturbating, we're left with only one other possibility.'

'Right,' Croaker said. 'There was someone else.'

They went further into the house. The smell of old paint, turpentine, wet and rot saturated the clotted atmosphere. The hall ended in an old-fashioned bathroom with tiny black-and-white tiles, cracked and smudged beyond the pale of any cleanser. A claw-footed bathtub, a square sink with some of the porcelain chipped off, no towels on the iron bars, the rustle of scuttling insects, it was as sad and desolate a spot as Croaker could remember seeing.

Lillehammer's mouth twitched again. 'Do you smell something?'

Croaker took the plugs out of his nostrils. '*Christ!*' he said, lunging for the door on the opposite side of the room. It was locked. He raised his left hand to the height of the lock. A thin metallic nail was extruded from the tip of the index finger. Croaker inserted it into the lock.

Lillehammer looked on in obvious fascination as Croaker turned the nail back and forth, feeling for the grooves. A moment later, there was an audible click.

'Well done!' Lillehammer said.

Croaker turned the knob and opened the door outward.

'Bloody hell! What?' Lillehammer took out a handkerchief, pressed it over his nose and mouth. 'This stench is worse than the one in the kitchen.'

'I think we've found our other person,' Croaker said as they entered the room.

On the bed was a young woman or, to be more truthful – what had once been a young woman. She was spread out in a star – the arms, legs and head making up the five points. Her torso had been incised – cut all the way through as finely and precisely as if it had been done by a surgeon. Croaker, circling the bed, counted the number of incisions. There were seven. Tucked neatly into the seventh cut was a white bird's feather, stained with blood.

Lillehammer, following him, said softly, 'Lord, she was a pretty thing, once.'

Croaker said, 'Another ritual.'

'Look at that!'

Carved into the center of her forehead was a vertical crescent, dark with dried blood. Lower down, where the navel had once been, was a dark hole across which something was woven. It had once been white, but was now stained dark with blood.

Croaker said, 'Is that some kind of bird feather stitched between the flesh and organ?'

'It looks that way. As soon as we're finished here I'm going to have it checked out with an ornithologist.' His gaze seemed rooted to the bloody feather. 'I'd better get the forensic team in here as quickly as possible.'

'I've always been a big believer in old-fashioned police work,' Croaker said, 'but in this case, I doubt it'll do any good. What we need is a sorcerer. Our murderer isn't about to leave fingerprints.'

'He left his semen,' Lillehammer reminded him.

'Yes, he did,' Croaker said thoughtfully, still examining the bloody crescent. 'It was a signpost, and look where it led us.' He turned to regard Lillehammer. 'But there's another question that needs to be answered: what in hell happened to Dominic Goldoni's head?'

Mikio Okami said, 'You see, Linnear-san, I came to Venice many years ago for a specific purpose. Here, I have been working to channel the old criminal Yakuza money into new legitimate businesses which will ensure the Yakuza's existence into the twenty-first century.

'As you must know, the Yakuza were officially outlawed in April of 1992. One can no longer assume the status quo will remain in effect. Myths are crumbling, even ones so powerful as those surrounding the Yakuza.

'About a year ago everything changed for me: friends, foes, alliances I have maintained for decades. This change was forced upon me by a growing disaffection within my own inner council. The result has been legion. One of my old partners was murdered, and now I have a very powerful enemy. He is a member of a group that calls itself the Godaishu.'

'Five Continents,' Nicholas said, unconsciously translating from the Japanese.

Okami nodded. 'The Godaishu's philosophy is diametrically opposed to mine. These *oyabun* feel terribly threatened by my plan to bring them within the scope of the law. These men revel in their lawlessness because it is the only thing that gives them community, status and influence. Without it, they feel they would be reduced to little people, and their fear of losing the status and privilege their old life affords them is all-consuming. They're power-addicts, unable to face a world stripped of the adrenalin rush their money, force and clandestine life provides. "What is the value of life without the razor's edge?" I've heard them ask this question time and again.

'It is vital – even essential – for Yakuza interests to expand. And by that I do not mean multiply from vice to vice. Yes, we are in the process of gaining a foothold in vices historically the purview of America's Mafia. These people are old and sick; the new blood is of a generation so removed from *omerta* and the other matters of honor that there is no more fabric for them to build upon. One don rolls over on another at the slightest pressure from Federal agents.'

He put a hand up, as if in some arcane form of benediction so that in an odd sense Nicholas was reminded of the liturgies he had overheard at the Church of San Belisario.

'Now it is time for the moral fiber of the Yakuza to take hold. The soil is ripe and ready for our strength of purpose. But this is not the Mafia's purpose.

'No, I am speaking now of legitimate businesses we partially control or wish to control. Buying into such conglomerates is not easy. We have the American SEC to contend with as well as numerous banking regulatory agencies. We must be so circumspect in our purchases that no suspicion whatsoever is focused in our direction.'

'Why would you tell me all this, Okami-san?' Nicholas asked. 'You must know that I am no friend to the Yakuza. I deplore how they prey upon the weaknesses of decent folk.'

'You have spoken frankly,' Okami said. 'So will I. You know nothing of what we do – or what we hope to accomplish. You would condemn us out of hand, as would our enemies.'

Nicholas gave Okami a wintry smile. 'On the contrary,' he said, 'I know at least something of the private lives of the *oyabun*.'

'But not mine.'

When Nicholas did not reply, Okami was forced to respond. 'Have you no hope that we could be involved in a beneficial enterprise?'

'Beneficial to yourselves, yes.'

'This was not how your father saw matters.'

Nicholas put down his cup. 'My father lived in different times. For him, a war was still on. He was involved in reinventing modern-day Japan.'

'You needn't elaborate,' Okami said softly. 'I was there with him.' Then he gave Nicholas a direct look. 'These harsh words pain me. The two of us needn't be at war.'

'Perhaps we are at war simply through ignorance,' Nicholas said. 'I have no knowledge of the origins of my father's debt to you.'

'That is a secret we swore would remain between the two of us.'

Nicholas said nothing; the silence was as much as telling Okami that they had reached a personal stalemate.

'Would you forswear your own oath to your father?' Okami said suddenly, sharply. 'Would you have me forswear my oath to him?'

'Your relationship with my father has its own life,' Nicholas said. 'Now you must deal with me. You and I must struggle toward our own understanding. Only from that can we expect a connection to evolve.'

Okami seemed surprised. 'You are speaking of . . . an alliance.'

Nicholas nodded. 'Perhaps, yes. But whatever our contact may eventually become you cannot expect to use me blindly as a huntsman draws his arrow.'

'But your father –'

'Okami-san, please try to understand. I am not only my father's son.'

Okami rose and, turning his back on Nicholas, went to the windows, there to stare out across the *rio*. His hands smacked one against the other as he pondered the problem. There wasn't much to think about; Nicholas had given him what amounted to an ultimatum: tell me how the debt came into being or I will not honor it. It was now, Nicholas knew, strictly a matter of face.

'Your father was an extraordinary man,' Okami said without preamble. 'He was extraordinary in many ways – some of which even you are not aware of. In a sense, your father was like an artist. What he saw was never strictly speaking reality, but rather what *lay beyond* the reality. Simply put, your father saw the *potential* in every situation – and he knew how to exploit the situation in order to turn that potential into a very real future.'

Nicholas noticed that Okami's back had straightened, the years seeming to slip away from him as he remembered his shared past with Colonel Denis Linnear.

'I met your father in a very odd way, because it was not through business. The truth was, my sister was crazy about him, and it was she who brought us together. She insisted I meet him – an *iteki* I thought. I hated him on sight, I thought. That was before I got to know him.'

Okami took a deep breath, as if steeling himself. 'You are no doubt aware that MacArthur's SCAP Command often liaised with certain members of the Yakuza. We were of use to them in combating the Communist incursions into Japan bent on subverting the new democratic order imposed by the Americans. At first, I – and others like me – felt as if we were caught between Scylla and Charybdis – trapped between two alien political systems both of which would pervert the basic fabric of Japanese life. But, of course, of the two Communism was by far the more feared and hated – so we found ourselves siding with the Americans. What else could we do? It was a question that we asked ourselves continually in those days – and one which your father and I debated endlessly.

'But the Communists were not the only threat. They were the overt enemy, and therefore easy for the SCAP command to identify. However, your father had ferreted out a far more subversive group, hiding deep below the surface of both our societies, and it was these people he recruited me to help him destroy.'

Okami turned round at last, sat on one of the pillows. He crossed one leg over the other, threw an arm across the windowsill. 'You must understand, those were lawless days, Linnear-san. The black market was flourishing, and any enterprising person could make a fortune in a matter of months – if he had the contacts and the merchandise to sell.

'It was even easy if, for example, you were an officer in the American Military Police. Then you had the virtual run of the country. You were the law.

'Your father had discovered a nexus of the black market in Tokyo. It was being run by a certain MP captain named Jonathan Leonard, who was as ruthless as he was unscrupulous. He was also so well protected that your father could never pin anything on him, despite all his best efforts. Meanwhile, Captain Leonard was supplying the city with everything it didn't need then: guns, ammo, weapons of every description – and drugs. Lots of drugs.

'Where was he getting this contraband from? Where was he storing it? Who was he using as a distribution network? Much to my surprise and rage I found certain Yakuza *kobun* involved on the street level. These were the disenchanted, the disloyal – soldiers who had been passed over for promotion or, more disturbingly, had been too impatient to work their way up the hierarchy.

'But who lay behind them? Captain Leonard? Why not? He was the one with the connections. Your father had done some further digging, and had discovered that Leonard had legally changed his name just before he had enlisted in the Army. The name he had been born with was John Leonforte.' Okami's head nodded. 'That's right, Linnear-san, he was the kid brother to Alphonse Leonforte, the Mafia don who terrorized the States during the war years and afterward. Alphonse single-handedly consolidated the East Coast Mafia's hold over the seaport of New York, as well as the construction and interstate trucking businesses, two areas whose growth in America would outstrip almost all others in the fifties.'

'Didn't I read in that biography published several years ago that Al Leonforte's kid brother died while he was in the Army?'

'That's right,' Okami said. 'I killed him.'

Nicholas studied Okami for some time. Then he got up, went to the sideboard and poured himself a brandy. He took it all down in one swallow, allowed the burn to reach his stomach before turning back to face Okami. 'Are you saying you murdered Johnny Leonforte on orders from my father?'

Okami took the last of his espresso in his mouth and swallowed it. 'Here's something you *didn't* read in that biography. Alphonse Leonforte's last official act before he retired was to order the murder of James Hoffa. And do you know why they never found his body? I'll tell you. The senior senator from New York at that time was a good friend of Leonforte's – I forget his name, but it doesn't matter. You can look it up in the biography, if you wish. In any event, this senator had a house – a summer house, I believe it was – on Shelter Island. Do you know that place, Linnear-san?'

'Very well,' Nicholas said with a sinking feeling in the pit of his stomach.

Okami nodded. 'I have not been there, but one day I would like to go. It is supposed to be very beautiful, very secluded.'

'It is all that and more.'

Okami inclined his head again. 'As I have said, the senator had a house there where he went to relax. Leonforte loved that place, although he was never allowed near it during daylight hours. Too dangerous for the senator, perhaps. But there was a pair of fine Japanese maples on the property – magnificent specimens, even back then. Leonforte was passionate about those trees, especially when their leaves turned scarlet in the autumn.

'Perhaps the senator had left the maples in a state of benign neglect and Leonforte felt them in need of some extraordinary compost. Or, again, he might have been playing a kind of ironic prank on his friend. At this

93

late date, who's to say? But that was where Leonforte directed his men to bury Hoffa, beneath the roots of the senator's maples. I am told the trees are there still, more magnificent than ever.'

Nicholas rubbed his forehead. 'And this is the guy whose kid brother you murdered.'

'Not murdered,' Okami said. 'No, not really. We got into a fight, he and I. I suppose I am guilty of engineering that fight, yes. I remember he was strong and tough and he certainly had the instinct for survival. But I was, in those days, a very fine martial artist, and those kinds of fights –' He shrugged. 'It is difficult to pull your punches. I think you know what I mean.'

Nicholas looked at his own hands, knowing very well what Okami meant. They had been responsible for a number of deaths. He looked back up at Okami. He wanted the old man to tell him outright if his father had ordered him to murder Johnny Leonforte, but he didn't think now that Okami would. He thought for a moment, said, 'And did Captain Leonard's death make a difference? Did the black market in contraband then dry up?'

Okami did not answer right away. 'For a while,' he said at last, which was as much of an admission as he was willing to put forth. 'But then to your father's surprise it began again. And this time neither of us were successful in tracking down its source.'

Nicholas stirred. 'Weren't you surprised as well?'

Okami gave the kind of smile a professor exhibits at a prize pupil's canny question. 'Believe it or not I knew a great deal more about the American Mafia than your father ever did. I had studied them, had even made a trip to Sicily' – he waved a hand – 'but that is another story. I knew that if one Leonforte was involved, others were, too.'

'You mean Alphonse?'

Okami shook his head. 'There were originally four brothers. One died in a boating accident at college. Well, one is never certain that the word *accident* exists in the world of these people, especially when it pertains to the man Alphonse was grooming to succeed him. In any case, Paul Leonforte died young, so that left the black sheep of the family, Francis. He migrated to San Francisco and stayed there – over the strenuous objections of Alphonse. But Frank was always his own man; not for him the shadow of his big brother. He knew no matter how much personal power he amassed he would always be taking orders as long as he stayed anywhere on the East Coast. He had no desire to lock horns with Alphonse, so he left to stake out his own empire on the West Coast, which he did with admirable success. He had three children, a daughter and two sons. One son, Michael, died a highly decorated veteran in Vietnam. The other one, Caesare, built on Frank's successes and is now the don of the western half of the United States. He is the East Coast *capo* Dominic Goldoni's chief rival.'

Okami grunted; it was half a laugh. 'Caesare is called Bad Clams. You think it's a joke but it's not. The way he made his bones in the organization is he was sent to assassinate a rival of his father. The man was eating dinner at a local restaurant. Pasta with fresh clams. The story is told that when Caesare had blown this man's brains all over his three-piece suit, he stood over him with the gun still smoking in his hand and said, "Look what bad clams can do to you."'

Okami gave a short, barking laugh, then quickly sobered. 'But I digress. Thinking about it, it seemed logical that Frank would have been John's ultimate source, but in order to confirm this theory either your father or I would have had to travel to San Francisco, where at the time neither of us had any connections. Besides, the Communist-instigated dock strikes in Tokyo soon took our attention elsewhere.'

Nicholas poured himself another brandy, then came and sat next to Okami. They both looked out at the dark water with its reflections of the *palazzi* across the Grand Canal.

'So the mystery was never solved,' Nicholas said at last.

'No, but today I find myself in a position significantly closer to its solution,' Okami said thoughtfully.

'What do you mean?'

Okami turned his head to look at Nicholas. 'Just this. While I have been trying to legitimize the Yakuza, someone unknown to me has been consolidating a link with the Mafia which I now suspect was forged during the days when Johnny Leonforte served as the Japanese point man.'

Okami's eyes glittered as they caught the nighttime reflections off the water. 'Linnear-san, it is my belief that this same someone – *one brilliant mind* – is behind the recent transformation of the Mafia. All the old dons with their sense of honor and family are being sold down the river, leaving behind the venal jackals, the button-down bean-counters who would sell their souls for another billion dollars profit – and it appears as if they've sold their soul to this one man who is forging the international conglomerate from hell, the Godaishu.

'Such a conglomerate – a sharing of underground contacts and resources throughout the East and the West; a kind of criminal *keiretsu* with arms that can encompass the globe – could conceivably gain more power over the world economy than the Governments of the United States and Germany do now. Have you any idea how much havoc such an entity could wreak? Legitimate business worldwide would literally be feeding it, allowing it to grow even more powerful.'

95

'But surely there are governmental agencies – the CIA, for example – that can deal with such a menace.'

'Ordinarily, that might be so,' Okami said. 'But recently I have been making enquiries along a specific line. It appears that the mystery of what happened with Leonforte in postwar Japan runs far deeper than your father or I had imagined. I believe that the alliances Leonforte made had, *at the very least*, semi-official links. Appalling as it may seem, Leonforte must have been operating under the aegis of certain individuals within the two Governments – Japan and America. The Godaishu is the end result. It is far more influential than you can possibly envision, its tentacles reaching all the way to the most powerful elements within Washington and Tokyo.'

'You mentioned needing time to initiate your own plans.'

'Yes. Over the last year, I have been trying to gather forces strong enough to stymie the Godaishu. It has been a formidable task, one that has exhausted me, taxing the limits of even the Kaisho's influence. Now I am in the final phase and I know it will be all or nothing. Either I will survive to destroy the Godaishu or they will become a force unstoppable by anyone or anything. You must buy me the time I need to bring the plan to conclusion. There is no one else who has the expertise, no one else I can turn to.'

Okami lit a cigarette but he quickly stubbed it out, unable to enjoy its taste. 'Frankly, Linnear-san, my desperation to stop the Godaishu has led me to make questionable liaisons with individuals who I cannot openly control or fully trust. I cannot say yet whether my actions will result in a brilliant coup or complete folly.'

He moved so that the lights from the *palazzi* across the canal played across his face, transfiguring it into the aspect of a Titian painting. 'One thing I do know: my actions have put me into deadly danger. Already I have word that one of my partners, Dominic Goldoni – the only one I *could* trust – has been murdered. And now I am convinced that my intimate knowledge of the Godaishu and my attempts to move against it have marked me for death.'

THREE

New York/Tokyo/Washington

Margarite Goldoni, with her daughter sleeping in her arms, had returned home to find that her husband had gathered an entire fleet of button-men to go after Robert. Tony was of the old school – very macho. Which was why Dominic had appointed him custodian of the Family business.

In fact, she had been dreading her return. And all her fears were borne out when Tony ripped open the door. He did not ask her where she had been taken, how far her culpability went in her brother's death, or even how she had made her way home. He asked her only one question: 'Were you touched?'

Not even *Did he touch you?* because Tony would not personify what in his mind had already occurred to her.

Because, in a very real sense, her answer did not matter to him. He had already decided her fate, seeing in his mind what she had become. The Madonna he had always wanted her to be was now soiled forever.

She told him no. She told him that Francie had been drugged, which was the truth, and that she had been blindfolded, which was, of course, not. But how could she admit to anyone – especially to him – what she had been coerced into doing? Committing the act was one kind of hell; admitting to it afterward, a wholly different kind she would not tolerate.

He heard none of what she said; he wasn't interested. He didn't even want to come near her, standing apart, his eyes cold, disapproving, as if she had caught leprosy on her strange journey.

Despite the fact that she was obviously despairing and emotionally exhausted, Tony had forced her into having it out with him about going to war with Robert. He wanted his revenge.

'For Christ's sake, Tony, we don't even know his real *name!*' she had exploded.

Tony had that cunning look he got when he was about to ram a contract down an adversary's throat. 'But we have you, Margarite. Now that the kid is safe with us, you can give the artist I brought in a detailed description of him. His face is all we need. He's a goddamned Asian. Do you think we won't be able to find him?'

She took a deep breath, said slowly and distinctly, 'Tony, I want you to listen to me. He said he'd be watching us, that if we did anything he would take Francie.'

Tony waved his hands in dismissal. 'Words, just words. He was trying to scare you, that's all. Think about it, Margarite, how the fuck is he going to monitor what we do? Even the Feds aren't too good at that, and look at all the manpower they have at their disposal.' He shook his head almost in pity. 'You're a woman. He knows he can intimidate you. Men like him do it all the time. Let me handle things. We'll get the bastard before he's had a chance to shit.'

She put the heel of her hand to her temple as if by that gesture she could slow her pulse, diminish the rising tide of panic. How like a child she felt, so impotent, exactly as she had with her father. In despair, she said, 'You don't know him. He'll take her. He can do it.'

She fought to keep her voice calm, but it cracked and the tears came. 'Francie's back safe with us. Jesus, just leave it alone now.'

'Leave it alone? You must be fucking nuts. Fagetaboutit! This sonuvabitch comes into my house, attacks me, humiliates me and leaves me to clean up the bodies he slaughters all over *my* house. This is sacred ground, Margarite. Not even that sonuvabitch Bad Clams Leonforte would dare violate my house.' His face was full of blood. 'Mary Immaculate, Margarite, he murdered your brother!'

She was silent before his power, his righteous rage so like her father's. Tony began to order his button-men around. Then he got on the phone, made some calls. He pounded into her bathroom, where she was taking a shower. 'Get packed,' he said. 'You and Francine are taking a trip.'

Margarite stared at him. 'She's already missed enough school, I don't want her –'

'Do as I say!'

She obeyed.

Tony finished his preparations, then came into the bedroom where she was dressing. 'Nobody knows where you're going except a few of my most trusted people here and the man I'm on the phone with. It's his house and he's Family so you don't have to worry about him.'

He had a man carry the bags she had packed downstairs. He took the sleeping Francine in his arms, following them downstairs. He had tried to pry Ryan, her favorite Teddy bear, out of her arms, but it would not come. Rag-tag and chewed, it was the sole remaining vestige of her childhood, the one even as a teenager she would not part with.

98

Outside, Margarite climbed into the Lincoln and he handed Francine in to her. They were surrounded by Family bodyguards both in the car and in cars in front and back of the Lincoln.

'I'll see you when this is over,' Tony said, slamming the flat of his hand down on the roof of the Lincoln.

It was only after they had left the compound that Margarite realized that he had not kissed her, had not in fact touched her at all since she had returned home.

Francine lay still clutching Ryan, her head on Margarite's lap, and she stroked her child's hair as she had when she was a baby with the croup. As they sped through the night, she could not help thinking of what Tony must be planning, and her anxiety grew. She tried to calm herself. She told herself that without her help he would not get his portrait of Robert, but deep in the night that seemed scant comfort.

They reached the stone house in New Hampshire an hour before dawn. The men in the lead car entered the house first, turning on lights, searching the place thoroughly. Only then did they signal to the Lincoln's driver.

Margarite had taken Francine into the bedroom herself, tucking her under the covers, propping Ryan against the wall within easy reach should her daughter turn over, looking for him in her sleep. Then she retired to the bedroom designated for her.

If she slept, she was not aware of it. Instead, she relived her waking death, her child's blank stupor, her hegira down the open roads through which she had wound. She saw herself as if through a looking-glass, already maimed beyond understanding, barely conscious, driven by the sole directive, an imperative from that primitive part of her that was still wholly functional to keep her daughter safe from the evil that stalked her. In this malignant state, her dream-imagining took the place of sleep.

She awoke near noon, her eyes gluey, feeling as if she had just fallen asleep. The adrenalin of anxiety rushed through her like a sickening wave, and she hurtled into the bathroom, made it to the toilet barely in time, bent double, her mouth and eyes full of fluid.

Later, she looked in on Francine, who was still asleep, then showered and dressed. In the kitchen she dawdled over a silent breakfast made by one of the bodyguards, a large man with raccoon eyes and a kind smile. She spent the time moving her eggs from one side of the plate to the other and assessing the extent of her loathing for her husband.

Francine emerged at last, rumpled and bleary-eyed, and Margarite had to explain to her where they were and why they were there.

'Of course,' Francie said dully. 'Tony.'

She wanted to go home; she missed her friends. Margarite did her best to console her daughter but it was a losing proposition; she could find no way to get through to her. At least, she got her to eat some breakfast. The strange drugs Robert had ground up and administered to her to make her sleep appeared to have had no lasting effects.

An hour later one of the bodyguards came into the house and spoke to the big man who had made them breakfast.

'What is it?' Margarite asked, anxiety turning to panic.

'Maybe nothing,' the big man said, but the smile was gone from his face. 'They've found a package outside. It's addressed to Francine.'

Francie looked alarmed. Jumping up, Margarite gave a little cry. 'I want to see it.'

The big man shook his head. 'That's not a good idea, Mrs DeCamillo. For the time being I think you'd better go to my room with your daughter. Sal will stay with you.'

From the small bedroom, she heard the big man on the phone with Tony.

He was there inside two hours. She heard the *thwop!thwop!thwop!* of a helicopter's rotors increasing in pitch and volume as it neared. She was allowed out of the room, but she left Francie behind with Sal.

The box sat on the entryway sideboard. Tony said nothing to her, directed one of his men to open it. Inside was a gaily wrapped package tied with a pink bow. This too the man opened, and they all peered inside.

Margarite gave a piercing cry. Nestled within, on a cloud of pink crêpe paper, was Ryan, Francie's Teddy bear.

She rushed into the bedroom where Francie had slept, stared at the bed with its ruffled covers, the empty space against the wall where she had put Ryan late last night.

'Mother of God!'

She put her knuckles to her mouth as Tony came in behind her. 'Tony, he was in the house; he was right beside her.' Her voice cracked and she had to stop, gather herself before continuing. 'I put it on her bed myself when we got here last night.' She turned, stared wide-eyed at Tony. 'Do you see now what I've been telling you? It's a warning. What good was it bringing us here? What good were the guards? I told you. All the button-men in the world aren't going to save us now. We can't hide from him. If we say a word, Francine's gone.'

'Calm down,' he said automatically, but she could see that he was pale beneath his sun-lamp tan.

'Please listen to me, Tony. I can't bear the thought of Francie being harmed more than she already has. God knows what she remembers from this nightmare; she won't talk to me about it. I'm pleading with you for our daughter's life. Let this go.' Was it purely desperation that gave her words such conviction that even Tony was moved?

And what else have I given you, Margarite? Now you know you have the strength of purpose . . . to do anything.

'All right,' he said at length. 'I take your point. But I want you and the kid in the chopper now. We're getting the hell out of here.'

Here's what it boils down to, Justine thought as she felt Rick Millar's muscular thigh press against the side of her leg under the restaurant table. *He wants me – not a part of me, but all of me.* And then came the thought, unbidden: *It's been a long time since I felt that from a man.*

Tears burned her eyes, and she had to turn her head away, quickly wipe her face with the back of her hand. She could not let him know just how vulnerable she was. What defenses were left to her were shaky at best, and she knew with a shudder of recognition that when – not if, but *when* – he put his hand on her she would not be able to resist him. Not tonight, not here. He had too much she needed. Feeling him so close to her she could imagine what it must be like to have been wandering delirious in the desert for weeks on end, then finally and unexpectedly stumble upon an oasis. She was so close to that clear, cold water. Who would blame her for drinking her fill?

'There seems to be no distance at all between us tonight,' Rick said as he poured more wine for them. 'Have you been treated so badly since I last saw you?'

'Was I always so untouchable?'

He leaned over her, covered her lips with his. She tasted him, felt the quick brush of his tongue and she felt her body melt against him.

'You're right,' he said breathlessly. 'I won't ask you again. When you're ready to tell me, to get it all out, I'll be here to listen.'

'I wonder,' Justine said, breaking away from his heat. 'Did you come here to seduce me?'

Rick laughed. 'My God, nothing could have been further from my mind. You, the Ice Maiden?'

'Is that what they called me at the office?'

'To my knowledge, only the guys who lusted after you. I think that included all of them – well, all the straight ones, anyway.'

Now it was Justine's turn to laugh, but she was flattered all the same. She put her head down. 'I feel as if I've been on another planet.'

'No kidding,' Rick said. 'As far as I can see Tokyo *is* another planet.' He put his hand over hers, squeezed. 'It's time you came home.'

When he returned her to the Hilton, she found that she did not want him to leave. That was not much of a surprise; all through dinner she had found her appetite for food suppressed by another desire just as basic. And by her tone of voice, the look in her eyes, the compliance of her body, she knew that she was seducing him. It was a good feeling. After years of being out of control, of being in a very real way subject to the whims of her alien environment – and to the frightening vagaries of Nicholas's tanjian heritage, she felt positively liberated at being able to exert her own personality. At last, she recognized how much of herself had been held hostage, had been subsumed within her fear of what her husband was becoming. Now she could see clearly that she wanted no part of his powers and his magic; these arcane things only made her uneasy, lying sleepless beside him at night, anxiety flooding her with adrenalin.

'Stay with me tonight,' Justine whispered in Rick's ear when the door to her room closed behind them.

'I want you to be sure this is right,' Rick said, as he held her.

I'm sure, Justine said to herself. *I need to have a normal life, to be productive in my work, to come home at night, make love with my husband, see friends on the weekends, take vacations twice a year.*

She tilted her head up, captured his mouth with her lips. Her lips flowered open and she moaned a little as she felt his tongue twine with hers.

She felt his hands on her body as he unbuttoned her blouse, slipped it off her shoulders, unbuttoned her skirt, pushed it down over her hips. She fell into his arms, as if she had passed out, her intense desire pushing them on. He scooped her up, carried her over to the bed.

There was only one lamp on and, through eyes slitted with lust, Justine watched his body appear as she disrobed him. She remembered parts of him from their time in Maui. Then she had seen him in a bathing suit that left little to the imagination. All the same, she found her heart beating faster than she thought possible as she slipped off his underpants. Naked, he stood at the side of the bed, looking down at her. Justine thought he had a beautiful body, slim-hipped, flat-bellied. Certainly, he did not have the unique musculature that Nicholas possessed, but, she reminded herself, this was an ordinary man and he was all that she desired now.

'Come here, darling.' She held her arms up to him.

Rick knelt on the bed, kissing her tenderly while he unhooked her bra, rolled her bikini pants down her legs. Justine was weeping when she felt his body on top of hers. It had been a very long time since she had made love with anyone other than Nicholas, and the unfamiliarity of his weight, form and smell excited her so that she bit into his shoulder as she jerked her hips up into his groin.

She could hardly breathe, and the hammering of her heart was all she heard amid the vertiginous swirl of her desire. She opened her legs, felt his hardness brush against her, gasped as she pulled his head down to her breasts. Her eyes fluttered closed as he laved her nipples, and she corkscrewed her hips to let him know how desperate she was for him.

He understood immediately, arching up over her so that she could guide him into her with her hand. Her fingers stroked his velvet flesh for a moment, then, because she could not help herself, her palm came down over his head and she squeezed. She heard him groan, his body shudder, and she lifted her legs, fitting him to her.

She was very wet, and he slid halfway into her in one stroke.

'Ohh!' Justine cried, canting her hips upward. She was already in a frenzy, and when, with his next stroke, his tip touched the core of her, she lost complete control, shouting out as her orgasm burst over her. She sucked on his flesh, wanting that taste of him to permeate her entirely.

'Oh, God, oh, God!' she chanted with each thrust of him inside her. Part of her knew that this was almost wholly her – her passion venting itself, needing this expression, this outlet. Her thighs were trembling, and she felt another orgasm building. She lifted her head up, whimpering in his ear, and she felt his hips give a ragged lurch inward, and then he was spasming into her.

Justine felt her orgasm flowering out. It was different this time, less violent but more intense, coming from deep inside her.

And when it was over she lay beside him, one leg thrown over him in abandon and, for the first time in long months, she slept the sleep of a child: deep and dreamless.

Ghosts.

There was something about Washington, Harley Gaunt thought, that was like no other city in America. Its wheel-spoke design, its wide, tree-shaded boulevards, its parks, the pillared stolidity of its major structures, all reminded him of Paris or London, of Europe, the Old World rather than the New World.

Also, the place fairly hummed with power. Gaunt could feel it as if the city were wired with overhead trolley lines. And that power, like the wide, tree-shaded boulevards, all led in one direction: to 1600 Pennsylvania Avenue. The White House sat in the center of Washington like a spider in the center of its web.

This city was full of ghosts.

Gaunt knew the capitol well, had many friends here. As the son of the former Democratic senator from Maryland, he had been born within sight of the Ellipse. He had been raised with the crackle of power in his ears, had burnt out on it quickly, more so than his father, who had hung on here past his time, dying in office.

Gaunt knew well that the power that fueled this city could be as malignant as nuclear radiation. The gamesmanship of deal-making had to it always the stench of power-mongering. Either you were In in Washington or you were nothing. This élite clique ran the country – the world's only remaining superpower – and that was justification enough to lie, cheat, extort, break every commandment in the pursuit of the amassing of power.

This power was like a virus, seeping into the players' bloodstreams, affecting their personalities, the whys and wherefores of decision-making. Gaunt had seen this virus so many times he could now recognize it like a fever lurking in the back of the eyes. He had had enough experience with it. He was convinced that his father had died of the fever, not old age or overwork. His father, an essentially good man, honest in the way most successful politicians learn never to be, had gradually changed. He had not been immune to the fever as Gaunt had been certain he, of course, would be. Gaunt's mother and sister had mourned Gaunt's father at his funeral, but Gaunt had mourned for him long before.

Every time he came back to Washington, Gaunt felt the ghosts whispering in the humid wind off the Potomac, hanging in the cherry trees near the Reflecting Pool, grinning from the heights of Capitol Hill. In a sense, his father had never left this place – the power kept him here, even after death.

The lobbyist Gaunt had chosen to run political interference for Tomkin Industries down here had been Secretary of State in a former administration. He was a middle-of-the-road conservative, highly regarded – he held the green fire of Potomac power in his closed fist. Unlike most, he had won his battle with the virus.

Terrence McNaughton had offices on G Street, hard by the Old Executive Office, a building that by its almost Victorian architecture looked haunted at night, and no doubt was, not by conventional ghosts out of a horror novel, but by the drudges of the current administration, who lived a near-spook existence executing 'Eyes Only' directives whose consequences never made the papers.

The imposing Federal façade of the stone building in which McNaughton plied his trade was like so many others in the capitol, bespeaking old money, influence and the presence of that green Potomac fire.

McNaughton was a tall Texan with leathery skin burnished a pleasing bronze color, pale blue eyes with sprays of squint lines at their outside edges and thick silver hair. His long, almost mournful face was redeemed by his Roman nose and a genuine smile he had perfected during the many campaigns of his youth. He was like an old glove, at once rumpled and comfortingly familiar.

He came out of his office the moment Gaunt was announced, extending his hand for a firm, dry shake. He wore a dark suit, white shirt and a string tie with a hand-made bolo of worked silver and turquoise.

'Come on in,' he said in his rich baritone. 'It's good to see you again, Harley . . .' He closed the door behind them with a kick of his tooled cowboy boot. '. . . though I wish to hell it were under kinder circumstances.'

Gaunt chose an upholstered chair, sat down. 'Just what *are* the circumstances?'

McNaughton grunted, opted to sit on the tatty sofa opposite Gaunt's chair rather than retreat behind his kidney-shaped desk, so old-fashioned it was in vogue again.

'The circumstances,' he said, folding his long body into the semblance of a sitting position, 'can be summed up in three words: Senator Rance Bane.'

'Bane wants me.'

'He wants Nicholas Linnear, but he can't find him,' McNaughton said. 'D'you know where he is?'

'If he's not in Tokyo, I have no idea,' Gaunt said.

'I hope that's so.' McNaughton steepled his long fingers, looked up at the ceiling. 'I've known Rance for ages. We grew up in adjoining towns. My brother dated his sister for over a year. I've been following his career for a long time, worrying. This man has an obsessive personality, and his current obsession is getting the Japanese out of large American businesses. For him, Tomkin's merger with Sato International has become a lightning rod, a symbol if you will, of all that he sees wrong with international takeovers.'

McNaughton stretched out his legs. Thus relaxed and comfortable, he eased the tension in his guest. 'Because Linnear's company is involved in a number of sensitive advanced computer projects, the Senator's anxiety level has reached the boiling point. He wants Linnear brought up on charges, he wants the merger terminated forthwith.'

'What kind of charges could he possibly hit Nick with?' Gaunt asked, alarmed. 'Nick has done nothing illegal.'

'Sure that statement can hold water? Can you swear that you know everything that goes on at Tomkin-Sato?'

'No, but I – I know Nick. He wouldn't –'

'Not good enough, son. I've heard rumors. Something to the effect that Tomkin-Sato has been using the technology they got from Hyrotech-inc to

105

make their own form of the classified Hive computer and are now selling it overseas to the highest bidder. Hive is the property of the US Government. Improper use of it would be a treasonable offense.'

Gaunt looked bleakly at the older man. 'C'mon, this is bullshit, Terry.'

'Davis Munch doesn't think so. He's the Pentagon investigator attached to Rance's Committee.'

'Pure raving paranoia.'

'Depends on what Munch and his ferrets have uncovered –'

'There's nothing sinister to uncover.'

'Eye of the beholder,' McNaughton said. 'It's how they go about making what they've found sound sinister.'

'Hey, this is America, Terry. People don't get railroaded like this. I mean, not on this scale – in the glare of the national spotlight.'

McNaughton leveled a jaundiced look at him. 'That's a mighty dubious statement, son, especially coming from you,' he said. 'But even if it passed scrutiny, we haven't had a mind like Rance Bane's in the driver's seat since – oh, well, I suppose McCarthy will do as the most odious example.'

Gaunt's anxiety level was escalating dangerously. 'So what are you saying,' he said, 'bottom line?'

McNaughton sat forward, punched a button on an ivory plastic console. 'Marcy, we'll have that coffee now.'

He sat for a moment, silent, tapping his fingertips together in an unknown rhythm. In a moment, the door opened and his long-legged assistant brought in coffee and Danish on an exquisite chased silver service.

'Much obliged, Marcy,' McNaughton said, as she set it on the coffee table. She asked if there was anything else and when he said no she left.

He stared fondly at the coffee service. 'Memento of bygone days,' he said. 'Thatcher gave it to me after I –' He gave a sly smile. 'But, no, even now I can't talk about that.'

He made himself busy pouring the coffee. He added cream and one teaspoon of Demerara sugar to Gaunt's – he never forgot anything. He took his own black.

'Danish?' he asked as he handed Gaunt his cup. 'Those prune ones are particularly good.'

Gaunt shook his head. At this moment, he doubted if he could hold anything in his stomach. He sipped his coffee, watched McNaughton select a pastry, bite into it with perfect white teeth.

It was only after the Danish had been eaten and he had poured himself a second cup of coffee that McNaughton answered the question. 'Bottom line we got a terminal problem. See, it's gone beyond a question of image. That's my meat, and I could turn something like that around on a dime.

106

But this is no go; believe me, I've tried. Rance's got his hooks into Tomkin and he's not about to let go until he's shaken it apart.'

'We've got to stop him.'

McNaughton stared at Gaunt and said, 'You're a scion of this city, son. Think about what you've just said.'

'But –'

McNaughton was shaking his head. 'No buts on this one, Harley. I've got power, so have my friends, but Bane is beyond us. Christ, he's beyond even the President's control. He's a man who scares this town shitless because he's got the kind of groundroots evangelical support that even the most entrenched politician isn't going to fool with. Right now he's a juggernaut under full steam and them that's in his way better step aside 'less they want to get crushed.'

In the silence that prevailed, Gaunt could hear Marcy or someone like her working her word-processor. A phone rang, was answered. A door slammed.

At last, Gaunt could procrastinate no longer. 'Terry, because this is so important,' he said, 'I want you to spell it out for me, chapter and verse.'

McNaughton nodded, drew his legs up under him so that his boot heels scraped across the floor. 'Okay, here's the way it is, son. You – that is to say Tomkin Industries – pay me a fair bit of change to do my best lobbying on your behalf – and that, I assure you, I've done.

'But now, the advice I'm going to dispense is personal. We go back a long way, you and I. I came to your college graduation when your father couldn't, up on the Hill fighting for a bill he had sponsored. I have only fond memories of him – and I think I've been a good friend to you.'

He leaned forward. 'As I see it you have only two options. One is to go before the Committee and answer all of Bane's blistering questions with the foreknowledge that you are going to go down with the ship. Because make no mistake, as sure as we're sitting here now, Tomkin-Sato is doomed.'

Gaunt's throat was dry, and he took the last of his cold coffee, almost choked on some dregs.

'What's the other option?' But he already knew.

'The other option is in my opinion the one you should take,' McNaughton said in measured tones. His eyes were fever-bright, and it seemed as if his mouth had lost its ability to smile. 'Bail out. Resign. Get clear of harm's way. Let the juggernaut have its day. Let it destroy what it will: Tomkin Industries and Nicholas Linnear.'

*

107

Margarite Goldoni's eyes flew open and her heart pounded painfully in her breast. Her clawed fingers filled with fistfuls of satin sheet. There it was again, she thought wildly, that awful sensation of falling.

She lay in her bed beside her softly snoring husband, her knuckles white with gripping, panting a little as she stared blindly up at the ceiling. Always it came as she emerged from sleep, slipping from her unconscious like some bitch in heat.

That curious sensation of falling.

Not down a flight of stairs or off the edge of a swimming pool, but into a kind of nothingness – a void filled only with her own terror.

And then she would come fully awake – as now – filmed with a cold sweat, filled with the certain knowledge that something precious had been irrevocably taken from her.

At first, the nightmares had been flicker-flashes of her unreal journey across America in search of her brother's death, heated, insensate emotions coloring the images like spray-paint madly spattered across a series of rooms. Then, she would dream of Dominic or, more accurately, his elaborate funeral, flowers everywhere, limousines parked fender to bumper, Feds videotaping everyone who crossed the street to the cemetery. And everywhere, as she stood beside the gleaming mahogany and cherrywood coffin, open mouths keening silently, turned in her direction until she could no longer bear the noise and she was forced to look down into the open grave, where Dominic lay, mutilated and headless, beginning to rise, broken skeletal fingers scrabbling at the loamy dirt, on his way up to where she stood, rooted to the spot with a terror that threatened to fill her lungs, her throat, her open mouth.

And waking from these nightmares, covered in sweat and shivering, she would tell herself, yes, of course, she felt a profound sense of loss, she had lost her brother, had been a party to that loss.

But, eventually, in the clear light of day, at a meeting at the office or later, with evening shadows spreading into the kitchen, as she fed Francie dinner, would come the knowledge from deep down in her unconscious that this loss transcended grief and guilt. It was something far more personal.

Margarite lay, tense and white, listening to the rasp of her own respiration, turning over this sense of loss as if it were a three-dimensional object. It put her in mind of the summer she was eleven. Her father and step-mother had taken her to see her grandmother – her father's mother – who, as it turned out, was dying.

The old lady was as crooked as a Venetian walking stick, bent as if she carried each year of her life on her shoulders. Her hair was white and pulled back tightly in a neat bun, and forever afterward Margarite was to

108

remember her plain black dress, which she wore in the hot sun without so much as a drop of sweat appearing on her brow.

She had trouble hearing, and she had few of her teeth remaining. Some time before, she had had her larynx removed, and her voice emanated from a small box, more of a vibration than true speech, so that Margarite had to bend close to understand her.

Her grandmother had fed the family and, afterward, she gave Margarite's hand a secret squeeze. She had led her granddaughter into her bedroom, which was filled with sepia-toned photos of herself as a child, her parents, her confirmation and her wedding in Venice. Margarite saw photos of her father and his sister, who had died of cholera when she was a child.

Margarite's grandmother narrated each photo, then went to the top drawer of her old walnut dresser. She took out something, which she pressed into Margarite's fist just before they left, murmuring in her ear as she kissed her, 'This is for you. It belonged to the forebear of my great-grandmother. She had it with her when she arrived in Venice centuries ago. She was a refugee and this was all that was left of her family, who had died in a great war that lasted twenty years.'

On the way home, she had opened her sweaty hand to see revealed there a carving in amber of the most beautiful woman she had ever seen. She had never told anyone of that gift, and when, months later, she stood at her grandmother's graveside, she clutched the carving in her hand to ward off the sensation that something irretrievable had been taken away from her.

Now, as she lay panting in her own bed, she was swept anew by a similar feeling. The death of her brother had been a blow to her, but her own part in it, extorted though it may have been, continued to torment her.

She had been forced by the man she knew only as Robert to effectively choose between her daughter and her brother. It was a hellish decision, one in which she had known she could not emerge unscarred. But what choice did she have save to bring him to Dominic Goldoni? Francine had to be safeguarded at all costs and, oddly, she had believed Robert when he had promised her that if she played her part well he would not harm her daughter. He had been true to his word, disappearing as if from the face of the earth after he had left her – and Francie – in the sleazy motel room off Highway 95, just outside Marine on St Croix, Minnesota.

Again, she asked herself now if he had somehow enchanted her. With a mounting sense of horror, she recalled all too clearly her desire, could feel now, though he must be very far away, the weight of him, his heat like an intensely erotic charge. The scent of him, rising.

No, I cannot think the unthinkable.

Involuntarily, she put her hands on her sex, felt the wetness there, and knew what sin lay like a stone in her soul. With an effort she wrenched her mind away, trying to concentrate solely on Dominic. *But what was it about Robert? What had he taken from her; and what had he given her in return?* Dominic: the one man in her life who had believed in her, who had seen beyond her femaleness to the mind that she possessed, had used her in secret and seclusion like a nun behind the ivied walls of her cloister.

These men are all like children, she thought, *playing at being Pope. Do they know they're living in the real world?* Beside her, Tony DeCamillo slept heavily, little grunting snores escaping from him in spurts. She felt as detached from him as if he were in London. She had never known how much she despised him until Dominic had hit upon his complex and audacious plan to use Tony as his successor. The idea of being a Family *capo* had immediately gone to Tony's head. Was it so surprising? He had an aptitude for influence – the Hollywood mentality, a legacy from his show business clients. Power was the only commodity worth a damn in the film business, and Tony had had plenty of experience amassing it for himself. When Dominic had opened the door to a whole new world, Tony had been only too delighted to step in.

Except that he had no concept of what that world actually entailed – only she and Dominic knew. Dominic had told him that she would be the conduit between the two; Tony's involvement with Dominic – even social – had to be kept to a minimum because of the nature of Tony's law practice.

Then Dom was murdered. Margarite remembered the moment when she was forced to tell Tony how it was going to be from now on, that his power and influence were only an illusion. It was all too possible, she realized in retrospect, to have predicted how he would react. That Sicilian thing came to the fore, his rage had been towering, and he had struck her so often that she ceased to feel his blows save as a form of numbing pressure that pinned her to the wall of their bedroom. She bit her lip. How much of that had Francie heard? Did it matter? All or half, it would have the same effect on the girl, an effect Margarite seemed incapable of reversing.

Why did Dominic make me his sole confidant? she asked herself. Her intense pride in their special and secretive relationship all too often warred with the crushing responsibility that was his legacy. She felt a brief moment of despair, an emotion with which the old Margarite was all too familiar.

Then Robert rose in her mind like the breath of the sea.

Lying now in her bed, listening to the night and to the film playing in her mind, Margarite knew that she had crossed some kind of Rubicon. Somehow everything was different when she had returned home; now she heard Robert's voice whispering in her mind, *And what else have I given you, Margarite? Now you know you have the strength of purpose . . . to do anything.*

Like it or not, he is the source of these profound changes, Margarite thought. *I know he took something from me and I hate him for that, but, oh God, what is this thing he has left me in return?*

Suddenly, as if he were a genie uncorked from a bottle, her mind was filled with him. And through the water of her unconscious she saw the stone, her sin lying at the bottom of her soul.

It was as if he was there, lying beside her, and she trembled with some unknown emotion. She knew now that he had given her the strength to continue with Tony along the path of their new future. Because there was more, and she turned her mind away from the knowledge for as long as she could. But, in the end, it came flooding back, but for this moment at least the new, emerging Margarite possessed the strength to shoulder the full weight of her brother's legacy.

Because of Robert. With a soft moan she surrendered to the thought that she wanted to see him again.

FOUR

Vietnam – Summer 1965

Truth to tell, Do Duc never knew his father. He surmised, from what he picked up around the house, that his father had been Japanese, but he never got this confirmed from his mother or anyone else. She would never speak of his birth or the germination of it at all, as if by this willful ignorance she could pretend it had never occurred. He imagined that the man who was his father was Japanese, because all the other alternatives were worse.

The 'house' was the compound in Saigon where Do Duc's mother worked. It was owned by a one-armed Frenchman. It was contained by pale-green stucco walls, this rambling horseshoe-shaped villa of sloping tiled roofs and lush inner courtyards. Around the villa were kaleidoscopic gardens full of bougainvillea vines and rustling tamarind trees which Do Duc sweated endless hours to keep pruned to the Frenchman's exacting specifications; encysted within it was a cut-stone patio floating an asymmetrical pool the shape of which reminded Do Duc of a water buffalo's head.

There was something about the pool that Do Duc loved. In the short hours he had for sleep he would creep off his pallet, slip naked into the clear water, and push himself to the bottom. There he would cling, sealed in this soundless world, his head cocked back, staring upward at nothing, thinking about nothing, and whatever had filled him, preventing sleep, drained away into the nothingness.

Here in the Frenchman's compound, the thrumming diesel clangor of Saigon and, especially, the war itself, could be kept at the distance of memory. Only the reflections of jets, momentary as dreams, rippling in the cool cerulean water of the pool, articulated the harsh reality outside the stucco walls.

Do Duc's earliest memories of the Frenchman were wholly spurious: a gentle man, religious in his own way, because he sang the *Nunc dimittis*, Simeon's prayer, every evening, and taught it to Do Duc much as a father would teach a nursery rhyme to his child:

Lord, now lettest thou thy servant to depart in peace, according to thy word . . .

To induce Do Duc to sing along with him – the words were unfamiliar and difficult for him to pronounce – the Frenchman fed him sweets, a recipe of his own concoction that was dark and rich, tasting of honey, cinnamon and cloves.

But that was long ago, when Do Duc was five, the age at which the Frenchman deemed him old enough to be put to work.

When he was very young, Do Duc was certain that the Frenchman was printing up money in his basement, so much of it was there constantly changing hands. Later, he came to understand that the Frenchman was in the business of weapons and dope, if not directly sanctioned by Uncle Sugar – the local cynical nickname for the US Government – then at least tolerated by this enigmatic, godlike entity which overstrode life in wartime Saigon like a Titan from the clouds.

Often, half drunk on Medoc, he would order Do Duc to inventory his war matériel. Once, a supplier, disgruntled at the Frenchman's resolve to keep his costs low, had left a live grenade wired to the inside of one of the crates of K-Fifties he sold him. In those days, the Frenchman, dogmatic on matters of security, had done all the inventorying himself. That was how he had lost his arm. Now he ordered natives to do that work. Do Duc discovered that he was the third young Vietnamese to hold this job.

Later still, when he, acting as houseboy-slave at one of the Frenchman's astonishingly extravagant parties, was told by a pair of giddy Swedes how his mother had been used at these parties years ago before time had etched her face and bent her frame, he experienced the auras for the first time.

Stoned on a combination of champagne and the peculiar opium-laced marijuana the Frenchman favored, they related to Do Duc with the kind of raucous vivacity that could not be faked certain events that had taken place twelve years before. His mother, who was serving them their particular brand of poison, stood stoically through the recital, her eyes focused on nothing, as opaque as the clouds in the night sky that blotted out the horned moon.

Do Duc could not make up his mind whether they were waxing callously nostalgic or being deliberately sadistic. How could they not know who he was, that this was his mother they were giggling over? But then, Caucasians had this disturbing propensity for seeing Asians as just another part of the exotic landscape, along with the Nipa palms, rice paddies and mangrove swamps.

As to the auras, this strange incandescence he saw emanating from people seemed to signify like stigmata upon the flesh the depth of the change he himself was undergoing. It was as if he were able to peel back the layers of rational behavior civilization had impressed upon people, divining in their auras their purely primitive essence.

The auras became for him a kind of trigger. And eventually, he came to believe that the release of his profound rage was akin to a state of grace. In that moment following the onset of the auras, the purity of purpose that moved him to action was of the utmost relief, after the knots of conflicting emotions he carried upon his back like the bones of the dead.

This was how Do Duc viewed the Frenchman: he was someone who had given his mother life after the man she had loved had been killed by the military for daring to speak his mind for the good of his people. Whatever schooled intelligence she had possessed, whatever stature she had once had, had perished with the man she had loved. But this fall from grace was fatal. Unlike most of her brethren, she had an inkling of what might have been. Now she could only stare dull-eyed like a cat at nothing while she leaned her heavy head against the side of the refrigerator.

Life, even for her now, meant a few piasters, a pallet on which to sleep (his mother's was in the kitchen so she could be ready to whip up a meal at any time of the day or night) and even, from time to time, the benevolence of the Frenchman's protection, for he was an exceedingly powerful man, even in the corrupt and treacherous waters of Saigon.

At the same time, the Frenchman treated her with the kind of contempt normally reserved for a disease-ridden cur. He did not see how he demeaned her, stripped her of all dignity; was pleased, in fact, by his benevolence, his one significant act in keeping this Vietnamese woman from becoming a whore, grubbing in some filthy back alley until she died of consumption or addiction. Instead, she became a whore in his house, and renowned she was for services to all nations whose representatives came and went beneath the Frenchman's roof.

Life? Do Duc often thought. What life? She was expected to be on call for the gluttony – in all things – of the Frenchman's many guests. He was particularly proud of his reputation for hospitality – his bit, he said, laughing, for off-setting the constant bad press given his fellow countrymen back home.

And yet without the Frenchman as guardian angel his mother would have had nothing, would have been used up by the street, died old before her time. And what of Do Duc? There would have been none. He owed his very existence – humiliating and shameful beyond words – to this man. Owed him, in fact, for everything that had any meaning for him. And yet . . .

The Frenchman's aura, as it happened, was different from that of the others. It was a sharp blue, almost metallic, and much later, upon reflection on many such incidents, Do Duc was to understand that this color signified the man's close proximity to death.

'*Gang-rape*,' Do Duc said as he took the bread knife to the Frenchman's sun-dried flesh. The party, like a sun that had waxed too bright, had burned itself out. All the guests were gone, or insensate in drugged slumber. 'They told me. Everyone grouped around, counting how many men could penetrate her before she passed out.'

The knife flashing like a cormorant in the sun as it rose and fell in a terrible rhythm. 'This is what you have done to my mother.' Blood on the Frenchman's hands, first, startling as a spilled bottle of his best wine. 'This is my birth, a humiliating party anecdote.' Then, in a great spurt, Do Duc's own hands were hot and sticky.

'Do you understand my mother's shame? She cannot even bring herself to speak of my birth.' His thin cotton shirt was wet and heavy with blood. 'No, you cannot. What can you know of shame?'

The Frenchman's eyes were wide and staring, muddy with an incomprehension as to what was happening, his life leaking out through the proliferating wounds as Do Duc stabbed him again and again.

'Each time she looks at me she remembers all over again what she is, what you have made her become.'

The Frenchman's mouth gaped wide.

'She knows how mean and bitter life is because this was your gift to her.'

He put his bloody hand out; it opened and closed on nothing, spastic as a machine-gun on rock 'n' roll.

'To her you are the Word, more than god or Buddha because these are indifferent entities. But you are here – flesh and blood. The man who made the world.'

The Frenchman had slipped to his knees, and now swayed this way and that in a rhythm dictated by Do Duc's attack. Finding his voice was difficult through the blood bubbling in his throat. 'I did nothing that you ... I saved her.' Incredulous, still, at the end, not even dissembling but, frighteningly, still righteous. And this innocence served only to enrage Do Duc all the more, although, later, when the auras died, it would haunt him, confusing him in a labyrinth of complex adult emotions for which he was wholly unprepared, because the Frenchman was entirely sincere.

'You saved her for *this* – misery and degradation. She would never touch you, never even think ill of you in her heart because that is her way. But not me. I am different ... different ... different.'

'Lord, now lettest thou thy servant to depart –'

115

Doc Duc slit his throat, unable or unwilling to allow this last obscenity – the word *peace* in the *Nunc dimittis* – to be uttered here in the peaceful isolation of a luxe fantasy that contemptuously denied the poverty and suffering at large in every quarter.

The Frenchman's last words were curdled in blood and bile, slurred by the inexpressible runes of death, but distinct enough to be forged into Do Duc's soul. 'There are . . . no evil thoughts,' the Frenchman vomited. 'Only . . . evil deeds.'

This last exhortation must have taken everything he had left, because his eyes rolled up and he collapsed, one leg jerking fitfully in galvanic response. Then his sphincter gave way, leaving a final epitaph Do Duc found particularly fitting.

Do Duc fled Saigon, fearing for his life. He knew how powerful the Frenchman was, and he understood that he was obliged to bury himself in order to remain among the living.

What he wanted most then was to fight, to climb into the cockpit of one of those jets he had for years seen only in reflection or at a far distance.

He hated the Communists as much as he hated the French and the Americans – more, even, because the Communists were his own people and they should know better than to turn on their own. What madness gripped them to try to commit genocide, to expunge their own unique history, was as yet beyond him to comprehend. All he knew for certain was that they were like a pack of rabid beasts who were best exterminated with all due dispatch.

However, joining the ARVN – the South Vietnamese army – at just this point might prove dangerous, as those looking for him might understandably search through the dossiers of recent recruits. Instead, he went into the mountains and changed his life forever.

At that time, the mountains were no place for a twelve-year-old boy. There, the rag-tag hill-tribe montagnards were forming; there, the Viet Cong were massing; there, blood was being spilled every minute of the day and night. But to Do Duc it still felt less dangerous than the life he had led in the Frenchman's walled compound in Saigon.

But there were others in the mountains, urged on by the Communists and the war, who had crept southward from their home in the highlands of North Vietnam. These were the Nungs, a wild, almost aboriginal people of Chinese descent who possessed their own primitive outlook on the world, their own ancient ways of preserving what was theirs.

Even the fierce VC were afraid of the Nungs, keeping their distance, shunning the areas where Nung tribesmen were sighted. In the mountains, Do Duc heard wild rumors and exaggerations about the Nungs – that they were disposed toward magic, that they wrapped themselves in the cured skins of their enemies while crouched before fires, eating their roasted flesh.

Far from frightening him, these tales merely aroused Do Duc's curiosity. He was intrigued by any people who could terrify the Communists. In the Frenchman's compound he had learned the only lesson worth remembering in Asia: that it wasn't money one sought in life; it was power. The Nungs had power while Do Duc had none. So he set out to find them. The way he figured it, all he had to lose was his life, which at this moment was just about worthless. What he had to gain, he felt, was limitless.

It was the best decision he ever made – and the worst. The old Do Duc, whomever he may have been, was dissolved among the Nungs, and a new Do Duc was born. Resurrection would have been too simple a term, but after the assimilation process, he would often go off by himself, climbing higher into the cliffs to look out into the deepening sapphire twilight and, quite without knowing it, sing to himself the *Nunc dimittis*.

Even after the old Nung, Ao, had examined him, told him that he had once been addicted to opium, Do Duc set aside a time each twilight to sing the prayer. Even after he worked out what must have been in the sweet the Frenchman had fed him besides the honey, cinnamon and cloves, even as he wondered at the cynical method the Frenchman had used to import loyalty to his compound.

'Lord, now lettest thou thy servant to depart in peace, according to thy word.'

The words, still only dimly understood, were of such comfort to him that he could not bear to forget them. Of course he had biological parents, he had known his mother, if only superficially, but she had never wanted to know him because in his face she could see reflected all that her life would now never become.

The hymn of the *Nunc dimittis* provided the only safety, the only true warmth he had ever known. Impossible to expunge that from his psyche, even after the training the Nungs gave him began.

They liked that he was an outlaw, the Nungs. The first night after he had come upon them just over a high ridgetop, they laughed at his tale, clapped him on the back and spit in the dust to show their pleasure at what he had done. All except Ao, the eldest man and most respected of the tribe. He crouched still and indrawn, his odd, ginger-colored eyes all but closed as if Do Duc's words were rays of light that might blind him.

Watching him as he spoke, Do Duc caught the impression that Ao was aware of his heartache; the rage, the bitterness, the revulsion as well as,

117

buried below like a fish in the depths of a muddy lake, the tenderness he felt for the man he had murdered.

After the others broke up, going their own way in the cool mountain night, he opened his eyes, studied Do Duc alone by the fire. A branch crackled, a sudden crack appearing as it settled deeper into the flames.

'People say strange things about the Nungs,' Do Duc said, suddenly shivering. He put his hands on his bent knees, almost a defensive gesture. 'They say you roast the flesh of your enemies and eat it.'

'I prefer to eat my meat raw,' Ao said. He waited what seemed a long time to break into raucous laughter. When his face had settled into its former pattern of lines and depressions, he said, 'You are safe with us, younger brother.'

This was how Ao, the stoic, opened his psychic arms to Do Duc, gathering him into the Dark.

He was an unusually big man, with a commanding presence. He knew all the Mysteries and he knew the ways of the Caucasian as well. For example, he knew how to break down an American M-60 machine-gun, clean it, and put it back together again, all in the dark. He knew the grades of plastique, how to use a white phosphorus mortar and a CS gas grenade; he was conversant with the principles of aviation.

One night he took Do Duc down the mountain into the green-and-black-striped jungle. It was so wet and dense it was like gliding underwater. Do Duc noticed that Ao, though old, made no sound at all. He seemed to be following some kind of trail, but try as he might, Do Duc could discern nothing, not even an occasional notch in a tree trunk, that might be construed as a path.

They continued this way, wending their way through the night. Utter darkness engulfed them, so that Do Duc, traveling single-file behind Ao, was obliged to put his hand on the old man's shoulder so as not to become lost. All around him were the night chitterings and cries of the jungle. The rank smells of moss and decomposing vegetation were as strong as freshly brewed black tea from the Iron Mountains of China.

Great whirring insects brushed Do Duc's cheeks and arms, and once, he heard the muffled growl of a great predator. The level ground changed, sloping steadily downward, and at last his eyes could begin to see the wash of pale moonlight drifting down through the jungle's canopy as it began to thin.

Ao stopped and, crouching down, wordlessly pointed straight ahead. At first, Do Duc could see nothing, then the wind changed direction and he heard like temple bells the deep musical tones of slowly flowing water.

The sounds directed him, and he began to make out the bank on which

118

they crouched and, just beyond, a mountain stream. He heard a sudden splash, and saw a great bulk sliding slowly into the water.

Ao made a peculiar noise in the back of his throat which made the hair at the back of Do Duc's neck stir. The bulk lifted its head, and Do Duc saw the furred head of a black leopard.

He had heard stories about such beasts, rare as they were, but no one he knew had ever seen one. They were said to possess magical powers that turned the orange stripes of their pelt black, as if singed by the force inside them.

Ao made the sound again and Do Duc shivered. Slowly, the black leopard turned, came toward them. Do Duc felt a rippling of his muscles, a firing of his nerves over which he had no control. His head seemed to have developed a tremor so that the beast, as it approached, went in and out of focus. He was so frightened he could feel a chill come over him as his blood drained from his extremities, pooling sickeningly in the pit of his stomach.

The black leopard emerged from the water. It was now close enough to be able to swat Do Duc down with one blow of its massive forepaw. Its body was perhaps eleven feet long, and its thick tail, flicking this way and that, added another three feet.

Do Duc could smell it, heavy, musky, an odor of power and of death. His mouth was so dry his tongue clove to the roof and would not move. The beast stared at them, unmoving, breathing in deep, purring sighs.

Ao pressed one hand flat against Do Duc's shoulder, indicating that he should not move. Then, suddenly, terrifyingly, he was gone, back into the jungle.

The black leopard's bulk was like a planet. His great chest billowed out and deflated. Its huge golden eyes regarded Do Duc with a peculiar kind of intelligence, but for all this it appeared slightly myopic. An American army colonel who was a frequent visitor at the Frenchman's villa had told Do Duc that leopards could not see or hear well, that they relied most heavily on scent.

The beast blinked and Do Duc started, despite his best efforts. The black leopard growled low in its throat and its head lowered. Do Duc felt as if his bowels had turned to water. He had to urinate in the worst way.

Ao returned, holding his left arm straight out in front of him. As he crouched down Do Duc saw the curl of a venomous krait wrapped around his forearm. Ao had its triangular head pinched between thumb and fore-finger.

He swung his arm out toward the black leopard, an offering of some

119

kind, and Do Duc saw the beast's nostrils flare as it caught the scent of the viper. When it moved its head it did so with appalling speed. Do Duc doubted whether even Ao could have gotten out of the way at such close quarters.

The great jaws gaped wide, engulfing both krait and Ao's arm. A moment later, Ao pulled his arm out. The krait was no longer wrapped around it.

The small sounds of the black leopard eating was all that could be heard for a time. Then the beast gave a little snuffle, and Ao made that eerie sound in the back of his throat.

He put his hands on Do Duc's shoulders, thrusting him forward, down the embankment toward the great beast. Those baleful eyes regarded Do Duc with that same myopic intelligence as he came near it. Urine trickled down Do Duc's leg, and the black leopard snuffled again, more interested now in the smell of him.

He could feel the heat of the beast emanating from it in waves. The animal musk surged upward, into his nostrils, so that he felt abruptly dizzy.

Behind the black leopard, moonlight veined the water, turning it into lapis lazuli, on which, Do Duc imagined, it would be possible to walk.

He turned his attention back to the beast and blinked rapidly in outright astonishment. The black leopard no longer crouched before him. Instead, he saw a slender woman with an exquisite face, thick black hair so long it ran in rivulets like the moonlit river behind her. She was in all aspects human in appearance except that her long fingers were the gnarled roots of a tree, and when she shifted her body, Do Duc could see that from the waist down she was a skeleton, no skin, no flesh at all, bones only, glowing palely in the fitful moonlight.

'Who – what are you?' Do Duc could not help himself; he had to ask the question.

'Don't you recognize me?' the exquisite woman said. She regarded him from out of golden eyes. 'I am your mother.'

Do Duc's heart was pounding so hard in his chest he felt as if it had been he, not the beast, who had swallowed the krait. 'Impossible,' he scoffed in a voice thick with terror. 'My mother is much older than you.'

'No,' the exquisite woman said, 'I am dead.'

'What?'

'The Frenchman's friends killed me because I would not tell them where you had fled.'

'But you did not know!' Do Duc exclaimed. 'You could not!'

'And yet, in my heart, I knew,' she said. 'There was only one place left for you to go. You, who should never have been born, whose life had been

120

a terrible mistake. In order to live you must die and be reborn. Your first life was a misunderstanding; now you have a chance at a second.'

He knew who she was now, and that she appeared to him as she had once been – young and exquisite – and now he could understand how they could all desire her, if only for one night, those travelers in the night who congregated like magpies beneath the Frenchman's roof.

'Mother,' he said, an unaccustomed wetness in his eyes. He had never once before this shed a tear for her or for anyone.

'Do not call me that; I was never such to you,' she said sadly. 'I was wicked, never finding the compassion inside myself to love you. You were pariah to me; the Frenchman no doubt loved you more than I.' Her head lowered, and her dark hair cascaded over her silvery face. 'It is good I am dead. I prayed to Buddha daily to let me feel the love I should have for you, but my prayers were never answered. My heart was already shriveled, a dead lump beneath my breast.'

'Mother, this was not of your doing.'

Her head snapped up, the cascade of hair falling from her face. Her eyes blazed pale fire, and the grimace she made contained within it the heart of the black leopard, baring its yellow teeth for the kill.

'No. Of course this is true,' she whispered fiercely. 'I am Asia, spreading my legs compliantly to be raped by the French, the Russians, the Chinese, the Americans. They have used us so carelessly, enslaved us to opium, turned us into water buffaloes to do their labor, and finally we are as mad as a rabid dog, turning on itself, chewing its own leg off in its insanity.'

She drew up, her skeleton-like fingers clawing the air. 'And I am mad, too, so insane that I lacked the capacity to love that which I should have cherished. You are my blood, Do Duc, and I looked on you as they look on us.' She shook her head. 'No, do not waste your time mourning for me. I have my *karma* and I embrace it. Now I am a part of the destruction of Asia. It may be horrible, but it is at least something.'

'But I have killed you!' he cried. 'Because of me –!'

The exquisite face shone. 'I would not tell them where you went. I kept your secret, Do Duc. Didn't you think I knew what the consequences would be? Yes, yes. I did it willingly, and it felt good to defy them. At last, oh!' She gave a sigh. 'This was the only meaningful act in my life. At the end, I found that my heart was still beating, beating for you.' The golden eyes caught him in their web.

'Now is your time, my son. Make the most of it.'

A cloud must have ridden across the sky because the moonlight faded, the darkness shifted and, blinking, Do Duc found himself face-to-face with the black leopard. Dizzy again with its musk, his eyes closed for a moment,

121

and when he opened them again, the beast had clambered down into the water, was swimming swiftly downstream, away from them.

He lowered his head and wept uncontrollably. Never before this had he been touched by love, and now here it was, so painful that he resolved never to allow it to touch him again.

The hand on his shoulder was firm and steadying. 'Yes, younger brother,' Ao whispered in his ear. 'Harden your heart until it is like unto a stone in your breast, for your path is as treacherous as it is arduous.'

Do Duc, crouched on the steaming bank of the mountain stream, felt these words rather than heard them, and they filled that nothingness inside of him, the emptiness that, back where he had once lived, he had exulted to feel at the cool, silent bottom of the Frenchman's pool.

When, at length, he raised his head, it was that peculiar hour just before the first dawnlight, when the world is devoid of color, etched with the grays of mist and night's last strands of shadow.

'We have been here all night?'

'Time is unimportant now,' Ao said. 'Forget time.'

'What happened?' Do Duc turned to face the old man. 'The black leopard, the krait, the ghost of my mother. Was it all a dream?'

Ao's lips curled into a sardonic smile. 'It is Ngoh-meih-yuht, the Crescent Moon,' he said. 'Now listen to me, and I will tell you about the Paau Dance:

'In the old days, when the civilization of the Nung was at its height, certain of our city-states revered the leopard. The Nung called the animal Paau and believed that it was a deity. But there were those who coveted the power of the gods and so set about capturing the Paau. This they did with rare courage and cool cunning, trapping it in a camouflaged pit of their own devising.'

Ao had a way of speaking that was almost hypnotic, as if by his voice alone he could conjure magic out of the very atmosphere.

'First, they broke the beast's legs so that it could not flee – even their evil had its limits, and they would not dare cage it and risk the wrath of the gods. But in breaking its bones they were assured that its soul would remain intact inside it and would eventually become a part of them.

'In the unbroken bones of man and animal alike resides the remnants of the "soul", from which a new life may be reconstituted by the proper rituals and prayers.

'Next, they fed it the living flesh of their enemies to make it strong and increase its divine power. After nine days, they slit the breast of the leopard, prying apart its ribcage in order to remove its still beating heart. They ate this organ, and, naked, wrapped themselves in the open, eviscerated body of the Paau as if they could absorb its blood. It was said the ghastly cloak trembled as it clung to their bare shoulders. This was the Paau Dance.'

The predawn mist steamed from the bank, obscuring the stream; even its sound disappeared into the opalescent atmosphere, so that they could have been anywhere, hanging suspended in time.

'They became united in this grotesque ritual, these men, and their power, whether real or imagined, grew. Their enemies were invariably found naked with their digits broken and turned backwards so that they could no longer hold onto their own power, and their feet could not function to make their escape.'

Ao's ginger eyes seemed to take on a peculiar cast. 'And, most important of all, their hearts had been ripped from their chests and sewn to their navels so that their souls could not emerge at the moment of death.'

His head swung away for a moment, and it appeared to Do Duc as if he stared through the walls of mist to another place, another time.

'The Paau Dance,' he said. 'The gateway to power and more power – this is what I will teach you because it is why you have come to me from the lowlands.' He lifted a hand. 'Now you must take a creature to represent you, to be your spirit familiar. Choose!'

Do Duc said the first thing that came into his mind. 'I want the white magpie.'

'The white magpie.' Ao turned his head in Do Duc's direction, and Do Duc could feel the heat in his eyes. 'Are you certain?'

Do Duc nodded. Oddly, he *was* certain, for the first time in his life.

Ao's expression was grave. 'You have spoken, let it be so. Your familiar shall be the white magpie.'

Ao's words seemed to penetrate Do Duc's flesh like a flurry of darts, making him twitch with momentary pain.

Ao's eyes were like black stones at the bottom of the river, smooth and unknowable. He hesitated but a moment. 'It is done! You will become Ngoh-meih-yuht, and by Ngoh-meih-yuht alone can you be tracked down.'

'What does this mean?' Do Duc whispered.

A sardonic smile curled Ao's lips. 'You will become another person. Does this frighten you? No? Good. For yours will be a thirsty soul. Soon – very soon – food and drink will no longer be of interest to you.'

'What will sustain me?'

'That will depend,' Ao said gravely, 'on what remains after you become Ngoh-meih-yuht.'

'But I will be mortal.'

Ao did not answer him at once. At length, he said, 'If you are delivered a mortal wound, then yes, you may die. In that sense, you will be mortal.

123

But you will be Ngoh-meih-yuht, and your body will possess remarkable recuperative and regenerative capabilities.'

'I will be close to immortality.'

Ao's eyes were hooded. 'In the end, that will be for you to determine.'

Now he was aware that Ao was studying him with keen attention. The old man held one hand out between them, palm up.

A bird called shrilly, its voice echoing through the jungle, against the walls of mist, with an eerie tone.

Ao was waiting for Do Duc to slide his hand over his. When Do Duc did, he felt Ao's grip all through his body. And when Ao spoke, it was already as if through a different kind of veil or mist.

'Are you ready to continue your journey from one world to another?'

Do Duc opened his mouth to speak, but Ao was nodding, as if already aware of the response forming in his mind.

FIVE

Venice/Tokyo/New York

Nicholas was awakened by the deep rumble of boats on the Grand Canal. He opened his eyes into darkness. He looked at his watch; it was not yet dawn. But as he padded across the room he could already see a thin strand of not-quite-darkness making its way between the wooden shutters. He threw them open to find a pale light of a color he could neither describe nor name staining the marble façades of the *palazzi* along the *rio*. In the water was the reflection of a sea bird, all too soon gone from sight. It left, cool and distinct, the sight of the Santa Maria della Salute.

He went into the bathroom, relieved himself, splashed cold water on his face, dressed and went out of his room. He had no idea where he was going; he only knew that he must walk the streets, breathe the air, feel the city on his skin like cloth-of-gold.

He pulled the collar of his jacket up around his cheeks as the first bite of the wind off the *rio* struck him. Then he went out of the small square, down a *ruga*, a street with shops. No one was around at this early hour and most shops were still closed. His nose led him toward a small bakery, where he purchased a cup of coffee and a delicious hard roll, which he munched on delightedly as he crossed over a small bridge that led to the Piazza San Marco.

He paused for a moment, as he liked to do, at the apex of the bridge's arc, looking down the *rio* at the play of light off the silken water. Commercial boats lay tied up, bobbing slightly, patiently awaiting their owners upon whose doorsteps they floated.

He passed over two more bridges without seeing a soul, then went beneath the arch that led to the piazza. Ahead of him rose the Doge's Palace and, to his left, the bell-tower which still struck the hours as it had for decades. The vast space, bordered on either side by arcaded shops and cafés with their outdoor set-ups, seemed so private at this hour, it was as if he had entered the drawing-room of the gods.

He walked out onto the cobbles and soon enough he heard the cooing of the well-fed pigeons that flocked to the floods of tourists who would begin to appear some hours before lunchtime.

All at once, Nicholas heard a voice raised in song. He listened, transfixed, as he heard 'Nessun Dorma', Prince Calaf's beautiful aria from Giacomo Puccini's *Turandot*. 'No man shall sleep,' the tenor sang, and coming toward him Nicholas saw a street-sweeper, pulling his wheeled garbage can behind him, his thick-bristled brush pushed rhythmically ahead of him. His head was thrown back as he sang, and Nicholas, hearing this aria in the sublime amphitheater of the Doges of Venice, felt that no matter what troubles he had left behind him in Tokyo, no matter what dangers he was about to face, on this morning, at this hour, it was good to be alive.

He saluted the *de jure* opera singer as he passed him, and the burly man smiled without missing a beat, moving on, his passionate voice resounding through the piazza.

Nicholas turned the corner, walking through the Piazzetta toward the wharf and the Grand Canal. The first colors of dawn had risen from the bosom of the ocean to stain the sky and the buildings along the water the same hue, so that there seemed no distinction at all between sea and land.

The quay – actually the Riva degli Schiavoni – was beginning to fill with schoolchildren climbing onto *vaporetti* bound for morning classes. Their high-pitched voices rang across the *piazzette* as they ran to buy their tickets and climb on board. There, they laughed and shoved each other, filling the narrow outside decks of the boats while bleary-eyed workers inside the cabins buried their heads in local papers.

There were few people about. The tourists were probably only now rolling out of bed to order their croissants and cappuccinos. He strolled toward the *traghetti* where the *vaporetti* pulled in and departed. To his right was the statue of Saint Theodore, to his left the famous winged lion. It seemed altogether fitting to him that the Doges of Venice should have chosen a mythical animal to represent their city.

Popping the last of the roll into his mouth and finishing off his coffee, he reflected that the longer he was here the more he understood how Venice was a true modern-day city-state. The people here might be Italians by nationality, but there it ended. Many areas within a country had their own argot such as the Venetians did, but none thought differently, as the Venetians did. Their way of life was unique unto themselves, and Nicholas found himself responding to that iconoclasm on the deepest level.

As he came closer to the statue of the winged lion he saw a young woman in a short, fur-collared jacket sitting on its base. The first wave of schoolchildren had been swept off along the Grand Canal and, for the time being at least, the broad arc of the *riva* was deserted.

The woman was quite striking. She had one of those long-nosed,

126

wide-mouthed Mediterranean faces that was just as much Phoenician as it was Roman: thick red hair drawn back off her face, her skin the color of a North African desert. As he drew abreast of her, Nicholas saw that her deep-set eyes were the color of aquamarines. Her cameo face, far from being perfect or even symmetrical, nevertheless possessed a kind of breathless ardor, as if it were the result of an enchantment. She sat with her knees drawn up, her elbows on them. She was holding a chocolate-filled pastry which she was eating with evident delight.

She looked up as Nicholas's shadow fell briefly across her, the sunlight firing the translucent blue of her eyes. Her smile told him who she was.

There were tiny smudges of chocolate at the corners of her mouth. 'Would you mind moving? I've been enjoying this view.' She spoke in English, but there was the hint of an accent that led him to believe it was not her primary language.

Nicholas sat down beside her.

'I've been waiting for you,' she said.

'Not for too long, I hope,' Nicholas said. 'It's a pleasant surprise to see you without your mask.'

She bit into her pastry, her smile broadening as she chewed. 'All Hallows Eve is past,' she said. 'In the daylight we can all be ourselves once again.'

'Even Mikio Okami?'

She gave him a sharp glance. 'Okami-san is under unbelievable pressure. This life would surely have killed lesser men by now.'

Nicholas said nothing. He rubbed his hands together to rid them of the early-morning chill.

'You *will* help him?'

'What was he doing in partnership with Dominic Goldoni, America's most powerful Mafia don?'

'Trying to save himself,' Celeste said. Then she added, 'Do you know anything about Goldoni other than that he was Mafia?'

'What more is there to know?'

She gave him a sad smile. 'For one thing, Goldoni was half-Venetian; that made him unique among the *capi* of the Sicilian-dominated Mafia. For another, he had a vision that went beyond anything the Mafia ever dreamed of. He saw that the days of Sam Giancana and the others like him were numbered, and he did his planning for a new era. His contacts in America were crucial for Okami-san to implement his plan to stifle the Godaishu.' Her clear eyes regarded him. 'Does this mean you won't help Okami-san?'

Nicholas was aware of the concern in her voice. 'Tell me,' he said, 'do

127

you know the identity of Okami's nemesis, who has forged the link between the Yakuza and the Mafia?'

'No,' Celeste said. 'I wish I did.'

'What could his power be – his hold – on all these other powerful men?'

Celeste was silent so long that Nicholas felt compelled to change the subject. 'What is Okami-san to you? Employer? Father-figure? Lover? All three, perhaps?'

Celeste laughed. 'How full of pride Okami-san would be if he heard you say that. Do you know he is over ninety?'

'I didn't.'

'Um hmm. Well, he's been here in Venice a long time now – and even before he moved here he's had – ah – ties to some of the important Venetian families.'

'I take it yours would be one of those.'

'My father gave his life for Okami-san.' She wiped her hands on a piece of paper. 'I imagine that sounds odd to you – and perhaps a little bizarre.'

'Not at all,' Nicholas said. 'I'm half-Eastern. I understand the meaning of debt.'

'Yes, of course.' She turned her head away, stared out at the sun rising over the lagoon. To their right, across the Grand Canal, the Santa Maria della Salute glowed in the shell-pink light, and above them, the wings of the Venetian lion seemed afire. 'My people, or some of them at least, came from Carthage,' she said after a time. 'They were seafarers but also philosophers and, it has been said, great scientists. Their home was burned, their city razed, so they set out on the only friend they had left: the sea. And, at last, they found themselves here, in Venice.' Her head swung round and she looked him full in the face. 'These are stories my grandfather used to tell. He swore they were true, just as he swore he knew where the boat they came in was buried beneath the palazzo you were in last night.'

'That was your house?'

'It is Okami-san's now,' Celeste said without a trace of melancholy or bitterness. 'I live elsewhere now – away from the Grand Canal where it is more secluded.'

'And the rest of your family?'

'Okami-san bought my mother her own apartment, one she could take care of on her own. As for my sister, she no longer lives in Venice.'

She turned her head a little, and the sunlight struck the bridge of her nose so that he could imagine her at the bow of an ancient ship, setting sail from Carthage, across the Mediterranean, heading for this sheltered place that would become Venezia.

'I suppose, in light of Venetian history, my family's fate is not so atypical. Here, we have learned to be adaptable, to the times, to fate and, most importantly, to politics.

'My father's business was fabrics: Fortuny velvets, laces, silks and the like. My grandfather invented a specific process for creating a certain kind of moire brocade that is still ours alone. Okami-san's people came from Osaka, and were once also in the dry goods business. He and my father understood each other right away. Both were honorable; both were pragmatic. My father's family was very Eastern, and he could see why Okami-san would want to buy his company. In the end, they worked out a partnership.'

'So the partnership was strictly legitimate, a perfect cover for Okami being here in Venice.'

'I am concerned only with what Okami-san has done for my family.' He could tell that she did not care for his tone of voice. Softly, she said, 'Please answer my question. Will you help him?'

He thought back to last night when Okami had told him that his life was in danger.

Here are the problems, he had said to Okami. *There is the question of identity: we don't know who will be sent to kill you. There is the question of time: we must assume that we have very little of it. Under these extreme conditions our options are severely limited. It will do no good to send you to ground because you need to continue to work and you cannot do that in hiding. It will do no good to guard you day and night because whoever is sent will have the advantage of setting the time if not the place, and I will be at a disadvantage. In these desperate circumstances I cannot afford any disadvantage. I am already at a disadvantage because I have no idea who I'm up against.*

Okami had looked at him bleakly. *What you're saying, then, is that we are checkmated.*

Not at all. What I am saying is that extreme circumstances require extreme measures. He had suddenly felt cold, as if a wind had swept through the palazzo. *In order to help you I am going to have to become a magnet.*

Magnet?

Yes. Call it a human shield. What I want to do is redirect the assassin's attention from you to me.

'I will do what I can,' Nicholas said now.

'Yes, I know,' Celeste nodded. 'Okami-san and I discussed it at length last night after you left. But I wanted to hear it from you. To be certain.' She looked out to sea for a moment. 'I need to tell you about the three men of the Kaisho's inner council, because one of them has ordered Okami-san's death.'

'The man Okami says is behind the rise of the Godaishu as an international criminal organization.'

Celeste nodded. 'The inner council consists of the *oyabun* who command Japan's three major Yakuza families: Tetsuo Akinaga, Akira Chosa, Tomoo Kozo.' She showed him photos of each of them. 'All of these men must be considered guilty until you can prove them innocent. I urge you not to trust any of them; one has betrayed Okami-san and all he has worked for.'

He stared at the photos, committing them to memory. Then he looked at her. 'Okami-san is not your lover, but he is very special to you. Before, you said the pressure he was under would kill a lesser man.'

'That's right.'

'And yet he is ninety.'

She rose abruptly. 'Let's walk. I'm cold.' She tucked her hand in her jacket pocket as they headed off down the *riva*. Pigeons rose and fell in concert, like the wing of a gigantic avian, and hawkers offering free rides to the island of Murano for an obligatory tour through the glass-blowing factories raised their voices over the heavy thrum of the boats. Pigeons, crying for food, swept low overhead, their wingbeats strong on the cool air.

'Now I will tell you what not even the men of the inner council know, a secret about the Kaisho: he possesses *koryoku*.'

Koryoku. The word burned itself across his mind. 'Mikio Okami has the Illuminating Power?'

'It's what has allowed him to survive all these years,' Celeste said. 'It answers many questions, doesn't it? Over ninety and with the strength and will of a fifty-year-old.'

Nicholas's heartbeat throttled up, and he had to slow his breathing. But his mind was racing forward. *Koryoku*, the nexus, the doorway into *Shuken*. If Okami did indeed possess the Illuminating Power he would be able to tell Nicholas whether it was possible for him to attain *koryoku*. His dream of finding the lost secret of his ancient race, the combining of Akshara and Kshira, Light and Dark, the two sundered hemispheres of Tau-tau, might at last be within reach.

If he could keep Okami safe.

'I've startled you at last,' Celeste said.

'I'm afraid you have.'

She turned her head, gave him a quick, sharp look. 'He doesn't want you to do it. To put yourself in the line of fire.'

'It's too late for that.'

'But what do you mean? I agree with him.'

'Keep walking, but pick up your pace a bit,' Nicholas said. He guided her away from the *riva*, into a side street. The hour was late enough for more stores to be open, and there was what might be described as a crush of people hurrying to work. Somehow this struck Nicholas as somewhat odd and a bit amusing; it was difficult to believe that anyone actually worked in this city of marvels. But, of course, beneath the treasures Venice was still a city, although hardly a mundane one.

'Neither Okami nor I have a choice now,' he said. 'We're both committed to this path. You must accept what happens.'

'*Karma*. This is your fate.'

He heard the cynical edge to her voice. 'Listen, Celeste, if you don't believe in *karma*, it doesn't exist.'

'Like *giri*.' She liked the surprised look that sprang to his face. 'Yes, I know about obligation, a debt that can never adequately be repaid.'

Seeing a small bakery, he pulled her in, where they stood in front of glass cases, staring at the breads and small cakes fresh from the oven.

'Are you hungry? We just ate.'

'I'd like to know if we're alone in this part of the city.'

Celeste watched him as he glanced in the mirror along the wall behind the clerk, a middle-aged woman with rosy cheeks and a cheery word for all her regular morning customers.

'What have you seen?'

'Maybe nothing,' Nicholas said, as the woman came over. He pointed at a huge, flat loaf of bread filled with black olives and fresh rosemary. He indicated the size of the slices she should sell him, but his eyes were constantly flicking upward to the mirror. 'Maybe something.'

'Has it begun?' Was that fear or excitement firing her face?

He dug in his pocket for some *lira*, took the white paper bag and his change from the woman and headed for the door. 'I'll leave you here. Wait five minutes then head back to the *riva*.'

'No,' she said. 'I'm going with you.'

'You're not involved in this.'

'Oh, but I am. Remember *giri*? I owe Okami-san. Besides, whoever is coming for him must already know about me. I'll no doubt be safer with you.'

Nicholas had no ready counter for that argument. He did not think she was the type to hide out at her mother's house until this blew over. He decided to say nothing, but he knew he would need to alter his plans slightly now that he would not be alone.

Back on the street, they headed away from the Grand Canal. The narrow streets were periodically filled with people, then almost deserted as these clumps of humanity dispersed at a cross-corner or a bridge.

All the while, Nicholas used the plate glass of store and restaurant windows to scan the street immediately behind them.

'What do you see?' Celeste asked.

'Right now, it's not what I see that bothers me,' Nicholas told her. 'It's what I *feel*. Someone definitely has us under surveillance.'

They went over a bridge, then turned left into another street.

'So it *has* begun,' she said. 'What do we do now?'

'We let whoever it is continue to follow us.'

'Why?'

'Because,' he said, 'the longer they have to shadow us the better our chances are of spotting them. And that's what I really want to do.' He gave her hand a squeeze. 'Are you up for looking your enemy in the face?'

She gave him a small smile. 'Under the circumstances I'd like nothing better.'

'Got a break.' Lillehammer made his way haltingly down the aisle of the Air Force jet, holding several fax sheets in his fist. His face was alight with excitement.

'It's about the mutilated girl,' Croaker said, setting aside his cup of coffee and capping it so it wouldn't spill.

'Right.' Lillehammer waved the faxes. 'She had a bridge. Unusual dental work, something about two adult teeth never coming in, so she had a bridge put in when her milk teeth fell out.'

'Some tooth fairy, huh?'

Lillehammer grinned, the spiderweb of pale scars waxing in his flesh. Outside the thick ovals of perspex, dark cloudbanks shredded and reformed, whirling upward at points in grand horsetails. They had needed a bit of oxygen, getting up above the storm blanketing central Minnesota. The plane was still shuddering in the aftermath of the major turbulence, on the eastern edge of the front, but pulling away from it now.

'The work was so distinctive the computers dug out her name in no time flat: Virginia Morris.'

What computer, Croaker asked himself, had such a vast databank and was so well coordinated it could orthodont-ID a victim in less than twelve hours? None that he had used, even the ones he'd had limited access to on occasion at the FBI. But maybe that was just because it had been a long time since he'd needed access.

Croaker was watching the storm streaming by below them while the

132

frame of the jet vibrated slightly. 'She the one with whom Dominic violated the WITSEC rules?'

'Looks that way. She's from Queens, his old stomping grounds. I spoke to the Federal Marshals handling his case and they had no record of her as authorized personnel.' He shook his head. 'I reamed them out, though. Dominic was always something with the women; he couldn't keep it in his pants for long.'

'So he imported his mistress all the way to Minnesota under WITSEC's nose. How'd he manage that?'

Lillehammer shrugged. 'He commanded thousands. It could have been any of them.'

Croaker looked away from the cloud-strewn sky. 'I doubt it. I know these guys. They don't make a habit of getting their button-men involved in their personal affairs. Who knows what enemies could get wind of that kind of vulnerable spot?'

'You have an idea who helped him?'

'Just considering your theory about an inside job.'

'What about it?' Lillehammer cocked his head. 'Who else but someone inside could have given the murderer Dominic's whereabouts?'

Croaker shook his head. 'I know you think someone inside the Government's rotten, but my instinct says there's another possibility and I want to follow it. See, Goldoni was murdered at that house. How did he get there? Was he snatched? I doubt it; he was too well watched. Besides, if it was an inside job and they knew where he was, they'd have just gone there. But what if he *deliberately* slipped his handlers to go to a rendezvous? It would be relatively easy; tell his wife he was going to the store for more toilet tissue or a T-bone steak, then take a detour at the last minute.'

'It's certainly possible.' Lillehammer seemed intrigued. 'But why would he do that?'

'It might be to meet someone,' Croaker said, 'who he trusted absolutely.' He looked at his watch. 'If we divert the flight plan from Washington to Kennedy in New York, what would our ETA be?'

'Let me check with the pilot,' Lillehammer said, reaching for the intercom.

When Justine awoke in the queen-sized bed at the Tokyo Hilton the first thing she did was reach over for the man who had fallen asleep beside her. Finding only bedsheets, her heart skipped a beat, and for a moment she was suffused with a dull, leaden ache, familiar as hunger.

Then she picked her head off the pillow and heard him in the bathroom, urinating. There was a kind of comfort in that purely male sound, the hard splash against porcelain.

'Rick?'

He appeared in the doorway to the bathroom, naked and grinning. 'Finally up? Good. I hope you're hungry, I'm about to order breakfast.'

Justine sat up and stretched. She was aware of his eyes on her, greedy and lustful.

'Do you know what that does for my id?'

She laughed. 'Your "id" seems to be preceding you into the bedroom.' She opened her arms to him as he took a leap, landed against her. He arched over her. She looked up into his face. 'What about breakfast?'

'I don't know about you, but I'm a lot less hungry than I was before you woke up.'

Later, after they had showered and dressed, they went down to the restaurant. He ordered bacon and eggs, a side of potatoes, a large orange juice, coffee and toast. Justine could not help but laugh – he was so American. Delighted and famished, she said she would have the same.

The juice and coffee came almost immediately. He took his coffee black. While she was adding cream and sugar to hers, he said, 'If you haven't changed your mind, when can you come back to New York?'

Justine looked across the table, took his hand in hers. 'I haven't changed my mind. When do you want me?'

'Now,' he said, pressing the back of her hand against his lips. 'I've waited too long to wait any longer.'

Justine smiled at him, caught up in his open enthusiasm. 'All right. But I'll need a day to pack.'

'Why? Is there anything here you really need – or want – to take with you?'

The food came, giving her some time to contemplate what he had said. Rick asked for strawberry jam. Justine munched her bacon, watching him spread his toast with butter and the jam. At last, she said, 'Thinking about it, I guess there isn't anything here I can't live without.' He looked up. 'I know what you mean. Starting over. Completely over.' She finished the slice of bacon. 'I think I'd like that very much.'

'Great!' He wiped his lips. 'I'll make the reservations right now.'

She watched him walk away, ask the maître d' for a house phone. She could not stop studying his face. She imagined herself in New York, married to him, back at her old job. She felt a vitality rush through her, a feeling that for so long she had despaired of ever having again. She was eager to return to work, to reestablish herself, to mount an assault that would regain her her old life, her self-respect, that would give her an identity.

134

At that moment, a waiter brought over a cordless phone.

'Mrs Linnear,' he said. 'Call for you.'

For an instant Justine sat frozen, terrified that somehow Nicholas had found where she was staying, through Nangi, perhaps. A ball of ice sat in her stomach, preventing her from breathing.

'Mrs Linnear?'

She nodded, gave the waiter the semblance of a smile, took the proffered phone.

'Hello?'

'Justine, it's Nangi.'

'Good morning,' she said with some relief.

'Are you feeling better? Did your visit with Millar-san go well?'

'Yes, very well,' Justine said. She was very conscious of how close Tanzan Nangi and Nicholas were. But Nangi was not tanjian; he had no special power to read her emotions, especially through the telephone. 'It was so good to see an old friend from the States.'

'I can well imagine,' Nangi said. 'Tokyo is the hub of Japan, but I often find myself homesick for the town where I was born. The feeling is natural.'

'Thank you, Nangi-san,' she said, 'for your concern.'

'Perhaps we can see each other soon.' His voice sounded melancholy. 'I do not know how long Nicholas will be away.'

'Have you spoken to him?' The moment she said it she knew it was a mistake.

'Haven't you called him?' Nangi asked. 'I asked Ito-san to leave his number with the concierge at the hotel.'

Had she received a message from Nicholas's hateful assistant? Justine could not remember. She thought desperately. Which lie should she tell? 'Yes, I got it. I tried him several times with no luck.'

'It's not surprising, I expect,' he said. 'I have been unable to reach him either. We'll just have to keep trying.'

'Yes, we will.'

'Call me any time, Justine-san.'

'I will, Nangi-san. Thank you again.'

She broke the connection with a profound sense of relief. She really did not like lying to him, but what other choice did she have? When she put down the phone, she saw that it was moist with her sweat.

Rick returned, a grin lighting up his face. 'All set,' he said as he sat down opposite her. 'We leave tonight. That will give you just enough time to take me around the city like the tourist I am.'

'No,' Justine said. 'I'm sick to death of Tokyo. We'll take a ride into the country where it's beautiful. I have to return the car to the house, anyway.'

They ate in silence for some time, and Justine thought that she had not enjoyed a meal so much in a very long while.

Over more coffee and another order of toast which Rick slathered with more strawberry jam, they spoke of their new life together.

'Where do you think you'd rather live,' Rick asked her, 'Manhattan or somewhere outside, like Long Island?'

Justine considered this. 'From what I've heard of Manhattan these days, I'd say definitely not there.' Her eyes clouded for a moment. 'But not the Island, either.' Too many memories of the house she and Nicholas had shared in West Bay Bridge. 'What about Connecticut?'

'Good idea,' Rick said, sipping his coffee. 'One of the firm's veeps lives in Darien and it's beautiful up there.' He grinned. 'We won't have to pay New York City taxes, which will be a relief.'

'You don't mind giving up the apartment?' She recalled Rick had a co-op on Fifth Avenue.

He shook his head. 'Not a bit. The truth is my ex-wife has been making my life miserable recently because she wants it.' He wiped his mouth. 'God knows why she wants to live in Manhattan. These days you're better off wearing a forty-five on your hip.' He shrugged. 'Anyway, this will simplify my life considerably. I can sell her the apartment and she'll owe me big.'

'You're sure you don't mind giving it up?'

Rick laughed. 'Are you kidding? I can't wait. We'll go house-hunting the first weekend we're home.'

That sounded so good to Justine she began to cry. House-hunting in Darien. America. Home. Oh, my God! It was almost too good to be true.

Rick took her hands in his, leaned across the table, kissed her tenderly on each eyelid, tasting the saltiness of her tears. 'No more pain, darling,' he whispered. 'I promise you.' His lips closed over hers, and he felt her inarticulate cry echo through him.

'Tony,' Margarite Goldoni said as she entered their bedroom, 'this Sicilian thing is *morte*.'

Anthony DeCamillo, newly anointed godfather for the Goldoni family, lay naked – save for a small white nylon bikini – beneath a sizzling sunlamp. White plastic goggles over his eye sockets along with the bizarre shade of his flesh beneath the lamp made him seem to Margarite like one of those cheap saints made of molded plastic which many New Yorkers stuck on their dashboards.

A timer rang and he stirred as the UV light switched off. He sat up, removed the white plastic goggles. He stared at her voluptuous figure clad in the clingy nightgown and began to get hard.

'Margarite, it's amazing, you look better now than you did ten years ago. Have I told you that lately?'

'Up until now, you've had no reason to,' Margarite said, coming toward him. She was massaging some of her own moisturizing cream into the skin of her hands.

Tony grunted, abruptly abandoning his attempt at a spurious reconciliation. 'You know, my brother told me I'd regret marrying a girl who wasn't Sicilian.'

'Your brother's an idiot,' Margarite said flatly.

He sat forward quickly. 'Hey, we're talking family here! Watch your fucking mouth!'

'I'm sorry, Tony.' She sat on the bed next to him and wondered if he would flinch away.

She felt split off, disassociated from herself. Part of her wanted desperately to undo the damage that had been done by her abduction, to make herself clean again in her husband's eyes. And all the while, another, less familiar part of her savored the loathing for him she had tasted when he had sent her and Francie away to New Hampshire.

'We both know you're in trouble,' she said. 'The Leonfortes are going to come east and try to take away what was once Dominic's sole province.'

'If I'm in trouble it's because of your fucking brother,' he said angrily. 'He never had a formal *consigliere*. He never confided in any of his lieutenants. He never allowed anyone to get close to him. He kept his own counsel. The secrets he used as leverage to influence all his high-powered contacts in Washington are history now.' Tony's hands flew through the air, describing complex arabesques. 'Mary Mother, how many times did I beg him to give those secrets to me for safekeeping? "If I'm to succeed you I've got to know everything," I'd say. "You can't tie my hands like this."'

He shook his head, sad and angry at the same time. 'I swear I loved him like a brother, Margarite, but he was a damned stubborn man, your brother. He left me with *ugatz*, and now I'm twisting in a fucking wind that stinks to high heaven of Bad Clams and his whole West Coast machine.'

'You have me,' Margarite said.

'That madman brother of yours, giving you all his secrets! A fucking woman!' He threw his hands into the air. 'It's enough that I've had to sit through meetings with Dom's contacts knowing you were the one who'd report to him, who'd make the decisions that came out of my mouth. Now I gotta live with the fact that Dom gave *you* everything!'

137

He got up, began to dress, throwing on a white shirt, charcoal trousers. He shook his head. 'I don't mind telling you, I got to hand it to the fucker. That sonuvabitch Caesare Leonforte finally got his wish. He's wanted Dominic dead so bad he'd probably incorporated it into his Sunday prayers. But I'm not gonna let him get away with it. I know he hired that bastard who you think has us under his thumb. I'm gonna –'

'You and I both know you're no match for Caesare. I think it's time you gave up trying to hypnotize yourself into believing you're really the head of the Family.'

Tony watched her for some time as he slid his belt through the waist loops. 'I'm gonna tell you something, babe. I know you've had a shock – especially since Dom's widow and kids have been spirited out of the country so the Feds can keep them under lock and key. I know it's been tough, them hanging onto the corpse and all – and us making like Dom's body was actually in that goddamned coffin we buried yesterday.'

She wondered if he was going to bring up the subject of Robert, actually had a bet with herself that after what had happened he wouldn't. She won.

'But for Christ's sake, ever since you came back from that Magical Mystery Tour to nowhere you've changed.'

'Of course I've changed.'

'No.' He shook his head, stepping into tasselled Italian loafers. 'You don't get it, do you? You're a different person altogether. The Margarite Goldoni I married doesn't seem to exist any more.'

'Your imagination's working overtime,' Margarite said, but she wondered as she heard another voice in her head: *And what else have I given you, Margarite? Now you know you have the strength of purpose . . . to do* anything. She shivered, but as much with anticipation now as dread.

'You think so? Before this your own business has always been enough for you.'

'Business is business, Tony. I've proved I've got a good head for business.'

He snorted. 'Well, I'll say this for you, you were never a girl to keep a bun stuck in her oven.'

Tears sprang to her eyes. 'Bastard, to bring up what I couldn't help. I had three miscarriages trying to give you the son you wanted so badly. The last one almost killed me.'

Tony shook his head. 'Maybe it was physical,' he said. 'And maybe it was psychological, too. You never wanted to be tied down by kids. Look at our daughter. Having her never slowed you down. Did you ever think of staying home with her when she was little?'

'Did you ever think of coming home at a decent hour to be with her?'

138

'That's different,' he shouted. 'I worked my balls off to afford an estate of substance for you and her, so I wouldn't be in your brother's debt. And where do I end up? Living on his fucking estate with a daughter who doesn't even know how to say hello to me properly.'

'I see. So it's okay for you to absent yourself from the family because you're the man?'

'We wouldn't be having this conversation,' he screamed, 'if I had a wife who knew what her priorities were regarding her child! If she knew how to be a mother!'

'Oh, Christ, I'm so tired of you and your bullying.'

He gave her a rude Sicilian sign. 'So leave.'

She put her head down, sobbing now. 'I just might.'

'You're fucking full of shit!'

Margarite's face went white and her head came up. 'Don't you talk to me like that! You don't talk to any of your men friends that way.'

'That's because none of them are fucking women!'

She tried to slap him, and he caught her wrist, slammed her back against the wall. The pain came. It was an all too familiar feeling.

He stood over her, menacing. 'I'm going to make sure that whatever's going on comes to an end.' He slipped his belt out from around his waist. 'It's been too long since I last gave you a lesson.'

But the next moment he was staring down the barrel of a snub-nosed .45-caliber pistol.

'You goddamned Sicilians only understand one thing,' she said, struggling to her feet.

'Margarite –!'

'And don't make the mistake of thinking I don't know how to use this.'

What new emotion had she felt then? Rage? No, she had felt that before, bottled up like a demon clamped tight against her soul. What then? She felt beneath the rage and the terror a kind of iron core she never believed she had, a will coalescing from out of the nightmare maelstrom that had become her life. She reached out and grasped it with the desperation of a swimmer exhausted past all limits.

A voice she only vaguely recognized said, 'For so long I've been – what is it? I've been afraid of you. *Afraid.* I say the word now and can hardly believe it. You hit me and I took it, silently bit my lip and said not a word, not even to my brother. Because I was *afraid.*'

Tony was backing up as she advanced on him.

'Now come on, babe. Chill out. You've been under a tremendous strain with your brother's death and this man breaking into –'

'And not a kind word to me when I came home, our baby in my arms,

139

no sympathy. I saw the hatred, Tony. You thought – no, no, you *knew* – he had raped me. In your mind I had been soiled. Just by *being* with him. You had that look on your face – oh, Christ, it crystallized everything inside me I'd refused to acknowledge; it made me feel like a piece of –'

'Babe –'

He stopped as she brought the gun up. She stayed far enough away from him so that he couldn't overpower her by sheer brute strength. There was a strange light in her eyes which frightened him.

'Margarite, you've made your point. Why don't you put that thing away before someone gets hurt.'

'No, Tony. No more "babe", no more screaming at me, no more beatings. All of that is finished. It's a new world order. Because I have the power to kill you now. I *can* pull this trigger; just give me one more reason, as if I don't have enough already. *That's* how I've changed: I've been given this power – no, it's been restored to me. My self-respect. You took it away, Tony, and God help me I let you.'

Tony licked his lips, his eyes flicking from the gun barrel to her face. 'Hey, come on now. I don't think you've really got a grip on what's happened to us over the past few days. I know you're upset about the kid. And the shock of Dom's –'

'You bastard, I know what's really happened here – to Dominic, to Francie and to me! But you'd never understand.'

'I understand how we've all been violated. My own home – my family –'

Her eyes blazed and she hit the side of her head. 'I get it now. This isn't about Francie or my brother or me. This is about you, you macho prick! You can't stand what he did to *you*!'

And now she knew: it was her brother's voice, coming out of her mouth. As part of her marveled at this seeming miracle, another part was remembering the time she had seen Dominic put a loaded gun to the head of Rich Cooper, her business partner. Margarite wanted to expand Serenissima, her cosmetics company, overseas, but Rich thought it was too risky. Dominic had spent all afternoon using every argument he could think of to persuade Rich to change his mind. To no avail. Afterward, with the signed contract in his breast pocket, Dominic had said to her, *You see, Margarite, there is a correct persuasion for every sort of man.*

Now, looking at her husband's respect for the weapon she held firmly in her hand, she knew she had found the correct persuasion for him.

'What we need,' Nicholas said, 'is a mirror.'

'A mirror?' Celeste asked as they broke out again along the *riva*.

'Yes. A place we can disappear into where we can look back at our pursuers.'

Celeste smiled at him as she took his hand. 'I think I know just the place.'

She took him over the Ponte della Paglia, the Straw Bridge, where, in ages gone by, boats filled with straw were unloaded, and past the Bridge of Sighs, where prisoners of the Doge were led to prison and, often, worse fates. They ducked down, going through a *sottoportego*, an archway leading into an underpass, and very shortly they came out upon a *campo* fronted by a stone church, rather unprepossessing by Venetian standards, and a secondary building.

'This is the Convent of San Zaccaria,' Celeste said, leading him out of the *campo* via the only other egress. 'It has an interesting history, since the sisters have historically embroidered the ceremonial hat of the Doge.' They made a sharp right at a tiny square, hurrying down a narrow street that bent like the back of an old woman around to the right. 'Since the ninth century the reigning Doge made a short pilgrimage here at Easter to vespers at the church.'

They broke abruptly out onto a wide *fondamenta*. To their right were houses and shops, to their left a wrought-iron railing beyond which was a *rio*, crossed by two small stone bridges.

'This was the reason the *campo* and the convent were so well fortified,' Celeste said, as they went down the *fondamenta*. 'You can't find another entrance to the church or the convent from the *campo*.'

Perhaps halfway down the *fondamenta* they came to an old doorway in a stucco building. The sign above read: SCUOLA ELEMENTARE ARMANDO DIAZ. After looking down the entire length of the *fondamenta*, Celeste drew him through this open portal.

They went through a stinking *sottoportego*, emerging on the other side into a grassy courtyard faced on three sides by fairly modern brownbrick buildings. The sounds of children could be heard behind the façades.

Celeste led him through a courtyard dotted with enormous Zelkova trees and brightly painted swings, tricycles and other paraphernalia of small children. Beyond this innocuous façade was a remarkable surprise: the rear of the San Zaccaria.

Celeste took him into the basement of the oldest of the brown-brick buildings. It smelled of ashes and urine. At the far end of a large boiler room was a wooden door, scarred and ancient. Celeste pushed it open and Nicholas could immediately smell *rio* water. He could hear the squeal of rats, see the ruby eyes in the dark.

141

The sound of their soles echoed off stone walls which Nicholas was sure were very old. They seemed to be in a network of tunnels.

This theory Celeste confirmed. 'The doges of Venice were a paranoid lot,' she said. 'They were made so by circumstance, I'm afraid. So they had these tunnels installed as a measure of security for their entrances and exits from San Zaccaria. Centuries later, the school was built on the bedrock just above, under the direction of the San Zaccaria nuns, who did not want part of their tradition destroyed.'

The dark air was alive and moving with stone dust and history. Ahead of him, Nicholas could see the bright wash of Celeste's hair as if it were a lamp leading him down the corridor of time.

The tunnel ended at a small wooden door bound by old, studded iron bands. She gave a soft knock in a curious rhythm and, almost immediately, the door swung inward. She slipped quickly inside, pulled Nicholas in after her. The door swung shut.

A torch flared and Nicholas saw a small woman in a nun's habit. Celeste spoke to her rapidly and softly in Venetian dialect, so that even if he had been within earshot Nicholas would not have understood the conversation. At length, the nun signaled with the torch, silently bid them follow her up a winding flight of stone stairs, worn to shallow arcs in the centers of the treads.

'Where are we?'

Celeste turned to him. 'You wanted a mirror. I've given you one.' She nodded. 'Over here.'

She led him to a shuttered window made of leaded stained glass. She set the torch in a wall sconce, pointed through the colored glass of the window. 'Look. The *campo* where we just were.'

Nicholas looked out and down and, indeed, he could make out the front of the convent.

'The power of paranoia; the imperative of Venetian politics. It was all like quicksand,' Celeste said. 'Some of the predecessors of those Doges I spoke of never returned to their palazzo, having been assassinated on their way from vespers at just this spot you're looking at. The Venetians, when aroused, could be astonishingly bloodthirsty.'

Like everything else in Venice, Nicholas thought, the darkness mingled with the light.

As he continued to peer down into the *campo* he saw a man appear. He was dressed as any modern-day Venetian might be, except that he wore an old-fashioned wide-brimmed hat which threw deep shadow across his face. From his elevated position, Nicholas could not make out his features.

'Is this our pursuer?' Celeste asked.

Nicholas watched as the man moved carefully across the *campo*. His hands moved expertly over the doorways and windows he passed, checking on whether they were locked or open. So naturally did he do this that anyone casually watching would think nothing of his movements.

'That's our man,' Nicholas said. 'Come on.'

They went back down the stairs, emerging into the gloom of the ground-floor anteroom. Nicholas moved to the door, put his hand on the wrought-iron lock. Now it was time to pursue the pursuer.

Together, they left their mirror, traversing the tunnel, the schoolyard, heading back down the *fondamenta*, away from the convent.

Up ahead, he could see the shadow of the man as he cautiously emerged from the *campo*, moved through the maze of streets. He was very good, Nicholas observed, methodical and careful not to overlook any possibility. More than once, he used existing glass surfaces to check the route behind him. The first time he did this, Nicholas was almost caught off guard, but he managed to flatten them against a recessed doorway just in time.

It became easier as he began to get a sense of the man's m.o., but at a certain point it would get very difficult indeed. When the tick found that he had permanently lost his quarry he would cease to be deliberate and would get himself back to his base as quickly as possible in order to give whoever was running him the bad news. At that point, Nicholas knew, they would have to be very quick as well as a little bit lucky in order to stay with him without being detected.

The tick took them back into the Piazza San Marco itself, filled now with tour groups and children running with their hands full of breadcrumbs, simultaneously attracting and scattering the platoons of pigeons which clattered and cooed across the square.

The man passed beneath an arch just to the right of the Torre dell'Orologio, the clocktower at the northern edge, and plunged into the narrow, crowded streets of the Mercerie. This shopping district, where once only the fantastic Venetian fabrics and dress goods were sold, twisted and turned all the way from the Piazza San Marco to the Rialto. Now it contained shops and restaurants of every description.

The light was dim here after the sun-splashed openness of the piazza, and possessed a mysterious quality, as if filtered by the gauzy veils of time. Even the shops of ultra-modern designers such as Gianfranco Ferre and Franco Zancan had about them a timeless quality.

The tick stopped at an antiques shop, stood just outside its open doorway, chatting with the woman owner. Nicholas grabbed Celeste, drawing her quickly into the recesses of the shop of a clothes designer, the Venetian Roberta di Camerino. There he directed Celeste to a display of fine woolen dresses in the Venetian colors of sea aquamarine and sky indigo, while he glanced through a corner window at the antiques shop across the street.

'He's stopped to make certain he isn't being followed,' Nicholas whispered to her. 'This man is very clever.'

A chicly clothed saleswoman was doing her best to get Celeste to try on one of the dresses.

'Do you recognize him?' Celeste asked.

'I haven't gotten a good look at his face,' Nicholas said as Celeste politely waved the saleswoman away. 'We're always behind him, and he's keeping well to the shadows.'

'It would be helpful to see his face,' Nicholas said thoughtfully. He extended his psyche, feeling the soft beat against *kokoro*, the center, the heart of the universe.

A sudden gust of wind seemed to beat up against the tick, lifting the bottom of his jacket. It took his hat, swirled it off his head, making it tumble crown first into the street.

And there was the face: bronze skin, Oriental features, but a mixture; not a pure Japanese face, the hard lines softened, perhaps, by a bit of Khmer or Burmese or Tibetan blood, the lips firm; a mole on his lip at the corner of his mouth. A memorable face, nonetheless, at least as far as Nicholas was concerned.

Without hesitation, the tick bent to retrieve his hat, snatching it out of the gutter. He was extended for a moment, and Nicholas saw the curvature of muscle and sinew in shoulder and arm, the absolute lack of fat along waist and pelvis, no tension in the face, none at all. And then he had straightened up, the hat securely back on his head.

'Come on.'

The tick was on the move again, weaving them through the fabric of the city. They followed him down a street, saw him disappear round a sharp turn to the left. When they reached it, they found themselves in a tiny courtyard of stone and twining bougainvillea, at the far end of which was the entrance to a restaurant. They went into what appeared to be the plushly appointed dining car of a train. A gleaming mahogany bar took up the left-hand side of the room, while three intimate banquettes were arrayed on their right.

'This place has another entrance,' Celeste said urgently.

They hurried down the passageway, through the small, velvet-covered anteroom to the restaurant, then through double doors onto another street.

'There!' Nicholas said, pointing to their right. They broke into a sprint, bolting down the narrow street.

'Christ, I think he's headed toward the Rialto,' Celeste said, after a time. 'That's bad news for us. There's always such a crush of people around the bridge we'll stand a good chance of losing him.'

Some moments later, as she had predicted, they broke out onto the quay surrounding the famous covered bridge, until the nineteenth century the only one over the Grand Canal. From its inception, the Ponte di Rialto had been filled with merchants' shops, and with its confluence of foreign goods and tongues more resembled an Arab *souk* than it did a Western bridge.

They caught sight of the tick, and Nicholas ran down toward the *rio*, Celeste right behind him. They wove their way along the *fondamenta* just in time to see him step onto the *imbarcadero* as a Number 1 *vaporetto* bound in the direction of the Arsenal nosed alongside the dock.

Nicholas and Celeste raced down the quay as he boarded the *vaporetto* along with a host of other people, and they pushed their way onto the *imbarcadero*, sprinting the last several feet onto the boat just as it was about to depart.

Nicholas kept them close to the side of the boat so that they would not have much space to cover should he get off quickly. The *vaporetto* passed the Fondaco dei Tedeschi, an enormous palace of 160 rooms, now the central Post Office, which was originally used by the Tedeschi family as their warehouse and a kind of hotel for visiting members of other merchant families.

They were headed toward the *Volta dei Canal*, the great curve where the Grand Canal begins to bend back upon itself. There, the four Palazzi Mocenigo sit, commanding the Grand Canal as befitted a family that gave Venice seven Doges. Celeste spoke to him of these bits of Venetian history as they pretended to be tourist and guide, enjoying a planned itinerary.

The tick swung off just as the *vaporetto* nosed into the Sant' Angelo station, and Nicholas and Celeste broke through the crowd, headed down the *imbarcadero* after him. They passed along the façade of yet another palazzo, this one more traditional than many others Celeste had pointed out.

The tick hurried around the Palazzo Corner-Spinelli, down a narrow alley, then into another street. There, a second palazzo sat, smaller and older, and he pulled open a side door, disappeared inside.

They waited a moment. The seconds edged by, and Nicholas could feel Celeste's nervousness as she stood close beside him in the shadows. The façade of the palazzo was brick over which traditional Venetian stucco of powdered brick and marble sand in a foundation of lime paste produced the rich rubiate hue so typical of the city.

At length, he signed to her, and they edged up to the door. He put his

145

ear to it, listened for a moment but heard nothing. What was waiting for them on the other side? Nicholas took a deep breath, pulled the door open.

They went inside, found themselves in a small courtyard filled with roses and a gnarled weeping willow, its thick green trunk looking like a marble column. In one corner, a lion of Istrian stone watched them with implacable objectivity.

Nicholas heard a soft sound from over their heads. Looking up, he saw an open loggia, not much different from the one in the Doge's Palace. An outside staircase of worn stone and red Verona marble surmounted a series of stilted arches inlaid with complex Byzantine reliefs. The staircase led up to the *piano nobile* which seemed suspended between sky and earth by rows of slender Byzantine pillars.

At the top of the staircase, they emerged onto the loggia. The floor was composed of tiles of yellow, burnt orange and pale green set in patterns that echoed its Byzantine predecessors. The inner wall was stucco, painted the color of buttered sweet potatoes. Opposite, the delicate dark-green *verde antica* stone columns were carved into spiral confections.

They looked about; they seemed alone.

Celeste stood very close to him, and he could feel a slight tremor go through her. They had come up onto a section of the loggia that had no doors or windows, a curious feature in a palazzo that, in the Veneto-Byzantine style, should have been more open.

They headed down the length of the loggia. Beyond the copse of helical columns on their left, the trees of the courtyard stirred in a faint breeze, heavier now. The sky was clouding up; a pearlescent light suffused the loggia, devoid of shadow or the kind of orientation sunlight provided.

They continued round a corner. They could see the wedge of a *rio* through a gap in the low buildings. The water had turned dark, a depthless gray that seemed to suck the light out of the afternoon. The roar of a *motoscafo* lifted and died, leaving them in silence.

Then they came upon the door, a heavy oaken affair with brass hardware weathered to a sea-green patina. It was the lone aperture in the stucco wall, and this continued lack of windows became all the more curious.

He reached for the doorknob, but she held him back. 'Wait!' she whispered urgently in his ear. 'I don't want to go in there!'

'We have to,' Nicholas said fiercely. 'We have to find out who's been following us.'

She clung to him, trembling slightly. 'There must be another way. I'm frightened of what might be inside.'

'Take my hand.'

146

She slipped her hand into his as he turned the knob and opened the door. They slipped inside as silently as smoke, closed the door behind them.

They were in utter darkness. There was the faint smell of ashes, and a heavy, bitter scent which was not readily identifiable to Celeste. They took several steps away from the door, and it was as if they had traveled miles. All sense of being in a room – of being *inside* – vanished. There was a rushing, as of a wind sweeping across a prairie, cold and desolate, and they experienced a quick, wrenching paroxysm of vertigo.

They heard – or perhaps more accurately felt imprinted on the membranes of their eardrums – a rising series of vibrations, becoming louder or perhaps only more distinct. Soon this evolved into a discernible rhythm which, after a short time, seemed to alter to its own cadence the very pulse of blood through their arteries.

Celeste stifled a shriek.

Ahead of them appeared as if through a viscous mist an arching bridge that seemed composed entirely of bones. They gleamed palely, with here and there a hint of red, as if only recently they had been picked clean of flesh.

The bridge seemed to connect the darkness, as if it were a central point, the only substantial structure in an otherwise amorphous and terrifying void.

Celeste, her fist jammed hard against clenched teeth, turned to try to find her way back to the door, but Nicholas pulled her back, close to him.

'I know this place,' he said under his breath. 'Or at least I recognize it.'

'My head hurts,' Celeste said. 'I'm having trouble breathing, as if we're under water.'

Nicholas stood very still, concentrating. Celeste felt a ripple in her mind, and the sensation of relief one experiences when poking one's head outside the door at the end of a long, bitter winter. Slowly, her head began to clear. She was about to ask him what had happened when he pulled her forward, toward the near end of the bridge.

It was, in itself, a frightening artifact, for the bones were certainly human. Now that they were only a step away from it, they saw that it was an exceedingly narrow affair. Certainly, were they to attempt to cross it, they would have to do so single-file, and then very carefully indeed, for its 'railings' were composed of ribs arching inward, whose ends had been honed to razor sharpness.

It seemed to be raining – at least the sound of rain could be heard, traveling toward them from some direction, passing across the plane of

147

their hearing, then falling swiftly beyond their ken, but they felt nothing.

'Where are we?' Celeste asked him. 'Is this an hallucination or are we dreaming?'

'Neither,' Nicholas said.

'Then this . . .' She shook her head. 'I refuse to believe this skeleton bridge exists.'

'It's real enough,' Nicholas said, gripping her hand. 'But that doesn't mean it couldn't disappear at any moment. Do you remember that smell as we came in here? It's the burning flesh of a kind of mushroom, the *Agaricus muscarius*.'

'Like peyote. Then this *is* an hallucination.'

'No,' Nicholas said. 'The use of hallucinogens is a corruption; they aren't ingested by the true mystic, whose trance is pure, manifesting itself solely from his own highly trained will.' He dragged her behind him as he stepped onto the bridge. 'This mushroom is used in certain rituals. It concentrates the ethereal power of the necromancer, allowing him to make real things that exist but are rarely seen.'

The 'floor' of the bridge was only nine bones in width, and the gauntlet of wickedly honed rib ends was scarifying. He could sense her fear as if it were a living presence, a third figure hanging behind them like a dangerous shadow, ready to impale them upon one of the points of the ribs. It was this fear that could prove deadly to them, he knew. He needed to distract her; to make her forget her terror.

'Celeste,' he said softly, 'I meant it when I said I know where we are. This is the Kanfa bridge – the center-point of the universe; the place where heaven and earth meet, where life and death collide.'

As he spoke he continued to move forward, drawing her carefully after him.

'On the Kanfa time ceases to exist – or at least to behave as you believe it does. It does not tick off in seconds and minutes; it does not move in one direction only.'

Another step, and she gasped behind him as she swayed slightly, her cheek almost brushing against one of the razor-sharp points. Nicholas paused, and gripped her hand more tightly.

'Here time flows in all directions at once, often overlapping itself, pooling and eddying, repeating like echoes the past, present and future, until they cease to be discrete entities, until they are merged into the ocean of time.'

He urged them on, but at a slower pace. Feeling her turning her head, leaning over between the ribs, he said, 'Don't look down. The Kanfa is built to the height of a hundred men. Below it lies the place that Christians have named hell, though the priests of Tau-tau know it by another, far more ancient name.'

Celeste looked straight ahead, at the back of his head. 'Is this bridge some form of Tau-tau magic?'

Nicholas found it interesting and curious that she should know about Tau-tau and that he was tanjian. He said, 'Only in the most peripheral way.' He paused for a moment. 'The Kanfa bridge is a creation of the oldest of the psycho-necromancers. They were known as Messulethe, and they are so ancient no one can say for certain where they came from. But perhaps it doesn't matter, because certainly they were nomads, braving the vast wastes of the Gobi desert, the steppes of what would eventually become Siberia, the high mountains of Tibet and Bhutan.'

The bones beneath their feet rattled and hummed, treacherous with curved surfaces made slick by the absence of flesh or sinew.

'They were bronze-skinned people with the heavy epicanthic folds and straight black hair of certain tribes who are now strung out through Northern China, Cambodia, Laos, Burma and Polynesia. But they all have one thing in common: a mark upon them, a blue vertical crescent, like the waxing moon, tattooed on the inside of their left wrist.'

It was very narrow on the Kanfa, and the rattling of the bones their passage set up was disturbing, triggering perhaps an ancient race-memory in the primitive brain of the death of the soul.

'It is said that their name, translated again and again into other languages, finally became Methuselah, and so the Messulethe – personified into a single ancient wise man – were woven into the fabric of the Bible.'

They were approaching the apex of the Kanfa bridge, and the way grew more difficult as the pitch of the arc increased.

'Centuries later, the Persian mystic Zarathustra came across records of the Kanfa and incorporated it into his teachings. In his version, the righteous, who believed in him, would cross the bridge and be lifted up to heaven by a guardian spirit.'

'What about the unbelievers?' Celeste asked.

'According to Zarathustra, crossing the Kanfa was an ordeal – something like an initiation into his faith. It symbolized the cosmic struggle for the soul of man. I think you can guess the rest. The impious were refused crossing. They were met at center-span by a demon out of hell who cast them over the side.'

Celeste started as she gave a little cry.

Ahead of them, the way was blocked by a figure. It was masked, a cruel face of bulging eyes, high brow ridges and a hideously grinning mouth.

There was about the whole a vaguely insectile aspect which played upon the deepest antipathies common to all humans, and behind him, Nicholas could feel Celeste cringing away, tugging on the bond of their clasped hands. He struggled to keep that bond whole, knowing instinctively that if it was broken their chances of stepping off the other side of the Kanfa would be virtually nil.

With the psychic extension of Tau-tau, he had known what was almost certainly awaiting them even before he stepped through the loggia doorway. Far from being daunted, he was intrigued – and puzzled. While he had read about the basics of the Kanfa, he had not been aware that it could actually be manifested by Tau-tau or any other form of magic currently known. The Messulethe had been subjects of intense study by the priests of Tau-tau, but the fact remained that even their knowledge of this ancient sect of numinous mages was at best incomplete and, often, contradictory.

He found it interesting that the Kanfa should manifest itself here in Venice. Interesting but not incomprehensible. Hadn't Celeste mentioned the Scythians at their first meeting in the Church of San Belisario? The Scythians, too, had practiced the ancient sorcery of the Messulethe, even before the time of Zarathustra. According to Celeste they were one of the refugee peoples who founded Venice.

Nicholas faced the masked demon. 'I know what you want,' he said. 'You won't get it.'

'You don't know anything.' Laughter, deep and booming, emanated from the ridged hole in the mask representing a mouth of some sort. The sound rumbled through the black space, creating a frisson against their skin.

Nicholas began to project outward with his mind, then abruptly stopped. Instinct warned him, and now he began to suspect the reason for the resurrection of the Kanfa bridge. He tucked away the powers of Akshara he had learned at the knee of Kansatsu – his Tau-tau *sensei* and his implacable enemy; the man he had been born to destroy. How he wished he possessed *Shuken*, the full range of Tau-tau – Akshara and Kshira – inside him, for he suspected he would be far better prepared for the mortal dangers to come.

He let go of Celeste's hand and, in a semi-crouch, rushed headlong at the masked demon. He feinted to his right with a vicious *atemi* – aikido's main percussive blow – whirled himself on the fulcrum of his left foot, moving as he did so from his semi-crouch to his full height.

The demon figure dodged the blow.

He feinted again with another *atemi*, swung his right leg inside the demon's stance. As the demon moved to counter his blow, he shifted his weight, slammed the side of his right foot into the inside of the demon's ankle.

Immediately, he jammed his elbow into the demon's right kidney, moving past him now and, swinging round and behind as the demon turned to face him. He drove the heel of his hand forward, missed, caught the demon an *atemi* on his lowest, and most unprotected, rib.

The demon let go an explosive breath, and Nicholas felt as if he were moving underwater. His lungs labored to breathe air suddenly thicker than silt. There was a buzzing filling his ear canals, boring into his mind.

He knew what this was. The Tau-tau adept was summoning his psychic power by exciting the membrane of *kokoro* at the heart of the cosmos. This was the rhythm they had 'heard' when first entering this place, the magic that had conjured up the Kanfa bridge.

Now his intuition was borne out. This was no demon drawn out of Zoroastrian hell, but a tanjian, the Tau-tau adept whom Celeste believed had been sent to murder Okami. And – somehow – he had access to the lore of the Messulethe!

He felt the rhythm of Tau-tau beating its incessant, hypnogogic rhythm upon his consciousness, but he refused to project his own power. Instead, he kept up his physical assault on the demon, while methodically shutting down the pathways for the adept's Tau-tau to work on him.

But something more than Tau-tau was at work here, and Nicholas felt it beginning to insinuate itself between the beats at *kokoro* and, like a vine or briar that uses a host plant to bring it into sunlight, he knew that the ancient magic of the Messulethe was now just blossoming like an evil flow, dense with putrefaction.

Celeste saw these two locked together, muscles bulging, the sweat running down them, in a titanic struggle. She broke out of the strange paralysis that had gripped her, and rushed to help Nicholas. As she neared them she felt a cold wind stirring, not against her bare flesh, but inside her mind, and she recoiled. And then she understood that this conflict encompassed not only the physical, but the mental as well.

A gale arose, gyring and shrieking through the skeletal bridge, so that Celeste stumbled back and was thrown to her knees. A furious burst of cold green light blinded her, and she screamed, believing her bones bleached, her soul seared beyond recognition. Then even that sound ceased as she fell, insensate, to the floor roiling with involute energy.

A dome of diffuse sunlight hovered over Tokyo like the immense turbine of a UFO. Shadows – pale, prone to disappear at a moment's notice –

followed Justine and Rick Millar as they left the thronged heart of the city behind them.

But perhaps shadows were not the only thing following them. While Rick continued a monologue about how the working relationship among the senior partners of the advertising agency would change once she was brought on board, Justine was watching her rear-view mirror, where a nondescript white Toyota was hanging three cars back.

She was not yet worried. Though she seemed to recall the same Toyota right behind her at one of the large Tokyo intersections, this car could just as well be one of a thousand others that were no doubt on the city's streets right now.

Still, she couldn't help feeling a sense of foreboding about this particular white Toyota. Was she becoming paranoid? It was not guilt that fueled her paranoia, but the past. *Well, why shouldn't I be nervous?* she asked herself as she checked her rear-view mirror again for the white Toyota. *With the dangerous people Nick deals with I should have a bodyguard with me all the time.* In fact, Nicholas had broached this very topic a number of times. Of course she had refused. She had had no desire to have her every move scrutinized by anyone, especially a stranger. This did not stop her from time to time looking over her shoulder when she went into Tokyo. Hence her heightened awareness of the white Toyota.

She kept on the highway, heading more or less in the direction of her house, where she would eventually leave the car. She had arranged for a limousine to pick them up there for the ride out to the airport. She checked her mirror again, straining to catch a glimpse of the driver, but the diffuse sunlight spun off the Toyota's windshield, making any kind of identification impossible.

'Honey, what's the matter?' Rick said, as her expression of concentration changed to one of concern.

'Probably nothing,' she said, changing to the far right lane and accelerating. A moment later, she watched the white Toyota pull out from behind a black BMW, and accelerate behind her. 'I don't want to alarm you,' she said, 'but someone might be following us.'

'What?' Rick swiveled round to peer out the rear window. 'Who?'

'See that white Toyota? I think he picked us up when we were still in the city proper.'

Rick gave the Toyota another look, then turned round again, straightening his jacket. 'But that's nuts. Why would anyone want to follow us?'

'I don't know,' she said. 'Maybe it has something to do with what Nicholas is doing in Venice. Everything bad happens because of what he is.'

Rick grunted. 'I think you're imagining things, but just to put your mind at ease let's give your theory a try.' He pointed. 'Get off at the next exit. Let's see if the Toyota follows us.'

Justine nodded, but as the signs for the exit passed them she made no attempt to change lanes.

'What are you doing?' Rick said. 'At the speed we're going, if we don't get over now, we won't make the – Jesus!'

Justine accelerated abruptly, sliding just in front of the grill of a truck, almost clipping its fender with the tail of her car as she switched lanes. The truck's air-horn sounded angrily. The exit was coming up very fast, and there was a Nissan sedan cruising sedately in the left lane. She jammed on her brakes, slid almost sideways across the one clear space in the exit lane and, burning rubber behind her as she pumped the brakes hard, hurtled onto the exit ramp at twice the advised speed.

She almost hit the outer verge, corrected, then slowed for the long arc off the highway. When they were on the local street, she said, 'Well, did you see whether the Toyota tried to follow us?'

'Are you kidding?' Rick said with a small laugh. 'I was too busy trying to keep my bladder under control.'

He turned round now. Justine had just made a right turn, and he could see the road was clear behind them. 'Nothing,' he said, giving her a kiss on the cheek as he settled back in the seat. 'See, I told you. But, sweet Jesus, you could have made the same point by taking the exit at a decent speed.'

'Oh, God, no!'

'What is it?'

He saw her staring into her rear-view mirror and, shifting, saw the familiar silhouette of the white Toyota come into view. 'Same car?'

Justine nodded grimly. 'Now what do you think of my theory?'

'Let's see if we can get him off our back.'

Justine nodded again. 'We're near the house. I know this area better than any other in Japan. If we can reach the road to our house without him too close I can lose him there.'

She took the next left with a sharp squeal of tires, accelerated dangerously through an intersection, then made another left. He could see that she was looping round, attempting to make the turns fast enough to switch positions with the Toyota and come up behind him, then veer off so that he would have no chance to follow.

He was dizzy after the sixth turn. There was also no sign of the pursuing car, and Rick was of a mind that her guilt at having cheated on her husband had begun to rub off on him.

153

'Coming up on the road I want,' she said. 'Any sign of him?'

'No,' Rick said. But he was concerned for another reason. She was obviously an excellent driver, but she was having to concentrate on a lot of things at once: finding the right road, remembering to drive on the left, watching for the white Toyota. And she must be thinking of Nicholas.

'Slow down,' he said. 'The Toyota's not following us – if it ever was.'

'No,' Justine said. 'I'm on the road now; I want to make certain he won't find us.'

This road was narrow and winding. Great Yoshino cryptomeria trees and massive evergreen hedges lined it so that there were no margins. He felt as if he were inside a gigantic maze. No wonder Justine felt safe here. It was almost like finding Eden after the concrete and steel megalopolis of Tokyo.

The turns were almost switchbacks. So sharp were they that many of the home-owners had installed circular fish-eye mirrors on tree trunks so motorists could see the oncoming traffic round the acute bends.

They flashed along the road, the sharp turns back and forth making him a bit queasy. 'For the love of God, Justine, slow down!'

She continued to consult her rear-view mirror; her face showed that she still felt they were being pursued by the wrath of God. 'Just a little more, until I'm sure we're safe.'

They sped into a turn sharper than most. There was no mirror here, and Rick experienced a moment akin to what he had experienced the first time he'd parachuted. Nothing below him but air, the ground coming up and he hurtling downward to meet it.

He heard the deep diesel roar of the giant earth-mover before his brain registered what his eyes saw. Justine was looking into her mirror for any trace of their pursuer and, shouting a warning, Rick grabbed the steering wheel.

The huge machine was bearing down on them as Justine, screaming, hit the brakes. The machine's air-horn exploded into the quiet afternoon, sounding as mournful as a funeral dirge.

Rick threw himself across Justine's seat, yanked hard on the wheel, but at that point there were less than two feet remaining between the vehicles.

What is thought, locked in an endless moment like this? Justine's mind was blank. She saw only a small wedge of cerulean sky, shining with a curious light behind the looming bulk of the crimson earth-mover. In that luminescence she could see reflected the entire breadth of her existence as if it were a single exhalation from the mouth of God.

The two feet were covered in a split second. The massive front end of the earth-mover struck her car almost head-on. The front crumpled like cardboard and the cracked engine, split dashboard and shattered windshield plowed like a furious juggernaut into the passenger cabin.

What was left of the car, now halved in length, was lifted like a matador, gored on the curve of a charging bull's horn, and thrown into the air. Upside down, it struck a pair of very old cryptomeria, instantly felling them. It hung in the air for a moment, while gasoline from the ruptured tank spewed out as if it were blood from an artery.

The appalled driver of the earth-mover smelled the rank odor of raw gasoline and jumped from his cab, running as fast as he could. Even with that, the percussive wave of the explosion blew him off his feet. Fetched up against the bole of a tree whose trunk had been sheared off either in the initial accident or the ensuing explosion, he looked dizzily up to see an oily fireball consume the car, the blue sky, and finally his consciousness.

10,001 Nights

Vietnam, Autumn 1971

Science Fiction, that's what they called the US Army Special Forces in Vietnam, and that nickname seemed just about right. These boys did all the nasty jobs that no one ever wanted to talk about, that were certainly never logged in on INTSUM, the weekly intelligence summaries on limited distribution at Pentagon East – the Military Assistance Command, Vietnam HQ at Tan Son Nhut. UWO, the Army called them: Unconventional Warfare Ops.

Even so, Do Duc was a kind of anomaly within Science Fiction. He was officially an E-9, a sergeant-major in the RVAF, the Republic of Vietnam Armed Forces, where he had served in the 3rd Ranger Command, where he gained his expertise in zippos – search and destroy missions. That was how he had come to the attention of Science Fiction.

He had enlisted in the RVAF at the age of sixteen, having lied about his age and his mixed heritage. It was easier to be Vietnamese only, so he had hidden away his surname, made up another, and no one bothered to check. South Vietnam was in a fight for its life; men, not paperwork, were paramount.

Sergeant-major was the highest rank an enlisted man could attain. He was officer material, no doubt about it, but he resisted with all his heart his superiors' suggestions in that direction.

Something of his nature had been forged in this mad crucible of war. Here, life was essentially a cut-and-dried affair. Men were sent out to kill one another, and women – well, they were around to bed in between missions.

In such a hellish atmosphere it was not surprising that human beings should lose their value. Life was reduced to a commodity, to be bought and sold, to be possessed or to be terminated. Hearts quickly became so callused that the wretchedness of existence could no longer be perceived.

In Vietnam, the jungle had a way of taking everything away from you. Inch by inch, the hive of horrors lurking there stripped away the veneer of civilization, exposing like a raw nerve all the dark things of humanity.

Quickly, the foundation of benevolence was subverted, so that in the end one doubted whether one had ever had a true sense of humanity at all. No wonder Do Duc's favorite song became the Rolling Stones' 'Sympathy for the Devil'.

Compassion was reduced to the remembrance of a dream; it was supplanted by the shark's peculiar imperative to continue to move. That meant missions: the fearful plunge into the jungle, the choking terror that you would make a mis-step and end up without your legs or be impaled on Punji sticks – fire-hardened bamboo spikes dark with a venom that would paralyze your central nervous system. The men in Do Duc's outfit often confessed to having nightmares of such happenstance. Curiously, these became a spur to volunteer for missions even when you were overdue leave.

Because what happened between missions? The shark's imperative needed to be met. Sex was okay as far as it went, and there were the drugs which provided the illusion of movement. But Do Duc needed more – much more.

This was how he struck up a relationship that was strange even for the strange days in which he was living. It began when a corporal named Rock was transferred into Do Duc's outfit. While with a grunt platoon in the Big Dead One, the First Infantry Division, elements of which were the first infantry in Vietnam, Rock had been bumped up from PFC via the courageous run he had made at a Viet Cong stronghold. He'd burned five of them before being shot in the arm. Then he'd dropped a grenade and had run like hell. That had earned him a field promotion and an impact award from a real live general.

But that was before Do Duc knew him, before he had been assigned by his own request to Do Duc's Science Fiction outfit. He had asked for the assignment in lieu of another impact award.

About the outfit: they called themselves Werewolves. They dressed like VC, ate like VC, and had as little to do with the soldiers around them as they were able. The Werewolves were a kind of semi-autonomous unit of madmen who were used on missions other outfits either couldn't or wouldn't undertake. Some of them, Do Duc believed, even the President wouldn't have abided had he been told of their planning and execution.

Who requisitioned these missions Do Duc never did find out, but the Werewolves' CO was a dour-faced colonel named Bud Powell, who came from the heartland of America. He had been a college professor in the sixties who had grown bored with his work and his deferral, so he had enlisted. Not that you could tell he had been a teacher from the zeal and cunning with which he employed his men to do the bloody bidding of the US Army. He was known affectionately among his men as Bowel.

157

It was Bowel who had first paired Do Duc with the cherry, Rock. 'This is one bad dude, so I'm given to understand,' Bowel had said to Do Duc just before the official mission briefing. 'How about this; he goes around with a LAW.' That was an M72 antitank rocket launcher which could blow open the side of any bunker Charlie could erect.

'Sounds like my kind of guy.'

Bowel had snickered. 'So I thought. I'm giving you a zippo mission to see what he's really made of.'

The two of them were sent to take out a VC 'vampire' patrol – one of those feared, lethal entities that stole through the lines at night, killing soldiers in their sleep. This kind of behavior on the part of the enemy was 'intolerable', according to Bowel, who ought to know since he was so well connected all the way up to Pentagon East.

The psychological effects of such raids were devastating, and they had to be stopped. The Werewolves were tapped to do just that.

But Bowel told Do Duc and Rock that he wanted them to do more than destroy the patrol. 'I want you to make an example of them. How you boys do that is strictly up to you.'

'Are you gonna tell us what's in bounds and what's out?' Rock asked.

Bowel had turned away from them. 'Son, I don't know what the fuck you're talking about.'

So Do Duc and Rock went vampire-hunting.

'Does Bowel really mean what he said?' Rock asked Do Duc as they made their way out of camp by the light of a sliver of moon.

'He always means what he says,' Do Duc said. 'Then again he always means what he *doesn't* say.'

Rock grinned. 'You guys've got yourselves a whole other war here. I think I'm gonna like this set-up.'

In the jungle, Do Duc said softly, 'I don't want to shoot these bastards, get me?'

'Cool,' Rock said. 'I'm already thinking of the thousand and one things that're better than shooting them.'

They camped in the jungle, sleeping one at a time for two-hour spells, until it was an hour before dawn. Then they tracked down the VC vampires – a unit of four – who were returning to base after a nightside foray.

They took them in their own makeshift camp, where four others waited for them, and not a shot was fired. They strung the eight VCs up by their feet, then slit them open from neck to pubis, a line of steaming humanity, and left them there to be found, a testament to the power of human hate and the corruption of the human soul, the true and lasting damage war inflicts on its participants.

Rock proved utterly fearless. If he hadn't known better, Do Duc would have assumed that he was merely too dim to feel fear. But there was nothing remotely dim about Rock. Do Duc quickly saw that Rock was intuitive about learning; he had an uncanny knack of sizing up a situation and making the best tactical advance into it.

The truth was that Rock was like those big city cockroaches at home which could live for a month on the residual protein in a human fingerprint. He subsisted on fear; the killing – which was the motivating factor for most of the Werewolves – was almost incidental. Bowel had been right in assigning him to this mission.

Afterward, of course, they were obliged to save themselves – from going mad or, perhaps, from savoring too intensely what they had done. Alcohol took care of that, for forty-eight hours, at least. By that time, they were horny as toads. Executing the release from life precipitated the need for that other release.

Do Duc had been with his girl, a sinuous Vietnamese who might have been as young as fourteen. Softly he stroked her thick night-black hair, ran his callused hands over her velvet flesh with such tenderness that she rose off the straw pallet to kiss the hollow of his throat in gratitude.

Do Duc heard a howl from the next room where Rock was with his girl. Thinking *Charlie*, Do Duc had grabbed his Marine combat knife, and ran to his buddy. What he saw in the next room turned his blood to ice. Rock had tied his girl with flex so tightly that her flesh bulged obscenely between the strips. Here and there, where the metal had bitten most cruelly into her, she had begun to bleed.

Rock, naked, was beating her with a length of bamboo. His erection stood out before him, red and quivering.

Do Duc, watching, flashed on the abattoir they had created in the jungle. He stood so still he could hear the sound of his own pumping blood over the rhythmic beat of bamboo against flesh.

'What happened?' Do Duc's girl said in Vietnamese from just behind him.

'Look at all this blood,' he said.

'So? It happens all the time,' she said. She reached her hand around his thigh, took hold of him. 'Ooo, your weapon is so hard. Why are you still standing here? Come back; it's fuck time.'

Do Duc, with his girl leaning on him, had taken one last look at Rock and the bleeding girl as if they were some tableau painted on a pagan temple wall which had survived the ravages of the ages. He was aware of a sensation in his mind that was akin to the ache one felt from a wound, very deep but so old it had been long forgotten.

159

Many years later, Do Duc would have cause to think again of that violent scene, the scent of blood, and the lost child's phrase reverberating in his mind, *it's fuck time.*

Two days after leaving their base camp, which was then approximately five hours by gunboat from Ban Me Thuot, the company was drenched in sweat, mud, and rice leaves.

There were six of them: Do Duc, Rock, a tattooed black giant named Riggs, a tightly wound explosives and ordnance specialist named Donaldson, so young the 'Dr Strange, Master of the Mystic Arts' comic he read over and over seemed the perfect medium for him, and a pair of CIDGs. This was an acronym for Civil Irregular Defense Group, Science Fiction-trained soldiers selected from various indigenous tribes who knew the local terrain. These particular CIDGs were anti-Communist Nungs who knew the target area inside out. The Nungs were among the men selected from the mountain hill-tribes of North Vietnam, who often provided Science Fiction with troops and intelligence to fight Charlie.

The Nungs were rail-thin, sunken-eyed creatures who looked to Do Duc like the wretched semi-human denizens of *The Island of Lost Souls*, but the only experiments being worked here were the discharge of ordnance that was systematically dismantling their country. They did not seem familiar to him, but rather, stripped from their environment, appeared to Do Duc as helpless as many of the Americans. How he pitied them.

Do Duc piloted a U-8F Seminole, a troop transport plane without weaponry of any kind, which Bowel had somehow procured. It arrived specially outfitted with a SLAR, a side-looking airborne radar unit.

Do Duc wondered why a defenseless aircraft had been requisitioned instead of a heavily armed gunship. Bowel had provided some clue.

'This is a God mission.' That was a Werewolf joke. God mission meant It Does Not Exist. 'I don't want any bushwhacking cowboys from AirCav in on our dinner, get me?'

'I sure do,' Do Duc had said.

Bowel had squinted at him. 'That's what I like about you, Do Duc, you know when it's time to go to work for Uncle Sam.' He took out the sad remnant of a cigar that had been chewed over for months. It was slimy and about to fall apart, but Bowel stuck it between his lips just the same.

'Okay,' he said, 'besides being a God mission, it's a Ten-thou.' That meant it was the worst. 'It concerns the fate of one man. He's officially listed as MIA. Either he's dead or he's been captured by Charlie, we don't know which.' Bowel chomped on his disgusting stogie, waiting for a comment. When Do Duc made none, he nodded, went on. 'Sounds fucked ten ways from every Sunday in the calendar but that's the shit-stick hand we've been dealt.'

'We've been dealt worse.'

'Yeah? Wait'll you get a load of what's out there. You're putting down into dead space.' That was very bad. Dead space was an area where covering fire and observation by backup was impossible. Because of the Nungs, Do Duc assumed it was somewhere in North Vietnam.

'Your objective's name is Michael Leonforte.' Bowel paused as if expecting a response. Not getting one he continued. 'This guy's on another plane of existence. He's a veteran of Poison Ivy.' The Fourth Infantry Division. 'He's a helluva soldier, commendations up the yin-yang, but he's also been in the LBJ Ranch twice, once for beating an indigenous civilian into a coma, a second time for knifing a girl he swears was VC.'

'They check that one out?'

Bowel's mouth twisted. 'They would've liked to, only the girl was already cold.'

'Mick sounds interesting. How come they let him out of Long Binh Jail?'

"Cause he's a VIP as far as certain elements of Pentagon East are concerned. They put him in the field – in charge of his own unit, no less. The group was inserted behind enemy lines – you'll find out where soon enough. They kept strict radio contact for five days; then the transmissions ceased and all attempts to raise them proved fruitless.'

Bowel's eyes flicked down to the 'Eyes Only' onion-skin sheet he held. 'That was approximately three months ago. When he was reported MIA, Pentagon East freaked. They rolled out a shitload of special pattern activity just for him.' Bowel meant detailed observations of enemy activity within certain sectors. 'They mobilized a goddamned division, for Christ's sake.'

'Just to find one Michael Leonforte.'

Bowel grunted, handed over a black-and-white photo. Do Duc was looking at a charismatic young lieutenant with a long face, wide-set black eyes and a scowl as deep as the Grand Canyon. Even in the picture Do Duc could discern the power emanating from that face.

'Heavy,' he said.

'Yeah.' Bowel took the photo back. 'That about sums up young Mick.'

'He should have had a CO at Pentagon East,' Do Duc said. 'Why didn't he lead a team in to find Mick.'

'Did just that,' Bowel said dryly. 'The team never came back out. It vanished just like Mick's.'

161

Do Duc mulled that over for a time. 'You know why Pentagon East has gone batshit over his disappearance? He have possession of classified intelligence?'

'Maybe. Maybe they have plans for him,' Bowel said, deadpan. 'But then again maybe it has to do with the fact that he's the son of Frank Leonforte, the hotshit Mafia godfather.'

Do Duc was silent for some time. *This guy's on another plane of existence.* He was watching Bowel's smirk and wondering how much more he knew about Mick Leonforte he wasn't giving up.

'What do we do when we locate this motherfucker?'

'If he's dead, you bring back the body. If he's alive, you are instructed to extract him from his hostile environment and –'

'Jesus, sir!'

'That's the language they used to tell me, son, so I'm only passing it on. I want to be precise about this. Quite naturally there's no paperwork associated with this God mission. None whatsoever.'

'Okay, let's say he is alive,' Do Duc said. 'I find him and hotel alpha.' That meant 'haul ass'. 'Then what?'

'You bring him to me,' Bowel said, 'that's what.'

Maybe it was then that Do Duc began to smell a rat. In any case, he said nothing.

Bowel had looked at him. 'I want him alive, alive-o, get me?' Do Duc said he did. 'I'm assigning you a complement of CIDGs. Where you're going, you'll need their expertise. My advice is to use these CIDGs when-ever practical. By the way, you won't be issued a prick. We don't want anyone eavesdropping on unauthorized transmissions.' A prick was a PRC-25, the lightweight field radio that was the Werewolves' standard issue.

Bowel stared at Do Duc. 'Like I said, it's a Ten-thou.' He cleared his throat. 'That's it, then. And, Do Duc, for Christ's sake don't crash the damned Seminole. What we don't need is hard evidence that we've been where you're going.' That was classic Nam doublethink, and it didn't pay to dwell on the irony of it. That kind of oxymoron wore thin pretty quick over here.

'One last thing, sir,' Do Duc said with his hand on the door. 'What if the objective resists extraction?'

For a long time Bowel said nothing. He stared through Do Duc as if he did not exist.

'In that event,' Bowel said slowly, 'you are free to use your own judgement.'

'Sir.'

Bowel's eyes snapped into focus, raked Do Duc's face. 'You bring this motherfucker back to me, soldier, one fucking way or another.'

They took off at night without Do Duc knowing where he was going, save for the initial heading Bowel had given him verbally at the final briefing. In the air, Donaldson, looking more tense than usual, worked the SLAR as if he had been born to it. Rock was right over his shoulder. Do Duc had given him the sealed envelope with their instructions on a kind of paper that melted in your mouth. It helped when you needed to eat the stuff after memorizing the information. Every few minutes Rock called out course corrections to Do Duc as if the SLAR itself was providing them. Riggs stared at the back of Donaldson's head as if he expected a psychic attack from Dr Strange. The two Nungs slept the entire way.

There was no armament aboard the aircraft, so it was clear they had been targeted for insertion in an area where there was little or no enemy air traffic or ground radar. That had sounded suspiciously like Cambodia, where Charlie had bunkered himself in and was rearming and resupplying before venturing back across the border to engage the US Armed Forces.

Despite being provided with directions piecemeal, Do Duc had a general idea where they were headed, and it was no surprise to him when they set down in a green LZ – a landing area free from enemy observation. It was the distance which threw him, and now he knew why he had been given the longer-range Seminole instead of a gunboat: as far as he could tell they were in the middle of nowhere; the map he had memorized and then eaten had given only one landmark besides the Mekong: a nothing village named Sre Sambor three klicks northwest of the landing site.

'We've flown halfway across Cambodia,' Rock said with some astonishment. 'What the fuck was Michael Leonforte doing here?'

Do Duc looked at him. 'The question to ask is: what was Pentagon East up to sending him in here?'

Cambodia, Do Duc knew, was an ostensibly neutral country in the war, but long-standing political problems with the more powerful Vietnamese caused Cambodia's leader, Lon Nol, to turn a blind eye to the Viet Cong incursions into his sovereign territory. As Do Duc suspected, they were headed straight for a hot zone, and prickless, they were working without a net.

Ten-thou, as advertised.

It was the wet season and there had been a great deal of rain – twelve straight days of it – before they had launched the mission. The wet season was not the best time to effect any kind of offensive action, Do Duc knew, and the fact that they were moving in now testified both to the significance and the urgency of what they had to accomplish.

The strip where he had been ordered to put down did not even have a shed attached to it. God alone knew how anyone had discovered its existence. Do Duc had no sense that there was anything remotely military about the strip, which was nevertheless well-maintained. By whom? he found himself wondering.

The strip was at the extreme edge of a vast area of terraced rice paddies to the east, into which they plunged directly they had unloaded their equipment from the aircraft, heading north toward the Mekong River. Looking back from the unprotected morass of the flooded paddies, Do Duc was not happy to see the Seminole disappear into the hazy distance.

The physical effort to get across the rice paddies was enormous. They saw no Viet Cong patrols. Indeed, to Do Duc's amazement, they saw no one at all. They remained alone, traveling on a flat, viscid landscape that dwarfed them no matter in which direction they looked.

The leader of the Nungs was an emaciated young man named Jin. On the ground, in the midsection of Cambodia, it was Jin with whom Do Duc consulted most often and to whom Do Duc deferred when there was a difference of opinion. Rock disagreed with this action, and it became a source of friction between the two.

'What the fuck're you doing?' Rock had said the first time Do Duc asked for Jin's advice and followed it.

'For Christ's sake, keep your voice down,' Do Duc said. 'The jungle can act like a cathedral, bouncing sound for yards in every direction.'

Rock glowered evilly at the Nungs, but he lowered his voice. 'Maybe they're Doubtfuls. If they've sold us out, Charlie already knows we're here.'

'Calm down. You forget even we didn't know where we were headed until we were in transit.'

'Yeah, maybe, but these sorry bastards would probably as soon have you for lunch as look at you.'

'You're misinformed,' Do Duc said. 'They're not barbarians.'

'The hell they aren't. Just look at them!'

'Their civilization's a lot older than yours or even mine.'

Rock snorted. 'What civilization? All these shits've been doing for centuries is killing each other.'

'And what've your civilized countries been doing?'

Rock gave him a hard look. 'You're a good one to talk. You were brought up where? In the middle of this fucking jungle, right? Sort of a stone age kind of thing, huh? Maybe that's why you can relate to them real well.'

Do Duc had bared his teeth at Rock.

Rock grinned. 'Shit! Look at you! You're a fuckin' tribesman just like

164

them! Hell, you even speak their dialect.' He laughed. 'So, okay, maybe you understand these shits better than I do.'

'Do you good to figure that out, Ace.'

Behind them, in the far distance, beyond even the southern horizon, the continuing flush of war could be seen if not, at this distance, heard. Man-made lightning in the form of aerial bombardment lit the underside of the clouds with the bitter rain of napalm and, in the fuliginous aftermath, dawn came unnaturally early in the kingdom of the damned.

Before the real dawn arrived they had pitched camp.

Rock did the work of three men, but he had a haunted look in his eye. As they took their horse pills to stave off malaria and ate their Charlie rats, what they called C-rations, he said to Do Duc, 'Where the fuck is Mr Charles?' He patted his LAW rocket launcher, slung at his hip like a six-gun of the gods. 'I can't wait to blow him away.'

'Patience,' Do Duc said. 'I got a nasty feeling we're going right down his throat. You'll get your chance.'

'Yeah, when? It's quiet enough to hear a lung collapse.' He spat, shook his head. 'There's a weird kind of isolation here, like we're dead and don't yet realize it.'

In a way, Do Duc thought he was right. 'Jin says we're in a hot zone but I don't understand it and there's just so much he's willing to say. Is Charlie really this far north in Cambodia?' He shrugged. 'We'll find out soon enough. At dusk we'll begin to move.'

'I'll tell you it won't come fast enough to suit me,' Rock said, spewing out a mouthful of his Charlie rats. 'Christ, I'd rather eat my enemy's arm.'

They slept the first day beneath a clump of dank foliage set on a knoll just above the water level of the paddies. Rock, who took the first watch, did not sleep well. There was not a dry spot on his body, and he had begun to itch in the most unfortunate places. *Where are you, Mr Charles?*

They broke camp at dusk. At this point, a visual sense of distance had to be abandoned. Jin advised them not to look at the horizon, but to concentrate on the immediate environment, which had become so monotonous that Rock found himself dozing off as he slogged on through the unending morass.

Toward midnight they stopped to eat a light meal. The sky was completely clear; starlight and the watery illumination from a half-moon fell upon them like fistfuls of diamonds. Rock went to relieve himself and, crouching down, stared into the muddy water. Slowly, the patchwork of light and dark ceased to swirl from the movement of his approach and a pattern began to coalesce.

Good Christ!

'Would you look at this!'

Do Duc and Jin, who were closest, came over. They stared down into the water.

Skulls.

Rock waded around in a circle, crunching human skulls as he went. Thousands upon thousands of skulls made up the floor of this flooded paddy. And here were bones: femurs, ulnae, sacra, ribs, scapulae; he was standing in a veritable graveyard.

Now Do Duc knew that Jin hadn't lied: they were in a hot zone.

'Ask the Nungs what the fuck happened here,' Rock said, as he danced a jig on a ribcage and a shattered pelvis. The proximity to so much death was like being shot up with adrenalin.

'You should learn to speak their language,' Do Duc told him bluntly before turning to speak to Jin.

Jin's face was unreadable. 'The North Vietnamese and Viet Cong are massacring the Cambodians in the same way they are killing my people,' he said in his peculiar dialect. His voice was very controlled so that it took Do Duc a moment to discern the choler hidden there. 'Here is our history. This is what will be left for our children – the ones who survive this war. And I ask myself whether they will be the lucky ones.'

Do Duc translated for Rock who, for once, was silent, his little jig at an abrupt end.

'Then Mr Charles is here and he must be close,' Rock said, fingering the firing mechanism of his LAW.

They pushed on, spurred now, Do Duc was sure, by the thought of the skeletons over which they were traversing, though no one spoke of the sea of horror they cracked beneath their boot soles with every step they took.

It was almost dawn by the time they could see an ending to the paddies. It had begun to pour again, as it had done off and on during the last part of their trek. The wind drove the warm rain into their faces, cutting visibility to several hundred feet.

The water level had lowered considerably. They trudged through the miserable rainswept landscape. Do Duc, on point, could make out a dark smudge on the bank of the last paddy. Beyond it should be the Mekong River up which they must make their way. They had been heading steadily east, and the river would take them almost due north, straight for the border of Laos. Laos lay like a concubine curled up against the back of Vietnam, arching from the southern end where they were headed in a northwesterly direction until it hit the borders of Yunnan in southern China and the Shan States in Burma, the area known as the Golden Triangle because of its production from the vast poppy fields covering its rugged mountain plateaus.

He thought about Pentagon East flying into a panic when Michael Leonforte went MIA in this hot sector. He thought about the first rescue party that had gone MIA, too. He thought about Bowel's directive to extract Leonforte and *bring him back to Bowel*. Not to his handlers at Pentagon East. Now, Do Duc thought, it was going to get interesting.

He picked up his pace, nearing the dark smudge. It was a makeshift pier: three rotting wood boards on creaking pilings that jutted out into a wide muddy river that snaked its way into the mist.

'This must be it,' Do Duc said, and Jin, plodding near him, nodded mutely.

They broke out the black rubber Zodiac boat, pulled a pair of rip-cords. It inflated very quickly, and they pushed it off the end of the pier.

'Keep your hands inside the boat,' Jin warned. 'There are plenty of crocodiles in the water. In this low light they'll look like drifting logs.'

They spent four nights navigating the river. As had been their m.o., they slept during the day, pulling the boat up across a muddy bank beneath the deep shade of the trees while they huddled in sleep. Once, the watch reported the passing of a Khmer boat, but its complement of soldiers did not see them and did not stop. Otherwise, they appeared to be alone.

'Where Charlie?' Rock asked, eager as ever to draw blood.

No one answered him because they didn't know.

They ate fish hooked from the opaque water by Jin and his CIDG companion. More than once the Nungs pointed out the ziggurat-studded backs of crocs, gliding silently through the currents and eddies. Do Duc watched the creatures with an expression that Rock could not define.

The river looked familiar to Do Duc, not because he had ever been there before but because he had memorized the map that had been in the sealed envelope Bowel had given him. He had since eaten all the directives and attendant intelligence, typed on the edible paper.

Near dawn of the fourth night, he directed them to pull into the left bank. The light was a glistening pearl, just lustrous enough to etch and limn but not yet bright enough to produce color.

'We're close now,' he said to Rock as they pulled the Zodiac into deep cover. 'Charlie must be here somewhere.' They were less than a klick from the border to Laos, and this was where their intelligence ended. Somewhere up ahead was where Michael Leonforte and eight other men went MIA.

Do Duc and Jin went on a perimeter patrol while the rest of the unit prepared camp beneath the trees. When Rock was finished, they still hadn't returned. He pulled out his LAW and went looking for them. It didn't take long. They were on the other side of the stand of trees.

'What's the problem?' Rock asked them.

Do Duc pointed. 'Crispie critter,' he said.

It was like being in a car, coming out of a fog at sixty miles an hour to find a semi coming straight at you. They stood before the naked body of a girl whom he judged to be perhaps ten years old. The corpse lay twisted, back arched as if she were pinned to the rotted-out bole of a tree. The skin over two-thirds of her body was scorched to a crisp; her legs were broken, the bones poking through the ripped flesh almost as if in a deliberate composition. She was missing the lower half of both arms.

'Fuck,' Rock said. 'What the hell hit her?'

Do Duc continued to stare at the girl.

It had begun to rain again, fat drops like the sweat off Buddha's brow. The air was as heavy as chain-mail. It took an effort just to breathe it in and out.

'She was smoked with jelly, for sure,' Riggs said as he came up behind them. He shifted his M60 machine-gun restlessly from one arm to another. 'But as for the rest of it . . .'

'Never seen anything like that,' Donaldson said, holding onto his M16A1 with white knuckles. 'Kinda makes your hair stand on end.'

'Fuckin' Charlie,' Rock said.

'Wasn't VC did this,' Jin said in decent English.

Rock's eyes widened and Do Duc smiled.

'You knew all along he spoke English, didn't you?'

'I told you to learn his language,' Do Duc said. 'He's learned yours.'

'Sonuvab –!'

Do Duc waved him to silence, said to Jin, 'Who, then, if it wasn't Charlie?'

Jin touched the dead girl with the end of his Soviet-designed AK-47 as he stepped over her, and Do Duc thought he saw his lips move in silent prayer.

Do Duc waved the others to stay behind as he went after Jin. He paused, stood for a moment on a small knoll, watching the Nung squat on his haunches, his machine-gun between his knees.

Do Duc crouched beside him, shook out a cigarette. They smoked for some time in silence. At last, Do Duc buried his butt in the mud, said softly, 'What is it about the situation back there I should know?'

For a long time, Jin did not answer him. He continued to stare out across the glade in the triple-canopied jungle as the rain began to hammer down full-force.

'When I was growing up, I used to play for hours in my grandmother's flower garden. How the sunlight lit up its delicate colors! How I loved to

168

run between its precise rows and circular beds!' He took a long drag on the cigarette, let out the smoke with a harsh hiss. 'Less than a year after she was killed by the Viet Cong, my duties led me back to the area of my youth and I took a short detour. The house was still intact, but the garden was overgrown, choked with vigorous weeds and thorny vines. It was ugly now.'

His mahogany-colored hand opened, palm upward, like a flower. 'I would like to think that one day I can come back home without needing one of these.' He slapped the side of his AK-47. 'But the longer I am a soldier the less conviction I have that this will happen. Every day a new atrocity springs up like a weed or a thorny vine.'

'Jin, I grieve with you,' Do Duc said, 'but I must know what happened to that girl.'

'Ask the Gwai.'

Do Duc swung his head around. 'The Gwai?' The word meant demon in the Nung dialect.

'The Gwai are Nungs, just like me, but not like me at all. They did this.' Despite his Buddhist upbringing he was unable to keep the bitterness out of his voice.

'I've never heard of the Gwai.'

'It's not what they call themselves, but what others in secret have named them.'

Jin seemed very uncomfortable. Do Duc wondered at this. Jin showed more emotion now over the death of this one child than he had over the thousands of Khmer whose bones they had cracked as they marched like ants across the riverbed of skeletons.

A sect of Nungs – the Gwai – had tortured this child? Do Duc again heard the warning bell that had gone off in his head during his final briefing with Bowel. Laos. The southern route from the Golden Triangle. All of a sudden, the rat he had caught a whiff of before seemed a whole lot closer.

'Do the Nungs – the Gwai – know where our objective is?' Do Duc asked. 'Are they keeping him for ransom?' That would explain some of the hysteria which had seemed to grip Pentagon East at Michael Leonforte's MIA report.

'I don't know,' Jin said, getting up and walking back into the canopied forest.

Daylight and the scent of fear. The sense of isolation had vanished. Rain thundered down, drowning all other sound in the maelstrom of its fury. They slept as best they could, which was to say not well.

Do Duc found that he could not close his eyes without seeing the image of the girl, lying like a sacrificial lamb against the drum of the rotted

169

tree. He was not disturbed by her death – what did one more matter?; there would be plenty more – but by the manner in which it had been carried out. He was remembering.

He got up, went back to where she lay. He hunkered down, staring at her, his mind turning over like an engine. It was like a picture, perfect in its own calculated way. The composition. The phrase 'sacrificial lamb' repeated itself in his mind like the tolling of a bell. Had she been a sacrifice? Is that what had gotten under Jin's skin?

Though he had carried out a score of missions when he had been no more than a heartbeat from death, and had become as familiar with the grip of fear as he was with his own body, he knew he had stumbled upon something utterly new. He didn't know whether to be terrified or excited.

He stayed where he was, his consciousness mesmerized by the sight, his unconscious stirred perhaps by the ethereal scoria of some strange alchemy. He passed the day in a semi-conscious dream state, in which visions, memories and fantasies combined to form the constructs of a new reality: an eternal war from which he wished never to return.

Armies of his imagining rose to challenge each other to mortal combat. Blood spurted from grievous wounds, soldiers fell, were trampled underfoot by their own comrades' inexorable progress across a plain composed of the slain.

Emerald twilight emerged from the heat of the colorless day. Sometime while they had slept it had ceased to rain, but it began again soon after they awakened. They relieved themselves, ate hurriedly, dutifully swallowed their horse pills and broke camp. Within an hour they emerged from the jungle only to be drawn to a series of flickering jewels in the near distance. These particular jewels were fiery.

'Laos,' Jin said from close beside him.

Do Duc nodded, said, 'Butterfly,' and the men spread out. The Butterfly was a patrol pattern revolving on multiple axes which gave the unit maximum protection as it progressed through unknown and presumably hostile territory. Despite their extreme vigilance they encountered no one.

The fires were less than a klick away, and turned out to be flickering in the remnants of a substantial village. They paused at the perimeter. Here and there, the fires still burned white-hot, impossible in this weather unless they were of a chemical nature. The buzz of the insects was startling, rolling over them like a net. Soon the stench of scorched flesh was overpowering.

'Napalm,' Do Duc said. He knew the effects of napalm when he saw them, and there was plenty to see. A sea of corpses confronted them, blind eye-sockets cast in incongruous directions, silent and accusatory. Clouds of insects lifted and fell in sickening waves, feeding off the carrion. He kicked over bodies, studying them as if they yet had a tale to tell. Viet Cong or Laotian, it was impossible even for the Nungs to tell them apart.

'What d'you think happened here?' Rock asked. 'US Army clean-up?'

Do Duc shrugged. He knew what Rock was thinking: was this another incident like the one Calley and his Butcher Brigade perpetrated at My Lai? 'As far as I know we don't have any units inside Laos.'

'Face it,' Rock said, 'neither of us know shit about where MI is operating or what it's up to.'

He meant Military Intelligence, and Do Duc found himself wondering whether the elements within Pentagon East who had given Michael Leonforte his mission had been MI.

The Nungs, AK-47s at the ready, patrolled the torn-apart streets of the village with closed faces. Do Duc's thoughts returned to Jin's assertion that the Gwai were operating inside Cambodia. Could they also be active within Laos? Each question he asked, it seemed, was leading him northward toward the Golden Triangle. Abruptly, the rat he had been smelling ever since Bowel had given him the final briefing had a distinct flavor: it was the odor of money.

At that moment, Riggs gave a shout and the unit ran toward the eastern perimeter of the devastation. Do Duc saw the concrete bunker. He and Rock went down into the natural hollow to take a closer look. The curious thing was that, though it had been only half hidden underground, the bunker itself was intact, the only thing spared utter destruction.

Do Duc motioned to Rock, who leveled his LAW at the bunker's locked door, pulled the trigger. Donaldson was the first man into the hollow echo after the explosion, tossing a CS grenade into the gaping hole the rocket launcher had made in the concrete. They all backed away from the hiss of the riot gas, then sat back on their haunches, waiting for the air to clear.

Do Duc and Rock ducked inside the bunker, took a look around. There were no personnel inside; it was an armaments warehouse. The curious thing was that what they saw stockpiled were K-Fifties, 7.62 submachine-guns, all Chinese Communist-manufactured. Considering Jin's warning, that was significant.

They explored the entire bunker, came up with more Chicom weapons.

'This doesn't look like Charlie,' Rock commented. 'This ordnance is so new I can see my reflection in the oil. He's never so well equipped.'

'You know about the Nungs?'

Rock nodded. 'Did a patrol or two with some of 'em when I was with Big Dead One. We were always on the cutting edge of the war.' He laughed. 'And I do mean cutting.'

'This look like them?'

'Fuck, they don't have the kind of money needed for this cache.'

'You ever hear of the Gwai – a rogue group of Nungs?'

Rock shook his head. 'No, why?'

'Jin mentioned them. According to him they're very bad news.'

Rock grunted. 'Fucking Nungs.'

Do Duc shrugged. The odor of money was becoming stronger. 'Who has the capital for this, then?' Do Duc said.

'Easy. Soviet Union. Or Uncle Sam.'

The two men looked at each other for a long time. At last, Rock said, 'You think this shit has anything to do with Michael Leonforte?'

'Maybe,' Do Duc said. 'Who knows what Pentagon East has on its mind.'

'If we bought this ordnance who are we arming?'

'Good question,' Do Duc said. 'At this point, I think Mr Leonforte is the only one who'll give us an answer.'

'If we can find him.'

'That's why we're here,' Do Duc said. 'But if he's dead I say we come back here and "liberate" this ordnance. We'd get big bucks selling it.'

'Done,' Rock said.

They got up to leave, and Rock put a hand on Do Duc's arm. 'Whoever owns this has got to be close; maybe they're already eyeballing us.'

They made their way out of the bunker. Both had the beginnings of a headache brought on by the last of the CS gas. Do Duc broke the unit up into teams of two, ordered them out on Cloverleaf recon, so that they would loop back, overlapping each other for backup in this obviously hostile environment.

Do Duc and Rock explored the area around the bunker. They found nothing of interest. Within ten minutes they caught sight of Riggs and Donaldson returning from recon across the destroyed village. It was at that moment that the mortars began to fall, the sky caving in, turning to hot lead in a paroxysm of death.

The first or second round caught Donaldson, hurling him into the center of another black and red plume. Do Duc, who had taken cover alongside Rock, could not see Riggs through the smoke and explosions. The Nungs were nowhere in sight. Do Duc hoped they were trying to find the source of the attack.

The silence after such an attack is eerie because it is deafening in its own right. Do Duc poked his head out from behind a crumbling wall, saw what was left of Donaldson, not much more than a smear on the pock-marked ground. Nearby, amid the rubble, he could make out the enormous

Riggs, who was propped up against another wall. He was staring down at the blood covering his lower body. His chest was heaving and shuddering.

'Ah, shit,' Do Duc said, as Rock pushed up beside him to take a look around.

It remained quiet. He still had no idea where Jin and his Nungs were or any sense where the incoming mortar fire had emanated from. He saw Riggs's chest moving in panting heaves, and he knew he had to get to him immediately.

'Cover me,' he said to Rock.

Taking a deep breath, he broke cover, zig-zagging his way toward Riggs. No sniper took a shot at him and he could see no sign of enemy infantry. He saw no evidence of the Nungs, either, and this worried him. What had happened to them? It was unlikely they had neutralized the source of the enemy fire since Do Duc had heard no weapons fire. Had they deserted?

He knelt beside Riggs. 'It's gonna be okay, Big Guy,' he said, breaking out an ampoule of morphine. 'Just take it easy.'

He was just beginning to assess the damage when the air turned thick with the peculiar whistling of incoming fire. Do Duc launched himself toward the relative safety of a cracked-apart structure, but he could already feel the oppressive weight of the shells streaking inward on their high arcs.

Where are those goddamned Nungs?

Then the world was collapsing in on him with the shriek and wail of matter rending itself. The ground rippled underneath his boot soles, then came up and smashed against his stomach.

He lay for a time, dazed and so shook up that he swore later that he had actually glimpsed the phantom armies of his previous day's dream on the march, the dread beat of their weaponry and armor shaking the leaves off the trees, his own helmed and masked silhouette striking down the last flames of the setting sun.

Then he blinked, saw Rock crouched over him, shaking him, shouting at him.

'What?' he said. 'What?'

'Let's hotel alpha!' Rock was shouting. 'I found the Nungs – or what's left of 'em. We're it from the first team!' He hauled Do Duc to his feet, steadying him. 'Goddammit, buddy, get your ass in gear now!'

Do Duc nodded, but now the shelling had started again, and together they staggered into the northwestern outskirts of the village, heading deeper into Laos, but that was all right for now because it was away from the barrage.

It seemed to Do Duc that night that he did nothing but dream. He lay beneath a palm tree, with the rain pattering all around, curled in a fetal position, exhausted and famished. He was in pain from the rubble that had landed on him, his skin was chafed raw, and he itched in so many places he had given up scratching. He took that as the best sign; he was still alive.

He slept . . . and dreamed, the images kicking in one after another as if his mind were a vehicle that had been thrust into high gear by the adrenalin-rush of the war.

He spoke with the ravaged girl on the bank of the rice paddy. She had no eyes, but her bare teeth smiled at him in a most disarming manner. The darkness of her blind sockets was lit by the phosphorescence of memory like anti-aircraft tracers.

The memories were not, of course, hers, but Do Duc's, played out upon the grisly stage of his childhood, mangled by the terror it generated, so that by the coming of dawn, when he opened his gluey eyelids, there remained no pleasant sanctuaries, no safe harbors for him to withdraw into. There was only the war, and the war was where he had chosen to be, as if it were a country into which he could disappear like some dissipated expatriate disgusted by life back home.

Which, in a sense, was just what had happened.

Do Duc had taken the first watch, but sometime during it he had fallen asleep, not to wake up until dawn. It was lucky that the enemy had not come upon them in the night.

Distance was obscured by clouds. It was as if they were in the Cardamom mountain range, thousands of feet above sea level, instead of being in the low plateau country.

'Where the hell are we?' Rock said.

'I don't know,' Do Duc said, doing some deep knee-bends. The movement had begun to work the stiffness out of his body. 'In this dense fog I can't tell east from west.'

He took out his compass, but it had been smashed sometime during the mission, probably during the barrage, and was of no use. He looked at Rock, who was sitting on a blasted tree stump, his menacing LAW braced on his right hip.

'I want to get something straight right now, so we both know where we stand,' Rock said. 'I don't much care whether or not I get back. In fact, thinking about it, I'd like it a whole helluva lot better if I didn't. The truth is I like it out here, away from all the bullshit of the Army bureaucracy.' He spat. 'You know and I know that the bush is where it's at when it comes to this war. The bush is where Charlie breathes and shits, and the bush is where we're gonna put his ass in a sling.'

'What about support?' Do Duc said. 'You can't wage war without it.'

174

'Fuck that,' Rock said. 'The kind of support we're getting from Penta-gon East can only get us killed. Count on it. Friendly fire or wrong coordinates on a drop or shit-stick intelligence about a green zone where Charlie is waiting for us Alpha bravo' – he meant an ambush – 'we're the ones who'll get it in the neck.'

'I can't argue with you there.'

'Then why go back? I'm out here in the deep bush and I'm thinking the longer I'm here, the farther out I go, the better I like it. And d'you know why? Because I feel safe here. I only have to rely on me and on you – not a bunch of ass-wipes in Saigon who do not know how to wage war. We do. And this is where we should be doing it from.'

Do Duc thought about that for some time. 'There's the mission to think of,' he said at last.

'You know this mission stinks to high heaven,' Rock said. 'Now that it's just us there's no harm in talking about it openly.'

'What do you mean?' Do Duc knew but he wanted to hear Rock's version.

'I think we've been put in the middle of a sensitive MI mission that fucked up in a major way.'

Do Duc nodded. 'I agree. But I still want to reach the objective.'

'Michael Leonforte. Well, why not? If he's still alive.' Rock took a minute to squash an insect between his thumb and forefinger. 'You know the odds are that this mission is no longer what it once was.'

'It's occurred to me that it never was what it was supposed to be,' Do Duc said.

'All the better.' Rock rose, grinning. 'I say let's get the fuck on with it.'

Just before noon, they stopped to rest in a depression between two long fingers of muddy ground which, before the war, had perhaps been farmland. Do Duc ached all over.

If anything, the fog had thickened, so that it was impossible to see even a meter in any direction. All sound was muffled but, in truth, there was little to hear. It had seemed to Do Duc as if they had been moving across a landscape devoid of any other life, as if they themselves had become as insubstantial as ghosts, flitting across terrain already beyond their ability to touch or change.

Sensory input dwindled until there was a minimum of sight and sound; even the rank stench of the semi-tropical foliage seemed far away, as if dampened by the heavy fog.

In this state somewhere between consciousness and dreaming it was easy to assess even the minutest change in their immediate environment.

Do Duc stopped. 'We're not alone.'

'In all this shit no one could see us, not even with Starlights or infra-reds,' Rock said. Nevertheless he hefted his LAW, planting the butt firmly against his right hip. 'I'll tell you one thing; if Charlie's here his ass is grass.'

Do Duc put a hand on his arm. 'Don't be hasty. It won't help us to blow Mr Leonforte to kingdom come.'

'If Charlie – or the Gwai or whoever the fuck *they* are – are holding him hostage they'll be sure to keep him well away from any incursion.'

Do Duc was certain that Rock was right – only he wasn't so sure now that they were working under the correct premise.

He pointed into the mist-shrouded trees. 'This way.'

The doleful drip of moisture enclosed them in a clammy embrace. They moved very slowly, as if they were underwater or on a planet where the gravity was many times that of Earth. Breathing became laborious, and they moved through the jungle with extreme difficulty.

'I imagine it's me you've come all this way to find.'

They stood stock still, watching as first one, then five or six shapes appeared as if conjured out of the trees themselves. Do Duc took a brief look at all of them – could they be the Gwai? – but quickly concentrated on the man in front, the one who had spoken.

'Michael Leonforte, I presume.'

The man smiled. 'Mick will do. You recognize me from the photos they showed you back at Pentagon East. I assume that's where you're from.'

'Not exactly,' Do Duc said, answering both questions. This Michael Leonforte was different than the one in the photo Bowel had shown him, though the more Do Duc studied him the more the resemblance became apparent. 'We're not official like the party Pentagon East sent. We're Were-wolves.'

Mick Leonforte grinned. 'Science Fiction Werewolves, huh? I've heard of you.'

He was surrounded by the lean Chinese faces of the Nungs, and he wore what they wore: surplus camouflage fatigues, high-topped paratrooper boots, web belts – all US WWII stuff. They were armed with the Chicom K-Fifties like the ones in the cache Do Duc had found in the bunker. None of them wore any insignia, not even Leonforte, but when he held up his left hand for silence, Do Duc saw tattooed on the inside of the wrist a curious image: a human face, the left side skin-colored with its eye open, the right side blue with a vertical crescent where the eye should be.

It passed like a flash as his hand came down. It had been small, less than three inches in height, but the power of it electrified Do Duc's mind.

176

'You guys've done some pretty heavy shit in your time,' Mick Leonforte said. 'It's gonna be a damn shame to kill you.'

Do Duc, feeling Rock shift against him, said nothing. He continued to study Leonforte, because it was essential now to figure out what had happened to him. He had heard of one or two cases of Marine officers in charge of CIDG montagnards out-country going native, but he suspected that was too facile an answer to the enigma. He had only a few disparate clues to go on, but he could see by the heightened tension among the Nungs that he had very little time.

'My CO sent us here to bring you back.'

'No surprise there,' Mick Leonforte said. He had let his hair grow. It was as black and lustrous as the hair on the Chinese mountain tribesmen who were his companions. His full beard was neat, but it hardly fell into the guidelines set by Army regs. His cheeks were a bit hollow, and there was something about his eyes, a clarity that bordered on the feral, which for sure would have disturbed the people back at Military Intelligence. 'My handlers have been trying to recall me ever since they realized they sent the wrong man to do the wrong job.'

'You were dragooned into MI, weren't you?' Rock said.

'Dragooned into MI and all the way through it,' Leonforte said. 'I came out the other side, and like Alice I found myself in Wonderland taking orders from someone called the Jabberwocky.' He laughed. 'Fucking spooks. They've all got names like that: Jabberwocky, the Mad Hatter, the Red Queen.'

'You're supposed to be a prisoner,' Rock exclaimed. 'What the hell –?'

'Forget MI. It was the spooks who sent you on this mission, wasn't it?' Do Duc said, overriding Rock's voice. 'That's why the Jabberwocky plucked you out of LBJ. He thought he had you over a barrel. You either did what he told you or he'd kick your butt back into jail.'

'And "lose the key for 10,001 nights", as the Jabberwocky put it.' Leonforte laughed, but he was looking more shrewdly at Do Duc. 'Yeah, that was the gist of it, more or less. Too bad he put the gun to the head of the wrong Joe. I was brought up to mete out threats, not buckle under them. My father taught me early how to handle arrogant bastards like that.'

He shrugged, made a gesture. 'What the fuck's the difference, anyway. They sent you for my scalp; I can't allow that.' The Nungs leveled their K-Fifties at Do Duc and Rock. 'Time to say your prayers, assholes.'

For Do Duc, it was time to gamble everything. 'We never had any intention of bringing you back.'

'That's a laugh.' Leonforte took a step toward them, ran a finger across Do Duc's forehead. 'Is this flop sweat I feel?' He made a hard sound in the back of his throat. 'Why else would you make the trek all the way out here to my territory?'

There it was, the confirmation he had been looking for. *My territory.* 'Why should we bring you back?' Do Duc said. 'That would be like cutting the throat of the Golden Goose, wouldn't it?'

The smile came off Leonforte's face like the shine off chromium. The ensuing silence gathered its own energy until it generated a kind of kinetic buzz that set the short hairs to stirring at the back of Do Duc's neck.

'Golden Goose,' Leonforte said in the exact tones in which Aladdin might have uttered 'Ali Baba'.

'Sure. That's what you're doing leading the Gwai – this rogue sect of Nungs.'

Leonforte's eyes opened a bit wider. 'What do you know of the Gwai, except rumor and hearsay? They're a deeply religious people.'

'Right now, I'm more concerned with the Golden Goose,' Do Duc said. 'I think that's an apt description for the man who's had the balls to appropriate a VC supply line into the Golden Triangle. How much could that kind of drug trade be worth a year? Speaking for Rock as well as myself, I can tell you we'd both rather have a piece of this than try to bring you back.'

'Listen to you!' Leonforte turned to the Gwai. 'Can you believe him? What a mouth!' He turned back. 'And speaking of balls . . .' He drew an American Army officer's .45 pistol and pressed its muzzle hard against Do Duc's temple.

Rock made a small move and a Gwai jabbed him with a K-Fifty in the small of his back.

'Don't even think about it,' Leonforte said, without turning his head.

'Lights out.' Gripping the .45, he squeezed the trigger.

Save for the sound of the hammer coming down on an empty chamber, nothing happened.

Leonforte, his face close to Do Duc's, grinned hugely. Then he removed the muzzle from Do Duc's temple and, at almost the same time, kissed him energetically on each cheek.

The Gwai, putting up their weapons, began to whoop.

'Welcome,' Michael Leonforte said, 'to the Land of the Dead.'

In that eternity between the instant Leonforte's finger pulled the trigger and the moment the hammer hit the empty chamber, a piece of Do Duc's past came rushing at him like a train out of control.

It began with the auras, light refracting from the people nearest him as if their skin and flesh had dissolved, transforming the remainder into lenses through which he now peered. He stared, transfixed, as if he could see in those pulsating shards of color their very souls laid bare like a corpse on a stainless-steel slab.

Then came the trilling of the white magpie, the bird's call expanding and echoing as if it were being simultaneously amplified and heard from a very great distance.

The magpie, big as a child, sat on his shoulder, preening its long, iridescent feathers while its gold and red eye peered at him with intense curiosity. If it spoke, Do Duc had the impression the entire episode would explode like a bubble or a dream, but it never did, and he remained under the spell of the auras.

Ao, the Nung elder, the initiator, the shaman of the tribe, would often take Do Duc down the mountain to the wide, muddy river where the Nungs fished. These seemed more like idyllic outings between father and son than pre-initiation rites.

Once, on a day so hot the sun seemed to sting Do Duc's bare flesh, Ao trapped a crocodile and, riding its ridged back while Do Duc had looked on agog with electric fear, he had pried open those mighty jaws, inserted a thick polished stick, and had rendered the beast harmless.

Ao settled Do Duc on the croc's back, placing his palms against the armor-like crests of its spine. Do Duc, his heart in his mouth, could hear the thunder of his heartbeat, the rushing of his blood in his inner ears. And then, for no good reason he could think of, Ao shoved him far over, so that his head was hanging just above the croc's face. He had peered into the beast's reptilian eyes.

What was it he was supposed to see there? Even now, recollecting the moment with utter clarity, he could not say for certain. Yet the suspicion remained: that he had been meant to seek out a kindred spirit in a beast because he could not find one among humans.

Others might find that to be a horrible notion, but not Do Duc. It had been he alone who had watched Ao plunge a knife into the croc's brain, midway between those eyes that regarded Do Duc, if not with outright curiosity, then at least with interest.

That evening, while watching the Nungs feast on the roasted meat which he had helped Ao strip from the bones, Do Duc felt the onset of the aura, and he remembered the white magpie crying in the trees as if offended by his hands ruddy with the reptile's blood.

For the first time since he had come to the Nungs, Do Duc disobeyed Ao, submitting willingly, almost eagerly, to the punishment he was certain the white magpie had meant for him.

It was the first time he became aware of sin – not the sin the loathsome

179

Catholic missionaries preached with such peremptory zeal, but a sin against the natural order. If the white magpie had not spoken to Do Duc there was in its eye the corona of desire, the halo of divinity, the thorned garland of sin.

And even when he went to his own priesthood with the Nung elders, he kept a secret part of himself free, pure for the holy trine the white magpie had tucked away in its heart of hearts.

At his initiation he had been required to hunt and kill a crocodile much as Ao had done thirteen months before. He was obliged to bring back its bloody meat in strips for the celebratory feast so that all of them – elder and initiate – could share in its strength.

Do Duc had gone alone, as was dictated, and he found his crocodile – a monstrous beast lying like a log in the still waters of the Song Ba. What a magnificent creature it was, utterly placid yet ready as a drawn bow to snap the bones of anything that crossed its path.

The stillness and the power: it was just this juxtaposition Do Duc was certain the white magpie meant for him to understand. What human could teach him this and other like mysteries? Not even the Nung priests. None.

Instead of killing the crocodile, he had spoken to it as the magpie had once spoken to him through its radiant eye, and he had climbed astride the croc's back, gliding with it through the leech-infested water until he came upon one of the Catholic missionaries who so badgered the lowland people with their talk of God and the Devil and Hellfire and eternal damnation. These missionaries who were so disdainful of the forest, so disconnected from their environment. Their world was Rome and nothing more.

The priest had come down the muddy bank to cool himself in the brown water, and the crocodile, launching itself forward with appalling speed, had caught his bare ankle, had held him long enough for Do Duc to stop his screaming by killing him. Languid once more, the croc had watched patiently as Do Duc skinned the missionary, cut slabs of meat off the chest and back. Only when he was finished did the beast roll what was left down into the water, dragging it beneath the surface.

What strange strength flowed into the elders that night as they feasted on the fresh meat Do Duc had triumphantly brought them? In Do Duc's ears the shrill cries of the white magpie reverberated like an aria as, smiling, he consumed the fragrant roasted flesh with the others.

'I could have killed you both,' Mick Leonforte said. 'Maybe I should have.'

'You won't be sorry we joined you.'

Rock said it with such conviction that Leonforte stared at him for a long time. At last, he said, 'You don't know the whole story. After you do, we'll see what measures have to be taken.'

'So we're on probation,' Rock said.

'You'll be stone dead unless you can accept certain precepts that may be hard for you to swallow. That's certainly been the case before.'

'Before,' Do Duc said. 'You mean the party the spooks at Pentagon East sent out after you.'

'See, I'm God here,' Leonforte said, just as if he hadn't heard a word Do Duc had said. He lifted his hands to include the Gwai who squatted with them in the bush. They were eating a simple midday meal of dried salted fish and cold sticky rice-balls, which to Do Duc and Rock tasted like manna from heaven after the Charlie rats. 'Just ask my subjects.'

Again, Do Duc saw that it would be easy for someone from Pentagon East to assign a madness tag to Leonforte. DWW, they called it. Dangerous When Wet. He had no doubt that this was how he was currently viewed by those in Saigon who were aware of him. That was a dangerously easy – and spurious – conclusion to draw. Maybe it was what had gotten the Pentagon East party killed. Do Duc knew that this conclusion would certainly get him and Rock dead right quick if he persisted in it.

'I liked what you said about the Golden Goose,' Leonforte said now. 'What do you know about the pipeline from the Golden Triangle?'

'Only what I've deduced,' Do Duc said. 'My CO told me jack-shit about it, although I'm now convinced he's at least aware of it.'

'What makes you say that?'

'First, he's very well connected at Pentagon East.' Do Duc paused a moment. 'I often wondered about that. I mean, he's not a career Army man, far from it. He was a college professor before he got bored with life and enlisted. What's he doing cozying up to the big honchos at HQ?' He licked salt off his fingertips. 'Second, my orders were to extract you from your environment and bring you back to my CO, not to Pentagon East.' He grunted. 'That also didn't sound kosher. Not until I met you and figured out you were on a spook run. Then everything started falling into place. If my CO had been a civilian spook – say, a recruiter for the Company on his college campus – it would all make sense: his being sent in-country, being asshole-buddies with Pentagon East, his outfit being given the assignment of bringing you back, wanting me to deliver you to him personally.'

A slow smile spread over Leonforte's face. 'You know, Do Duc, I believe I made the right choice not blowing your brains out.' He got up, brushed kernels of rice off his fatigues. The Gwai followed suit.

Do Duc, rising with them, was more acutely aware than ever of being under Leonforte's control.

181

'Let's get going,' Leonforte said. 'There's something back at base I want you to see.'

They arrived just before sunset. Color was lavishly splashed across the cloud-swollen sky, and the treetops appeared to be swords of stained glass. Birds flitted nervously among the branches and, some distance away, Do Duc could hear the low warning growl of a large predator – a tiger, perhaps.

Leonforte's camp was both more and less than he had imagined. While it was composed of houses rather than pitched tents, these hootches were ramshackle and mean in a way that spoke of poverty and suffering plainly beyond Western understanding. The stench of refuse and offal was so strong it soon became an acrid taste in the back of their mouths.

Almost immediately, and without a sign from Leonforte that Do Duc could see, the Gwai broke up. Only one stayed with them as Leonforte led them toward one hootch that seemed more substantial than the others. Do Duc assumed this was Leonforte's own place, but he was wrong, and it was the last time he allowed preconceived notions to cloud his assessment of the man.

The hootch was, in fact, a jail. It was occupied by one man: a Caucasian in black VC pajamas. Though he was obviously without the insignia of rank, it was most obvious by his posture and mien that he was a military man.

'This the spook?' Rock asked.

Leonforte nodded. 'The Mad Hatter.'

The man stared at them mutely, defiantly. He was tanned and fit. Tall and thin, he seemed a bit put out by the low ceiling of his jail, but that was all. His piercing blue eyes studied them seemingly without prejudice, but Do Duc did not mistake this mask for indifference.

'He led the first party to come looking for me.'

Do Duc was going to ask what happened to the rest until he realized this man was the answer. He was the only one in Leonforte's jail; the others had never been heard from again. They were dead.

Do Duc understood then the mortal line which Michael Leonforte had crossed, and the enormity of the step he and Rock would be taking should they decide to link up with this man. No wonder he thought of himself as a god; he had transgressed the law of man with a vengeance. To do that it was imperative he know he was beyond the law.

'What are you going to do with him?' Rock asked in that almost gentle tone that Do Duc had come to identify as his killing voice.

'I haven't decided yet.'

Rock took a step toward the cage within which the Mad Hatter was imprisoned. Looking him hard in the eye, he said, 'I have an idea.'

Do Duc did not object to what Rock had in mind because it would cement their relationship with Mick Leonforte. Leonforte himself was impressed with the plan because it at once increased the power of his spell over the Gwai and therefore the pipeline, while it bound these two to him in a manner that was as close to irrevocable as the human condition could get. It also appealed to him for the kind of message it would send back to the Jabberwocky.

'When they get a load of this,' Rock had said, 'they'll think twice about sending anyone else after us.'

He instructed the Gwai to tie the Mad Hatter to a rectangle of bamboo. Then, squatting over him, he had begun asking him questions. This was something of a ruse. Rock suggested that they make the Mad Hatter believe that they wanted access to the spook secrets filed in his brain. The fact was they wanted simply to make an example of him, to alter him significantly enough so that when he was dumped onto Pentagon East's doorstep the Red Queen would take immediate notice.

'We could kill him,' Rock had told them, 'but that's so final – and the message could be misconstrued. Who's to say that Charlie didn't do this to him? No, we need to send a stronger message, pack him up like a party favor and deliver him from evil so that he's got a story to tell the Red Queen, so he can mislead them about what we're up to – he'll be able to do it far more convincingly than we ever could.'

Do Duc was impressed with Rock's thinking. It would drive the spooks crazy to think they were out in the boonies setting up their own business in heisted military secrets. Commerce was the one thing spooks understood better than anyone else. It didn't matter if you were a capitalist or a Marxist, a Fascist or an anarchist. It was the prime directive of spookdom: commerce transcends ideology.

So he and Michael Leonforte watched in fascination as Rock went to work on the Mad Hatter, interrogating him for hours on end, using light and sound in concert, in between bouts of intense pain persuasion. Absorbing the process, which Rock conducted as if it were a medical protocol, Do Duc felt an odd sensation stirring the short hairs at the back of his neck.

No way had Rock learned this discipline in the Big Dead One, his former infantry outfit. He felt as if a supposedly well-trained pit bull had suddenly slipped its leash and was now gnashing its teeth in the nearby underbrush.

Apparently, Leonforte had the same thought, because on one of their breaks from their newest spectator sport he said to Do Duc, 'He learn this shit in the Werewolves?'

183

'*I* never learned it in the Werewolves,' Do Duc replied.

They were at the latrine, urinating into the damp morass below them.

'I bet your CO knows how to slip between the slats of consciousness like this.'

'Bowel? I don't see that. Why would he have a small Science Fiction outfit and not be with the other honchos at Pentagon East?'

'Spook-think,' Leonforte said, buttoning his fly. 'He'd be nearer the action, able to move on any mission he needed to without questions being asked. Also, no one would suspect who he really was.'

'Maybe,' Do Duc said, adjusting his trousers. 'And maybe you're seeing spooks hanging like bananas in the trees.'

'Let me tell you something,' Leonforte said as they turned back to the hootch where Rock was tirelessly trying to slip between the slats of the Mad Hatter's consciousness. 'In the business you and your pal just bought into you'd better be looking for spooks in the trees. Otherwise, you're liable to be court-martialed and executed before you can invent a defense.'

They returned to the hootch. The stench of fear, sweat and fecal matter hung in the air like a spider's web. They could see Rock's back. He had taken off his blouse and his heavy muscles were oiled with sweat, bunched as he performed his work.

Do Duc could see that he had a small blade in his right hand and, with a surgeon's precision, was making incisions in the Mad Hatter's face.

Hearing them enter, Rock said, 'I want to make sure he never forgets what we wanted from him.'

There was a peculiar sound, a kind of spine-chilling susurrus that resolved itself into a soft sobbing interspersed with an animal's panting. As he moved closer, Do Duc got a full view of what Rock was doing. The Mad Hatter's teeth were clenched, and as Rock worked on him, they ground together as puffs of agonized sound distended his cheeks.

That was as much as Do Duc cared to see. He nodded to Leonforte and, together, they moved out of the miasma into the sticky late afternoon light.

'Let's make arrangements with the Gwai to get him back to Pentagon East,' he said.

'Your friend Rock's certainly a workaholic.'

'You don't know the half of it,' Do Duc said. 'But it seems all of us here like this work more than your average Joe.'

Leonforte laughed. 'It's like my father says: nothing beats the capitalist spirit.'

'For Rock, I think this enterprise transcends money or power. It's somehow spiritual, like the Holy Grail.'

184

'Yeah, I know what you mean,' Leonforte said, wiping his forehead with his sleeve. 'I get the impression he could work on the Mad Hatter another couple of days.'

'I don't think that's such a hot idea,' Do Duc said. 'What would be left?'

'To tell you the truth,' Leonforte replied, 'I don't want to find out.'

Do Duc watched him as he spoke to the Gwai; it was decided they'd take the Mad Hatter back in-country at first light tomorrow.

'Now let's get down to business, partner,' he said when Leonforte had dismissed the Gwai. 'I want to know exactly how you cut Charlie out of his own drug pipeline.'

Leonforte threw his head back and laughed long and hard. He said, 'You still don't get it, do you?'

'What the fuck d'you mean?' Do Duc was already a little pissed off being made the butt of a joke he didn't get.

'You stepped into it big-time, Do Duc. This pipeline from the Shan States is the motherlode. It isn't Charlie's, never was. It's being run by Uncle-fucking-Sam. The whole stinking war's being funded through this mother.'

'You mean the United States Government owns and operates an opium pipeline? You must be out of your mind.'

'If by the Government you mean Congress or the Joint Chiefs of Staff, no. That *would* be an insane notion,' Leonforte said. 'No, I mean a clique of high-level officials from all branches of government – the military, judiciary, legislative, executive – a sub-rosa organization at work for their own purposes.'

'Which are?'

'Power,' Leonforte said. 'That's all any of them care about: possessing the power to manipulate events, people, governments, economies. Power and the circumvention of the law. The group's even got a name. It calls itself Looking-Glass.'

'How d'you know all this?'

'I was sent out here to monitor this motherlode for Looking-Glass, but I got one look at it and decided this was the opportunity of a lifetime, so I liberated it. I don't think Looking-Glass should have all the goodies for itself.' Leonforte laughed again. 'Why d'you think the Jabberwocky's so damned anxious to bring me back?'

'This is all bullshit,' Do Duc said. 'You with your record would be about the last person Looking-Glass – or anyone else, for that matter – would trust with monitoring the biggest drug pipeline in Asia.'

Leonforte's eyes sparked as he laughed. 'I've got friends in high places,'

185

he said. 'Or, at least, I did. And I've got a brother who watches over me like a guardian angel.'

Do Duc stood very still, the sweat running down him in rivulets. For a long moment, his mind was paralyzed. He felt numb with the implications. He noted with interest that Leonforte had said 'brother', not 'father'. What of the famous 'hotshit' Mafia boss, as Bowel had referred to him – Frank Leonforte?

'And now you've fucked these guys in a major way. Why?'

Leonforte shrugged. 'This jungle does something to you. As a Vietnamese, you should understand because you've been close to it all your life. There's *power* in these mountains. It infects the blood like the bite of a vampire. And I thought, why should I be an errand boy for Looking-Glass when I can be monarch of this realm.' He laughed again. 'Besides, Do Duc, it's a rush to fuck with people's heads when you know there's nothing they can do about it.'

Do Duc said, 'If what you're telling me is the truth, Looking-Glass won't let you get away with it. They'll bring in an entire division to weed you out.'

Leonforte smirked. 'Really? Tell me, how many regular Army units would have to be rerouted? How many officers would get wind of a mass movement like that? And in a priority-one out-country hot zone like Laos? No way.' He was smiling now. 'Besides, I got a deal going with my brother. It's no sweat.'

Do Duc was thinking this through. He thought of how batshit Pentagon East had gone at Leonforte's MIA sheet, how they had brought out pattern activity surveillance on a massive scale to get a line on this one man. And how they had chosen Bowel's élite Werewolves to go in and bring him home. And then he thought of Bowel's directive to extract Leonforte by any means possible, and he knew something had gone wrong.

He took a breath, said, 'I want you to know something. My orders were to bring you back, one way or another.'

'Looking-Glass,' Leonforte said, nodding. 'They sent this other bastard after me, too. So what?'

'I don't think it *was* Looking-Glass,' Do Duc said. 'See, my CO was very specific. He told me I had to deliver you to *him*, not to the people at Pentagon East. I thought it odd at the –'

Leonforte stared at him for a moment. He blinked as if he could not believe his ears. At last, he said softly, 'Who gave you those orders?'

'My CO, Bud Powell.'

'My brother,' Leonforte said, as if invoking one of the 10,000 names of God. 'Powell works for my brother inside Looking-Glass. My fucking brother has turned against me.'

He turned away for a moment, his shoulders hunched as if against a chill wind only he could feel. When he turned round again, he seemed in some subtle way changed. His eyes glittered and burned as if reflecting firelight, and, seeing this, Do Duc listened with all his attention when Leonforte said to him, 'This changes everything, including your role in this deepening shadow-play.'

BOOK 2: ANCIENT ENEMIES

*The truth about a man
lies first and foremost
in what he hides.*

André Malraux

SIX

When Celeste awoke, the demon and the Kanfa bridge had vanished. She took a deep, shuddering breath, and blinked like someone awakening from a nightmare. She found herself sprawled on the cool stone floor of a vast windowless room that seemed to have been hewn out of the heart of the palazzo. There was no furniture in this space, but seven enormous brass candelabra ringed them, the ash of hemp, or perhaps the mushroom of which Nicholas had spoken, mingling with the muddy residue of yellowish tallow.

She saw Nicholas, his back to her, crouched and silent in the center of the room where the apex of the horrid bridge had been. He was naked to the waist, as if his battle had stripped him of his shirt and jacket. She could see the bunched muscles of his shoulders and upper back, the faint expansion and contraction of his ribs.

'Nicholas?'

He did not answer her.

Slowly, her breathing returned to normal. She became aware that the walls were hung with ancient Flemish tapestries, depicting hunting scenes. In one, the prey was a delicate, silvery unicorn; in another, it was a horned dragon, spitting bright, acidic flame.

For a long time she stared, dazed, at the powerful mounts of the hunters, their round eyes wild with fear and the scent of blood.

The tragedy of it is, Tanzan Nangi thought, that it ends here, in Tokyo, a place that was alien to her, a place she could not understand, let alone like, the place that finally came between her and Nicholas.

Nangi stood looking down at the closed coffin, which lay in the side chapel of St Theresa's, the single Roman Catholic church in Shinjuku, four blocks west of the wide Meiji-dori. This was Nangi's church, the place of worship he had introduced Justine to when she was at a low ebb in her life.

For a while, at least, it had seemed some form of solace for her, but

191

not lately. Lately, it appeared, she had taken up with her old friend and boss Rick Millar.

Justine's face, composed, relaxed now in death as it hadn't been for many years in life, acted like a mirror, reflecting facets of recent history which, until the moment he had watched the police and fire units disentangling what was left of Justine and Millar from the charred remains of the car, had eluded him. How was he to know that Rick Millar, asking to find Justine again, had wanted to take her back with him to America? How was he to know that, after spending the night with him, Justine would accept?

Nangi tried to look away from her face, but could not. Just as he tried to hate her for what she had done to his friend, and could not. Not simply because he was a devout Christian, or Shintoist, but because he so well understood the many layers of human relationships. Because he also had to ask himself what Nicholas had done to her to drive her into another man's promises of love and protection.

He stirred, hearing a taped choir begin its ritual of psalms, no less holy or beautiful for being prerecorded. Of course, he knew part of the answer: Tau-tau. He had sensed what Nicholas had perhaps not: that Justine was profoundly terrified of what Nicholas would become once the legacy of his mother had been revealed to him, once he took the first step down the path to becoming tanjian. Even Nangi had little knowledge of the mysteries to which Nicholas had been exposed up on the Hodaka, that sheer face of ice and snow in the Japanese Alps, where he had been taught by his mentor and his enemy, Kansatsu. Nangi only knew that, whatever transpired there, Nicholas had returned a changed man. He was ready now to burrow into himself, to find the secret of his people, no matter how dark, how terrifying. Nangi and Nicholas spoke of many things, were close friends, shared secrets and fears and triumphs without reservation – save the Tau-tau, whose workings were forbidden to outsiders.

Nangi could understand this, even admire the bonds of discipline that veiled Nicholas's inner heart from even those closest to him, but he was quite certain that Justine could not. Nicholas trusted her as he did no other, and so he had taken for granted that she would understand – just as he had been sure she would come to love Japan as he did. That he had been wrong on both counts was not so much a surprise as a tragedy.

And here, Nangi thought now, as his gaze caressed the form inside the coffin, is the ultimate result. This was her *karma*. I should have seen it. He felt tears burning his eyes, but he would not lift a hand to wipe them away. He wanted to feel their heat, their weight, their slightly acid sting as they slid down his cheeks, not only for himself but for Nicholas, who was not here and must never know the true nature of his wife's last thirty-six hours.

He leaned a bit more heavily on his walking stick, its carved dragon's head digging into the palm of his hand. *I did see it*, he thought now, *and I did nothing.* But what was there to do? Who would listen? Who ever believes their own fate? What happened was meant to happen.

The choir swelled to a passionate crescendo, the trained voices magnified by the stone chapel and the clever acoustics that brought to the sharp ears of the priests even the clandestine whispers of sinners.

Nangi became aware that he was no longer alone in the chapel with Justine. He turned, his leg paining him, and saw Seiko, Nicholas's assistant. She somehow made him think of Gelda, Justine's sister and only living relative. He had tried all morning to locate her in the States, to no avail. She had apparently dropped out of sight.

Seiko came silently toward him only when she was certain that he had recognized her.

'Pardon me for disturbing you, Nangi-san,' she said, bowing, 'but you wished to hear news of Linnear-san as soon as we received any.'

Nangi listened intently, aware that she averted her eyes from the coffin. Was it merely the Buddhist's abhorrence of burial rather than a clean cremation, or was there some other reason? Because he had been Justine's friend and sometimes confidant he knew of her suspicions that Nicholas and Seiko were having an affair. He did his best to calm her, assuring her of Nicholas's loyalty to her, but sensing the depths of Seiko's anxiety here, he could not help but wonder where the truth lay.

'Linnear-san is no longer in Venice,' Seiko said.

'What?'

'He checked out hurriedly late last night.'

'What forwarding address did he leave?'

'None, apparently,' Seiko said. She was worrying her lower lip with her small, white teeth. 'The hotel's concierge has no idea where he went.'

Nangi watched her for a long moment, and this scrutiny made her all the more nervous. Perhaps she would have preferred to continue this conversation out on the impersonal, sunlit street, but Nangi, only now becoming aware of how much he had missed immersed in the minutiae of business, would not allow it. Tension, he had invariably found, was a fecund medium for inadvertent revelation.

'How often did you leave messages for him?' he asked.

'Three times.'

'And he never answered?'

'No, sir.'

193

'So the last time you had any communication with Linnear-san was when he left the office the day of his departure for Venice?'

He caught the slight hesitation, turned it over in his mind as if it were a vintage wine ripe for tasting. 'No, sir. I met him at the airport just before flight time.'

'Was this at his request?'

'No, sir.' Seiko shifted from one foot to another. Her deep brown eyes moved, and in their movement was revealed the wall between herself and Justine. 'After Linnear-san left for the day, I received a coded fax from Vincent Tinh in Saigon. It seemed urgent enough to get it to him before he left for Venice.'

Nangi noticed that Seiko had begun to perspire, though he felt no particular heat inside the chapel. In fact, it was quite cool.

He held out his hand and she put into it a copy of the coded fax. He read it twice without comment, as he always did any document that entered his purview. On the surface there seemed nothing alarming. Obviously, Nicholas had agreed since he had not contacted Nangi about it.

'What do you make of this?' he asked abruptly.

This time Seiko was ready for him. 'In Linnear-san's absence I faxed Vincent Tinh to ask for clarification on this one point regarding the shadow government in Saigon,' she said. 'I got no reply.'

'As to that I'm not at all surprised,' Nangi said, though he was pleased with her initiative. This was just the kind of action Nicholas was training her for. 'Tinh surely wouldn't have had time to follow up on the rumors.'

'That is not what I mean,' Seiko said, licking her lips. 'I have received no return fax at all from Tinh-san.'

The voices, all sopranos now, were building to another crescendo and, mounting it, the confluence of heavenly sound, repeating ever more slowly, began to die away, until at last it was held in the air only by acoustics and echo.

Nangi took his time digesting the possible ramifications of this bit of unsettling news. 'I think,' he said, 'we had better return to the office immediately and see if we can locate Vincent Tinh.'

It was bright outside, the sky a lusterless white without shape of cloud or brilliance of sun. It was as if they were inside a glass sphere, entombed within a post-modern megalopolis that lay beyond the glass and reinforced steel skyrises all around them.

Still, they were obliged to squint even for the short walk across the sidewalk to Nangi's chauffeur-driven BMW limo. He stood there with her for a moment while the driver held the rear door open.

Justine had confided in him her fears about an affair between Nicholas and Seiko. Nangi had done his best to reassure her, but Justine had seemed oblivious to rational argument.

And why should she be? He knew from experience that love was not so ephemeral a thing as most people supposed. It was solid, even weighty, with its own imperatives which, like a layer of make-up, drew transformations from out of thin air. The areola of love was like the kiss of an angel, invisible in itself, yet discernible by the intimations of its eminence.

The tangled expression on Seiko's face was articulate even if the rest of her was not. All at once, he understood Justine's concerns, could view them as something more than fictional. Seiko's relationship with Nicholas was something more than assistant to boss. What it was he was powerless to say, but its mere existence was evidence enough that he should be attentive and reactive.

He turned to Seiko. 'If there is a problem in Saigon I'm going to need your expertise. I want you to be prepared.'

She gave him a curiously formal bow. 'I am honored, Nangi-san.'

Inside the car, as it drove off, he handed her a small filigreed sterling-silver pillbox. It was of English manufacture, a fine example of Western turn-of-the-century silversmithing. It had been a present from Nicholas, and it was important to him. But not as important as a human being.

Seiko held the pillbox in her open palm, her eyes filled with its beauty. She knew of its existence, even something of its history, and her hand trembled slightly to hold it.

'Seiko-san,' Nangi said, 'I want you to take care of this for me.' And when her eyes met his, questioning, he went on. 'For some time it has been empty. I no longer need the pills it used to hold, and I think you will agree it is not the same without something to fill it up.'

The car slowed in heavy traffic. A haze was building as the shortening afternoon blurred into an early winter twilight, blue and gray and umber. Somewhere a police siren sounded, cutting through even the efficient soundproofing of the BMW.

'It seems to me that you have something of significance with which to fill this box,' he said into the growing silence. 'Something precious, something as yet tentative that requires its own time, its own place. Something to put away, yet not to forget.'

He knew by the expression in her eyes that she understood all the implications: that he had divined her love for Nicholas, that he did not necessarily disapprove, that she must nevertheless ensure that it did not interfere with what she must do for Nicholas – and for him – at Sato International.

With a great deal of reverence, Seiko slowly opened the pillbox, stared down into it for long moments, before swinging closed the lid. She put the box carefully away.

'Words cannot adequately express my feelings, Nangi-san,' she said quietly.

And both of them were so caught up in the moment that they failed to notice the white Toyota that swung in behind them as they lurched through the intersection at the Meiji-dori, and which followed them all the way back to the Shinjuku Suiryu Building, Sato International's headquarters.

It was not going to be easy getting in to see Davis Munch, Gaunt decided, after his third hour of the Federal bureaucratic runaround. Even with all his ins – and knowing the right people to go to to cut through the red tape – he was having no luck.

Munch, the Pentagon special investigator seconded to Rance Bane's Strategic Economic Oversight Committee, was a busy man. Not only that, he had apparently decided that he did not want to see Gaunt. That was something of a deterrent, but in the end, Gaunt had already vowed, it wasn't going to stop him from seeing Munch. Nothing was.

He had taken some time after his thoroughly unpleasant meeting with Terry McNaughton to review his options as the lobbyist had outlined them. He had headed down to the C & O Canal towpath in Georgetown, always his favorite spot, to clear his head of the political doublespeak and figure out a plan of attack.

It was peaceful there, reminding him of the best times he had spent in this citadel of influence, the real reason he had wanted to make a life for himself in government, and how that reason had gotten submerged in the day-to-day power struggles endemic to Washington. This was shark city, where even people who purported to be your friends would turn on you at the first sign of political pressure.

He had walked along the Potomac, deep in thought. Despite McNaughton's dire warnings, he was not yet about to abandon ship. Leaving a friend – and he certainly considered Nicholas Linnear a friend – to the wolves was just not his style. For one thing, what would his father have said? For another, he owed Nicholas plenty for believing in him when he supposed even he had given up on himself. Nicholas had found him some time after a rather nasty political purge had flung him out of his cozy White House sinecure.

Stupidly, he had taken it personally. Against convention and sound advice as old as George Washington, he had tried to mount a counter-attack. In the process, he had made several high-powered enemies who had closed

196

the doors of State and Commerce to him, departments which would have otherwise remained open to take this particular political orphan in. Only a minor post in Defense, bean-counting third-world arms sales, was offered him, a job too mean and humiliating even to contemplate.

Those were the days in which, as far as he was concerned, Washington was the only town that mattered. Nicholas had proven him wrong. Now he wouldn't take a political post here for anything. Only in hindsight did he realize that he had been quit here even before Nicholas had convinced him to move to New York. How ironic that, in Nicholas's defense, he was obliged to return.

He stared into the slow-moving waters of the Potomac and knew he couldn't jump ship. He also knew that McNaughton's second option, going down with the ship, was out of the question. So where did that leave him?

Only one path to tread, and he was on it now: searching for Davis Munch.

He found him, eventually, hiding out in a Vietnamese restaurant in Falls Church, Virginia. After a contact at the Pentagon had told him that Munch had logged out to State for the afternoon, Gaunt had looked up an old acquaintance of his, Josie Rand, who worked for one of State's myriad deputy assistants. She was able to determine that Munch had a meeting with the Assistant Secretary of East Asian and Pacific Affairs, but as far as she could determine the two were not in the building.

It had taken Gaunt a good twenty minutes to work out his approach to the Assistant Secretary's office and make his preparations. State was like a tiny medieval fiefdom, the momentary Solons jealously guarding both their power and their perquisites. Outsiders were invariably treated with either derision or suspicion or both.

The Assistant Secretary's junior assistant was a young man, fair-haired and fresh-faced, who was just learning which ropes would swing him across the quicksand and which would bring him down into it. He was just the man for Gaunt, who approached him in that manner only someone who had been inside the corridors of power could summon up. He remembered to put that slightly Southern drawl he had all but lost during his time in New York back into his voice.

'Brock Peters, presidential attaché,' Gaunt said, thrusting out his hand to the junior assistant while giving him a steely eye. He had patted a battered briefcase he had borrowed from Josie Rand. 'Papers from the POTUS for the Assistant Secretary.' POTUS, an acronym for President of the United States, was used only by White House staff and those closest to the President.

197

The junior assistant had jumped up with such alacrity that Gaunt had had to stifle a grin.

'The . . . the Assistant Secretary is currently unavailable,' the young man stammered. 'If you'll log in I'll take possession of the material.'

That steely eye from Gaunt froze the junior assistant in his tracks. 'Son, these papers are Eyes Only. Scare up the Assistant Secretary for me pronto.'

The junior assistant swallowed hard. 'But the Assistant Secretary's not currently in the building. I've had no call from the White House alerting me –'

'To Eyes Only documents?' Gaunt sneered. 'Don't be ridiculous, son. The White House is not in the habit of broadcasting dissemination of Eyes Only material.'

The junior assistant was all but standing at military attention now. He was very frightened. 'Yes, sir. But I don't –'

'Son, you'd better get this through that thick skull of yours. When the POTUS sends out Eyes Only material he expects it to be read. Immediately. Do I make myself clear?'

Gaunt had. Within fifteen seconds he had been given the name and address of the Vietnamese restaurant at which the Assistant Secretary was being treated to lunch by Davis Munch.

The place, a vine-covered stone building that had once been some kind of mill, was situated in a picturesque setting amid linden and alder trees. A brook burbled merrily, hidden behind the trees, but the top of a wooden water-wheel was visible above a low wall of arborvitae. The path from the parking area to the restaurant itself was lined with oleander and clematis.

Inside, the restaurant was unnaturally dark with a low, beamed ceiling and a heavy stone floor. Buddhas and other Vietnamese artifacts peppered the walls.

The Vietnamese maître d' glided up and Gaunt asked for Munch, who he imagined had made the reservation. It was well after the prime lunch hour, when almost all the diners were on coffee or just bullshitting while the tables were cleared.

'I am so sorry. Mr Munch cannot be disturbed,' the maître d' said portentously in a heavy accent. He did not look as if he was in the least sorry.

'He'll see me,' Gaunt said, slipping the maître d' a fifty-dollar bill.

'Ah, of course,' the Vietnamese said, smiling. He nodded toward a table in the far left corner, then promptly disappeared into the kitchen.

Gaunt stopped at the bar, ordered a beer, stood drinking it for a time while he watched the two men at the table. The Assistant Secretary was easy to spot. He had that polished look so coveted at State, a tall man with close-cut graying hair, a hawk nose, and the blue eyes of the patrician. His companion – Davis Munch – was short and dark, with the body and mien of a prizefighter. His shoulders were hunched, his head stuck forward as he spoke. The intensity he emitted was apparent to Gaunt halfway across the room. Gaunt thought he would much rather have to take on the Assistant Secretary.

He waited, patient as the Buddha sitting cross-legged on a wall niche not far from where the two men talked. Once, the Assistant Secretary reached into his attaché case, pulled out a sheaf of onion-skin paper with the telltale blue filaments running vertically through it. Eyes Only documents. He pushed the sheaf across the table to the investigator, who scanned them quickly. Apparently, at the Assistant Secretary's instigation, Munch stopped at the fourth sheet, read it more carefully. In a moment, the Assistant Secretary began to answer a battery of questions.

At last the lunch was over. Munch put the sheaf of onion-skins away, called for the check. He paid in cash, asked for a receipt. The two men rose, shook hands. The Assistant Secretary went off to the men's room and Munch went out to find his car.

Gaunt followed him out the front door. Halfway down the path, he called to him. Munch stopped, turned to look at Gaunt as he came unhurriedly down the path.

Gaunt introduced himself. His name brought a smile to Munch's thin lips.

'What brings you to Washington a week before the Committee sits in judgement of you, Gaunt?'

Gaunt could see that Munch wasn't going to make it easy for him. But then why should he? He was in the business of rubbing people's noses in their own shit. He probably thought of it as a perk of the job.

'Talking to you would be one of the reasons,' he said.

Munch grunted, turned and began to hurry down the path. 'Bad timing, I'm afraid. I'm on my way back to a high-level meeting at the Pentagon. You should've gone through my office.'

'That would be fruitless. Your assistant said you were permanently in a meeting.'

'You would have done well to listen to him.' The parking lot was still and quiet. Not a breath of air was stirring, and a kind of heavy somnolence had invaded the late autumn, as if time had reversed itself and summer had returned. But there was no sound of insects or birds, and this lack gave the whole a peculiar surreal quality.

'But I didn't and I'm here now.'

'I'm wondering how you pulled off that particular trick, but no matter.' He took out the keys to his government-issue Ford. 'I have nothing to say to you, except that you pulled a losing hand this time.'

He inserted the key, opened the door. Leaning past him, Gaunt slammed the door shut.

'Get out of my face,' Munch said.

Gaunt put himself between the investigator and the Ford. 'Not until I get some answers from you.'

'Ready to take me on?' Munch said, taking a stance. 'I was Golden Gloves champ in the service.'

'If I have to I will,' Gaunt replied. 'But I'd rather buy you a beer.'

Munch came in low, leading with a left jab, and Gaunt blocked it, felt a numbing pain in his lower forearm. He countered with a quick uppercut that snapped Munch's head back, and he was cheered.

That was before Munch made a helluva feint to the right, lashed a counterpunch to his ribs. Gaunt felt the breath whoosh out of him, but he battled on, landing a soft, ineffectual punch on Munch's shoulder while missing entirely Munch's movement inside his guard. The next moment he found himself flat on his back, looking up at Munch. He had no memory of the blow that had landed him there, but there was a pain in his jaw.

Munch laughed, relaxing suddenly. He offered his strong, callused hand, pulled Gaunt slowly to his feet. 'Yeah, well, what the hell,' he said, 'I'm out here five minutes and I'm already thirsty.'

Inside, at the bar, he said, 'I'll tell you something, Gaunt, it's been a long time since I found someone willing to stand up to me. Believe it or not, these days the Government's full of pussies.'

Gaunt rubbed the side of his jaw, which was still somewhat numb. 'Not like when I was in harness here.'

'White House staff, right?'

Gaunt nodded, winced at the resultant pain, as they poured their beers. 'I liked it well enough until I got caught in the gears and couldn't see it for what it was.'

'I know what you mean,' Munch said. 'My sister was in the Navy. Got caught up with a bunch of drunk Tailhooks, got slapped around, groped, God knows what else by a gauntlet of the Navy's finest.' He gave a harsh laugh. 'She got caught in the gears, too. A real career-killer. Nobody likes a whistle-blower.'

They downed long draughts, were silent for some time. The sounds of the waiters and busboys going about their duties hardly intruded.

Gaunt felt a sudden pain in the side of his jaw where he supposed Munch's knockout punch had landed and, feeling around in there, discovered he was bleeding. He excused himself, went to the men's room to wash out his mouth and take a look in the mirror. It looked like the gum, not a tooth.

'You okay?' Munch asked on his return.

'Just a little bleeding,' Gaunt said, gingerly touching his cheek. 'Nothing to worry about.'

'If you say so.' Munch ordered them another round of beers. 'I know why you came to see me. I wasn't going to tell you dick, but we have something in common, you and I, and because of that I'm going to tell you to turn tail and get the hell out of your company now, while you can get clear.' He held up a hand. 'No, don't interrupt me, I won't answer questions.' He finished off his beer, sat staring straight ahead at a photo of Saigon as it had been in the 1950s.

'Here's what I can tell you. We'd heard persistent rumors that a version of the Hive computer that your company and Hyrotech-inc were working on had begun to appear on the black market in Taiwan, Bangkok, Singapore. We were able to get our hands on one, and I traced the item back to Saigon, where it was manufactured. There, I lost the trail. I don't have the contacts I need there – no one in this fucked-up Government does. One of our problems.'

He saw Gaunt still worrying the side of the jaw where he had hit him, handed over a handkerchief. 'Press it against the bleeding,' he said. Then, 'Anyway, we've vetted everyone at Hyrotech-inc – it's a small concern, so no trouble there. It was a waste of time and I knew it. Hyrotech-inc doesn't have the capacity or capital to manufacture these computers here, and especially in Southeast Asia where it has no presence at all. That left Sato-Tomkin, which opened facilities in Saigon.'

'Opened a year ago,' Gaunt said. 'Hardly enough time to ramp up any computer to market – let alone something as technologically advanced as a Hive clone.'

The investigator ignored him. 'This meeting I just had with the Assistant Secretary for East Asian and Pacific Affairs at State was the clincher. He provided me with copies of coded faxes from the Sato-Tomkin HQ in Saigon to the home office in Tokyo. State spent six days breaking the code. All the faxes concern the Hive clones, which Sato-Tomkin has dubbed the Chi Project.'

Now he turned to look at Gaunt, said, 'I don't need you to confirm what I already know: that the Chi Project is under the sole control of Nicholas Linnear.'

SEVEN

Venice/Tokyo

The head sat upon an eighteenth-century Palladian armoire, its dark, intelligent eyes staring straight at the man who stood, slightly stooped over, hands in his pockets, studying the object.

'Dominic Goldoni,' Leon Waxman said, allowing a bit of awe to creep into his voice, 'Madonna, I've dreamed of seeing you like this: so quiet, drained of fluids, embalmed like a trophy – by God, you *are* a trophy! Dominic, if only you could see the *Gim*, the sacred crescent in the center of your forehead!' His laughter shivered off the walls of the hotel room.

'You taught me all about the *Gim*, Do Duc, when you defected, came in from the jungles of Laos where Michael and Rock were reaping what should have been mine! When I became head of Looking-Glass I thought I could finally regain control of those deserters.' Waxman was silent for a moment, but his body shook dangerously with emotion. 'But Michael and Rock are still out there, running things in their floating city. Even you can't find them.' He bit his lower lip.

'I had a hell of a time getting it here,' Do Duc Fujiru said, indicating the head. He wanted to get off the subject of his failures. 'It was ironic, really. I set the thing in a bed of nails – one of many such crates in a shipment of construction materials.'

Waxman turned and a slow, strange smile crept over his face. 'Primo Zanni. Dominic would have appreciated the name I gave you – the clever, chameleonesque Venetian servant. Yet another reflection of Looking-Glass.'

It was a curious thing, Waxman's face, like an artifact one discovers quite by accident in a long-lost temple. The wide, round eyes were so deep set they seemed ringed with purple flesh. Above a shallow, sloping forehead, a widow's peak, dark as night, thrust as aggressively as the jaw at the opposite end of the face.

'I see Florida was good for you – all that sun and surf and American girls. After what you've been through, you deserved the R and R.'

202

'I'd rather have been in Laos.'

'Yes. You did leave rather a mess behind in Hollywood.'

Despite its obvious age, there was nothing brittle about Waxman's face, nothing dried up or slack. But for all the strength there, it was a grotesque face, lop-sided with severed nerves in one cheek and under one eye.

'The woman I married was cover. I did what was necessary.'

Waxman seemed to accept the explanation. 'You had no trouble getting to Goldoni?'

'As it happens, it was simple.'

'When it came to Dominic Goldoni nothing was ever simple.' Waxman's eyes opened wide for a moment. 'You'd do well to remember that.'

'Why? He's dead and it's over.' Do Duc lounged against an overwrought Louis XV credenza which fairly dripped gilt. The extreme luxury of this hotel suite made him uneasy.

'Dead, yes,' Waxman said. 'But it's not over yet, not until I have access to the power he possessed.' He reached out a hand and, as he did so, his naked wrist slid out from the cuff of his shirt. On its inner side was a tattoo of a human face, the left side skin-colored with its eye open, the right side blue with a vertical crescent where the eye should be.

'Those fucking Goldonis just don't want to give it up.' Waxman withdrew his hand. 'But he's the last male. Who's left? Two sisters and his daughters. Nothing.' He was moving now, walking to one side of the armoire, peering again at the head from that direction. 'I like it better when he's looking right at me,' he said, moving back.

Do Duc said nothing. He understood. The goddamned head still had an aura, faint and growing fainter all the time, but even so . . . The thing was dead.

'Dominic was a murderer – and a betrayer. He deserved this fate.' He shrugged and his teeth clacked together, a sound that unnerved most people. 'But what does that matter now? I've done what had to be done, what others said was impossible. But I knew him better than most, yes, how volatile he could be, how – above all – he loved his sister Margarite, and his goddaughter – better than his own children perhaps. Strange. But, then, that was Dominic.'

His teeth clacked together in a kind of atonal rhythm. 'I would have given five years of my life to see his face when our informer delivered the message that Tony D. was not only beating Margarite but Francine as well.' Waxman grunted. 'Lucky for us he didn't have a stroke on the spot. But he wanted to see his beloved sister and goddaughter and the WITSEC rules be damned. I knew he would . . . I felt it here' – he pounded his chest – 'where he felt it. I *knew*.' He turned again to look at the head. 'That's how I got you, bastard. Love became your end.'

Do Duc said nothing, merely regarded Waxman with lambent, half-closed eyes.

'You got the information from him?' Waxman said, with that abrupt change of subject even his closest associates found disconcerting.

'Eventually, I got the real name of his source,' Do Duc said, and when Waxman gave him a glance, he added, 'I bled him like a grape. He gave me all he had.'

'Then I'm in.' Waxman laughed as he resumed his contemplation of the head. 'Think of it! Goldoni's secret, the source of all his hidden power,' he whispered, the awe returning to his voice.

'I'll say this for him,' Do Duc said, 'he led us a merry chase.'

'Bastard!' It was shot out of Waxman like a mouthful of bile. 'Fucking Goldonis – too much was never enough for them. That sonuvabitch Dominic – what kinds of fucking dreams did that rat bastard have, that he decided to turn on us? What he leaked to the Feds when he was in WITSEC! The new *capi* Dom betrayed – nothing, compared to what he did behind my back, the sonuvabitch. He betrayed me, made a deal with Mikio Okami, and the two of them set out to cut Looking-Glass off at the knees.'

Waxman abruptly turned away from the head, impaled Do Duc with his gaze. 'But that Dominic, I gotta admit he was some kind of genius. He fooled all of us. First, he makes us believe he's a part of Looking-Glass, then, when we negotiate to expand Looking-Glass worldwide, he becomes a part of the Godaishu.'

He whirled on the head, his face red with fury. He struck the head a heavy blow, sending it careening into the corner of the room, where it lay grotesquely on its crown. 'What the fuck happened to you, Dominic? What were you and your partner, Okami, planning? Why did you betray us?'

Memory and emotion combined to make him tremble as if he were ill. Then he turned away, while Do Duc retrieved the head, set it back on top of the armoire. Upside down, with its aura, it disturbed him.

All at once Waxman's expression softened. 'I can see from the *Gim*,' he said, staring into Dominic Goldoni's dark, intelligent eyes, 'that you did your thing with him.'

'Yes.'

He chuckled. 'Must be scaring the shit out of Lillehammer right about now.'

'I wouldn't doubt it,' Do Duc said.

'Watch out for him. He'll want to skin you alive.'

204

'I'm counting on it,' Do Duc said.

'I know. That's why I chose him to head the investigation. The two of you need to meet again.' Waxman grunted. 'And you had fun,' he said. 'I suppose it hasn't changed any.'

'No.'

'Rituals never do, that's part of their strength – and a measure of their comfort.'

'You're wrong,' Do Duc said. 'I don't need comfort.'

Waxman pursed his lips. 'We all need comfort, now and again. Only the dead can forgo it.'

He was right, of course. There had been the girl. Do Duc would never say a word about her existence or what he had done to her, that wouldn't be smart. She had been a risk – a risk for more power. But Do Duc lived with risk, thrived on it as others did peace and quiet. Because he didn't have to concentrate with her in the same way he had had to do with Dominic Goldoni, the ritual he took part in with her was different; he hadn't needed to dissect her mind and extract information. She became Kshira: the Path. With Goldoni he had had to placate the gods, damp down the psychic engines to avoid a backlash. But with her, just the opposite: he had feasted on her soul and it had increased his power.

'Blood's going to spill, and plenty of it,' Do Duc said, 'before I get all the way to the man who provided Goldoni with his secrets.'

'Hey, I don't give a rat's ass what you do as long as you do it quickly.' Waxman gave him a warning look. 'Remember that even the dead aren't powerless.'

'You know all about power,' Do Duc said.

Waxman nodded. Then, carefully, as if handling an extremely deadly serpent, he gripped Do Duc's left arm.

'We both do.'

Waxman clasped Do Duc's arm tighter, one Roman centurion to another, turned it slightly, opened his fingers to reveal the wrist beneath. And there it was:

The face split down the middle, its right eye open and staring just like Dominic Goldoni's, the dark left side scarred with the *Gim*, the sacred crescent.

Their eyes held for a long time.

'Now, tell me, who was Dominic's source?' Waxman said at last. 'Who was feeding him the information he was using to control his contacts in government and business?'

'Linnear,' Do Duc said. 'Nicholas Linnear.'

*

'What he was doing was trying to draw me out,' Nicholas said.

Celeste, her long red hair whipping against her cheek, stood very close to him. 'I don't understand.'

'I think you do.' Nicholas put his arm around her. It was cold here on the outer deck of the *vaporetto*, the wind clawing its way along the snaking Grand Canal. The shirt and jacket they had bought for him were inadequate to the temperature, but he did not want to go inside because the color of the water was a curious, enigmatic green, the same hue, precisely, as the finest Murano blown glass.

But was the chill the only reason he wanted some of her warmth? He did not want to think about that, just as he did not want to call his office or speak to Justine. What would be the point? Immersed as he was in the enigma of Okami and the Messulethe, he would be of no use to either Nangi or Justine. Best to wait. Nangi would get all the help he needed from Seiko if Tinh had run into a bit of trouble. And as for Justine, he suspected the longer he waited until their emotions cooled down the better.

Sunlight, punished by zinc-colored clouds and a bitter, harbinger wind, fell upon the water, turning it into an ancient copper mirror. Celeste said nothing. She was staring out at the *palazzi* as they drifted past. A police launch raced by and, in its rough wake, a postal boat chugged, making its rounds. Rain began to pucker the water, making of its rich reflections pointillist impressions.

Looking at her face he had no idea of her reaction to his touch or his proximity. It was as if she had lost a piece of herself during the encounter with the Tau-tau adept and was now only partially there.

'Celeste, you're so quiet. What are you thinking?'

'I'm surprised you have to ask.' For an instant, her eyes blazed. 'God in Heaven, we were almost killed back there!'

'You may be right.'

She shuddered heavily, but her face was full of scorn, a fitting mask perhaps for her own terror. 'Well, look at you, as calm as if we'd just come back from a stroll along the Lido beach! What's the matter with you? Is this a common occurrence in your world? Because if it is, I want nothing to do with it.'

'You must have known there'd be danger in associating yourself with Okami-san.'

'Oh, yes. Bullets and sword blades,' Celeste said. 'Those kinds of danger I can deal with. But this –' She shook her head. 'This is something out of my ken.' She turned to face him as the *vaporetto* began to nose into a station. 'Frankly, it scares the hell out of me. Some bastard with God alone knows what kind of powers almost kills us with . . . with what? Magic?'

She shuddered heavily, turned away from him, and thrust herself into the temporary security of the crowd disembarking from the boat.

Nicholas hurried after her. Ahead of them was the Accademia with its footman, the splendid wooden bridge. But now it reminded him of the Kanfa of the Messulethe.

They were near Okami's palazzo, and he saw this was where she was headed.

'Yes,' he said, catching up to her. 'Tau-tau is a kind of magic. But it's as explainable as physics.'

'Not to me it isn't.'

'Celeste, listen to me, I let us walk into that trap.'

That got to her. She stopped, whipping round to glare at him. 'You did *what?*'

The rain was in her face, strands of deep-red hair plastered to one cheek. She looked very beautiful, and at that moment terribly vulnerable.

'I felt him in there – in that palazzo. In so confined a space he couldn't hide what he was from me. He was already summoning his power – that strange rhythmic pulse we heard in there – remember?'

Celeste put her arms around herself as if to ward off a chill. 'I couldn't forget even if I tried.'

He pulled her into a doorway, out of the rain. The eternal morning lineup for the Accademia was gone; budget cutbacks dictated that the museum close just after lunchtime. Now just a few students in backpacks and Nikes sat on the front steps, waiting for the rain to let up. 'You've got to understand. I had to find out what we're up against. I had to test him just as he tried to test me. He tried to draw me out, to get a measure of my powers. I wouldn't let him.'

'Good for you.'

She began to turn away, but Nicholas grabbed her elbow.

'You don't understand.'

'The hell I don't!' she flared. 'You let us walk into that trap. You had no idea how strong this man was. He could have beaten you; he could have killed us both. Christ, what kind of person are you to take such extreme risks!'

'Whatever risks I took were worth what I learned,' Nicholas said.

'No risk is worth –'

'Please listen to me,' he said carefully. 'Whoever is coming after Mikio Okami isn't your normal Yakuza hit-man.' He projected his inner mind outward, forcing her to concentrate on what he was telling her. 'You're right about one thing. This man who trapped us is very dangerous. He possesses the knowledge of the Messulethe, the most ancient race of

207

magicians. Their particular form of sorcery emanated from the mind. They were psycho-necromancers. Do you understand what I'm saying?'

There was a light in her eyes, akin to the one seen in that moment just before a fulgent sun crosses the eastern horizon.

'According to legend the Messulethe were able to access the elemental energy of the cosmos, the god-stuff from which the universe was created.'

Celeste seemed to be trembling. 'Are you mad? You're talking of gods.'

Nicholas nodded. 'As close to gods as we can imagine.' He gripped her hard. 'And one of these people has been sent here. What for? If Okami-san is right, it's to kill him.'

'Oh, my God!'

They ran all the way to Okami's palazzo. Celeste used her key to unlock the front gate and they raced through the portico. The canal was very close, the water as black as ice at night. The cold rain felt as hard as buckshot, and the wind took the branches of the pear tree, whipping them back and forth. The petals of the bougainvillea and the roses were strewn across the courtyard like droplets of blood.

Celeste's fingers shook as she unlocked the front door.

'Okami-san!' she called as they went inside. The palazzo was dark.

'Christ,' she said, 'we're too late!'

They headed up the stairs to the second floor with its long, leaded windows overlooking the Grand Canal. It was chilly in the living-room; the windows were open, and one of the panels was banging against the frame.

Celeste ran to the raised section at the far end and, kneeling on the cushions, stuck her head out the window, peered down.

He would have said, Do you see him?, but there was no need.

With a convulsive gesture, she withdrew from the window, closed the panel. Then she turned to face him. 'He's not there,' she said. 'But you knew that already, didn't you?' She said it in an accusatory tone.

Nicholas nodded. 'I would have felt the Messulethe if he had been here. If he had murdered Okami-san, the atmosphere would have remained in a state of excitation for some time after he had left.'

'You say that so matter-of-factly.'

'Celeste, it *is* fact.'

She looked at him for some time, and he could feel her bitterness toward him, but not fully understand it. She got up, went down the three steps to the main area.

'I'll take this floor, you search downstairs.'

'There's no need.' Nicholas watched her as she turned back to face him. 'He's not here, Celeste.'

Color crept into her face, and her hands clenched into white fists at her side. 'Is he alive or dead? What does your magic tell you?'

So that was it; it was not only the Tau-tau that terrified her. It was him. 'You don't understand,' he said. 'I don't know.'

'Well, you sure as hell better find out what's happened to him.' She was shaking, the veins standing out in her long neck.

He came down off the raised area to stand beside her. 'We'll find out, together.'

She looked up at him with an enigmatic expression. 'So much power,' she said. 'How can I ever trust you?'

They went into Okami's bedroom first, but there was nothing there to guide them. The bed was made, his clothes hung in the closet; in his dresser they lay folded, the corners neatly aligned. His personal items were in their appointed places in the adjoining bathroom.

'Well, at least he hasn't run off,' Celeste said, pointing to his luggage stacked on the top shelf of a deep closet.

'But he might have been abducted,' Nicholas said as he searched the darkest reaches of the closet. 'Didn't Okami-san have bodyguards?'

'And draw more attention to himself?' Celeste shook her head. 'Besides, despite his age, he was still very good at defending himself.' They went back out into the hallway. 'God knows he's had enough practice; he's been doing it almost all his life.'

Nicholas glanced over at her. 'And then he had you.'

'Yes, he had me,' she admitted, as she pushed open the door to his study. 'He had to practically break my arm to get me to stay with you.'

'That's comforting.'

'I didn't want to leave him.'

'Now I see why.'

He pushed past her into the maelstrom of Mikio Okami's study. The room was a whirlwind of papers, pages ripped from books. The heavy burlwood desk was overturned, its drawers out and splintered, its back peeled away from the frame like skin from stewed meat. Framed etchings had been pulled from their places on the walls, the backing torn away. There were holes in the plaster walls where they had once hung.

'Good God,' Celeste breathed.

Nicholas, down on one knee behind the desk, said, 'What the hell were they looking for?'

'I don't know.' She knelt beside him, pushing a raft of papers away from her. 'As far as I know, whatever Okami-san was working on he kept entirely in his head. He was too experienced and too clever ever to commit anything of substance to paper.' She looked at Nicholas. 'Do you think he was taken?'

Nicholas was busy moving the desk over an inch. 'What's this?'

Wedged beneath one of the desk's legs was a square of thick paper folded over twice into a small package. It was a black-and-white photo. It was grainy and full of grays, and its subject was Celeste in her Domino costume. The background clearly showed an area of the interior of the Church of San Belisario, just outside the *schola cantorum* where Nicholas had been taken to wait for her.

The thing was already open, being picked over by the tekkies, like a cadaver being examined by pathologists. The analogy was apt, Nangi thought as he was brought the sterile coat and shoes that were a requirement for all people on the fiftieth floor.

The Chi Project.

Masamoto Goei himself was waiting for Nangi. He was all but wringing his hands in his despair.

'Where was it found?' Nangi asked as he made his way to the zinc-topped table where the thing was laid open, all its guts exposed – fiber optics, silicone chips, copper shielding, minute diamond relays.

'On the Asian black market,' Goei said, hurrying to keep pace with Nangi as he strode across the room with the help of his cane. Masamoto Goei was one of the Chi team directors, a theoretical language technician, one of the whizz-bang tekkies who had thought up this computer without software.

'Is it the Chi?'

They had come up to the table, stood staring down at the orderly tangle of the open computer.

'Well, yes – and no,' Goei said. He pointed. 'There, to the left, you can see three neural-net boards which are our proprietary technology, but the rest of the thing – I don't know what it is. The only thing I can say for certain is it's not ours.'

'But part of it is,' Nangi said. 'How did it get from here to – wherever this thing was put together? And who is responsible?'

He was met with only silence. Even the tekkies who had been busy autopsying the thing had stopped, were staring at the two men.

Nangi motioned for Goei to follow him out of the lab. Outside, he stripped off the cleansuit, said to Goei, 'What else is there?'

'The clone – although that's not strictly speaking the right term – was assembled somewhere in Southeast Asia. My men spotted that right away. My best guess would be Hong Kong. Tiny businesses are up and running, out of business the same month, no one pays attention. Virtually anyone could rent the space and hardware without attracting much notice.'

Shit, Nangi thought. Nicholas has dropped out of sight and his pet project has blown up in our faces. He wanted to get back to his office. Now he had even more of a need to speak to Vincent Tinh. In Saigon, Tinh would be closest to the action. He should have spotted this bastard machine on the black market. Why hadn't he?

'Keep me informed of your progress,' he said tersely to Goei. 'And make that thing a priority.'

He took the chairman's elevator back up to the executive floor.

'Has Vincent Tinh gotten back to us?' Nangi asked as he strode past Umi's desk.

'No, sir,' she said, pulling together several files from her desk and following Nangi and Seiko into his office.

'Any news of Linnear-san?' he asked.

'Nothing.' She waited until he put his walking stick across his desk before she said, 'But I have some related news.'

'Oh?' Nangi lifted a hand. 'Before you go on, Umi, write an electronic memo to all senior directors. As of today Seiko Ito has been promoted to Director of Corporate Liaison. In that capacity she will be an extension of my authority throughout the organization.'

Umi's head lifted momentarily to look at Seiko, then she continued with her shorthand.

'Make sure that gets distributed immediately.' When Umi nodded, he continued.

'Now, what I want you to do –'

The phone rang and Umi got it.

'I'm in a meeting,' he said.

She spoke into the receiver for several seconds. Nangi, who was talking to Seiko, paused. Umi's face had gone ashen.

With a shaking hand she pressed the hold button, and said, 'I think you had better take this call, Nangi-san.'

Curious, Nangi took the receiver from her.

'*Moshi-moshi*,' he said, curtly.

'Tanzan Nangi?'

'Speaking.'

'Chief Inspector Hang Van Kiet here. Mr Nangi, I am with the Saigon Police. I have the unhappy chore of informing you that your employee, one Vincent Tinh, has met with an unfortunate accident.'

Nangi was aware of just how tightly he was gripping the receiver. There was a cold spot forming in his belly. 'How seriously is he hurt?'

'I am sorry to report that he is dead, Mr Nangi.'

Nangi listened to the ululating tones of interference on the line sounding far away, isolated from reality. Tinh was dead. He found that he had to remind himself of what those words meant. He said a silent prayer, then he gave free rein to his analytical mind.

'May I ask what kind of accident Tinh was in, Chief Inspector?'

'It was an odd one. It seems Mr Tinh was inspecting a warehouse out in the northern district and he –'

'We have no warehouses in the northern district,' Nangi said.

'Indeed,' Van Kiet said, and by the inflection of that one word Nangi was made aware that he already knew. 'Your Mr Tinh was trespassing.'

'Who owns the warehouse?'

'There seems to be some confusion about that. We're running an inquiry now.'

Nangi put his fingertips to his forehead over the spot where a headache was forming. He knew these people, how parochial and clannish they could be in times of crisis. They closed ranks against outsiders. From Van Kiet's reply he doubted whether he would ever get an answer to that question.

'Go on,' he said.

'From what we can reconstruct from on-site analysis Mr Tinh was up on a plank catwalk. His foot plunged through a rotten spot and he lost his balance.'

There was a silence that contained the strange electronic singing of inadequate long-distance cables.

'Yes, and . . . ?'

'He fell,' Van Kiet said, 'into a barrel of sulfuric acid.'

'Did you say sulfuric acid?'

'I did, sir.'

'And this barrel of acid just happened to be in the spot where he fell?'

'There were many barrels in this warehouse, Mr Nangi.'

'What were their contents?'

Van Kiet hesitated a moment, and Nangi thought he heard the rustle of papers being shuffled.

'Salt, gasoline, bicarbonate of soda, potassium permanganate.' Anger, frustration and resignation could all be heard in the Chief Inspector's voice.

Nangi felt his headache growing with each pulse of his heart. 'In other words this warehouse was a drug factory,' he said.

'That conclusion seems inevitable,' Van Kiet said. 'Have you any knowledge of Mr Tinh –'

'My employees do not deal drugs,' Nangi said stiffly.

212

'That must be a comforting thought for you so far away in Tokyo,' Van Kiet said dryly.

The last thing Nangi wanted was to get into a verbal boxing match with this police official. For the moment, he was Nangi's only connection with Saigon and the growing mystery of Vincent Tinh.

'How have you concluded it was an accident?' he asked.

'Pardon?'

'In this situation how could you have possibly ruled out murder?'

'Frankly, Mr Nangi, I haven't. Nevertheless, the death will be considered an accident. There were no witnesses and there are no overt signs that anyone else was in the warehouse at the time that Mr Tinh was there. And, of course, because of the circumstances of the death, the body itself can offer us no clues.' He sighed. 'I regret to inform you that I am grievously understaffed and underfunded. By any standards the crime rate here is shocking, and it just keeps escalating. I am afraid from where I sit, Mr Nangi, it is clear that capitalism breeds contempt for the law.'

'Are you telling me there's nothing you can do?'

'I must ring off now, Mr Nangi. I regret the loss of your employee.'

'If you could spare a moment more, Chief Inspector, I'll put my secretary on so that arrangements can be made for the body.'

'But, my dear sir, the arrangements have already been taken care of by Mr Tinh's family.'

'Mr Tinh *has* no family,' Nangi said. 'Who had the body picked up?'

'Let me see. A man claiming to be Mr Tinh's brother. He gave as reference a company called Avalon Ltd in London.' Van Kiet grunted, as he gave Nangi the man's name. 'Now I really have overstayed this call. Good day, Mr Nangi.'

Nangi stared at the receiver, now as dead as Vincent Tinh.

'It looks like this was taken the night we met,' Nicholas said of the photo of Celeste in her Domino. 'Did you know this was being taken?'

'No. I would have bet my life we were alone. I made certain you weren't being followed.' Her voice was shaky.

'It's a surveillance shot.' Nicholas pointed. 'Look at the heavy grain and the grays – that's from using a long lens and high-speed film.'

'But what's it doing here?' Celeste asked. 'Was Okami-san aware of it?'

'It's possible – perhaps even probable,' Nicholas said. He stood up, completed a thorough search of the study, then came back to where the photo lay. He studied it again.

'There's something odd here. The entire room is a mess. There isn't

213

one item in here that hasn't been either ripped apart or shredded. Except this photo.' He glanced at her. 'I can't believe that it was overlooked.' His fingers ran down the creases. 'And see how carefully it was folded, almost like an *origami* sculpture.'

'Then the only explanation is that it was left here deliberately.'

'Exactly.' He folded and unfolded the photo. 'What if it was left behind – by Okami-san? If he was abducted he'd be clever enough to manage to leave us a clue as to where he was being taken.'

'If he knew.'

'Celeste, he knew he was a marked man. I'm beginning to think he knew who was being sent after him. I have to believe he knew where he'd be taken.'

She stared down at the photo. 'But what is this telling us? All I see is me.'

'Have you gone on a trip recently for Okami-san?'

'He has some business on Burano. Every once in a while he'd ask me to go there for him.'

'Okay,' Nicholas said. 'Burano's a possibility.'

'Not a good one, I'm afraid,' Celeste said. 'Okami-san has too many friends there. And it's not a large island. All the fishermen know one another. I don't believe anyone could hide him there.'

'What else do you see in the photo?'

'Well, I'm standing in the church of San Belisario.'

'Right. I think it's worth a look.'

It took them twenty minutes to reach the Campiello di San Belisario. Their route took them through the Jewish Quarter, which Nicholas had heard described as the poorest part of the city. He found it to be rather the most austere, but this was only natural. Compared to the Gothic and the Byzantine *palazzi* and churches elsewhere in Venice, the buildings and synagogues here were plain structures which could easily be construed as mean and shabby by those who had little understanding of how the Jews had been forced by history to internalize all their joys. The Jews' most sacred scripture, the Torah itself, warned against public manifestations of wealth.

Here, stripped of the encrustations of the Gothic and the Byzantine, one could feel the pulse of the people. The weight of centuries hung, unadorned, like curtains of the finest linen on which were painstakingly embroidered depictions of their endless wanderings.

The small square of San Belisario was empty save for an old, emaciated man on the opposite side from the church. He glanced at them briefly, smiled wearily before disappearing behind a wooden door.

'All I can say for sure is that we weren't followed,' Nicholas said. 'As for whether Okami-san is inside the church –' He shrugged.

'This way,' Celeste said, leading him back down an alley toward a *rio* and its bridge. He recalled emerging from the hidden entrance to the church from beneath this bridge. This was the route they now took, letting themselves into the church through the oldest of its doors.

The weight of the ages pressed in upon them as they moved through the gloom. The air was heavy with myrrh, frankincense and mold. It was damp and chill this near the water, and parts of the stone floor were greenish near the edges.

Celeste led them unerringly down a short, dark corridor dense with wooden beams, then up a flight of stone stairs. They emerged onto the main level beneath the ogival arcade, quite near the *schola cantorum*. She led him around until they reached a certain spot. She took out the photo, looked at it briefly, then held it up for him to see. 'This is the spot where I was standing when this was taken,' she whispered.

Nicholas nodded.

'What do you feel? Any sign of Okami-san ... or the man who was following us before?' she asked.

He stood very still for a long time, attuning himself to the minute vibrations of the church. As if a set of slides had been slipped into a projector, he could feel the age of the place, the succession of peoples who had built it, then rebuilt it from the ruins of previous incarnations: the Cycladians, the Phoenicians, Greeks, Romans, the myriad peoples of Asia Minor who in time came to call themselves Venetians.

This had been a holy place for all of them; he could sense the lines of power running toward this spot like spokes radiating from the hub of a wheel. They were ancient, now all but forgotten by the priests who went about God's business in the modern world. And yet this was no less a holy place now than it had been in centuries past. The power abided, scented of ripe fruit and heated embers, like the breath of a slumbering Leviathan.

He was drawn here. This was Nicholas's thought, riding unbidden on the tide of the elemental vibrations. *He, too, has felt the force, and wants to be part of it.*

'Blood,' Nicholas said suddenly. 'I see blood.'

Celeste drew a sharp breath. 'Where?'

'This way.'

Nicholas took them into the *schola cantorum* and through it. On the other side was a set of small rooms – no larger than cells – hewn out of the cyclopean stone blocks. The flickering light from reed torches grew dimmer as they went from room to room. The first one held a cot with a

215

straw mattress over which were drawn undyed muslin sheets and a thin wool blanket. A cell, indeed. The second room was obviously used as a kind of storeroom. Piles of hymnals and musical scores for the choir lay atop crates that contained candles, holy wafers and bottles of sacramental wine.

The third cell appeared to be empty save for thick shadows pouring down its walls and across the small square of floor. The ubiquitous smell of mildew was absent, replaced by the astringent odor of a strong disinfectant.

'There's nothing here,' Celeste said.

Nicholas closed his eyes. 'Nevertheless, the smell of blood is stronger.'

'Was that why the disinfectant was used?'

He nodded. 'Perhaps.' He walked away from the center of the cell where they had been standing. As he did so he seemed to vanish into the deep shadows at the back of the cell.

'Nicholas?'

The silence seemed to stir the silken hairs at the back of her neck.

'Celeste, come here.'

His voice was watery, echoey, as if it came from a great distance. She followed the sound, saw him then at the rear wall. For an instant, his image flickered, as if it were only a reflection. Then she was beside him, and it was as if she had stepped through a translucent opening in the iris of an enormous eye. She turned to glance behind her, and was certain the far side of the cell appeared yards away.

Nicholas's arms were up, the palms of his hands flat against the stone. 'Something here.'

She heard him grunt, then she gave a little start as the wall began to move. Or, more accurately, a part of the wall. A moment later, the two of them stepped through the hidden doorway.

They found themselves in a minuscule garden. Flowering clematis clawed its way up the stone walls which rose on all sides, brocaded with purple-blue flowers, dark-brown vines and small green leaves. Birds twittered in a ginkgo tree, white-barked as a skeleton, whose upper third could be seen above the far wall.

The ground was damp, exacerbating the stale smell of autumn, but the rain had ceased. Ashen sunlight fell as if exhausted, broken apart, so that it seemed as if they were in a deep forest glade far away from all civilization.

An ancient wrought-iron bench stood in the center of the garden, facing away from them. The ground was green and spongy so that Celeste knew they were walking on moss, not grass. Close at hand, a bird sang, and then was still. It was so silent here they could make out the faint lapping of a *rio* somewhere beyond the high walls.

'Look!'

Nicholas pointed as they came abreast of the bench. Lying on its seat was a Venetian mask, broken in half. It was covered in blood that had already dried.

Celeste gave a little cry, said in a whisper, 'That's the Domino, the mask Okami-san gave me to wear when I met you.'

'How can you tell it's the same one?' Nicholas asked. 'There must be over 10,000 Dominos in Venice.'

'Mine was not mass-produced. It was signed by the maker,' she said. 'Look there in the corner on the underside.'

Nicholas peered at the part of the mask she pointed out.

'Nicholas, what is this doing here, covered in blood? Whose blood is it? Okami-san's?'

'I wish I knew.'

He crouched down, took out the photo of her they had found in Okami's study. Celeste crouched down beside him.

'Here, you're wearing this Domino costume, and now we come upon the same mask,' he said. 'Perhaps it's the Domino which holds the answer as to where Okami-san has been taken.' He thought a moment. 'What did you tell me about it that night?'

'Let's see, I said that the name came from the Latin *benedicamus Domino*, meaning Bless the Lord. I think it was a kind of joke the ancient Venetians played on their putative Papal masters. At Carnival, after all, whoring was one of the prime activities.'

'Latin. So the Domino was one of the archetypal Italian characters.'

'I don't think it was,' Celeste said. 'But I don't know enough of the *maschere* history to say for sure. There is someone who can tell us everything there is to know about the masks of Venice and my Domino mask in particular. The man who made it.'

EIGHT

Old Westbury/Venice

Lew Croaker's first sight of Margarite Goldoni DeCamillo was across the long expanse of lawn – still summer-green. Perhaps this color, glowing, almost incandescent in the full sun of noontime, was what lent the scene its intensity, as unforgettable as an object that defies the law of gravity.

He saw the mass of dark, curling hair which spoke to him of cool jazz and double espressos at some long-forgotten Greenwich Village club. Then she turned at his approach up the flagstone walk, and he saw the strength and tenacity in her jawline, her prominent nose. Her eyes regarded him coolly. Not with the hostility or suspicion he had expected, but with a genuine curiosity.

'You're out of luck,' she said as he came up to where she stood in a multi-color woven wool jacket. She wore black leggings and ankle-high boots. Her ears were adorned with earrings made of old Roman coins, and there was a large diamond solitaire ring on her marriage finger.

'Why is that?'

'My husband's not home.'

'He assured my office when they contacted him that he would be.'

She shrugged. 'Tony's Sicilian. Either he respects people or he doesn't.'

Croaker looked at her, wondering what she thought of her husband. She had said that one word *Sicilian* through clenched teeth, as if it were an epithet. 'Meaning he doesn't respect me.'

'You're the cop.'

'Used to be,' he said with a smile. 'NYPD. But that was some time ago.'

She cocked her head. 'What did you do in the used to be?'

'Detective,' he said. 'Homicide.'

'Just your meat, then.'

'What do you mean?'

She laughed in his face. 'Come off it, Detective or whatever the hell you are now, you want to talk to Tony about my brother's murder.'

'But he's not here,' Croaker said. 'Maybe I ought to talk to you.'

'I have nothing to say on the subject. Dom's dead, that's the end of it.'

'Not to me it isn't.' Croaker watched a wise guy walking the perimeter of the estate, a powerful-looking young man who watched him from the corner of his eye. 'I'm charged with finding out who killed him and bringing him in.'

'Dead or alive?' she said, staring at his bio-mechanical hand.

'Well, now, that depends,' he said, lifting it up and flexing the articulated fingers, 'on how he reacts when I find him.'

She examined each finger, touching them in the way an artist would an armature on an incomplete sculpture, as if imagining the effect the finished design would have on the viewer.

'These look lethal.'

'I can also do the most delicate work with them,' Croaker said, extruding a steel blade from the tip of one finger.

She looked into his face. 'Has it changed you?'

'What?'

'This . . . hand.'

'Why would it?'

Margarite abruptly shifted her attention and the moment was gone. She watched the wise guy as he lit a cigarette. 'Hey,' she called to him, 'remember to put the butt in your pocket.' Then to Croaker: 'You're very sure you'll find him – the man who murdered Dom.'

'I'll find him.'

She looked at him for a long time, the sun in her eyes so that he could not tell whether she was merely curious or there was something deeper there.

'I think I'll stay a while,' he said.

She turned, began to follow a branch of the flagstone round the side of the house. 'Don't expect an invitation inside. I have workmen sanding a new tongue-and-groove wood floor and there's plastic sheeting and saw-dust all over the place.'

'No problem.'

She put her hands in the pockets of her jacket. 'You mentioned your office before. Just who do you work for?'

'Damned if I know,' he said, then grinned at her look of consternation. 'Federal bureau,' he added, obscurely. 'This case has national reper-cussions.'

'Don't bullshit me,' she said, swinging round on him. 'My brother had national repercussions. The FBI kissed his ass for years.'

'Funny. I thought it was the other way around, in the end.'

'Hah!' She had stopped to look at a sheared azalea which was looking none too healthy. Her fine-boned hands moved through the tight tangle of branches with deftness and precision, and he guessed this was how she proceeded with everything she did. 'For a Fed you sure don't know much.'

'Maybe, but I'm eager to learn.'

She straightened up, peered at him oddly. 'That's more than I can say for most of them.' They began to walk again. 'They all have their own agendas, I've found.'

'You mean like inter-agency in-fighting?'

'Hell, no,' she said, pushing her fingers through her hair. 'It's all personal with them. They see these wise guys they're following day and night walking around in 3000-dollar suits, riding in BMWs, living high off the hog, and it sticks in their gut like a knife. So they decide they're going to take this one or that one down.' Her face twisted into a wry smile. 'You know, it's like they tell you about watching sports events: they're boring unless you pick one side and root for it. Make it personal. That's what these Feds do. To beat the boredom, they pick a target and make him a personal priority.' She glanced at him. 'You think I'm making this up.'

'No, I don't.'

They had reached the back of the house. In the distance beyond the covered pool Croaker could see a couple of men in among the trees. They were clones of the pair who had stopped him at the front of the property: hard-muscled wise guys, ex-cons, most likely, with cynical eyes and quick reflexes, made for guard duty. One had a young Rottweiler on a length of thick stainless-steel chain. It strained at the leash, interested now in Croaker, who was so close to one of the people it had been trained to protect.

As he watched the dog, Croaker was thinking of the dossier on the DeCamillo family Lillehammer had pulled up for him on the computer in the Air Force jet.

There was a scent in the air which transcended autumn. The bittersweet odor of crushed leaves could not quite hide the smell of change. He said on impulse, 'That's not the same dog, is it?'

'I beg your pardon?'

'You had a Rottweiler named Caesar, but that one there is a new one.'

'What if it is?'

'What happened to Caesar?'

Margarite said nothing, but she was staring at the Rottweiler in a curious manner.

'Caesar died,' she said. 'I think he must have eaten a field mouse that was poisoned.'

'That must have been tough.'

She rounded on him, her cheeks suddenly flushed. 'My brother's murder was tough. This –' She lifted an arm, let it fall. 'This was just a fucking dog.'

The Rottweiler had stopped in its tracks, its head swung round. It had been Margarite's sharp tone that had caught its attention, but it was Croaker those malevolent yellow eyes were fixed upon.

She looked from the dog to Croaker, abruptly amused. 'If you make a move now, you're dead.'

'Thanks for the warning.'

She made a sound in the back of her throat and the Rottweiler backed down. Its flanks were still quivering, and Croaker did not much care for the look in its evil eyes.

'It's okay now,' Margarite said, beginning to walk again. 'But you'll want to be more careful.'

'I'll remember not to startle you in the dog's presence.'

They went on, into the estate, over a small knoll, heading toward a wisteria-covered pergola. There was an ornate stone statue of the Greek god Poseidon, king of the sea. The tines of his trident looked very sharp. The wise guys and the Rottweiler followed at a discreet distance, like a duena in Madrid with her high-born charge.

'I don't believe my husband wants to talk to you.'

'Evidently not,' Croaker said. 'I don't blame him.'

They reached the pergola. Sunlight slanted through the gaps in the twisted, woody vines, spilling over stone benches green with moss on their bases.

'But you're braver than he is. You're talking to me.'

Margarite laughed. 'It was fate,' she said. 'You caught me at home.'

She sat on one of the benches while he leaned against the main stem of the wisteria.

'I guess, being the *capo* now, Mr DeCamillo feels he can run his own investigation into who iced his brother-in-law.'

'My husband's a legitimate lawyer. Just ask any of his clients.'

'I don't have to,' Croaker said. 'Half of Justice and the FBI have already gone over that ground.'

She squinted up at him, making her appear more vulnerable than she actually was. 'Then what ground are you on?'

'I told you. I want to get your brother's murderer.'

'Why? What's in it for you? Get your kicks rooting around in other

221

people's grief? Or are you a Mafia groupie like three-quarters of the Feds?'

'Well, I'll tell you the honest truth,' Croaker said. 'Every now and again when I feel bored I like to right a wrong.'

'This is New York: a murder-a-minute city. Go solve one of those. You're in over your head here.'

'No,' Croaker said softly. 'Your brother's murder was different.'

'So that's it. The notoriety.' She seemed disgusted. 'He was a Mafia don – the biggest ever in WITSEC. I can see your point.'

'No,' he said. 'You can't.'

She was staring at him. Behind her he could just make out the Rottweiler at the end of its taut chain. For the moment its handler was out of sight behind a large beech.

'Did anyone tell you how your brother was killed?'

Silence, shocked and vibrating, like that after the report of a gun.

'Anyone show you the pictures of what was –'

'Shut up!' She stood up abruptly and the Rottweiler made a whining sound.

Carefully, Croaker reached into his jacket, extracted a manila folder.

'I think you ought to see these.'

'No! I –' The Rottweiler's forepaws struck the hard ground glancing blows as it began to rear up. 'No.'

But she would not take her eyes off the folder. 'Don't you think I want to see my brother's killer brought to justice?'

He knew he had to be very careful here. 'That's just the question I was asking myself when I first started talking to you. But now I believe I know the answer.' She was smarter than he had been prepared for.

When she took the folder from him he noticed that her hand did not tremble. She sat back down, put the folder in her lap, closed her hands over it.

'I said it, didn't I?' she said almost to herself. 'It was fate that I was here when you came.'

Croaker would have liked to have kept his eyes on the Rottweiler, but he concentrated on her instead.

As if they belonged to someone else, her hands unclasped the envelope, pulled out the photos. She glanced up at him, almost, he thought, as if for support. Then, with a convulsive gesture, her head went down.

It was the first one, with the heart sewn into his navel, and she gave a little cry.

The Rottweiler, growling, was coming, pulling its handler toward the mistress it believed was in distress. It was right.

'Mrs D.?'

'It's all right, Joey,' she called. 'Leave us alone.'

Croaker heard the jingle of the chain as Joey gave it a hard jerk. The Rottweiler was back to whining again.

There were tears upon the photo, glistening in the sunlight. She had gone through them all, and now seemed paralyzed, shuffling them slowly over and over as if to relinquish them now, terrible as they were, would require saying goodbye to him again.

'Why did you show me these?' she breathed at last. 'They're so – beyond any logic of human behavior.'

'Yes,' he said. 'Now you know why I'm here.'

Her fingers were as white and rigid as bone. 'I only agreed to talk to you because –'

'Because I'm a cop.'

Margarite shook her head. 'The Feds seem to believe I owe them some kind of debt for taking Dom into WITSEC. Well, they're mistaken because they didn't live up to their end of the bargain. They didn't protect him.'

'That's one side of it,' he said. 'The other side is that Dominic Goldoni violated the rules of WITSEC and that breach got him killed. You forget that no one's ever gotten to a WITSEC-protected person who hasn't violated his contract.'

'WITSEC never had my brother before.'

Touché, Croaker thought.

'You know how the modern world works, my detective,' Margarite said in a voice less brittle and more fragile. 'No one will admit responsibility. But then I never expected the Feds to say to me, "Sorry, we fucked up". It's too potentially embarrassing for the program. The inmates will get spooked, try to bolt, and some of them will get their brains splattered all over the place.'

He thought that was an accurate assessment of the situation, as far as it went.

'See, here's the thing. What did Dominic Goldoni do to get himself killed?' He watched her now, as carefully as if she were the Rottweiler ready to strike. 'He brought his mistress – a woman named Ginnie, Virginia Morris – out from Queens to be with him where WITSEC stashed him.'

Margarite had her head down. She was wiping her tears one by one off the photo of her dead brother.

'Ginnie was murdered, too, in the same spot where we discovered your brother.' Her head jerked up so fast he could hear her vertebrae crack. 'I came here because I'm trying to figure out what got Dominic to break the WITSEC rules. My theory is he wanted out of his relationship with Ginnie, she didn't want it to end, and in the sensitive situation he was in, I think he called someone – probably your husband – to help him with the problem. The call's maybe what got him killed, someone tracing it back to him – to where he was stashed.'

'Tony won't help you. He wouldn't help a crippled cop across the street.'

'Did *you* know Ginnie?'

'What?'

Something she had said or the way she had said it had triggered the thought in the back of his mind. She and her brother had been very close, and this, after all, had been a female problem.

'Well, you must've known your brother fooled around on the side, you two being close.'

She got up abruptly and the photos slid to the ground. Croaker bent to retrieve them, slid them into their folder as he hurried after her.

'Yeah, maybe not,' he said when he had caught up to her. 'That Sicilian thing. Women and business don't mix.'

'Dom's sexual appetite had nothing to do with business,' she said curtly. 'Besides, the Goldonis aren't Sicilians, which is more than I can say for my husband. Our family comes from Venice.'

'But you and your brother are half-Sicilian.'

'His mother,' she said. 'Not mine.'

The Rottweiler had moved so quickly it had almost pulled its handler off his feet. Now it stood, its rear legs apart, its forepaws holding a small animal, a chipmunk or a vole, perhaps. The Rottweiler began to gnaw on it with increasing vigor. There was a small but distinct *crack!* as it crushed the animal's skull. Margarite stood regarding the scene with no particular fascination or revulsion, merely curiosity. It was the same expression she had had on when she had first seen him.

Croaker said, 'So you knew Ginnie Morris.'

'I didn't say that.' She looked around as if someone on this heavily guarded estate might be eavesdropping. 'But the fact is I did. I knew all his mistresses. I was the only one he could trust to confide in.'

'Then you knew where WITSEC put your brother.'

'No. I only got Ginnie ready for the move. The rest Dom did on his own.'

'Good Christ.' He could see why she had been crying over the photos: she had helped her brother violate the WITSEC rules, and that violation was what had gotten him killed.

'Dominic was . . . different, in many ways,' Margarite said. 'As far as his womanizing was concerned he was like John Kennedy – he couldn't help it. I think there's a medical term for what they both suffered from: satyriasis.'

'You mean your brother was an addict for pussy.'

'I've heard it put that way before,' she said, watching the Rottweiler devour the creature at last, but then she turned to face him and her face was set in a cool expression. 'You're here now as my guest, detective. I suggest in future that you treat my brother's memory with respect.'

He had wanted to shock her yet again, to elicit an uncalculated response. When he had first driven up, he had been ready to dismiss her as just another piece of Italian window-dressing. But she had proved to be much more than that. And now he began to see that perhaps his basic assumption regarding these three – Dominic, Tony and Margarite – was totally off base.

He had assumed that, boys being boys, Tony DeCamillo must have been Dominic Goldoni's confidant. On the face of it, this typical scenario had made sense: it was Tony whom Dom had designated his successor. But the longer he talked with Margarite the deeper his conviction became that the two men had never really been that close. Now the one question nagged at him: if Margarite had been his confidante regarding his mistresses, what else had he confided in her?

'I've been living alone too long. I guess my manners aren't what they used to be.'

'You mean on the streets of New York?'

He couldn't help but laugh at that. 'I take your point, Mrs DeCamillo. I apologize. But I wish you'd call me Lew. Detective sounds so . . .'

'Generic?'

He laughed again, suddenly happy to be in her company.

She turned to him. 'Why don't I call you Lew and you can call me Margarite?'

'Fair enough.'

'I'm hungry,' Margarite said. 'Let's get something to eat.'

She drove him in her Lexus coupé. A Ford Taurus was on their tail the entire time. Croaker, glancing in the rear-view mirror, hoped the wise guys had left the Rottweiler at home.

Margarite drove quickly and efficiently. She knew where all the cop cars were lying in wait along the back roads and the highway's service road, ready to pick off speeders. Ten minutes later, they pulled into one of those elaborate diners with the fake gold stone façades, an enormous six-page menu and food that appeared to have been prepared at some vast central kitchen that serviced all like-looking establishments in Queens and Long Island.

The owner, a dark-complexioned man who could have been from virtually any country on the Mediterranean, hurried up as they slid into a booth large enough to accommodate six oversized adults. It was covered in turquoise vinyl.

'Good afternoon, Mrs D.,' he said deferentially. 'What can we get you today?'

'Order pasta,' Margarite said to Croaker without opening the menu. 'It's the only thing made here.'

'And a bottle of Valpolicella, on the house,' the owner said, beaming as he scurried away.

They ate pasta all'olio with hot, crusty Italian bread. Margarite put a handful of crushed red pepper flakes into hers. Croaker had been in Marco Island so long he had forgotten what really good pasta tasted like.

Margarite drank most of the wine.

'Why exactly did you agree to let me be your guest?' Croaker asked halfway through the meal.

'Curiosity,' Margarite replied in that very direct way of hers that was so disarming. 'When you drove up you were just another cop sent out here to give us grief. But then I talked to you and found my basic assumptions about you were all wrong. I was operating on stereotypes.'

Croaker laughed. 'That's exactly what happened to me. I thought that you being Tony D.'s wife, you know . . .' He broke off suddenly, oddly embarrassed.

'The Sicilians have a saying, Lew. Women are for cleaning, cooking and making babies – preferably sons – every two years. I'm not Sicilian; I fit none of those parameters.'

'Yet Tony the Sicilian married you.'

She dabbed oil off the corners of her mouth. 'I was very young and he was drunk on sex. He loved to fuck me.'

'And you? What did you love?'

'About Tony? He was like a white knight – strong, handsome, powerful. He was older and he knew what he wanted and how to get it. For a young girl, that kind of direct force can be a potent aphrodisiac – especially when every other boy you know is floundering around not knowing what he wants to be.'

Croaker poured her more wine and she smiled. 'You can't get me drunk, Lew, don't even try.'

'So you got married early,' he said, ignoring her remark. 'Then what?'

'Then . . .' She paused, frowning, took up her glass of wine, studied it. 'Christ, then life – real life, not fantasy – came crashing down on me.' She sipped the wine. 'All of a sudden I was no longer Margarite Goldoni.

226

I was Mrs Anthony DeCamillo, Tony's wife. And then I realized that that was all he wanted me to be and it was such a shock –' She broke off again, put the glass aside, smiled at Croaker.

'But you have your own business.'

'Oh, yes. But only by the good graces of my brother, who interceded for me with Tony. That was a mistake, because Tony lost face and he has made me pay for my business every day since.'

'You mean he takes a piece of it.'

'No,' she said coolly. 'He takes a piece of me.'

The mask-maker's shop was only a short block from the Grand Canal – a small, dingy workspace filled with flour and magic. The ceiling was made up of thousands of masks, hanging face down, overlapping one another, the colors by turns harmonizing and clashing, creating a sea of emotions trapped within the confines of their wire bones, papier-mâché flesh and enamel skin. These masks, so alive, reminded Nicholas of Circe, who confined the souls of her visitors in the bodies of animals so that they might form a compendium of living art.

His name was Marin Fornovo. He was a smallish man of middle age, with the absent-minded demeanor of the artist whose inquisitive mind finds the bounds of the mundane world too restricting. His hair was thinning but it was as fine as spun gold. Now and again, as he moved back and forth behind a scarred marble counter littered with the detritus of his art – bowls of flour, coils of wire, pots of lacquer and the instruments with which to meld, contort and apply these – light lanced off the round lenses of his gold-rimmed glasses, blanking out his eyes and making him appear as comical as a cartoon.

'Celeste, *bellissima!*' Fornovo pushed aside the litter, leaned over his counter and kissed her on both cheeks. 'There isn't a day that goes by when I don't think of your father, and miss him. I tell you, Venice is the worse off now that he is gone.' He spoke slowly and formally, as if he were still part of the Doge's court of long ago.

Celeste introduced Nicholas, and Fornovo gave him a penetrating look before nodding to him with a small smile. When he returned his attention to Celeste, he said, 'What mischief have you gotten yourself involved in now, my darling?'

Celeste laughed. 'I could never hide anything from you.'

'Neither could your father,' Fornovo said, frowning. 'I wish he had taken my advice that day, *cara mia*. If he had, I believe he would be alive today.'

'That's all in the past.'

227

'Ah, yes, the past.' Fornovo sighed deeply. 'But in the past are hidden all our sins. And our sins are what, in the end, lead to our undoing.' He clucked his tongue against the roof of his mouth. 'You would do well to remember what your father forgot, my child. I do not want to see his fate become yours.'

'I will remember. I promise.'

The little man grunted, as if, possibly, he did not believe her.

'Marin, we need your help,' Celeste said. 'Do you remember the mask you recently made for Okami-san?'

'The Domino,' Fornovo said. 'But of course! A magnificent piece of work.' He scowled. 'It has not come to harm?'

'We need some information on the Domino itself,' Celeste said, adroitly sidestepping his question. 'I seem to remember that it wasn't one of the original Venetian characters.'

'No, no, of course not. The Domino was introduced into Venice in the second half of the sixteenth century,' Fornovo said, as he began to mix a color in a shallow bowl. 'It is actually French in origin. The Domino was the name the French gave to the long, thick capes their monks wore, and which, when their noblemen and ambassadors traveled here, they brought into Venetian fashion.'

The color was becoming clear now, a deep cerulean which even in its dull pot appeared luminous. 'The mask itself is a kind of joke, however,' Fornovo continued. 'The Venetians were forever irreverent when it came to their Popes.' He lifted a thick tear-shaped drop of the pigment into the light, eyeing it speculatively. 'It was a Pope who declared Venice a threat to the rest of the world, you know.' With vigor he smeared the pigment onto the cheek of a naked white mask. 'That damnable man. But why should we decry him? We Venetians refuse to contemplate the past unless it is beribboned with ritual. But this is what makes us Venetians great.'

He daubed the other cheek, the ends of the eyeholes, the lips, and now, by some alchemical process, the mask had become a face. '*Morte ai tiranni!* That has always been our battle cry! Death to the tyrants of Rome! Whether they be Popes or Caesars. Our Republic was the only one to survive the fall of the Roman Empire; that was no happenstance!'

He set the mask carefully aside, winked at Nicholas. 'Here, in Venice, we have always been free. That is why the Jews fled here from their persecution in less enlightened lands. The Ghetto was invented here just after 1500, and for many years Venice became the heart of rabbinical study in Europe.'

He took up another pot, began to mix a color that might eventually become a shade of scarlet. 'The truth is we understood the Jews, and they

228

us. We were the same, really: enigmatic, brilliant, eminently practical – the scholars of business. When the rest of the civilized world was feudal, we were not; the Jews, who could not abide feudal thinking, appreciated this most of all. We were, all of us, capitalists from time out of mind.'

Yes – scarlet, bright, startling as newly drawn blood. He looked at the mask he was working on, nodded, as if satisfied with the magic he had wrought. 'Of course, we made the Jews pay for their sanctuary. Why not? They could afford it – and they had nowhere else to go. And we marked them by decreeing that they wear red hats.'

He began to apply the scarlet, sparingly, almost, one might say, compassionately. 'Was that cruel? Why should anyone say so? We treated them no differently than we treated our own Doges. We isolated the Jews in their Ghetto just as we incarcerated the Doge in his magnificent palace in San Marco. His oath of office became longer each year because we kept adding to the things he was enjoined from doing.'

He lifted a forefinger, waggled it at them. 'Of course, from time to time we paid a heavy price for our successes. Like the Jews we were often despised and envied for what we were. In 1605, when Pope Paul V accused Venice of heresy, didn't we reply that we were better Christians than he? Who fought the Turk in the name of Christ while Rome sat idly by? Why, Venice, of course!'

'Marin,' Celeste broke in gently. 'About the Domino.'

'Yes, yes,' he said almost irritably. Again, he put the mask aside to dry. 'I'm coming to that. Did you think I'd forgotten?' He gave Nicholas another sharp look. 'We Venetians have a saying: When history is inadequate, myth will do.' He smiled at his own enigmatic joke. 'Well, there is a myth concerning the introduction of the Domino into the Carnival and it is this: it was not French noblemen and ambassadors who brought this ironic, irreligious character to Venice, but the Jews fleeing the anti-Semitism in France.'

He turned abruptly, went through a beaded curtain into the rear of his shop. A moment later, he returned, cradling an item in his hands as if it were as fragile as a new-born baby.

'The Domino!' Celeste exclaimed. 'But that's impossible.'

'Hardly, *cara mia*, because here it is.' Fornovo gave her a crafty smile as he held it out for them to examine. 'But this is the original – the oldest mask in my own private collection. I am showing it to you as I did to Okami before you.'

'Did Okami-san know of the origins of the Domino?' Nicholas asked.

'But of course,' Fornovo said, frowning deeply. 'Did you think I would be so remiss to sell him one of my prized Dominos without making him cognizant of its history? What kind of a Venetian do you take me for?' He made a face. 'Besides, *this* Domino is special, because it was *made* in France – Paris to be exact – and brought here by the Jews fleeing persecution.'

Carefully he turned the mask over so that they could see the underside. 'Here is the name of the maker: A. Aloins.' He pointed with a thin fore-finger. 'And here, just below, is the stamp of the company under whose aegis M. Aloins toiled. It is the oldest mask-maker in France, which is saying something. And it still exists.'

He lifted the mask toward them so they could read its name:

Avalon Ltd.

In the ensuing silence the crash of a dish slipping out of a waiter's hand was stunning, but Margarite's eyes never left Croaker's. There was a defiance there that made him believe this was the first time she was con-fessing this horror.

'He beat me and what's worse I let him do it. I didn't complain, didn't go to Dom, didn't take my daughter Francine and leave. Instead, I stayed and submitted.'

'Why?'

She smiled, but the brittleness had returned, and he had the impression that if he reached out and shook her now she would shatter into 10,000 pieces.

'That's the billion-dollar question, isn't it?' She dabbed at her lips again, but there was no longer anything to wipe away. 'Maybe I felt I deserved it, marrying against my brother's wishes.'

'Dominic was against the marriage?'

'Very much so.'

'Why?'

Margarite shrugged. 'Maybe he knew Tony better than I did. But I was determined then. I thought I knew it all. Or maybe I was hell-bent to defy Dom. Who knows any more?'

'Yet Dominic named Tony his successor.'

Margarite watched him with her wide-apart eyes. 'I'm going to have to start calling you Detective again.'

He smiled at her. 'It's what I do, ma'am. Detecting's in my blood.'

That made her laugh. The owner came with more garlic bread, but she declined, and he cleared the plates away. She ordered espresso for them both.

Because he didn't think she was going to answer his previous question, Croaker said, 'If I might ask, what's the current state of your marriage?'

She was thoughtful for some time. Her eyes were leveled at him, and he could see now that they were the color of amber. 'We co-exist. But I think that's the state many married couples find themselves in.'

The noise level in the diner rose as a bunch of high-school kids slouched in, gangly-legged, jeans-clad, Walkman-armored. The espresso came, along with cordial glasses of Sambucca, compliments of the owner. Margarite turned and caught his attention right away. She blew him a kiss, which caused the widest smile Croaker had ever seen.

She turned back to him, said abruptly, 'I think Dom had a love-hate relationship with Tony. He could admire the legitimate practice he had built up all on his own while still recognizing all of Tony's faults.'

'Which are?'

She toyed with her espresso cup. 'He's impulsive, often too aggressive; he has an inflated sense of his own importance.'

'And what about your brother? What were his faults?'

'The Feds I've talked with think they know more about him than I do,' she said.

'Lucky for me I don't come with that bias.'

Those amber eyes regarded him in that very intimate way. 'You're the first man I've met since Dom who thought my opinions were worth a damn.' She plucked a coffee bean out of her Sambucca, placed it into her mouth, bit down on it without wincing. 'Dom was a devil and an angel, all in the same breath,' she said. 'You know it never made a difference to either of us that he was my step-mother's child. When my father officially adopted him, that was it. I had a brother. It didn't matter that he was thirteen years older than I was.'

Her eyes shifted over his shoulder and her expression changed in some subtle way. Croaker was careful not to turn his head in the direction she was looking. A moment later, he was aware of another presence.

'Hi, Mom!'

He turned to see a red-haired girl who was just as beautiful as Margarite. She was slender, a long-legged colt with that impossible to duplicate ungainly grace, the sole province of teenagers. This must be Francine. He was stunned to think of her as Margarite's daughter. How old had she been when she had given birth to this nymphet? Nineteen or twenty, no more. He thought about what Margarite had told him of her marriage.

'Francie, what are you doing here?'

'I'm with Doug and Richie and Mary,' Francie said, pointing to a group of teens taking a booth in boisterous fashion.

'I told you about going out alone.'

Francie made a face. 'I'm not alone, Mom. I'm with the guys. Besides, Richie's father –'

231

'I know all about Richie's father,' Margarite said quickly.

Croaker glanced over at the other booth, saw that another wise guy had taken up station in the diner. The place was crawling with them now.

'Who's this?' Francie was looking directly at Croaker.

'Francie, this is . . . a business acquaintance of mine,' Margarite said, thinking fast. 'Lew Croaker.'

'Howdy, ma'am!' Croaker said, making her giggle. He extended his hand and she stared at it.

'What happened to you?'

'Francie!' Margarite exclaimed.

'No,' Croaker said, 'it's all right.' He looked up into Francie's face. 'I lost my hand in a fight. A sword sliced it off. Surgeons in Tokyo gave me this one, instead. Like it?'

She took it gingerly in her own. She was clearly fascinated, and he asked her to join them for a moment.

'I don't think that's a good idea,' Margarite said.

Francie gave her a quick look before sliding in beside her.

Was it his imagination or did Margarite seem uncomfortable as her daughter sat beside her?

Francie put her elbows on the table, ordered a double bacon-cheese burger with extra cheese, a large order of fries, and a Diet Coke. With a child's unconcern, she seemed to have completely forgotten Croaker's hand. She leaned over, took a sip of her mother's Sambucca. Oddly, Margarite said nothing. Her unease increased.

'What kind of business are you in?' Francie said, impaling Croaker with her large pale eyes.

'Does it matter?'

Francie nodded. 'Sure. You make Mom laugh.'

His gaze just touched Margarite's for an instant before sliding away.

He said, 'The truth is, Francie, I came to talk to your mom about your Uncle Dominic.'

Her Diet Coke arrived, and she abandoned the Sambucca to slurp it through a straw. A moment later the food arrived, and she attacked it as if she had not eaten in a week.

'Would you like to tell me about him?'

Margarite's agitation increased exponentially. 'I don't think that would be –'

'I miss him,' Francie said around an enormous mouthful of food. 'He was good to me.'

Croaker, listening to her answer, kept hearing echoes of what she might be feeling and not saying: *I miss him; he was good to me – not like my dad.*

'Did you see a lot of him?'

'Sure,' Francie said, pouring more ketchup on her fries. 'Mom would take me when she went to see Uncle Dom.' Chomp chomp. 'He always had a freezer full of ice-cream – neat new flavors he was testing out. It was cool.'

'I'll bet,' Croaker said, wondering about Margarite's palpable distress. Up until Francie arrived she had been very much in control. No, that wasn't quite true, he thought. She had cracked when he had mentioned the Rottweiler Caesar's death, and then again when he had shown her the pictures of her brother. 'So you all sat around eating ice-cream.'

'Uh uh,' Francie said, cramming her cheeks full of fries. 'I'd eat the ice-cream while Mom and Uncle Dom talked in the library.'

Croaker gave Margarite a quick glance, but her attention was concentrated on her daughter.

'Didn't your dad ever come along?'

'Uh uh,' Francie said, wiping her smeared lips with a napkin. She began to edge out of the booth. 'You'll have to excuse me now.'

Then she was walking very quickly through the restaurant. Croaker watched Margarite follow her with her eyes as she passed by her friends' booth, made her way to the ladies' room.

'Excuse me, Lew, while I go powder my nose,' Margarite said. Her face was white.

She disappeared into the ladies' room and something clicked in Croaker's mind. He was up, almost running through the restaurant.

At the door to the ladies' room, he paused for a moment, then said, 'What the hell,' and pushed it open.

He found Margarite in a stall on her knees beside Francine, who was bent almost double over a toilet. The teenager was vomiting in great heaves.

Margarite became aware of him; the distress on her face was acute.

'Get out of here, will you?' She was on the verge of tears.

Croaker went into the room, letting the door close behind him. 'She isn't sick, is she?' he said. 'At least not with a virus or the flu. She's bulimic.'

Margarite said nothing, continued to hold her child's head while she rocked a little, crooning to her. At length, she looked at him again. 'Why are you still here?'

'I think I can help her.'

'Leave us alone.'

'I don't believe either of you want that now.'

He went over to her, took Francie gently by the shoulders, led her over to the sink, ran the cold water for her. Behind him, he heard the toilet

233

flush several times. Then Margarite emerged from the stall, stood looking at the two of them.

'Her father doesn't know; he wouldn't get it.'

'Do you?' He held her while she put her head under the stream of water.

'She's bulimic, Lew. Of course I get it. She's in therapy.'

'Is it doing any good?'

'These things take time.'

But by her resigned tone he knew she was answering by rote. 'Margarite, this is Francie's fight, not yours. She needs to want to get better, otherwise she never will.'

He pulled Francie out of the water, dried her hair and face with a wad of paper towels. Her complexion was so pale he could clearly see the blue veins at her temples.

He bent down, turning her around to face him. 'Francie, what –?'

But he never got to finish the question because her pinched face stared up at him and she cried out: 'I'm going to die! I'm going to die! I'm going to die!'

Lillehammer, exhausted from a particularly frenzied bout of accoutremental sex with Doug, his very secret current flame, sank into a deep sleep. Doug was wild, unpredictable, which was his appeal. Neither man knew the other in real life – business or social. They came together essentially as ciphers, mindless bodies intent on sating themselves in the most bizarre methods available. In that respect, Doug was ideal. A restless spirit by nature, he was happiest getting something different going every time they met, the more grotesque and outlandish the better.

As Lillehammer sank into slumber, even the taste of Doug evaporated, until all that was left was darkness. And, from out of the darkness, emerged the Dream, until it surrounded him in the walls of its own peculiar universe.

Lillehammer rarely dreamed, but when he did it was usually the Dream. At least, this is what he had come to call it. Not that the Dream was always the same, but certain fundamental aspects never changed.

There was the jungle, first, last and always: the triple-canopied tropical trees dripping moisture, rank fruit and deadly serpents. No doubt about it, it was a nightmare vision of the Garden of Eden, and Lillehammer knew that the Fed shrink he had been forced to see after he came back from 'Nam would have had a field day with the symbolism of it – if he had ever told her, which was, of course, out of the question.

The Dream was like tripping over gravity, falling upward instead of down, slamming the top of your head against a cage of fire-hardened bamboo. And that was another of the fundamental aspects: an impression of being in a zoo – the stench, the cramped space and, most of all, the uncomfortable sense of being constantly observed.

In the Dream as in memory he paced back and forth across the area of dirt floor too small for him ever to fully stretch out on. He'd had to sleep sitting up, not that he got much sleep. That was part of it. Darkness, the heavy lull of the insects' buzz, and then the bright lights would stab behind his closed eyelids and he'd be jerked awake. This happened over and over again in the Dream as in memory, until sleep became yet another freedom denied him.

The idea was perfectly sound, deriving from the basics of interrogation: strip the subject of a sense of time, of place and, finally, of himself. The end result was pliability. In the same way a baker kneads dough to the right consistency, so his captors sought to break down his psyche.

To what extent they were successful he would never know. And that was the worst horror of all. Not knowing.

At first, when the Dream began, Lillehammer was hopeful that it would answer the question that had been haunting him ever since he returned from 'Nam: had he been broken? In hospital, while his wounds were slowly healing, he'd had much time for contemplation, and even more when he had returned to the States and the shrink was loosed upon him.

Actually, he had liked her, Madeleine, had even fallen a little in love with her. That was only to be expected, she had explained to him one day. She had showed him the only real kindness since his incarceration in the bamboo zoo somewhere in the bush of Laos.

Christ, what a fuck-up he had made of things. But Madeleine had disagreed with him and, in fact, had proved to him that the reverse was true. They could not have broken him, she said, because none of the intelligence with which he had been entrusted had been compromised. Not a code, man or network had gone down. *Don't worry about memory*, Madeleine had assured him. *In these cases, memory is thoroughly unreliable.* Which was why she had been loosed on him, to pick through the rubble and unearth what he apparently could not.

You're fine, she had told him at his last session, *whole and functioning, able to return to what you were doing before. Whatever happened is in the past.*

He wanted to believe her. And he would have, of course, had it not been for the Dream. Even as he saw that she had not lied, that he was still trusted, and now revered among his élite compatriots, the Dream was lodged in his memory like a stone.

In the Dream as in memory the smell of blood and excrement was always with him, the sweat of fear coating him like a malevolent second skin. They came for him in the zoo, and did things to him, unconscionable, unmentionable even to Madeleine, whom he loved and even trusted a little bit.

As much as he could trust, because that is what the zoo did to him, if not, as Madeleine had assured him, depriving him of his humanity, then crushing his ability to trust in his fellow man.

In the Dream as in memory he was alone, abandoned by his compatriots, those with whom he had sworn undying friendship. The zoo was his alone to endure. No one came charging over a thickly foliated ridge, no one stole into the zoo in the dead of night to rescue him.

He existed inside the zoo, prey to endless indignities and torture. The suffering of life was punctuated only by the hallucinations of his own mind, at which point he was left alone the short length of time until he was returned sufficiently to the real world for the process to begin all over again.

His mind, under extreme pressure, telescoped time, bent it back upon itself until it disappeared entirely. He found himself again at the moment when he was being inducted into Looking-Glass, the shadow society that was pledged to embrace him as a blood-brother for just so long as he was of use to it.

But now he was peering at himself and his brethren through his own self-made looking-glass, aware at last of the shifting of reality and unreality, of the unsettling truth that lay behind the comforting façade of loyalty and fealty, that those behind the Looking-Glass had sold him lies as effectively as they sold everyone else around them. This was the frightening world that lay behind this modern-day Looking-Glass; and it was not so different from the one that Lewis Carroll had created more than a century and a half ago.

Much later, when he was back in Washington and working again, he discovered that if he had not been dumped unceremoniously on their doorstep in 'Nam, they would, indeed, have been prodded into action. They would have sent out a solitary Ranger – a sniper who would have had orders to put a bullet through his head in order to keep their secrets safe and sound.

In a way, he didn't blame them – in their position, he supposed he might have contemplated the same thing. But in another way, he could not help but blame them: they had lied to him, his blood-brothers, and they had failed him. Their betrayal taught him a profound lesson in the manner in which human beings treat one another. After that, he discovered that he didn't like humans much any more.

He forgot about Madeleine or, more accurately, his love for her; that was far too painful to dwell on. Instead, he turned himself into a kind of automaton. There was a familiarity that comforted him in going through the 10,000 rituals of his trade and getting it all spot on. There was a satisfaction that this veil he had woven was invisible to his comrades, that they had adjudged him well and whole as well as a hero. He was promoted, given far greater powers and leeway in initiative than he'd ever had when he was in 'Nam under the command of the Jabberwocky.

In those days he'd been known as the Mad Hatter – a nickname he believed even more appropriate now than it had been then.

Whatever else had been washed away from that era, the sobriquet of the Red Queen had remained. He and the Red Queen had toiled ceaselessly under the marshal glare of the Jabberwocky, even through the embarrassing mishap with Michael Leonforte.

Somehow, the Red Queen had sidestepped the fallout from that fiasco, and had risen in rank so that now he inhabited the ultimate position of power which the Jabberwocky had occupied for decades.

How had the Red Queen done it? He had dislodged the Jabberwocky, a man whom Lillehammer had been certain would only be taken from his position of power feet first. The Red Queen had an asset named Nishiki, it was rumored. Nishiki's intelligence was so compelling, so accurate and at such a consistently high level, that it became a sword with which the Red Queen cut a swath, rising through the hierarchy, mowing down unbelievers, political and ideological enemies as he went.

As he did so, Lillehammer the opportunist rode his coat-tails. These days, he was the Red Queen's eyes and ears, the only man, he believed, whom the Red Queen explicitly trusted. The Red Queen claimed that not even he knew Nishiki's real identity or even his nationality. The intelligence was always sent to him by some form of dead drop which was changed at frequent though random intervals. But if all this were true, what was the Red Queen's relationship to Nishiki? What was their connection? What was Nishiki's motivation for providing this flow of high-level intelligence?

Did Lillehammer care very much about the answers to these questions? In these veiled days filled with memory and the Dream he found it easier to follow his superior's orders than to seek answers to politically loaded questions. He had chosen a side long ago – or it had chosen him, what did it matter? – and now morality had no part to play in his current actions. He found some form of dim pleasure in succumbing to dumb rote.

Short-circuited, he was disconnected from the consequences of his actions. He flew through the nighttime skies of the world dispensing what the Red Queen called justice, and did not imagine there might be a different reality. He was hermetically sealed behind his mask, peering out at the world with incurious eyes.

But man – even a man such as Lillehammer had become – could not exist on the familiarity of comfort alone. Disconnection from the world around him did not mean that the synapses had ceased to fire. He was alive, after all. Damaged, but alive.

It took him a good deal of time to work out what, really, was driving him in the new life he had made for himself. And, in this regard, the Dream served him well as a path backward into memory. The Dream showed him why he was still breathing, why he had not slit his wrists in his Philippine hospital bed or defenestrated himself from his Washington office. It was because the Dream brought him, like detritus washed up on a far shore, the faces of those who had run the zoo. Like acid on metal, these faces were forever etched upon his memory; their faces, lit crazily by floodlight and sunlight, rode herd upon him, crouched like cruel ghouls upon his shoulders, driving their long bamboo nails into his flesh, slouched beside him in noisome fury as he walked or ate or defecated. In the Dream as in memory.

And, at last, Lillehammer had come to the conclusion that he had been saved from the jaws of death for one purpose: to find his cagers and destroy them, as they had destroyed him. And to that cadence, and that cadence alone, did his heart beat.

NINE

Paris/Old Westbury

Entering Paris was like emerging into clear water from the incantatory flux of a whirlpool. The charism of Venice's Byzantine brocade was broken by the effulgent flood of lights streaming into the cloud-clotted sky.

The Parisian night was a bouquet of vibrant façades, broad boulevards, massive fountains guarded by lions, cherubs and gods, glittering whitely, bathed in light.

Fingers of light illuminated the Arc de Triomphe, rising from the fulcrum of the Place de l'Etoile, nexus of a dozen major avenues, radiating like the veins on the back of a hand. Geysers of light spilled over the Place de la Concorde, where Louis XVI and Marie Antoinette, Danton and Robespierre, felt the terminal kiss of the Revolution's Razor; the Place Vendôme, where monuments to Napoleon rose and fell and rose once again. Arcs of light burst against the strong artery of the city which crossed from Right Bank to Left, with the Grand Palais and the Petit Palais on one end and the great gilded dome of Les Invalides on the other, while between them, lit by clusters of lamps, rose the magnificent bridge across the Seine named after Alexander III of Russia.

Through this urban landscape, white as snow beneath a full moon, Nicholas and Celeste were driven from Charles de Gaulle airport. Entering the city of light, they felt like pilgrims who had been cast into the wilderness for transgressions unknown and unforgivable, and who now were re-entering Western civilization.

They crossed the Seine from Right Bank to Left, entering a world still somewhat bohemian, certainly younger than that across the river, filled with art galleries, trendy clothing boutiques and food kiosks of all description.

They found lodging a block and a half from the Boulevard St Germain at a hotel with a white and black façade of sand-blasted stone and wrought iron. The rooms themselves were small, post-modern, neat, comfortable, with views of Paris's justly famous rooftops, aglow with an astonishing aura, the pyramid of energy surrounding the Eiffel Tower.

Inside their room, a small, neat space, a VCR attached to the TV was already displaying the black-and-white images of Humphrey Bogart and Lauren Bacall, in a scene from Raymond Chandler's febrile *The Big Sleep*. Electronic shadows on the wall, iridescent flickers like the blinking of an eyelid, the beating of a heart.

Sleep . . .

Avalon Ltd is a company with an interesting history, Fornovo had told them. *Originally a house that manufactured costumes for traveling theatrical troupes, it gradually metamorphosed as the renown of its mask-makers grew. At one point – who knows when, perhaps around the time of the French Revolution – the mask-makers themselves wrested control of the company from their overlords, who – the story goes – were, because of their notoriety, forthwith guillotined in the Place Vendôme. The name was changed to Avalon et fils because the artisans had come to think of the company as their home.*

And so it remained virtually unchanged by the passing years until perhaps five years ago when, after falling on hard times, it was bought by a foreign firm and the name was changed again, to Avalon Ltd.

Who bought the company? Nicholas had asked.

Now that's the curious part, Fornovo had said, setting the Domino aside. *No one seems to know.*

Nicholas awoke to sunlight spilling through the window. He turned over in bed, found Celeste sleeping beside him, her clothes still on. Her face, extraordinarily beautiful, was cast half in sunlight, half in the blue shadows of the dregs of night. The TV was still on but, the tape having finished hours since, was spewing out a soundless spray of gray and white particles, like a beam from some science-fiction weapon.

He looked down, found himself also fully clothed. He could not even remember lying down. Exhaustion, complete and blessed, had overtaken them without warning.

He lay where he was, too content for the moment to move. He knew he should call his office; Seiko must be frantic by now. But why should he let her know where he was? She would only want to give him an update on the Saigon situation, and he had no desire to hear it. Besides, she and Nangi would be able to take care of anything that arose.

These excuses, he knew, were old and wearing thin. Slowly, almost painfully, like the progress of a degenerative disease, the truth was dawning on him. He was fleeing a marriage that had come apart, a relationship that had run so far off course he was powerless to set it right. Guilt had done its best to strangle the truth, to keep alive paper-thin fabrications that were laughable in the pragmatic light of day.

But, as another facet of the truth was revealed to him, he knew it went deeper than that. He was running away from his old life: his retirement

240

into marriage, a supposed family, a settled job, the minutiae of responsibility settling upon his shoulders like soot. He was being buried alive.

The profound sense of freedom he had felt the moment he had donned the Bauta mask was exhilarating. He did not want it to end. He wanted his old life back.

Carefully, he turned his head, staring into Celeste's sun-struck face. And then there were his growing feelings about this wondrous woman. If he were not married, he knew he would be falling in love with her. And then, the truth, writhing and extending itself like a scar upon flesh, revealed yet another facet of itself: what did his being married have to do with it? The concept of love precluded outside circumstance. He *was* falling in love with her.

He sat up abruptly, got out of bed. Soundlessly, he padded into the bathroom, stripped and stood under a scalding shower for five minutes. He soaped up, then turned the hot spigot off, felt the chill of the needle spray puckering his skin like the first barometric drop of an incoming storm. He turned his face up into the torrent, as if the water could scrub his mind as well as his body clean.

Wrapping a towel around his waist, he returned to the room to discover Celeste rummaging through her small suitcase.

'Christ, I slept like the dead,' she said.

He went quickly by her, not trusting himself to speak or even be near her at the moment.

Bearing her clothes, she disappeared into the steamy bathroom. The room seemed immediately small and meanly impersonal without her presence, and without thinking too much about it, Nicholas pushed open the door into the bathroom.

Celeste was in the tub, soaking. He crossed to a small wooden stool at the foot of the tub, opened the French windows, then sat down.

Celeste was wearing a mask. It was composed of dark mud and minerals, another luxe perk offered by the hotel. Her eyes were closed and her face was in repose.

'Have you come to seduce me?'

'No,' he said, tasting the lie on his tongue.

Her eyes opened, their aquamarine color all the more startling contrasted against the mud. 'Can you feel Okami-san?'

'The future is blank, Celeste.'

She regarded him silently for what seemed a long time.

'I'm frightened, Nicholas.'

'Yes, I know.'

'I'm not used to that.'

He nodded. 'Perhaps all we need is to help one another.'

She turned on the hot-water tap. 'I need to wash off this mask. If you stay, you'll get wet.'

Twenty minutes later, she emerged from the bathroom. Her hair was still damp from the shower, plaited into a thick French braid. This more tempered style contrasted sharply with the lush wildness of how she had worn it in Venice, a city of excesses. It made her seem less impetuous, and also more introspective, melancholy. In Venice, a city many thought of as melancholy, she had been as exuberant as sunlight on the water. What would she be like here? he wondered.

She wore black leggings, a sapphire-blue suede blouse, a puffy-sleeved silk jacket embroidered with a phoenix on its back. Her feet were clad in sensible black flats. They had had two and a half hours before their flight from Venice, and she had made good use of the time, stuffing a soft-sided weekend bag with everything she thought she would need.

'Ready for espresso and *petit pain*?' she asked, on the way down in the minuscule elevator. It had glass sides so that they could see the curving marble staircase through whose heart they descended. Nicholas, so close to Celeste, was aware of the smell of her, subtle hints of frangipani and cinnamon beneath rosemary and peppermint, the aromatherapeutic scents of bath gel and shampoo. It seemed to him that he was drawn toward her in an almost tidal pull, an ebb and flow as familiar to him as the pulse of his own blood through his veins.

To stop himself from pressing himself against her, he thought of Justine. Distance had put clarity to their relationship. Sadness and suffering, long withheld, had given birth to resentment and anger. He recognized now that they had both been wounded by the death of their infant daughter, though it must have been in vastly different ways. In insisting they stay on in Japan, he saw that he had taken away a part of herself, when his only thought was to add to it. But was that the whole truth? How much of an element was his own selfishness, his burning desire to get to *kokoro*, the heart of his own natural history? The revelations of Tau-tau consumed him, he knew that – but now he had to face the consequences of that obsession. The price of truth was always high.

In the lobby, they made their way to the small restaurant with its pale ash tables, ebony chairs, steel and leather banquettes. Just to the right of where they sat was a tiny courtyard into which spilled sunlight unfiltered by either tree branch or roof eave. The pale pebbles, rearing, water-racked boulder and miniature Hinoki cypresses conjured up Japan in the deliberate methodology of the Western gardener, more homage to form than understanding of substance. And yet its easy confluence of natural elements caused him to become instantly nostalgic for the East, where the tao of emotion was swathed in layers of ritual, custom and symbolism.

'I don't feel like real food, do you?' Celeste asked.

'Not really.'

She ordered for them; her French was excellent.

The truth had given Nicholas a sense of liberation. His sadness for what had been, and what might have been, was slowly being supplanted by his excitement at being close to the edge again. The perilous journey was what fueled him, what made life worth living. He was just realizing now how far from his personal center he had drifted these past years.

'How far?'

'What?' Instantly, his attention refocused on her.

'I was wondering how far away you were.'

He smiled, less startled now that she had explained her comment. For a moment, he had thought she had been reading his mind. He drizzled marmalade over a broken crust of his *petit pain*. 'I think I'd like another espresso,' he said.

He felt from her a desire to push him, to open him up as she might an expensive compact in order to gaze at herself in a new mirror. But was her interest in him merely curiosity? It was most odd, but even after their experiences together he felt in some respects as distant from her as he had the night they first met behind their Venetian masks. He was used to reading people, getting behind their façades, but with Celeste he was finding that for every step he took toward intimacy, he was in some manner shoved back a corresponding step.

He slipped two small cubes of sugar into the black depths, stirred the espresso, sipped it delightedly.

She licked bread powder off her fingertips, put her elbows on the pale ashwood and, leaning close to him, said, 'Do you really think this Avalon Ltd is a clue left behind for us by Okami-san?'

He thought of her on the *vaporetto* in Venice, cold wind in her face so that she blinked back tears, her thick hair streaming from her face. The anger she had expressed then caught him in a viper's grip and, aware that he knew nothing about her, he wondered whether it had truly dissipated.

'Follow the sequence of what we found carefully folded in Okami-san's study and where, step by step, it has led us. Okami is a meticulous man – and a supremely clever one. I would say, yes, it's a deliberate message for us.'

'What if it *is* a clue but it wasn't left by Okami-san?'

'That possibility has occurred to me, but we won't know until we arrive at Avalon Ltd itself.'

She looked down at the remains of their breakfast. 'Don't you think,' she said, 'that if the assassin got to him he would be dead by now?'

'Only if Okami's enemies want nothing more from him than his demise.'

She seemed to be vibrating now, but from fear or exhilaration he could not say.

'You told me he never wrote anything down,' he said. 'Whatever he has been working on is all in his head. It stands to reason his enemies would want his secrets before they have him killed.'

'Are you sure?'

'It's what I'd do in their place.'

'Christ, you're cold,' she said, looking away from him at the deep, lustrous green of the miniature Hinokis, and again he felt this peculiar attraction/repulsion from her mind which he could not fathom.

'Look, Celeste, if we aren't able to think clearly and without emotion we have very little chance of helping Okami.'

She nodded mutely, her eyes dark and unreadable.

He felt that it was time to go. On the way out he asked the concierge for the address of Avalon Ltd. The concierge looked it up, wrote it down on a slip of paper, handed it over along with a folding map of the city. On the back of the map was a schematic of the Métro, and the concierge drew the route they needed to take.

At the rue du Bac Métro station, they took Line 12 north three stops to Concorde. They were now on the Right Bank. They transferred to Line 1 heading east.

'How much do you know of this alliance between the Yakuza and the Mafia which Okami-san spoke to me about?' Nicholas asked her.

'I suppose if I knew as much as Okami-san does,' she said, 'I'd be a target too.' She swung her head to look past him, at an ad for Galeries Lafayette, the Parisian department store. 'He told you about the Godaishu?'

'Yes.'

'Did he tell you that the Godaishu was his own creation?'

Nicholas stared at her. 'He didn't.'

'The Five Continents seemed a fitting name for an international conglomerate that spanned the globe,' Celeste said. 'It was to be legitimate in all ways, the path that Okami-san had seen to keep the remnants of the Yakuza from being annihilated by increasing government controls and crackdowns.

'By the power of his personality and his office he convinced the inner council of *oyabun* to go along with him, but some were unsure, others clandestinely hostile to the idea.'

'Yes, Okami told me that they were afraid of losing the enormous influence and power their lawlessness gave them.'

Celeste nodded. 'There was talk that the Kaisho had grown old beyond his usefulness, that he was increasingly bound to a world of his own imagining.'

'You mean the council believed him senile.'

'Someone was promoting the tale, in any event,' Celeste said.

'The man who now controls the direction of the Godaishu.'

She nodded. Clearly, she did not believe that Okami was senile. 'Their growing estrangement caused Okami-san to rethink his own path. Someone was consistently undermining his orders, so in desperation he shifted alliances, made deals behind the Godaishu's back, began, in effect, to work against their growing conviction that they needed to preserve their illegal empire.

'Now the war is in the open.'

'Do you have a suspicion who has ordered Okami's death?'

'It disturbs me that I don't,' Celeste said. 'But I have a recurring nightmare. In it I discover that *all* the *oyabun* of the Godaishu are in it together – and even Okami-san does not have the power to beat them down.'

'Is that possible, now that the hostilities are in the open?'

'I doubt it,' Celeste said. 'Some of the *oyabun* are weaker than others, and there are sub-alliances based on *giri*. No, I believe there is one *oyabun* persuading the others that Okami-san must be destroyed. He is the one controlling the Godaishu, because despite my paranoid nightmare I can't imagine all the *oyabun* of the inner council moving against the Kaisho no matter how much they disagreed with his plans.'

Nicholas considered this. 'It seems logical, then, that this *oyabun* is the one controlling the Godaishu, Okami's nemesis.'

'Yes.'

'Then I'll have to find him,' Nicholas said. 'And for that I'll have to return to Japan. But not before I've made sure that Okami is safe.'

'But can't you tell if Okami-san is all right? I mean, you're psychic.'

Nicholas was beginning to understand her approach to him and, suddenly, he had what seemed like the answers to questions he had been asking himself. 'Let's get one thing straight. I'm not psychic,' he said immediately. 'I don't see the future or perform exorcisms; I don't bust ghosts down to size.'

'But you can see things – feel them,' Celeste said. 'You knew Okami was not in his palazzo; you saw the bloody Domino mask before we found it.'

245

'What I am able to do,' Nicholas said, 'is to tap into certain elemental laws of nature. They're light-years away from quantum physics or solid geometry or any of the other sciences mankind has created so it can make order out of chaos.'

The train slowed into a station; the usual exchange of passengers made talking difficult for a moment. When they were on their way again, he said, 'Perhaps Tau-tau comes closest to mathematics, which man created by unconsciously translating the heartbeat of the universe into a language he could understand. Music – which is universal to all cultures – is merely a matter of mathematics.'

'The rhythm in the air just before the Kanfa bridge appeared,' Celeste said.

'That's right.'

They got off at the St Paul stop. Emerging onto the street, they found themselves in the heart of the Marais.

Celeste was silent, but Nicholas could feel emanating from her a disturbing sensation akin to throwing the transmission of a car from drive to reverse and back again.

The Marais had a fascinating history. It had been shunned during the Middle Ages because it straddled an arm of the Seine that turned its ground swampy, thus its enduring name, which meant marsh; disease was rampant here. In the thirteenth century, monks devised a way to drain the water away, making the area habitable. A century later, it was taken over for a time by Charles V, and it came into vogue. But when during the First Empire the nobility moved out for posh residences in the Faubourg St Germain, it fell into decline, and the Jews took over, transforming it into an area of tradespeople.

All this Nicholas related to Celeste as they walked toward the Place des Vosges, the most famous spot in the area.

'How do you know so much about Paris?' she asked.

'I spent a year here, setting up the French office of the advertising agency I was working for.'

'You, in advertising? I can hardly imagine it.'

'Believe it or not,' he said, 'neither can I.'

They walked in silence for some time. At length, she said, 'That was a difficult year for you, wasn't it?'

He was startled by the accuracy of her comment, but then he knew people invariably emanated all manner of unintentional signals via their tone of voice, their facial and body expressions. No doubt she had picked up on a number of these.

'Yes,' he said thoughtfully, 'but it had nothing to do with business.'

246

'A woman.'

He looked at her. 'Maybe you'd like to tell me about her.'

She laughed, coloring. 'God, no. I have no idea . . .'

'You said it was a woman.'

'Any female would have known.' But she seemed distracted now, almost uncomfortable. They were a little more than a block from the Place des Vosges, and the working-class food markets were giving way to trendy clothing and shoe shops, post-modern stationery-as-art boutiques and the occasional antique store.

All at once Celeste started, clutching at him. 'It's him!' she said hoarsely. 'There! The man who was following us in Venice. He's hiding down that side street! The one we followed, who almost trapped us on the Kanfa bridge.'

Nicholas turned, heading into the street she indicated. He was not yet concerned because he was certain she was mistaken. Surely if the man were there he would have picked up the emanations of his Tau-tau-trained psyche.

The narrow thoroughfare contained a tangle of shoved-together shops and shadows. Sunlight touched the upper floors of the buildings but left the street itself in deep shadow. Nicholas wound his way through the pedestrian traffic, his eyes and mind searching for the Messulethe. He had a clear picture of the man in his mind, from when his hat had blown off and he had bent to retrieve it: chiseled Oriental face, bronze skin, the lips firm; a mole on his lip at the corner of his mouth. He saw no one fitting that description. He felt nothing; there was no sign of any disturbance, physical or psychic.

After a thorough search up and down the street proved fruitless, he returned to where she stood, fingertips pressed hard against her temples. They were white with strain.

'I couldn't find him,' he said. 'Are you all right?'

'Just a slight . . . headache.' She shook her head. 'Sorry. I must be seeing goblins.' But her eyes were clouded – with pain or doubt? he wondered.

Extending his mind toward hers, he felt her emotions swept away from him like fog scuttling along the ground on a cold, wet morning. He could not tell what she was feeling.

He took her hand, led her back toward the wide rue St Antoine where sunlight and crowds beckoned gaily. He could tell she was shaken, and he wanted to do something that would shift her mood, bring her back to where she had been before. He decided to tell her about that year in Paris, so long ago.

247

'Her name was Mylene,' he said as he propelled her along, 'the woman I met here years ago. Red hair just like yours. I fell in love with her and almost married her.'

'What happened?' She looked at him, and he could see that the translucence had returned to her eyes. Happily, he had re-engaged her attention.

'The relationship spun out of our control,' Nicholas said. 'Neither of us understood ourselves, let alone the other person. As a result, we were either making love – at all hours, in any venue imaginable . . . and a few that weren't – or we were at each other's throats. In the end, we exhausted each other emotionally and physically. We had nowhere to go.'

'How did it end?'

He could see the arch that led to the Place des Vosges, a magnificent square of park, recently remodeled, surrounded by attached residential buildings of varying shades of pink and sienna, colonnaded on the street level, where shops and restaurants plied their trades.

'Badly,' he said. 'There were tears, flying fists, clashing ids, screams and, finally, a ferocious coupling. You couldn't exactly call it making love; we'd finished with that emotion some time before. We were driven by rage and, I imagine, a good dose of fear. What would we do without one another?' He smiled at her, though the memories, so long held in check, were particularly painful. 'Live, of course. But in those days neither of us knew how to do that very well.'

'It sounds like a film.'

'Perhaps so,' he said. 'We were torn from one another as if by a hurricane.'

'And you never heard from her again?'

'No.'

They passed through the south entrance into the Place des Vosges and, in that moment, the whole of bustling Paris vanished behind them in a mist. The studied calm of the colonnaded park embraced them. Children ran along the paths, laughing, and, near one fountain, a group dressed in suits and gowns flowed together as a photographer took pictures. The young couple in the center giggled just as the flash went off, and everyone began to laugh, ignoring for the moment the photographer calling them to attention.

'Oh, look,' Celeste said, 'a wedding party!'

They watched from a discreet distance as the young couple kissed chastely for the camera and then, urged on by their friends and family, spontaneously embraced as the photographer's flash went off again and again.

'This reminds me of my sister's wedding,' Celeste said. She seemed more relaxed, as if, secreted away here, she could forget the disturbing

248

mirage of the Messulethe. 'It was held outdoors. I remember it rained in the morning and we were all despairing. But then an hour before the ceremony was to start, the clouds broke and the sun came out. There was a rainbow, briefly, and the photographer caught them with it in the background.'

The wedding party broke up, wending their way out of the square, and Nicholas and Celeste began to walk toward one of the colonnades.

'I often think that golden afternoon was the high point,' she said, sober again. 'Everyone seemed so blissfully happy, but perhaps I'm misremembering it.' She shrugged. 'The truth is, I don't think she has a very successful marriage.' She smiled wistfully. 'But then my sister is extremely willful – and you know how Italian men are. Women in their place and all the rest of it. "Your sister's too smart for her own good", that's what my father used to say.'

'And what did he think about you?' Nicholas asked.

'Oh, he'd say, "You're different, Celeste. You're clever. Now cleverness is a trait a man can put up with in a woman."'

Nicholas laughed, but he could see that for her it wasn't funny, and for the first time he got an inkling that her relationship with her father had not been perfect.

'So in some ways your father was Old-World Italian.'

'No, he was Venetian, and that's not the same thing at all. There was Carthaginian blood in him, Cycladian – who knows what else. From what I could gather from him he relied on my mother's advice. She was an extraordinary woman, so my father loved to tell me, filled with ambition for him . . . and for herself.' She put her head down, but not before he noticed her eyes going opaque. 'She died in a fire. There were many – my father's rivals, superstitious women whom she had frightened by her inversion of what they saw as the natural order – who believed that her life was taken by God or by the priests, that she died like a heretic at the stake.'

'When did this happen?'

'Barely a year after I was born.'

Shadows from beneath the colonnade striped their faces, stitched long shadows to their feet. All around them, set into the colonnade, were tea and antique shops, bistros, small businesses. One of them was Avalon Ltd.

Nicholas, looking across the square, could see its façade. There was nothing remarkable about it – just another storefront with scrollwork lettering on the window: *Avalon Ltd. Masks Designed and Hand Made.*

Celeste was watching the door into Avalon Ltd. 'He might be there,' she said. And then, after a long pause, 'Isn't there anything here – a rhythm – that will tell us if Okami-san is alive?'

Nicholas, hearing the desperate tension in her voice, considered lying to her. But what good would that really do? Instead, he said, 'Think of me as a hunter. Sometimes, when the wind is right, when other conditions allow it, I can smell the prey before I come in sight of it. But it's not all the time, and I'm not always in control of those conditions.'

'Then he might be already dead.'

'Let's hope not. There will be little satisfaction in bringing his murderer to justice. It has occurred to me that Mikio Okami must know more about what has been happening to him – and to us – than he revealed to me or to you.'

Here and there, leaves fell, tumbling through the air. A police car turned in through one of the entrances, proceeded to make a slow patrol around the perimeter street. It stopped for a moment, its engine idling, then moved on, at last disappearing through the opposite gate. A middle-aged couple strolled in. The woman read her guidebook while the man took some pictures of the fountains and the pigeons. They didn't stay long.

All the while, Celeste's gaze had not wavered from the storefront across the colonnade.

'Time to see what's inside,' Nicholas said.

'I'm afraid. I have an intuition Okami-san is in there, dead.'

'Celeste, one way or another, we have to find out.'

'Just give me a moment, okay?' She had that distracted expression he had seen earlier when she had had her false vision of the Messulethe.

As she wended her way to the nearby bistro at the corner of the colonnade, Nicholas contemplated her enigmatic life. What she had revealed to him had had a searing impact and yet, quite unexpectedly, he found that he knew as little about her as he had before. He found that quite extraordinary.

He was just thinking of the odd approach/avoidance emanations coming from her when he saw her emerge from the shadows at the side of the bistro and slip out a side entrance without looking in his direction.

He went after her. She was headed out of the Place, through the north arch. Immediately, she turned left, heading up the rue des Francs-Bourgeois.

The pre-lunchtime streets were more crowded now, and Celeste had picked up her pace. Then, like a twig pulled inexorably on by a stream's current, she disappeared round a corner, and Nicholas broke into a run, because now he felt the darkness, the sinister pulse of the silent chorus at *kokoro*, the chant that set up black vibrations like the desperate pulse of a fly caught in a spider's web, reverberating . . .

The Messulethe!

Nicholas swung round the corner, almost collided with a middle-aged woman with her hands filled with netted bags heavy with groceries. He excused himself and, already looking past her, swerved out of the way.

Down the street he pounded, feeling Celeste in his mind moving closer to those malevolent reverberations, following her path with his mind's eye, his tanjian eye, using Tau-tau now, because he knew he must in order to save her, but also knowing he was alerting the adept to his own presence by the extension of his power.

He knew he was playing a very dangerous game. He had only come up against two tanjian adepts and both of them had come near to killing him. This one was, of course, different: he had tapped the numinous power of the Messulethe and the profound sense of the unknown here was like a yawning abyss whose size and depth were veiled in mystery.

He could feel him more clearly now, and that sense of the rhythm, the silent beat against the membrane of *kokoro*, at the heart of all things, began to fill his mind with its hideous strength. It was the primitive cadence that made things happen, that brought what others thought of as magic out of the realm of the mind and into the physical world. The excitation of *kokoro* set into motion the networks by which Tau-tau gained its strength. It was a mentally fatiguing act, this excitation of the membrane of *kokoro*, and it was only now when he was so close to the adept that Nicholas understood, and his blood ran cold.

As he at last caught sight of Celeste at the far corner of the crowded street he knew what made this adept different – and so very dangerous: he was able to keep the rhythm of *kokoro* going endlessly. No conjuring it up from time to time when it was needed for him. That was for lesser tanjian.

Then the horror of what he had discovered was blotted out. Nicholas felt the pressure in his mind as the adept increased the tempo of the cadence, saw with his special sight the extension of Tau-tau, like a liquid shadow that entwined itself through all the shadows of the street, unnoticed by passersby, by Celeste herself, who was standing stock still at the street corner, her head moving from side to side, her eyes wildly darting in every direction.

He launched himself forward, darting between angered pedestrians, his way encumbered, slowing him down when he had no time to spare. He caught sight of the Messulethe and, to his shock, did not see the face he was expecting. This was a different Messulethe than the one he had seen in Venice.

His path was made more difficult now because of the sudden press of people. The sidewalk was narrowed by the stained wooden planks of a construction crew repairing gas mains below the ripped-up pavement. As he pressed on, he became aware of the Tau-tau shadow detaching itself

251

from his hiding place, flashing with black light directly toward Celeste. To Nicholas it represented pure malignancy, and he knew he would never reach the Messulethe in time. He smelled the acrid stench of sulfur, knew he was the only one around who would, and his psyche expanded.

Like a great beast it wrapped itself around Celeste just at the moment the shadow struck her. The sheer force of it staggered her, thrusting her off the curb and into the street, but Nicholas's protection held.

The pressure in his mind was so great now that all vision was distorted. Rainbow colors smeared themselves like auras around every living thing that moved in his field of vision, and he experienced that disconcerting sense of sliding sideways, outside the grip of time, so that it seemed as if he could see himself in the struggle with the Messulethe.

The Messulethe redoubled his efforts to get to Celeste, to crush her mind with the force inside him. Nicholas staggered with the enormous effort required to protect her. Battered by unknown forces, he felt a rushing in his ears, and he was blind, fully inside Akshara, time-slipped, acutely, painfully aware of its shortcomings.

If only he had *koryoku*, the access to what he knew had once existed and could again: *Shuken*, the whole of Akshara and Kshira, the power of the Dominion.

All at once, the rushing in his ears became a howl, and the cold sweat broke out on his goose-fleshed skin because he knew that Akshara was not enough to win this battle. The reverberations the Messulethe had set in motion at *kokoro* were so powerful that they were threatening to tear him apart, and he knew he had to get them away, now, or they would both be finished.

Already he could feel his protection cracking, slipping away from Celeste, leaving her open and vulnerable to the Messulethe's assault. The most appalling noise filled Nicholas's mind, making rational thought impossible. He knew he was at the limits of his power; he felt weak and ineffectual against this malignant power which drove against him with the force of a piledriver.

In seconds, he knew, it would be over. He would be overwhelmed and Celeste, stripped of his protection, would be killed.

He did the only thing he could.

Stripping himself from Akshara, he closed his tanjian eye and, returning to real time, opened his physical eyes. He saw the Messulethe, concentrating, his face lined and sweat-beaded with effort.

His protective force had been withdrawn, and he knew he had only precious instants to act before Celeste's mind would be pulverized beneath the Messulethe's relentless assault.

He reached down, hefting a chunk of concrete from the rent sidewalk and, without conscious thought, hurled it as he would a *shuriken*, a steel throwing-star.

The Messulethe must have heard the whirring of the missile as it neared him, but he was time-slipped, his focus narrowed to the diameter of a filament as he concentrated his psychic power.

Awareness came too late. The concrete slammed him backward, throwing him off his feet.

Nicholas raced toward Celeste, on her knees in the street. Traffic blared as a taxi bore down on her despite the driver desperately applying his brakes.

The harsh squeal of brakes, the smell of burned rubber, accompanied him as he charged through the throngs, leaped between a pair of thick iron posts, driven into the pavement to prevent Parisian drivers from parking along the corner.

He left his feet because it was the only chance now, the taxi terribly close. He could smell its exhaust, see the front tires as they left marks on the street.

Tucking his head down he rolled in a ball, increasing his momentum, came up beside her after one revolution, put his arms hard around her waist, yanked her up and over one shoulder, his head toward the far side of the street.

The taxi, brakes screaming, went through the spot where she had fallen, screeched to a halt some feet beyond. But by that time Nicholas had regained his feet, had scooped Celeste into his arms, and was carrying her away from the curious crowds, the blaring horns, the stunned cab driver, and the scorching psychic afterburn like the stench of the flowers of evil.

Francie giggled. 'Gotta go, Mom, but could I have fifty? We're hitting the movies later.'

Then she began to sob, still lying in Croaker's arms.

Margarite's face was a mask of agony. 'Francie, darling –'

'Oh, God, oh, God!' The tears whipped off Francie's face. 'I can't go on like this.'

'Come on, Francie,' Margarite said, reaching for her. 'I'm going to take you home.'

'No!' The girl shrank away, into Croaker's chest. 'I'm not going home. I'll die at home!'

'Francie –' But she stopped, looking into Croaker's eyes. Margarite could read him, knew what he wanted to do, knew from speaking to the

253

psychiatrist that sometimes a stranger could be of more help than a family member, particularly a parent.

'Francie, I'm not going to do anything you don't want,' Croaker said. 'I'm going to pick you up and take you out of here.'

'We're not going home!' she cried. 'I don't want to go home.'

'Not home,' Croaker said. 'Somewhere where you and I can talk. Okay?'

Francie looked down at his biomechanical hand. 'I want to hold that,' she whispered, her eyes wide.

Croaker closed his fingers into a tight fist and Francie wrapped her hands around it. 'Now no one can hurt me,' she said, almost to herself. She nodded and Croaker scooped her up in his arms.

'Is there a back way out of here?' he asked Margarite.

She had been about to protest, control stripped from her, but she could see that her daughter was already calmer.

She nodded. 'This way. I'll take care of the bill – and alert the bodyguards so they don't break your arms.'

She met them a moment later beside the Lexus coupé. The bodyguards had kept a discreet distance but they had not yet piled into their car. Margarite came hurrying up, unlocked the Lexus. Croaker took the back seat with Francine.

'Where should we go?' she asked.

'Why don't we just stay here for the moment,' Croaker suggested. 'Okay with you, Francie?'

She nodded, silent, tearful, snuggled against his muscular shoulder. She began to sniffle.

'Now I want to ask you some questions,' he said softly, 'but I want you to remember something. You don't have to answer any of them.'

Margarite sat behind the wheel, half turned round, staring at Croaker and her daughter in the rear-view mirror.

'Can you tell me why you felt like you were going to die back there?'

'I still feel that way.'

'You do? Why?'

She shrugged. 'I just feel that way.'

'Okay, what's it feel like?'

'Blackness. Just . . .' Words failed her and she squeezed her eyes shut. She was weeping again, silently this time.

Croaker did not touch her, did not in any way acknowledge she was in distress. 'Francie, who's your favorite actress?'

'Jodie Foster,' Francie said, wiping her nose.

'Okay, pretend you're Jodie Foster,' Croaker said. 'You're on the set of a movie. Let's see, *Terminator 4*.'

The girl giggled. 'That's silly. Jodie Foster wouldn't be in *T4*. Linda Hamilton would.' But she had stopped crying and definitely seemed more alert.

'What if they couldn't get Linda Hamilton? Maybe they'd pick you. Okay?'

'Yah.'

'Now think of what happened back in the restaurant as a scene from the film. Think of the feeling as a *thing*, as something to scare you so you can bring back what you felt back there. Get the picture set in your mind. Now describe it to me.'

Francie closed her eyes. 'I'm in a car, not like this one, but bigger. Riding through the country. It's night and very dark. I'm supposed to be ... asleep, but I'm not. I'm awake, lying in the back seat, listening to the voices, staring out at the night sky.' Her lids fluttered. 'That sky, so close and black ... blacker than black – like being under a thick blanket in the summertime ... no stars, no clouds ... stifling ...'

She gave a little gasp and her eyes flew open. They were terrified.

'It's okay,' Croaker said, holding her tight. 'You're safe here with your mother and me.' But he followed Francie's gaze, saw that Margarite was sitting with her head lowered, her hands over her face.

'Mom?' Francie said tentatively. 'It was you I heard ...'

'Hush, baby.'

'You and that ... man.'

Margarite's fingers closed into fists, and she said in a strangled voice, 'Oh, my detective, how I wish you had never come into our lives.'

'He said he knew more about Uncle Dom than you did, Mom.' The girl obviously needed to talk now, to free herself from the unconscionable trauma that had been crippling her. 'He said that you held my life in your hands, and you said, "You don't have to keep threatening me, I understand the situation". Then, later, as we were pulling into one of those motels along the highway, he said, "Right now you think of me as the Devil but later, months after it's all over, you'll know the truth", and when he got out of the car you began to cry.'

Margarite was crying now, her shoulders hunched, the sobs torn out of her in racking spasms.

Croaker waited a moment before he asked, 'What man?'

'He's why I'm going to die.' Francie looked at him. 'He's going to come back and kill me. The man who killed Caesar and then killed Uncle Dom.'

TEN

Tokyo/Paris/Venice/Old Westbury/Washington

Nangi tried to decide at what point he had become aware of the white Toyota. Had it been when his driver had accelerated away from the traffic light in Shinjuku or even before that, when they were closer to the office?

He tried to clear his mind. 'Tell me what you know about Vincent Tinh,' he said to Seiko.

'I've known him for years,' she said. 'He used to date a friend of mine. That's how we met. It was at a party, I think. Singapore. Well, it was a long time ago, but I remember he impressed me right away. He was very clever and not at all the trusting sort. You can't afford to be trusting in Southeast Asia.'

'So you've followed his career, more or less?'

Seiko shook her head. 'Not really, but it seemed I couldn't avoid him. His name kept popping up as he brokered billion-dollar deals – electronic factory start-ups in Kuala Lumpur, computer manufacturing in the Philippines, high-tech import-export work in Vietnam. But solid deals, leading-edge stuff. He was the wizard middle-man. It seemed to me he not only knew all the right people but knew how to handle them. So when Linnear-san asked me to recommend someone for Saigon I automatically thought of Vincent.'

'Did you hear of anything illegal he was involved in?' Nangi asked.

'Illegal?' Seiko seemed startled.

Nangi nodded. 'The Saigon police inspector intimated that Tinh might have been dealing drugs, that this activity might have been the reason for his death.'

'But you said Vincent's death was accidental.'

'That's what the police are calling it but, reading between the lines, Chief Inspector Van Kiet privately felt it was murder.'

'It's all so strange,' she acknowledged. 'There was the matter of someone claiming to be a family member picking up the body. I did as you asked, got the telephone number of Avalon Ltd in London. The person I spoke to there assured me he had never heard of the man.'

'Well, that was to be expected. What business is Avalon Ltd in?'

'High-tech import-export,' Seiko said.

'Just as Tinh used to be,' Nangi mused. 'Curious, but I'm certain it's just a coincidence.'

Seiko lowered her head. 'I take full responsibility for Vincent Tinh, Nangi-san.'

'Nonsense. You did what you thought was right. Besides, at this point there's no proof that Tinh was involved in anything illegal.'

But part of his mind was back at the office where Masamoto Goei and his Chi team were still dissecting the neural-net clone computer, trying to discover what technology made it run besides the section of Chi boards Goei's men had already identified. A sense of foreboding darkened Nangi's thoughts every time he called Goei for an update and was told no substantive progress had been made, except that the other boards were of American design. Where had this clone come from, and who had spirited out technology to reproduce the Chi boards?

The white Toyota moved in the periphery of his vision.

'Still, I – what is it?' Seiko saw the peculiar twist of his head.

'We're being followed,' Nangi said.

Seiko turned round, peered through the BMW's rear window. 'Which one?'

'Wait,' he said, 'and watch.'

He leaned forward, tapped his driver on the shoulder in a particular cadence. At once, the BMW swerved to the left-hand lane, took the first left with a screech of brakes and protesting tire rubber. A moment later, a white Toyota turned the corner, and Nangi said, 'That one.'

'Can we get away from them?' she asked nervously.

Nangi folded his hands over his dragon-headed walking stick, said, 'Why on earth would we want to do that?'

Seiko gave him a curious look. Her hand closed with some pressure over the door handle. 'We're slowing down.'

'That's right.' Nangi opened his door even before the BMW had come to a complete halt. 'Perhaps now we'll begin to get some answers.'

The white Toyota screeched to a halt just in front of the BMW, its rear end angled outward, blocking the other car's way. Nangi emerged from the BMW in time to see a tall, slim man unfold from behind the wheel of the white Toyota. He wore a dark sharkskin suit and black wraparound glasses. This rather insectoid creature waited with the open door between him and Nangi. Nangi could see his pistol bulging beneath his jacket. Yakuza.

257

Slowly, the front passenger-side door of the Toyota opened and a burly man appeared. He had a pock-marked face and blunt mouth, and eyes that quartered the environment every fifteen seconds.

He bowed, paid his respects in formal Yakuza fashion, giving his name, place of birth and his clan affiliation.

The Yamauchi, Nangi thought. He had met Tomoo Kozo, the *oyabun*, only once. What could this man want with him?

The burly man rose, and said, 'Please send the woman away with your driver. You will be in our care today.'

Nangi's driver moved and the insectoid's gun was out in a flash.

'There's no need for this,' Nangi said.

'I have my instructions to bring you,' the burly man said. 'The method is entirely up to you.'

Nangi nodded. He bent down, said something to his driver, then slammed his door shut.

Seiko's pale face was in the window. 'Nangi-san –'

'Go home,' Nangi said. 'Nothing will happen to me.'

'How can you trust them?'

But he was already limping toward the white Toyota, relying more than he had to on the dragon's-head cane. When he came abreast of the Toyota, the insectoid opened the rear door for him. He got inside, and the burly man joined him in the back seat. Then the insectoid slid behind the wheel, slammed into gear, and the white Toyota took off.

Nangi sat back against the cloth of the back seat, his hands curled around the carved head of his cane.

'Where are you taking me?' he asked.

The burly man turned his pock-marked face toward him. 'Today is not the same as yesterday,' he said with a smirk. 'Your protector may no longer be among the living.' A gold tooth flashed. 'Mikio Okami is missing.'

Celeste was screaming.

She came awake with a violent shudder, as if forced from theta to alpha, from sleep to consciousness, by a clawed fist. Sitting straight up in the bed, her forearms crossed protectively over her face, she screamed.

Nicholas, who had been sitting very close to her, came and pried her forearms apart, imposing himself into her field of vision, trying with the force of his mind to exclude the nightmare image, dredged up from the swamp of her subconscious, that swam with sharp teeth and razor-tail behind her eyes.

258

Celeste.

He spoke with his mind, to calm her, and because she would not hear him over her screams. But, oddly, this made her all the more frantic. He let go of her wrists and, when he was certain she was focused on him, moved back off the bed. In the end, he stood quite still, breathing slowly, in and out, until she was finished, until her mind, lagging in the aftermath of severe shock, could surface on its own from the depths of the nightmare.

When she had stopped screaming, he picked up the phone, spoke quietly to the day manager to assure him that everything was all right, it was Mademoiselle remembering how close the taxi had come to hitting her, she was fine now, *merci*, but perhaps an *infusion menthe* to calm Mademoiselle's nerves.

He replaced the receiver, said to Celeste, 'It's all right. You're safe now.'

But she was shaking her head, fear a dark stain, widening, in her eyes. 'No. It's not all right. You're still here.'

And then he understood it all, and he said, 'Celeste, it's time you told me about yourself.'

She turned her head to the wall.

'You can't hide from me, you see.'

She wrapped her arms around herself for warmth, for shelter.

'Celeste, I'm not the enemy.'

'Everyone is the enemy.'

Of course, he could see how she would think that. There was a knock at the door and, opening it, Nicholas took the tray from the waiter, put it on the desk. He signed the check, closed the door to the room.

When Celeste had accepted the mint herbal tea from him, he said, 'It's so simple, isn't it? You knew what an awful time I had spent here years ago; and you knew it was because of a woman.'

Celeste said nothing, instead put the edge of the cup to her lips. She would not look at him, but it didn't matter now.

'But more than that, you foresaw the Messulethe adept's appearance in the Marais. It was only the street you got wrong.'

The cup fell from her lifeless fingers and its steaming contents spilled onto the bedcovers. She seemed unaware of anything but the sound of his voice. He reached out with his psyche to enfold her in his protection, but she flinched and cried out.

'Keep away from me!' Her voice a dry rasp. 'We're two of a kind, aren't we?' She shuddered. 'Dear God, what dreadful irony that I should call on you for help!'

'You're wrong,' Nicholas said, and something in his tone made her turn her head. 'You and I are quite different – the talents we possess –'

'Talents!' There were tears standing in the corners of her eyes and her body was vibrating with a series of tiny spasms. 'You call this a *talent*, this . . .' She shuddered again and, for the first time, looked down, saw the mess on the bedspread in front of her. Her eyes flicked up at him. 'So you'll understand, I did not tell you the whole truth about my mother.' Down again at the wet stain because she could not now maintain contact as she was drawn backward in time.

'She died when I was six. We had – how shall I describe it? – a *difficult* relationship. She and my father were always at odds, or so it seemed to me at the time. *At the time.* That's all that matters, isn't it? In the reverse telescope of memory, I understand what an insufferable brat I was, how cruel I was to her. But only now; not then. Then I only knew that she hurt my father and that in return I must hurt her.'

There was a long silence. Nicholas could hear her breathing, would perhaps have sensed what was going on inside her, but in prudence kept his psyche well heeled inside himself.

At length, Celeste drew a deep, shuddering breath and her eyes closed. When her lips moved, her whispered words had a ghostly quality. 'I *saw* what was going to happen to her: the fire, her death, *everything*. I saw it in my mind like a film and I said nothing, *did* nothing to help her.' Her eyes opened and, looking into his, they had a haunted aspect; they were magnified by tears. 'I could have saved her. Why didn't I?'

So this was the truth: not only fear of herself but a crippling guilt as well.

'You were too young,' he said and, in response to her withering look, added, 'Look at yourself, Celeste. You're still too young to understand, let alone control, your talent.'

'That word again.' She squeezed her eyes shut, shuddered. 'You can't control a gift from the Devil. It just *is*.'

'Whatever it is,' he said softly, 'it's a part of you.' He came and sat on the edge of the bed. 'You were six, Celeste. Can you say with all honesty that you knew what you saw was the future? That it was actually going to happen to your mother? Or could you have thought that it was an idle wish?'

'A wish, yes. I –' But the words caught in her throat, and she began to gag, so that Nicholas reached out to hold her close to him, and only this near her could he hear the tissue-thin keening of her words, forced at last from her throat:

'But maybe not just an idle wish, a passing fancy, but an . . . evil desire that . . . with this thing, this *power* . . . I caused to happen.'

260

She was sobbing now, and Nicholas rocked her, holding her tight, all the fear and tension sluicing from her as her heart broke open and poured forth the blackness she had been holding in check for so many years.

'Celeste, listen to me,' he said in her ear, 'no one, not you or me or that Messulethe out there – *no one* – can create the future. What you saw was happening, perhaps even as you saw it. You were six, Celeste, a small child. Think. Even if you had gone to your father and told him what you had seen, would he have believed you? Why would he? You must accept the fact that at six you were powerless to help your mother.'

'But I didn't want to help her.' Her head on his shoulder, a child again.

'That feeling you must deal with,' he said, stroking her hair. 'But that's another matter, entirely.'

'I don't want to spend the rest of my life hating her.' Her breath was slowing as she calmed. 'I want to love her.'

'Then you've got to forgive her ... and forgive yourself.'

She slept then, for a while, curled in a ball, her face to the windows, where the gauzy curtains filtered the last of the late afternoon sun as it fell into the green copper lake of the rooftops. Nicholas put on a light jacket of black cotton, slipped out the door.

Margarite drove very fast, overtaking cars and trucks at will. Croaker was glad he had his seatbelt fastened. She had become quite distraught and he wanted to know why.

She turned through the gates of her estate, nodded to the two goons who were lounging around smoking and keeping their hands warm in case, Croaker supposed, they needed to grab their guns quickly. A spray of gravel was left in their wake as she kicked the Lexus round the last curve to the house.

In the silence after she switched off the ignition, Croaker could hear the Rottweiler barking forcefully. The dog and its handler came into view. It was up on its hind legs, its mouth open, tongue lolling wetly. As soon as Margarite stepped out of the car it came down on all fours, snorted, then returned to its panting and restless padding.

Croaker looked at Margarite over the low-slung car-top as she drew Francie out beside her.

'I want Francie out of this environment right now. I can see how Tony and I are destroying her. I've got a friend in Connecticut who she can stay with.'

'Tony won't like it,' Croaker warned.

'Fuck Tony,' she said, as her daughter slipped her arms around her waist. She kissed the top of Francie's head, said quietly, 'Darling, go inside

261

and ask Mikey to help you pack.' Still the girl was reluctant to part from them. 'Go on, sweetie,' Margarite said.

Francie stood staring at Croaker. At length, she said, 'Will I see you again?'

'Promise.'

She gave him one last look, then turned and ran up the front steps, into the house.

'The Rottweiler ought to go to Connecticut with her.'

'What for?' Margarite said. 'He's already killed one dog – he'll just do it again if he wants her.'

'I don't want anything to happen to her.'

She gave him an ironic smile. 'What an extraordinary thing to say, my detective.'

A wise guy appeared at the front door to the house. 'You want Francie to get packed, Mrs D.?'

'That's right, Mikey,' she said. 'Do it now before Mr DeCamillo gets home.'

The wise guy seemed uncertain, then nodded, went back inside.

For a moment, Margarite was silent with indecision. Unknown emotions flickered in her eyes. At last she said, 'What am I going to do, Lew? He was here. He killed two of my staff and Caesar.'

Croaker felt his heart thudding heavily against his chest. 'But that isn't all he did, is it, Margarite?'

'No.' Her voice had dropped to a hoarse whisper. 'He went after Francie, threatened to kill her. He would have; I saw that much in his eyes. God, no wonder she's so freaked out.' The estate had acquired a preternatural stillness, the kind beneath which a trained ear could sense the first onset of electrical energy that presaged a major storm.

'He drugged Francie, hung her upside down in her room as an example for me to see.' She took a deep, shuddering breath. 'Then we sat and waited for the phone to ring. He told me Dom was going to be calling and that I was to set up a meeting without his WITSEC handlers. That was easy; it's what Dominic wanted. He'd been told that Tony was beating up on Francie.' The amber eyes seemed haunted, like a roomful of mirrors.

Croaker went on when it was clear she couldn't. 'Then Robert forced you to take him to your brother – all the way to Minnesota.'

Her head went down. 'Oh, Christ, what he did to me.' She was shaking with the memory. 'He made me an accomplice to my own brother's murder.'

Gaunt was waiting in a dingy bar on the outskirts of Chinatown. He was nursing a Jack Daniels and feeling like hurling himself into the Potomac.

262

Was there such a thing as death by pollution? Sure, it happened every day: death by exposure to radon, plutonium, radar guns, microwaves, even above-ground high-tension wires. Who said living in the country was healthier than the city?

Gaunt, seated in one of the booths in the bar's rear, stared into the amber corn liquor and contemplated his current situation. Strictly No Exit.

He knew enough about the Chi Project to be frightened by what Davis Munch, the Pentagon investigator, had told him. The Chi Project was supposedly still in the development stages, but that could mean anything from 'We've got shit-all' to 'We're about to roll out a production model and beat the competition six ways from Sunday'. He also suspected that the Chi technology roughly paralleled that of Hyrotech-inc's Hive computer. Nicholas, prescient as usual, had embarked on his own project when it became clear that his bid to buy Hyrotech was going to be stymied. From the limited knowledge disseminated within Sato-Tomkin, Gaunt understood that the Chi computer would be several steps advanced from the Hive technology.

At this time of the day, somewhere between dinner and drunk-as-a-skunk, the bar was crowded. A beery, smoky smell permeated everything, killing all color, all sense of time and place, which was just the sort of atmosphere that attracted the denizens of this kind of watering hole. In his current mood, Gaunt felt perfectly at home here.

Had Nicholas somehow managed to steal proprietary elements from Hive or was someone neatly trying to frame him with Senator Rance Bane's Strategic Economic Oversight Committee? Perhaps it was the Senator himself, or was it merely that Bane had an agenda, and Nicholas fit neatly into it?

Men in business suits, women in skirts and slacks, lounged up front at the boomerang-shaped bar, half slurring comments between overloud, horsey laughs, leaning in that way, intense and nonchalant, that only seasoned drunkards can achieve. Gaunt watched them with a jaundiced eye, trying very hard not to be reminded of his mother.

He knew that whichever scenario turned out to be the truth, McNaughton was right in urging him to walk away from Sato-Tomkin and his ties to Nicholas. Of course, he was already technically in the mess since the Committee had served him with a subpoena, but he was an old political hand and he could decipher McNaughton's code. If he walked away now, McNaughton could still save him. There was still a limited amount of time for him to flex his political muscles before the Committee sat at its first session at the beginning of next week. After that, Gaunt would be strictly on his own. Once the Committee got to him, there was no string

McNaughton could pull that would be sufficient. Gaunt would, as McNaughton had said, go down with the ship.

Gaunt, who had been diligently watching the front door, did not see the figure until it slipped into his booth.

'They make Emergency Exits for people like me,' the figure said to him.

'Timothy Delacroix?'

'That's me.' The man sitting at right angles to him did not offer his hand, but then again neither did Gaunt. He was a sandy-haired man in his mid-forties who at some time or other had gotten more than his fair dose of sun and wind. As a result, the skin of his nose, cheeks and forehead seemed permanently flayed, red and deeply lined as would flesh that had been wounded many times over without having had time to properly heal. Delacroix's eyes were so pale as to appear colorless, and he licked his lips incessantly. His face possessed a great deal of character, like T. E. Lawrence's – not hard, but reconstructed by curious and scarifying adventures.

'You're a friend of Munch's,' Delacroix said.

'We know each other.'

'Whatever.' Delacroix shrugged. 'He told you to ring me so you must be in bad fuckin' shape.'

Halfway back to Washington his gum had started to bleed again, and Gaunt had reached into his pocket for the handkerchief Munch had given him to stanch the flow. Something had dropped out, onto the floor of the car.

He had not been able to pull over onto the shoulder of the road until he was in the city. Then he had bent down, retrieved a scrap of paper with a name and a phone number scribbled on it: Delacroix's. Well, what do you know, he had thought, the investigator's more sentimental than he let on.

'Okay,' Delacroix said now as he tapped the none too clean tabletop with his forefinger and licked his peeling lips, 'I get distress calls like yours 'bout seven or eight times a year – more 'n' you thought, huh?' He winked. 'Well, don't you worry. Assuming you've got the shekels, I can do anything, and I do mean anything. You need transpo no one can catch? Believe it or not, I've got a mint-condition Lockheed SR-71. Hits mach 3 while other jets are still on the runway. Or how about an F-15? You heard me right. An F-fucking-15! You got an East Asian dignitary flying into Bangkok you want blown out of the sky, you need to break into some concrete and lead-lined cache somewhere in Africa, you want to keep a local uprising in Eastern Europe going' – he spread his hands wide – 'I'm your man.'

'Pardon me?' Gaunt said, abruptly disoriented.

264

Delacroix was waving his hands as if he expected to take off any minute. 'Okay, not your scene. I get it. Something more subtle is required here. I can do that, too. You need a Python-600 hand-held mortar, a Badger laser-sighted, infra-red lock-on flamethrower? What?'

'What in the name of creation do you do, anyway?'

'You mean Munch didn't clue you in?' Delacroix looked offended, his yellow teeth playing with the skin on his lips. 'I don't get it. Everyone else he sends me knows who I am. They're only too happy to pay for my services.' He grunted unhappily. 'It's not like people in my line grow on trees, you know.'

'And your line is . . .' Gaunt asked hopefully. His mouth was throbbing again and he held it tight, tasting his own blood.

'Christ, man, I have it all. I have access to any weapon or machine of war imaginable – within some limits, of course. I can't get a Stealth bomber, but neither I guarantee can my competition, despite their claims to the contrary.'

'But I don't need –' Gaunt stopped, trying to reason it out.

'Oh, great,' Delacroix said, throwing up his hands in disgust. 'I suppose I won't even get a free dinner out of this.'

'Don't worry,' Gaunt said hastily. 'We'll go wherever you want that's open this late. It's on me.'

'Jeez, I don't know,' Delacroix said, pointedly looking at his watch. 'In a trade like mine, time is money.'

'I have money,' Gaunt said, swirling some Jack Daniels around his wounded gum. 'Now I just have to figure out how you're going to earn it.'

He ordered a Jack Daniels for Delacroix, and they finished their drinks together.

'First things first,' Delacroix said pragmatically, when they had settled themselves into a Chinese restaurant two blocks away where everyone appeared to treat him like a long-lost brother. 'Just what is the nature of your problem?'

Without waiting for an answer, he then turned to an expectant waiter and proceeded to spew out a long stream of what might have sounded like invective except that it was Cantonese. Had Gaunt not just seen these two men treat each other as intimates, he could have mistaken this conversation for an argument.

'We're having whatever's fresh, that had better suit you,' Delacroix said, as the waiter scuttled away and he turned back to Gaunt.

'It doesn't matter,' Gaunt responded. 'I'm not hungry.'

The hands flew. 'While you're at my table, you'll eat.'

Gaunt would have pointed out that he was paying for this meal, but this man's enthusiasm seemed to have gotten to him. Somewhere between here and the bar his depression had lifted.

He said, 'The problem is this: I have four days to figure out if my boss is masterminding a huge computer swindle – which, I will admit, I cannot believe.'

Those waving hands again. 'Fuck what you believe or don't believe. You have this problem – you're probably in a position to know dick about what he's doing.'

Gaunt hated to admit it but Delacroix was right. He said, 'The other possibility is that someone – probably someone high up in the US Government – is trying to railroad my boss by planting false info for others to find.'

'That it?'

'Stripped to its bare bones, yes.'

'Um hum.' Delacroix sat with his head on a pedestal made from his fists. 'You don't need me. You need some kind of wizard investigator, which I'm not, though I've got to say in all honesty there was that time in the Sudan when –' The hands again, whirring in the air. 'But that's neither here nor there. See, this isn't my thing. I'm into more of a wham-bam-thank you-ma'am kind of thing, know what I mean?'

'Firepower.'

'Yeah. Right. I deal in nice little wars. The breakup of the Communist bloc's meant a bonanza for people like me. All these ethnic minorities chafing to flex their ethnic and religious muscle, ready to bash the other guy over the head with whatever's available. That's where I come in. I make sure the weapons of war and destruction are on hand. For instance, I got this computer-guided gunship. I'm talking state-of-the-fucking-art, Persian Gulf War in your face kind of thing. None of that surplus 'Nam stuff my competition's running specials on. I mean, man, this baby's loaded with weapons that can put some mean *hurt* on you.'

'Given that,' Gaunt said, stepping in before Delacroix gave him an offer he couldn't refuse, 'I'm trying to figure out why Munch gave me your number.'

The food came, looking wet, gooey and not very appetizing. Smelled good, though, Gaunt thought.

Delacroix was busy spooning what looked like blue-backed crabs in some kind of thick white sauce onto two plates. 'You mean he didn't say?'

'Uh uh.'

'Then for Christ's sake stop dicking around and ask him!'

'Not possible,' Gaunt said, watching his plate fill up with scallops, squid

266

and sticky rice. 'If he'd been able to tell me I'm sure he would have. No, he's on the opposition's side. I've got to figure it out on my own.'

At Delacroix's behest, beer came, a whole copper cooler full, at least a dozen bottles of '44 stuck in shaved ice.

Delacroix popped a couple of bottles and waded into his food. 'That boss you were talking about, he in deep shit with the Feds?'

'You could say that.' Gaunt stared at his plate, daunted. 'In four days a Senator Rance Bane's Committee will convene in a session that could convict him of treason and shut down the entire American division of Tomkin Industries.'

Delacroix picked his head up. His lips were greasy and a tip of blue crab claw was sticking out of his mouth. He spit it hastily out. 'You mean Tomkin, as in Sato-Tomkin?'

'Yeah. Why?'

Delacroix's pale eyes were big and round as he goggled. 'Christ, I deal with those people all the time,' he said. 'That's fucking why.'

ELEVEN

Paris/Washington

Night. A glaucous fog descending like the gauzy wings of an angel. The threat of rain, bringing with it the intensified odors of automobile exhaust and soot.

Below him, Nicholas could see the horse-chestnut trees sheared into the shape of the letter 'L' at the four corners of the Place des Vosges. He looked up into the Parisian sky, which was filled with garish fire from streetlights along the wide boulevards and circles, the spotlights around the Eiffel Tower reflecting off the low-hanging clouds like smears of rouge on a tart's over-made-up face.

The rain, when it came, was a friend because it helped hide him, but it was also an enemy because it made the patinaed copper tiles of the mansard roof treacherously slick.

In the midst of taking a cautious step he froze, crouched down in low profile as, below him, a cop car made its slow circuit of the square. At the corner bistro, there was more activity now than there had been during the day, young people spilling out into the colonnade and beyond, onto the street. Some of them could see him if they looked upward. He must give them no cause to do so.

The roof was at a forty-five degree angle, good for keeping the inside of the building dry, but extremely difficult to negotiate without a roofer's secured platform.

Directly ahead and slightly below him was the dormer window, his entrance to the building that housed Avalon Ltd. The problem was that the window was closer to the square side of the roof than he would like. He calculated he would need perhaps twenty to thirty seconds to get the window open and lever himself in, more if there was an alarm system. During that time he would be fully exposed to those passing below in the Place des Vosges. It would be foolhardy to assume that no one would chance to look upward during that time; in fact, he was going under the assumption that someone would. The trick was to present a silhouette that would cause no questions to be raised.

268

Nicholas was dressed all in matt black. Before he had left the hotel room he had confiscated Celeste's kohl, and now he applied it to his cheeks, nose, forehead, and the edges of his ears, the backs of his hands. From his pocket he drew out two objects he fitted over his palms. These *nekode*, which he had designed and made himself, were a kind of lightweight ridged chainmail which covered his palms, allowed him to grip slick surfaces.

Then he stretched himself head-first along the roof and, placing his palms firmly against the roofing, began to edge his way down.

Rain pattered on the copper, spitting bright bits upward into the glare of lights. The brittle tang of the metal was in his nostrils. He moved as he had been taught as a young boy, in a motion known as *kagiri nishiki*, where only one limb was moving at any time. Distance was crossed in painfully slow fashion, because breathing was prolonged to meditation rhythm, the entire body going slack for stretches of time. In this state, the prone human form, already distorted by the shadows of the night and the angle of the roof, appeared to dissolve, the parts flowing in different directions, so that it lost the aspect of a human form altogether.

Anyone glancing up on the roof would need to stare fixedly for quite some time at the spot where Nicholas lay in order to discern movement. Even then, that movement would most likely be mistaken for pigeons huddling out of the wet weather or rain sizzling off the copper roof.

Time ceased to have any meaning for Nicholas. He was in the semi-conscious state that Tibetan holy men attained when walking on fire or nails, when the conscious mind was pulled inward, sensation dulled throughout the body.

In this fashion, he reached the corner of the dormer without incident. A tendril of his mind pulled free of its centrism as his right hand explored the face of the dormer where the frame of the window met the sash of the dormer itself, and he was immediately alerted.

Wire.

An alarm system. But now, a blind man in the dark, he could feel a frayed edge of the insulation and, just a bit further on, a break that had been ineptly mended to make it appear as if the system was still intact. The two ends had come apart, and now Nicholas was certain that whatever connection had once been made was broken.

Using a *shuriken*, a thin sliver of edged steel, he popped the old-fashioned semi-circular lock. For a long moment, he lay still. He heard the city sounds all around him: the drift of voices from the bistro across the Place, the crunch of footsteps on gravel, the hiss of passing cars from beyond the enclosure of the square, and, closer, the intermittent coo of roosting pigeons.

269

He lifted the window a centimeter at a time, then slithered toward it. His head and shoulders were already in when his peripheral vision caught a bright flash and he froze.

He stayed that way, allowing his pupils to adjust to the darkness. He moved his eyes toward the left and picked up the flash again as if it were reflected off the curvature of his iris, and then he knew.

His chin was three centimeters from a wire-thin laser beam, more sensitive and reliable than infra-red. If any part of him intercepted it, an alarm would sound. No wonder the occupants had allowed the outmoded wire alarm to deteriorate.

Below him, the sill dropped away three feet to the wooden floor; he could see the dusty board gleaming in reflection from the ambient streetlight filtering through the dormer. If he could get down to the floor, and could drop to a prone position, he'd be underneath the laser wire. The problem was he had no room in which to maneuver – he was right up against the wire.

Now time was as much his foe as the lack of space. Half in, half out of the dormer, he was at his most vulnerable. He could not go down, he could not go forward, he could not stay where he was.

So he went up.

Raising his torso up on his palms, he brought his legs slowly through the open window by drawing up his knees against his chest. He was now in what was essentially a ball, and he shifted an infinitesimal amount in order to get his feet flat on the surface of the sash. In the process, his nose almost touched the laser wire. All movement ceased. His heart hammered in his chest, the flow of adrenalin escalated, and with it the lethal possibility of inadvertent motion.

He sought *prana*, the slow, cleansing inhalation and exhalation that brought oxygen all the way to the bottom of the lungs. He closed his eyes, concentrating on what he must do. He opened his tanjian eye, re-imagined the room, its dimensions clearer to him now than they had been with normal sight impaired by the intense gloom.

There was a cross-beam, so he had perhaps three feet of clearance above the laser wire. Always before, when he had tried this maneuver, he had had at least that much space. Now he knew he would have to use up no more than two and a half feet, or part of him – his forehead or his feet – would break the laser wire.

He gathered himself, sinking deeper into Akshara. Time shattered into 10,000 fragments and, like moonlight on water, became insubstantial. He could feel the pulse of *kokoro* as he summoned those forces of the universe locked deep inside him. He could feel the pulse running through him, like fire in his veins. More and more slowly the pulse beat until it ceased to throb at all.

Now.

He launched himself up and outward. Tumbling, he felt his head graze the top of the ceiling, a split instant, but enough to minutely change his trajectory. His arc was foreshortened and, with his tanjian eye, he could foresee the disaster of one foot breaking the laser wire.

He reached up, the *nekode* secured to his palms digging into the ceiling's cross-beam, swung there for a moment like a mad monkey, legs drawn up. He heard a creak, felt a trickle of sawdust: his temporary perch was sagging.

He took a desperate chance, holding on long enough for his momentum to swing him in another backward arc. He dropped a bit lower as the beam, rotten from past roof leaks, started to give way for real.

Then he was swinging forward and he let go, tumbling out into the blackness, the laser wire below, flashing past his whirling vision, a ruby needle, and then he was past it, on the other side, as he fell, tumbling still.

He hit the floorboards with a soft thump, rolled over on his back, his head tucked between his shoulderblades, as he came up on his haunches.

He was in.

It's not my mother I need to forgive, it's my father. This was Celeste's thought as she awoke into darkness. She had started up in bed, in that curious middle state suspended between living one life and another. Which was real, which the waking state and which the dream? For a long, uncomfortable moment, she could not decide.

The life she had been living was the one before her father was killed. Sacrificed, was it? as Okami-san had explained it to her. What she hadn't told him, what he would never understand, was that no amount of explanation would be sufficient to accustom her to her father's death. She didn't want explanations: she wanted him back.

Her father had been so Eastern that often Okami-san said jokingly to him that he was more Japanese than Venetian. He looked at problems from the inside out, and his solutions often baffled his competitors and helped him amass a small fortune, even by today's inflated standards.

Celeste stirred in the darkness of her Paris hotel room, not yet willing to acknowledge the reality of her present surroundings. What she wouldn't give to have her father alive and standing beside her. Anything. Even, she knew, Okami-san's life. She was pledged to defend him now, because this was her father's wish, but the truth was she despised Okami with a vitriolic passion. Only a true Venetian could understand how it could abide deep beneath the surface without showing its ugly face.

It was Okami who had come into their lives so many years ago, ensnaring them in a nest of vipers, a world largely of his own making filled with bitter enmities, ancient as oak.

His affinity for her step-mother, a schemer in her own right, had been instantaneous. Celeste had never trusted her step-mother, had hated and feared her. For one thing, as a Sicilian, she was an outsider; for another, she seemed to possess a dark power, an ability to weave a web of scandal and deceit that destroyed anyone who stood in her husband's way.

When Celeste grew older, she understood that Okami had helped her. Together, they had built a base of power which her father, alone, could not have done.

Celeste's world had revolved around her father. She had grown up with her older sister, sharing secrets in the dark, until, gradually, a pattern of knowledge she could not share with her sister overtook her.

She recalled the first time this had happened, she and her sister lying on their backs on a beach in the Lido, a sultry summer's day when the throngs in the Piazza di San Marco made movement all but impossible, when the walls of history all but disappeared behind phalanxes of human heads.

Staring up at lazy clouds, her sister seeing a griffin, an amorous couple, a stampeding horse within the billowing masses. Celeste had concentrated, trying to see the fantastic forms her sister was describing.

What she saw was the drowning, the air engulfed in darkness, a small, black-haired head, turning face upward as it bobbed in the ocean, then the wave coming down with such vivid clarity that Celeste had gasped, as if she, too, could no longer suck air into her lungs.

Then she was up and running, her mind reeling, her equilibrium as cock-eyed as a drunkard's, racing along the wet shoreline, stumbling over bathers who turned their sweating, oiled faces to stare open-mouthed at her.

Where was she running to? She had had no idea, except that the faster she ran the closer she seemed to come to . . . the Event. As if her pounding strides were crossing not distance but time, drawing her nearer to her vision, the drowning.

In the distance she could make out a commotion, young men wading into the breakers, shouting to one another, leaving their feet to knife their bodies beyond the place where the waves crashed in white spume, out to a dark spot in the water. The drowning.

Celeste felt like she wanted to vomit. The sense of death was so palpable that, for a black instant, it seemed more real than life. An intense sense of dislocation struck her so that she stumbled, living for a moment in eternity,

272

in two places at once and, being fully in neither one, she fell, her limbs no longer receiving the correct commands from her numbed brain . . .

'Nicholas!'

Celeste, in the bed of the Paris hotel, reached out in the dark for the body she expected to find beside her. She looked at the empty space and . . . in the dislocation that followed she saw him, knew precisely where he was because she, too, was there, in that way she had come to fear and abhor. And, in the last crystal instant of the dislocation, she became aware of the enemy not more than eight feet away, across the city, crouched and waiting in the darkness for him.

'Nicholas!'

Nicholas crouched in the darkness of the building that housed the offices of the mysterious firm of Avalon Ltd. All around him, the old building seemed to respire as if it were some being alive in light slumber. He felt that it would be perilous to wake it.

He crept out of the attic room into which he had dropped from the roof. He found himself on a narrow wooden landing. He opened his tanjian eye, and saw the steep pitch of the stairway directly in front of him. He descended, silent as a cat, faced obliquely down so that his feet were placed almost horizontally along each tread, distributing his weight more evenly and over a wider area of the tread. His balance was centered, so that his weight was at all times evenly distributed between both feet.

Halfway down the stairway he stopped, crouched motionless, listening with his ears and his tanjian eye. He could hear the rain beating against windowpanes, an occasional slap as the wind took a loose shutter against the face of the building, nothing more.

He was frightened now. He could recall with a suprareal precision the power of the Messulethe, and he knew he was no match for it. He had been lucky the last time, taking the Messulethe by surprise; he had no illusions about being able to do that again.

There was a time when nothing frightened him. But that was before the advent of Tau-tau, before a tanjian had gone to work on his brain, turning him *shironinja*, blocking all his powers. He was physically healed, had, in fact, learned of his tanjian heritage because of it. But there was embedded deep inside him a shadow on his soul. He understood now – as he had not when he was younger and more ignorant – the power of the Unknown. His *sensei* – the one man he had trusted with his very life – had turned out to be his enemy, and at the very core of him lingered a terror that what Kansatsu had taught him was in some way he had yet to understand inimical to him.

273

The Unknown.

The Messulethe was the Unknown, and he was out there, somewhere in the rain, in the Parisian night, waiting. The encounter this morning had confirmed a suspicion Nicholas had harbored ever since the Messulethe had led them to the palazzo where he had conjured the Kanfa bridge: the Messulethe had another agenda. Perhaps he had, indeed, been dispatched to murder Okami as Celeste believed. But, though Okami was missing, there was as yet no sign that he had been killed. Moreover, the Messulethe seemed to be concentrating on them. Of course, now that Okami was in one way or another out of the way, it might be natural for him to attach himself to the people pledged to guard him.

But the incident with the Kanfa bridge may have occurred before Okami had disappeared. This one possibility had stuck with Nicholas, making him wonder. The more he turned it around in his mind, the less sense it made, given the overall set-up within which he had been operating.

To go back to the beginning, if Okami was marked for extermination by a traitorous Yakuza *oyabun*, then why on earth was the assassin going after Nicholas and Celeste? Why waste the time and expose himself to potential danger? He had Okami out of sight; why not kill him and be done with it?

Two chilling possibilities occurred to Nicholas: either the Messulethe's assignment had not been to murder Okami, or the Messulethe did not have Okami. One possibility meant that Okami had lied to him, the other that he had totally misread the situation. Either answer would surely lead to a dire conclusion.

Filled with apprehension, he stepped onto the landing of the floor below and began a thorough exploration of the rooms there. What he discovered startled him. There were no workshops for mask-making, none of the paraphernalia one would normally expect in the business of supplying hand-made masks. In fact, if he'd had to guess, he would have said he was inside a company specializing in investments.

In the half-light coming in through the windows from the Place des Vosges he could make out banks of phones, faxes, computer work stations arrayed like sentinels, silent and ghostly. Desks, lamps, chairs, all the accoutrements of an office, except one thing. Files. There were no filing cabinets.

Nicholas stepped up to a computer terminal, turned it on. He stood there for an instant, transfixed by the blinking orange characters. A password code was required to get into the system. That, in itself, was hardly out of the ordinary. What was was that he was staring at a line of *kanji*: Japanese characters.

He turned off the computer, certain now that Avalon Ltd was not what it purported to be. He recalled Fornovo telling him that the company had been sold five years ago to a foreign company no one seemed able to identify.

What was it now?

He had no idea, but it was clear that it had been sold to a Japanese concern.

Nicholas froze. Something in his peripheral vision, the hint of a movement, reflected off the slightly curved fascia of the computer screen. Slowly, as if his body had turned to smoke, he sank to his knees. As he did so, he twisted until he was half facing the direction from which the movement had come. Nothing.

Slowly, he quartered the area, taking in each shape, identifying it if he could, coming back to it when he couldn't. In this methodical way, he took in the environment. He stayed in this uncomfortable position for a very long time, waiting.

He saw the movement again, this time nearer the center of his vision. It had reflected off the dark computer screen and now he could see it for what it was: a tangential spark from the headlights of a passing car. He gripped the edge of the work station's desk as he raised himself and felt the difference in surface texture on the underside beneath the pad of his thumb.

Moving beneath the desk, he tilted his head upward, saw the square plastic button, set flush into the melamine of the desk surface. He reached up, pressed it. It would not give. Then he saw beside it a lock, countersunk into the melamine so that it would not protrude.

He extracted another *shuriken*, inserted the sliver of steel into the lock. A moment later, the button gave beneath his thumb. Nothing seemed to happen. Then he rolled the chair away, moved the plastic pad and found an opening in the carpet. He drew out a box of a dozen 3½-inch floppy disks. On the box was written a numerical sequence.

He turned the computer on, took the first floppy, inserted it into the A drive. When the prompt for the password came up, he typed in the numerical sequence. The system rejected it. He reversed the order with the same effect. The computer flashed a warning that unless the correct password was entered within thirty seconds an internal alarm would sound.

He closed down the computer, sat staring at the blank screen, thinking of how to get in. He translated the numerical sequence into letters of the Western alphabet, turned on the computer to try that.

The computer booted up, the screen changing. He had forgotten to take out the floppy from the A drive and the computer was reading it first

275

instead of booting up from the C drive hard disk. The screen prompted him for a numerical sequence and Nicholas typed in the one he'd found on the box of floppies.

He was presented with a directory of files. He called up the first one, had perhaps ten seconds to read what appeared on the screen: dates of delivery for shipments of Chinese F-type fighter planes, Russian Tupolev-22M bombers, T-72 tanks, SAM-13 antiaircraft missiles, American F-15 fighters, Lockheed SR-71 supersonic jets, Badger computerized flame-throwers, Python-600 mortars, Deyrael hand-held antitank bazookas; the list seemed endless. It appeared as if Avalon Ltd was a clearing house, a middleman between suppliers, identified with numerical codes, and buyers in Iran, Iraq, Afghanistan, the Balkans, the new ethnic battlefields of the world where bitter warfare was just beginning in earnest.

And then, at the end of the list, he saw a short line of curious icons. He pressed the Help key and the icons resolved themselves into two words: ON ORDER. Meaning not yet available?

He scrolled to the end of the icons, pressed the Enter key, and saw: TORCH 315.

What the hell was that?

Ten seconds and then his world came crashing in.

The collapse was soundless, a kind of psychic implosion, and he thought, *I didn't sense him.*

The Messulethe!

He had not heard the beating against the membrane of *kokoro*, had been reasonably certain that for the moment, at least, he was safe.

He staggered beneath the assault, swinging around, thrusting his tanjian eye this way and that in a vain attempt to discover the location of the Messulethe. As before, he believed his only chance to survive the encounter was to come within physical proximity of the Messulethe. Arm's length would be preferable, but close enough to throw a live terminal at him would do.

But, as he had suspected, the Messulethe wasn't about to allow that to happen. Nicholas groaned as he went down to his hands and knees. There was a black weight in his mind, freezing his synapses, robbing him of the ability to string two thoughts together. The world was reduced to chaos, and then, shrinking still farther, was forged into a spike of gleaming steel whose point began to pierce the lobes of his brain.

He was going to die without even looking his antagonist full in the face. He did not know his name or who he was, could not even conjure a reason for this assault. But death was coming; that became the only surety in the closeness of his collapsed universe.

Nicholas!

He tried to center himself, to gather his forces at *kokoro*, but the path was blocked, strewn with barbed wire that repelled him as he tried to beat the drumhead at the center of the universe.

Akshara was inadequate and, again, the self-doubt crept through him, as insidious as a virus: Kansatsu's training contained within its very essence the seed of Nicholas's destruction. It would have been like Kansatsu, whose soul had been deformed by Kshira, to plan for the eventuality of defeat. Kansatsu had been the great deceiver, the spinner of schemes within schemes, and it would fit him to have devised a way to destroy Nicholas from beyond the grave.

Nicholas!

Akshara taught that there were seven paths to *kokoro*. All were blocked, and now the crushing pressure in his brain turned him blind and deaf. A great howling, as of a pack of hungry wolves, was making his ears bleed. Breath was coming hot in his lungs, as if he had been thrust into a furnace.

Red shapes moving against the black scrim of his maimed vision, eerie dreamscapes distorted as they were projected through his fevered brain, preternatural images from the dawn of man, race-memory glimpsed through a forest of pain and crushing pressure.

Nicholas!

Water running, the bell-like tones, working their way through the howling, the rising wind-storm. A filament of silence, iridescent and insubstantial as an insect's wing. Blindly, he reached for it, missed, and the howling increased, the fury of the wind-storm threatening to engulf him entirely, the cold hand of death laying its skeletal fingers on his breath, robbing him of . . .

Nicholas!

He heard her, understood its nature, spoke to her with his mind, though he was dizzy and sick unto death.

Here . . . It was all he could muster.

And the filament came down, a lifeline in the chaos, running through the core of him, wrapping itself around him, brushing aside the skeleton's grip, lessening the din of entropy, pulling him back from the abyss that had opened beneath him, the abyss beneath *kokoro*.

And now he saw what his antagonist's attack had blinded him to: he was directly underneath *kokoro*. This was why the seven pathways had been blocked, and he reached up, began the ritual tintinnabulation, setting the rhythm at the center of the universe that would transmogrify thought into action.

He allowed his tanjian eye to sleep, knowing now that the Messulethe's

277

psychic storm had rendered it dangerously unreliable. He opened his physical eyes and saw Celeste, crouched and shivering with terror, but there nonetheless, extending the psychic filament that had saved him.

And, behind her, the Messulethe.

In this excruciating moment of crisis, the last facet of the truth he had been withholding from himself made itself manifest: he couldn't let anything happen to her. He had been struck, crippled by love.

That was when his ears caught the susurrus, as if an insect were caught in a web. His attention diverted for an instant, his eyes picked up the bright flash, desperately transferring messages to his brain. And then the dagger, thrown directly at his chest, came hurtling out of the dark.

In all ways Renata Loti was an impressive woman. She was in her mid-seventies, tall, stately, evincing none of the outward infirmities which the years brought to other women her age. Her back was not bent, there was no tremor in her hands, no fragility in the way she moved. A slight but noticeable limp did nothing to deter her maneuverability or her stamina.

She's smart and *clever*, Delacroix, the arms dealer had told him, *which is hard to find in anyone, let alone a woman. She's an influence-peddler of rare distinction who specializes in the Asian theater. She's your man.*

Gaunt met her on the corner of Constitution and 17th Street, across from the Ellipse that fronted the White House. There was that odd sense, prevalent throughout the capital, of being in a countryside park rather than in the middle of an urban bustle, the broad, open spaces serving as a brilliant setting for Washington's primary contrasting elements of sky and imposing stone and cast-iron edifices.

Behind him rose the Renaissance splendor of the OAS building with its triple-arched entrances, massive bronze gates and curious statuary, a mish-mash of the Americas, North and South, which served as a reminder of how essentially incompatible the two cultures were.

Renata Loti had the strong, determined face of a woman who knew her way around the corridors of power, who had a clear sense of herself and of her purpose in life. If she had ever lost her credulity to the disillusionment of reality it would have been a great many years ago, but she evinced none of the world-weary cynicism or the unconvincing jingoism that pervaded Washington's political circles. Her jutting nose, high cheekbones, deep-set cerulean eyes and strong jawline made her a woman to be reckoned with wherever she went. She wore her hair in a short fringed cap. It was platinum, perhaps a touch wild for a woman her age, but certainly in keeping with her powerful personality.

She was dressed in a black, slubbed-silk suit, black alligator shoes and

278

matching handbag, and was wrapped in a stylish three-quarter-length black suede coat. She wore no jewelry save a glowing cabochon ruby ring on the finger where a wedding band would have been.

'Mr Gaunt?'

He nodded, and she smiled, showing just a flash of tiny white teeth.

'It's good of you to meet me at such short notice,' he said, shaking her hand.

'I knew your father. He was a man to be proud of.' She gave a little laugh. 'Besides, I was at a very dull play. When you paged me, I was already thinking about leaving. This gave me a good excuse.' Her head cocked at an angle, a young girl sizing up the new boy in class. 'You said you got my number from Timothy?'

'Timothy Delacroix, yes,' Gaunt said, as they began to walk. Renata indicated that they should sit on a bench just outside the OAS gardens. 'He said that you might be the only person in Washington able to help me.'

'How flattering.' But her face grew serious. 'I've known Timothy a long time. He never exaggerates.'

Gaunt filled her in concerning Senator Bane's interest in Tomkin Industries and Nicholas in particular. He ended up by saying, 'Now Delacroix tells me he's had dealings with Sato-Tomkin through our Saigon director, Vincent Tinh. If that's true, if we've been involved in some way with arms shipments, then I suspect Bane's Committee already has proof of it. The company is a dead duck. And Nicholas is liable to wind up in a Federal penitentiary for the rest of his life.'

'I know all about Tinh,' Renata said. 'I thought it intriguing that he'd become the Saigon director of Sato-Tomkin, and always wondered who set that up.'

Gaunt's ears immediately pricked up. 'What do you mean?'

'Tinh is very bad news – the worst, in fact. He's slick, gets things done on time and right, which is impressive in Southeast Asia. But he's a real entrepreneur in the worst sense – he'll deal in anything and everything if he sees a profit in it.'

'For the company?'

'For himself,' Renata said. She considered for a moment. 'I don't know Mr Linnear personally, but you can imagine in my field I've heard a good deal about him from a great many people. They say he possesses what the Japanese samurai called *bushi no nasake*, the tenderness of a warrior.' Her eyes, which were clear and lustrous, their color unfaded by time, looked out at the traffic on Constitution as she gazed inward. 'I am told he has excellent instincts. Do you agree, Mr Gaunt?'

'Yes. Absolutely.'

279

Renata nodded, as if receiving an answer already divined. 'I find it unlikely he would have hired Tinh on his own – someone very good must have sold Tinh to him.'

'It's interesting you'd say that,' Gaunt said excitedly. 'I've had a suspicion all along that Nicholas and the company have been set up to be guillotined by Bane.'

'Rance Bane is like a cancer racing through a sick body,' Renata said. 'He's a commanding force now, despite Senator Branding and the opposition's best efforts to control him. He has an unshakable power base, which means even those who despise him are forced to defer to him, so I'd be careful whom you talk to and what you say. Bane has many friends in Washington at the moment, not all of them out in the open.'

Gaunt nodded. 'Thanks for the warning, but I'm an old hand here. I know when to keep my mouth shut.'

'You're still in danger if you are determined to pursue the Vincent Tinh angle,' Renata said. 'Timothy doesn't know half of what Tinh's been into. Stolen arms shipments are only the top strata, if Tinh's past is any indication. Drugs, banned chemical weapons, high-tech military secrets, he's been involved in them all – and made a fortune at it.'

'If that's the case,' Gaunt said, curious, 'what was he doing taking a legit salaried job with Sato-Tomkin?'

'Undoubtedly opportunity,' Renata said. 'The legitimacy of the business and the set-up work he's doing for the company – and I would guess doing it quite well – would provide a perfect mask for his own business. These days it pays to be a bit less flamboyant with the kind of work Tinh loves best.'

'If someone set us up, I've got to find out who he is,' Gaunt said. 'That's the only chance we have of getting out of this alive.'

Renata was silent for such a long time she started to make him nervous. 'What are you thinking?'

She sighed, turned to look at him. 'I'm aware of too many eyes. Let's take a walk.'

It had begun to rain, but Renata, buttoning her coat, seemed undeterred. They left the Ellipse behind them, crossed over Constitution into West Potomac Park. As the ground began to slope downward, Gaunt was aware that they were heading toward the black duolith of the Vietnam Memorial. He could scent the Tidal Basin, south of the Reflecting Pool, and it brought back all sorts of memories, good and bad, of his previous life in this city.

The hissing of traffic along the wide avenue on their right gradually gave way to the night wind whispering in the last of the leaves on the trees.

280

Beside him, Renata Loti had no difficulty negotiating the incline. On the contrary, she clearly enjoyed the exercise, and they moved at a steady pace. Underfoot, the mulch of dead leaves provided a comforting susurrus that made him think of wet autumn days, steam coming off the ground, mixing with the layers of burnt orange and gold leaves to create a unique confluence of earthy odors.

He thought of his dead father, his stature in this city, knowing that he had beaten this place before it had risen up to beat him. There was a kind of solace in that knowledge, and for the first time since returning here, he was grateful that fate had dictated that he return, against his will.

Renata, her head down, her hands jammed in her pockets, seemed totally lost in thought. Droplets of rain glittered in her hair like diamonds. At last, she said, 'It seems to me that in your case, taking the most direct route may be the only way for you to find out who touted Nicholas on Vincent Tinh.' She paused, and he could see the breath steaming from between her half-opened lips. 'The problem is it's also the most dangerous.'

Delacroix's tip had been a good one, he suddenly decided. This was a special person. He felt confident with her, balanced in the net of her agile mind, and he felt a brief twinge of envy for whoever had been her husband or lover.

'I think there's someone in Washington who will know,' Renata said, 'but it will be exceedingly dangerous to approach him on the matter.'

They were at the first wing of the wall, gleaming black marble engraved with the names of the fallen. Rain struck the memorial, individual drops sliding down its slick face like tears down a cheek.

Renata stopped, stood staring at the wall for a moment. At her feet, a tiny American flag planted at the memorial's base fluttered in the wind, and rose petals torn from a bouquet lay scattered on the stone walk.

She swung toward him, very close, so that her exhalations fell upon him in tiny puffs. 'Remember I told you that there were people in Washington who supported Bane clandestinely? This man is one of them. He's high up in Bane's hierarchy but, like a spook, he publicly espouses another philosophy.'

Her eyes, dark and reflective, seemed hewn out of the same black rock as the memorial behind her.

'He may be vulnerable because he is sometimes indiscreet in his sexual life. I have only very recently come into a few excellent photos. I have been waiting for the most judicious moment to use them against him. So, it seems, our meeting is most fortuitous.'

In the rain-filled night, sheen and halo – the one indirect, the other ephemeral – made her appear many years younger. Gaunt found her both

281

desirable and inspiring, a potent combination. Seeing her in this glitter, he was reminded of a portrait he had once seen of Lucrezia Borgia, Caesare's sister. Both were illegitimate children, and a popular theory had it that this fact played a dominant role in their subsequent lust for power. Gaunt found himself for a moment swept up in the role he imagined for her.

'This man is connected to the nerve center of Rance Bane's machine,' Renata continued, 'and if you use the information I give you, he will tell you what you need to know.' She used a strong, working woman's forefinger, its clear-lacquered nail cut to a man's length, to wipe her cheek free of rain. 'And, who knows, perhaps because of this the whole of Bane's foul machine will begin to unravel.'

A chance to save the company! Gaunt was dizzy with the possibilities. Just a few short hours ago he was contemplating throwing himself in despair into the Potomac, and now look what his one-man investigation had turned up: the probability of a frame and a way to prove it.

'Tell me,' he said a little breathlessly. 'What's the man's name?'

The rain, striking her face, made it seem as if her pale skin was carved from marble. She said, 'William Justice Lillehammer.'

TWELVE

New York/Tokyo/Washington/Paris

'I want to confess everything,' Margarite said. 'But to you, not to the Federal Government.' She looked up into Croaker's face. 'Of all the people in my life, I only trust you.' She put her head against his shoulder. 'My God, how pathetic that sounds, even to me. You're the next thing to a complete stranger. What have I made of my life?'

'You told me when you got married you knew exactly what you wanted.'

'Oh, I did! Who am I now? I don't even recognize myself. Everything I've ever wanted has been rendered meaningless.'

They were in her Lexus, somewhere in the Connecticut countryside, after having dropped Francie off with Margarite's friend, a divorcee with her own at-home consulting business and an intelligent Scottie named Muirfield. She was a golfing enthusiast, and promised to teach Francie the game.

'I want to thank you,' Margarite said. 'Your effect on Francie has been extraordinary. I was worried back there that she wouldn't let you go.'

'She's a strong girl,' Croaker said. 'After all she's been through she still wants to live.'

'I'm afraid I've made quite a mess of both our lives.'

They drove in silence for some time. Because it was what was on his mind, he told her about his friendship with Nicholas. He recounted how they had met when they had both been tracking the man who had turned out to be Nicholas's cousin, the ninja Saigo, how they had been reunited in Japan when Croaker had lost his hand. As he did so, his words reconstructed the electrifying past for him to live all over again. But it was a mixed blessing; he found that he missed Nicholas with an almost physical sense of pain.

'I envy you that kind of friendship,' Margarite said wistfully. When she saw that they were headed toward Old Westbury, she said, 'No, I don't want to go home. I can't be there now.'

'But your husband –'

'My husband doesn't count,' she said carefully. 'I see now that he never

283

did.' She ran her hand through her hair, pulling it back from her cheek. She turned on the seat to half-face him. 'Lew,' she said, 'I'm going to tell you something that I never imagined I'd tell anyone. But then I could never have imagined this future for myself, and I'm so frightened now that I know I have to do something *tangible* to try and disperse my terror, otherwise I know it'll consume me.'

'You're frightened that your brother's murderer will come back for you?'

'No,' she said with a voice quavery with emotion. 'I'm afraid he *won't* come back for me.'

They waited at a light, hanging in the midst of stalled traffic, the flow cut off until the signal changed, and the surge began.

Croaker blew air out of his mouth in order to clear his mind. 'I think you're going to have to explain that.'

Margarite nodded. 'That and many other things,' she whispered. 'But for now, drive, Lew, drive until you run out of road.'

All the way out to Montauk Point she seemed to sleep, lying slumped beside him, her head tilted back, her hair folded softly around her, her skirt hiked partway up her thighs. She seemed like the girl he had dated his one summer out of Hell's Kitchen, part of a program for disadvantaged kids he'd lied to get into in order to escape the city's intolerable August heat. Somewhere in Pennsylvania, outside a small town with an Indian name that seemed funny to a kid his age, he had come upon her in the dusty, fly-blown interior of a tiny general store. They had drunk five-cent Cokes from a red-and-white vending machine, and the afternoon had seemed miraculous even then.

Innocence was a precious commodity for a blazing youth like Lew Croaker, who routinely cracked heads and defended himself with a scarred baseball bat on New York's ferocious West Side. Innocence, for him, had been a dream, a quality too far out of his ken to recognize before he had met Rebecca. And, of course, he didn't recognize it, not that summer, anyway, not until many more years had passed.

Croaker woke her when they were east of Amagansett, passing through the gorgeous desolation of sand, beachplum, stunted black pine and the occasional wild rose bush that was Napeague. This was the narrow neck that connected the east end of the Hamptons to Montauk. Another Indian name, he thought.

'We'll be running out of blacktop soon,' he said as she stirred. 'Are you hungry yet?'

'Let's wait,' she said, staring out the window at the hypnotic rise and fall of the dunes.

He stopped at a ramshackle clam bar on the edge of a ragged field of beachplum to call Lillehammer. He wanted to bring him more or less up to date, but he also wanted to know if Lillehammer had gotten the lab reports back from the crime scene. The assistant who answered the number Lillehammer had given him told him to wait when he gave his operation name. He got the impression that she was beeping Lillehammer who was God knows where, doing God knows what.

'You were right when you said we'd need a sorcerer,' Lillehammer said when he finally came on the line. 'No prints – not even smudges – except those of the two victims.' His voice sounded metallic, as if some electronic gizmo was tearing his voice apart and putting it back together. 'If this was a science-fiction novel we'd clone this sonuvabitch from his own DNA, grow him up in accelerated fashion, and not only find out what he looks like but send him out after the original.'

'Very funny.' After the events of the day, Croaker was not in the mood for levity of any kind. 'What's this DNA-mapping going to do for us?'

'Forget it. Modern science's not going to ride to our rescue on this one. But I did get a line on that feather stuck to the girl's front and it's interesting. It's from a white magpie. Very rare avian, according to the Smithsonian expert I scared up. So rare, I had to go through six ornithologists before I got the ID. Its habitat is the highlands of Southeast Asia. No zoo or rare bird breeder in this country has one. How is your end progressing?'

Croaker gave him an edited account of the inroads he was making with Margarite.

'This is great news, far more than I expected. Keep at it. She says this guy Robert is Oriental; the white magpie's from Southeast Asia. It fits.' He paused for a moment, the hollow sound of the secure line ticking like a bomb. 'Ishmael, if the DeCamillo woman's right and the murderer has some kind of affinity for her, she's our best friend right now. Hold on tight. And don't take shit from her husband. If Tony D. gives you trouble, I'll give you whatever backup you need. He's no Dominic Goldoni; we know how to take care of gavones like him.'

'I'm going to need an rdv as soon as I'm finished with her. That'll be tomorrow. Where do you suggest?'

There was a brief silence while Lillehammer considered the options. 'Book seats on a commercial airline and I'll meet the two of you myself at Washington airport. Advise me of the particulars, okay?'

Croaker said it was and broke the connection. He got back in the car, cruised the rest of the way into tacky Montauk village. They ate outside of town, at Gosman's, once a medium-sized restaurant overlooking the wharves where the fishing boats came in, now a sprawling institution of eateries, shops and walkways, a community unto itself.

They were seated at a table near one of the oversized plate-glass windows overlooking the harbor. At this time of the year, the vast restaurant was nearly empty, but the seagulls, grown bold and enormous from being fed by Gosman's customers, swooped and called raucously across the dark water as if it were the height of summer.

They sat drinking in companionable silence for some time. Despite his eagerness to get closer to finding Dominic Goldoni's murderer, Croaker held himself in check. It wasn't easy. Here, sitting opposite him, was the single link anyone had to the man who had murdered Goldoni. He had an intuition, bred of the jungle of New York's streets, that if she could not, or would not, help him, the man would never be found, despite his and Lillehammer's best efforts. He knew she wanted to tell him everything she had been sitting on since she and Francie had been abducted, but these were terrible, tragic events. Who knew whether she had the fortitude – or the depth of trust in him – required to dredge them up again into the light of day? He was not at all sure, if their positions were reversed, whether he would be able to do it.

Margarite drained her drink, sat staring into the empty glass. 'After he let us go,' she said in a slow, almost emotionless tone, 'after it was all over, his – what he did to Dom . . . when I brought Francie back . . .' Her pale eyes swung up to meet his. '. . . I knew then that it wasn't over.'

She swallowed, and he could see that she was mentally sinking her toes into the ground, as one physically does at the shoreline to keep from being pulled out on the tide.

'You see, something happened between him and me that . . . I don't think he anticipated. He came here to use me, to get to Dom, and in that he succeeded. But there was something else, on the road one night, a kind of – I don't know how to put it – a transference.

'He allowed me the opportunity to kill him and I took it. It was false; he'd switched razors and the one I used had no sharp edge, but that didn't matter, he told me, and he was right. I tried to kill him; I would have, and that was important for me to know. That act . . . unlocked something inside me, some inner resolve I never knew I had.'

She licked her lips, and Croaker called for another round of drinks. When it came, he said, 'You said something about a transference.'

She nodded. 'Yes. You see, it was as if he gave me this – strength, and in return took something from me.'

'What was it?'

She took a sip of her drink. 'I don't know. At least, I didn't. Now I'm beginning to suspect what it might be and it has me terrified.' She drank

286

again, almost compulsively, and Croaker resolved to order them food as soon as he could catch the waitress's eye.

Margarite's head was in her hands. 'I've got to talk to someone about this. To keep it bottled up any more is . . . intolerable. But who would understand? Not my husband or my daughter, and I can't talk about any of this to my friends.' Her head came up, and her eyes searched his face. For what, he wondered – understanding, absolution? 'That leaves you, Lew, because I don't know what you are to me – or what you will become. You're as unknown as what my life has become.'

'Margarite, what is it you're afraid he's taken from you?'

'My ability to hate him.'

He saw that she was terrified he would laugh in her face as, almost surely, her husband would have done had she confessed this to him. After what he had seen of Dominic Goldoni's body, this particular fear did not seem at all funny to him. On the contrary, it seemed chilling.

'It's as if we're bound together at the soul. I can't get him out of my mind – I don't mean his face or . . . But in the dead of night I can *smell* him, *feel* him close to me as if he's actually beside me.'

Croaker caught her eyes with his. 'Margarite, I want you to understand something before we go any further,' he said. 'This man who abducted you and Francie, who murdered your brother, is so extremely dangerous that I think quite literally you're the only one who can help me track him down. Without you I'm nowhere. I've got to know I can count on you in this. If you're this conflicted about –'

'I want to help you,' she said, a bit too quickly. 'I *need* to, to prove to myself that he hasn't . . .' She shook her head, unable to go on.

Croaker snagged a waitress, ordered them steamers first, then lobsters. The local clams came almost immediately, redolent of brine and seaweed, in bowls so large they were daunting. Margarite, eating the sweet flesh slowly and deliberately, gained color in her face and seemed to recover a modicum of her composure.

'What I keep thinking about is how I've changed since he let me go.' She was finished with the steamers, and she pushed the bowl away from her, licked her fingers one by one, fastidious as a cat. 'My marriage was, to be frank, a dismal failure. Tony and I don't communicate – with the advantage of hindsight I don't believe we ever did. As far as women are concerned, Tony does his communicating with his cock and his fists. He communicates with other men by negotiating – that's life to him. When I spoke up he beat me. I suppose, Sicilian that he is, he's been pissed off at me ever since Francie was born. What, no son?' She tried to smile but it came out a lopsided grimace.

287

The waitress came to clear the plates. She handed them foil packets of Handiwipes. Margarite said she wanted a beer, and Croaker ordered a pair and the waitress bustled away.

'The thing is,' Croaker said gently, 'you took it. The beatings, I mean.'

Margarite leveled her gaze at him. 'You're not a woman. I don't expect you to understand.'

'I'm doing my best,' he said. 'I'm listening.'

She digested that for some time, staring out at the darkness coming down over the water. A fishing boat, running lights ablaze, navigated the channel outside, moving from left to right across the plate glass as if it were a television screen.

'Give me your hand,' she said quietly. 'No, the other one.'

He put his biomechanical hand in hers.

She sat looking down at the confluence of skin and man-made elements.

'A man's world is violent,' she said at last. 'A woman's world – well, a woman wonders why violence is part of the equation at all.'

'But passivity –'

'You're still thinking like a man.' She smiled kindly at him. 'Passivity doesn't enter into it. Men make the mistake of thinking that because women can't see the sense in violence they must be passive creatures. It's just not true.' She cocked her head. 'In one important way, at least, men are the passive sex. Given a choice, they will always opt for the status quo. They hate change of any kind, and they fight against it constantly. On the other hand, what women want is stability, which when you stop to think about it is a very different animal.'

The lobsters came, along with the beers. They were given plastic-coated bibs which tied behind their necks. Margarite picked up a nut-cracker, began to go to work on the bright orange-red shell.

'Having said that, I've come to understand that there is something else at work within me. Robert – that's what he called himself – proved that to me. I was prepared to kill him. Coming back from that, I am here with you. I am at last able to say to my husband "Fuck you", and feel its validity. I can see how screwed up my life has been, staying with him. It was the wrong decision, to want stability – for me *and* for my daughter. She's bulimic for a damned good reason. She's not stupid and she's no longer a child. She sees what goes on around her, she feels the vibes more acutely than any adult. Maybe I've damaged her more than anyone else. Can you see as I do that it was Robert who allowed me to understand this important truth?'

Croaker was silent for some time. The steamers had filled him up, or the emotions of what had happened – what, possibly, would begin to happen here and now if he handled things right – had suppressed his appetite.

'You have a decision to make, Margarite. I think you've decided to help me find Robert. Do you want to see him again? What, possibly, can be gained from that? He's a murderer – brutal, cunning, perhaps demented, but in any case dangerous in the extreme. You survived one encounter with him. Who can say what will happen the second time?'

'He won't hurt me.'

'How can you be sure?'

She used her fingertip to tap the place just over her heart. 'I know in the same way I eat or breathe. There's a connection on some level so deep it bypasses conscious thought. Certainly, there's no logic to it. Nevertheless, I'm sure.'

The thing was, he believed her. Looking into her clear eyes, he saw a truth there that was profoundly disturbing. He felt the hairs at the back of his neck stir, as if this man, who called himself Robert, could suddenly appear behind him. He shifted in his chair, abruptly uncomfortable.

Thinking of the scene he and Lillehammer had come upon in the house in Marine on St Croix, Croaker said, 'Perhaps you should concentrate on what Robert did to Dominic.'

'Do you think I can forget?' Margarite, too, had had enough of food, and Croaker signaled the waitress to clear the table. Margarite waited until she had gone before continuing. 'But there's more to it than just Dom's death, and I've been thinking about this aspect ever since I got back from Minnesota.' She wiped her hands of brine and tiny flecks of pink-and-white lobster flesh. 'I told you I wanted to confess everything. That wasn't a theatrical gesture. I meant it.'

She leaned forward, a certain intensity in her face. 'Remember Francie telling you about her visits to Uncle Dom's, how she often went with me, spent time in the kitchen sampling the contents of Dom's ice-cream freezer?' She nodded. 'I wonder if you've asked yourself what I was doing there so often.'

'You were brother and sister – family,' Croaker said.

Now a genuine smile spread across Margarite's face. 'Christ, Lew, that's what Dom always told me when I worried we were spending so much time together. He'd chuckle at my anxiety and say, "Of course, *bellissima*, we're family. Who will wonder about the time we share? Not Tony, and certainly not the Feds!"'

She paused for a moment to drink the last of her beer, but Croaker harbored the suspicion that she was gathering herself. He was right.

'You see, Lew, I believe now that my brother knew he was going to die. He was preparing for his death two years before it happened.'

He knew she was giving him clues, wanting to see if he could put aside

289

logic, make the leap of faith necessary to solve the riddle. He did not think she was being deliberately obtuse, but genuinely needed to find a man who could take her brother's place, who might rely on her for what she really was, not be swayed by her beauty, be fooled by her gender. She was so innately intelligent that she –

Good God! He was struck momentarily dumb as the thought hit him, a bolt so weird, so wild, so inconsistent with logic that he had a strong suspicion that it must be true.

'It was you,' he said. 'It was you all along. Ginnie Morris didn't mean anything. Dominic broke the WITSEC rules in order to stay in touch with you.'

'Yes,' Margarite said, clearly delighted that he had worked it out. 'I confess. It was me Dominic picked to be his successor. He wanted me to work behind the mask of my husband, who Dom officially designated his heir apparent. That was what my visits with my brother were all about. I was learning his business, using my own company as a front to meet his contacts and, under his aegis, transferring his influence to me.'

'But as a woman in a sacrosanct man's world, wasn't that all but impossible?' Croaker asked.

'It was a difficult and time-consuming project, since I had to deal with Dom's contacts in business, politics and law enforcement in an entirely different manner than he had. I was always Tony's wife, because Tony was the mask behind which I needed to hide. But I was the one who Dom confided in. I was the one who provided Tony with the information he needed to keep Dom's contacts in line.'

Even having worked out the gist of this bizarre arrangement, Croaker needed some time to digest the details. 'I don't get it,' he said. 'I'm a cop and you've just confessed to –'

'Continuing my brother's legitimate consulting business,' Margarite said with an ironic smile. 'Let's not get lost in legalities when there's a more important aspect to deal with.'

'Which is?'

'Let's return to logic,' she said. 'I now believe Dom was aware he was a marked man, that his murder was inevitable. I've come to the same conclusion. If we extrapolate from that beginning, we see that he began to plan for this future two years ago. He picked me, a woman, to transfer his power to. Why? It was perhaps the most difficult of his options. A woman has never had power in his business – *ever*. Why would he try for it now? The answer is because no one in his business would ever suspect a woman – even Dom's sister – of having the secrets of his contacts, the intelligence

– dirt, if you will – he had amassed over the years, which he used as leverage.'

Her head moved closer to his over the table, and her voice, already low, dropped to a reedy whisper. 'There is a war going on, Lew. A war in the corridors of power, locked away from the sight of most people. And it isn't just a Mafia war – Goldoni against Leonforte – although I have begun to suspect that this is an element more important than even I can as yet understand.'

'Isn't this sounding a little melodramatic?'

'Don't forget I have access to all of Dom's intelligence,' she said. 'The rollcall of powerful people he can force to his will would take your breath away, so I know the arena in which this is being played out.'

'Use the source of your brother's information,' Croaker said. 'Surely he can help us.'

'But I don't know the identity of Dom's contact; I merely receive periodic information at a dead-letter drop that is changed each time. It's a one-way conduit; I have no way of contacting him.'

She shook her head. 'What I am sure of is that this is a war of a far, far wider scope than just the Mafia. It involves the heads of the largest corporations, Federal law enforcement agencies, governors and congressmen – even, perhaps, the White House. And, right now, Robert is our only way in to its center.'

The thunderclap of his hands coming together, the chainmail nodes of the *nekode* ringing musically as they struck the dagger's blade, was the only sound in the shadow-shrouded room.

Celeste shrieked.

The point of the dagger held fast three centimeters from his heart as he clamped his palms on either side of it. He slapped it down as he would an insect, looked past Celeste into the gloom. He recognized the face he had glimpsed in Venice: deeply planed Oriental features, a mole at the corner of the firm lips. Then, like the moon disappearing behind clouds, it winked out.

Nicholas, gaining strength every second from the rhythm of Akshara, rushed toward the precipice of physical combat. He kept his tanjian eye firmly closed, understanding that this enemy had the power to use Akshara against him. He must trust in his earliest martial arts training, trust his own hands, his *te-gatana*.

His mind was open as he spotted the Messulethe in the shadows and, lunging out, grabbed his right wrist with his right hand. His open mind had chosen *sokumen irimi-nage* because he needed to end this quickly. The

Messulethe's psychic attack had shaken him to the core, had brought him to the very brink of death, and he was unsure how long his reserves of strength would carry him.

He turned the Messulethe's wrist inside out and went for *suwari-waza*, stiffening his fingers, tilting his left hand upward, slamming the heavily callused heel of it into the Messulethe's jaw. When he heard the sharp crack as the head snapped back, he swung his left arm back and down, using the Messulethe's own momentum to sweep him off his feet.

The Messulethe's body cartwheeled as Nicholas whipped him over, and he caught a flash of the inside of the figure's wrist. The Messulethe hit the floor chin first, and his head snapped back.

'Shit!' Nicholas said, bending over the crumpled form.

'What is it?' Celeste had come up behind him.

Nicholas showed her the inside of the man's left wrist. 'We've got the wrong man. You see, there's no blue crescent tattoo. He isn't the Messulethe.'

She looked up. 'You mean someone else is here?'

'Is,' Nicholas said, letting go the man's wrist. 'Or was.'

He went back to the computer monitor he had been studying, but the screen was blank. He reached for the floppy drive slot, but it was empty.

'Damn, he's taken all the Avalon files I found.' He showed her the cut-out in the floor where the box of floppies had been hidden.

'What's this?'

She pulled out a piece of paper, showed it to him.

What do you want to know? Where Okami is? Or why his death is necessary? Which question is more important to you? Who Okami controls? Or who he is?

Now is the time for decision. Come *alone* to the parish church of the Hill of the Martyrs. Two p.m. tomorrow.

Not surprisingly, it was unsigned. Nicholas stared at the words, reciting them again as if they were a prayer. The scent of the snare reached him even from this distance, but he had to ask himself if it mattered. What was important was that whoever wrote this knew which questions to ask – and if there was even a ghost of a chance that he knew the answers to those questions, Nicholas knew he had to be at the Hill of the Martyrs at the appointed time.

'Mikio Okami is missing,' the little man said. 'Missing and presumed dead.'

This was Tomoo Kozo, the *oyabun* of the Yamauchi clan. He was in

292

his sixties, but looked a good deal younger; he kept himself fit with a rigorous daily regimen of open-hand and small-blade martial arts. He had a long, pinched face, as if at birth some sadistic doctor had put his head in a vise. The top of his head was shaved, shiny with oil, save for one spot at the back where his silver hair had been left to sprout out in a ponytail. He wore a pair of suit trousers held up with suspenders, but his shirt was open at the collar and his sleeves were rolled up enough to reveal the edges of wings and clawed feet – colorful *irizumi*, the unique tattoos of the Yakuza. His small, black eyes, not unlike those of a rat, peered suspiciously at everyone and everything, as if at any moment he expected to discover a new conspiracy.

Nangi watched, fascinated, as he moved restlessly around the room. This was as singular as its owner, no doubt reflecting Kozo's personality. The wood floor was as highly polished as that of a martial arts *dojo*. The walls were gray ferro-concrete, interspersed with steel girders, half-emerged from the walls, like sentinels or body-builders. An oval shape was cut out of the center of the floor. It was lined with glass, filled with water, water-lilies, aquatic grasses and the most astounding array of rare koi. The gold, black, copper and white-spotted fish swam serenely, lit from above by a kind of crystal-shaped skylight, oval itself, so that a muscular shaft of sunlight struck downward onto the pool. There were no other windows in the room, so that the corners were left in shadow.

'I don't feel an overabundance of distress at his passing,' Kozo said as he circled the pool like a cat waiting for his moment to pounce. 'I felt he had gained too much power. I had always held that the Kaisho was just another way to usurp power. We *oyabun* have always ironed out our differences at council.' He peered into the depths of the pool, at his prized collection. He placed one finger in the water, perhaps testing the temperature. 'Yes, there was the occasional disagreement. But war and bloodshed, history has shown, invokes a positive influence on mankind. Survival of the fittest, that should be the Yakuza motto, *neh?*' He giggled like a child. He wiped his hands. They were preternaturally large; Nangi had the odd, fleeting thought that they had come from some American lumberjack and had been grafted onto Kozo's wrists.

Kozo stopped abruptly, looked up at Nangi, as if remembering he was there. 'The advent of the Kaisho changed all that. The power that had been the council's flowed to one man: Mikio Okami. That kind of concentration of power too often brings with it its own peril.' He put his hands behind his back, nodded. 'The management of power, there's the riddle that has baffled mankind throughout the ages, *neh?*'

Nangi stood, his feet apart, slightly braced, his hands wrapped around the dragon's head of his cane. He had been offered neither a seat nor tea. This was Tomoo Kozo's way: interview by intimidation.

Kozo shrugged now. 'Perhaps Okami-san received a message. Who knows?' He took his hands from behind his back, rubbed them together. 'In any event, I have a message for *you*, Nangi-san.'

'Is it from you?'

'From me?' Kozo appeared startled. 'Nangi-san, I am merely the humble messenger.'

'Then you have used curious means to bring us together.' Nangi was watching the men who had brought him here, stationed in the shadows at the corners of the room. He did not yet know how hostile Kozo might become, but the fact that Okami was missing, perhaps dead, was a very bad sign. 'You could have phoned me.'

'Phoned you?' The small man giggled again, a high, disconcerting sound. 'But, oh no, that would not have done. We don't publicize our relationships, do we? And then, of course, there is my principal, for whom the tightest security is of the utmost importance.'

'And who might that be?' Nangi said.

'Do you not recognize us?' said a voice.

Nangi became aware of a figure moving out of the shadows toward the ellipse of filtered light generated through the skylight.

In a moment, a slight man with the ramrod-straight bearing of a military officer pierced the curtain of light which, falling upon him from above, gave him a rather frightening mien.

'Ushiba-san,' Nangi said in a hushed voice.

Naohiro Ushiba bowed slightly – a man in his mid-forties, fit and hard, with a face that could only be called beautiful. In other cultures he might be described as effeminate and, therefore, be an object of derision. In Japan, the opposite was true. There was, in fact, a history of Japanese heroes, known as *bishonen*, young Adonises, who were invariably taken under the wing of an older protector.

As like a *bishonen* as he was in many ways, Naohiro Ushiba needed no older protector. Though it was true that in Japanese society power resided in the aggregate rather than the individual, perhaps Ushiba was the exception that proved the rule.

He was Daijin, Chief Minister of MITI, the Ministry of International Trade and Industry, the controlling and coordinating body for all of Japan's export policies for which Nangi himself had worked many years ago before 'retiring' from the bureaucracy into the business sector.

Against Kozo's unconventionality, Ushiba's almost painfully austere formality was striking indeed. He was dressed in a black silk and wool

294

suit, polished black wingtips. Against this background, his snow-white shirt positively glowed, and his tie, a stylized black-and-white spiral with a dot of red near the bottom, set off everything around it. His salt-and-pepper hair was cut close to his temples, almost straight across the top.

And then there was his beautiful face, graceful as a girl's, with no sharp edge or heavy plane to mar the almost fragile whole. The full lips, the curving cheek, the sculpted nose, the heart-shaped jawline, the long-lashed, wide-apart eyes, all contributed to the curious sense of beauty that transcended gender.

'There are those in MITI who still speak of your many accomplishments, Nangi-san,' Ushiba said carefully, 'though those occurred many years ago.'

It was just like Ushiba, Nangi thought, to couch a rebuke inside a compliment. 'Watch out, old man,' he was saying. 'I know you were clever, but that was a long time ago.'

'I am grateful that something I did has stood the test of time.' Only Nangi himself knew his smile was artificial.

'We often think of contacting you,' Ushiba said from across the expanse of the glittering koi pond, 'for a quiet lunch somewhere out of the way' – he shrugged – 'but our schedule is so impossible . . . well . . .' – he smiled in the Japanese manner, without showing his teeth – 'perhaps you have forgotten what life inside was like.'

The insult was like a blow across Nangi's face. He kept his composure, however, for he knew to have this man as an enemy could be an insurmountable obstacle to his business.

'Once inside,' Nangi said, his voice neutral, 'one never forgets.' His smile matched Ushiba's. 'There will come a day, I have no doubt, when the Daijin will understand better than he does now. I was in your position, once, and I can tell you from experience that there is ignorance inside, as well as out.'

Ushiba's smile widened an inch, and his beautiful head dipped just slightly in recognition of Nangi's cleverly barbed reply. Perhaps he is not my enemy after all, Nangi thought. But then he saw Kozo staring fixedly down into the depths of his koi pond and he was not heartened.

'We can only agree,' Ushiba said, his smile stitched to his face, 'if only because we must deal with such ignorance every day.' Like a star in a film production, the Daijin had chosen his key light well. Flushed with the sunlight streaming down through the lens of the skylight, he stood out in the dim atmosphere of this strange, disturbing room.

'We have much to discuss,' Ushiba continued, his lips pursed. 'About the Hive computer, which is so important to us, and the reasons for its being stalled. About charges of the most serious nature being leveled against your company and, especially, Linnear-san.'

It was as if he were deliberately thrusting himself into Nangi's full attention, and Nangi was instantly suspicious. He continued to listen to Ushiba while keeping Kozo well within the range of his peripheral vision, because he believed now that the *oyabun*'s reactions could tell him far more about what was happening here than the Chief Minister's words.

'We find all of this utterly distasteful,' Ushiba said with all the pain of a teenage girl who has been jilted by her lover. 'Disgraceful, actually. We had counted on Linnear to obtain for Sato the contract for the American Hive computer and then absorb Hyrotech-inc. A coup for Japan, in the area of international public relations as well as technological advance. Now, however, we must begin to formulate other plans – without the inclusion of Sato.'

'But Linnear-san has done all that and more,' Nangi said.

'Then why has the United States Government blocked Sato's attempt to buy Hyrotech-inc? Why has your American representative, Harley Gaunt, been subpoenaed by the most powerful and feared congressional committee to answer charges of illegal business practices and treason? Why is Linnear himself currently in hiding so that he will not himself be served with a subpoena?' Ushiba moved his beautiful head from side to side. 'These are questions of the most serious nature, Nangi-san. They cannot be made to disappear with a few clever sentences.'

'Linnear-san is not in hiding,' Nangi said, knowing his words seemed as transparent as paper.

'No?' Ushiba skewed his head around, and sunlight flooded across his face.

'His journey out of the country is entirely unrelated to the American subpoena.' Nangi knew that no one would believe this now.

'Ah, I am heartened to learn this fact, Nangi-san. Tell me, where is he? Do you know? Can you present him to me today, tonight, tomorrow, even the day after that?' He grunted. 'How could you? Elements of the American Government have been looking for him ever since your office responded to their subpoena.' A look of satisfaction made his face effervescent – a girl with her new boyfriend, crossing paths with her old beau. 'Ah, yes, they have been keeping us fully informed of their enquiries. Why not? I am certain their congressional committee will want our cooperation in their investigation of Sato-Tomkin, and I am fully prepared to give it to them.'

The light put a crease in Ushiba's features, making it seem more than ever a two-dimensional paradigm, an illustration in some glossy fashion

296

magazine. 'You see, Nangi-san, we are in the midst of an exceedingly delicate game of perception with the United States, and it is one we are determined to win. If, to do so, we are obliged to sacrifice a pawn here or there – or even a rook or a bishop – we will do just that.

'At this moment, Sato-Tomkin and Nicholas Linnear are what the Americans want to tear down. We will say, Let them. And why not? Sato has disappointed us. It has turned a potential coup into a full-fledged disaster.'

'You're ignoring what is really happening behind the scenes,' Nangi said rather more desperately than he wanted. 'Linnear-san believes that the US Government –'

'None of that concerns me,' the Daijin said flatly. 'This is strictly a matter of perception. We must avoid at all costs any negative repercussions with the Americans.'

The Chief Minister struck a pose, as if news cameras were trained on his face. Beside him, Kozo had found a fascinating koi to hold his attention fast. 'Public relations, Nangi-san, is a game we have come into late in the day. But it is a game we mean to master in the quickest possible order. Whatever has to be done to make this possible will be done, believe me. In fact, it is being done, even as we speak. The American Senator, Rance Bane, is receiving all the dossiers he has requested from us, and we are transferring them in the most public manner.' Ushiba raised a hand. 'Photo ops are primary to our strategy. The more open and helpful we are with the senator, the more wind we take out of his anti-Japanese sail while showing the entire world how we have changed.'

Nangi was appalled. His blood ran cold at the thought of what the Daijin – all of Japan – was in the process of doing to him and to Nicholas. 'So you're throwing my company – my entire life – to the dogs.' It was a pathetic statement, so impotent it filled Nangi with disgust and self-loathing.

Ushiba must have caught a whiff of that. 'How bitter you sound, Nangi-san. But of course we will take care of you. You are an ex-minister of MITI, after all; you have been one of us. Linnear, however, is another story.'

The Daijin was an exemplar of icy calm, the eye of the cyclone that swung out from him, extending its wicked arms to smash Nangi, Nicholas and all they held dear into shards. And, with a sinking heart, Nangi knew there wasn't a damned thing he could do about it. Still, he knew he must try.

'What has Linnear-san done to deserve this grossly unjust fate? He has fought many times, taken on great personal risk against the enemies of Japan, both in the United States and in Russia.'

'We are aware,' Ushiba said. 'And there are those inside who have fought to try to save him, in memory of his father – and what he has done. But, in the end, the present must overweigh the past. This is our judgement.'

Nangi was filled with a sudden dread. He had a presentiment that they had now come to the core, the real reason Ushiba had sent for him in such humiliating fashion. 'The present. What do you mean?'

'We are speaking now of the Chi Project, the secret program, the brainchild of Linnear-san. It is up and running, Nangi-san, without your knowledge. Its products have been built and assembled in Sato's own Saigon facilities, and your own man, Vincent Tinh, has quite quietly been selling them to the highest bidder for several months now.'

Nangi felt his heart lurch. The Daijin knew of the Chi prototype. 'I know nothing of this,' he said.

'Unfortunately, there's more,' the Daijin said coldly. 'The Chi technology has turned up in a new generation of computer-controlled guided missiles bound for Iraq, Syria and Afghanistan. Thanks to the Chi technology, these new weapons of war your company is selling are able to think, to out-maneuver the cleverest evasive action by even the fastest target.'

Nangi opened his mouth to say something but not one word emerged. This was news of the very worst kind.

Ushiba's line of reasoning was inexorable. 'The Chi Project is directed by Linnear; that fact has been highly publicized. Now you can see how sacrificing Linnear to Bane and his Committee will be of extraordinary psychological and public-relations use to us. He is, when we stop to think about it, the perfect scapegoat, and we shall ride him all the way down until he disappears from sight, digested by Senator Bane and his very nasty Committee.'

Holding the .38-caliber handgun, Harley Gaunt recalled the times his father would take him hunting. Crisp autumn weekends, the smell of woodsmoke and burning leaves in his nostrils, the rustling peacefulness of the forest in the Virginia hills, the golds, bitter oranges, ochers in the trees and underfoot, a sweet odor emanating from the springy forest floor which his father once told him was decay.

Manny Mannheim, a fat, balding man with a two-day growth peppering his jowls, and trousers so low the top of his butt stuck out, said, 'You okay with this, Harl? I've never seen you with a gun before. Hate to think you'd pull the trigger and blow your toe off – or some part slightly more vital.'

Gaunt smiled as he looked around Manny's pawnshop. The place hadn't changed much from the time he had first followed his mother in here. By then, drink had changed her so much that she was selling things precious to her – the diamond and platinum Tiffany necklace Gaunt's father had given her on their tenth wedding anniversary, the heirloom sapphire brooch left to her by her mother, even, once, her gold wedding ring. When Gaunt's mother had begun to drink heavily she had lost her job and, humiliated, she had turned to pawning her possessions rather than allow her family to know what had happened.

Gaunt had met Manny so many years ago – a youngish, gawky young man helping his dad out in the pawnbroker business – and the two had become, if not quite friends, then something more than acquaintances. They took pleasure in helping one another out in times of need. Manny had seen to it that none of the items Gaunt's mother had pawned were sold. Years later, he had come to Gaunt because thugs were threatening his father; Gaunt had spoken to a couple of his friends in the FBI and Manny's father was never bothered again.

Manny blinked myopically in the pawnshop's mean light. 'Gun's in excellent working order. I cleaned it myself.' He laughed, pushing his glasses back up a nose that had been broken many times. 'The skills you acquire in my trade.'

'Don't worry,' Gaunt said, as he carefully loaded the .38. 'I know how to use this.'

Manny's nose twitched. 'Now don't for Christ's sake get into any trouble, okay? Promise me.'

'I promise,' Gaunt said, stowing the .38 away inside his jacket. 'Chances are I'll never even fire it. It's just for effect, really.'

Manny sniffed, coming round from behind his glass counter, swinging open the metal cage door, and walking Gaunt to the front door, a fly-blown oblong of cracked glass embedded with wire mesh.

'Now you're back for a little while let's have dinner.'

'Sure, Manny,' Gaunt said, slipping out the door into the Washington twilight. 'I'd like that.'

He had spent the night in a motel in Bethesda, going over the photos Renata had given him, deciding how best to present this evidence to William Justice Lillehammer. He had spent the day considering all the prudent alternatives to what, in the end, he knew it must come to, discarding them one by one. Late in the day, he had gone out to make his preparations. His last stop had been Manny's pawnshop.

They call themselves Looking-Glass, Renata had told him on their nighttime walk around the Vietnam Memorial. *Who they are or under what aegis they operate I can't say – I doubt if even the President could tell you. They have a great deal of influence, very deep pockets, although I haven't a clue as to how they're funded. They were very active during the war in Vietnam – perhaps for a long time before.*

What's their purpose? Gaunt had asked.

To reshape the world in their image, Renata said. *To slowly bring their people to power – and then to keep them there, to replace them, when the time comes, with others sympathetic to their goals. They're basically conservative, protectionist, xenophobic, utterly righteous. They believe in what they're doing, even though they inhabit a world that circumvents all existing law.*

Someone once said that a mind becomes a detriment when it acquires more intelligence than its integrity can handle. I think this can be applied to Looking-Glass. They have worked for so long in their lawless labyrinths of power they can no longer distinguish right from wrong, justice from injustice.

It took Gaunt an astonishingly short time to emerge from the shabby section of Washington where Manny's pawnshop was located to the mani-cured sweep of Dupont Circle, with its Victorian mansions and black iron gates. The rain of the night before had washed the streets and sidewalks, making the contrast between the shabby slums and the patrician town houses even more shocking. It was a curious fact of urban life that such violent and amorphous decay could co-exist with upscale neighborhoods, patrolled and, for the most part, peaceful.

He took New Hampshire Avenue to M Street, swinging right there, heading across the bridge into Georgetown.

Lillehammer lived in a large Palladian-style town house overlooking Dumbarton Oaks and, above, the US Naval Observatory and the Vice-President's house.

This short section of S Street, the last street before the generous expanse of parkland, had therefore the aspect of a small-town road, the outskirts just before lush countryside reclaimed the landscape. There were no cars here, no pedestrian traffic either, at this time of day, with the darkness coming down, and the air growing very chill indeed.

Gaunt steered his rental car slowly by Lillehammer's house, saw the lights on, an American station-wagon illuminated in the granite driveway. He pulled into a parking space near the corner, and walked back.

The house stood back from the street. It was built of white stone, its colonnaded porte-cochère and columned façade making its four stories seem far larger and grander than they actually were. It was framed by a pair of stately Bradford pear trees which shot up above its rooftop, drew the eye toward the entry, making it more dramatic.

The semi-circular driveway sloped steeply upward. The sweet, earthy scents of the emerging evening reminded Gaunt of those long-ago hunting

300

expeditions with his father. He went up the steps, knocked on a carved wooden door painted a glassy black.

It took a long time before the door opened, but when it did, he saw a tall, thin man with ruddy cheeks, dark eyebrows, and piercing blue eyes which evaluated him with a mixture of curiosity and studied calm. He was wearing deep-blue wool slacks and a white button-down-collar shirt with the sleeves rolled up his forearms.

'Yes?'

'William Lillehammer?'

Lillehammer nodded. 'What can I do for you?'

Gaunt introduced himself. He noted in Lillehammer's bearing a rigorous military training, and adjusted his speech accordingly, using precise, clipped phrases. 'I hope you have a moment to spare me. I've come a long way to talk to you about Senator Rance Bane and his Committee's vendetta against Tomkin Industries and Nicholas Linnear in particular.'

Lillehammer's eyebrows lifted just a fraction. 'Bane's motives aside, how is it you think I can be of help with a congressional hearing? I have no connection with the legislature.'

'Oh, but you must,' Gaunt said, steeling himself by closing his right hand over the butt of the .38 tucked neatly into the waistband of his trousers. 'You're part of Looking-Glass, aren't you?'

In the ensuing silence, Gaunt thought he could hear the wind rustling the tops of the Bradford pears, the distant hiss of traffic along Wisconsin Avenue.

'I beg your pardon?' Lillehammer blinked, as if Gaunt had thrown a bright light into his face.

'I think you understand me,' Gaunt said, his grip tightening on the handgun.

Those clear blue eyes were like X-rays, searching his face as if for a weak spot. 'Yes, indeed,' Lillehammer said abruptly. He smiled, stepped back into the entranceway. 'Won't you come inside?'

There was no strain evident on his face, no sense of tension about the man at all as he led Gaunt past the curving Colonial staircase of polished maple, down a carpeted hall lined with prints of comfortably masculine scenes of fox hunts and other equestrian activities.

Renata had told him that Lillehammer lived alone, and Gaunt could detect no hint of a female presence – neither in color nor in style. The furniture was on a massive scale, made of leather, suede, metals, some covered in heavy cottons of richly colored patterns reminiscent in an impressionistic manner of animal hides.

The study into which he was taken overlooked the small, manicured

301

conifer garden at the back of the house. It was a high-ceilinged room with wide panels of forest green interspersed with decorative wooden mock pillars painted the color of clotted cream. The ceiling was a shallow dome, festooned with scrollwork in high relief.

Lillehammer went past a pair of grand leather sofas, to a mirrored wet bar.

'Drink?'

'A beer would be fine,' Gaunt said.

Lillehammer bent, extracted an amber bottle from a half-refrigerator below the bar. He popped the cap, carefully poured the beer down the side of a pilsner glass. Then he made himself a whiskey and soda in an enormous old-fashioned glass.

He came back to where Gaunt stood, handed him his beer, then went behind his gilt-encrusted escritoire, sat in a high-backed chair.

Gaunt, left to fend for himself, glanced at the nearest chair, a rather uncomfortable-looking slingback affair of welded bronze and wide interlaced leather straps the color of honey. He chose to stand.

The room, carpeted and snug, was warmly lit by a series of copper-hooded wall lamps in sconces, giving the whole a distinctly homey, old-fashioned atmosphere.

Lillehammer put his glass down on his bone-colored blotter, said in an avuncular tone of voice, 'My dear chap, you really must tell me how on earth you came by the name Looking-Glass.'

Gaunt debated with himself whether to play against Lillehammer's chosen defense – this rather interesting technique of reversing the process of interrogation – or to rudely thrust it aside and go for the jugular. It was, he knew, more a judgement of Lillehammer's personality than it was of his own nerves.

Gaunt set his own glass aside. 'Let's cut the chummy bullshit, shall we?' he said. 'You're part of Looking-Glass. How I know that is irrelevant to the situation.'

'But of course it's relevant,' Lillehammer said emphatically. 'In the course of my rather checkered career I have made my share of enemies. We all do in this town, sooner or later.' He chuckled as if bringing Gaunt into his confidence. 'And if it's one of my enemies who's been feeding you stories I'd very much like to know who so I can set the record straight.' He spread his hands wide. 'You wouldn't begrudge me a chance to refute this accusation, would you?'

Gaunt saw the flash of metal in Lillehammer's left hand too late. His right hand was bringing the .38 out of his trousers when the first bullet from the small .25-caliber pistol struck him in the forehead. He felt nothing more than if a woman had slapped his face. He blinked, could not remember why his hand was around the butt of a handgun.

He stared into bright blue eyes, incurious, almost stoic, a hero's pose, certainly, reminding him of the bronze statue of the noble soldiers overlooking the Vietnam Memorial. He knew he had seen it recently, had been there with someone. Who? It had been raining, cold rain on his face now.

The small explosion caught his attention, and his head snapped back. He slipped to one knee, as if the footing had become abruptly treacherous. Cold rain; could there be ice on the ground?

There was a throbbing behind one eye. He felt nothing more, a slight headache, more light-headed really, but he could no longer see. That was curious. His father would never have taken him hunting in the dark. Too dangerous. Dad was always lecturing him about how dangerous firearms were, about how careful you had to be around them at all times, even when you were positive they were unloaded, especially then, he would say, because that's when you'd get careless.

Where am I? Gaunt thought. In the forest at night. Where's Dad? He tried to call out but no sound emerged from his mouth. There was a loud report at close range, and he was slammed over, the stink of cordite in his nostrils mixing with the lovely earthy sweetness of the forest floor in autumn, giving up the last of its loamy richness before the first frost of winter put everything to sleep – the deer and quail, the cedars and the larch, the maples and the . . .

Bang!

'Good God, man, I've got to have a chance to defend myself against charges,' Lillehammer said as he bent over Gaunt's prostrate form, where beer and blood mingled indiscriminately. 'Why, that's the American way.'

Montmartre. The Hill of the Martyrs. Its parish church – St Pierre de Montmartre – lay just north of the Place du Tertre, once the outdoor theater for Paris's most celebrated artists. Now it was infested by the type of hustler for whom the sight of tour buses was like honey to a bear.

From the outside, St Pierre was nothing much to look at – certainly insignificant compared to its close neighbor, the renowned Sacré Coeur. Inside, Nicholas knew, it was another story. It had been built upon the ruins of a beautiful seventh-century Roman temple. Originally a Benedictine nunnery, fires had caused rebuilding several times over, and eventually the Benedictines had moved further down the hill, allowing the parish to establish operations in the church.

Nicholas saw someone close to the shadows thrown by the church and, as the figure's head turned in his direction, he recognized Okami's face.

He wondered whether there was surveillance here – or how much. But the imperative to reach Okami overrode any sense of caution.

He began his approach on the oblique, using the cover of a cluster of Germans arguing over who was going to get his portrait painted first. Then, at the last minute, when he was quite close to the façade of St Pierre, he broke cover, racing toward Okami.

He reached him in three long strides, grabbed him.

'Okami-san –'

Okami grimaced, twisted his body with unexpected strength. He broke free, lurched away from Nicholas, racing into the Place du Tertre where he was instantly whirled into a current of tourists and busy would-be painters indefatigably hawking their dubious wares. A cheerful Nigerian tried to sell Nicholas a ten-foot balloon with 'I Love Paris' printed in pink all over its sausage-like skin. He ran on.

Nicholas looked toward the position he had told Celeste to take, up the hill toward the Butte of Montmartre. He saw her standing, pointing in the direction Okami had taken.

Nicholas turned, saw Okami darting in among the crowd, plunged in after him. He fought through the throngs of Japanese and Germans, broke past a line of tour buses. Okami disappeared around the corner, onto rue Cortot. Nicholas, following after him, saw him turn another corner, head right onto the wider rue des Saules. He got there, saw it was a street of steps, flights and flights of them, heading down off this end of the Butte.

There was Okami, racing downward, and Nicholas took off after him. The steps were divided into flights with broad landing areas. On either side, squat white-stone apartment buildings rose, following the steep slope of the side of the Butte down to the broad rue Caulaincourt, with its bustling shops, thick traffic and Métro stop. Nicholas knew he had to catch Okami before he disappeared into that urban forest where no footprint or spoor would remain.

Their shoes clattered against the stone steps, resounding off the façades of the buildings, and a cloud of pigeons, disturbed in their afternoon meal, rose into the air, swooping in a great black wing.

Nicholas opened his tanjian eye, and heard the silent beat begin against the membrane of *kokoro*, setting thought into motion, psychic impulse into reality.

He hurtled down the stairs, his eyes on the fleeing figure below him, while with his tanjian eye he searched the wider environment for the snare he had felt all along would be there, waiting for him.

As it had many times since he had seen it, the image of the Messulethe in Venice, bending down to pick up his hat, crossed his mind like a cloud across the sun. What was wrong with the image? Something disturbing, something out of place, as if it were a film rather than reality.

He hit one of the landings, took a leap down the next set of steps. He was gaining on Okami. Below them both he could see the wide rue Caulaincourt, the buses lurching forward, the thick lines of traffic, the dense swirl of pedestrians. The city was down there, with a labyrinth of escape routes.

Okami swung like a monkey past a pair of lovers, who broke their tender embrace to look at him.

If he was Okami. Even if Okami did possess *koryoku*, he was too old to be moving with such speed and agility.

At that moment, Okami stumbled. He was halfway down the flight of stairs just below Nicholas. He went down, rolling, then tumbled head over heels down the lower half of the flight.

Nicholas, putting on a burst of speed, sped across the landing, then leapt down the next flight. He landed beside Okami's prostrate form, reached down to turn him over, saw the edge of something along Okami's jawline.

He explored with his finger, felt the stickiness of the spirit-gum, then, digging in, saw the skin begin to wrinkle up in a wholly unnatural manner, exposing the edge of an unfamiliar jawline, and he knew he was looking not at human tissue but at a highly advanced form of acrylic resin made up of a silicon-polycarbonate hybrid of the kind his research and development people had designed for the Chi Project.

Abruptly, the present collided with the image he had been carrying around with him of the Messulethe, the wrongness as he bent to retrieve his hat *and no blood rushed to his cheeks*. Of course not. Then, as now, he had been wearing a mask!

It was the shock of this interior collision of sight and memory that slowed Nicholas's reaction. The inert body abruptly rolled into him, and he found himself staring into the mask of Okami's face. The lips were partly open, a small 'o' framing out the center of the space.

His tanjian eye opened; Nicholas knew what was to happen, saw the ruse, knew it for the snare, felt its jaws snapping shut, and he began to react.

Phut!

But he was too late. Even a moment was too long a time. As his muscles responded to the danger, the mini-dart was already on its way at point-blank range.

It struck him in the neck and he immediately felt his throat begin to close up. He struck out, but part of him was already struggling with the

305

disorderly shut-down of his autonomic nervous system, and there was little strength behind it.

The figure rolled again, cutting Nicholas's feet out from under him, and he began to collapse forward. He tried to break his fall but somehow his limbs had ceased to respond to his brain's command.

For the space of a heartbeat, control of his mind was all that was left him as the toxin spread through his system. Then that, too, was snatched from his grasp.

He felt the sun like a weight upon his back. Its light streamed past in a dizzying array of rainbow colors, then winked out as all consciousness died.

Six Monkeys

Tokyo, Spring 1947

'*Omerta*, the law of silence,' Mikio Okami said. 'If you do not understand this about the Sicilians you understand nothing.'

Colonel Denis Linnear closed his eyes, felt a bead of sweat crawl slowly down his cheek. It fell with a soft *plop* into the steaming water in which he and Okami were immersed.

'It's odd to hear a Japanese speaking of ancient Sicilian law.'

Okami took the time to inhale the scented steam beating up off the water. He knew very well that the Colonel meant a Yakuza *oyabun*, had only used the term 'Japanese' because he was not an *iteki* – a barbarian, as Okami had assumed when his sister had insisted they meet. She was crazy about this man. Foolhardy, Okami thought, because he is Western; even more foolhardy because he is married; most foolhardy because he is happily so.

'My study of these particular Sicilian families began some time ago.' Okami felt his own sweat brought to the surface with the deep rhythm of the heat. 'The logic of it is simple: these people found a way to cross international borders at will. We will have to do no less if we wish to survive in the new world Japan and America together will construct. The Yakuza has always been a strictly *national* organization; like the country within which we exist, we have been unaware of the world at large.'

'*Omerta* and *kyokyaku*,' the Colonel said as if he were alone. Some believed the *kyokyaku*, local heroes, such as firemen, who were appointed by the Tokugawa Shogunate to help keep order in the seventeenth century, were the origins of the Yakuza's mythic credo of honor among thieves, nobility alive like the spark of life within the underworld. As society as a whole grew more corrupt, so too did the *kyokyaku*, until they themselves were absorbed into the shadowland of gambling and prostitution.

No wonder, the Colonel thought, the Mafia has caught Okami's fancy.

'I speak of *omerta* because it is a necessity,' Okami said. 'Because I perceive a threat to my world and it is up to me to do something about it.'

The Colonel was a tall man, handsome and commanding, with piercing blue eyes. He stirred slightly in the hot water. Soft echoes from the other baths in the *furo* were an almost rhythmic counterpoint to their conversation. 'There are others – older than you – who could take up this burden.'

Again, Okami was impressed by the Colonel. He had used the Japanese word for 'older' when what he meant was 'more powerful'. His sister was right: he knew the ways of Japan almost as well as a Japanese.

'In any other society that might be true,' Okami acknowledged. 'But the Yakuza is a closed book. The elders are – arthritic in their thinking. They see the past as future. Whereas I see the future as present.' He lifted a hand briefly to scratch himself. 'I believe you and I are similar in this regard, Linnear-san.'

The Colonel opened his eyes, inclined his head slightly toward Okami. 'You are kind to say so, Okami-san.'

Okami smiled to himself. 'Kind' when he meant 'wise'. 'But we are similar in another regard,' he said. 'We are both men of honor. In my experience this is rare among Westerners; it is a potential to be treasured.'

'Word and deed, Okami-san.'

'Just so.' So he knows, Okami thought with a quickening of his pulse. In Japan, words meant next to nothing. It was deeds that mattered, nothing else.

'I understand how you must have felt, having Kisoko insist that we meet' – the Colonel paused for effect – 'especially given my status in Occupation HQ.'

'You have Douglas MacArthur's ear.'

'Especially given how your sister feels about me.'

Okami did his best not to laugh outright. How he loved the way this man orchestrated conversations! He wondered at how much pleasure he derived by being in the Colonel's company. Two months ago that thought would have profoundly disturbed him. He was grateful for his ability to tolerate change – in himself as well as in others.

'You had every reason to hate me on sight,' the Colonel said. 'And perhaps you did. Lord knows, I couldn't blame you.'

Okami said nothing. Like a chess master he was thinking of what moves the Colonel was bent on making.

'But now we have reached a certain understanding. We know what it is we need from one another and, because of this, we have learned to respect one another. Give and take, Okami-san, that is the dynamic of any successful ongoing relationship.'

'The Yakuza and the United States military,' Okami said. 'You do not find a certain ironic dimension to this alliance?'

A small smile played around the Colonel's tanned face. 'Listen, Okami-san, I believe the human race has an infinite capacity to rationalize dreadful events, unspeakable acts, unholy alliances. What one must sort out for oneself is the ultimate line across which one must never, ever venture.'

Okami stared into those blazing blue eyes. 'As for myself,' he said, 'I am bound by a code of honor no less stringent than *bushido*, the code of the samurai. Anything that does not contravene that code is permissible.'

The Colonel laughed. 'You sound just like a Sicilian.'

At last, Okami permitted himself a smile. 'So we return to the subject of John Leonard, also known as Johnny Leonforte.'

'And, apparently, your beloved *omerta*.' The Colonel steepled his fingers. 'This man Leonforte is making a market in every sort of contraband imaginable: not only US Army matériel, but Russian weaponry, prescription drugs and illicit drugs. The real problem is that no one we've picked up with the stuff will talk.'

Okami nodded. 'Even Yakuza *kobun*. He has been using foot soldiers disenchanted with our alliance with the Occupiers to house and distribute his contraband. Mysteriously, they won't implicate him, either. But I have picked up a name – Leon Waxman. But that's all he is – a name. I have been unable to find anything else about him. It's as if he's being protected.'

'By Leonforte?'

Okami shrugged, and the Colonel sighed, closed his eyes again. 'Someone,' he said, 'has to have a talk with Johnny Leonforte.'

Truth to tell, the aspect of the situation that disturbed Okami the most was the fact that street Yakuza were betraying their oath, bonding themselves to an *iteki*. What strange power did Johnny Leonforte possess that he could command the loyalty of elements of the Japanese criminal underworld?

This was the central question that Okami kept worrying on his way to see the Military Police captain. Of course, the Colonel was too well known to do more than pay Leonforte an official visit, and both of them agreed that this would be more apt to cause problems than solve them. Besides, the best thing about the alliance between Okami and the Colonel was that no one would believe it could exist. Confronting Leonforte with another criminal type could elicit information from him he'd rather die than divulge to someone in the Colonel's position.

Captain Jonathan Leonard spent much of his off time in the small, crowded apartment of a woman he was sleeping with – an Army nurse named Faith Sawhill with a narrow waist and clever eyes. She had the legs of a model and knew how to show them off. She had never seen line duty, but instead belonged to a general with a chronic ulcer who coveted her with the avidity of a religious zealot.

Knowing the Sicilians as he did, Okami doubted that Leonforte had included his inamorata in his business dealings, but on the other hand he worked his magic out of her place so there must somewhere be an overlapping of business and pleasure.

All of this went through Okami's mind as he stood in the open doorway to Faith Sawhill's cluttered apartment. Sawhill was just kissing Leonforte goodbye as she went to serve her general. As she brushed past him, Okami smelled sandalwood. She flashed him a wide, white-toothed smile, and then was gone, her heels click-clacking down the stairwell.

'Mikio Okami.'

'*Hai*.' Okami bowed slightly, saw in his peripheral vision that Leonforte did not return the bow. Well, he was used to such treatment by the conqueror. All the personal rancor had been burned out of him in the aftermath of the war, which he had hated and had fought against while such sentiment meant anything. In the end, he had joined in it, simply because he was a patriot – he loved his country, even when it acted on decisions that were near-sighted and bellicose. But he was no war criminal, and was now doubly glad that Kisoko had introduced him to the Colonel, because he had some debts outstanding and Denis Linnear was his path to settling them.

'Come in,' Leonforte said. 'This is Vincent Alba.' He waved an arm in the direction of a rugged-looking individual with the dark, close-set eyes of a predator, short-cropped hair and large, hairy hands. While Leonforte had on his MP uniform, Alba was dressed as a civilian in a well-fitting and expensive suit of silk and lightweight wool.

'Make yourself at home, put up your feet, whatever,' Leonforte said. He was a tall, lean man, handsome in that dark Mediterranean way, with thick black hair, cut short in the military style. Okami could imagine it long, curling over his forehead and the back of his neck like a Roman senator's.

While Okami perched himself on the edge of a curved love-seat, he went to a small, drop-leafed table set against a wall. 'How about an anisette? Maybe a Sambucca. I got fresh coffee beans to float in it.' He turned round to Okami. 'You know about the Italian custom with Sambucca? No? Then you gotta try it.'

Okami accepted the clear liquid with two dark beans floating on top. He noticed that Alba had not moved. He neither asked for nor received a drink. In fact, Leonforte treated him as if he did not exist.

'Here's looking at you,' Leonforte said, clinking his glass against Okami's. He took half his Sambucca in one shot. 'What d'you think? Good, huh? Better than sake, am I right?'

Okami did not like his first taste of the liquor, but he persisted, willing

310

his palate to adjust. He also willed himself to smile. 'It's excellent,' he said. 'May I have some more?'

While Leonforte was refilling his glass, he took a look around. Every available horizontal space was covered with stacks of books, mostly medical texts, but also, he saw in other piles, tomes on international law and economics, as well as the dynamics of philosophy from Nietzsche to Kant to Socrates. He wondered if Faith Sawhill did all the reading in this dyad.

Leonforte handed him his glass, sat in an oversized chair, crossing one leg over the other. 'What can I do for you? I admit, I wasn't surprised when I got your call. You guys are always asking for favors.' He winked. 'I've looked the other way plenty of times while your goon squads fleeced the public at large. Long as I get my cut, what do I care what you do?' He put his drink down on an old chest which served as a coffee table. 'What's it this time? Gambling? Whore house? Or maybe you want to be enfolded within my benevolent protection so you can make a run at a rival family. These days that kind of shit happens more often than I can count.'

He laughed. 'To tell the truth, I like that best. You guys, with your territories, killing each other off. More room for me.'

'I understand your pleasure,' Okami said. 'It's just like back home, isn't that right, Mr Leonforte.'

Leonforte hardly missed a beat. If Okami hadn't been watching for it, he would never have seen the left eye twitch. 'Why did you call me that?'

'Did you think I would come here without doing my homework?'

'There's homework and then there's homework.' For the first time he glanced at Vincent Alba, who stood rather like a forbidding grandfather clock near a print of a Roman battle scene. 'I figure people who take the time to do some digging on me I got to watch out for – they could be dangerous.' He picked up his glass again, and Okami was aware without having to look at him directly that Alba had subtly changed his stance. 'I respond quickly and instinctively to danger, know what I mean, Okami? I don't fuck around. That way I don't have to worry about digging a bullet out of my gut.'

'You've made yourself all too clear,' Okami said. He deliberately finished off his Sambucca. 'This really is quite good.'

'Glad you appreciate things Italian,' Leonforte said shortly. 'Now tell me what the fuck you want.'

'All right.' Okami put down his glass. 'I propose we do a deal. I have a good idea of the commodities you're trading in . . .' – he held up his hand – 'Please don't bother to deny it. I have in my men a distribution network par excellence. My people know every back alley in Tokyo. I know

311

where your commodities will fetch the highest prices – and where it won't be worth your time going. In short, we could make an excellent team.'

Leonforte produced a hard laugh. 'You hear that, Vinnie? He wants I should give a piece of the action to a snot-nosed gook.' He jumped up with such force that the glasses on the trunk shook. 'Who the fuck do you think you are, slant-eyes, to come in here drink my Sambucca and then demand a piece of my action? If I were back home I'd horsewhip you, but since I'm in a foreign country I gotta show some restraint, ain't that so, Vinnie? Oh, yeah.' He pointed to the door. 'So get the hell out of here and count yourself a lucky buck.'

'The other man – Vincent Alba – is his bodyguard,' Okami said, 'no doubt about it.'

'The two of them sound like quite a pair,' the Colonel said. He dipped his pipe into a leather pouch, stuffed it with tobacco. His fingers curled lovingly around the rough-sided bowl; the pipe was a kind of talisman. It had even saved his life and the lives of his unit in Singapore in early 1945. Because he was looking for it he had held his men from advancing into an open area where, a moment later, an enemy bombardment began. 'With those epithets he's using I have no doubt he's in need of one.'

The two men sat in the cramped back room of a late-night bar off the Ginza. It was a perfectly legitimate place and therefore safe for them to meet. They did so, however, only at night, and entered and exited the place through the service entrance off a grimy, deserted alley. The owner himself served them; the Colonel had saved his establishment after a notorious black-marketeer was caught here and the MPs threatened to close it down. The Colonel, always the futurist, saw in this place just what it had become – a safe house for him, where he could operate securely.

'I need to do something about the inroads he's making by recruiting from the Yakuza ranks,' Okami said. 'The fact that he almost threw me bodily out of the apartment when I offered him a deal makes me suspicious.'

'Indeed,' the Colonel said. 'He's certainly not stupid. I would say on the face of it he's already got a deal.'

Okami contemplated the Colonel for a long time. The sounds of glasses clinking, low voices and, once, a bright spray of drunken laughter drifted in to them. The owner entered and, without a word, replaced their empty beer mugs with full ones.

At last, Okami said, 'If that is the case we both have a serious problem on our hands. For you, it means that Leonforte is just about untouchable. For me, it means that my world has suddenly gone out of control. Leonforte has a deal with another *oyabun* and I should have known about it by now.

312

That I don't means there is a Yakuza boss making secret deals with foreigners.'

'Like you.'

The Colonel's response was not a rebuke, merely a reminder that one's power was never absolute, even though as it grew it conveyed the illusion that it was.

The Colonel turned his head slightly, the ghost of a smile appearing and disappearing in the lamplight. 'Something has happened, Okami-san. We've touched a nerve somewhere.'

'What do you mean?'

'I was called into Willoughby's office today,' the Colonel said. Major General Charles Willoughby was, along with the Colonel himself, one of MacArthur's most influential aides. He was also head of G-2, the intelligence section of the Occupation, and a constant thorn in the Colonel's side. 'I got what amounted to a dressing down.'

Okami kept a keen eye on the Colonel. He seemed relaxed, almost contemplative; Okami took that as an excellent sign.

'Apparently Willoughby's people have got wind of the ad hoc investigation I've been doing. Thank God he's still got no idea of your involvement.'

'I've been exceedingly careful,' Okami said.

For the past three months he and the Colonel had been looking into why certain key officers in the former Imperial army and navy of Japan had not appeared on the rolls of the war-crimes tribunals. Okami himself had identified these officers to the Colonel as people whose excessive zeal and power had led them to commit acts of calculated brutality that now required the most extreme punishment.

The Colonel had submitted the names of these officers to the adjutant general's office, along with documentation Okami had amassed on them, but to date he had received no satisfactory answer to his numerous queries. Clearly, someone was stonewalling.

'Willoughby wondered aloud why with all I had on my plate I was taking time to go off on what he characterized as a wild goose chase. Do you know what that is? – a useless search. "If you're bored with your job," he told me, "I'll be more than happy to write you a letter of recommendation for any other that would fit your requirements."' The Colonel's blue eyes were frosty. 'I marked how careful he was being. At no time did he mention the subject of my investigation or any interest he himself may have had in it.'

The Colonel tapped the cold dottle out of his pipe, began to fill it up again. 'I began to wonder how I'd managed to step on Willoughby's toes while looking for your war criminals.' He struck a match. 'Of course, it would take someone of extraordinary muscle to pull the jackets on these officers and hustle them away from the adjutant general's office.' He stuck the pipe in his mouth, began to draw the aromatic tobacco through it. When he had it going to his satisfaction, he said, 'After the meeting, I had copies of the documentary evidence you had provided sent to him by messenger. I ordered the messenger to make certain that Willoughby himself signed for the sealed package. I now have his signature.'

'Willoughby will do nothing with the information,' Okami said.

'Then I will have my answer,' the Colonel replied. 'I'll know he's taken these men into custody for some security reason of his own. There needn't be anything sinister to it. Perhaps they are privy to sensitive intelligence MacArthur doesn't want transcripted during an open tribunal.'

'Justice must be done.' Okami's expression was set in stone. 'I *will* have my vengeance, Linnear-san; that was an essential part of our alliance.'

'I understand completely.'

But later that night, on his way across war-torn Tokyo, Okami had his doubts. It could be that the Colonel and Willoughby were cut from the same cloth. They were both Western, after all, and who could trust Westerners? Okami shook his head. That was a dangerous path; he knew part of him was still thinking as the other *oyabun* did.

Sometimes, as now, Okami felt positively schizophrenic. He knew in his heart what had to be done. This was a new world – the war in the Pacific had seen to that. If the war had taught him anything it was that Japan could no longer depend solely on itself in the coming decades. It had come down on the wrong foot in the war – had destroyed itself and ravaged its people – because of its history of isolationism. *It was our lack of understanding of Westerners – especially the Americans – that defeated us*, he thought. *We underestimated their strength, discounted their resilience, and misunderstood their resolve. We cannot afford to do that again.*

His own resolve to see his businesses flourish in the decades to come was what had prompted him to form his alliance with the Colonel. And, the fact was, he liked the man. And this attraction was strange to him, for he, like a vast majority of his fellow Japanese in those days, felt a profound disconnection from the other societies of the world outside Asia.

Strange to him, the Japanese, to find in the Colonel an understanding of Shintoism, Zen, Confucianism and the legion of martial metaphysics which together made up the ethos of Japan. Extraordinary, he thought now as he stared out into the sodium glare of nighttime Tokyo.

No, he decided, he trusted the Colonel implicitly. But he was disturbed that the Colonel was willing to give Willoughby the benefit of the doubt.

But, to be fair, in his position, it was easier for Okami to smell a conspiracy than it was for the Colonel. Okami had already learned from bitter experience that one was the last to become aware of disorder in one's own house.

Okami had come of age during that time seven years ago when his father had been betrayed by his own brother, who had sold out to another family which coveted the lucrative Okami territory in the heart of Tokyo's business districts. Okami's father had been slain by members of this rival family as he lay alone in his bed, Okami's mother having left that day to visit her ailing mother outside Hiroshima. Acting on detailed information provided by Okami's uncle, these men had slipped into the house, bypassing guards, to plunge their swords into Okami's father's abdomen.

At the funeral, Okami had stood between his mother and his uncle, knowing nothing but sorrow. Two weeks later, while drinking in a late-night bar with his girlfriend, he had overheard a drunken conversation among a large group of young Yakuza *kobun*. Two happened to be the ones who had slain his father, and they were recounting to the delight of their compatriots how they were able to slip into and out of the house unseen.

The next morning, Okami took his father's *katana*, secreted it beneath a long raincoat he wore. He went to his uncle's place of business and asked to see him. After fifteen minutes or so he was ushered in. His uncle, imagining himself by his perfidy amassing money and prestige by the minute, smiled broadly as he introduced his nephew to those Yakuza toughs around him. His uncle, always flamboyant, enjoyed having an entourage. His mind was mired in his country's feudal past, when élite warriors ruled the land and commanded lesser mortals.

As was the custom, Okami bowed to these men, who stood while Okami's uncle sat behind his massive wood desk, extending his right hand, palm up. When he straightened up, his uncle asked him why he had come.

Okami promptly took a step forward. As he did so, his unbuttoned raincoat parted and, as he leapt upon his uncle's desk, he drew his father's sword. Before any of the startled bodyguards could react, he raised the *katana* above his head and, with all his might, slashed it obliquely downward, neatly severing his uncle's head from his neck.

A fountain of blood exploded upward, catching two of the bodyguards as they began to react. Okami's uncle's headless body jerked galvanically. The head lay upside down on the bloody desk, its eyes open wide in disbelief, its quizzical expression frozen as if on a well-crafted mask.

Okami slammed the butt of his *katana* into the nose of one bodyguard, then whirled, his blade carving into the shoulder of another. A gun fell to

315

the floor as the man howled in pain and, collapsing, tried vainly to stanch the flow of blood.

There were two others. Swords were out. There was no question now of using a gun; the man who did so would lose so much face by dispatching Okami without honor that he would no longer be considered Yakuza. Cast summarily out of this curious, tightly knit band of outsiders, he would have nowhere to go; he would have lost the only world that would accept him.

Okami feinted right, went left, leaping off the desk. He drew his legs up beneath him, slashed right as he hurtled past the third bodyguard. His swordblade tracked across the man's chest, curling open fabric, skin and muscle. The man dropped his *katana* from nerveless hands.

Okami felt a quick numbness as he landed and, turning back toward the fourth man, the searing pain came and he knew he had been wounded. He clamped down on the pain, blocked a second blow from the man and, kicking out into his knee, used the break to get inside the man's defenses. He smashed the butt of his sword into the man's right ear, then lunged forward, felt the tip of the blade slide in and out of flesh. The fourth bodyguard crumpled head-first to the floor.

This is how Mikio Okami became *oyabun* of the Okami clan.

Before he left the office, Okami had the presence of mind to take up his uncle's head by its damp hair. For six weeks afterward it hung by a leather cord in the courtyard of Okami's house. Everyone who he summoned over that time – the underbosses of his family, as well as the *oyabun* of the other Tokyo families – were obliged to pass it on their way to meet with him.

The last *oyabun* Okami summoned was Seizo Yamauchi. He was a bull-shouldered man with a long, pouty face and a righteous air about him. He was forever decrying the loss of traditional values among the new recruits to the Yakuza ranks, but he was a usurer par excellence, squeezing the old people in his territory who increasingly came to him for help, as the specter of war crept over the land and conscripted their sons on whom they had been dependent.

The two *kobun* Okami had overheard in the bar were from the Yamauchi clan.

As Seizo Yamauchi made his way across the courtyard he stared long and hard at the shriveled, crusted head of Okami's uncle. He shook his head disapprovingly as if he were regarding the handiwork of some anarchist.

'Filthy days,' he said to Okami when the ritual introductions had been made.

'I couldn't agree more,' Okami said, reaching over the hibachi to make tea for his guest. He could feel the older man's tension like a pressure-drop

316

in a descending elevator, and he fought to keep his own anxiety in check. He had a long way to go, and there could be nasty surprises lying in wait for him.

Neither man said another word until the cut leaves had been placed in the bottom of the cups, the hot water poured over them, the whisk taken up, making the pale-green froth on top. Okami watched as Yamauchi put the cup to his lips; only then did he take his tea. Yamauchi nodded, pleased at the younger man's manners.

'This is why I asked for this meeting,' Okami said in his sweetest voice. 'Now that the traitor to the Okami clan is taken care of, I would seek an alliance with the Yamauchi.' He poured more tea for them both. 'These times are, indeed, filthy. War is coming; I can feel it in the same way an old man feels the onset of rain – in my bones. Now, more than ever, we need to band together, drop our various territorial feuds, forsake revenge. For survival, Yamauchi-san.'

He put down his cup. 'And for another reason, if I may speak freely.' The older man nodded, more at ease now. 'I am a young man. Perhaps – as some no doubt have said – I am as yet too unseasoned to become *oyabun* of such a large family as mine. But I have been merely reacting to circumstance, so perhaps I can be forgiven the abrupt . . . elevation in rank. However, I am not unaware of my precarious situation and, thinking it over, I see that it would be to my benefit if I were to have a mentor, someone older and wiser than I am, to whom I can turn for valued advice and counsel. In return for this expenditure of time and effort, I am willing to share the wealth of the Okami. How does this idea strike you, Yamauchi-san?'

Yamauchi made a show of mulling this offer over, but Okami could feel his elation as if the sun had appeared from behind a cloud.

At length, Yamauchi said, 'What you propose has merit. It shows me that despite the rashness of youth that some *oyabun* condemn, you possess a wisdom others in your clan did not.' He nodded. 'I accept your proposal.'

'Excellent,' Okami said. 'And to seal the arrangement I ask only that you find the two perpetrators of my father's murder and put them to death by your own hand.'

Yamauchi said nothing for a long time. He did not move; did not touch the remainder of his tea which was growing cold in its cup. After a time, he said slowly, 'I have had enough tea. Please bring a bottle of Napoleon brandy so that we may each in our own private way celebrate this historic union of the Yamauchi and the Okami families.'

*

317

Three nights later, Okami welcomed Mitsuba Yamauchi to the back room of the late-night bar that served as a Yakuza safe house. Mitsuba was one of Seizo's underbosses and one of his two chief expediters; he was also Seizo's nephew.

Mitsuba was wary, as Okami would have been in his place. He was a thin man with no hips and the long legs of an arachnid. He had a nervous habit of stroking the side of his jaw with his thumb. His face was carved into flat planes, and was dominated by a thick-lipped mouth he worked into an ingenuous-looking smile for friend and enemy alike.

After the ritual greeting, Mitsuba unbuttoned his jacket, sat at ease across the small table from Okami. As he did so, Okami saw the butt of a .38 arching up from the waistband of his trousers. Hovering in the main room of the bar were a pair of Mitsuba's soldiers, alert as hunting-dogs who had been given the scent of prey. Okami was alone, deliberately so.

For thirty minutes or so the two men drank fine black-market scotch and spoke in polite banalities. The sounds of the bar up front were muted. A radio played a jaunty American pop song and some drunk sang along with it for a few bars before going unalterably off-key.

At length, Okami said, 'What is your opinion of the proposed merger between my family and yours?'

'You have an interesting manner of expressing what is already a fact,' Mitsuba said.

Okami nodded sagely, though a bit ruefully, 'I, too, believed this to be the case,' he said. 'Until today when this was delivered to me.' He rose, went to the back of the room, switched on a 16-mm film projector. 'I would ask you to watch this film in its entirety, Mitsuba-san, and then render an opinion.'

The film had already begun to run as Okami slipped back into his seat. Out of the corner of his eye he watched Mitsuba's reaction to the grainy but perfectly clear black-and-white film capturing with professional skill Seizo Yamauchi shooting to death two members of his own clan. They were, of course, the soldiers who had murdered Okami's father.

The spellbinding film ran its course. Okami briefly left Mitsuba to turn off the projector. He poured more scotch for them both.

'Where –' Mitsuba paused to clear his throat. He swallowed half his whiskey before continuing. 'Where did you get this document?'

'From a source of mine in the Tokko.' This was the notorious 'thought police', who were so powerful they were even feared by the Yakuza.

'So the police already have this evidence against Seizo-san.'

Okami noted that he hadn't used the term 'my uncle'. He said nothing, wanting to see in which direction his pinch in the buttock would cause Mitsuba to jump.

'This will cause chaos in the ranks,' Mitsuba said almost to himself. 'With Seizo-san gone . . .' He turned his gaze on Okami. 'May I confess something to you, Okami-san. I have for some time been disenchanted with Seizo-san's long-range . . . plans. In fact, I bitterly opposed several decisions he made most recently.' His eyes held Okami's, and they both knew Mitsuba meant the directive to murder Okami's father.

'I appreciate knowing this,' Okami said. 'Perhaps something of the alliance between our two families can yet be salvaged.' Then he rose, indicating the interview was at an end.

An hour later, this same scenario was replayed with Katsuodo Kozo, a brash, swaggering man, Seizo's other chief expediter. Kozo had a hard-edged, brittle personality which had made him almost as many enemies as his clear-eyed, logical mind had made him admirers. Unlike Mitsuba, he had come alone.

He sat still and silent through the film, absorbed Okami's spiel without comment. When Okami was through, he said, 'You know, these two boys who Seizo-san shot are the ones responsible for your father's death.'

'They were the weapon, that much is true,' Okami said with some emphasis. 'But it was Seizo-san whose hand directed that weapon.'

Kozo considered this for some time. 'I don't believe Seizo-san would have taken retribution on them had it not been a stipulation of the alliance.'

'Old debts must be settled,' Okami said, 'before new liaisons can be consummated.'

Kozo made a steeple of his fingers, stared at them intently. 'It seems that Seizo-san made a serious miscalculation.' Now he stirred a little. 'I cannot speak for Mitsuba, but as for myself I believe the best course for the Yamauchi family is to forge its own path which runs parallel to the Okami.'

Well said, thought Okami. 'There is bound to be no small turmoil within the Yamauchi in the coming weeks,' he said. 'There are those who will disagree vigorously with your philosophy. This turmoil may spread to the other families. There may even be talk among the *oyabun* about interven-ing in their own self-serving way. I do not believe this to be the best course for the Yamauchi. It no doubt would prove dangerous for whoever is seeking control.'

He leaned over, poured whiskey for them both. 'The Yamauchi family has lost its way. My wish is for the Yamauchi to regain the stability it once had. As of now I consider it a danger not only to the Okami but to all the families. Rest assured I will do everything in my power to see that this stability is established and maintained.'

Okami could see that Kozo understood precisely what he was proposing. He lifted his glass in a Western toast. 'To stability,' he said with the ghost of a smile.

A week later, responding to an anonymous tip, the police discovered the bodies of Seizo Yamauchi and his nephew Mitsuba in the living-room of Mitsuba's residence. From the position of the bodies, the angles of the entry wounds on both bodies, it was clear that the two Yakuza had had a disagreement which had led each to use deadly force against the other. And if there were one or two minor discrepancies, the police were more than willing to overlook them. After all, the main thing was that there were two less Yakuza to worry about. Maybe they would all rub each other out – now, there was a policeman's dream come true.

In the ensuing weeks, the bodies of various Yamauchi soldiers and underbosses were found, until Katsuodo Kozo had weeded out all his enemies and had consolidated his power. As Okami had predicted, the degree of bloodshed unnerved the other *oyabun*, and there was some talk of moving in concert to establish order within the Yamauchi. True to his word, Okami protected the peace and Kozo by keeping the other *oyabun* at bay until Kozo had established control.

The outcome not only increased Kozo's standing in the underworld, but also cemented Okami's. From then on he was seen increasingly as a visionary who could guide the families through difficult times.

This was the beginning of Okami's rise to the position of Kaisho, the mysterious commander, *oyabun* of all *oyabun*.

It happened that General Willoughby had an adjutant who had come to the attention of Okami's people. This was because he had a taste for young men, and the underworld into which he was obliged to slip in order to slake his particular thirst was the province of Okami's family.

His name was Jack Donnough. He was a youngish man, quite handsome, with sandy hair, a high forehead and green eyes. He was thin-lipped and intense at work but, according to Okami's sources, just the opposite during his nightside forays.

Now, as Okami made his way across nighttime Tokyo, he thought he might have use for Donnough. He had his driver change course, head into Shinjuku, where establishments of the water trade, as the Japanese so eloquently put it, flourished like mushrooms beneath a tree.

The owner of The Iron Gate ushered him inside, bowing so often and so deeply her head must have begun to spin. She was a tiny woman in a black and orange kimono. Her hair was elaborately coifed in the style of the old geisha. Huge tortoise-shell pins held it in place. Her face, though lined, was still an elegant reminder of times when she had been both beautiful and desirable.

Jack Donnough was indeed plowing the fragrant field, she told him matter-of-factly as she pointed out the room upstairs in the back. Okami thought it interesting that Americans had such a strict taboo against sexual liaisons between men; in Japan, it had been an accepted part of life for centuries.

Curiously, Donnough insisted on this one room, the owner said. She didn't know why but, after a swift perimeter inspection of the building, Okami did. The window of Donnough's trysting place gave out onto the corner alley which was dark and easy to get lost in in the event of a police raid or other disturbance.

Okami went back inside The Iron Gate and was about to mount the stairs when he saw the Army nurse he had encountered when he had gone to see Johnny Leonforte – Faith Sawhill – walk in.

He stepped quickly back into the shadows of the hallway that led to the kitchen, watching her as she went straight for the stairs and up them. It was interesting that she was here, even more so that she apparently knew her way around.

Okami approached the owner, asked her if she knew anything about the American woman.

'She comes in from time to time,' the woman said, concentrating. 'Perhaps one time in every three or four that Donnough does. She's never here when he isn't. What she does in there with the two men I have no idea.' She shrugged. 'I told Donnough the first time it happened that I expected more money from him. He paid it without question.'

Fascinated, Okami went silently up the stairs after Faith Sawhill.

At the end of the corridor he paused, considering his next move. On impulse, he put his ear to the door which was, in this kind of establishment, thin enough.

'Are you sure it's safe?' Sawhill's voice came through the door.

'I told you,' a male voice, undoubtedly Donnough's, said, 'he doesn't speak English.'

'This whole thing gives me the creeps.'

'Which whole thing,' Donnough said icily, 'sex between men or running for Alba?'

'You're awfully flip for someone playing so dangerous a game,' Sawhill said. 'If Willoughby finds out what you're doing . . .'

'He won't,' Donnough said flatly. 'The little Fascist is too busy exercising his Jap colonels' brains. He wants to turn them into spies.' He gave a low chuckle. 'Well, I suppose work is hard to come by if you're a full-blown war criminal.'

'Those men should be behind bars,' Sawhill said. 'I know some of the atrocities they're responsible for.'

'So does Willoughby, I can assure you,' Donnough said. 'He has no trouble sleeping at night. But that's because he's got the Communists on the brain. His idea is to use these Jap officers as the nucleus of a new military general staff for a rearmed Japan. "The Soviets," he likes to say, "are only spitting distance away."'

Okami could hear the sound of his blood rushing in his inner ear. His heart was pounding and his mouth was dry. What had he stumbled into? He had been right about Willoughby. But what was Sawhill running – as Donnough had put it – between Donnough and Alba? And why Alba and not his boss Johnny Leonforte?

'I'm late,' Sawhill said. 'Let me have it.'

Her voice was abruptly louder and, with a start, Okami realized she was nearer the door.

'Here it is,' Donnough said. 'The latest poop on Willoughby's group of fifteen. This ought to make Alba's day.'

Okami heard a rustling, and he pulled away from the door, turned and sprinted back down the corridor. He was heading quickly down the stairs when he heard the door open behind him and the click of high heels in the corridor above him.

He was sitting on a black lacquer bench, waiting for her when she came down the stairs.

'Miss Sawhill,' he said, rising and smiling at her as she reached ground level.

Faith Sawhill turned in his direction. Her cool dark-blue eyes appraised him as if he were an interesting handbag in a shop window.

'And you are Mikio Okami. I remember you.'

'That's good,' Okami said. 'I wonder whether we could have a drink.'

'I'm afraid that's out of the question,' Faith said, frowning. She tucked a manila folder she had been clutching under her arm. 'I'm already late. Jonathan doesn't like to be kept waiting.'

'Don't you mean Vincent Alba?' Okami said.

For the first time, Faith appeared briefly startled. 'Why, yes, under the circumstances I think I can spare a minute or two.'

Okami took her to an *akachochin* down the street. Its red lantern swung cheerily in the darkness. Inside, it was boisterous and so smoky they couldn't see the far end of the long, narrow room. Unconcerned by the din, Okami pushed his way to the bar, ordered two scotches without asking Faith what

322

she wanted, then led her to an empty booth at the rear of the place.

'You and Alba have a nice little racket going,' Okami said as soon as they were seated.

'I beg your pardon?'

'Maybe you two are sleeping together behind Johnny's back.'

Faith laughed. 'Yeah, and maybe the moon is made of green cheese.' She laughed again. 'The guy's an ape.'

'An ape you're working for.'

Faith turned her head. Her dark-blue eyes sometimes had the uncanny ability to take on the tone of her surroundings. Right now they possessed the fugitive translucence of smoke. She smiled. 'You're either clairvoyant or a good eavesdropper.'

'What's he got that Johnny doesn't?'

'Alba? He's absolutely loyal. And he knows how to take orders.' Faith picked up her glass, sipped the whiskey. 'Johnny's erratic, a hothead. His schemes of conquest aren't always in line with reality.'

'So Vincent Alba is his shepherd.'

She nodded. 'That's as good a way to put it as any.'

Okami spent the next several minutes studying this woman. She was exceedingly beautiful, with an oval face, cat-like eyes and a rich bow of a mouth which reminded Okami of a particularly memorable geisha he had once known. Besides that, however, she knew how to conduct a conversation, and this above all else made her intriguing.

'Who does Alba work for?'

'Right now you're better off not knowing,' Faith said in such a serious tone that it gave Okami pause.

'Perhaps I should be asking Major Donnough these questions.'

To her credit, Faith didn't even blink an eye. 'I can see the drift of this conversation,' she said. She arched an eyebrow. 'Am I to assume Vincent and I have a new partner?'

'It's as easy as that?'

She shrugged. 'When in Rome . . .' She saw his perplexed look, added, 'This is your country so you have us at a disadvantage. Besides, if you blow the whistle on Donnough we're all down the tubes. My decision's simple. Two-thirds of the pot is better than none at all.'

He considered for a moment. 'What's Alba doing with the information on Willoughby's group of war criminals?'

'Nothing, that I know of,' Faith said. 'He's merely passing it back to the States.'

'And you two have no idea of its use?'

'None.'

Okami decided this was getting him nowhere. 'And what if I put a gun to Vincent Alba's head while I ask him these questions?'

Faith snorted and her eyes turned dark. 'Jesus, you slobs are all alike, aren't you? Everything's settled by a weapon.'

Okami found himself pricked by the note of scorn in her voice. He held out his hand. 'Let me see what Donnough passed on to you.'

Faith gave him a curious look, as if she were seeing him for the first time. 'I can see you've given me no choice.'

He quickly scanned the intelligence reports Donnough had copied. Willoughby had been a busy boy. Lieutenant-General Arisue, former chief of Military Intelligence for the General Staff and several of his officers had already been incorporated into G-2's historical section, where they were providing Willoughby with up-to-date reports on Soviet troop movements in the Far East, as well as evaluating other intelligence. Colonel Takushiro Hattori, who had been chief of the First Section of the General Staff's Ops Division, was now in charge of Japanese military demobilization. That was appalling on two counts. A war criminal was in charge of weeding out other war criminals and, should Willoughby's plan for Japan's rearming become a reality, Hattori would be in charge of remobilizing the army.

This is infamous, Okami thought. It took some concentration to stop himself from shaking with rage. These men, whom he now saw paraded before him like a chorus line in a dance hall, had been elevated to some perverted form of celebrity, instead of being condemned to the seven levels of hell as they deserved.

'You seem a bit tense, Mr Okami,' Faith said. 'Perhaps I should order us another round of drinks.'

Okami, wrestling with his personal animosity, was beginning to ponder the larger implications of this report; namely, of what possible use was it to Vincent Alba's boss back in the States? Whoever he might be, he was certainly a Mafia *capo*. Why would he find it interesting that elements of the US Army were employing war criminals in their own intelligence network?

The scotches came and Okami drank his straight down. He no longer cared what Faith Sawhill thought of him. The revelations of Donnough's report had made her irrelevant. She was, despite her beauty and her cleverness, only a woman, whose role in this game he already knew. She was a minor player, like Johnny Leonforte – what had Donnough called her? A runner. He and the Colonel had wondered if someone was backing Leonforte, and now he had his answer: Vincent Alba's mysterious *capo* Stateside.

He looked up. 'Tell me, Miss Sawhill, what's your role in all this? The Mafia's strictly a man's game.'

'And you know all about men's games, don't you, Mr Okami.' She smiled so sweetly when she said this he might have been her lover. She looked down for a moment before continuing. 'The truth is I have a restless soul. I'm a good American. I came out here to do my duty for my country to the best of my abilities.'

'And just happened to fall in with the wrong crowd,' he said skeptically.

'I fell in love with the wrong man.' Sadness and remorse filled her face. 'I admit to being stupid, falling for Johnny, for his manic energy and his crazy dreams.' She lifted a hand, let it fall to her lap. 'Why did it happen? It's the aftermath of the war, or maybe it's this city – Tokyo – so alien and strange and devastated. I – got sucked into everything.' That smile again, so disarming. 'I'm as curious as a cat, you see. Even Vincent and Johnny couldn't hide their work from me for long. Vincent, when he found out, was all for throwing me out, but' – the smile broadened – 'I wrapped my thigh around Johnny's and he let me stay. So I got involved like a tree caught up in a twister – a powerful storm.'

Okami wondered whether to believe her. Then he realized that it didn't matter – she didn't matter at all. Only the intelligence purloined from Willoughby had consequence here.

He rose, the report still in his hand. 'I'll make a copy of this. You'll have it back by morning.'

Faith looked distressed. 'Vincent will have a fit.'

'Let him,' Okami said. 'He'd better get used to having a new partner.'

'This report is invaluable,' Okami said. 'It's the weapon I've needed to get my revenge.'

The Colonel was studying the papers while he and Okami walked in Ueno Park. The Colonel gave no sign that he saw the brandy bottle Okami carried and from which he took a swig from time to time. Okami had not been to bed. He was drunk, had been drinking ever since he had left Faith Sawhill, his elation mounting with each step he had taken, because he now saw a way to crush those he hated most.

It was early morning, fog still curling in off the Sumida River. A china-blue sky was peeking out from the dregs of night like a baby robin out of its shell. Below, the Yoshino cherry trees were bursting with sprays of pink blossoms so pale they were almost white.

There was a scent in the air which Okami always associated with his childhood. In those days, he had seen very little of his father, but each spring his father would take Okami and his brother to Ueno Park for cherry blossom viewing. The sweet, ethereal scent reminded him of holding his father's hand. It was hard and dry and comforting. He had felt happy with the tall figure towering over him.

'Look at the cherry blossoms above your head,' he could remember his father whispering in an almost reverential tone. 'They bloom so quickly, and then at the height of their beauty, fall to the ground and die. This is why we love them so, because all men are like these blossoms; we have their beauty inside ourselves, we're one with them. *Shizen*' – nature – 'is a word that was imported from China because here we had no word for it. Why did we need it? Aren't man and nature one and the same?'

Years later, when Okami had been summoned to his father's house the night he was killed, he had knelt beside the bed, waiting for his mother's arrival. He would not allow any of his father's men into the bedroom, though he could not stop them from swarming around the house and grounds, and guarding him. Later, he would deal one by one with those who had been remiss in their duty to his father. But for this moment he had bent his head and, taking his father's cold hand in his, had out of season smelled that soft, sweet scent of cherry blossoms at the height of their brief, effulgent life.

Now, walking again in Ueno, Okami inhaled deeply that miraculous scent, redolent of metaphysics and memories. He glanced over at the Colonel, who was going over the reports again and again, mostly without comment.

Okami said, 'If you take this intelligence straight to MacArthur –'

The Colonel looked up sharply. 'What makes you think that he isn't already aware of Willoughby's plans?'

Okami had no ready answer for that.

'Here among the cherry trees,' the Colonel said softly, 'we must take time to look at this picture calmly.' He took several deep breaths and Okami was reminded all over again why he liked this Westerner so much.

'I know what these men are capable of,' the Colonel went on in that same soothing tone. 'I know they gave the orders to execute your brother.'

'He was a pacifist,' Okami said in a strangled voice. 'He was the brave one, not me. He spoke out for what I was feeling in my heart but never said aloud.'

'Perhaps he was a bit foolish, too,' the Colonel commented. 'Those were not times to speak your mind if it went against the majority.'

'No, no, don't you see, he was true to himself. A hero.' The bitterness in Okami's voice was like poison lacing a goblet of wine. 'And I was the one who was decorated – a joke, surely, because I did what I did out of fear for my own life; my captain would have shot me in the back if I had not obeyed orders. But I should have risked that.'

326

Perhaps because he was drunk, he added, 'Aren't you going to ask me *why* I should have risked being shot in the back?'

The Colonel stopped, took the empty brandy bottle out of Okami's hand. 'I know why,' he said. 'For glory. *If only we might fall, like cherry blossoms in the Spring – so pure and radiant!*'

At the Colonel's recitation of a poem a kamikaze pilot had written just before flying to his death, Okami began to weep. He was drunk, and among friends, so this was permissible – desirable, even. The excruciating internal pressures of holding all emotion inside oneself required periodic exorcism.

'General MacArthur can't possibly condone what Willoughby is contemplating,' Okami said as he wiped his eyes. The cool, fresh air was dissipating his drunkenness despite his best efforts to keep it going. 'Rearming Japan now would be a diplomatic disaster for your country and an economic one for mine. If Japan can't find a way to forge a new economic foundation based on peacetime commodities there will be no future at all for us.'

'I agree,' the Colonel said. 'And so, I believe, does MacArthur.' He clasped his hands behind his back, slapping one against the other rhythmically. 'But we still have no idea where this information is being funnelled or who might now have access to it. Who is our enemy now, Okami-san? I cannot see them, can you? And I have a growing suspicion they may be powerful – and they may be legion.'

'I see no time for this . . . contemplation.' In his state, he spat the last word. 'You must go to MacArthur –'

The Colonel shook his head. 'No, listen to me, my friend, we must defuse the scenario Willoughby has in mind – but we must be circumspect. MacArthur detests any sense of rift between his people – he's got his own problems with the President and the allies, and he's wary of anything that could be turned into negative publicity. And we must gain a sense of those arrayed against us. Tell me, Okami-san, would you draw your *katana* while you are deaf, dumb and blind?'

'I would if I had to,' Okami said dully. His heart was burning with the last of the effects of the alcohol and his need to see vengeance done.

The Colonel paused, turned toward Okami. They were beneath an ancient cherry. Enclosed within its ethereal, fragrant bower, they might have been gods on the summit of Mt Fuji, discussing the fate of the mortals below them.

'You're not the suicidal type. I know you better than that,' he said tartly. He shook his head again. 'We have Alba and his Stateside *capo* making inroads here – not merely in the American black market but also among your own Yakuza. The Mafia and the Yakuza in bed together is a daunting concept. *This* is our main problem. Willoughby's scheme is merely part of a larger picture, one that we must bring into focus before we know which way to move.'

'I suppose this is the time for me to pay Alba a visit.'

'No,' the Colonel said. 'I believe that would be a mistake. As yet, we cannot know who is our friend and who our foe.' They commenced walking again. The sun felt warm on their shoulders, and the early-morning breeze had died. The Colonel had to maintain silence while they passed a pair of armed soldiers. A child ran up to him, his arms heaped with cherry blossoms he had scooped off the grass. He threw his arms up, scattering the blossoms like snow. His laughter rang through the park as he scampered away.

'The prudent course of action now is to confront Johnny Leonforte,' the Colonel continued when it was safe. 'From what you've been able to gather, he seems to be the weak link in this chain. If so, he'll be the easiest to crack.'

'It might take some kind of force.'

The Colonel's face was solemn. 'Okami-san, it is vital that we know what kind of a situation we are confronted with. The future of your country – and perhaps mine – hangs in the balance.'

Okami chose the time and the place with great care. He spent three days shadowing Johnny Leonforte so that he could get an idea of his routine. In the end, he decided to take him on his way to Faith Sawhill's apartment.

Okami had discovered that, by and large, Leonforte kept his evenings clear because that was the time he did his most lucrative business. Okami watched from the shadows across the street as Leonforte pulled up in his motor-pool jeep.

Pressing once the flat hilt of his *wakizashi*, his long, slightly curved knife which lay close against his belly, Okami headed quickly across the street.

'Johnny!' he called as he neared the other man.

Leonforte's head turned so fast Okami could hear the vertebrae in his neck crack.

Leonforte's eyes narrowed. 'You! I told you –!'

Okami's right hand shot out, catching Leonforte a powerful blow in his solar plexus just where the major nerves bundled beneath the muscles.

'Aagh!'

Leonforte sounded as if he were gagging. He began to topple forward, but held onto the seat back with one hand, fumbled for his officer's .45 with the other. Okami reached out serenely and squeezed a spot on his upper arm quite near the shoulder. Leonforte's entire right side went numb.

Okami dragged him from the jeep, swept him into a narrow, wind-blown alley at the side of Sawhill's apartment building. Propping him against the grimy ferro-concrete wall, he slapped Leonforte's sagging face a couple of times until his eyes began to clear.

'I'm sorry it's come to this,' Okami said, kneeing him hard in the groin.

Now Leonforte began to retch in earnest. Okami stepped deftly away to avoid being spattered. He hauled Leonforte roughly further down the alley, away from his own mess.

'I want to know what's going on.'

'Go to hell!'

Okami cracked him so hard on the side of his head he heard bone splinter. Leonforte moaned, shook his head. Tears were standing out in the corners of his eyes. 'I'll kill you for this!' he hissed between bloody teeth.

'I can see you're hungry for the chance,' Okami said. He slapped Leonforte's .45 into his hand, stepped back. He touched the hilt of his *wakizashi*. 'Here it is.'

Despite the battering, Leonforte was fast. The muzzle of the .45 came up in a blur, Leonforte's fingers squeezing the trigger. But Okami had already stepped within the perimeter of his defense, and the honed tip of the blade was pricking the skin of Leonforte's throat.

'Do it,' Okami whispered. 'Pull the trigger.'

Leonforte looked hard at Okami as if he were a man just waking up from a dream. 'What –' He swallowed hard. 'What d'you want?'

'Tell me what Vincent Alba's up to.'

Leonforte blinked. 'Vinnie? What d'you mean? He's a fuckin' bodyguard.'

'Uh uh. He's here to see you don't get into trouble.'

'You're outta your fuckin' mind, ace.' But Okami could see that he was thinking it through; he might be hot-headed and uncontrollable, but this was not a stupid man.

'Then Jack Donnough's crazy, too, because he's who I heard it from.'

'Madonna!' Leonforte exclaimed. Then he began to laugh. His body began to shake, his eyes to water. He spat blood, but he appeared beyond caring. He tried to catch his breath as the pain of the beating kicked in, but the laughter bubbled out all the faster. It built and built until it hung on the precipice of hysteria.

Okami slammed the heel of his hand into the bridge of Leonforte's nose just to stop the sound. In disgust, he turned away from the unconscious man, went swiftly and silently out of the alley.

*

329

If Faith Sawhill was surprised to see Okami, you couldn't tell by her face.

'Mr Okami, won't you come in?' she said, smiling as she opened the door to her apartment.

Okami stepped across the threshold, pushed the door shut behind him. Faith Sawhill was still in her military uniform. Okami looked at the major's bars pinned to her epaulets, found himself astonished by her rank. But then everything about her astonished him.

'Would you care for a drink?' Faith asked him as she headed for the drop-leaf table. 'I don't know about you but I've had a helluva day.' Her strong hands were deft as they went about their work. 'At 0600 hours the general's ulcers began bleeding and now I think an amoeba's involved. What a mess his insides are!'

She handed him a scotch, clinked rims, sipped hers. She curled up on the love-seat, pushed her shoes off her feet.

He was aware of her sexual magnetism, her deliberate use of it. Then he centered himself, said, 'Where's the boss? Where's Alba?'

Faith regarded him evenly. 'Out.'

'I'll wait,' Okami said, setting aside his glass. The cold of the ice was chilling him. 'I ran into Johnny downstairs. He didn't look so good.'

Faith sat up straight. 'What have you done?'

Did he detect the color of fear in her beautiful eyes? 'I did what I had to do. Besides, Johnny was begging for a fight.'

Faith rose, looked over his shoulder to the door. 'I hope to Christ you killed him, because if there's an ounce of life left in him –'

At that moment, the door flew open and Johnny Leonforte, in a spray of blood and sweat, rushed into the room, .45 at the ready.

'Okami, you bastard, I'm gonna fuckin' kill you!'

Okami ceased to think. He allowed his body to respond to the deep-seated instinct for survival. In the mind-no-mind that was the essence of his martial training, he threw himself headlong behind the love-seat where Faith stood, her attention for the moment on Leonforte.

'Johnny –'

'Shut up!' Leonforte cried. 'What're you two doing together? Plotting against me like you did with that fuckin' spy Alba? Or just having a two-bit affair?'

'Don't be stupid.'

That was the wrong thing to say.

'Either way, it's at my expense!' He spat out words and saliva together like a madman. 'Get outta the way, Faith, or I'll plug you too!'

Too late she tried to appease him. 'Johnny, look at this reasonably . . . there's nothing going on between Okami and me. If you'll just calm down –'

'I'll calm down,' Leonforte snarled as he squeezed the trigger, 'when Hell freezes over!'

Explosions, one! two! three!, ripped through the back of the love-seat just as Okami pulled Faith down. One bullet slammed into her left thigh.

'Uhh!' she grunted through teeth clamped together in pain and shock.

Scrambling over her, Okami crawled the length of the love-seat and took a quick look from behind his makeshift cover. Leonforte stood spread-legged, his arms rigidly in front of him in the classic marksman's stance. He squeezed off a shot that ricocheted past Okami's left ear so close it hurt.

'I know where you are, fuckers, and I'm going to blow your brains out!'

Okami had no doubt that Leonforte was going to make good on his threat. He had never thought about death, but now he was obliged to stare it in the face. He did not care for what he saw. He felt the blood pounding in his veins, the strong muscle of his heart contracting and expanding. He had life in the palm of his hand. He wanted to give nothing up, and he resolved that should he emerge from this alive he would never again allow himself to be in such a position of weakness.

'Ready or not, here I come!'

Okami braced himself to move, for to remain behind the love-seat would mean certain death.

At that moment, he heard the tangle of voices raised in anger. The explosion of shot, when it came, did not penetrate the back of the love-seat.

He risked another peek, saw to his astonishment Leonforte slamming the butt of his gun into the bloody head of Vincent Alba. He had already put two bullets into Alba and was now in the process of battering him to his powerful knees.

Breaking cover, Okami whipped round the end of the love-seat, launched himself at an oblique angle to where Leonforte stood. As Okami had guessed, Leonforte saw movement at the periphery of his vision. Busy in blood-heat, he was slow to react and, when he did, he assumed Okami would head straight for him, and broke off two shots in that direction.

That was enough time for Okami to change course from the oblique. As he leaped toward Leonforte he saw the man swing his .45 round, and he knew that he would only get one chance. His *wakizashi* was out, leveled in a horizontal plane.

It sliced across Leonforte's face into his chest at the moment he fired for the third time. Okami felt the force of the percussion as the blade hit Leonforte's ribs, then slid between them.

Leonforte staggered, his eyes opened wide. His mouth dropped open, perhaps to utter a final epithet, but by that time his eyes were already rolling up and his legs lost their strength. He tripped over the bull-like form of his latest victim, one hand slipping across Alba's crimson face as if it were a sheet of ice. He crashed backward into the liquor table, shattering bottles everywhere.

The cool astringency of the liquor combined with the cloying sweetness of death. Okami, bloodied, his knife in his hand, stood staring down at Leonforte. He tried to summon up any feeling of remorse but could not.

After a moment, he turned, made his way back to where Faith lay half under the overturned love-seat. Okami put aside his *wakizashi*, lifted the love-seat off her.

'How much blood?'

She meant how much had she lost. He went into the kitchen, found a thin towel, came back and, kneeling beside her, tied off the thigh just above the wound.

'Not enough,' he said. He meant not enough to die.

'I can't feel my leg.'

'Isn't that to be expected?'

She looked up at him. 'I don't know. It's not my field.' She tried to laugh. 'I went all through the war and never saw a wound.'

'Some war,' Okami commented.

'Johnny?'

'Dead,' Okami said. 'But not before he killed Alba.'

'Oh, Christ,' she whispered. Her eyes closed and her lips moved. 'Let me think.' Her eyes opened suddenly, and they seemed as red to him as the blood sprayed all over the room.

She licked her lips. 'There's a place I want you to take me,' she said.

'I know where the Army hospital is.'

'No, not there.' She waited a moment, but when he made no reply, she added, 'I don't know whether I can trust you.'

'But I don't believe you have a choice,' Okami said. 'We both need to get out of here before the cops or the MPs get here.'

He stuffed his knife into the waistband of his trousers, scooped her up in his arms. She was surprisingly light.

She directed him to the side entrance that led out onto the alley where he had confronted Leonforte, and it was a good thing he used it because from the shadows into which they emerged he could already see the reflections of the red and blue lights of cop cars and MP jeeps.

Okami turned, raced down to the far end of the alley, emerged onto a street, turned left. Hurrying to his car, he unlocked it and bundled her in. He tried to ignore her gasps of pain. He got behind the wheel, started the engine, and they got out of there.

*

332

She told him to head west, toward the warehouses that lined that part of the Sumida River. It was a dilapidated neighborhood, suffering as much from neglect as from the ravages of the war. Far away, Tokyo was being rebuilt, but here the old pre-war structures were still intact, rotting against the somnolent waters of the river.

With a voice made weak by pain and shock, she directed him down a narrow street that dead-ended at the water. Much to his surprise, Okami discovered what appeared to be a private dwelling wedged between two long warehouses.

'Stop just there,' Faith whispered, indicating a spot outside the private dwelling. 'Now leave me here.'

Okami sat with the engine idling. He looked out the window at the building, then back at Faith. She was slumped in the back seat, her eyes almost closed.

'You've lost a lot of blood, Miss Sawhill,' he said. 'If I don't help you inside you're not going to make it on your own.'

'You've done the good samaritan bit.' She struggled to a sitting position, but almost immediately fell against the door. Her hand fumbled with the handle.

Okami got out, opened her door, lifted her gently out of the car.

'You mustn't be seen here,' Faith whispered. Her head lolled against his shoulder, and he could see her rapid, shallow breathing. He knew he had to get her inside right now. 'It's dangerous . . .'

He took her to the front door, hit it several short but powerful kicks. The resulting noise was like the boom of a kettle drum, and he realized that the door was made of metal, probably steel.

It opened quickly, giving him the distinct impression that they had been observed drawing up. He was confronted by a delicate Japanese woman of no more than eighteen.

She bowed to him perfunctorily, then said, 'This way, please,' in the terse, terribly efficient manner of a doctor or a nurse.

She led him down a long corridor lined with cherry-wood paneling. At the end of it he was conducted into what appeared to be a brightly lit operating theater, albeit on a modest scale. A doctor was already scrubbed and waiting. He directed Okami to place Faith on the table and then leave.

'Anako will show you where you can wait,' the surgeon said as he began his preliminary work-up on Faith. 'I'll join you when I can.'

The young woman named Anako ushered him into an adjacent room which had been set up as a library. Bookshelves lined the walls, a crystal chandelier hung from the center of the vaulted eighteen-foot ceiling, a

jewel-toned Persian carpet covered the floor. The comfortable furniture –
a pair of facing oversized sofas, two chairs with ottomans – were leather.
Between the sofas was a bronze and glass coffee table on which sat a small
clock. In one corner a French secretary stood with its surface entirely free
of objects, polished to a hard gloss. Okami had been in museums with
more dust.

Curious, he went to the bookshelves. He was startled to discover that
almost all the volumes were in Japanese, save for an impressive section on
historical warfare, which was in English and French. Elsewhere, there were
histories and horticultural books in profusion, but most of the library was
given over to philosophical texts, so obscure that even Okami, who by dint
of his martial training was learned in that field, had never read them.

He took one of these volumes over to a chair, sat reading it for some
time. Illumination came solely from the chandelier and several green-
shaded lamps scattered around the room. Thick curtains were pulled tight
across the high windows, and when he rose to part them, he discovered
only blank wall behind them.

Recalling Faith Sawhill's warning about the danger to him here he was
abruptly restless. Leaving the book on the chair, he went to the door and
opened it. The hall was dim and so silent he could hear the muffled
tick-tock of the clock in the library behind him.

This end of the corridor was comprised of three rooms. Two of them
he had already been in: the surgery and the library. Now he crossed the
hall, put his ear against the third door. He could hear nothing.

Grasping the knob, he turned it, pushed inward. He found himself in
a smallish room. It was altogether anonymous, rather like a doctor's waiting
room: white walls, a gray low-pile carpet, a pair of steel engravings of
turn-of-the-century clipper ships on the walls. One desk, three chairs;
nothing more.

He went to the chair closest to the desk because he saw draped over
it Faith Sawhill's blood-stained uniform. Now that he had come this far
he could see there was another door which he guessed led directly into the
surgery.

He bent over the chair, stared at her uniform for some time. Then he
carefully went through it. He found nothing but a matt-gray pen clipped
to the inside breast pocket of her jacket and, within the same pocket, a
short list of items to purchase.

It was when he was carefully replacing the list that he noticed something
odd about the pen. It was thicker than an ordinary writing instrument and,
now that he looked at it more closely, he saw that it was made of a substance
he could not identify.

334

He plucked it from the pocket, turned it over and over as he scrutinized it. He pressed the button on the top and a tip clicked out. Then he noticed there were a series of bumps along the spine of the oversized clip.

He pressed the top one, heard a barely audible whine. He put the pen to his ear. Something was going on inside it. He pressed the second button and again heard the whine. The third button stopped the whine, and now he was beginning to get it. With a mounting sense of excitement, he pressed the fourth button, and heard Faith Sawhill's voice emanating from the pen – which, as it happened, was also a miniature wire recorder.

'Report from Tokyo. 17 April. We've hit the motherlode of intelligence. Donnough has proved an exemplary source; see accompanying microdot. Unfortunately, I've run into a rather complex wrinkle. A Yakuza *oyabun* named Mikio Okami knows more about our operation than is healthy. I've offered him a partnership which, for now, is the best of a bad set of options.'

There was a slight pause, then her voice began again.

'I told him that Vincent was here to monitor Johnny, which was the truth, as far as it went. He has no idea that Vincent was here to monitor me, as well. Well, even Johnny didn't know that, but then Johnny didn't really know much at all, did he? But that's how you wanted it because, in the end, Johnny only cared about Johnny.'

Again, a slight pause.

'Okami believes Vincent was running the show over here, which is kind of funny, but certainly helpful from our point of view. I don't believe Okami knows who we're dealing with here, which is a relief. But he's smart and tenacious – and I think he must have some kind of American backing of his own, which is alarming. I need to pump him but in such a way that he believes he's pumping me. Not so easy but don't worry, I can handle it.'

Silence, while the remainder of the wire unspooled itself. Those were the only entries, but as far as Okami was concerned they were more than enough. How foolish of him to have underestimated Faith Sawhill. She was a woman, and he had seen her wholly in that light – and had dismissed her out of hand. He wouldn't make that same mistake again.

He ran the wire back to the spot he guessed it had originally been at, then replaced the pen. He went silently out of the room, back across the hall and into the library.

He sat for some time, the book he had selected open and unread in his lap. His first instinct was to take Faith Sawhill down, but in a moment he saw the foolhardiness of such rash action.

If the Willoughby plan were brought to fruition they were all sunk –

especially Japan, which desperately needed breathing-room to regain its economic feet and build a base from which to haul itself from the ashes of defeat.

Even the Colonel would be helpless in such a doomsday scenario as Willoughby was preparing. Rearming Japan was about the last thing the country needed to heal its wounds and get on with its future. Being America's point-man against the Communists in the Pacific would keep Japan under its thumb for decades to come. That was absolutely unacceptable.

With a profound sense of unease, Okami realized that the Colonel's prudence was correct. He now had the opportunity of a lifetime. Whatever Faith might say to her as yet unknown employer, she was going to make him a partner in the black market scheme here. Now he knew what she wanted from him, he would be prepared. He knew that he must protect the Colonel from her at all costs because her employer would undoubtedly see him as an enemy and do his best to destroy the Colonel.

That meant either trying to outwit Faith, or – an appalling thought – trying to come to some form of truce with her. Because Okami knew her employer held the key to stopping Willoughby's plan to rearm Japan and reinstate its most heinous war criminals to their former positions of power. Not only was he in possession of the top-secret intelligence that could destroy Willoughby, he was also, with his high-powered contacts inside Washington, in a unique position to overcome those in the military and the US Senate who were siding with Willoughby.

Also, he knew the physical nature of her reports. This, he sensed instinctively, was his biggest edge. Because, sooner or later, he or the Colonel would be able to trace those wire recordings and those microdots back from Tokyo to their final destination in the United States, and at last they would know the nature of their enemy.

At that moment, the door to the library opened and the doctor strode in. 'She's going to be fine,' he said. 'Though perhaps a small limp is inevitable since some nerve damage occurred.' Then he smiled. 'Would you come with me, please? She would very much like to see you.'

Faith Sawhill was lying on the table as if she were dead. Okami, staring down at her, thought she looked very pale. Her eyes opened, and he was startled to find them as dark as his.

'You're still here.'

'So far my stay has been uneventful.'

She licked her dry lips, and without being bidden, he poured her some water, slipped the straw between her lips as he lifted her head up, watched her drink her fill.

336

When she was through she thanked him. 'Have you seen anyone here?' she asked with some anxiety. Her voice was hoarse and still weak.

'Just the surgeon – and Anako, of course. I've been alone in the library.'

Faith nodded, and her face appeared to relax. Her eyes held his. 'The alliance that Johnny wouldn't grant you, I'm prepared to guarantee.'

Okami studied her for some time. 'How did I get so lucky?'

'I'd rather have you as a partner than an enemy.' She gave him a tiny smile. 'Besides, you did me a big favor, getting rid of Johnny. Vincent told me he was becoming increasingly uncontrollable.' She licked her lips again. 'He had only contempt for women.'

'I'd be a much better partner,' he said. 'I only underestimate them.'

Faith tried to laugh.

'Is it real this time?' he asked. 'You know, you said it was at The Iron Gate, but we both know you didn't mean it.'

'This time I do.' Her hand sought his. 'So what do you say? Deal? We can be very helpful to one another. I need all the help I can get out here now that Vincent's gone. Who knows when there'll be a replacement and, anyway, until then, you would benefit from Vincent's contacts.'

He appeared to consider this for some time. At length, he said, 'Do you know the story about the Six Monkeys?'

'I don't believe I do.'

He ignored her puzzled expression. 'There was once an old man. He was very wise, and over the course of his long life many people sought his counsel. What was most interesting was that almost everyone who came to him asked the same question. "How," they would ask, "do I understand myself?"

'To this the old man gave the same reply. He brought out a curious cage constructed of bamboo. It was oblong and contained six windows. Inside the cage was a monkey. "Choose a window," he counseled them, "and then call the monkey. Observe closely his response. It will be a reflection of your own inner self." '

For a long time there was only the sound of her breathing, supplemented by the methodical engines of medical science.

'Am I supposed to understand that?'

He shrugged. 'Yes and no. It's a Zen riddle. It's meant itself to be a pathway for thought and meditation.'

Faith screwed her face up, thinking. 'I think I get it,' she said. 'The monkey responds differently to attitude and tone of voice.'

'I'm sure that's true.'

She looked up at him. 'Which one of the Six Monkeys are you?'

'That's for you to discover,' Okami said with a brief smile.

337

He clasped her hand in his. It was warm and dry, and unaccountably made him think of his father. 'In the meantime, my dear Miss Sawhill, we should have green tea to properly seal this pact.'

'You won't regret your decision.' Those dark eyes smiled up at him. 'Partner.'

BOOK 3: ENDLESS TRUTHS

The autumn wind:
for me there are no gods;
there are no Buddhas.

Masaoka Shiki

THIRTEEN

Tokyo/Washington

Naohiro Ushiba, Daijin of MITI, had heard it said that some called Tomoo Kozo the mad *oyabun*. There were many stories about him. One was that his penis was entirely covered in *irizumi*, the exquisitely wrought tattoos that all Yakuza wore on parts of their skin. *Irizumi* was applied as it had been done for centuries, with sharp bamboo dipped in colored inks. The pain, it was said, was formidable.

As Ushiba stared into Kozo's face, he said, 'From the moment you decided on your own to put a shadow on Nicholas Linnear's wife, you set us on this very dangerous course.'

Kozo took a drag of his cigarette, his tiny black eyes moving over Ushiba's face. 'It was a smart move. Linnear had disappeared into the mists – at the behest of Okami. Should we have done nothing to keep track of him?'

'What about Nangi?'

Kozo shook his head. 'The wife was his link. She always has been. And, believe me, the moment Okami entered his life Linnear was not about to confide in Tanzan Nangi. How could he? With Linnear's professed hatred of the Yakuza, how could he tell Nangi that he was going to become the Kaisho's lackey?'

Ushiba lit a cigarette, kept pace with the restless Kozo as he circled the koi pond. 'You may have fooled the other *oyabun* of the inner council, but not me. I think you instigated this attack on Okami merely to pit yourself against Linnear.' For Ushiba, aggression was often more gratifying than introspection. Besides, if Kozo truly were mad, perhaps he could be provoked into revealing his private motives for this decision to oust the Kaisho. 'I'm right, aren't I? It's just the kind of crazy challenge you can't resist.'

'What nonsense!' Kozo circled the pond like a predator in a cage. 'You know the dangers Okami represented as well as I do. We've rehashed them time and again. There's no room any more for the Kaisho. The kind of power he wielded is too dangerous to be left in one man's hands. Simply put, the Kaisho has been supplanted by the Godaishu. Our network spread

341

all around the world will work far more efficiently and with far more checks and balances than it would have being directed by one man.' He blew smoke up toward the skylight. 'All of Okami's arguments against the Godaishu are scattered now like cherry blossoms in the rain. Okami should have foreseen his demise as Kaisho and planned for the eventuality of its passage into history. I know I would have.'

'But without Okami's intimate knowledge of the Mafia, the Godaishu would never have come into being. He, not you or I, is its true father.'

Kozo shrugged. 'More's the pity for him that he turned against us. *Karma*. He chose his own path, no one pushed him.'

'You did your best.'

'I was once Okami's most trusted ally, everyone knows that. But when his path changed I noticed and became suspicious, and I was proved right. At the end, I fought him tooth and nail – and why not? He did not believe in what the Godaishu had become. He betrayed the Godaishu, betrayed our trust in him as the Kaisho. He made his own deal with Dominic Goldoni, and now we're left with picking up the pieces.'

'He and I were always the best at dealing with the Americans, but I must admit that he understood them better than I do.'

Kozo said, 'That will soon change. I'm working hard to understand the *iteki*.'

'You see what I mean about challenges?' Ushiba said. 'You just can't resist them. But your determination to destroy Linnear is senseless – worse, it's downright dangerous.'

'Not senseless,' Kozo said. 'I initiated my actions on the basis of some astonishing information. Linnear is Nishiki, the secret conduit who had been supplying intelligence to Dominic Goldoni and Okami.'

'Ridiculous,' Ushiba said. 'Linnear's strict moral code –'

'The history of Japan teaches us that the espousal of righteousness is the securest refuge for corruption, *neh*?' He smiled. 'Think it through, Ushiba-san. Linnear has the kind of mind and the range of expertise to destroy all of us.'

'But that's only part of it, isn't it?' Ushiba said shrewdly.

'Daijin, you will not draw me into a personal confession.' He shook his head. 'Look, by going after Okami now we take down two birds at once. We agreed that the Kaisho's day was over. And by deliberately letting him find out his days were numbered we forced him into a corner. He had to draw on the Colonel's promise to him that his son would come to his aid. Linnear did not fail his father, and now we are able to pick the time and place of our confrontation. I'm convinced the only way to defeat Linnear

342

is for us to choose the killing ground. As Sun Tzu has taught us, that will be our advantage.'

'Us. You mean *you*.' Ushiba stared at him a long time. 'I was right all along. You *are* going after Nicholas Linnear.'

Kozo laughed. 'Daijin, I'm doing better than that. I'm about to get him.'

'It has come to my attention that you are indulging in a bit of extra-curricular activity.'

The Red Queen stretched, relieving the tension that had built up between his shoulderblades. He cracked the knuckles beneath his gloved hands. 'You're costing the Government of the United States of America money it can ill afford to spend. Tell me why.'

'You know why,' Lillehammer said. 'Dominic Goldoni was whacked under our noses.' And when confronted by the Red Queen's implacable silence, he was compelled to add quite unnecessarily, 'Inside WITSEC, for Christ's sake.'

'Goldoni was operating – isn't that how it's put? – inside WITSEC. What did you expect?'

Lillehammer watched the Red Queen pick his way through the remnants of his double bacon cheeseburger and jumbo fries. Why did they always have to eat at a fast-food joint? 'I expect we won't let whoever it was get away with it.' It was surreal having these discussions amid the cacophony of kids, working stiffs and people marking time until they could place their next bet at the OTB across the street.

The Red Queen, pushing aside his coated paper plate, was not amused. 'I need another Coke.' He got up abruptly, went across the red and yellow plastic restaurant. He was wearing an English-made tweed suit with a hand-cut doeskin vest. His tie, its pattern as voluptuous as it was gaudy, was, however, strictly American.

When he returned, an enormous paper cup of soda in his hand, he said, 'Don't get coy with me. I took a good long look at those photos of Goldoni. I know Do Duc did the Goldoni hit. And I know how badly you want to put his nuts in a meat grinder.' The Red Queen sucked a bit of cheeseburger from between his teeth. 'But I'm giving you a direct order to cease and desist.'

Lillehammer sat very still. He wondered if this was the moment of severing, when the granite of which he had been a part for years was cracked in two. 'I'll need a very good reason,' he said quietly.

The Red Queen's face was laden with a frown. 'What do you think? Should I get a sundae?'

'Here? The sundaes taste like plastic, just like everything else.'

'Really? I never thought so.' He shrugged and patted his stomach. 'Oh, well, I suppose all that's left is to leave the busboy a token of our appreciation for a clean table.' He took out some change and placed it on the plastic tabletop. As they were getting up, he said softly, 'Your personal rage won't help us now. If it doesn't get in the way of ops, it'll get you killed. I want your word. Forget Do Duc and attend to current business. God knows there's enough of that.'

Lillehammer turned his head to stare at a little boy with ice-cream all over his face. 'You have my word,' he said. 'I will not go after Do Duc. Does that satisfy you?'

'I want you to keep an eye on Davis Munch. Bane tells me his prosecutor was seen with this man Harley Gaunt shortly before Gaunt showed up at your house. Bane may be paranoid but he's not stupid.'

The Red Queen patted the little boy on the head as they passed him. Outside, he leaned toward Lillehammer in an uncharacteristically avuncular gesture. 'Madness is born of the meditation on revenge,' he said. 'It will do you good to remember that.'

Manny Mannheim was staring at the thickly stuffed manila envelope when the buzzer sounded. He turned, hastily shoving the envelope onto the shelf beside the sawed-off shotgun he kept loaded and ready. Peering through the gap in the wire mesh he watched as a tall figure came through the front door.

The man, wrapped in a dark wool tweed coat with its collar up, did not immediately look at him. Instead, he spent a good deal of time peering at the larger pawned objects Manny had hanging on the walls or lining the dusty wooden floor: glittery electric guitars, a full set of classic Louis Vuitton luggage, a green and silver mountain bike, a pair of Chinese celadon vases, a gleaming black and cream Harley-Davidson Softail, autographed by Johnny Cash to someone named Ferdie Francis.

The man took his time, so Manny had a while to size him up. The more he did so the more nervous he became. Actually, he had become nervous the moment Harley Gaunt had come in a second time, handing him the thick manila envelope with instructions as to what to do with it if he did not contact Manny within twenty-four hours.

That was two days ago, and Manny had to assume that something had happened to his friend. He did not want to think about what might have happened to Gaunt, but he dreamed about the possibilities when he went to sleep at night.

The man who had walked into Manny's pawnshop was broad-shouldered, ham-fisted, intimidating. As he turned this way and that, examining each item before moving ever closer to where Manny stood behind his wire screen, Manny could see the scars on his face, the nose that had once been broken, the clever eyes that saw every scratch and defect in whatever they were examining.

A light sheen of sweat broke out on Manny's forehead and upper lip, and he shifted uncomfortably from one foot to another. An itch began just below his right shoulderblade as a droplet of sweat snaked its way down his back.

Christ, what had Harley been involved in that could have gotten him killed? Manny wondered. Curiosity and terror waged a battle inside him. How many times had he picked up the envelope after the twenty-four hours had passed? Too many to count. Once, his curiosity getting the better of his common sense, he had decided to slit it open. But at the last moment either his courage failed him or he had come to his senses.

But today he had scrutinized with excruciating concentration every customer who walked into the pawnshop, because he had started awake this morning, his mind filled with a terrifying possibility: what if Harley had been followed to the pawnshop, and somebody knew he had given the envelope to Manny?

The man lifted his shoulders, let them fall as he ran his hands over the Louis Vuitton luggage. He gave a quick glance toward the front door, then back at the cage where Manny stood, rooted to the spot. The thick, callused fingers upended the steamer trunk, large enough to hold a human being if it were curled up. He snapped it open, lifted the lid, contemplated the interior with a diligence Manny found highly disturbing.

Manny's first thought had been to burn the envelope, to be rid of the evidence of Gaunt's visit, to avoid the responsibility his friend had thrust upon him without asking his consent. In the end, he could not even light the match. Perhaps he was less of a moral coward than he had thought. However, seeing the man now replace the steamer trunk and move toward the motorcycle, closer to the wire cage, Manny could believe that he had made a grave mistake.

Yet how could he abandon his one true friend? His relationship with Gaunt, inconstant though it had been, was important to him. They were the kind of friends who, though not having seen each other for long periods of time, could pick up their conversation as if the intervening years had never passed. People like that were rare in life, especially Manny's life, which had never amounted to much of anything.

The man in the tweed overcoat cleared his throat and Manny jumped. His right hand automatically sought out the butt of the sawed-off shotgun

345

he kept within easy reach under the counter. His finger eased around the trigger.

'Yes?' Manny said, not liking the high squeak in his voice.

'Nothing,' the man said, glancing his way. 'Only . . . how much d'you want for this?'

'Twelve thousand,' Manny said. 'It's a classic –'

'Softail,' the man finished for him. 'Yeah, I know.' He put his hands in the pockets of his overcoat, turned to stare at Manny. 'You always stay inside that cage?'

Manny was terrified now. Of course the man wasn't interested in the Harley, he never had been. He was here to take the envelope Gaunt had left, and to kill Manny in the process.

'Did you hear what I said?'

Manny, shaking mightily, tried to get his tongue unstuck from the roof of his mouth. 'Ulbg!' was all he managed to say.

'What?'

'I've – had some, uh, you know, trouble over the years,' Manny stumbled. 'So I –'

The man took a step toward him. 'You packing a gun back there?'

'Don't come any closer!' Manny said, trying vainly to get saliva back into his mouth.

The man stared at the sawed-off shotgun leveled at him. 'You gonna use that if I ask if you'll take ten-five cash for the Softail?'

'Huh?' Manny blinked, swallowing hard.

'I want the Softail,' the man said, taking his hands out of his pockets and spreading them wide. One held a thick roll of bills. 'You gonna sell it to me or you gonna shoot me?'

Manny felt his heart in his throat. Nothing seemed to be registering. He was locked into an assumption that was immutable.

'Come on, buddy,' the man said. 'I know you said you'd had trouble here, but gimme a break, would ya, I just want to buy the damn Softail.'

Manny wiped his face with a tremorous hand. Jesus Christ, he thought, this isn't my kind of life. I'm seeing bogeymen coming out of the walls. Any more of this cloak-and-dagger shit and a heart attack or a nervous breakdown is not out of the question. He put the sawed-off away. His muscles were spasming so heavily he had to grip the counter with both hands in order not to fall down. His desire to urinate was very strong.

The man waved the bills over his head. 'How about you come out here with the keys and we'll do this transaction one-two-three?'

Manny opened the door to the cage, stepped out. 'You got a license?'

'Sure,' the man said, reaching with his free hand behind his back.

346

That was the moment Manny knew he was a dead man. It was a moment one only experiences in dreams, when momentous actions occur all around you while you watch, helpless to intervene. His thoughts were gelid with a kind of existential morbidity. Why did I leave the cage? he wondered. Why did I put away the sawed-off? Why didn't I listen to my instincts?

Manny watched, impotent, as the man pulled out his wallet, put the wad of bills on the saddle of the Softail, extracted his license. He held it out to Manny.

For a moment, Manny stood frozen. His heart clamored inside his chest like an out-of-control subway train, and he was having a good deal of trouble breathing.

"S'matter?" the man said. 'Don't you want to do the deal? These days how many people come in here offering you ten-five cash for the Softail?'

Woodenly, Manny held out his hand, took the license. Somehow, it fell through his fingers and, as if in a dream, he bent down, retrieved it. Then he got the paperwork, went through it like a zombie. He hardly heard what the man said. Mac Divine, the driver's license read. He took receipt of the ten-five without counting it himself. Divine had done that with great care right in front of him.

'Man, my neighbor's gonna shit his pants when he sees this baby in my driveway,' Divine said, with a grin. 'He's been looking for one of these for three years.'

After he left, wheeling the Softail as if it were his son, Manny leaned against the door, panting heavily. He was drenched in sweat. He hurried back to his cage, slipped on his coat, sliding the thick envelope under it. Then he went outside, locked the door, and pulled down the gates, padlocking them. It was only three in the afternoon, but he'd had it for the day.

On rubbery legs, he went to his bank, made a night deposit of the cash in the till, including the amount Mr Divine had given him, then he set off to do what he should have done this morning: follow Gaunt's instructions.

The tolling of the bell reverberated deep inside him, like a raspy voice spoken in the small hours of the morning when the senses are blurred by a melancholic stupor born of a furious rush of reckless emotion, now spent.

The tolling continued like a heartbeat or a sermon, a spoken text of words indistinguishable as a flight of sparrows after sunset.

If he was alive he did not yet know in what state it might be. His thoughts, still chaotic as the molten magma of the universe, seemed to exist

347

wholly on their own, without the confines of brain or corpus, a pinpoint of light flickering uncertainly in the cosmic night.

No past, no present enriched these thoughts, and this lack of context made logic as evanescent as a dream. There was no evidence of breath, of blood pumping, of an urgency for movement. How could movement exist without brain or body to give thought density and substance?

But the tolling of the bell continued – not a sound, for he had no ears with which to hear, but a pulse, an atonal voice belonging to neither man nor machine, an implication that somewhere in the vastness a context did, indeed, exist.

Light, a shadow upon the soul. So he did exist after all.

He was born into a house of metal. It seemed to be somewhere underground, a vast conical space filled with sapphire light and the sharp echoes of industry. He inhaled the scent of metal, hot and amorphous, cool and oiled, but at least he was breathing.

His eyes, learning to focus all over again, saw being constructed at different automated stations arms, legs, feet and hands, torsos, hydraulic fingers and infra-red eyes. Slowly, before his still bleary gaze, the perfect beasts were being formed. It was as if he were witnessing Creation, somewhere between God's mind and Vulcan's forge.

Or maybe it was just a robot factory. By which deduction he was at least able to make an educated guess as to his current whereabouts. He wasn't dead, he was in Tokyo. How in the world had the Messulethe got him here?

No other humans here, just the precise movements of metal cylinders through shadow and light. The hive-like thrumming of engines, the heartbeats of 10,000 disembodied souls, the happy operatic singing of life being fabricated from steel, titanium, high-density plastics, silicon chips and fiber-optic cables.

He inhaled, enjoying the sensation as another fragment of evidence that he was indeed alive. The air-conditioned, triple-filtered atmosphere was cleaner than any country air could be, but was nevertheless redolent of the foulness of machines. It seemed to hold a static charge like clouds filled with incipient thunder, and far away an effulgent flicker of lightning pawed the air like a restless animal.

Abruptly, an intense, disorienting stab of vertigo replaced the light and sound barrage, and the world closed into a pinpoint of undifferentiated gray. His eyelids fluttered closed.

A sharp pain jerked him back to consciousness.

'Wake up! You've slept too long as it is!'

The voice sounded disturbingly familiar.

He started, a shiver racing down his spine as he recognized his own face bending over him. His own lips curled into a smile, his own eyes crinkled in delight.

'Welcome to your new life.' His own voice reached his ears like an hallucination. 'It will be a short one. But I promise you it will be full of surprises.'

Nicholas passed out.

FOURTEEN

Montauk/Washington/Tokyo

Croaker watched Margarite as she stood in the shower and soaped up. He could see nothing but a vaguely outlined silhouette, yet he could not take his eyes off her. Here they were in a run-down Montauk motel, in the same room together because she had insisted that she did not want to sleep alone. What was it she feared more, Robert's imminent return or her husband's?

He had checked the scene out the window as soon as she had gone into the bathroom: oil-stained blacktop, only a few cars parked where, in summer, would be a sea of painted metal and chromium, and, across the street, the odd kind of fast-food place existing only on the East End, with its tacky red and yellow plastic sign, 'CHICKEN & SEAFOOD, open late hours', lit up by frosty fluorescent lights and a Bud Lite sign, its neon leaking vivid color into the darkness.

It was by this illumination that he had spied the wise guy, burly body, bland, oval face, coming out of the store, a cardboard box filled with two coffees and some sandwiches balanced in one hand rather than two. The free hand hung loosely at his side, as he had been trained, ready for a quick draw or anything else that might come his way.

Croaker watched him as he got into a black Ford Taurus parked more or less in front of the fast-food joint. The inner light came on briefly, and Croaker got a glimpse of a second wise guy.

He was quite certain that these were Tony DeCamillo's men. He was unsurprised. They would not have been difficult to locate, especially for a man with Tony D.'s resources. After all, they were using Margarite's Lexus with a known license plate. Under those conditions, Croaker knew it was virtually impossible to keep your whereabouts secret for long.

Croaker had turned away from his contemplation of the Taurus and its hulking occupants when Margarite partially opened the door to the bathroom. It was already overheated in the room, with no way to lower the thermostat, and the steam from the shower was making the bathroom unbearable. The smells of mildew and surf drifted like dust in the air. The

350

wise guys wouldn't make a move until Tony D. arrived, and that wouldn't be until morning. Croaker had all that time to figure out how he was going to handle the confrontation without anyone getting hurt.

Staring at Margarite's shifting outline, he knew he had other matters with which to occupy himself for the time being. He still found himself having to adjust to the new reality, that she, not Tony D., was heir to Dominic Goldoni's domain and all that implied. She had in her hand the power of Goldoni's shadow world, where governors, police chiefs, justices, congressmen would all do her bidding.

He saw now how Goldoni had outsmarted them all – the Feds *and* his enemies. He had given up vital information to WITSEC, yes, had rolled over on those around him, beneath him, so that they would believe he was helping them dismantle his empire. But he had given the Feds nothing of himself or how he ran his domain. In the end, he had not even retired to the soft life they had created for him in Marine on St Croix. And, as for the Leonfortes, his enemies, their sights were set on Tony D., a false target.

If he were being truthful – and he believed tonight was a time for ultimate truths – he was both frightened and elated by Margarite's intelligence. He had never met anyone like her, had, further, never even imagined anyone like her could exist. Perhaps this was a failing in him, he wasn't sure, but certainly his being with her had the profound effect on him of a close encounter of the third kind. Margarite was as alien and as marvelous to his way of life as if she were an extraterrestrial.

She emerged from the bathroom wrapped in a towel. She appeared to have no inhibitions. *You know my soul,* she had said when she had undressed in front of him. *Why should I hide my body from you?* Then she had laughed. *Tony insisted we turn out the lights when we made love.*

Perhaps that bastard Tony D. was only being practical, Croaker thought, not caring to see the aftermath of his brutal handiwork, weals and black bruises in scattered constellations over her flesh.

Looking at her now, Croaker thought he could love this woman in a way he had loved neither Gelda nor Alix, but immediately he was suspicious of the emotion. It was all too easy for men to confuse love with lust at the outset of an affair, to convince themselves they felt something in their heart, when the stirring occurred quite a bit lower.

It was said that men coveted beauty in their mates, and women power. How many men had Croaker come upon in his time in Homicide who were intimidated by women with power? There was an almost instinctual reflex mechanism at work. He had always been interested in the fact that he had never felt it. True power in a woman was so rare, so precious, he found it

351

an aphrodisiac. This, too, could explain the feeling welling up in him.

Night and Margarite.

'Why are you looking at me that way?' Her eyes, luminous in the steamy glow from the bathroom light, appeared so innocent of guile or subterfuge that for a moment Croaker could almost believe that their conversations of today had never occurred, that she was just a battered housewife – beautiful, desirable, lonely – who needed refuge and protection. Everything would be so simple, then, all his decisions made for him without the shadow and light of a far more complex reality.

He cleared his throat, began to walk past her toward the bathroom.

'I need a shower,' he said thickly.

She reached out, put her arms around him, and he could smell the delicate scents of soap and freshly scrubbed skin.

'It's too soon,' she said, 'to take a shower.'

She lifted one shoulder and the towel unwound itself from around her body. He could feel her dampness through his shirt.

'You smell like an animal,' she whispered as she drew his head down.

Her lips blossomed under his, soft and passionate, her tiny tongue curling against his teeth. He thought he should say no, thrust her away from him now, at this moment, the only moment it would still be possible, but instead he circled her in his arms.

She let out a throaty moan, and her legs drew up, her bare ankles crossing and locking over his buttocks. The bed seemed far away and, suddenly, superfluous. Her breasts flattened against him, and the heat broke from her in waves.

Their lips parted for a moment, and he said, 'Tony –'

'I don't want Tony,' Margarite breathed, her hands busy at his belt. 'I want you.'

He had the presence of mind to know he must be gentle with her, no matter how passionate she became. He understood the importance of that, as he knew, eerily, that Robert had been with her. Robert, who had mutilated and murdered her brother; who had given her back her own life.

She kicked with her heels, and his trousers slid to the floor. She tore at the buttons of his shirt. His arms ached from holding her, as the blood and strength began to pool in the area below his waist.

He picked her off him, placed her on the floor, knelt over her. For a long moment, he stared into her huge, liquid eyes, witness to her true nakedness – her desire for him, her need for Robert, her rapture at being on the threshold of her empire all wrapped up into one shifting pattern, so complex and numinous that all at once he felt himself drowning there. It was too much to contemplate the transcendent become immanent, and he sought to lose himself in the heavy pulse of his blood.

He lowered his head to her breasts. Light from the bathroom picked out the peaks of her, leaving dark and mysterious the soft curves and sweeping dells. There was a scent rising from her. He inhaled it like incense as he licked her hard, dark nipples, as he circled her navel, slid his lips down the center of the slight curve of her belly.

She groaned deeply, gripping the sides of his head, her fingers stroking and caressing him as his tongue slipped into her. Her legs drew up involuntarily, her thighs splayed wide. He could hear her ragged breathing, and this, more than anything, fired him. It was the only sound in the room, rhythmic, deeply erotic, almost a sobbing torn from the very core of her being.

'Oh, God, oh, God, oh God!' A chanting in the darkness as her head whipped back and forth, as her muscles tensed, as she lifted her pelvis up toward his lips and tongue, then jerking in erratic motions, her legs locked around his back, trying to draw him closer, to have so much of him inside her when –

The spasms, when they came, were so intense that the entire lower half of her body arched up off the floor. Her sex expanded like a flower, her sweat mingling with other, more intimate fluids. And then, in the aftermath, her panting, ragged and muffled by one arm thrown across her face.

Then, as he knelt there, he heard her slither around. She knelt in front of him, her heavy breasts hanging so delectably he reached out to cup them. She put her hand over his bio-mechanical one. She kissed him deeply, then licked her own fluids off his face.

Her head lowered, her mouth at work on his nipples, then lower and lower, nibbling, teasing, until the incredible liquid warmth engulfed him.

But, almost immediately, he drew her away as gently as he could. Aware as he was of her bruises and what they represented, he could not bear to see her in that position, bent over him, submissive. He wanted other things for her – and for himself.

He lay on his back, drew her over him until he felt another kind of wetness engulf him. She arched her back, breasts thrust upward, riding him, a bit awkward at first, but increasingly ecstatic in this unfamiliar position.

The feel of her on him as he was in her was indescribable. He held her breasts, staring up into her face, drinking her in, the light across one cheek, firing the planes of her face, making her appear both more and less than she did in the full flood of sunlight, turning her into an embodiment of the secrets she held so vigilantly inside her.

The air rushed out of her, and she took his hands from her breasts, spread his arms wide on the floor as she pressed her torso against him, as if holding him down as her hips rose and fell on him. Her fingers twined with polycarbonate, graphite and titanium.

Her eyes were wide, her face very close to his. He licked her, and she whispered with a kind of awe creeping into her voice, 'I'm going to come again. I can't . . . It's . . .' Her eyes closed, her fingers caressed his neck, little noises in the back of her throat as she worked over him.

'Please,' she gasped. 'Please . . .'

He could hold himself back no longer, didn't want to any more, but abandoned himself to his own pleasure, his buttocks clenching, all his strength gathered in one spot, then released like a pent-up stream rushing over descending rapids.

They crawled onto the bed, slept in sticky exhaustion, twined one around the other, no beginning, no ending, one.

Wan daylight, the color of an old oyster shell, opened their eyes.

'My detective.' Margarite smiled, kissed him tenderly. They unwrapped themselves slowly, as if reluctant to shed the aura that like night and shadow had protected them from the vicissitudes and hard decisions of real life.

In the shower together, Margarite said, 'I've been telling myself that last night was just a fling, a hunger made irresistible by frustration and gratitude.'

'Is that what you believe?'

'No,' she said, washing the soap from her body, 'but I wish I did. It would make the future so much simpler.'

She was about to step out when he took her in his arms, turned her to face him. His flesh-and-blood hand covered a large black and blue mark on her thigh. She looked at the back of her hand for a moment before taking his bio-mechanical hand between hers, pressing it against her breasts.

They had nothing to dress in but their old clothes. The buttons of Croaker's shirt were scattered over the floor, testament that last night's passion had not been a dream.

'There must be somewhere in town we can buy jeans and shirts,' Margarite said.

Croaker watched her draw on her clothes. 'You're never going home again, are you?'

She looked at him. 'How could I? The old Margarite is dead.'

'I guess the only problem is Tony doesn't know that, and you'll never be able to convince him that it's the truth.'

'Don't worry about Tony,' Margarite said, as she stuck first one foot then the other into her shoes.

'I don't think either of us has a choice right now,' he said. 'A couple of his wise guys have spent the night across the street.'

Margarite clacked across the floor to peer out the window.

'The black Taurus to the left of the chicken and seafood place.'

'Yeah,' she said. 'There's a Lincoln Town Car with it now.' She turned to him. 'If you're ready, let's go.'

Outside, a chill, wet breeze from the water swept across their backs, stirred Margarite's still-damp hair. As they set off across the deserted street the front doors of the Taurus opened and the two wise guys Croaker had seen last night emerged. He was pleased to see that their clothes were as rumpled as his, and they weren't half as relaxed.

The one who had bought the coffee and sandwiches went to the Lincoln, opened the rear door. Out popped Tony DeCamillo. He stood, legs slightly spread, shooting his cuffs, eyeing them as they headed in his direction.

Croaker had a weird, almost suprareal sense of being in the middle of a Western shootout, the climax to a wild and woolly tale of hatred and revenge.

When they were halfway across the street, the two wise guys made a move, but Tony D. turned, put his hands flat on their chests, said something to them under his breath. They halted, contented themselves with glaring at Croaker, their hands hanging loosely at their sides. He expected they blamed him for their long, uncomfortable night.

On the far side of the street, Margarite turned to him and, as he suspected her husband had done with his men, said, 'Stay here. Let me handle this alone with Tony.'

It was not so much bravery that motivated her, Margarite thought as she and Tony came together, but an innate sense of practicality. She knew that the worst thing she could have done was to have them all meet, Tony with his wise guys, she with Croaker. Then the situation would be defined in male terms, would degenerate into a macho thing, and violence would almost inevitably follow. She would not allow that.

'Babe,' Tony said, his dark eyes sliding from her face to stare at Croaker. 'You spend the night with this jamoke?'

'Why would it matter to you?'

'Jesus H. Christ. Because you're my fuckin' wife is why!'

Not 'Because we're married'. The difference said it all about their relationship.

'Then look at me,' Margarite said sharply. 'Not him.'

His eyes flicked to her. 'I got problems that have to be solved.'

'We'll solve them.'

'You walked out on me. You stashed the kid – '

'Francine!' She almost lost it then, raising her voice so that Croaker and the wise guys could hear. 'Our daughter's name is Francine.'

'Yeah, yeah.' His lips pursed. 'I'll find out where you stashed her. You think I won't?'

Margarite could only wonder at the changes at work inside herself. The force of his familiar intimidation now only served to harden her resolve.

'Oh, I have no doubt of it,' she said. 'But by then I'll have moved her. And I'll do it again and again.' She shook her head. 'No matter what you think now, Tony, you'll never get her. And, d'you know something, the harder you try the more she'll hate you, and then you'll have lost everything.'

There was a small silence. In the interval, she could hear his breathing, and she wondered briefly how high his blood pressure had shot up. Behind her, she could hear intermittent traffic start up, and, closer, the sharp scrape as Croaker shifted uneasily from one foot to another.

Tony leaned in so his face was very close to hers. He was wearing too much cologne and hadn't shaved. She was glad to see evidence of the haste with which he had made the trip here.

When he spoke again, his tone was lower, more conciliatory. This was the soft Tony. 'You know you're acting nuts, babe. I don't know what to make of it, but you're making me look bad in front of the boys. What with recent events and rumors of the Leonfortes making a move, I got to tell you morale is kinda on a slide. I need you back home, babe; you belong at my side.'

'The only one who's acting here is you, Tony,' Margarite said. 'Macho Tony, tender Tony. You've shot your load now; you're finished. That's all you ever had. It took me all this time to face up to the fact it's not nearly enough for me. Now it's time for you to face up to reality.'

He squinted at her, not knowing what to make of this curious creature.

'Cut the bullshit,' he said menacingly. 'What it boils down to is you don't need me as an enemy.'

'Oh, Tony, I don't want us to be enemies. But we can never go back to the way it used to be.'

'That's the only thing I want, and I'll move heaven and earth to make sure it turns out that way.' Now he sounded like a petulant child.

'I'm not going to divorce you, so don't worry about that,' Margarite said. 'At least for now there's one compelling reason not to leave you, because we need each other. It's what Dominic counted on, you being the mask for me. Without your male façade, I can't work effectively continuing Dom's work. Without me, you're without Dom's contacts. Six months from now, at the outside, the family will abandon you and you'll be a pariah.'

'The hell I will!'

She said nothing, knowing that he needed time to digest the truth, find a way to make it palatable, to save face.

'Ah, shit,' he said at last. 'The truth is, I've already had trouble with certain factions of La Famiglia. The Infantes, the Dellarcos. I'm used to overcoming corporate infighting to save a client's ass. This is a whole other ball game. These fuckin' greaseballs –'

They both laughed, the first time they had done so in a very long time.

'Yeah,' Margarite said, 'these fucking greaseballs can be a handful and a half when they get out of line.'

'Maybe we do need each other.' But his dark eyes were wary. 'You coming home now?'

'Not yet,' she said. 'There's still some business to be settled.'

'With him.' He gestured toward Croaker with his chin.

'He's part of it.'

'Well, shit, babe, I don't know. I ran a check, got all the skinny on him. Your friend's not a Fed.'

'I know. He told me. He's an ex-cop. NYPD, out of Homicide. He's even a little famous in the annals of the city.'

'Christ Almighty, babe, I hope you know what you're doing.'

Margarite felt the double flip of her heartbeat. 'So do I.'

'This is the kind of jamoke your brother always warned me about.' He reached out, was about to touch her, then apparently thought better of it. His hands hung loosely at his sides. 'I want you to be very careful with this man.'

'Don't worry.'

'How can I help it? Something about you with this lawman makes my hackles rise, you know what I mean, like the time I just knew Warner Brothers was going to screw Eddie Mentor on that seven-figure contract. I saved Eddie's mil-plus, but here' – he shook his head – 'I don't know.'

'I can take care of myself.'

'Yeah. You've made that clear.'

Margarite wanted to say thank you, but it wasn't time yet; there was too much hurt he had made her bear. With a certain pang, she recognized that perhaps sadly for him the time might never come.

'About the families,' she said. 'The Infantes have a son, Joey, who's been sneaking around seeing Kate, the Dellarcos' youngest daughter. They're in love. Talk to them; broker the marriage.'

'Holy Mother,' Tony said, 'the two *capi* will kill each other – if they don't murder me first.'

357

'The marriage will be the best thing for everyone,' Margarite said. 'You'll see – the children's love will heal the rift. Within six weeks the two families will be the best of friends.' She looked at him. 'It's what Dom would have done.'

She was about to turn away when he said, 'What about the kid?'

She looked at him for a very long time. 'Leave it alone, Tony. Francie's ill. She's bulimic, and we – you and I – did it to her. What we've done to each other did not happen in a vacuum. Our little psychodrama had the gravest consequences for Francie. She's suffering from radiation burns from that fallout. My best guess is she needs a vacation from both of us.'

'Yeah, well . . .' He put his head down. 'Shit.'

Margarite nodded. 'That about sums it up.'

Croaker watched her walk away from her husband. She did not look back, but Tony D. stared after her until a moment before she rejoined him, then he turned on his heel, barked a sharp command, and slid back into the dark comfort of the Lincoln Town Car. Engines started up.

Croaker cleared his throat. 'How'd it go?'

'It went,' Margarite said. 'That's all I can say.' She seemed tired, drained of the bravado that had put a bounce in her step on her way to meet Tony.

'Let's get some breakfast,' he said, guiding her down the street. 'By the time we finish, White's Drugs and Department Store over there is bound to be open.'

She nodded wordlessly. Croaker, studying her, found himself wondering what effect Tony had had on her. He remembered the odd moment when they had laughed together, so incongruous. He was dismayed to realize he was anxious to know what had allowed them that kind of intimacy again. He longed to ask her, but he knew he could not, and her silence all through breakfast warned him that she was not going to tell him.

They arrived in Washington on the 4 p.m. shuttle. As promised, Lillehammer met them at the airport. He looked freshly scrubbed, as if he'd just bounced in from his health club, and very dapper in a coal-black suit and crisp white shirt. He had on a tie with a bull's-eye pattern.

'Good flight?' he asked, his piercing blue eyes already on Margarite.

'An interesting couple of days,' Croaker replied. 'This is Margarite Goldoni DeCamillo.'

'Charmed,' Lillehammer said. He introduced himself. 'A terrible shame about your brother.'

'I understand,' Margarite said. 'A blot on your record.'

'Not at all.' Lillehammer did not miss a beat. 'All of us in government who knew Dominic came to admire him. For doing what he did, stepping

358

forward, naming names, putting his life on the line. That took real courage, and as a former soldier I, personally, respected him.'

It was an interesting speech, even a good one, Croaker thought. But he did not believe it had fooled Margarite.

'Well, thank you,' she said sweetly.

The pleasantries over, Lillehammer guided them through the crowded terminal, out onto the pavement where a large sedan with government plates was waiting for them, its engine idling. From its deep, throaty pitch, and the unmistakable sound the doors made when they slammed home, Croaker knew the car had been bullet-proofed.

'I can't pretend to understand how difficult it is for you to agree to this meeting, Mrs DeCamillo,' Lillehammer said, apparently sincerely. 'But my colleague here feels that you are our single best lead to finding the man who murdered your brother and, believe me, we are very anxious to do that.'

'Why?'

'I beg your pardon?' Lillehammer shifted in the seat.

'I asked why, Mr Lillehammer.' Margarite looked at him candidly. 'Why is it so important that you find Dominic's killer? Can it be merely a matter of pride, a kind of – how shall I put it? – altruism toward a man you came to admire and respect even while you were crucifying him?'

Croaker expended a great deal of energy keeping the smile off his face, but Lillehammer had gone red.

'Jesus Christ – pardon me, ma'am,' he said, struggling to contain himself, 'but your brother controlled all the construction, produce and meat packing, private sanitation, gambling, prostitution, and God knows what else on the Eastern seaboard. The Mayor of New York couldn't take a crap – pardon my French – without getting an okay from Dominic Goldoni. So I don't really believe righteousness is the proper attitude for you to take with us. At the risk of offending you, your brother died for his sins – we didn't have anything to do with it.'

Croaker said nothing, watched Margarite bite her lip before putting one hand up over her face.

The car came to a halt and they climbed out. They were in Washington but Croaker had no idea where. Lillehammer led them into the side entrance of a monumental granite and limestone building, one of so many throughout the city their sheer number had the curious effect of making these imposing, grandiose structures humdrum.

He offered up a plastic-coated ID card, obtained from the uniformed guard temporary cards for each of his guests. No one else accompanied them in the elevator that took them from the echoing marble lobby to an anonymous, fluorescent-lit room along a nondescript hallway. Somewhere the sound came as of beetles chewing wood, computer operators clicking nails against keyboards, but no one was in evidence.

The cubicle contained one metal table, six straight-backed chairs, a water-cooler, a stack of ruled pads, a clutch of pencils, and a small window that looked out on a sooty, lightless airshaft.

'Marvelous,' Margarite said, looking at Croaker, not Lillehammer. 'It's almost like being in jail.'

She went over to the table, discovered there a mass of black-and-white prints of the murder scene: Dominic Goldoni and his sometime mistress, Ginnie Morris.

'Not a pretty sight, is it?' Lillehammer said. 'But I've had to pore over these until my eyes hurt.'

Jesus, thought Croaker, but he knew what Lillehammer was up to. He wanted Margarite to get another jolt of what had been perpetrated, just in case her proximity to the Feds had begun to change her mind about cooperating.

Margarite seemed not to have heard. She was staring at the evidence as her hands mechanically sifted through each photo. Croaker saw her pick up one of Ginnie Morris – these were photos he hadn't let her see before – where that weird ladder pattern of cuts, overlayed by the bloody white magpie feather, was the focus of the photographer's lens. She stood very still for so long it began to worry Lillehammer.

He went to the water-cooler, filled a paper cup, set it on the table beside her.

'Perhaps it will be easier if we all sit down,' he said. When they were seated, he drew over a notepad and pencil, then went on. 'My colleague has filled me in on the gist of what occurred just before the murders, but I'd like to hear the details directly from you.' He pulled out a pocket cassette recorder. 'Do you have any objection to my taping your statement?'

Margarite shook her head.

'Would you mind stating that for the record?'

She did, then began to recite her encounter with the man she knew as Robert. It was very cut and dried, without any of the deep emotion she displayed when she had told Croaker what had happened. To him, her voice, like her actions, had an eerie, monotonal quality, as if she were not quite there. Lillehammer, engrossed in the bizarre events leading up to the murders, apparently failed to notice anything amiss. But then he did not know Margarite as Croaker now did.

When she was finished, Lillehammer glanced at a few notes he had jotted down, asked a string of questions, all of which Margarite answered in the same tone of voice.

When Lillehammer was satisfied, he said, 'I'm now going to ask you to do something extraordinarily difficult. In all probability it will be quite dangerous, as well. But, from what little we've been able to glean on our own and from what you've told us here, I'm convinced – as is my colleague – that the only way to catch this exceedingly clever murderer is if we use you for bait.'

'Wait a minute,' Croaker said before Margarite had a chance to answer. 'I never agreed to any such insane idea.'

'Uhm.' Lillehammer appeared to give this outburst due consideration. 'But that's not the impression I got from your telephone call.' He tapped the recorder at his elbow. 'I taped the conversation. Shall I play it back for the lady?'

'Whatever I may have implied then isn't relevant now,' Croaker said. 'Putting an innocent in certain harm's way seems to me totally unacceptable.'

Lillehammer looked at him quizzically. 'Are you telling me you never used this tactic when you were with the NYPD?'

Croaker risked a quick glance in Margarite's direction. Her eyes were lowered as she stared at the mass of carnage Lillehammer had left out for her to see, the grisly remnants of her brother and his mistress. He could well imagine the war of emotions going on inside her – repulsion for what Robert was capable of, attraction to what he represented to her new life. He did not envy her.

'I can't say I never used another human being as bait,' he said at length. 'But I always felt uneasy about it, and I always did it with me – and only me – as sentinel.'

'I imagine I should translate for the lady,' Lillehammer said. 'A sentinel is the professional who backs up the bait, sees she comes to no harm while the trap snaps shut on the quarry.'

Still, Margarite seemed oblivious to his words.

Lillehammer looked at Croaker. 'You'll admit it is a strategy that has a high percentage of success.'

'When the circumstances were dire enough,' Croaker said grudgingly. 'When our backs were to the wall.' He did not care for the position that Lillehammer was putting him in.

Lillehammer spread his hands. 'Well?'

'Mortal risk,' Croaker said hotly. 'That's what we're talking about.'

'Stop it!'

Margarite's voice, loud and shrill, left them both in astonished silence.

361

'Stop it, the two of you!' She looked from one to the other. 'You're talking about me as if I weren't here, as if I were a commodity to be negotiated over.' She stood up abruptly. 'I need some fresh air, Lew.'

'I understand,' Croaker said. The two men stood. 'Your further involvement should not have been brought up.'

'No. Mr Lillehammer has made a good point.'

Croaker was stunned. 'You're not seriously considering –'

'I may do it. I told you I'm sure Robert won't hurt me,' she said. 'But if it happens it'll be my decision, not yours or the Feds'.'

'Fair enough,' Lillehammer said. 'That's all I can ask of you.' He gave Croaker a quick nod as he pulled open the door for them. He smiled, the scars at the corners of his mouth standing out like graffiti. 'Thank you for taking the time, Mrs DeCamillo.'

In the doorway, she turned, smiling sweetly back at him. 'By the way, Mr Lillehammer, you were wrong about what you said before. You and the others like you had everything to do with my brother's death. If it weren't for racist cops there never would have been a need for Dominic Goldoni; if it weren't for cops eager to be bought, Dominic Goldoni never would have flourished; if it weren't for cops looking to make a name for themselves he never would have died how and when he did.'

When the alarm in Nangi's ear sounded its shrill warning he was fast asleep. He opened his eyes into the dead of night. He stirred, fumbling for his cane. He had fallen asleep on the upholstered chair in his living-room. As he stood, the sheaf of papers he had been reading fanned out onto the carpet at his feet. He bent down, ignoring the pain in his leg. Facts and figures on Avalon Ltd were arrayed in neat columns, pie graphs and fiscal summaries. On the surface, none of it amounted to much.

It had taken a great deal of legwork and favors exchanged just to get this much. Avalon Ltd as a privately held company was not obliged to make public any of its business.

He shuffled the papers together and, leaning on the dragon's head of his cane, stood up. He put the papers aside, went into the front hall and grabbed his tweed overcoat.

Outside, in the car, he switched on the defroster, watched the rime slowly disappear from his windshield. He had not bothered to wake his driver. The whine in his ear changed pitch and he pulled out of his driveway. The pitch changed again, and he picked up speed, guided by the miniature receiving device in his ear.

Not that the information he had received was in all ways useless, he reflected, as he made a turn into one of Tokyo's wide nighttime boulevards.

If Avalon Ltd did a lot of business, it nevertheless generated no profit. What business could long afford that kind of balance sheet? Unless it was a shell corporation, set up essentially to funnel capital from one source to another.

Pink and silver neon lights lapped at the sides of his car, lacquered the faces of those pedestrians still about, tourists mainly, peering into windows filled with futuristic electronic gadgets and antique kimonos, seeking to drink in as much of the bewildering metropolis as they could in as short a time as possible. What use had they for sleep?

Nangi thought for a long time as he drove. Given the premise that Avalon Ltd was not what it was purported to be, the most burning question was not what Avalon Ltd actually was, but why he was being directed to it. The mysterious man who had claimed to be Vincent Tinh's brother when he had come to collect Tinh's corpse had given Avalon Ltd as his company. Why? Why not give a totally fictitious corporation where any inquiry would lead to a certain dead end. That's certainly what Nangi would have done in the man's place. Why hadn't he?

Faces of teenage models and platinum-haired pop stars, stories high, animatedly sold soft drinks or cosmetics. Their presence, gigantic and extortionate, broke apart reality, put it back together in a whole new way.

The pitch in his ear changed yet again, and Nangi turned off the boulevard, into a string of streets that became increasingly narrower, darker, meaner. Garbage littered the alleyways, and yellow dogs, conspicuous by their overly prominent ribs, stalked the intimidating shadows in search of offal.

Someone wanted Nangi to link Avalon Ltd to Tinh's death, to point him in a certain direction. Was it the right direction or a false lead meant to obscure the true circumstances of Tinh's murder?

Nangi, his window rolled down, could smell the Sumida River, a bouquet of salt and decay, as of a neighborhood long past its prime, too long buried in the earth. Anonymous concrete houses, thrown up and torn down within a week, were giving way to blank-walled warehouses, somber reptiles slumbering beneath a horned moon. The bizarre machinery of heavy construction crews squatted like sullen beasts in the temporary shelters provided by the ferrous bones of beams and girders.

Too many questions without answers, Nangi thought, and I only have one path – uncertain at best – into this riddle. The alarm in his ear was fairly shrieking now and he slowed to a crawl. Long before, he had dowsed his headlights, using streetlights and then what ambient glow emanated from the city itself to guide him.

Through a gap in the buildings he saw the Sumida, moonlight defining

363

its puckered skin, dancing on the wavelets set up by a barge like strings plucked on a *koto*.

Then he was past the gap, and that shimmering view was lost in darkness and the stench of putrefaction. The alarm in his ear was a dull shriek, and he rolled the car to a stop. Further down the block, he saw an older car's lights go out. It was parked in front of what strangely appeared to be a private dwelling wedged between two huge warehouses.

As he watched in silence and shadow, Seiko got out of the car, hurried up the stairs, and rapped quickly on the door. It was opened almost immediately by an old woman dressed in traditional kimono. Her dark hair was up, elaborately coifed, set with long pins. With a quick, furtive glance around, Seiko passed across the threshold, and the door closed behind her.

Nangi pulled the miniature receiver out of his ear and, opening the carved dragon's head of his cane, dropped it into the hollowed-out interior. The other half of it – the transmitter – was lodged in one of the filigreed lines etched into the silver pillbox Nangi had given Seiko in the car on the way back to the office from Justine's funeral.

What had made him suspicious of her? It would have been un-Christian of him to doubt her motives simply because she had spent so much time in Vietnam, had had a torrid affair with a Vietnamese equities trader. Just as it would have been un-Christian for Nangi to have succumbed to the Japanese bias against the other, so-called 'lesser' Asian cultures, which, in more bellicose days, the Japanese had sought to subjugate.

The truth was this sort of prejudice ran deep within the Japanese psyche. Adherents and critics alike saw this bias as cultural, but Nangi suspected it was more an imperative of being a resource-poor island nation whose inhabitants were terrified of relying for their continued existence on – and therefore under the thumb of – societies on the Asian continent.

It pained Nangi to think that he might harbor un-Christian attitudes even while he understood that these errors affirmed his humanity.

In any event, he had run a check on Seiko's ex-lover and had pulled from the deep several intriguing nuggets of information. For instance, the man was suspected of running a highly complex scam on the Hang Seng, the Hong Kong stock exchange, that made his clients tens of millions of dollars, and lined his own pockets with a tidy percentage of the profits. These clients, on further investigation, turned out to be a nexus of holding companies which Nangi knew, from his own contacts, to be owned by the Yakuza. On another occasion, this Vietnamese had made a killing for clients in several Japanese ministries on a curiously rapid and unexplained downdraft in a favored real estate stock.

Seiko might have been perfectly innocent, unaware of what her lover

364

was up to, but Nangi could not help but wonder whether she was ignorant, as well, of what kind of man he was. It was his experience that women were more astute judges of character than men ever gave them credit for being. Even considering that she might have been momentarily blinded by love, he could not countenance for long the idea that such an obviously whip-smart person could be deaf, dumb and blind.

And while he was perfectly willing to give Seiko the benefit of the doubt – especially for the benefit of Nicholas – he knew, deep down, that he had put her on a kind of probation, at the end of which he might be forced to act. The homing transmitter had been that act, plucking his suspicion out of the theoretical amber into which he had temporarily consigned it.

Even so, he might have been obliged to shelve his distrust forever, had she not overstepped her hand. The work she was doing for the company was unarguably first-rate, and her expertise in Vietnam – and Saigon, in particular – was proving invaluable.

But then she had homed in on Nicholas. Perhaps she could not help herself. She was, Nangi had observed, a highly sexed young woman. But this insensitivity to Justine – and to Nicholas himself, for that matter – spoke of a certain dark current in her personality. Also, the ulterior circumstances again aroused his suspicions. Nicholas was her key into Sato International. The Vietnamese expansion was strictly his idea, and she knew that.

With the illuminating lens of hindsight, Nangi could appreciate just how astute a woman she was. She had sensed Nicholas's troubles at home, and she had quite willfully played upon that, imprinting herself more and more strongly on his psyche.

And when Nicholas was gone, how smoothly she had segued herself into Nangi's life. Far from hating her, he found himself filled with admiration. Far too rarely, one found an extraordinary, Machiavellian mind like Seiko's. The question was what to do with her now that she stood naked before him. Should he banish her or take her like a serpent to his breast?

'Don't lie to me, Lew,' Margarite said. 'Don't tell me you haven't been thinking about the possibility of using me to trap Robert since I told you what happened.'

'Thinking about something this risky and acting on it are two separate things,' he said.

She nodded. 'That's right. But risk is your stock in trade, isn't it?'

There was no use in denying it, and he kept his mouth shut. They were sitting at a table in Terrazza, an Italian restaurant on King Street in the Old Town section of Alexandria. The government-issue car had taken them to a nearby hotel where Lillehammer had arranged rooms for them. The driver said he was at their disposal during their stay in Washington, but Margarite was understandably uncomfortable with the arrangement, and Croaker had dismissed him. Margarite had wanted to eat Italian food, and the hotel's concierge had recommended Terrazza. They had taken a cab to Alexandria.

Croaker, sitting across the small table from her, smiled now.

'What's so funny?'

'I don't know,' he said, tearing off a piece of crusty bread, 'I was just thinking how much I admired the way you ended the interview with Lillehammer.'

'Before we can go on – before I can make any kind of commitment to put my life in your hands – I've got to know where your allegiance lies. Do you owe it to him?'

The waiter came up, perhaps to take their order, and Croaker glanced down at his menu. But Margarite waved the young man away. She apparently did not want any distractions.

'Lew, you'd better think this through.'

'I'm working for him,' Croaker said. 'He's counting on me to break this case.'

Margarite's gaze would not let him go. 'Let me tell you something. The Feds allowed Dom to keep running the organization through Tony from inside WITSEC. That was part of the deal from the get-go.' Her eyebrows arched. 'Do I have your attention now? Good. These Feds are more corrupt, more venal than any of the municipal law enforcement people Dom dealt with. That's because these bastards are closer to power – real power. That's what this city is all about.'

'There's a pleasant thought,' Croaker said.

'People like Lillehammer are different, Lew. They wield enough power to make every dirty trick stick. You've already seen a bit of what he's capable of, but I wonder whether you understand the levels of his psychological games. That jailhouse room of his. I know he took us there just to give me the willies, to show me who holds the power. Dom warned me about people who play convoluted psych games and now I'm warning you.'

'I've no doubt your brother was right on target,' Croaker said. It was astonishing to him how much influence a dead man still exerted on their lives. He was just beginning to appreciate Dominic Goldoni, and regret that he had never had the chance to meet him.

'I know something about Lillehammer, and can surmise a bit more,' he said. 'He was a POW in Vietnam. Did you see the scars around his

366

mouth? He told me something about how he got them. He was tortured. Who knows how long he was under pressure and what the circumstances of his escape were.' He shook his head. 'It seems to me men like that have no easy road ahead. Something has been broken inside them. Perhaps it's not what the enemy wants – Lillehammer claims he never gave them what they wanted – but under that kind of pressure you emerge changed. Men I've known who have been in similar circumstances seem to have lost some basic ability of judgement.'

Croaker tore off more bread, then, his appetite gone, did not know what to do with it, so he twisted it into a design with his titanium and polycarbonate fingers. 'Maybe it's simplistic to say that commitment becomes complicity but, nevertheless, it seems true. The victim inadvertently falls into the trap of protecting the time his psyche was under siege, until everything else becomes distorted in order to preserve the fiction he has constructed of that time. In effect, he and his torturers have become allies because they caused the fiction in the first place.'

'It's clear he's desperate to track down Robert,' Margarite said. 'Robert got to Dom through me, but how did Robert know that Dom would call me and precisely when?'

'Inside job? Lillehammer told me he couldn't trust his own people, that because Dominic was murdered he suspected a leak somewhere in the Fed system.' Croaker squeezed his eyes shut. 'But since that first time Lillehammer's made no mention of the supposed leak.' His eyes flew open. 'What if he knows Robert?'

Margarite was already shaking her head. 'It doesn't make sense. If he knows Robert of course he'd go after him himself. He'd know Robert's habits, where he liked to hang out, who he hung out with, it'd be a snap to find him.'

'Not if he hadn't seen Robert in a long time,' Croaker said. 'Like not since Vietnam.'

'What?'

'You told me Robert looked Oriental, not Japanese or Chinese, but like a mixture, copper skin, part Polynesian, almost. You could be describing a Vietnamese.' Croaker nodded. 'Yes,' he said slowly. 'It would make some kind of twisted sense.' He tapped his finger on the table. 'Who tortured Lillehammer, the Viet Cong? I assume so. Could Robert have been one of them? If so, being the good soldier that he is, he'd know the risk of going after Robert himself. If Robert caught one glimpse of him he'd bolt down a hole so deep Lillehammer would never find him. But Robert doesn't know me from Adam. An ex-cop, Homicide detective, proven to the Feds – I'd be perfect for the job.'

Margarite seemed to be holding herself tightly in check. 'I don't like this man Lillehammer.'

Now he could feel the tension coming off her in waves. 'This isn't just about Lillehammer,' he said.

'No. It's about something I saw up in that jailhouse room of his.' She shuddered. 'You hadn't shown me any pictures of what Robert did to Ginnie so I had no idea.'

'I didn't see the need.'

She nodded. 'I understand. But now that I've seen them I know there's someone here in Washington we have to see. Someone who knows about those wounds Robert inflicted on her.' She looked at him, her eyes bleak. 'You see, Lew, Ginnie's death was part of an ancient ritual. I don't know much about it, but I know someone who does. And I think once she tells you what she knows we'll be so close to Robert we'll feel his breath on our faces.'

Davis Munch, Pentagon special investigator on loan to Senator Rance Bane's Committee, didn't look anything like Gaunt had described him to Manny Mannheim.

If I don't come to collect this in twenty-four hours, Gaunt had told Manny late in the afternoon when he had returned to Manny's pawnshop before setting out for Lillehammer's home, *I want you to take this envelope to a man named Davis Munch. He's to get them to Nicholas Linnear at my company in Tokyo.*

Shit, Manny had said, already frightened for his friend, *I can do that for you, Harl – assuming it needs to get done, which I don't believe it will.*

Listen, Manny, Gaunt had said. *Munch is DIA, a Pentagon spook troubleshooter. He'll know what to do. I can't take the risk of this stuff going through the mail or being opened by anyone but Nicholas – or, failing that, Tanzan Nangi. Promise me you won't do anything stupid. You'll take it straight to Munch. He'll find a way – an official courier – to get it to Tokyo.*

If anything happens to you.

Promise me, Manny.

Manny had promised. Which was what he was doing here in the middle of the night, on a rain-swept Washington street, keeping his face out of the flashing red lights on top of the half-dozen squad cars blocking off an area of the street.

A siren sounded, approaching very quickly, and as Manny watched from the shadows, an ambulance was waved through the police roadblock, came screeching to a halt beside the body.

368

So much blood. Manny, deep in his lined mackinaw, shivered. Good Christ, he thought, what was Harl mixed up in?

He had phoned Davis Munch at home, using the number Gaunt had given him, left a message on the answering machine. Maybe he shouldn't have done that, maybe someone had Munch's phone bugged. But who? Munch was with DIA, the Pentagon spooks. Who would bug one of *them*, for Christ's sake? Manny shook his head as he watched the paramedics at work. Even at this distance he could tell that their presence was useless. Munch was dead, shot through the head with a high-powered rifle. Manny squeezed his eyes shut.

Gaunt had cautioned Manny not to leave his own number even if he spoke to Munch in person. In his message, Manny had decided to use the number of the pay phone in the bar downstairs from his apartment. He had eaten dinner there, then, ordering beer after beer, had waited for the phone to ring.

Mention the Golden Gloves boxer to him, Gaunt had said. *He'll know who you're talking about.*

Gaunt had been right. After dinner, Munch had gotten back to him. No names had been exchanged. Munch had agreed to meet Manny near the FBI headquarters on 9th Street, at the site of the former Lone Star Beef House. The Feds had been compelled to take over the place – a topless bar, no less – back in the seventies, after confiscating it from a particularly enterprising member of the Department of Transportation, who had acquired it with, as they say, i.g.g. – ill-gotten gains – embezzled from his employers.

What kind of bullet could make the back of a head explode like a melon hitting the ground? Manny wondered as he watched the paramedics get out the body bag while a bunch of spooks in suits took photos of Munch from every conceivable angle. A couple of them got down on their knees in the rain to snap the close-ups. Manny felt the contents of his stomach coming up into his throat again, and he gulped, sucking in damp air, rain, anything not to vomit. He closed his eyes again, but he could not blot out the sight of Munch's brains spewing out behind him ten feet or more. He'd still been in the shadows when the impact of the bullet had slammed Munch against the building's façade, still been across the street.

There had been a building fire between the bar and the rendezvous point, and the cab had been bogged down in traffic, blocked off streets, and clogged detours. In the end, Manny had hopped out early, half run the last leg. He had still been fifteen minutes late.

The spooks, finished with their iconography, signed for the paramedics, and soon Munch was cocooned inside the glistening body bag. Safer there, Manny thought, than on the streets this night.

That fire had saved his life. He turned away. With the departure of Munch, his reason for being here had slipped away. Or had it? Beneath his mackinaw he clutched the envelope tighter against his chest.

Hurrying home, he stayed just long enough to pack an overnight bag, take a wad of hundreds from beneath the floorboards of his bedroom. What was he forgetting? His passport! He went on a frantic fifteen-minute search, the sweat pouring off him, before he dug it up. It was still in the inside pouch of the cheap vinyl flight bag the tour company had provided for his trip last year to Israel. He stuffed some personal items into the bag, then got out of there. After what had happened to Davis Munch, he wasn't comfortable in his apartment or, truth to tell, anywhere in Washington.

Spending the night at Washington International airport, watching his reflection in the darkened plate glass of closed trinket shops, calmed his overwrought nerves, but not by much.

Margarite and Croaker arrived precisely at midnight. The house – more like a Georgian-style mansion – was perched like a magnificently plumaged crow on the crest of a hill, one of many in this emerald-green countryside. Rolling down the window, Croaker inhaled the rich scents of horses and hay. This was Potomac, Maryland, the middle of hunt country.

He leaned forward, peeled off a fifty-dollar bill, handed it to the cab driver. 'You'll wait for us,' he said.

'Yes, sir,' the cabby nodded. 'No problem at all.' He crossed his arms over his chest and, slouching in the seat, was soon fast asleep.

Croaker could see six or seven cars parked in the driveway by the side of the house – Jaguars, Rolls, large BMW sedans. If there were chauffeurs they had not been left to fend for themselves in the autumnal chill.

'Whose house is this?' he said.

Margarite continued to stare into the cloudless night. A horned moon, pale as butter, rode in the sky like a spectral ship or a catafalque. She stirred, but did not move, weighed down by the morbid thoughts that invariably assailed her when she returned here.

'Margarite?'

'Shhh,' she whispered. 'Don't speak, don't move, otherwise I will have to think about what comes next. Perhaps it's inevitable, like one second coming after another, but for this moment, let me dream of us together alone in the night.'

Croaker smelled her and the horses. Surprisingly, he had no trouble imagining her with their musky, muscular odor clinging to her thighs as she popped a booted foot out of a stirrup, swung off a smooth leather saddle. He thought he heard in the night small ghostly sounds: the creak of leather, the jingle of metal against metal, the soft snort of the beast. Then he blinked, and only the sounds of the cabby's heavy, rhythmical breathing, the slow, tempered tick of the engine cooling, came to him.

'I used to ride here,' Margarite whispered through dry lips, 'when I was younger.'

He looked at her concentrating as if in the endgame of a chess match, and he wondered by what hallucinatory process he had been given an auditory glimpse of another time, another world.

Margarite leaned forward, slumped against the door as if exhausted or acquiescing to the dreadful before she opened it, got out. Following her, Croaker heard the crunch of her heels on the crystal-cut gravel, white as milk beneath the moonlight.

The mansion was built of pinkish-brown brick. The windows were neatly bracketed by shutters the color of clotted cream, and the imposing front entrance was surmounted by a stained-glass fanlight that must have been at least a century old. Behind them, the sweeping driveway was lined by sheared cherry trees and, closer to the main house itself, spear-like magnolia and crescent-limbed hemlocks rose toward the slate roof. The brick steps up to the entrance were set between beds of annuals, now bare, the black soil streaked with compost the color of straw. A thin, penetrating wind blew through the layers of dark-green dwarf Hinoki cypresses which ascended with them as they mounted the steps.

As he walked, he scanned the environment. He had been careful when they had left the restaurant in Alexandria, remembering that the concierge at their hotel had recommended it and, therefore, knew where they were going. Margarite, apparently of the same mind, had insisted that they walk some distance from the restaurant, and then not take the first cab that cruised by. The directions she gave the cab driver were exceedingly circuitous. She did not want anyone to know where they were going.

In front of the carved wooden door, Margarite turned to him, said, 'I want you to understand something, Lew. I'm not responsible here, for anything. This place is something more than private property.'

He stared at her, trying to fathom the strange transformation she had undergone from the moment she had seen the photos of Ginnie Morris spread out on Lillehammer's mean government table.

She touched him gently on the wrist, tried to smile, then used the brass knocker. In a moment, the door opened, and a beautiful woman dressed in black wool trousers, a cream silk blouse, and an embroidered Spanish crop-waisted black jacket stood before them. The outfit, which would not have looked out of place on a runway model one quarter this woman's age, accentuated her slim, long-waisted figure.

'Margarite! Thank God you've come!'

The woman's smile, metallic as the ticking of the cab's engine outside, caused Croaker to give her a harder look. Lines crinkled her face, at the corners of eyes and mouth, along her upper lip, and he could see the years weighing on her, not heavily as they might in many other women, perhaps because of the indefatigable spark in her cerulean eyes, but lurking nonetheless.

By this smile alone Croaker knew she was a dangerous woman. And now he could scent like the discharge from a pistol the fear and reluctance that marked Margarite's decision to return here.

'Come in, darling,' the woman said, closing the door behind them. She embraced Margarite, kissing her on both cheeks in the European fashion. 'It's so good to see you. Nothing's been the same, it seems, since Dom died. Despite my best efforts to pull strings, even with the senior senator from Minnesota, who owes me a raft of favors, I've come up against a stone wall in trying to find out what happened to Dom.'

'I think we can help each other on that score,' Margarite said tightly.

'Darling, that's the best news I've had in weeks,' Renata said. 'Trust you to know the score. Dom always held you in the highest regard.'

As she held Margarite at arm's length, she frowned, and Croaker could see more lines appear like writing in invisible ink materializing under the influence of an infra-red bulb.

'But, my dear, you've come with a stranger. Where is Anthony?'

Margarite turned to him and he could clearly see the struggle in her eyes. Pain and half-heard heartache swirled like dark colors muddying an artist's best work.

'Lew Croaker,' she said. 'I'd like you to meet my step-mother, Renata Loti.'

Renata smiled sweetly, extending an astonishingly firm hand which gripped Croaker's strongly. 'Do come in. My daughter is being uncommonly kind,' she said. 'I've been known by many names in my day. Renata Loti is the one Washington knows and it serves me well. But in times past I was known as Faith Goldoni. You know that name, don't you, Mr Croaker?'

This is Dominic Goldoni's mother, Croaker thought, stunned. *Good God!*

She did not invite them to take off their coats, but turned immediately, led them down a long pearwood-paneled hallway. Croaker noticed her slight limp. She made no mention of it, and he could see by the way she moved that she did not consider it a handicap. On the contrary, she had adapted herself to it so that her stride appeared, if not quite natural, then at least uniquely hers. They passed double doors behind which the sounds of a sedate party discreetly emanated.

'The main house is alive with guests tonight,' she said. 'Knowing my daughter, I'm certain we could use some privacy.'

They entered the sweet-smelling pantry, then went through a vast tile and stainless-steel kitchen, redolent of fresh sage, olive oil and red wine. A young chef in white apron and *toque de cuisinier* gave them hardly any notice as he worked on a pear tart.

Renata took a fur-lined black vinyl slicker off a wooden peg, draped it over her shoulders. The rear door gave out onto a tiny herb garden and, to the left, a wood and brick loggia down which Renata Loti led them. Thick wisteria and woody grape-vines protected them from the chill of the clear November night.

The yeasty scents of the kitchen were soon supplanted by the sharp, heady reek of horses, hay and manure. Renata reached out, turned on a light, opened a wide door into the stables.

Horses snorted and stamped, and Croaker was reminded of the hallucinatory moment in the cab, as if he had been eavesdropping on Margarite's memories.

Huge dewy-brown equine eyes regarded them with agitation and distrust. There were several high whinnies, as the horses adapted to the new scents.

He scanned the interior, as he always did, taking in details. 'Odd,' he said. 'There's a gun in here.'

Renata looked at the revolver in its old, scarred leather holster hung on the far wall. 'It's a Colt,' she said. 'I keep it in perfect condition. I bought it when I put in these stables. Just a couple of miles from here I'd seen a horse with a broken leg suffering for over an hour while someone tried to find a gun, some humane way of putting it out of its misery. When I decided to ride horses, I vowed I'd never let any of mine suffer that way.'

Croaker studied her for some time, putting in sync the information she'd just provided with the elegant physical presence of the woman. 'Frankly, you've taken me completely by surprise,' he said after a moment.

'Oh?'

'I was under the impression . . . I think the Feds are, too, that Faith Goldoni died some time ago. I saw a xerox of the death certificate myself in the file I was given on the Goldonis.'

'I don't doubt it a bit,' Renata said. 'I *did* die some years ago. At least, Faith Goldoni did. Then Renata Loti was born and moved here within shouting distance of Capitol Hill, where she could do the most good.' She leaned against a horse stall, unraveling a piece of tack with her expert fingers. Hers was a body that apparently had never experienced arthritis. 'Of course, taking different identities is nothing new for me. I served in the US Army during World War Two under the name of Faith Sawhill.'

Croaker was shaking his head. 'Assuming all of this is true, why are you letting me in on it? If even the Feds I work with don't know who you are, why risk telling me?'

'First, you're not a Fed,' Renata Loti said. 'Second, I know who *you* are.' Her piercing blue eyes slid from Croaker to Margarite. 'Third, my daughter brought you here.' She made a curious sound in the back of her throat that made the horses' ears prick up. 'Why, she doesn't even do that with her husband.'

Apparently, Margarite had had enough of this because she pulled out a thick, folded piece of paper. As she handed it to Renata, Croaker saw that it was a photo.

Wrapping her fingers around it, Renata looked into her step-daughter's eyes as if already alerted to the extraordinary nature of their visit.

'Ginnie Morris,' Margarite said woodenly. 'Her body was found in the same house with Dom's. There was a vertical crescent carved into her forehead.'

'Dear God,' Renata Loti breathed. 'No wonder you came.' She was no longer leaning nonchalantly against the stall, but was gripping the folded photo with fingers made white with tension.

'I suppose you know who Ginnie Morris is,' Croaker said, suspecting the answer but needing it confirmed.

'I don't believe my son had any secrets from me,' Renata said with a voice that made plain the burden of sharing another life. 'In all ways, he was an exceptional man.' Her eyes flickered to Croaker's. 'Whatever opinion to the contrary you have already formed, he was a man for whom the word Fidelity should, in all cases, be capitalized. As to his sexual peccadillos, he couldn't help himself.' She gave a small, crescent smile. 'Who among us can?'

Croaker, watching her in the manner in which he had been trained to study potential suspects, felt a peculiar chill go through him, as if it might be possible that she knew that he and Margarite had made love.

'There's more,' Margarite said softly, 'than just the mark carved on her.'

As Renata unfolded the photo, she studied the thoroughly unpleasant sight of a woman's torso slit with seven evenly spaced horizontal wounds. Tucked into the lowest, and seventh slash, was the feather of the rare white magpie.

'Does something in that photo look familiar to you?' Croaker asked.

374

Renata had not taken her eyes from the photo. Croaker tried to read her, but her expression did not change. The horses shook their heads in the increasingly restless atmosphere. Perhaps they smelled a storm coming.

'The Soul Ladder,' Renata said at last.

'Pardon me?' Croaker said, leaning forward to hear her.

'This is part of a ritual of a people known as the Messulethe,' Renata said. 'Psycho-magicians older even than the Chinese civilization. Some say they were Cycladians, roamers of the seas, descendants of the Titans, others –'

She shrugged and pointed to the photo. 'You see, there are seven cuts. In the lore of the Messulethe, there is a belief that the human soul must pass through seven levels in life and in the after-life. The Messulethe priest often creates this Soul Ladder in, for instance, very ill people, by making seven incisions along the torso in order to help the soul to continue its journey.'

She licked her lips, the only sign she had made that she was in any way distressed. 'In times of extreme hardship – like drought, when it is believed that the cosmic order is impaired – an animal is often sacrificed this way so that the balance can be restored.'

'So it's some kind of ritual – what? – voodoo?'

Renata's lips curled into a sardonic smile. 'It is Ngoh-meih-yuht,' she said flatly. 'That's a phrase in an obscure Chinese dialect which means literally the crescent moon. But of course that is not its meaning here. It is almost synonymous with another word, Gim, which is a kind of two-edged sword. The Gim is the symbol of the Messulethe priest: the vertical crescent, dark with woad.'

Croaker, listening with mounting fascination, said, 'How on earth do you know about these people?'

Renata shrugged. 'When one lives in Venice, Mr Croaker, when one exists for so long suspended between the sea and the land, in a lagoon of mist and magic, one feels compelled to explore the beginning of things. Especially when one is not by birth Venetian and is reminded of that fact every day of one's life.' She was not looking at Margarite, but Croaker had the feeling it was to her step-daughter she was directing her reply.

'One might say that I am by nature acquisitive, an acquirer of knowledge.' Her eyes had turned dark. 'Also, I explored the myths of these beginnings through my late husband, Margarite's father. He was Venetian. Through him, through Margarite's mother, and so through her, flowed the blood of the Cycladians, or so they maintained.' She shrugged, somehow managing to impart hidden meaning to even this most nondescript of gestures. 'I may say that many ancient cultures claimed to have been the founders of Venice, even the last scholarly remnants of the Trojans, fleeing before the wrath of the brothers Menelaus and Agamemnon and their Achaean armada.'

Croaker, fascinated though he was, kept Margarite in the corner of his vision. He noted, as Renata spoke, that she turned her face more and more into shadow. It was as if these two had a long history of psychological conflict, pitting the force of one personality against the other. Was this why Margarite found it so difficult to return here?

'I don't expect you to have heard of them,' Renata continued, 'but in the highlands of North Vietnam and Southern China live hill-tribes called, collectively, the Nungs. These Nungs practice Ngoh-meih-yuht, the way of the Messulethe. They are not headhunters or cannibals, per se. But it is their conviction that in the unbroken bones of man and animal alike resides the essence of the "soul", from which transcendental enlightenment – energy and wisdom – may be reconstituted by the proper rituals and prayers.'

Renata had a way of speaking that could make the most fantastic tale sound credible. Not that Croaker believed for a moment that she would be giving this particular account to many people.

'The Nung priests believe that Ngoh-meih-yuht is the one true path to nirvana. Others have seen in their lore an ancient path to power that can be implemented in the modern world.' Her head swung away for a moment, and it appeared to Croaker as if she stared through the walls of the stable to another place, another time.

'Like this man who killed Dominic and Ginnie.'

Renata nodded.

'I'd appreciate it if you'd give me some details,' he said. 'For instance, what meaning does the white magpie feather have?'

'So you have done some research.' She shifted as if abruptly uncomfortable. The stallion next to her stamped and whinnied, as if scenting with its primitive brain the intimations of evil. 'Should I tell you about the feather?' she asked rhetorically. 'I suppose once having begun I am obligated to finish this.' She turned her head in Croaker's direction, and he could feel the heat in her eyes.

What is Margarite thinking? Croaker wondered, watching shadows like spiderwebs steal across her cheeks. *She must have known. She brought me here.* She'd known the moment she saw the seven wounds, the feather of the white magpie. *Perhaps it's inevitable, like one second coming after another,* she had whispered in the moment before they had come inside.

'In Ngoh-meih-yuht,' Renata said, 'the white magpie holds a singular status. You must understand that in every culture of the world, flight is one of the greatest of shamanic powers. The bird is a symbol – not only of flight, but of the transformation of man into God.'

Croaker considered this a moment. His experiences with Nicholas had prepared him to believe in the fantastic. He knew, first hand, that another rarely glimpsed and often misunderstood reality existed beyond the façade of the ordinary. Besides, he could sense like a navigator intuiting currents a confluence in what she was saying and the highly disturbing aura at the murder scene. This curious form of double vision like that associated with a migraine occurred in him when the previously unexplainable suddenly acquired both context and meaning.

'How does this transformation relate to Ginnie Morris?' he asked.

'It doesn't,' Renata said. 'It is – how shall I put it? – a signature.'

'A signature?'

'Yes.' Renata nodded. 'The white magpie is significant because of the practitioner, not the sacrificial victim.'

Croaker took a step forward, his heart thudding heavily in his chest. 'You mean that this feather can tell you who committed the murder?'

'Precisely,' Renata said. 'The Nung priests are known to take animal familiars upon their initiation. I would think none of them these days take the white magpie.' She turned away, worried her lip with her small white teeth.

'If you know who murdered your son, you must tell me.'

Renata passed fingers over her forehead as if brushing away wisps of hair. 'Among the Nungs the white magpie is a bird of exceptional power. It is a bird through which God speaks to the priests. It is divine. The one who uses its feathers . . .'

The silence seemed to roll over them like a newly tarred road, sticky with portent. Croaker began to say something, thought better of it as he glanced at Margarite. She was silent, eyes half closed as if against a bright light that was in danger of blinding her.

Renata took a deep breath, seemed to be gathering herself. 'As I have said, the white magpie is a bird of singular power, but taking it as one's familiar is, almost invariably, catastrophic. Quite simply, it invites destruction by the gods.' Her nostrils flared briefly, as if she inhaled a new scent. 'In Nung history, those who sought the voice of God through it were driven . . .'

'Mad?' he finished for her.

There it came again, that curious crescent smile. 'No, the result of the transgression was not madness. It is something far worse,' Renata said. She half turned so that the stallion could see her as well as scent her, put her hand upon its withers, stroking rhythmically.

377

'What could be worse than madness?' Croaker wondered out loud.

'Listen to me. There is a logic to this,' Renata said, continuing to focus her attention on the horse, as if by the motion of her hand on the animal's withers she could manufacture tranquility out of foreboding and dread. 'Those who wish to be divine are slowly skinned alive, layer by layer stripped of their humanity – their ability to feel emotion, to be affected by the world around them. Slowly, they slip into a shadow world where, though they are able to affect the world around them, they are unable themselves to be touched by it in any way. They are like the walking dead.' She looked at him somberly. 'Here we have the origins of zombies, vampires and the rest of mankind's names for the undead.'

Renata's eyes were like colored jewels through which Croaker imagined he could glimpse the dangerous shadow play of another world. 'This is not an ordinary person who committed these murders.' She hesitated but a moment. 'He will not be tracked down by ordinary methods.'

'I need to do more than track him down,' Croaker said. 'I have to stop him.'

'That may be impossible.'

'I can't accept that.'

A sardonic smile curled Renata's lips. 'You have not met this person. You and Margarite and I, we live on the flesh of animals, on the grains of the earth. This one is different, I assure you. He gains his sustenance from more ephemeral sources.'

'But he is mortal.'

Renata did not answer him at once. At length, she said, 'If you put a bullet in his brain or a knife in his heart he will die. In that sense, yes, he is mortal. But he is also Messulethe, and if you do not kill him at once you will be in mortal peril.'

'You mean he will be able to function wounded better than I could.'

'What I mean for you to do is to remember what I have told you about the white magpie and its powers.' Renata momentarily dropped her eyes to the photo of the Soul Ladder. Then she looked up, cocked her head. 'You don't seem skeptical.'

Croaker shook his head. 'I'm not.' Thinking of Nicholas, he added, 'I have a friend who has a similar kind of control over his body.'

Now he was aware that Renata was studying him with keen interest. She had ceased to stroke the horse.

'What is this man's name?' Croaker asked.

'He goes by many names,' Renata said. 'Let me see. In this country he has used Donald Truc and Robert Ashuko.'

Robert, Croaker thought, glancing at Margarite. But her head was bowed, darkened by a veil of hair and shadow.

Renata stirred. 'His Vietnamese mother named him Do Duc. He took a Japanese surname, Fujiru, when he fled Saigon after murdering his employer, a French arms dealer who more or less raised him. God alone knows his true surname. His father was an unknown entity; it may be only wishful thinking on Do Duc's part that he was indeed Japanese.'

Croaker took some time to absorb all this. 'May I ask how you know as much as you do about this man?'

'He was a friend of Michael Leonforte's in Vietnam. The two of them – along with a man named Rock – got into some very nasty business over there.' She held up a hand. 'Please don't ask me how I have so much information on the Leonfortes. That is privileged information.'

'But, as you have said, you know who I am and you know that Margarite trusts me enough to have brought me here.'

Renata nodded. 'True enough, Mr Croaker. But, on the other hand, you are reporting to William Justice Lillehammer.'

'What of it?'

Renata brushed her hands together to get off them whatever was left by the horse. She regarded him levelly. 'I wonder how much I should trust you.'

'Are you going to tell me that Lillehammer has his own agenda I'm not privy to?'

'Why should I? You obviously already know.'

'I suspect as much; that's not the same thing,' Croaker said. He shrugged. 'Anyway, whatever Lillehammer's real objective, I'm in too deep to turn around. I have Margarite to think of now.'

'Margarite is a married woman,' Renata said crisply.

'You forgot the adjective "happily".'

Renata did not blink. 'I did, didn't I?'

There seemed to be a kind of curious contest of wills going on here, but Croaker was unable to fathom its basis. What role was the older woman acting out here besides the protective mother?

Croaker intuited he had to be careful, otherwise this invaluable interview would be prematurely terminated. 'She needs Tony D.,' he said. 'I wouldn't take her away from what she has to do.'

Now Renata did blink, and he knew he had scored an important point.

'Why don't we go outside?' Renata said.

The pale moon hung in a sky clear of rain or mist. The wind had picked up, but they were protected within the viney shadows of the loggia.

379

Beyond, moonlight fell like a curtain of silver lace. They stood very close together.

'Margarite's destiny was sealed by my son's death,' Renata said. 'Do Duc murdered him and it was surely done on Caesare Leonforte's order, but there is a reason Caesare chose Do Duc. He didn't merely want Dominic dead. He wanted what was in Dominic's mind.'

Now Margarite turned into the moonlight, and Croaker could see that she had been silently weeping. Her agony stabbed him through the heart.

'Are you saying Dominic was tortured before he was killed?'

Renata nodded slowly, her gaze on Margarite. 'There can be little doubt. The question is how successful was my son in holding out against Do Duc?'

Croaker said, 'You know this man better than we do. You –'

'Whatever Robert wanted to get out of Dom you can be sure he got it.' The words seemed forced out of Margarite's mouth.

Renata had gone quite white, and Croaker could see that she was holding on to her equilibrium with a good deal of effort. At length, she gathered herself sufficiently to say, 'You met him.'

'Yes.'

Croaker found it interesting that Margarite did not elaborate and Renata did not ask her to. After a long time, when only the horses stamping in the stable seemed capable of movement or even breath, Renata turned her head toward Croaker. 'If this is the case, then we must assume the worst. Mr Croaker, you must get to Tokyo as quickly as you can.'

'Why? What's so urgent?' He looked from the enigmatic face of one woman to the closed face of the other.

'Dominic's source of information is in Tokyo?'

Renata nodded woodenly.

Again, he thought of Nicholas, as he had ever since he saw the evidence of the eerie ritual of Dominic Goldoni's murder. Surely, Nicholas would be able to help him now that he would be going to Tokyo. His heart leapt at the thought of seeing his friend again.

'I'd better report all of this to Lillehammer.'

'I think that would be most unwise,' Renata said flatly. 'He's unlikely to have your open-mindedness and understanding.'

'True, but in any case I'll need a passport, funds and backup. Without Lillehammer's support in a country as foreign as Japan I'll be dead in the water.'

'I can provide everything you need,' Renata said, so breathlessly Croaker at once understood how critical this change in his status must be to her. 'In addition, I can protect you from him.'

'Who? Do Duc? With what you've already given me I think I can take care of myself.'

Renata was shaking her head. 'I was speaking of Will Lillehammer.'

She produced a rolled up copy of that day's *Washington Post* from beneath her jacket, handed it to him.

'COMPUTER GIANT EXEC FOUND SHOT TO DEATH', the headline read and, just beneath the banner, was a photo of Harley Gaunt, Nicholas's number-one man in the States. According to a highly placed Government source unnamed in the story, which Croaker read with mounting dread, Gaunt, Nicholas and Sato-Tomkin itself were about to go under the spotlight of Senator Rance Bane's Committee. Also, according to the story, Gaunt had decided to cooperate with the Committee. Apparently, its star witness's murder had blown the lid off the entire investigation. Nicholas Linnear had been subpoenaed from Tokyo in order to answer serious but as yet undefined allegations of misconduct, but had refused to comply. Now Gaunt, a man presumably with inside knowledge of all of Sato-Tomkin dealings, and ready to spill it all to the Committee, was dead. The inference made by yet more unnamed, high-ranking Government sources was clear. Linnear, from his sinecure in evil Japan, was suspected of ordering Gaunt silenced.

He looked up at her, saw the moonlight glinting in her eyes. What could he read there – a surreptitious intimation of satisfaction, an absence of grace?

Renata took a deep breath, said, 'The night before Mr Gaunt was murdered he came to me. I gave him certain information on a man – incriminating evidence. The man was Will Lillehammer. But I . . .' – for the first time she faltered, a crack forming in her demeanor – 'I never dreamed the result would be Gaunt's death.'

'You had this incriminating evidence and didn't use it yourself? Why not?'

'I felt I was helping Mr Gaunt. He appeared ill with desperation and I . . . seemed to be the cure.'

There was a momentary pause, during which Croaker monitored her physical signs like a cardiologist observing a patient in ICU. 'Tell me, what was Gaunt doing coming to you?'

'I was recommended to him,' Renata said. 'You know how it works in this town. Your contacts are everything, and God help you if you're stupid or naive enough to confuse them with friends.

'I told Mr Gaunt that Lillehammer worked clandestinely for Senator Bane's Committee. This seemed just the lead Mr Gaunt was looking for. I armed him –'

381

'If you were arming him you should have given him a howitzer.' He looked at her as if she were a cobra just popped out of a wicker basket. 'With your arsenal you should have gone after Will Lillehammer yourself.'

'If it was just Lillehammer I was after I promise you I would have,' Renata said. 'But my enmity goes far deeper than that.'

'So you used Gaunt to –'

'Stop it!' Margarite had come between them before Renata could reply. She stared at Croaker. 'I didn't bring you here to rip at each other.' And in a quiet voice so only he could hear, 'We all have our private motives, Lew, don't we?' Her amber eyes were lambent in the skittish moonlight. 'Listen to me,' she breathed. 'Even detectives are not immune to emotion.'

'You'd do well to listen to her,' Renata said. 'She is alight with the wisdom of her forebears.' She smiled, almost shyly, and Croaker thought he could see her as she must have been when she was a stunning young woman of twenty.

She touched his arm, said so softly even the trees spoke more loudly, 'Here is the last secret my son left with me, the identity of the man who was his strength, his source of intelligence.' She leaned in closer, put her lips against Croaker's ear. 'Even Margarite doesn't know. I promised Dominic I would never repeat what he told me in confidence, but now events dictate that I speak his name in order to save his life.

'Nishiki is Mikio Okami, the Kaisho, the head of all *oyabun* of the Japanese Yakuza.'

FIFTEEN

Tokyo/Washington

When Do Duc slipped the silicon-polycarbonate mask over his head he felt as if flesh and blood, skin and bones had been fitted over a face composed of smoke and dreams. He felt, in a word, safe.

I want, he said to himself, *to feel*.

Feeling was, after all, what Ao the Nung shaman had taken from him during the long, arduous initiation ceremony in the mountains of Vietnam. Not that the young Do Duc had been aware of it at the time. But even if he had been, would he have objected, considering the glittering new world Ao was offering him? It did not matter. This question, essentially metaphysical in nature, would never have occurred to that young Do Duc.

Feeling was, after all, what he tried so assiduously to suck out of his victims, most recently the late Ginnie Morris and Margarite Goldoni DeCamillo. But, even he had to admit in a fever of reckoning, that Margarite had been different. He could not kill her; could not because he did not want to. For the first time, Do Duc had understood an essential truth of nature, although for the moment he understood it in this most particular of cases as it pertained only to Margarite – that to kill another human being was in some mysterious way to diminish the nature of one's own soul.

Often, in the days since he had let her go, he had felt her close to him – her soft skin, the heady perfume of the flesh beneath her arms, the backs of her knees, the coral folds between her thighs. At first, he was able to convince himself that this connection existed because of what he had taken from her in stealth without her knowing, secreting it inside him as an oyster enfolds its growing pearl.

And like a pearl the luster of what he had extracted from her sustained his fantasy of what had happened between them as it contained the panic, slippery as an eel, riding just below the level of consciousness.

Neither wild beasts nor necromancy frightened him, but the growing realization of his connection with Margarite certainly did. For one thing, he was no longer alone in the universe; for another, his thoughts of her were often so intense that he forgot everything else. These existential aspects of reality were wholly foreign to him, as absurd and terrifying as the magic he possessed was to others.

His hands came up, making minute adjustments in the fit of the mask. The adhesive, a compound of his own manufacture, had the effect of bonding the polymers to his skin with such perfection that he could touch the skin of the mask and feel it as his own. This was as it should be. What good was a mask unless it changed you?

He stuck his tongue out, seeing it in the mirror. He licked his lips or the mask's lips. In any case, Nicholas Linnear's lips. He would get the information his masters wanted from Linnear and then he could do with his captive whatever he wished. What a stroke of luck to come upon a Tau-tau adept! The moment Do Duc had discovered Linnear's true nature he had trembled inside with the thought of breaching the unknown, of taking a path even ancient Ao had shunned.

Do Duc would call upon his familiar, the sacred white magpie, and with its help open the forbidden Sixth Gate. He would shed his own doomed soul and don Linnear's, sucking it right out of him, leaving behind only a dried husk with Do Duc's face.

In this way he could annihilate his own history.

But his thoughts of triumph were short-lived as Margarite's ghostly presence reasserted itself. He fell to his knees. 'Ah, Buddha, help me,' he whispered through lips that were not his own. What should he do? All of his power, his magic, was useless in banishing the memory of her. But it was more than memory; he had been struck down by an engine of unknown design.

His need for her transcended lust or desire. This notion alone baffled and enraged him. His infuriating sense of shattered apartness had been replaced by something far more horrifying: a growing intuition that without her he could no longer pull breath into his lungs.

It was time to quit the mirror. He pulled himself to his feet, summoned up all his energy to banish the iridescent vapor of Margarite twining itself about his soul, and moved on wooden legs to the metal cage he had constructed within the robotics factory.

As soon as he had unlocked the door and stepped inside, his mind became filled with the tendrils of Nicholas Linnear's dreaming brain.

Do Duc switched on the halogen spotlights and, directing them against Nicholas's face, slapped him hard on one cheek, then the other. No wonder he was dreaming on and off, Do Duc thought. The amount of toxin he had pricked him with in Paris had been enough to bring down a team of water buffalo. But with the power of Nicholas's mind, Do Duc had felt he had no choice. In this case, overmedication was far better than the opposite.

He placed his fingertips on Nicholas's forehead and cheeks, checking the fit. It was truly amazing what computers could do these days. A series of photos extrapolated into a holographic image, that three-dimensional icon reduced to a complex formula of zeros and ones, fed into a computer, whose software metamorphosed that formula into a Virtual Reality replica of the real thing, which was then formed into a mask, extruded from the brain of the computer just as, he supposed, Athena had emerged full-blown from the head of Zeus.

The fit was perfect, the bonding agent setting up nicely. There were pores, hair follicles, blemishes, melanin discolorations, the works. The feel and texture was so lifelike even a lover wouldn't be sure it wasn't skin. As long as the seal was not broken, you could swim in this thing, take a shower or make love. It made no difference.

Nicholas's eyes were fluttering open, beginning to focus, and Do Duc arranged the mirror behind him so that his captive could see his own face.

Just as Nicholas's dark eyes settled on him, Do Duc felt a disorienting bout of vertigo, and he dug his fingers into his captive's biceps in order to keep himself from again falling to his knees. All he could smell in his nostrils was Margarite, as if she were a horse into whose winter coat he had buried his face. Consumed by a vision of her, he gritted his teeth, exerting the mental discipline Ao had taught him, and bound her intrusive image to a tree in the forest of his mind. If someone had plunged a blade into his chest at this moment he would be in less pain than he was experiencing now. He felt himself a creature who looks in a mirror only to discover that he has become a rotting corpse.

In an agony of horror he said in Nicholas's voice, with Nicholas's face, 'Now that you've realized you're alive, it's time you see who you have become.' He shifted half a step to his left to reveal the reflection of Nicholas in the computer-generated silicon-polycarbonate mask.

He felt the galvanic response go through Nicholas just as if he had put a live wire to his testicles. The spasm of the muscles in the grip of his hands calmed him, affirmed the place he had made for himself in the universe, for the moment sprayed black ink onto the magnificent face of his terror.

He bent his face low so it hung with the force of a god at the periphery of Nicholas's gaze.

'See who you've become.' His whispered voice echoed like a hawk's piercing cry over the treetops. 'Can you believe it? Yes, believe it. You are me and I am you.'

He could scent like perfume the perspiration forming on Nicholas's skin, feel his own palms slippery with it. Putting his ear to his victim's warm

385

rib cage he could hear the flurry of his heartbeat like a wild bird trapped against a pane of glass. The sound warmed him to his bones like the first break of spring sun after a long, cold winter.

Then Nicholas passed out again and Do Duc was alone with the robots, the black ink melting like snow in sunlight off the image of Margarite, revealing her closer to him than he had thought possible.

He remembered a story his mother had told him when he was very small, of a young farmer who met and fell in love with the woman of his dreams, a girl of ethereal beauty, an orphan from a neighboring village. They were wed and lived a joyous, perfect life until she contracted a winter illness and, despite all the farmer's frantic efforts, died. He buried her himself beneath a cherry tree, its bare, pale branches scraping a cloud-swept sky.

So overcome with grief was the farmer that he was certain he would die without his love. Darkness came and, ignoring the entreaties of his friends and family, he curled up beside the newly dug grave of his wife. He could not bear to leave her, and he wept bitter tears through the darkest hours of the night.

Then, in that pearly hour just before dawn, when the world is composed of mist and silence, he heard a small stirring at the edge of the woods. In a moment, he saw emerging from the damp shadows a magnificent red fox.

The fox was so delicate, so mysterious and magisterial, with its coat glazed with cloud and hoarfrost, that for an instant the farmer forgot his misery and ceased his weeping. All at once, the fox's ethereal beauty reminded him so piercingly of his dead wife that he burst into tears again.

The fox sat with its forepaws crossed in peculiarly human fashion and, looking directly into the farmer's eyes, asked him why he wept.

The farmer, brought up on stories of the magic of the foxes of this region, answered him.

'You speak of your wife as if she were love itself,' the fox said.

'And so she was,' the farmer replied in a sigh. 'Love died with her, and without love I surely cannot survive.'

'Love is all around you,' the fox assured him, but the farmer only shook his head in misery.

'Not for me.'

'Then you must have your wife back,' the fox said, 'so that you may learn all there is to know of love.'

'But that is impossible,' the farmer said.

The fox raised one of its forepaws as if in strange benediction. 'Sleep now,' the fox said. 'Dawn comes soon, and with it, your wife.'

At the fox's urging, the farmer put his head on his arms, certain that

386

he would not sleep. But, strangely, the moment he closed his eyes, he fell into a deep, dreamless slumber.

He awoke with the new day's sun in his eyes as it slanted through the branches of the cherry tree beneath which his wife's body was buried.

The farmer blinked, sat up with a start, his heart beating fast in his breast. He was alone, the fox was gone. Had he dreamed its appearance, the fantastic dialogue he'd had with it? That must be it, he thought, as he picked himself up, dusting leaves and twigs off his trousers and shirt.

Then he felt her, not beside him, but in his mind. His beloved wife was alive! He hadn't dreamed the fox's existence. It had come and worked its magic on them.

He felt his wife's spirit moving in his mind and he was overjoyed, anticipating a kind of intimacy he could not have imagined when they were both flesh and blood. How wonderful life would be with their love wrapped inside him, never to be lost again!

But within the month, the farmer's family found him dead, slumped over his wife's grave, his bloodless fists gripping a hunting knife he had plunged into his own belly. Curiously, the ground over the grave was greatly disturbed by deep, frenzied slashes. The local police puzzled over this. They agreed that it was as if the farmer had been trying to reach his wife's corpse in the last moments before he took his own life. They further agreed that the farmer had been driven mad by his grief, and sadly buried him beside his beloved wife before they went on to other, more pressing, matters.

In the months that followed, relatives visited the graves once a week to leave small gifts and to pray, but otherwise the place remained deserted. Except on the night of the full moon when a fox appeared from the snowy shadows of the forest to pad about the stone markers with a grave and canny face.

And perhaps it was only the fox who knew the truth: that the farmer had learned more about love than he had ever wanted to know. Loving someone was a far cry from having them steal through your thoughts and memories like a wraith in the night. Sharing a household was wholly unlike sharing a mind, where there were no secrets, no respite, and never, with two people sharing it, any silence at all.

Silence and the shallow sounds of robots being assembled, the same ticks, squeaks and hums night and day, in numbing procession, were Do Duc's only companions now.

Why had he recalled that unspeakable story now? How it had terrified him as a child. Each night, afterward, he would try but fail to sleep, imagining that when he did someone he might have loved would have secreted themselves in his mind like a demon. Finally, in desperation, he would crawl into the Frenchman's bed, unmindful if the Frenchman was sleeping alone or with a female companion. The Frenchman had allowed Do Duc to snuggle against him, cradled in safety, and had never said a word about it.

Why didn't I go to my mother? Do Duc asked himself in the amniotic glow of the robotics factory. *Why did I go to the Frenchman?* He stared at his own face adhering to Nicholas's before he could ask himself the next and final question. *Why did I kill the one person who had offered me –*

He turned away from his victim and, grabbing blindly for the bars of the cage, pressed his forehead against the metal until bright stars of pain exploded behind his eyes.

Could he articulate the word, even to himself? How could he? Didn't the story of the farmer's wife prove the ultimate danger of it? Didn't all the hard, bloody lessons he had learned growing up prove it, too?

Love was death.

Yes. But he loved Margarite.

There, he had said it and now surely he was damned. He moaned, despite himself.

Beyond him, outside the cage, bodies slick with oil were being formed, extremities being tested and attached to sockets with ball-bearing fluidity. Infra-red eyes glared into infinity, seeing beyond time and space into another reality free from pain and terror. And love.

Nicholas, damn his soul to hell, was unconscious, wholly unaware of Do Duc's terror, his sense of helplessness in the face of the Margarite of his mind. Like the farmer's wife, her essence refused to let go despite distance or the passage of time. She held on with tenacious talons, inside him, picking through the mire of his past, peering at his sins, loving him still.

He could not bear it.

He threw his head back, uttered a hoarse, inarticulate cry filled with pain and anguish. Outside the cage, the steel servants were being born at intervals as regular as clockwork.

Then he gripped Nicholas's shoulders, tried to shake him awake. When that didn't work, he leaned forward, bit viciously into the flesh of Nicholas's upper arm. Nicholas stirred, his eyes snapped open. The sapphire light arced and flickered.

Do Duc said, 'Wake up! It's time to die!'

'That sonuvabitch Munch,' Lillehammer said.

'Save your ire for someone who can feel it.'

With an effort Lillehammer kept himself from shivering. With the air conditioning turned up full it was as cold as the Arctic tundra in here. Lillehammer, who missed the heat and humidity of Southeast Asia, had a difficult time keeping his lips from turning blue during these interviews.

The Red Queen leaned back in his swivel chair, shot the barrel cuffs of his Turnbull & Asser orange-and-blue-striped shirt so that they extended a half-inch beyond the sleeves of his cashmere blazer. 'I haven't pulled a trigger on a long gun in quite some time. Tell me, how did it feel?'

You could see the little clouds of their breath, for Christ's sake. Their images were reflected in so much stainless steel Lillehammer could believe he was in the cold-room of a morgue.

'It felt like heaven.'

The Red Queen smiled. 'I had a bet with myself. I knew you'd say that.'

Stainless-steel desk, chairs and lamps, stainless-steel wainscoting below walls lacquered a shiny ice-white, a color which set Lillehammer's teeth on edge. Or maybe it was his own agenda, eating at him like a cancer; he no longer slept for more than an hour at a time. The enormous strain of running an operation expressly forbidden by his superior was weighing on him.

'Should have waited.'

'What?' Lillehammer leaned forward.

The Red Queen looked him full in the face. 'If you'd waited you could have put both of them down.'

'If I'd waited,' Lillehammer said, 'I wouldn't have gotten Munch. Something was making him skittish. Thirty seconds more and he would have disappeared. And you know guys like Munch; once they go to ground it takes a major effort to flush them. This way, I made sure he was neutralized.'

'I don't like loose ends,' the Red Queen said, 'and we've got one now. What the hell were the two people you're running doing at Renata Loti's at midnight last night?'

'How many tails did we have on them?'

The Red Queen laughed. 'Just the one you assigned. But he reported to me as well as to you.' He laughed again. 'It's not that I suddenly don't trust you, you understand, but I can fully appreciate how a . . . creature like Do Duc Fujiru can get under your skin.'

'If you think I've lost my professional detachment –'

'Not yet,' the Red Queen said sharply. 'You kept your head all through 'Nam. But that was before the Zoo, wasn't it?' His cold eyes glittered. 'You need to run this man Do Duc to ground, Will. But take my advice, and now that you're getting close don't get overanxious. I don't want to have to go down to our morgue and assign you to a zipper bag.'

'Yes, sir.'

'I want you to take a run over to Renata Loti's, find out what your people were doing with her.'

'I'd better step carefully. Loti's got a lot of powerful friends on the Hill.'

'True. But she's no friend of Rance Bane's so she's had to pull in her horns a bit lately. I must say, though, for a lady she's been a helluva deal-maker among the old hands in the Senate. She's brokered many a stalemate into compromise bills that have made everyone involved look sterling.' The Red Queen lifted a hand, let it flutter to the stainless-steel desk. 'You'll know what to do. Use a little diplomacy or whatever. But watch out, she's smart as the devil himself.'

Lillehammer nodded. 'On the topic of Davis Munch,' he said, 'with Gaunt, the Committee's star witness, discovered dead and now Munch iced, Senator Bane has gone ballistic. That could be very dangerous at this stage. If he makes one of his patented public displays it's going to be like the pit bull taking a shit all over our best carpet. Maybe I should –'

'You leave Rance to me,' the Red Queen said icily. 'I've fed him everything he's ever used on anyone. I brought him along, bought elections for him, established contacts for him, manufactured influence, made sure the good old boys on the Hill made him one of their own before I set him loose on them like a rabid dog. Now they don't know whether to fawn or piss themselves when he walks into a room.' He shook his head. 'Rance Bane is my creation, so you leave him strictly to me. Dust to dust, eh, Will?'

'Still, Bane could become a loose cannon. Why don't I waltz him out a window?'

The Red Queen gave him a cool stare. 'Sometimes, Will, I truly think that the only thing that makes you happy is a war zone.' He tapped a finger against the side of his nose. 'Don't worry. Rance Bane doesn't need the extreme prejudice of your silver hammer. I built him out of fear, prejudice and ignorance. By those attributes he rose to power and by those will he fall, I promise you. But only when his usefulness to us is at an end.' He made a wry face. 'We will terminate no pawn before its time, eh?' He laughed at his own joke as Lillehammer left the room.

Outside the sealed electronic surveillance-proof room, Vesper sat in one of her many newly purchased winter suits. This one was a high-fashion number by Armani in a wine-red chalk-stripe worsted wool. She must be hands down the best-wardrobed working woman in Washington, Lillehammer thought. Well, what else did she have to do with her time? Though she handled all the travel scheduling, personal armament procurement, monetary allocation, and false document manufacture for Looking-Glass, even though she knew where every field agent was at any given moment of the day or night, Lillehammer was willing to bet a year's salary that she had no idea what was actually going on. How could she? The Red Queen was such a security fanatic he didn't even tell his asshole when it was time to take a shit.

Lillehammer spent some time admiring Vesper's long, sleek legs while she was at her computer terminal, working his bonuses through the bureaucratic maze illuminated in pulsing green icons on her screen. Her rather odd name came from her father, she had told him once, who had been a great Ian Fleming fan. Vesper was the name of James Bond's first love.

Vesper's cornflower-blue eyes regarded Lillehammer coolly as her long coral-lacquered nails danced over the keyboard. Her thick, pale blonde hair swept down over one peach-colored cheek. After the hibernal bleakness of the Red Queen's sanctum, it was a relief to spend time in her office, which was painted in the soft colors of the American West. Even better, the temperature was sufficient to sustain mammalian life.

Vesper's forefinger pressed ENTER and she said, 'Oh, hell,' with a slight frown. 'I can't get the money out of Accounts because their software is back-logged. Damned outdated system. If we'd been on line now with the Hive Project hardware I could have gotten your bonuses to you in no time.'

'Bonus' was the euphemism for wet-work overrides, extra money Looking-Glass received for successful terminations. The Red Queen, taking the moral high ground, defended this rather mercenary custom by pointing out that hazardous pay was a time-honored institution in many industries. Why not this one? Besides, it made sure that every agent in Looking-Glass was Strac – ready in the best possible condition.

'No problem. I'll wait.'

'By the way, I think he's getting his period again.'

Lillehammer, internally switching gears, began to listen very closely.

'The paranoia in that office was very thick this morning. He was on the phone with someone named Loti.'

'Renata Loti?' Lillehammer asked, wondering why the Red Queen hadn't mentioned this. The antenna of suspicion was up.

'Uh huh, that's the name,' Vesper said. 'I'd say it was far from a friendly conversation.'

This was not the first time Vesper had given him tips from the inner sanctum. They invariably panned out, earning him the respect of his enigmatic boss.

'In fact it degenerated into a holy screaming fight. I don't know what about, but I did overhear something about the name Douglas Moon and the word blackmail. That's when he went ballistic.'

Lillehammer thought he would pass out. Renata Loti knew about him and Doug? Good Christ! Unconsciously he put his hand up to his cheek, felt the quick, heady surge of blood. He jerked it away, as if his own skin had burned it. But how could she know? He'd been so terribly security-conscious, even over Doug's constant complaints that his elaborate preparations destroyed any sense of spontaneity their couplings would otherwise have had. A homosexual affair was bad enough for a spook – the potential security compromises were endless – but then there were the things he and Doug did together. Who would understand or countenance such radical behavior save the perpetrators? How had this happened?

And then he thought in a rage, *That fucking bastard Doug got bored and has blown the whistle on me!*

'Anyway,' Vesper chattered on, 'it seems clear to me he wants something done about her.'

'I don't know.' Self-preservation was warring with prudence inside him. 'The heat from the fallout might be intolerable. She's got friends in high places.'

'Is that so? I wonder. What were his exact words after he slammed the phone down? "Somewhere there's an accident waiting to happen to that woman."'

Lillehammer suddenly needed some air. 'How are we doing with my bonus money?' he asked innocently.

Vesper glanced briefly at her computer screen, gave him a dazzling smile. 'At last! Accounts has caught up with its back-log. Your checks are being printed up now.'

A moment later, the checks spewed out of a slot in her printer. Vesper smiled sweetly at him as she handed them over, and Lillehammer stumbled out into the hushed, anonymous corridor beyond the immense and bizarre corner office complex.

Nangi presented himself at the private dwelling wedged between the two huge warehouses. This area near the Sumida appeared wholly different in daylight. Laughing children played where by night the mangy, vaguely menacing dogs had restlessly prowled, and the incessant flurry and clamor of business perhaps hid – or at least recolored – the worst of the neighborhood's depressing shabbiness.

A young woman opened the door in response to his knock. She was chunky, quite plain in appearance, with a thick mane of black hair she had frizzed in a voguish but unappealing style.

392

'Yes?' she said, peering from around the thick door.

Nangi bowed, handed her a business card, one of a dozen different ones he periodically had made up. This kind of foray – clandestine and incognito – had become over the years an inherent part of his life. He had discovered that one most often acquired valuable knowledge when hiding behind the mask of another – anonymous – identity.

It was astonishing, really, Nangi thought as he waited for a response from the young woman. What people would never consider telling to Tanzan Nangi, chairman of a major *keiretsu*, they would readily confide in a feed salesman, a product engineer or a metalwork foreman, someone to whom they could feel superior.

This morning he was Seizo Abe, a representative of the housing ministry, purportedly doing a survey of area buildings over twenty years old. It was an all too plausible story which gained him almost immediate admittance to the house.

He was let into a small oval foyer dominated by a central staircase and a crystal chandelier. Lustrous brown and a rich melon color predominated. A striped marble console held a bowl with a spray of fresh flowers, hothouse-grown at this time of the year. The young woman took his shoes, led him down a cherry-wood-paneled hallway. Off it, to the right, a set of pocket doors were open. Beyond, Nangi could see a library with floor-to-ceiling bookshelves, a crystal chandelier, a smaller version of the one in the foyer.

The young woman signed for him to enter. A threadbare Persian carpet lay on the floor like an exhausted memsahib. To the left, a pair of high-backed upholstered chairs were set facing a velvet-covered couch. In the opposite half of the room, a glass cabinet along one wall displayed a magnificent torso of early seventeenth-century samurai armor. It had been placed adjacent to a burlwood French secretary so that whoever sat in the chair behind the desk could have an unobstructed view of it.

Alone, Nangi looked around. This was obviously the room of a scholar, an orderly, erudite mind that had worked out the role of each element in life.

'I see by your card that you have changed professions.'

Nangi started, hearing the soft female voice emanating from his left. He turned.

'I beg your pardon.'

'And not for the better, I might add.'

He bent forward, his forehead creased in concentration. He knew that voice, but he was certain he hadn't heard it in quite some time.

393

'Well, what are you waiting for?' the female voice said. 'I've had tea prepared.'

Nangi limped toward the high-backed chairs and, as he came round the side, saw that the one nearest him was occupied by a petite but noble-looking woman with pale, translucent skin, planular cheekbones and black, fiery almond eyes. It was only because he knew her that he could say with any certainty that she was in her early seventies.

'Kisoko!' he said, astonished despite himself. 'You are the last person I imagined I'd find here.'

'Often, I have discovered, the real world can be disarmingly like the one depicted in *Alice in Wonderland*!' There was the rustle of heavy brocaded silk as she moved her arm and the wide sleeve of her kimono slid against her porcelain skin. Pink, white and coral cherry blossoms were strewn across the breast and upper sleeves of her kimono, tossed by the indigo wind of the artist's imagination.

Kisoko retained every ounce of enchantment she had possessed ten years ago. He was stung all over again by the longing he had felt upon first seeing her a decade ago. How he had wished he had known her in the magnificence of her youth. The heavy-lipped, bow-shaped mouth that maintained promises all on its own, the smoldering, guileless eyes, the precision and economy of motion that rendered palpable grace and intelligence were all as he remembered them. But the ultimate attraction of this slightly asymmetrical face was its subtle hint of indulgence and, deeper, benediction. Nangi, rolling over in bed with the morning light streaming through gauzy curtains, had often imagined her as a Catholic nun, a secret fantasy of years past that was so forbidden it was unutterably delicious.

'Kisoko,' he said now, his head filled with the scent of memory, 'I have heard that Mikio Okami is missing. Do you know anything about this mystery?'

Those incandescent inky eyes looked up at him. 'I have no news of my brother,' she said flatly. 'For the moment, if you will sit, I will prepare the tea.'

He sat on the chair on her left hand, watched mesmerized as she made the green tea. When they had both drunk their first cups, she said, 'I do not know whether my brother is alive or dead, only that his enemies have made their move against him. What will happen next I cannot say.'

She put her cup aside, placed her forefinger on the business card he had given the young woman, pushed it across the polished ebony table toward him.

With her fingertip still on the card, she said, 'You have come under another name for a purpose that is surely false. Tell me, Nangi-san, what am I to make of this?'

'I did not know whose house this was, Kisoko. You know my way. My own name is too well known for me to obtain the truth in certain situations.'

Kisoko regarded him for some time. Nangi heard the stertorous ticking of an ormolu clock, the creak of timbers above their heads. But no sound from outside penetrated the library's walls. It was as if the world did not exist. Only in here, between the two of them, did life go on.

'And what truth did you expect to find under the guise of Seizo Abe?'

Ever since he had recognized Kisoko, Nangi was wondering what to make of Seiko coming to the house of Mikio Okami's sister. Perhaps he had been wrong to suspect Seiko; perhaps her involvement with Vietnamese of dubious repute was incidental to Vincent Tinh's treachery and subsequent murder. In any case, with their shared history he did not – could not – suspect Kisoko of duplicity.

'I came here this morning wondering about an employee of mine, Seiko Ito,' he said at length. 'I am ashamed to say I followed her here last night. She is troubled and, perhaps, in trouble. I wanted only to help her if I was able.'

'Without letting her know.'

'She would not, I fear, react well if she did.'

'I see.' Kisoko's finger tapped Seizo Abe's business card as if it possessed real weight and history. Nangi could see that she was turning over something difficult in her mind.

'Kisoko, I want to reassure you that my concern for Seiko is quite genuine.'

Kisoko nodded.

'She has become an increasingly important member of my staff. Now there is an opportunity for her to be sent to Saigon to take charge of my affairs there. You can see why I must be absolutely certain I can count on her.'

Kisoko laughed. 'But this is wonderful news, Nangi-san, and from my point of view the best thing for her.' She sighed. 'Such a sad creature. But so talented! She comes here because she believes she is helping me, which she is. But I am also helping her. She has a good heart, Nangi-san, but I fear that often her heart has betrayed her.'

'So you have taken her under your wing?'

A telephone rang somewhere in the house. Kisoko made no move to answer it. In a moment, it had ceased to ring.

'Oh, nothing quite so formal,' Kisoko said. 'Seiko would never tolerate that.' She shrugged. 'I suppose she has become used to being alone, to keeping her life shielded from others.' She smiled wanly. 'In that she is not so different from the rest of us, *neh*, Nangi-san?' She shook her head. 'The best I can do is to provide her with an arrangement. She gives me investment strategies and I provide her with whatever emotional base she can tolerate.' Kisoko gave him a small, deprecating smile. 'She has no family, you see. No one to turn to but me.' She shrugged. 'The trade-off, I believe, is a fair and useful one.' She cocked her head. 'Have I eased your mind?'

Nangi nodded. 'The truth is nothing like I imagined. Frankly, I'm relieved.'

'Good. I believe Seiko will thrive beneath the responsibility. Saigon will be good for her.'

'Then it's done,' Nangi said.

The doors to the library opened. Nangi, turning, saw a wide-shouldered man sitting in a wheelchair. His heavily muscled chest, arms and shoulders were clad in a form-fitting polo shirt. He regarded Nangi with soft brown eyes. There was something unspoken, perhaps a sadness that predisposed his long, handsome face toward a brooding introspection.

'The phone call is for you,' he said to Kisoko in a deep, well-modulated voice.

Kisoko said, 'Tanzan Nangi, meet my son, Ken.'

Ken, studying Nangi's cane as if it were a written sentence to be parsed, abruptly inclined his head.

'Son?' Nangi cocked his head. 'I never knew you had a child.'

Kisoko smiled, and he imagined he could hear the ice melting in the kitchen freezer. 'Ken was not with me when we . . . knew each other. He was away at school. I saw no reason to speak of him.'

She was right, of course. His affair had been with her, not with her family.

She rose with a rustle of silk, brushed his hand with hers. 'I must take this call. I won't be long.'

Nangi and Ken were left watching each other warily like sumo wrestlers before a match. Nangi dutifully kept his gaze away from Ken's nerveless legs, tried to keep the pity he felt off his face.

'It's been a long time since your mother and I saw each other.'

'I know.'

Nangi made a show of looking around. 'This is a beautiful house.'

'Mother inherited it.'

Ken said this with a clipped anger that took Nangi aback. 'She was lucky, then,' he said.

'Do you think so?'

Nangi, concerned by the distance between them, limped across the carpet to where Ken sat, still as ice. 'Well, I just meant . . .'

Something seemed to happen to Ken's face. He peered at Nangi curiously, as if Nangi had just changed color or sex. Watching Nangi lean on his cane, he said, 'Mother never told me. Does it hurt much?'

Nangi did not need more than that cue. 'Sometimes. At others, it's quite bearable.'

Ken seemed to think this over for quite some time. 'You know, I used to dream about you. Yes, it's true. I always imagined I hated you, yet, curiously, now that I've met you I seem to be unable to summon up that hatred.'

'I appreciate that,' Nangi said. 'I may have hurt your mother but I never stopped loving her.'

'Perhaps that's so,' Ken said. 'You were the second man she was crazy about who hurt her. Maybe neither of you meant to.' He shrugged, his muscles rippling. '*Karma, neh,* Nangi-san? My mother engendered certain responses in men. They could no more help it than she could.' He closed his eyes. 'She's still so beautiful.' They snapped open. 'I'd like to show you something.'

Nangi nodded and they went out of the library, past a set of back stairs. Ken opened a narrow modern door, seemingly out of place in this house. They went into a small elevator car, and Ken pushed a button marked '3'.

The elevator came to rest and Ken opened the door, led him down a carpeted hallway wallpapered in a pattern of cabbage peonies, large as human heads, joined by arabesques of thorned vines. The hall held the smell of steel and oil.

Ken opened the door, wheeled himself through. Nangi, following, found himself in a *dojo,* a martial arts gym. It was a windowless room, the light spilling down from a skylight in the center of the high ceiling. Arrayed around the four walls, from the tatami floor to perhaps hip height in an average man, was the most astonishing collection of steel-bladed weapons Nangi had ever seen. From the oversized *dai-katana,* the traditional weapon of the samurai, to a series of normal-sized swords – *katana, wakazishi,* the long knives used, among other things, to commit *seppuku,* ritual suicide, antique iron war-fans with tesselated edges honed to razor sharpness, *manrikigusari* – spike-and-chain weapons, all manner of *shuriken* – small, pointed projectiles most often used by ninja.

Ken sat at the edge of the tatami. 'I think you'll appreciate one of those. It's from the early 1600s.'

Nangi, knowing that the wheelchair could not be rolled over the tatami, considered telling Ken he wasn't interested. But he suspected that Ken would take that as a terrible loss of face.

Ken twisted his torso without, somehow, moving his legs. Nangi watched with a combination of fascination and horror as Ken dragged himself off the wheelchair, arranged his inert legs on the tatami. He began to crawl in a curious way, using his powerful shoulders and arms. Nangi limped after him on stockinged feet.

Ken reached the wall where a succession of *katana* hung in scabbards of lacquered leather, hand-tooled with silver. Those deep brown eyes began a contemplation of his collection. Then he took one down, slowly, lovingly drew the blade out into the light. The steel, so finely honed that the very edge seemed invisible, rippled as Ken moved it, seeming not a solid object at all but a river of light, ardent with intent, as if it were a Zen *koan*.

'It's curious,' he said. 'When I was whole I never thought twice about weapons. It was only afterward that they came to mean something to me.'

Reverentially, he replaced it in the scabbard, handed the whole to Nangi, who examined it as closely as a museum curator.

Ken, clearly pleased by this scrutiny, said, 'Somehow, I knew you would appreciate the swordmaster's art.

'They were part artist, part Zen philosopher, those ancient masters.' His eye followed the flow of light over the blade, like mist upon a frozen lake. He lifted the point, and the light rushed down toward the hilt. 'The *katana* is the representation of the artist and the picture, the higher self and the lower self, love and will as distinct from habit and memory.' He cut the air with the blade as if slicing through a body. 'The Way to modify the past with the physical will of the present.'

Ken's smile, tender and beatific, made him seem like a little boy, rather than the man in his forties he must be. He seemed content at last.

'Time seems to stand still here in this house,' he said as he took the *katana* back from Nangi in a motion that was close to a formal rite. But, grasping the precious *katana*, he frowned, as if remembering a recent bad dream.

'Nangi-san,' he said, lifting his head, 'you came here because of Seiko Ito.'

'Yes. I did.'

Ken nodded. 'I am concerned about her. She is a willful woman with, I believe, a self-destructive bent.'

Nangi, looking from the *katana* to Ken's handsome face, said, 'What makes you say that?'

'You know she holds herself responsible for her brother's death.'

'I had no idea.'

'It's a terrible secret she must bear. He was retarded and he lived with her. She left him unattended in the bath while she made love with her boyfriend who had just returned from a three-month trip to Vietnam. Her brother slipped under the water and drowned.'

Nangi felt unaccountably hot, as if Seiko's shame had somehow become his.

'That was six years ago,' Ken said, 'and I don't believe she's been the same since.'

'How do you think she's changed?'

Ken shrugged. 'So many ways. For one thing, she began to hang out with dangerous people.'

'How do you mean dangerous?'

'People no good for her. People who would do anything, commit any crime in order to make money.'

Nangi stood very still, listening to the blood sing in his veins. 'Is this true now?'

Ken nodded sadly. 'I wonder whether I am betraying her by telling you this.'

'Perhaps you're saving her,' Nangi said. 'Can you give me any names?'

Ken's dark-brown eyes gazed up into Nangi's face. 'There is one man she has mentioned. Masamoto something . . .'

'Masamoto Goei?' Nangi asked, his heart almost coming to a full stop.

Ken snapped his fingers. 'Yes. That's the name. Do you know him?'

Goei was the team director for the Chi Project who had contacted him concerning the neural-net clone. As a theoretical language technician, he should have been able to completely analyze the clone by now. And yet Nangi was still awaiting his final report. Now there seemed a good reason for Goei's procrastination.

Nangi's eyes ached. He felt a pounding headache coming on. With considerable effort, he pulled himself together. 'Tell me, Ken, does your mother know anything about Seiko's . . . associates?'

Ken gave an ironic smile. 'You know Mother. She absorbs everything she wants to absorb. As for the rest' – he shrugged – 'it doesn't exist.'

Nangi nodded. Yes, that described Kisoko up to a point. 'I think I'd better be getting back. I expect she'll be wondering where I got to.' He looked down at Ken, pitying him despite his resolution to keep that suspect emotion well buried. 'Thank you for the information,' he said. 'I'll do what I can to help Seiko.'

Ken nodded wordlessly. He was staring at the *katana* laid across his thighs. Perhaps he had already forgotten that Nangi was still there.

Nangi left him there, dreaming amid his useless weapons.

Back in the library, Kisoko was waiting for him as dutifully as a wife. 'Ken respects you. He rarely lets anyone see the *dojo*. It's his private space. Even I scarcely go there.'

'I'm sorry about him.'

'Oh.' She turned briefly away from him, fiddled with the teacups, now cold. 'He's adjusted well to his disability. You of all people can appreciate his courage.'

'Yes.' He waited some time, but she seemed incapable of continuing. He felt abruptly sorry for her, taking in a stray like Seiko, wanting her to be something she obviously was not. Needing, perhaps, a child who was physically whole, even one who was emotionally damaged. There is always in the human heart the hope for transformation.

Kisoko stood very close to him and whispered, 'I have missed you. My heart wishes . . .' She looked away for a moment. 'Ah, but I must not humiliate myself again. Once was enough suffering.'

'Kisoko –'

She lifted an arm as if to ward him off, but when his fingers gripped her shoulder, he immediately felt her weight against him, the consequence of his rejection of her. She had wanted marriage, something he could not give her. She longed for marriage with all her heart, but he could not imagine it, with her or with anyone else. He was one of those rare men who preferred the hardy silence and utter calm of a solitary existence. His life was complicated enough, he felt, without permanently adding a female to the equation.

But it was times like this when he profoundly regretted the path he had chosen for himself.

'If I hurt you,' he said, 'then surely I hurt myself as well.'

She was weeping, slow, silent tears running from the corners of her eyes.

'Why should I cry,' she whispered, 'for you?' She shook her head almost immediately. 'No, not for you, or for me, either. But for love. Only love.'

She had had a great hurt sometime in her youth, that much he knew from fragments of their talks after making love, intimations gleaned from her reactions to him and to certain intimate situations. That it had forever left its wound deep inside her he had no doubt.

He had thought it immensely brave of her that she would again seek love after the first disaster, despite all the years that had passed. That he had shot an arrow into her most vulnerable spot was unforgivable, but he was too much in love with her not to tell her the truth as soon as it became apparent to him. But in seeking to minimize her hurt he had committed the sin of being cold, cutting her dead. At the time, he believed a clean break to be the best course of action. Only later would he live to regret his decision, when she would not speak to him in private and in public turned her face in the direction of others.

'Ah, Kisoko, how I love you,' he said with her cheek against his. 'But how quickly that love would have turned to bitterness and resentment had we wed. In my life, I cannot be beholden to anyone else for decisions.'

Her arm came up, her fingernails caressing the nape of his neck. 'How lonely it must be for you.' And drawing closer still, 'For both of us.'

'If I had given in to you, even what we once had would have been destroyed. At least, this way, we were left with the memory.'

She closed her eyes. 'I wish you had told me this years ago.'

'Yes,' was all he could think to say.

Then she dropped her arm, pushed herself away, as if it were important to show him that she could stand on her own. She dabbed at her face. 'Isn't it curious how blind one becomes when one cries.'

She led him back down the cherry-wood hallway in silence, but the weight of the atmosphere when she was near him disturbed him still. Caught in an emotional eddy, he wondered whether he was safe in a protected harbor or about to be swept into white water.

He was struck again by the marvelous silence of the house, the security of its walls against the world outside. He wondered if Okami might be here, then hoped not. It might be too obvious a place for his enemies to look, and Nangi could not bear the thought of Kisoko in danger. He calmed himself. She had always remained wholly apart from her brother's world, and there seemed no good reason why the relationship should change now.

Gradually, he became aware of an ache inside him, as if a muscle had ruptured or a tendon had snapped. The pain, almost but not quite physical, made him long for scalding tea, a bit of sticky rice on the end of chopsticks, a magazine to read, anything mundane to take his mind from the extraordinary reverberations this leave-taking was inciting in him.

'My curiosity brought us together again,' he said when they had returned to the foyer. 'I must believe there was a purpose in that.'

Kisoko turned her dreaming face up toward him. 'Do you still live in the same house?'

'Yes.'

'I remember the garden in back. Do you still take great pleasure in pruning your shishigashira maple?'

'It's a permanent passion, I'm afraid.'

Her eyes caught his, glittering. 'There is one here I planted five years ago that is in desperate need of your attention.'

*

401

'I'm sorry, he's not here.'

'Where is he, then?'

'Pardon, who did you say is calling, please?'

'Croaker. Lew Croaker. Calling from the United States for Nicholas Linnear.'

Silence. Then that terribly formal voice made tinny by electronics and distance: 'May I take your message for Linnear-san?'

'I want – I need to speak to him now. Dammit, it's important!'

'I can take a message, please.'

Croaker put a splay of fingertips to his forehead. He had promised himself he would not lose his temper. But these damned Japanese and their symbolic formality could drive you around the bend when you wanted to get something done asap.

'I need,' he said slowly and distinctly, 'to speak to someone who can help me.'

'One moment, please.'

He stared down at the copy of yesterday's *Washington Post* he had found lying in front of their door with the photo of Harley Gaunt staring out at him. The late Harley Gaunt. Poor bastard. Croaker had never met the man, but he could recall the fondness with which Nicholas spoke of him.

He glanced at his watch. What would it be? Just after three in the afternoon there?

'Yes? Mr Croaker, may I help you?'

'I sincerely hope so,' Croaker said. 'I'm a friend of Nicholas Linnear's. Can you tell me where he is? I need to speak with him. It's urgent.'

'I'm afraid I can't help you.'

'Who is this?'

'My name is Seiko Ito. I am Linnear-san's assistant.'

'And you can't get me through to him? Do you know who I am?'

'Yes, Mr Croaker, I do.' There was a pause. 'The truth is, no one knows where he is at the moment. We're all very concerned.'

Croaker let go with a small sigh. *Christ.*

'How about Nangi. Can I speak with Tanzan Nangi?'

'I'm afraid Nangi-san is in a meeting. He left strict orders not to be disturbed. May I take your number so that –'

'Never mind that,' Croaker snapped. He looked up, saw Margarite standing by the hotel window, her torso striped by the blinds and the sodium streetlights. The room was drenched with elongated triangles of light like moonlight on water. 'Please give Nangi a message. Tell him that Lew Croaker is on his way to Tokyo. I'll be there tomorrow at 4 p.m. and I expect to meet with him as soon as I can get in from Narita. Got me?'

'Pardon?'

Croaker massaged his forehead. 'Just tell him, all right?'

'Yes. I will give Nangi-san the message as soon as his meeting is –'

But Croaker had already cradled the receiver. He rose, went to where Margarite stood. He touched her and she shivered.

'I can feel him,' she said in a reedy whisper, 'just as if he's in the room with us.' She turned her head toward him so that the sodium light fired her eyes. 'No, no. Put your arms around me. Hold me close. I don't know whether I'm hot or cold.' She put her head on his shoulder. 'He's inside me, Lew, and there's only one way I'm going to get him out.'

A taxi went by, hissing. A couple came round a corner, shoulders hunched, went quickly out of the wind into the hotel entrance below them. A cop car cruised past, its red light flashing but its siren off. Particles of dust, hanging in the air, turned blood-red, then vanished.

'I have to see him again.'

Plane trees, their branches bare as nails, rose from grilled openings in the sidewalk, a ghostly reminder of a summer long since past. He was staring at them because, apparently, he couldn't bear what she was about to say.

'I'm going to agree to Lillehammer's plan. I'm going to offer myself up. We're going to become target and sentinel, you and I.'

He felt a tiny tremor in his arms. 'I wish you'd rethink this.'

'Oh, Lew, what good would it do? Whatever has happened can't be changed. Whatever the link is between Robert and me can't be broken by any other means.'

'He'll know you're coming,' he said. 'Faith said as much. I can't imagine what will happen when he sees you again.'

'You'll kill him.'

'My job is to take him in.'

He could feel her head moving back and forth. 'No. You'll kill him. Or he'll kill you.' She turned round in his arms so that she faced him. 'Those are the only possibilities.'

He stared down at her, trying to see into her. 'Life is so much more complex than that.'

'Not this. Not him.'

He accepted her judgement, just as, he realized, he accepted her ambivalence toward Do Duc.

'In any case, we'll be in Japan tomorrow, and we'll see.'

Silence and the hum of the hotel's heater. Something, perhaps only a gust of wind, rattled the windowpane, and he could feel her tense, look

403

quickly over her shoulder, then sigh. In relief or in disappointment, he wondered.

'Tell me something,' she said. 'Why did you accept my step-mother's help?'

'Isn't that what you wanted me to do?'

'Yes, but it's important for me to know why you agreed.'

Just below the window, flags cracked and furled, ensigns of influence and command, seeking something unexplainable in the night.

'If you're looking for a rational answer I'm afraid I don't have one. All I can tell you is that right now I don't trust anyone. My sense all along was that Lillehammer was lying to me or – at the very least – not telling me everything about this case. As I told you, I didn't believe for a minute he needed someone outside his official agencies to do the field work. A man like that without people he could trust or call on in an emergency? Not likely.'

'And you believed my step-mother?'

'I believe what she told me, yes.'

'I hear a but.'

He smiled into the darkness. 'It wouldn't surprise me to learn that she has her own agenda.'

'Why go after Do Duc at all? Why not just walk away and forget him, Lillehammer, and my step-mother?'

He saw her eyes searching his, and he knew they were not the eyes of a married woman. Whoever ruled her heart would be blessed.

'There are so many reasons I couldn't begin to list them,' he said. 'I accepted Lillehammer's offer knowing it wasn't what he made it out to be. But, as he anticipated, I was bored running a charter boat out of Marco Island. I was getting boozy and soft. I needed to change that.' He could hear her breathing, just like an animal in the jungle. 'I was intrigued with Lillehammer, and Dominic's murder. It wasn't merely that he had been killed but how it had been done. I wanted to solve all the puzzles: who killed your brother and why, and who Lillehammer was and why he was so desperate to get Do Duc. Then, as you've told me, this thing just got bigger and bigger, like ripples in a lake.' A crown of thorny vines was in her hair for just a moment. The triangles of light were moving, as if alive, but it was only headlights which, now and again, came and went with unknown intent like spies in utter darkness. 'And then there's you. Even after what I've told you I could walk away from it all, but you can't and I won't have that.'

'Then I was right.'

His smile widened. 'Yup. Once in a blue moon emotion finds its way through even detectives' thick exteriors.'

He felt her shift in his arms, get more comfortable. She put her arms around his neck, sighed. She rested her forehead against his chest.

'I'm tired,' she said. 'I never realized before how power could exhaust you.'

'It's hidden in the definition,' Croaker said. 'As close as you two were, I doubt that would be something Dominic would have shared with you.'

'He was in power for a long time,' she said. 'I don't know how he did it.'

Croaker knew what she really meant was she didn't know how she was going to do it. Maybe she wouldn't. But maybe that was just wishful thinking.

'I'd better call Lillehammer and tell him you've agreed,' Croaker said. 'We don't want him getting suspicious at this late date.' He picked up the phone. 'He'll be delighted, I'm sure.'

He dialed a number, heard the hollowness just before the operator answered. He gave his code name and she put him on hold. The connection cut in abruptly and he heard the faint click of the solenoids as the anti-surveillance system kicked in and through the wavefronts of all the electronic junk he heard Lillehammer's voice.

'We're on,' he said into the mouthpiece. 'She's agreed to go ahead with it.'

'Excellent,' Lillehammer said. 'What do you need?'

'Documents,' Croaker told him. 'We're going to Tokyo.'

'Tokyo?'

'That's right. That's where he is.' He gave Lillehammer the particulars of their flight. 'Just get us on it,' he concluded.

'I'll have everything you need messengered over to the hotel within three hours. I assume that's where you are now.'

'Uh huh, fine,' Croaker said. 'And, Ahab, we need to meet at the airport just before flight time.'

'Roger.'

He hung up the phone, felt the sweat breaking out on him. *Now it's well and truly done*, he thought. *No turning back*. He turned to see Margarite watching him in the semi-darkness.

'How many ways is he going to try to fuck us, in the end?' she asked.

'I hope I'm not going to give him the chance to try.'

He walked across the room to her. He was already feeling contaminated by the phone call. He stood in front of her and she lifted her arm, such a simple gesture, pulled a lock of hair off his forehead.

'Tell me something,' he said after a time. 'What is it between you and Faith?'

405

'You don't know anything about her,' she said flatly, 'so you have no right to ask that question.'

'Don't you think the way we feel about each other gives me the right?'

Margarite, looking up at him, opened her mouth to say something, closed it almost immediately. Behind her, the street was entirely deserted, wide, wind-swept, solemn, with its looming, square-shouldered buildings in commemoration of something, the home of mythical beings.

All at once, her shoulders began to shake and he thought she was weeping. A stifled gasp told him he was wrong; she was laughing.

'God must be playing this joke on me for my sins,' she said, still laughing. 'Married to a despicable Sicilian who is regardless indispensable to me, duty-bound to carry on my brother's business behind my husband's male mask, I'm nevertheless hopelessly in love with an ex-cop working for the Feds.' Her laughter had a bitter edge sharp as a knifeblade. 'What is to become of me?'

What answer could he give? What answer did he want?

Life was so full of unclear choices and wrong turns that he wanted this moment to be different – the choice unclouded, the chance they were both taking correct. But how could he be sure? The answer was simple: there was no way.

Her arms went taut, her hands behind his neck pulling his face down until his lips covered hers. They were salty, and now he knew that she had been weeping silently in the shadows as she had at Faith's stables.

'You want to know what is between me and my step-mother,' Margarite whispered when she pulled her mouth from his. 'All right, I'll tell you. I suspect her. Of what? Of making what I am certain was in her eyes a simple business decision. When my father was no longer able to conduct his business, when he became a liability, she killed him.'

Croaker, feeling her heart thudding in her breast almost as if it were his, held her gaze for some time.

'Killed.' In this context the word seemed obscene, even though in his line of work he had used it so many times he thought he had become inured to its effect. 'As in murdered?'

'Yes.'

'Have you any proof?'

She smiled through her tears. 'My detective, ever and always.'

'I can't help it. That's how I see the world.'

'One day, I'd very much like you to get to know my step-mother.'

There was a peculiar timbre to her voice, and Croaker knew she said this as a way of acknowledging his own statement.

'Then I'm sure I will.'

When he held her like this he could not imagine ever leaving her. But it was a fantasy whose end made breathing painful.

Her thick hair brushed his cheek. 'Hold me tighter.'

He did, his nostrils filled with her scent and her breathing. Cars hissed by outside, one, two, then the street was again gripped in a monumental silence.

SIXTEEN

Tokyo/Washington

There were mice running over railroad tracks.

Nangi lay in the cramped darkness, thinking.

Seiko and Goei.

Betrayed at home and abroad. Lord Jesus, he and Nicholas were done for.

The mice were running again, and he returned his attention to the sounds coming through the thin wall of the capsule, trying to make sense of them. They reminded him of the sound he had heard as a child, of mice running over the rails of the tracks outside his house. These sounds in the darkness seemed as inexplicable as they had the first two times he had heard them, like bursts of static from an old-fashioned radio, the bleeps and squawks of machines in garbled conversation with one another.

He had spent hours following Seiko all over Tokyo before he came to the conclusion that she and Goei were too clever or too practiced to meet face to face.

That was when he switched his surveillance to Goei himself. At dusk, after his work was finished for the day, Goei had come here, to the Nakagin Capsule Tower in the neon jungle of the Ginza. The building was made up of modular capsule offices, eight by thirteen feet, so these modules could be transported by truck. The building's configuration changed continually as tenants came and went, adding capsules to enlarge space or subtracting them to conserve it.

To take his mind off the enormity of Seiko's betrayal, he went over for the thousandth time everything in the material the American Manny Mannheim had delivered to him this morning. But thoughts of Mannheim brought with them another wave of sorrow for the death of Harley Gaunt. Gaunt had been a first-rate administrator, both canny and compassionate. He had grasped what Nicholas and Nangi were involved in and had thrown himself wholeheartedly into the mysterious business of production and innovation for the future. He would be sorely missed.

The revelations of Gaunt's material had been legion. The most alarming of them had been that the US Government – and that meant Senator Rance Bane's accursed Committee – had pulled a so-called Chi clone out of the Asian black market and had concluded that the machine was using Hyrotech-inc's proprietary Hive technology. This, along with the copies of the coded faxes from Sato's offices in Tokyo to Saigon, meant they had concrete evidence which in their minds at least linked Sato-Tomkin to the theft of Hive technology. Since Hive was the hardware chosen by the American Government for use in all its agencies – even the top-secret ones – that theft could be considered treason.

Now it all became clear. The Hive technology, which Nicholas had quite rightly been eager to acquire, was the sole property of Hyrotech-inc, the American company with which Nicholas had been negotiating a buyout.

No wonder the American Government had put that merger on ice – Nicholas had been right about that, as well. The Americans were out for Sato International's blood, and they were going for the vulnerable spot: Sato-Tomkin, the American arm of the *keiretsu*. Except that Nicholas, Nangi and Sato International were innocent of wrongdoing. It had been that bastard Vincent Tinh, whom Nangi had never trusted, who had engineered all of this.

Of course, Tinh could not have done it alone. Someone in headquarters had been in collusion with him to steal the breakthrough technology of the Chi's neural-net computer, and Tinh had used his expertise, contacts and, most galling of all, Sato's capital and facilities to get a prototype of the softwareless Chi ramped up and manufactured.

Someone high up in the Chi Project had helped him. Naturally, the Americans suspected Nicholas. He was in charge of Chi. And, for many of them, he was a traitor the moment he merged Tomkin Industries with Sato International. And then to make matters worse he had abandoned Sato-Tomkin's New York office to move to Tokyo.

Now Nangi had cause to mourn his myopic insistence that Nicholas stay in Tokyo to help educate the Japanese corporate leaders on how American business and government ran and how to deal successfully with their American counterparts. Nicholas, ever the seer, had perhaps foreseen this moment in time, and had wanted to return to the States to argue his case for Japan, Inc. and Corporate America to work hand in hand.

But, according to Gaunt, there were elements within the Government who had their own agenda and they had been active for some time. The man whom Gaunt had gone to see, who had, it seemed clear, murdered him, was William Justice Lillehammer.

That name sounded oddly familiar to Nangi. Where had he heard it before? Hadn't Okami mentioned it once? But in what regard? He racked

409

his brain but could not recall the context of the conversation. An 8-mm video Gaunt had enclosed with the material lay warm next to Nangi's breast. He had viewed it once already, but was looking forward to studying it frame by frame.

The sounds were like bursts of energy, given off in the blackness, and in between, the silence of offices abandoned for the night. Nangi adjusted himself so that his ear was more firmly against the electronic eavesdropper. Unconsciously, he put one hand on his bad leg, rubbed it to invite warmth and better circulation. He smelled only plastic and the gummy dust of neglected machines. He held his nose to keep himself from sneezing.

How ironic, Nangi thought. Nicholas, the hero, was feared in Japan and reviled in America. Without him, Nangi wondered where Sato International would be now. Certainly not on the cutting edge of computer and telecommunication technology that would make the *keiretsu* one of Japan's top three corporations in the 1990s. If it survived. From what Minister Ushiba had threatened, and from what Nangi now knew from the explosive allegations and evidence sent over from Harley Gaunt, Nangi seriously doubted they would survive.

Unless he discovered who was responsible for draining the Chi technology. Vincent Tinh, the mastermind, was dead at the hands, no doubt, of any one of his numerous unsavory enemies. Luckily, Nangi had found a first-rate private investigator and had hired him to go to Saigon immediately and find out the extent of what Tinh had been into, and who had killed him. The entire Sato Saigon complex was temporarily on hold while he struggled to find a replacement for Tinh. As he had told Kisoko, there was, of course, a logical replacement already in the company.

Seiko.

But Seiko had been working for Tinh, and was doing her best to destroy the *keiretsu*.

The electronic gibberish from behind the capsule wall was coming in organized bursts. Part of Nangi's brain had been working on the problem, and now he began making rapid mathematical calculations as he kept his eye on the luminous dial of his wrist chronometer. What did these organized eruptions most remind him of? He racked his brain. Right. It was like telemetry. Or coded faxes being sent off into the ether.

He put the flat of his hand against the eggshell-thin wall, and thought, *If I put my fist to it I will surely break through to the other side.*

Who was in the capsule on the other side of the wall? Not Goei. He had only stayed a few minutes, then departed. Precisely seven minutes after he had left the building the mice began walking across the rails.

Nangi took his ear from the listening device, rolled away from the wall.

410

He rose with some difficulty and, ignoring the pain in his leg, limped out of the module. He was careful to pop the lock on the way out so that when he closed the door behind him, the office was once again sealed.

He went down the narrow corridor, lit by a single tube of fluorescent light. He adjusted the gloves on his hands as he stood outside the door to the office Goei had entered.

He could feel the measured beat of his heart, his accelerated pulse rate. He took several deep breaths, calming himself. Then he slid a thin metal tool with a hooked end into the lock in the center of the steel doorknob and began to probe for the interior ridges. One by one, he negotiated their contours. His other hand, on the knob itself, felt the resistance disappear, and he silently turned it as far as he could.

The door was open a crack and the telemetry or whatever it was became clearly audible in the dense silence of the corridor. Nangi slipped without a sound into the capsule, closing the door behind him in order to keep the level of ambient light from changing.

As it turned out, he needn't have worried. There was no one in the office. In fact, it wasn't an office at all, but a bare space with only a fax machine and a telephone on separate lines to show that it wasn't unrented.

Leaning on his cane, he lowered himself in front of the fax, took the sheets of paper out of the hopper. He turned them over in the light of the one black metal lamp. They were blank. Then, as he held them closer to the light, he saw the sparkles of metallic thread, pressed into a discernible pattern on the sheets.

Code.

He folded the sheets, put them in his pocket and stared at the fax machine in the semi-darkness.

The mice had completed their run across the tracks.

Transmission terminated.

The tolling of the bell was nowhere within the hive-like robotics factory. Electric blue arcs spilled across the interior cement, stainless steel and delicate copper-sheathed components, cold fire which ripped aside the veils of unconsciousness.

Still, Nicholas did not open his eyes. Instead, he kept his breathing deep, slow and regular, as it would be if his brain was still deep in theta.

He listened to the tolling of the bell, far off, as if in another universe, and amid the chaos that awaited him just beyond the paper-thin perimeter of his closed eyelids, he held on to that deep, rhythmic sound as a drowning man will grasp for any piece of flotsam to keep himself from going down again into the ultimate stillness of the deep. It was not a conscious decision,

411

but made at some primitive level, at his core, in the no-thought of his training.

Even at the edge of death there was this. And only this.

The tolling of a nonexistent bell.

If he focused on anything else, the pain would overwhelm him, plunging him into an abyss of despair. The figure with his face had slowly and agonizingly inserted what felt like long needles, shining with liquid fire or black toxin, into his flesh. Deep, deep they went into the heart of his pain centers.

Except that they weren't real, these long knives, these steel talons. They came from the mind of the Messulethe, invoking the dark side of the Tau-tau – Kshira. Nicholas never before had longed so profoundly for *koryoku*, the Illuminating Power, the pathway to Shuken, the dominion where Akshara and Kshira were safely integrated in one mind. It was clear that the dark side had destroyed the mind of the Messulethe.

As the pain grew so did the irony, for it became clear that what the Messulethe wanted from Nicholas he could not give him even had he lost all the will to resist. There was a link between Okami and the American Mafia don, Dominic Goldoni, a secret conduit code-named Nishiki feeding intelligence and incriminating evidence on friend and foe alike to the two men. Somehow the Messulethe had gotten the idea that Nicholas was Nishiki.

If he could have laughed he would have, but death was all around him. Not the physical kind – that was not what the Messulethe planned – but a kind of mental disintegration, shock upon shock to the synapses of the brain until the whole turned to jelly. The exchange of faces had been only the very first volley. Then the burning needles had been pushed home by the mind of the Messulethe while Nicholas's psyche, in shock, without recognition of place or of self, was pinned in darkness like a moth to paper, unable to access Akshara, the defenses at *kokoro*, the heart of the universe. Nicholas's mind was mute, paralyzed, cut off from any possibility of escape. This the Messulethe had planned for most assiduously and successfully.

Except for the tolling of the bell, which rang in echoes down the screaming synapses of his mind, a web glittering with endless pain.

If not for the tolling, resonant and steady, his mind would have been gone by now. Sanity was a sound he could identify and, on the edge of an abyss beyond imagining, desperately cling to.

He knew what the tolling was. At last, he was able to exert the energy that would connect one thought with another, as if he were an infant learning all over again how to think and, thinking, integrate thought with action. The veil of shock and paralysis was still firmly in place, but beneath it he had managed for an instant to stir.

In the face of the psychic barrage, he opened his tanjian eye, saw the color of the tolling, a clear, translucent green like the hillsides of Nara in springtime, and he felt her near him.

Celeste.

Celeste with the untapped power of her mind. This was the plan they had hit upon back in Paris when Nicholas had smelled the scent of the snare. She had tried to talk him out of it, had begged him, in fact, not to do this terrible thing: walk into the center of the snare. But what choice had he had? Could he have walked away from his oath to his father, his obligation to Okami? Another man, perhaps, whose terror so soaked his soul that he would forsake who he was to turn and run away. This was impossible for Nicholas. He could not turn, but only go forward, through the fire that surely was waiting for him.

But I will not go unarmed, he had told Celeste just before they had made their way to Montmartre. *You will be my secret weapon.*

She had looked at him quizzically, then, understanding dawning on her, with an expression of mounting dread.

No, she had said, *you can't mean it. My mind is untrained – for the love of God, I am afraid of what is inside me!*

And Nicholas, opening his tanjian eye, enfolded her in his psyche, at once calming her and showing her the Way – the path of Akshara by which she could link herself psychically with him, and maintain that contact.

But won't the Messulethe feel this connection?

No, he said. *I am providing you with the pathway of Akshara. Everything comes from me, and that is all he will be aware of – Akshara and my efforts to stop him. You with your untrained mind will become lost in the psychic mask of my defense.*

The one danger, which he did not bother to tell her, was if for some reason she should lose the psychic link he was now establishing. He did not know whether she would have the discipline to re-establish it. In order to do that, she would have to confront her fear of herself, would have to sink into that fear, go through it and, coming out the other side, see in her mind how to find his psyche again.

This, then, was the tolling in his mind, the one link to sanity in the maelstrom of the Messulethe's snare.

Celeste.

She was here, somewhere in the mad universe of magic and robotics, where faces were being stripped and re-applied like wrapping-paper over raw flesh.

He stirred once more, exhausting himself in reassurance of the link between them, the psychic thread that might pull him through this.

And so was unprepared for the blast of psychic energy that plastered him back into utter paralysis. He sat, slack-jawed, a fly in amber, caged and figuratively beaten and bloodied beyond recognition, for he had Do Duc's face, and his inquisitor, bending over him, placed his thumbs over his eyelids, gently at first, then more firmly as the chanting excited the membrane at *kokoro*, as the incantations made physical that which was moments before only a part of the transparent metaphysical world that enwrapped the reality that most men knew.

Pressing hard now on Nicholas's eyeballs, Do Duc opened another door in the Six-Sided Gateway at *kokoro*. It was a gate shut for long centuries, forbidden even to those who came after the Messulethe and had learned their dark and tragic secrets. It was the Sixth Gate, the only one sealed by spells and incantations which even Zarathustra would not attempt to sunder.

But even Zarathustra had not chosen as his familiar the white magpie, the messenger of the gods, the harbinger of their eventual doom. And it was the white magpie upon whom Do Duc now called, incanting the words that he had squeezed from Ao's mind, after the Nung shaman had foolishly refused to render it to him. What were the warnings of an old man, turned into a fearful woman by age, compared to the power he would unlock at the white magpie's calling?

And so the forbidden Sixth Gate was opened, and Do Duc was bathed in the baleful radiance and fearful asymmetry which lay beyond it. He took one step toward it and heard the cawing cry of the white magpie as clearly as if he were back in the mountain wilderness of his home among the Nungs.

He could not make out what was before him until the white magpie, clutching his shoulder with powerful talons, spoke in his ear. Then he understood.

He saw the asymmetry for what it was – yet another reality that stretched out beyond the metaphysical cocoon within which the physical world resided.

And now, reaching out for it, he used it, plunging it like a sword from heaven, into his victim's mind.

Nicholas, pinned by the sudden blast of psychic energy, intuited the outcome. He had been wrong. The switch of faces had not been merely for shock effect. The Messulethe had a far more terrifying motive in mind.

The pressure on his eyes became so intense that his pain receptors overloaded, shut down, and his whole face went numb. And then he was pierced by an awful radiance, and he knew what was about to happen.

It wasn't merely his face the Messulethe wanted – it was his very essence, drawn out of him by this connection, both physical and metaphysical, that was entering him now. And he would be gone, in a puff of smoke, leaving only a dead husk that would appear to anyone who found it to be the Messulethe himself.

Now, as the radiance streamed in through the Messulethe's thumbs pressed hard against his eyes, he summoned his last ounce of energy and, opening his tanjian eye, began to reel in the shining thread, the lifeline Celeste was providing, the reserve of psychic energy he would need.

But then, in horror and despair, he stopped.

The tolling, the pure-green translucent light, had vanished.

'Final instructions.'

'This man – Robert,' Lillehammer said. 'You get him and bring him to me.'

'From Japan?' Croaker said. 'What about the formalities?'

'There *are* no formalities when it comes to my people.'

The place stank of stale cigarette smoke and fear, just like an interrogation room. But this was a small cubicle, one of the airline's storage rooms at Washington National airport, that Lillehammer had commandeered.

'So I bring him back.' Croaker said it again so there would be no mistake.

'Right.' Lillehammer squinted. 'The messenger get you everything you need?'

'IDs, passports, currency in yen and dollars, tickets and prepaid rooms at a Tokyo hotel. Everything.'

'What about armament?'

Always the soldier, Croaker thought. 'I'll take care of that myself,' he said, raising his titanium and polycarbonate hand, clicking the needle-like nails together.

Lillehammer nodded. 'That's it, then.'

'I guess so.' Croaker turned away, then swung back as if drawn by an afterthought. 'Just one thing. Why didn't you tell me you knew who murdered Dominic Goldoni?'

Lillehammer, ever the cool customer, did not miss a beat. 'Who have you been talking to?' he said quietly.

The atmosphere in the cubicle was really quite vile. Maybe the ventilation wasn't working, Croaker thought.

'It doesn't matter.' He put his face close to Lillehammer's. 'Did you think I was toothless? That I'd let all my contacts drift away?'

415

'None of this concerns you. I don't know what's got under your skin.'

Croaker took a step closer to the other man and pointed. 'Tell me, was Do Duc the one who did that to you? Carve your face into a mask? That's what this is all about, isn't it?'

'That's about enough of that,' Lillehammer said flatly. 'Just shut up and do your job. Don't fuck with me.'

Croaker said, 'I'm not afraid of you.'

'Then you're stupid.'

'Not stupid,' Croaker said. 'Just prepared.' He gave Lillehammer a fierce grin. 'You ever hear of walking backwards? No? We did it all the time in the NYPD, had to otherwise you were liable to find a knife sticking out of your back. Not from the perps you were running down or you'd put away in times past, but from Internal Affairs, an asshole precinct captain, an overeager looie out to suck his way up the ladder, DAs with a political axe to grind, anyone and everyone who you worked with or for. Sure, we looked out for our own. But we also fucked our own six ways from Sunday. And let me tell you something, you never forget all the *very* nasty ways of keeping that knife from being stuck in your back.'

Lillehammer held up his hands. 'Let's back away from the precipice, shall we?' He looked away. 'Ah, shit!' And swung his head back. 'Okay, look, I need you to find this bastard for me. I didn't lie to you about that. I *do* know him – from 'Nam. He was one of three people who put me into a cage, worked on me, yeah, did *this*.' He brushed his lips with his forefinger.

'One of the bastards was a crazy shit of a guy named Michael Leonforte. He'd gone native in Laos. I was sent out by my unit to get him back but I was captured. Leonforte was commanding a group of Nungs – Chinese hill tribesmen. Then he recruited two more – a wacko named Rock and his buddy Do Duc.'

Lillehammer, brimming with the manic energy of memory, began to pace back and forth. 'Rock worked on me while the others looked on, asked me questions I wouldn't answer.' His eyes slid away from Croaker's. 'You know the drill.' He shrugged his shoulders. 'Anyway, there was no cavalry that day. No one to save me. They carved me nicely and neatly, then wrapped me up and delivered me back to my people as a warning. A fucking warning.' He blew his breath out hard.

'That was a long time ago but I never forgot.' He stamped his feet as if he were cold.

'Then Dominic gets whacked and I take one look at the mess and I know who did it. This bastard Do Duc, who'd been hired by Michael Leonforte's brother, Caesare, Goldoni's rival.'

416

'What's really behind the vendetta between the Goldonis and the Leonfortes?'

'If I knew that I'd be inside the mob. *Omerta*, get me? Anyway, Do Duc was an obvious choice. His allegiance to the Leonfortes goes all the way back to 'Nam.'

Lillehammer stopped pacing to face Croaker. 'That fucking blue crescent Do Duc carved into the Morris girl was tattooed on all of Leonforte's Nungs. Now I have number two on the line but not yet in my sights. For that I need you, because I know that Do Duc won't let me get within a mile of him. He'd smell me as sure as we're both standing here. He's half-animal.'

'Why didn't you tell me this from the beginning?'

'That it was personal? Would you have signed on?'

'I may be your Ishmael, but Do Duc's your white whale.' Croaker showed his teeth. 'No, I wouldn't.'

'You see? I couldn't take that chance.'

Croaker waited a moment. 'That's all of it?'

'The whole bloody thing,' Lillehammer said. He glanced at his watch, then pulled open the cubicle door. 'Now you'll have to do some running,' he said, 'in order to make your flight.'

The radiance came down like a veil from heaven. It was like watching yourself being eaten alive. Every muscle in Nicholas's body was contracted with pain and fear. The mask from the other side of time was settling over him. In a moment, it would begin to slice up his essence like meat upon a butcher's bloody table.

Frantically, he searched for Celeste – the shining thread by which he might pull himself loose from the settling of death, like radioactive rain, penetrating skin, flesh, bone, dissolving him from the inside out.

Where was she? What had happened? The psychic link had been broken and his one fear had come to pass: she was now unable to re-establish the link with him. Without the edge she provided, he knew he was finished.

The radiance, sinking deeper into him, provided an asymmetrical pulsation which upset the natural rhythms of his body. And with it, as if written in his own secretions, flaming runes of an incomprehensible language. The hideous cadence grew stronger and, as it did, his own diminished. In a moment, no thought would be left him, no essence, no life.

Then the pressure came off.

He felt it lift from his eye sockets, and immediately the radiance paled, the flow of incomprehensible language blurred. And in that moment, his tanjian eye snapped open. Freed from the paralysis that had gripped it, it shone straight through to *kokoro*, beating upon the membrane, summoning the energy that was thought and would now be action.

Nicholas opened his bleary eyes, saw the face that was his stretched in a grimace. The body of the Messulethe was arched backward, his hands at his neck. He was jammed back against the bars of the cage and, as Nicholas began to move, he saw the glint of the stainless-steel wire wound tightly around his neck, digging deep into the flesh of his throat.

He moved off his chair like a dead man reanimated, his arms and legs working in quick, spastic motions, his muscles jumping as he strove to re-establish brain-muscle coordination. The synapses of his brain were still on fire, but the rest of his body was free of pain. The physical connection with the Messulethe had been broken.

The man with his face gave out a cry, his hands leaving the makeshift garrotte, moving in a blur through the bars, grasping hair and flesh.

Celeste screamed.

Celeste!

And in an instant he saw what had happened. Sensing what was about to take place, he had taken the initiative, and the physical act of going after the Messulethe caused her untrained mind to break the psychic connection.

The Messulethe had her head in his hands and he slammed her forehead into the steel bars of the cage. Celeste staggered backward, her grip on the shining garrotte easing, and the Messulethe pulled free. He unwound the bloody thing from his neck, threw it aside.

Celeste was on the floor just outside the cage. Was she conscious or –?

Nicholas felt as if he were wading through water. His thoughts came so slowly, an agonizing jet of pain every time he tried to string one thought after another.

A wind was rising around him, and the heat of a blazing furnace. He was thrown backward, head over heels, smashing into the chair on which he had been sitting, breaking it apart. The side of his head hit the bars of the far side of the cage, momentarily stunning him.

Nothing was working.

And here came the man with his face.

Then the tolling began, deep inside him, and the green, pellucid light began to spread over him.

He opened his tanjian eye.

He connected with *kokoro* and began the basic litany of Akshara taught to him by Kansatsu, his Tau-tau *sensei*, his implacable enemy.

But the heat was rising again, the scent of white-hot cinders in his nostrils, his hair, crawling along his skin. The tolling, the translucent light,

418

his connection to Celeste, his secret weapon, withering beneath the assault of the Messulethe.

Akshara – everything Kansatsu had taught him – was useless. The man with his face made the two strides across the cage, hauled him to his feet.

And then, in an instant's flash of insight, he understood. He let go of the basic litany, abandoned all the lessons of Akshara he had so assiduously learned and, instead, listened only to the tolling of the inner bell.

Unpinned, bathed in the radiance emanating from his tanjian eye, he broke the hold on him. He struck with a quick *atemi* which the Messulethe easily swept aside. Nicholas, abandoning aikido, dropped to the level-horse stance, smashing the outside of his forearm into the Messulethe's right hip. The Messulethe struck out in an appallingly swift kite, striking Nicholas a glancing blow on his shoulder, struck out again.

This time Nicholas had lowered himself far enough so that one knee was on the ground. Very fast now, he intercepted the blow with the callused edge of his left hand and, rising up, swept the Messulethe's extended arm out and away in an unnatural arc intended to break bones.

The Messulethe moved with astonishing speed, twisting his torso into the attack so as to negate the unnatural position of his arm. At the same time, he delivered a vicious kite meant for Nicholas's kidneys.

Nicholas, in the right-angle horse position, directed a snap-kick to the Messulethe's groin. Both blows struck almost simultaneously, and both men went down. But Nicholas rolled and, angling his knuckles down, struck the Messulethe, delivered a short *twan ch'uan* to the Messulethe's forehead.

His own head snapped back, but he was already caught in the vise-like grip of the Messulethe's powerful legs. Kneed in the stomach, he tried to twist away, and caught another kite on the jaw.

He slumped back, and the Messulethe, on one knee, stamped at his armpit, extending his arm out, twisting it. Nicholas felt the tendons being strained beyond tolerance, and his left hand scrabbled under his body. His fingers closed around a broken chair leg and he smashed it into the side of the Messulethe's head just above his ear.

The Messulethe staggered, his grip on Nicholas broken, and Nicholas was up, kicking him a glancing blow. He fell on him, knowing he had only moments in which to kill him before his superior psyche reasserted itself. He used the heel of his hand, in an *atemi* meant to splinter the nose cartilage, send it directly into the brain. It was invariably a lethal blow, and the mind had to be absolutely centered, the organism in mortal danger, the resolve wholly unimpaired, because once committed there was no turning back; death was the only possible result.

Nicholas was certain he had that resolve in him, the conviction that this soul must be dispatched, that there was no other option available, that without this singular attack his risk was intolerable.

But the blow never landed. The heel of his hand stopped perhaps a centimeter from its objective, hanging in the air. Then the muscles of his wrist and forearm began to spasm as if he had plunged them into a bed of live coals.

Nicholas, deep in mind-no-mind, continued to resist the Messulethe with his upper body, even while his left leg kicked out, mindless, as if in galvanic response. The toe of Nicholas's shoe caught his enemy on the point of his hip, where the flexor muscles covered an important nerve nexus for the lower body.

The Messulethe fell and, as his concentration shifted, the numbing force of his psyche lifted. Nicholas slammed the edge of his hand into the spot between and just above the Messulethe's eyes, a crucial point in the line of the major conception meridian. The Messulethe's eyes crossed, and Nicholas could feel the almost total withdrawal of his psyche as he hovered at the point of unconsciousness. Still, Nicholas felt the squirming of his enemy's powerful mind, trying to break through the temporary paralysis, and he knew he had only moments in which to act.

He threw himself headlong across the enervated form, ripped the key from the Messulethe's belt and, leaping at the doorway, unlocked it.

A fusillade of needles scourged his mind as the Messulethe, recovering with appalling rapidity, lashed out with his psyche, trying to keep Nicholas from leaving the cage. Nicholas stumbled, fell to one knee, almost in Celeste's lap. She wrapped her arm around his waist, and together they loped awkwardly away from the cage. Celeste looked back, terrified, but the Messulethe was still lying on the ground. Had Nicholas killed him? She hurried them on.

Once, Nicholas fell heavily, bringing them both down, and Celeste cried out, blood on her palms as she skidded, feeling the creeping along her nerves of not only what had been done to him, but what was coming after them, the heat through the vivid electric discharges, billowing along the reinforced concrete floor, a low mist with form and substance, the lethal rhythms of the Messulethe reaching out for them.

But, with a heavy grunt, she hauled him to his feet, propelled him on, and kept him at it, with that *thing* so near her mind she could feel it singe her like a bright leap of flame. The terror running through her, but she kept him at it, out across the ferroconcrete beehive of the robotics factory with its spinning blue lightning arcs, its scents of hot metal and fused plastics, the presence in her mind growing stronger, seeking to fill her limbs with lead, as they stumbled past lines of stainless-steel heads being fitted

420

onto blocky inhuman shoulders. Infra-red-lensed eyes stared unblinking as the running shadows struck them and were gone. Kept him going in this cold crucible where machines created more machines, where the miracle of creation in a manner inconceivable even decades ago was occurring every minute of the day and night.

Down! The voice in her head confused her. *Get down!*

And Nicholas struck her a swift blow behind her knees so that she went down in an instant. She was aware of him, of his body spread over hers, and of a great heat like a concentrated beam running along the backs of her legs where they were exposed.

Crack like a bolt of thunder and she whimpered, the percussion shaking the floor, and then Nicholas was dragging her to her feet and, as she was pulled past a section of wall, she stared wide-eyed at the ovoid indentation in it, as if it had been struck by a gigantic fist.

He hauled her round the end of the wall, and the light dimmed. They were in a corridor and, up ahead, she could see a set of stainless-steel doors, which he hit full tilt, using his shoulder and his momentum to slam them open.

They found themselves in a wide service entrance, and they ran as best they could up the long ramp, through another set of metal doors, onto a loading platform, deserted save for a heavy-duty truck.

Nicholas jerked open the door, slid behind the wheel. He looked under the floormat, above the sun visor for keys. Not finding them, he used a screwdriver he found on the floor to pry open the steering column.

Watching him hot-wire the truck, Celeste felt her stomach rebelling. It was eerie seeing the face of the Messulethe, knowing because she was linked with it that Nicholas's mind lay beneath it. Still, she had thought she would pass out the first time she saw his eyes staring at her from out of that face she had learned to fear above all others.

'Nicholas!'

She shook him and he groaned, his forehead coming up off the steering wheel, his fingers resuming their work on the wiring.

Celeste looked up, shivering. At the edge of her mind was that awful sensation, as if some beast were snuffling obscenely through her innermost thoughts. She felt the onset of the heat, rushing up the ramp at them, and she screamed wordlessly, her terror an anodyne for her nausea.

The engine barked to life and Nicholas slumped back in the seat, near exhaustion.

'Celeste, you'll have to drive.'

'But I've never –'

'Get behind the wheel!'

He slid over, displacing her, and she settled herself, her feet feeling for the pedals.

Celeste gunned the engine just as the metal doors blew open with such force that one of them was ripped free of its hinges. She pressed herself back into the seat as she banged the gears into reverse and, with a squeal of tires, launched the truck out of the loading bay, swinging it round, a whoosh behind them which Celeste, rigid in her seat, refused to look at.

Then she slammed the truck into first, gunned the engine, hitting second a little early, the gears grinding in protest, then kicking in as the speed came up, and they were on the road.

'Wrong side!' Nicholas shouted. 'Get over to the left!'

An air-horn sounded so close Celeste jumped as they veered crazily away from a semi coming in the opposite direction, Celeste cutting it way too close, the wail of metal scraping against metal, paint strips whipping by, and the rumble, heavy as an earthquake, as the sides of the two trucks hit once, twice.

And then they were past, Nicholas slumped beside her, the truck roaring like a wounded animal as they accelerated away from the killing ground.

SEVENTEEN

Tokyo

The shapes, humped and bestial, like the Leviathan and the Devil, moved in grainy silhouette until they moved sufficiently into the one light, an unshaded photographer's lamp which threw off light with the violence of heat.

Nangi sucked in his breath as the true nature of what the two men were doing to one another became apparent. Nangi, part of a culture where the traditional Western taboo against homosexuality was nonexistent, was nevertheless shocked. Not by seeing the men naked together, but by what they were perpetrating on one another.

So this was William Justice Lillehammer, the older, taller one. The young blond, energetic, intense as a method actor, with the astonishingly supple body, seemed born for this kind of reckless abandonment.

Nangi leaned forward and, directing the remote at the VCR, rewound the images to a certain sequence. He had already watched the 8-mm tape Manny Mannheim had brought from the late Harley Gaunt through several times, and now he was taking notes.

The phone rang.

'*Moshi.*'

'Nangi-san, I have been able to trace the phone number you gave me.'

This was Jisaku Shindo, the private investigator Nangi had engaged, and he was speaking of the number Nangi had copied off the ghostly fax machine he had discovered in the capsule office Masamoto Goei had rented in the Ginza.

'It's here in Saigon, all right,' Shindo said, 'in an office building directly across the road from your own office complex.'

'Who owns it?' Nangi asked.

'A company that's nonexistent, as it turns out.' Nangi could hear the PI shuffling through the pages of his notebook. 'It appears as if your own man Vincent Tinh paid the rent every month.'

Nangi closed his eyes for a moment.

423

'Nangi-san? There's quite a bit more.'

'I'm listening.'

'Okay. A friend of a friend of mine works in the coroner's office, so I got to take a look at the autopsy report on Tinh. He was burned in sulfuric acid, all right, just like Van Kiet told you. But they also dug twenty-five bullets out of him.'

'*Twenty-five?*'

'Right. From the caliber of the bullets and the pattern of the wounds I'd say he was on the wrong end of some kind of heavy-duty machine-gun. A military weapon would be my guess, but I'm following it up.'

Good Christ, Nangi thought.

'There's one more thing,' Shindo said. 'The friend of a friend was on duty when the body was picked up. He claims the man was Japanese. He also swears he was Yakuza.'

Nangi's mind was reeling. 'How could he know that?'

'Little finger of the man's left hand,' Shindo said. 'The top joint was missing.'

Yakuza often cut a digit in such a way in order to swear allegiance to an *oyabun* or to atone for a committed sin, to affirm their subservience.

'Good work.'

'Thank you, sir. I've used my contacts and I've managed to get an interview with Inspector Van Kiet tomorrow morning. The idea is to find out what form of persuasion will work best on these people. They're all utterly corrupt.'

'I trust you'll be successful. Keep me informed.'

'As always.'

Nangi broke the connection, sat back on the couch in his study. It was very quiet in the house, something he dearly loved, but now, abruptly, he longed for sound – a radio playing rock music, or a woman's voice. He found himself again at the same gate, thoughts of Kisoko curling around him like mist.

But there was no time for her now. Tomorrow, Lew Croaker would be here with God only knew what news. Before then, Nangi knew, he had much to do.

Part of his mind chewing over what Shindo had told him, he began again to watch a certain section of the video in slow motion. This time, however, he ignored the main attraction, the two bodies coupling so oddly. Instead, he watched the extreme upper-right corner of the frame where his eye had caught a flicker of movement.

He saw it come and go and return, like the shadow of a flame cast upon a wall, and he switched on the digital enhancer. Immediately, the images shot into focus, all traces of fuzziness and motion-smear – a consequence of shooting in the low light – vanished.

And Nangi found himself staring right into a face.

The face was turned slightly away from the lens of the video camera, calmly observing the sexual acrobatics as if they were a tennis match.

Nangi hit the digital freeze button, stared for a long time at the face. It was partly in shadow but, curiously, the sections of darkness helped define and reveal the features of the face.

The odd thing was that he recognized it.

And it was the trigger his memory needed to pull up Okami's reference to William Justice Lillehammer.

Nangi could recall the conversation as if it had occurred yesterday instead of two years ago. Okami had been in Tokyo on one of his infrequent visits. Nangi remembered the place – the Meiji Shrine. It had been spring-time, when everything was shedding the somber colors of winter. The air had been perfumed with the heady scents of budding flowers.

I am on the edge of a great precipice, Okami had told him. *I must make a decision either to live and die as I have up until now or to make a great leap into the unknown.*

Do you need help, Okami-san?

No, no. Curious now in retrospect how Okami's agitation seemed so much more significant. *I don't want you involved in this at all. Not in any material way. But I seek your advice.*

Whatever I can do, Nangi had said.

There is a man with whom elements within my inner council insist I deal, and there is much about him that concerns me. But even though I have a profound sense of foreboding I nevertheless feel that I must take this path. I know it is the wrong one, Nangi-san, but I must make this attempt to appease the other oyabun *if there is to be any peace among the clans. I do not want a full-scale war on my hands.*

Okami had paused to watch several children playing and daydreaming in the grass. Who knew what was in his mind at that moment? Perhaps he was thinking, as Nangi had been, of the terrible price one paid for adulthood.

This man, whose name is Lillehammer, works for someone who I believe is known to you, so I thought we should meet.

They had moved on, leaving the children to their play, coming upon strolling lovers, hands linked, faces turned toward one another, blessed by the sunlight.

Leon Waxman.

Yes. I know him, Nangi had said. *We met here in Tokyo several years after*

425

the Occupation began. Let's see, perhaps it was in '47 or '48. In any case, I met him in hospital. I was doing work for the building ministry at that time, I believe, and there was some structural damage at the hospital. I was sent out with a team of engineers to see what needed to be done.

Waxman was an American, but he was recuperating in a Japanese hospital.

That's right, Nangi had said. *The hospital specialized in neural surgery. His wounds were extensive so I assume a number of operations of that nature had to be done.*

What kind of a man did he seem to you?

Curious, Nangi said. *He seemed to have two personalities. One, canny and bright, the other, terribly suspicious and dark. The nurses I spoke with said he was so prone to violent nightmares and night sweats they had gotten in the habit of sedating him right after dinner.*

And after he got out of hospital you kept in touch?

Yes. For one thing, he was hungry for contacts in Tokyo. For another, he actually helped me move upward into MITI.

How did he manage that?

The lovers had vanished with the sun, and now the two men were in an area populated by punks in pink and green spiky Mohawk hairdos, black leather jackets, insectoid sunglasses and black and chromium Kawasaki motorcycles. They sneered at the passersby, and gunned their engines. Muscular, bass-heavy rock music blared.

Apparently, he wasn't without contacts already, Nangi said. *He had been in public liaison when he had been in the Army, so he had done plenty of interfacing with ministry personnel, especially the Ministry of Commerce and Industry which would eventually become MITI. He desperately wanted contacts in the business world and so we bartered favors. I remember being impressed with how well he understood the Japanese way.*

So he wanted to become a businessman.

Apparently.

Well, he's in an entirely different line of work now, Okami said. *He's the head of a spook network that's buried deep inside the American Federal bureaucracy.*

They had come to an area of the park under construction. Now even the punks were left behind and, for the moment at least, they were alone. Pale-budded trees, their rootballs wrapped in burlap and twine, lay heeled over against an iron fence, awaiting planting.

I can see how he'd be drawn to that kind of life, Nangi said. *Waxman always impressed me as being someone who saw designs in shadows. Besides, even though he had a knack for it, my impression was that business bored him. It was too easy. 'Like shooting fish in a barrel,' he once told me.*

426

Okami said, *Waxman's network is so deeply buried even the American Congress has never heard of it.*

That can be good or bad, Nangi said.

There's more, Okami said. He put his hands behind his back and frowned, deep in thought. *Waxman has risen to the top of a loosely knit group of men who call themselves Looking-Glass.*

Looking-Glass. I've never heard of them.

I'm not surprised; virtually nobody has, Okami said. *These men seek power and control over their Government's political and economic policies. We speak here of an exceedingly dangerous man.*

Okami came to a halt, stood facing Nangi, and Nangi knew they had come to the crucial moment.

Waxman is the end of this particular path for me, Okami said. *If he proves untrustworthy I fear that I will have to take my great leap into the unknown. I have my own agenda which I will implement despite the extreme danger to me. I apologize for involving you in this crucial decision, Nangi-san, but there is no one else I can trust.*

I remember Waxman as being smart, Nangi had said that last time he had seen Mikio Okami, before he had abruptly disappeared. *Perhaps too smart for his own good.*

What do you mean?

Just this. His intelligence made for a restless soul. And I, personally, can never fully trust restless souls.

Now, as Nangi stared at the digitally enhanced still-frame of the 8-mm video, he knew he was looking at the face of the man he hadn't seen in so many years, observing in cool objectivity the sexual burlesque of one of his agents: Leon Waxman.

Tomoo Kozo covered his mouth as if, without that commitment, he would articulate to the world his hatred for Nicholas Linnear. Kozo stood naked in front of a full-length mirror staring at the movie of his body. The prismatic *irizumi* told a story of loss, revenge and death, to Kozo's way of thinking the three cornerstones of honor.

Loss, revenge and death were all that concerned Kozo now. He stared down at the phoenix that girdled his penis with its wings. Its fierce head was tattooed on the helmet. The phoenix grew as he did, spreading its curious wings in ardor.

Loss, revenge and death defined not only honor but Kozo's relationship with Nicholas Linnear. The two had never met; perhaps Nicholas did not even know of Kozo's existence; but Kozo knew Nicholas, intimately.

Despite the lies he had told Minister Ushiba, Kozo had deliberately

427

put the white Toyota on Justine Linnear and her lover – yes, Kozo had known who he was the moment he had landed at Narita, long before Ushiba or the other *oyabun* of the Kaisho's inner council had. And because of that Nicholas Linnear's wife was dead.

Loss.

Katsuodo Kozo, Tomoo's father, had once played a role in the rise of Mikio Okami, but Okami had outlasted him. Of course. Okami had the Colonel.

Kozo was sick to death of the Japanese deification of Colonel Linnear. Even many of the *oyabun* held him in high esteem because of what they saw as his efforts on behalf of their clans during the early years of the Occupation. Kozo had no doubt that the Colonel was more Japanese in his thinking than he was Western. In his opinion, that was what had made the Colonel such a dangerous creature. It was what had killed Katsuodo Kozo.

Kozo believed it was Colonel Linnear himself who had murdered his father, who had been found floating in the Sumida River with not a scratch on him. But Katsuodo could not swim and the Colonel knew that; Kozo had heard them speaking one hazy summer afternoon when the sweat collected on the skin like rain in the treetops.

A week later, Katsuodo's blue-white body was fished out of the Sumida and Kozo had lost a father.

An irreparable loss.

It was only years later that Kozo began to glean the nature and the context of the terrible incident. Almost from the beginning Katsuodo and Okami were at loggerheads over Yakuza policy. Okami was for accommodation with the Americans – especially since the Occupation forces often turned to the Yakuza to help quell riots instigated by Communist infiltrators. It looked better for Japanese gangsters to be banging the heads of Japanese workers than it did for the American military to do it. But Katsuodo argued vehemently against any association with the Americans. He despised being used by the Americans for any purpose – even the supposedly virtuous eradication of the Communists from Japanese soil.

The disagreements between the two *oyabun* finally erupted into open warfare. Until Katsuodo's body was discovered floating in the Sumida. Because no marks were found on him no blame could be assessed, no revenge taken. Okami and the Colonel exerted their influence. Order was restored.

But nothing could return Tomoo Kozo's life to the way it had been, and he never forgot. In true Japanese fashion, he took Okami as a mentor, studied under him, became a true and loyal friend, consolidated his power as Okami rose through the ranks. And when Okami became the Kaisho, Kozo was his staunchest and most vocal supporter. He had stood by Okami's side at the rite of ascension, because of his clandestine investigation into the history surrounding Katsuodo's death hating him and his connection with Colonel Linnear all the while.

The Colonel had died before Kozo could exact his revenge. That left the son. But the son was a ninja, powerful in his own right. Even the *oyabun* feared him. And then there was the memory of the Colonel, a reverence that Kozo could not fight. So he bided his time, patient as a spider whose intricate web is destroyed by wind, rain and frost, but who nevertheless respins it time and again.

Revenge.

Kozo turned away from the mirror, began methodically to dress. It was time to see Do Duc.

Time to recall honor and mete out death.

Nicholas, pale as ash, lay among the fallen maple leaves as if he were in a bed of fire.

Celeste, kneeling over him said, 'The house – *your* house, isn't it? – is just a hundred yards further through the trees.'

His eyes, clouded with pain, stared up at her as if she were a stranger. Celeste's heart skipped a beat. What had the Messulethe done to him? Why had she waited so long to act? But she knew. The terror that had gripped her from the moment he had established their psychic link was like nothing she had ever experienced before. Always in her mind lurked the shadow knowledge that beyond the world she could see with her eyes, hear with her ears, lay another, more ephemeral one with which her mind intersected in times of extreme stress or dreaming. Being so directly connected to it had scoured her nerves raw. But look at what her terror had wrought.

'Ah, Nicholas.'

She bent over him and tenderly placed her lips over his. She thought she heard him moan, and she jerked away, afraid she had somehow hurt him.

They were beside a stone basin filled with water that seemed to bubble up from below the ground. There was a single Japanese *kanji* carved into the stone, and across its top lay a bamboo ladle.

Nicholas, whispering in a reedy voice, bade her let him drink from the ladle. She scooped up the cold, clear water and, lifting his head, put the ladle against his lips.

He drank slowly and noisily for some time, his eyes closed, as if the water defined his world. He put his hand flat on the carpet of leaves, sat up.

'Home,' he said. 'Did I direct you here?'

'You don't remember?'

'No.'

She put her hand against his cheek. 'Nicholas, how badly are you hurt?'

'I don't know.' He looked around. 'This is where Justine and I buried our daughter – little thing, so tiny and white, she had no chance at life.'

He put his head down, and Celeste drew him into her arms, rocked him gently while he softly sobbed.

'It's all right,' he said after a time. 'That was a long time ago. Another life, really.'

Celeste closed her eyes for an instant, bit her lip. 'Nicholas, I'm afraid.' They stared into one another's eyes. 'I think at the end the Messulethe understood. I think he became aware of me, of how I helped you.'

It was true. Through the haze of pain and shock Nicholas understood that he could no longer shield her in that way. He had used her and now they would both pay the price. It had been a desperate gamble, putting his head into the jaws of the Messulethe's snare, but in a way it had paid off. From the interrogation he knew that the Messulethe did not have access to Okami. Otherwise, he would have known that Nicholas was not Nishiki, the conduit between Okami and Dominic Goldoni.

That meant Okami was alive and most likely in hiding.

'Nicholas.'

He looked up into Celeste's eyes, and suddenly he felt her psyche emerging from its shell, enfolding him in warmth and light. She put her hands on him, at first gingerly, then, as her sense of her inner self grew, more firmly. With the physical touch her strength flowed into him more fully, a floodlight illuminating shadowed depths.

'You have the hands – the mind – of a healer,' he said through cracked lips.

Automatically, he began the silent chanting of Akshara. Abruptly, he stopped.

Celeste said, 'What is it?' She had sensed the change in him. 'This is all so new to me. Have I done something wrong?'

He shook his head. 'No, it's me. I was taught the part of Tau-tau – Akshara – by a certain man. I trusted him for many years, but, in the end, it turned out that he was my enemy. He had learned both Akshara and its dark counterpart, Kshira. Without *koryoku*, the Path, and Shuken, the protection of integration, the dark side had corrupted him, as it has corrupted the Messulethe.'

430

Nicholas signed for more water, and she placed the ladle to his mouth. He drank in silence. The wet scent of leaves and rich soil perfumed the air. Birds flitted in the branches, calling sweetly to one another. This far from the winding road, there were no sounds of traffic.

Celeste did not want to think of the nightmare of navigating the truck, driving highways, then perilous, snaking roads on the left, past signs she could not read, banging and shearing the gears, Nicholas half-slumped beside her.

'This man, my *sensei*, taught me everything I know about Tau-tau,' Nicholas continued when he had slaked his thirst. 'Seeing how ineffective it was against the Messulethe, I began to wonder. And then in the cage, between consciousness and unconsciousness, my dreaming mind conjured up this man again, and I saw him – *I saw him, Celeste* – deceiving me. He was teaching me only those things he wanted me to know.'

Something stirred in the brush beyond the stand of bare ginkgo trees, and they both turned their heads. But it was only a small animal, foraging for fallen nuts.

Nicholas arranged himself so that his back was against the stone basin, as if he drew strength from contact with it. 'This man was exceedingly clever,' he said after a time. 'I took his teachings at face value even after I unmasked him. I'm now astonished that I could have been so naive.' He looked at her. 'Celeste, I think what he taught me wasn't simply Akshara. I believe now it was an incomplete combination of Akshara and Kshira. What if this dark side of Tau-tau has begun to change me?'

Celeste smoothed his dark, damp hair off his forehead, kissed him gently. 'I'm sure you're wrong,' she said reassuringly. 'The effects of being in that cage with the Messulethe can't be shrugged off so easily.'

He knew what she was saying, that the shock of the drugs and the interrogation had made him prone to paranoid delusions. But she was wrong. He could not shake the terrifying feeling that Kansatsu had somehow sabotaged him. He remembered how Kansatsu had told him that Nicholas had come to see him high up on the Hodaka many times, though Nicholas knew that moment had only occurred once.

Time, Kansatsu had said, *is somehow akin to the ocean. There are tides, currents, eddies which at certain nexus points overlap, creating a kind of whirlpool of events that repeat like ripples until, having spread sufficiently outward, they are spent upon a rocky shore.*

Nicholas, who had only begun to journey outside time, knew better now than he had then what Kansatsu was speaking of. If Kansatsu was able to live and relive moments in time, he might easily have foreseen his own death at Nicholas's hands, just as he would have understood the inevitability

431

of it and, accepting it as *karma*, had gone about exacting his revenge by planting a kind of psychic time-bomb inside Nicholas's head. The question Nicholas faced now was how to get it out.

There was a way, but it was so dangerous, so filled with unknown pitfalls, he did not know whether he dared take it. He wondered whether he had a choice.

It was at that moment that the birds ceased their songs, and Nicholas and Celeste, their eyes meeting in recognition, both knew that he was coming for them.

The Messulethe.

'Dead?'

'I'm afraid so. It was tragic. An automobile accident.'

'Jesus God. Justine dead.'

Lew Croaker stared into Tanzan Nangi's face. He looked older, his face more lined and weary than Croaker had remembered it.

'Does Nicholas know?'

Nangi shook his head. 'As you have heard, he has been out of touch for some time.'

Croaker sat down and Margarite put a hand on his shoulder. He had told her all about Nicholas and Justine on the flight over. They were bleary-eyed but not as tired as they could have been. They had shared a sleeping-pill Margarite had found at the bottom of her cosmetics case, and so had slept soundly for six hours.

They were in the living-room of Nicholas's house outside of Tokyo proper. Massive cedar beams criss-crossed the ceiling, and the late autumnal light spilled into the large room through enormous plate-glass windows. Thickly padded couches and oversized chairs filled the central tatami space, two steps lower than the surrounding wood-floored area. Along the walls were ranged Western artwork and brilliantly colored textiles from France and Italy. The house smelled of oiled wood, straw and rosemary.

Nangi felt this was the logical place to come. When Seiko had given him the message, he had been furious that she had not interrupted his meeting. But he quickly put his anger aside, and did some fast thinking. Seiko had given him Croaker's message verbatim, and that, along with a thorough cross-examination of her, had given him enough clues as to Croaker's tone and attitude to understand the urgency of the trip.

Considering his own current situation – as well as that of Sato International – he did not want anyone to know of Croaker's presence in Tokyo. That ruled out the office as well as his own residence. Neither did he want to take the chance of meeting them in so public a place as a hotel lobby.

Since Justine's death, Nicholas's house had remained empty, save for the cleaning woman. Nangi had keys to the place and its remote location made it ideal. He had taken his car to the airport, had met Croaker – and his companion – himself, driving them directly here.

But not before he had gotten rid of Seiko. She was the only person in the office who knew of Croaker's arrival, and he did not want her around while the meeting was taking place.

He had assigned her to Vietnam to temporarily take over the Sato Saigon office. He gave her Jisaku Shindo's name, but told her the private investigator was a production consultant hired to help integrate the relatively new overseas office with headquarters. He instructed her to help Shindo in any way she could.

The whole idea of providing her with so much freedom was risky, but Nangi was used to risk. He phoned Shindo, told him she was on her way and that she was suspected of working against the company. He knew this was the best he could do for now. He had no real evidence of her perfidy, except hearsay, and he was not prepared to act prematurely. Besides, she was less important than the people she reported to. If she was guilty. Perhaps her sense of freedom in Saigon would be her undoing. If so, Shindo would be there to document her fall.

Goei, the Chi Project leader, was another story. He had damned himself with his coded fax and, although Nangi's people were still in the process of deciphering it, Nangi had no doubts as to his guilt. In the best of all possible worlds, Nangi would have preferred to keep him in place and under twenty-four-hour-a-day surveillance. But he did not have that luxury. He knew that the moment he handed Goei over to the authorities he would at the very least mitigate Senator Bane's allegations against Nicholas and Sato-Tomkin and, with luck, destroy the case against them: Goei was the one who had leaked the Chi Project technology to Vincent Tinh in Saigon, not Nicholas. And because Goei could now be directly linked to Tinh, who had proved himself a renegade ready, willing and able to betray Sato-Tomkin, the *keiretsu* would be exonerated as well. So he had had Goei arrested and had handed Seiko her new assignment.

She had seemed thrilled. Also relieved, which disturbed him. He had packed her off to Saigon that morning with a weekend suitcase of clothes, promising to have the rest of her things sent as soon as possible. She had not protested, understanding better than most the emergency Vincent Tinh's death had created. Whatever misgivings he had about letting her go were soon submerged by Croaker's arrival and the subsequent revelations of events that had taken place in the United States.

Nangi listened closely as Croaker told him about being brought in to solve Dominic Goldoni's murder by Lillehammer, his growing suspicions that Lillehammer was more than he made himself out to be, and the subsequent revelations that Lillehammer had his own personal agenda to pursue against the Vietnamese assassin Do Duc Fujiru. Croaker was intrigued to learn that Nangi already knew about Harley Gaunt's death and its aftermath, but he surprised Nangi when he recounted Margarite's relationship with her step-mother, Renata Loti, with her brother Dominic, and revealed the legacy he had left her of running his empire.

When Croaker finished telling him of Margarite's suspicion that the war between the Leonfortes and the Goldonis was far more than a simple blood feud between Mafia families, Nangi turned to Margarite, said, 'You have told Croaker that your brother gave you access to the secret information he held on high-ranking officials of government and law enforcement. Where did this information come from?'

'A secret source,' Margarite said. 'His name is Nishiki.' Abruptly restless, she got up from her seat, walked tensely back and forth over the tatami.

'Did your brother ever allow you to meet this Nishiki?' Nangi asked.

'No. I . . . My impression was that Dom never met him himself. He was just a voice. But my step-mother knows who he is. She sent us over here to protect him from Do Duc.'

'So Croaker-san has said.' Nangi looked shrewdly at Margarite Goldoni DeCamillo, wondering if she could be trusted. He trusted Lew Croaker, Nicholas's closest Western friend, but that was all he could afford to take for granted. 'Did your step-mother give you a name?'

'Yes,' she said. 'We're supposed to see a man named Mikio Okami.'

Nangi stood very still for some time. 'Okami is the Kaisho, the head of all the *oyabun* of the Yakuza,' he told them. 'But his enemies have already moved against him; he's missing. Now you tell me that you believe he himself is Nishiki – Dominic Goldoni's source.'

'Faith seemed certain of it,' Margarite said. 'But what if he's already dead?'

'That thought had crossed my mind as well,' Nangi said, 'until I started putting some clues together. Regarding the allegations against Nicholas and Sato-Tomkin, I have found the traitors inside the company. One of them, Vincent Tinh, was murdered last week in Saigon. It seems he was involved in just about everything you can imagine that's illegal. But who murdered him? The Saigon police were of no help. But the curious thing is his body was claimed by a man purporting to be Tinh's brother. He had no family at all. And this man said he worked at a company called Avalon Ltd.

'I've done some checking. Though Avalon Ltd claims no knowledge of this man, it is an exceedingly strange concern which appears to be a conduit for transferring money across international borders. Now I have discovered that the man who came for Tinh's body was Japanese and Yakuza. It seemed clear that I was being deliberately directed to Avalon Ltd.

'All these factors lead me to one conclusion – that Mikio Okami is alive and in hiding, that he is secretly sending clues concerning his enemies to those who can best help him.

'You see, members of Okami's inner council were compelling him against his will into an alliance with a man named Leon Waxman, a man I knew in Tokyo many years ago who had subsequently become a major player in the shadows of Washington.

'I think Okami must have rebelled. I told him I thought Waxman was unreliable, and so Okami secretly abandoned the Godaishu, forming another alliance he had been secretly cultivating for years – one with your brother, Ms Goldoni. Dominic was murdered because of this alliance, and Okami has been driven into hiding.'

'But is he safe?' Margarite asked.

Nangi looked at her. 'Even if he is,' he said, 'there is so much power arrayed against him, I wonder how long he can survive.'

EIGHTEEN

Washington/Tokyo

When Faith Goldoni opened the door to her house, Lillehammer smiled and said, 'Will Lillehammer, Mrs Loti. Charmed to meet you at last. May I come in?'

Faith, staring at the working end of the pistol he was pointing at her heart, said, 'But of course.'

As she led him past the grand foyer and into the hallway, she heard him say, 'There's no one else at home, Mrs Loti. I checked.'

'I'm sure you did.'

He nudged her along. 'The kitchen and then out the back door.'

She could tell now without him saying anything that they were headed for the stables. She knew what that meant. In a way, she wondered that this moment hadn't occurred some time ago. It was only recently, when Lillehammer's lover Douglas Moon had sold her the videotape and she had viewed it, that she had recognized the man observing them as Johnny Leonforte. He looked very different, to be sure, what with the passage of time and the lopsided face, but this was a man with whom she had been intimate, and the moment she had seen the image she had known who he was. It had been long ago, but truly not far away. Those days in Tokyo during the Occupation had set the scene for everything that was to come. Those days were etched into her memory as if with a laser.

How long had Johnny known who she was? She did not live in the shadows as he must and, although she had had some subtle plastic surgery done in Los Angeles while getting her tucks, she was still Faith Goldoni. Johnny would have recognized her.

Johnny alive!

At first, she had found it inconceivable. But she had survived against all odds, why not him? And he had an innate advantage over her – he was a man.

'Open the door.'

She did, and smelled the pungency of the horses, the manure, the silage. The animals turned their heads in her direction, snorting.

'Don't worry,' Lillehammer said, 'I'm not going to shoot you. Too many questions that way.' She turned round, her back against one of the stalls. 'You're going to be kicked in the head by one of these.' He gestured at the horses.

Faith could feel the tackle against her back, moved a little to ease the pressure. 'Nobody will believe that,' she said. 'I'm too good a horsewoman.' Not only to ease the pressure, but to get a grip with her left hand on the leather and steel.

'They'll have to believe it,' Lillehammer said, moving closer to her and the horses, 'because it will be the coroner's findings. There won't be another mark on you. No sign of foul play.' He smiled. 'Believe me. I'm a master at this.'

'Why are you doing this?' She did not expect an answer; she wanted merely to reinforce his sense of control.

'Here's a big stallion.' He gestured with the pistol. 'Open the stall door.'

It was what Faith had been waiting for. She opened the stall door with her right hand while, with her left, she lifted the tackle off its hook, flung it with a practiced flick of her wrist. It acted much as a whip would, the thick leather and steel slapping into the side of Lillehammer's face and neck, drawing blood.

He roared, staggering, and kicked out, catching Faith on the point of her hip. She screamed, went down on one knee. The horses, terrified, banged into the sides of their stalls, whinnying, eyes wide, nostrils flaring, catching whiffs of her own fear and pain.

'Bitch!' Lillehammer shouted, freeing himself from the tackle and reaching for her.

He was right in front of the open stall door, and Faith slammed her shoulder into his knees with all the force she could muster. Lillehammer lost his balance, falling backward into the stall with the panicked stallion.

Lillehammer struck the stallion's side with such force that the horse reared up, its forelegs clawing the air. The beast, clearly terrified out of its mind, brought its hooves down squarely on Lillehammer, who was in the process of rising. He crashed into the side of the stall, the noise and confusion further panicking the stallion, whose hooves beat a steady tattoo on the creature that had attacked it.

Faith, rising to her feet, could smell the blood.

'Oh, Mr Dominic,' she said to the horse. 'Poor, poor frightened baby.'

The stallion, his eyes still rolling, caught the tone of her familiar voice. He turned his great head, his left eye staring at her. She continued her cooing sounds and he came down on his four legs, snorting, shaking his head. Like her, he did not care for the smell of blood.

She moved to the open doorway of the stall, reached up to stroke the place just above his nose. She put a cube of sugar in his mouth as she held on to him. He was quieting now, responding to her ministrations. It was only then she looked to her left, saw the red pulp that had been William Justice Lillehammer, crumpled against the stall wall.

'Ah, Mr Dominic,' she whispered, kissing the stallion, nuzzling it. 'Everything's all right now.'

'I'm afraid you're being a bit premature.'

She turned, knowing that voice, seeing the man she had spotted in Moon's homemade video. He was truly hideous now, seeming in real life less like the Johnny Leonforte she had known than he had in the video. Ironically, she thought he could have been seated next to her at a restaurant or the opera and she might never have recognized him. Unless she happened to be looking at him as the lights went down, and in the shadows and half-light the man he had once been had emerged, as he had in the video, part real, part memory.

'Hello, Johnny,' she said. 'You've come a long way since I saw you last.'

'We both have,' he said. 'And it's been a hard, painful journey.'

'For one of us, at least.'

Johnny Leonforte tried to smile, but the nerves on one side of his face didn't seem to work, and the result was grotesque.

'Your friend Okami cut me up real good,' he said, 'but I'm too tough to kill.' He moved slightly with the movement of the stallion. 'Really, Faith, I'd be much obliged if you'd move slowly out of the stall. Observing first-hand the rapport you have with these creatures, I see it was a mistake on Will's part to think he could maneuver you and them just right.' He kept moving. 'Besides, we don't want you getting your hands on Will's weaponry, do we?'

Faith, who had already thought of that, said, 'Mr Dominic is still agitated. I think it'd be best if I stayed here with him.'

Johnny took out a .357 Magnum. 'Where should I put the bullet, Faith; just below the horse's right ear?' He aimed at the stallion's head.

Faith broke her contact with the stallion, stepped out of the stall. 'All right,' she said. 'Now what?'

'Close the door to the stall,' Johnny said. 'We don't want to be disturbed.'

She did as he said, moved down the stables, away from the stallion.

'What are you doing?'

'I don't want any mistakes,' she said. 'I don't want you suddenly deciding to shoot Mr Dominic.'

Johnny made a grimace. 'Named after your not very dearly departed son, eh, Faith? Big mansion, stables, horses, more money and influence than you know what to do with. Jesus, what a life you've lived.'

She looked at him mutely.

'*It's* my *life you've been living, you queen bitch!*' The ferocity of his scream made her flinch. She could see all the rage and envy pent up over the years, swimming in his eyes like a school of ravenous sharks.

'You took everything away from me! You and that Jap sonuvabitch Okami. You schemed it all along! Fucking Goldoni, masquerading as Faith Sawhill. And I bought it. You threw your body at me and I took it!'

'It hurts, doesn't it,' Faith said, 'to know that in the end you were just a man – like all the rest of the men I've known. I opened my thighs at will, took a slab of your flesh in my mouth and everything I wanted followed as easily as saying "Open Sesame"!'

'I'm gonna fucking kill you!'

'*Now* you sound like the Johnny Leonforte I used to know,' she said as she backed down the stables away from his threat. 'Not the Red Queen, who conned all of Washington's mightiest minds. Speaking of influence, how many presidents did you manage to manipulate? Imagine! A Sicilian thug like you, an actor!' She laughed. 'Why do you hate me, Johnny? I did you the biggest favor of your life. You were born to the shadows and acting. Remember how bored you were with the business side of things? You even talked about me taking over the bookkeeping. Remember?'

'You took *life* away from me, Faith! Look at my face. I was handsome once. I had to change my name, undergo so many operations I lost count. And the pain! And then I had to hide myself away; yes, in the shadows but without a house, a family, the admiration of bluebloods, all the things I ever wanted in life. You took them all!' Johnny's face was so flushed it was as if she could see every venal emotion that drove him, crawling along his skin like maggots. He came after her, his shoulders hunched as if against the words she flung at him like knives.

She laughed again, a cruel edge coming into her tone. 'Nothing's changed, Johnny. I'm still doing your bookkeeping!'

'No! You and Okami and Dominic were intent on putting me out of business!'

'You made bad friends, Johnny, when you decided to play both ends against the middle. To the Feds you were the Red Queen, playing the deep-cover governmental spook, a hero to his country. But secretly you were running Looking-Glass toward your own ends, handpicking Mafia men, using your nephew, Caesare, to move them up the Family ranks until they became dons, beholden to him and to you. You were hero *and* villain, wrapped up in one unholy package.'

She was against the far wall now, and she moved to her left, her body blocking his vision of what hung there on the wall. 'And now you're doing it again with the Godaishu. You linked Looking-Glass up with the Godaishu to undermine the Feds, circumvent their laws and expand your network into business worldwide. Only this time, you're out of your league. Those boys in the Godaishu don't care one iota about you. You thought you and Caesare were going to remain their partners? Sorry to disillusion you. They were using you. You and Caesare were their meal ticket into all the restricted areas of America.'

She brushed the softness of the scarred leather with her back, and it comforted her. 'Think of it – the Mafia and the Government in an alliance. It was an irresistible combination to the Japanese Yakuza.' She moved her right hand, felt the leather with her fingers. 'But after the Godaishu was well established here, what do you imagine they'd do with you and Caesare?'

'I have protection against that possibility,' Johnny said. 'It was intelligence passed to me by a powerful source code-named –' He paused, then said, 'But why shouldn't I tell you now. What good will it do you? You'll soon be dead.' He tried to smile, and Faith shivered. 'My source is code-named Nishiki. His intelligence allowed me to rise in rank, to become the head of Looking-Glass.'

'Idiot,' Faith said. 'Nishiki is Mikio Okami. He only passed you intelligence that he and Dominic wanted you to have.'

'No! It can't be! You lying bitch!'

The Magnum came up, but Faith's hand had already drawn the old revolver out of the scarred leather holster – the Colt she used in case a horse went down with a broken leg.

She smelled the oil, felt the hickory grips solid against her palm. She leveled the barrel and fired, once, twice, the stench of cordite filling her nostrils as the revolver bucked in her hand.

Later, she would remember Johnny Leonforte's astonished expression, the stretched 'O' of his mouth, so like a little boy's. He staggered backward amid the rearing, stamping, whinnying horses, fell to his knees. Faith, in full possession of her wits, fired into his face, and he slammed backward onto the straw-covered plank floor.

'Not so hard to kill, after all,' she said, standing over him.

Just because you are supremely talented, Kansatsu had said, *does not mean that you are capable of fully* comprehending *that talent.*

440

Just how ironic he was being Nicholas could not appreciate until now.

A now that had perhaps been occurring over and over like ripples in a lake, expanding outward, affecting everything in its wake. A now that was as inevitable as taking another breath.

What had Seiko said to him at Narita airport in the last moment before he had flown to Venice, with something akin to panic in her eyes? *You will be different – so different that no one will recognize you.*

Yes. It was happening now.

Celeste, her heart beating fast at the knowledge of the Messulethe's approach, held his hand, but he could not feel it. All his senses were turned inward to make this one great leap of faith. He had to abandon everything Kansatsu had taught him. He had to have faith now – not in his training, not in those who had trained him, whether in good faith or in bad, but in his own innate talent.

He used *haragei* to center himself, to bring his breathing, his pulse, down to almost nil. The color drained out of his face, but Celeste did not utter a sound, though her heart skipped a beat. He had warned her.

Blood and energy pooled in *hara*, the center of intrinsic energy inside the body, as he returned himself to that moment in the cage when he and the Messulethe had been both physically and psychically linked, when the Messulethe, calling upon the help of the sacred white magpie, had summoned the opening of the Sixth Gate.

Nicholas had absorbed the incantation then, and now with the aid of *haragei*, he recalled it, pronouncing the strange syllables just as the Messulethe had done at the robot factory. The gate opened, and Nicholas, freed of Tau-tau altogether, entered the forbidden Sixth Gate.

'Dear God! He's here!'

'Margarite!'

But she was already running down the hall, throwing open the front door, disappearing outside as Croaker, taken by surprise, ran belatedly after her.

A hundred yards away, through the stands of trees, he saw the other woman, rising up as out of the ground itself, looking toward Margarite as she ran. Racing after Margarite, he could make out her features. The thick red hair, the oval face with its beautiful, aggressive features, and his own instinct, told him who this woman must be.

'Celeste!'

He could hear Margarite calling the woman's name and, a moment later, he saw the two sisters embracing.

There was no doubt in his mind that the red-headed Celeste must be the sister she had alluded to. He came upon them, still clinging to one another, in tears.

'Lew,' Margarite said, 'my sister Celeste has been with your friend Nicholas.'

'Nick! Where is he?'

And now he could see the despair in her eyes as she wiped the tears off her cheeks.

'Nick and Do Duc –'

'Which way?'

'Lew,' Margarite said, 'I have to go with you.'

'No!' Celeste cried. 'You don't know what the Messulethe's like, what he's done to Nick.'

'You don't know what he's done to me,' Margarite said quietly. 'Celeste, he murdered Dom.'

'Ah, God!' It was a quiet wail, but it stirred the hairs at the back of Croaker's neck. Celeste gripped her sister. 'All the more reason for you to stay away.'

But Margarite shook her head. 'He won't harm me. There is something unspoken that must be done.' She looked hard into her sister's beautiful face. 'You understand what I'm saying.'

Croaker was aware of a subtle shift in the light and he shivered. He saw Celeste nodding. Then she said, 'If you must . . . The two men are masked. This was Do Duc's doing. He has Nicholas's face and Nicholas has his. I think in some eerie way Do Duc wants to become Nicholas.'

'Let's go,' Croaker said to Margarite as Celeste indicated the direction in which the two men had set out. And to Celeste: 'There's a man named Tanzan Nangi in Nick's house. He's a friend. You can trust him with your life. Stay with him.'

Celeste nodded uncertainly, watching them as they headed toward the stand of bare ginkgo and what lay beyond.

How many sins had he committed in his lifetime? He could not say. Either he had lost count or he no longer recognized the definition of sin. Except one.

He had murdered Ao.

For the one secret that Ao, in his wisdom, would not divulge to his student: the incantation that would open the Sixth Gate. Ao, who had taken in a homeless, frightened boy, had accepted him when, perhaps, the other elders of the Nungs would have done otherwise. Ao, who had tutored him, initiating him into the magic of the Messulethe, who had made him privy to the power of the ages.

442

Perhaps, Do Duc thought as he struck out through the woods in pursuit of Nicholas, he had known he would sin in that singular, unforgivable way. How else to explain why he had chosen the sacred white magpie as his familiar. Had Ao an intimation of the future as well, at that moment? Do Duc could see his face, the astonishment etched upon it at his pupil's choice of the white magpie. Perhaps, in that moment, he scented his own death on the wind; perhaps the white magpie whispered it in his ear.

Ao, who had loved him, now dust.

Do Duc had pulled what he had wanted most from the depths of Ao's dreaming mind and then, taking his insensate form down to the river, had closed his eyes and pushed the head beneath the water. There had been nothing else to do. He had violated every code of the Nungs. He had invaded the mind of their head shaman and so was marked for death. He had had to kill Ao.

And, in the moment of Ao's spirit passing out of his ancient body, the sacred white magpie, alighting on Do Duc's shoulder, had spoken to him for the first time.

He stirred Ao's body in the muddy current. Immediately, there was a stirring from the far shore, and two crocodiles slithered into the river, swimming directly for him.

They hit the body almost simultaneously, tearing great strips of flesh from the carcass. The water began to boil and change color. It became viscous. And, as the beasts ate, Do Duc did as the white magpie directed him, and joined in the feast.

The sky had been quite clear, he remembered that. And the sweetness of the air − it had been like slipping from the birth canal, taking air into the lungs for the very first time.

Now, running up the small grassy knoll, he felt the weight on his shoulder, heard the white magpie speak to him again, whispering the path that Nicholas had taken.

He crested the knoll, saw the slope downward to the lake. On the far side, a pair of cranes, perhaps sensing some disturbance, lifted off from the glassy surface, took to the sky.

In that moment, Do Duc's nostrils flared and he turned back the way he had come, uncertain. He scented Margarite. Not her body, but her soul close to his and coming closer.

He crouched like a cornered animal, his spirit torn by utter despair and a love he could conceive of only in the form of a butcher's bloody knife rending him.

He saw her, breaking through the stand of tall ginkgo, catching sight of him, coming still, unafraid, terrifying him.

'Margarite,' he whispered.

He shivered as she came closer. 'I want,' he said. 'I want . . .'

'I know what you want,' Margarite said. She was so beautiful, framed by the high, white trees, the lowering sunlight caught in her eyes. 'I've always known.'

'You're the only one.'

His breathing was ragged, and he longed to tug the mask off him so that she could see his real face. But it didn't matter; he was naked before her as he had been all the time they had been on the road together, heading toward Minnesota, those days and nights he had never wanted to end.

She saw him – all of him – and she did not flinch or look away. She had seen clear through the beguiling mask he had donned for all his women. And, just as astonishing, the essence that had once been Do Duc – before all the deaths and the incantations and the sin – did not wither beneath her gaze.

'I knew the moment I met you that you would be the end of me,' he said. 'I saw you and somewhere deep inside I knew I could no longer go on being what I had spent my whole life becoming.' He felt himself beginning to lose control. He was battling emotions so clotted it felt like inhaling water. 'I have learned to kill so easily, but the thought of harming you is intolerable. I would rather destroy myself.'

'I know. We're inside one another.'

He was moving closer to her, wavering, the old and the newly birthed, half-formed, frightened thing inside him vying for control. 'At first, I thought I wanted you to fear me as everyone else fears me. But you wouldn't, fierce woman that you are. You defeated me, ended me, brought me down by piercing my armor, and now they're all around me, the baying hounds who will tear me apart.'

'It doesn't have to be that way.' She reached out a hand to him. 'It's over now. I can protect you, save you. If you'll come with –'

But in a forlorn flash he saw that he could never have her, that he would never again experience the inexpressible emotion he felt at this moment, and he made a snakelike lunge for her and was struck broadside by a great weight. He moaned as Margarite gave a sharp scream.

'No! Wait! I can –'

He crashed to the earth, dirt in his eyes and nose, rolling, the weight alternately crushing and releasing him. The proximity of Margarite blinded him. He wanted to call out to her, to reach for her, to tell her . . . He had been so close to taking her hand, to making contact in that moment when all things but her had ceased to have meaning for him. He was a stag caught in the headlights of a speeding car, in the wrong place at the wrong time.

444

Or perhaps not. Perhaps this was his time, the moment to choose between life and death. But how could he make that choice? Life was a desperate war to keep at bay those disenfranchised emotions he knew would destroy him, and death for a Messulethe was inconceivable.

He cried out as something needle-sharp pierced his flesh and, looking down, he saw a mechanical hand, the articulated alloy fingers surmounted by steel nails. With another cry, he pulled himself free, then kicked out once, twice, heard the heavy grunt, the thick body going down, and he drove his elbow into the midsection, pulling away, staggering a bit as he turned inward, his mind searching for Margarite.

But, as he had known, the moment was gone forever.

The man with his face came out of nowhere, struck him a blow close to the carotid artery in the side of his neck and, out of blind instinct, he countered with a sword-strike to the major nerve bundle just below the sternum.

Both men hit the water at once. In this part of the lake, the bank was steep, leading out onto a shallow strip perhaps two feet wide where the floor of the lake came up, so that the water level was shallow. From there, a precipitous fall-off brought them immediately into the deep water.

Nicholas, half paralyzed by Do Duc's sword-strike, went immediately for the head. He knew he needed a killing blow, but the water worked against them both, slowing them down, making traditional percussive *atemi* ineffectual.

Nicholas tightened his hold around Do Duc's head, began pressure with the heel of one hand against the spot where major nerve meridians converged. He drove his hand into Do Duc's upper lip and nose.

Locked together, their legs churning, they spun out of control, further and further into the lake. Darkness and light interspersed with air and water, until they found themselves in a kind of twilight world between the air and the land, aqueous, chill and darkening.

Do Duc, dizzying with the pressure on his face, struck again at Nicholas's sternum, took possession of his own hold as they flipped over, went down beneath the silver surface of the lake.

They fought each other, fought to keep sufficient air in their lungs, but their extreme exertions and the chill of the water were taking their toll.

They kicked out, but could no longer keep themselves afloat. Down they drifted into the chill, unnatural night, locked together. They seemed to be moving but Do Duc could not understand where. He was concentrating on his hold, the pressure he was putting on Nicholas's windpipe.

He felt Nicholas's hands scrabbling at his body, perhaps some pain,

445

but he exerted the power of his psyche, blocked out everything but the pressure he must maintain on the windpipe.

He could feel the pressure building in his ears as they sank, but he had no time for that. His mind was filled with red blood, with the magic of the Messulethe, and the one thought that he must rise out of this blackness to get to Margarite, who was waiting for him on the near bank.

Nicholas knew he was drowning. The fact was, they were both drowning, but he doubted now whether the Messulethe was even aware of that. He could feel the concentration of the Messulethe's mind like a dark star, dense with abnormal gravity and lethal emissions.

He had led the Messulethe here to the lake quite deliberately, for he knew what lay within its depths, what he had thrown there so many years ago when he and Justine were just starting out, full of love and hope. Now he must not only survive the assault on his mind and body, but he must move them closer, closer to what lay within the purling shadows of the lake bottom. He could feel it. He could . . .

Dimly, as if through the veil of dreams, his battered mind had picked up the Messulethe's breakdowns at the robot factory. He could hear his sobs like echoes, almost see the image of the woman who swam in his thoughts like a prehistoric beast. And now it had happened again, stronger this time, as if the icon had appeared in the flesh. He could, for the first time, sense all the muddled and compressed emotions coiled within the Messulethe's mind like a basketful of cobras.

He had been set to use the power he had found beyond the Sixth Gate, he had been fully prepared to blast the Messulethe with a fireball of psychic energy. And then they had come together and he had felt it all, burning there, like rubble from a disaster.

It had made him hesitate, compassion momentarily overcoming his rage for revenge. And now he was paying for that hesitation. He was drowning.

He looked inward, opening his tanjian eye, stepping through the Sixth Gate, ready now to summon the power to break away from this demon and destroy him. But he found the essence of the Messulethe already there, inside the gate, at the same place, and all either of them could do was to block the other's access.

Stalemate.

Deeper into the lake they sank, Nicholas kicking out at regular intervals, propelling them further toward the center until, during one of their slow revolutions, he saw the vague humped shadows of the lake bottom. He prayed as he kicked out, prayed that he had calculated correctly because he had only one chance now for life, one chance to keep the water out of his nose and throat, keep it from filling his lungs, all the breath going out of him, the end.

And there it was.

Illuminated by pale light like the ghostly finger of God was the tip of the samurai's *dai-katana* his father, the Colonel, had given him. Its name, *Iss-hogai*, meant For Life.

His eyes began to roll up and darkness began to flicker at the periphery of his vision. He kicked out with his legs, propelling them toward the long keen blade of the sword which he had thrown into the lake, thinking never again to need it. The heavy hilt had struck the lake bottom, embedding itself into the soft silt, and now there it was, the blade shooting up at an angle from the lake bed.

Do Duc, sensing Nicholas's weakness, tightened his hold, and now Nicholas did not believe he would have the energy to get them the last six feet to the tip of the blade. His hands moved upward, clamping onto Do Duc's face – *his* face. His fingertips sought the edge of the mask, finding it. He dug his nails into the adhesive, getting purchase, lifting a minute strip of it, breaking the seal. The lake water soaked the adhesive, and he lifted more of the mask away from the Messulethe's face.

He moved it, so that the acrylic resin slipped across the Messulethe's nostrils and mouth, covered his eyes. The Messulethe reacted and, as he did so, Nicholas drove his legs in a powerful scissor kick.

They rolled, and for a moment Nicholas was dangerously close to the blade point. Then their momentum rolled them again, and the Messulethe's back was coming up on the point.

Nicholas drove his legs one more time, beating them down toward the lake bed. He saw – and felt – it happen all at once. There was no expression he could see on the Messulethe's face, hidden as it was beneath the grotesquely twisted mask, but the point of the *dai-katana*'s long blade popped through the Messulethe's breastbone, piercing him all the way through.

The Messulethe's legs kicked and churned, the muscles spasming as clouds of filmy blood drifted upward like kites upon a summer's breeze.

Nicholas pressed downward, the blade rising upward as if itself alive, eager to rend flesh and bone. He felt the pressure come off his windpipe, and dizzy with lack of oxygen, he immediately struck upward for the surface.

But he did not move.

He looked down, saw the Messulethe's hand gripped tightly around his left ankle. He tried to jackknife his body, in order to reach the death grip, but the angle was so acute it took all his energy just to get his fingers on the Messulethe's. Then he found he could not release the grip.

So Nicholas hung there, exhausted, staring into the leering face, at the blue crescent tattooed on the inside of the powerful wrist, and into his mind blew the last, scattered memories of his antagonist . . .

. . . the river in the jungle, sunlight filtering through the triple-canopied trees, heat and a black leopard speaking runic promises and portents . . . an old man, his face weathered by time and magic, and the blue-white bloat of death . . . crocodiles lazily swinging their tails in the hot sun, jaws opening to feed . . . the taste of a man's brain . . . a white magpie screaming in triumph as it rises, burning, into a copper sun . . .

Hung there, dying slowly with the Messulethe, whose deteriorating mind shed ardent thoughts like bubbles rising to the roof of this aqueous graveyard.

. . . incantations of the earth and the air . . . and a beautiful dark-haired, amber-eyed woman . . . Margarite, I want to tell you . . . magnificent in your terrible beauty . . . tell you that I . . . like Circe . . . that I . . . more powerful even than Gim, the Blue Crescent, all the ancient rituals of the Messulethe . . . I can't touch you . . . this is all that is left me . . . in this one moment . . . that I love . . .

And then Nicholas was alone in the utter silence and stillness of the deep.

Time seemed to have come to a halt; even his heartbeat seemed to flicker and slow. Blood turning to ice. And then, through the darkness of near-death, he felt a stirring of a current against his cold cheek. His head turned slowly, wearily. He thought he saw a shape emerging from the dimness, saw a man approaching, his cheeks puffed out as he held air in his lungs.

Air!

He blinked. It was Croaker, swimming quickly and efficiently, cutting through the water. His hand was extended as if in greeting – the bio-mechanical hand of stainless steel, titanium and polycarbonate, the replacement for the one he had lost helping Nicholas. Nicholas had never forgiven himself for being the cause of his friend's disfigurement – though Croaker had himself forgiven him. And now here Croaker was, offering that hand. Nicholas wanted to take it in his, in friendship, ready at last to forgive himself.

He watched in a haze as Croaker's hand took the Messulethe's fingers and, bending them back one by one, snapped the joints, broke the death grip.

Croaker grabbed him around the waist and, kicking powerfully upward, brought them both through the increasingly paler layers of twilight, out of the icy night, out of the graveyard, to the surface and the last light of day.

448

EPILOGUE: NEW YEAR'S DAY

Ah! To be
A child —
On New Year's Day!

Issa

Tokyo

With an ear-rattling rumble, the 747 jumbo took off, leaving behind it an ashy cloud that clung to the air like gauze to a wound. Through it, the bloated sun was stained the color of dried blood.

'I want you to know something,' Margarite said. Her amber eyes were leveled on Croaker. 'If I never see you again I'll shrivel up and die.'

'Maybe you really are the siren Do Duc thought you were.' He smiled, trying to make light of it, but she swung her head away.

'I felt it when he died,' she whispered. 'I felt him call my name.'

'Why did he do it, Margarite? Murder Dom, all the others?'

'I think it's all he knew,' she said. 'To him life was death. There was nothing else. He was just trying to survive.'

'Poor bastard.'

'I wonder,' she said, raising her voice as another jumbo roared down the runway, 'what he would have done if you and Nicholas had let him grab me?'

'Who knows?' Croaker said. 'But my guess is even he didn't want to know. He made the move to provoke us because there was no other way out for him. He said the hounds were out for him and he was right.'

She turned back toward him, and he could tell by the look in her eyes that she wanted to put the topic of Do Duc to rest.

'I meant what I said before.'

'I know you did,' Croaker said. 'But I also know where you're going now – back to Tony D.' He paused for a moment, as if he did not want to go on. 'It would help if you gave me the procedure for contacting Nishiki.'

Margarite shook her head. 'That was Dom's only legacy, the perpetuation of all his power. I won't jeopardize it – even for you.' She gave him a desolate smile. 'Business,' she said, taking his face in her hands. She kissed him hard on the lips, and he held on long enough to taste her tears.

'Come home soon,' she said when at last she broke away. 'Francie will already have begun to miss you.' She hefted her bag. 'Will you walk me to the gate?'

451

He looked at her. 'I've come as far as I can, Margarite. It's farther than I ever thought I would go.'

She nodded, turned away toward the terminal. A moment later, she looked back at him over her shoulder. 'When will you come home?'

'When this is over,' he said. 'When I can.'

'And then?'

'It's up to fate, isn't it?'

She seemed uncertain for a moment, then she smiled. 'For the moment, at least, I suppose it is.'

'I should never have thrown it away,' Nicholas said. 'That was an act of arrogance, like a slap in my father's face.'

Behind him, on the wall of the living-room, *Iss-hogai*, the great *dai-katana*, was hung in its temporary leather scabbard. A new one, of hand-made lacquer, tooled silver and cured manta-ray skin, was being made for him in the traditional manner by a man of ninety years who Nicholas had known for some time.

'This place wasn't the same without it,' Croaker said. There was a silence for a time. He looked from the long sword to the pair of armatures Nicholas had made himself to display Do Duc's two masks. It had seemed grotesque at first that Nicholas should want to keep these grisly reminders of a man who had almost killed him. But then, as he had learned from Margarite, nothing was ever so cut and dried in life; evil as well as good wore many different faces.

At last, he said, 'Have you gone to the grave?'

Nicholas knew he meant Justine's grave. 'Not yet,' he said. 'It will take some time before I can reconcile her death in my mind. I don't want to go there until that's settled, until there's a kind of peace between us.' He put his hands together. 'There's still part of her spirit here, restless. I feel her every morning at dawn when I wake up to do my exercises. I think she needs to be free of this place, Lew.'

Croaker nodded, understanding. 'Give it time, Nick,' he said, and sighed deeply. 'At least Senator Bane's no longer a force to deal with. When the Red Queen died his power base collapsed. It wasn't difficult for Faith Goldoni to get those who had feared him to join his enemies in denouncing him.'

'But the Godaishu still lives,' Nicholas said. 'And whatever we've accomplished, I have a premonition we've so far only scratched the surface. Where is Okami? What happened to him? Nangi is convinced he's still alive. Certainly, the threat to him still exists – and now there are some hard questions he needs to answer.'

Outside, there was snow on the ground. Tomorrow it would be New Year's Day, a time of renewal, when all things were possible.

'What I'd like to know,' Croaker said, 'is what Okami and Dominic Goldoni were up to.'

'We only have to follow this maze far enough,' Nicholas said.

'If we can get that far.'

'I'll start with Tetsuo Akinaga, Akira Chosa and Tomoo Kozo, the three *oyabun* in the Kaisho's inner council. One of them is responsible for plotting his death. And then there's Avalon Ltd. They're suppliers of every kind of war matériel you can name. It's relatively easy to buy Chinese and Russian weapons, but they also have access to American F-15 jet fighters.'

'Waxman – the Red Queen – would have been able to provide that access,' Croaker said.

Nicholas nodded. 'True. I just hope he's the only one who did.'

Croaker poured himself some coffee from an insulated pot. 'Why do you think Dominic gave Do Duc your name as Nishiki's identity?'

Nicholas shrugged. 'Who can say? Maybe Okami led Dominic to believe I was Nishiki in the event of the kind of disaster that actually occurred. Okami knew I'd be the only one who'd be able to stop Do Duc.'

Nicholas looked out the windows at the deep snow. The silence of winter had stolen over the countryside like fog obscuring the stars.

'Right now what worries me most is Torch 315, the codeword I found embedded in the Avalon software in Paris.'

'I've been thinking about it ever since you mentioned it,' Croaker said. 'I'd bet the farm it's some kind of experimental weapon they're trying to get their hands on. If that's so, it's better than even money it's one of ours. I'll check that out.'

Nicholas was silent for some time. 'I agree that's the most likely possibility,' he said. 'But there's another one we dare not ignore.' He tapped his fingertips together thoughtfully. 'What if 315 isn't a number but a deadline?' he said. 'That would be two and a half months from now. Ides of March.'

Nicholas shook his head ruefully. 'If only Okami were here. I have a feeling he'd be able to tell us what Torch 315 was.'

'Nangi seems to think Okami's been trying to give us clues to follow.'

'Right. Avalon Ltd. And then there's this international arms dealer, Timothy Delacroix, who Harley Gaunt mentioned in the material that Manny Mannheim delivered. According to Harley, Delacroix claimed that Sato was one of his suppliers. That means the late Vincent Tinh was one of his suppliers.'

The two men stared at each other, and the look they exchanged brought no words to mind, only memories.

'You put Margarite on the plane?' Nicholas asked.

'Late yesterday evening.'

He looked at Croaker. 'Sure you made the right choice?'

'Not in the least.' Croaker grinned at him, but it felt false and he put it away. 'I can't let her walk out of my life, Nick, but what else was I supposed to do? I'm a cop, for Christ's sake. I've always worked the right side of the law.'

'Are you certain she's on the wrong side?'

Croaker looked at his friend, astonished. 'What are you talking about?'

'This is one hell of a woman, Lew.'

'She's the fucking Mafia, buddy.'

Nicholas, his hands laced in front of him, said softly, 'Mikio Okami is Kaisho of all the Yakuza. Two months ago, I would have cheerfully turned him in if I'd been given even half a chance. Now I can't be that certain of things.' He looked from the snowy landscape outside to his friend's bleak face. 'Let me ask you a question, Lew. Is Margarite an amoral person?'

'I –' Croaker stopped, not knowing what he was going to say. In what gray landscape did the truth lie?

'We all wear masks,' Nicholas said, 'to hide what is most important to us.'

There was a silence again, and the two men heard the hushed crunch of footfalls from outside. Nicholas stirred and said, 'You know what you're going to have to do.'

'Yeah. Nangi and Faith Goldoni are convinced that Okami is Nishiki. If that's the case, Margarite is going to know how to contact him. Even the indirect route he set up with Dominic Goldoni will be better than what we have now, which is nothing.'

Croaker sloshed the coffee around in the ceramic mug. 'What if they're wrong? What if Okami isn't Nishiki?'

'We still have to try to find Okami. Are you up to it?'

Croaker examined his bio-mechanical hand as if he'd never seen it before. He knew what he was being asked to do: spy on Margarite long enough so that he could follow the elaborate chain of cut-outs back to the source: Nishiki. 'I love her, Nick. But we both know the rules. We know who we are and what roads we've chosen to travel.' He looked into his friend's dark eyes. 'It isn't simple, but it's all either of us has.'

The front door opened, then closed softly, and Croaker rose, went toward the kitchen. 'Dinner in an hour?'

'Fine,' Nicholas said, grabbing his Thinsulate jacket. 'Don't bother cleaning up. Sashiko will be in first thing in the morning.'

Celeste was waiting for him in the hallway. She silently watched him

454

put on his boots, then slipped her fingers through his as they went out into the twilight.

Blue shadows lay everywhere. Beneath a cedar, wreathed in snow and its copper-fringed winter coat, he could see rabbit tracks, a bright blur of fur bounding swiftly into the underbrush.

They went through the stand of ghostly ginkgo, up the small knoll, and then down toward the lake. It was almost all frozen over, bright patches of ice like stained glass.

'In the spring,' Nicholas said, 'I'll take a dive.'

'Are you afraid he won't be there?'

'No. But his soul needs company. It never had any during life.'

Celeste squeezed his hand in hers. 'This man was a cold-blooded killer. I can't understand your attitude toward him – or my sister's.'

'Then I can't explain it.'

'Neither could she. It's just as well.'

They turned back, went up to the crest of the knoll. From here they could see across to the other side of the lake, to houses huddled together as if for warmth. A dog barked while men worked assiduously pruning trees into knobby, precise globes. The Japanese, Celeste had learned in her short time here, did not like to leave anything to chance.

'What about *koryoku*, the Illuminating Power?' Celeste asked. 'Do you still think it's so important?'

'I'm planning to ask Okami that when I see him,' Nicholas said. 'But, yes, I think it's more important than ever.' He had been thinking of the gift he had found beyond the Sixth Gate. Perhaps this was why he felt so close to Do Duc. Do Duc had given Nicholas and Margarite very precious things which had changed both their lives. The power beyond the Sixth Gate was still by and large a mystery; what it would portend Nicholas could not yet say, except that, as Seiko had predicted, he was no longer the same.

He broke his train of thought, looked at her. 'You didn't leave with your sister.'

'We're two different kinds of Goldonis,' Celeste said. 'I need to find Okami before memory and obligation can be laid to rest.' A wind off the lake caught her hair as she shook her head. 'Besides, I could never live in America. I'd miss the water and the light – the weight of Venice, the significance of history. Now, in winter, all the beautiful colors are muted by cloud and rain, until that magical moment in late afternoon when a thick shaft of sunlight breaks through, turning the *piazze* to Byzantine gold.' Her eyes had a faraway look. 'Soon, it will be time for the Carnival, and the masks will be born again.'

In silence, they began to walk slowly back to the house.

455

In time, Celeste said, 'I know you're angry with me.'

'Am I?'

'Yes. You think I should have told you in the beginning that I was a Goldoni. But the truth is, Nicholas, that I doubt you would have trusted me had you known. Okami knew your personality, and he warned me to keep my true identity hidden from you.'

'Mikio Okami continues to haunt me like a specter,' Nicholas said. 'His *bête noire* – the mastermind of the Godaishu – has become mine.'

They paused at the front porch to stamp the snow off their boots. Nicholas opened the front door and they took off their footwear.

'Please don't be angry with me,' she said. 'It hurts too much.'

Shadows in the night. The moonlight, sliced into pieces by the bamboo, swept across Nicholas as he lay on his futon. He should have been asleep hours ago, but his body betrayed him, vibrating in blood and heat, wanting the woman in the next bedroom.

He knew he should get up, go and lie down beside her. He knew that was what she wanted – what they both wanted – but he felt paralyzed.

Images of Justine haunted his mind. He knew – not because anyone had told him, but because he simply *felt* it like moss upon a rock too long without sunlight – that she had died because he hadn't been there to protect her. And if they had grown apart in the last years, if in fact their love had not survived, he knew that this, too, was his doing – his and Japan's.

He heard a small sound as the *shoji* – the rice-paper screen – to his bedroom was slowly drawn back in its track. He saw a shadow stepping lightly and without any sound into the room. It avoided the slivers of moonlight, keeping to the deep shadows in the corners of the room.

It stood very still for a moment, watching him. Then, like a wraith, it shed its kimono and, with a soft sigh, slid beneath the covers of the futon. He smelled Celeste's scent, as exciting as he remembered it in Venice and Paris. Whatever happened from this time forward, he knew that he would always remember her in that first electric moment, masked in the *schola cantorum* of the Church of San Belisario, robed in enigma and power, the currencies of Venice.

'I can't be her.'

'I so much don't want you to be,' Nicholas said.

'Do you mean that?'

'Look inside me.'

'I don't want to do that with you – ever.'

This was one of the things he loved about her. 'I see only you when I look at you.'

She sighed again, but this time it was because he had enfolded her in his arms. His lips came down over hers, and he found them trembling as they opened, as her tongue twined with his. And then it was all right, their bodies melting together as if they had been made for each other.

At dawn, Nicholas arose. He did not want to leave Celeste, but his body and mind needed to flex. It was New Year's Day. Outside, another snow, silent and deep, was coming down, obscuring all but the large trees nearest the house.

Nicholas meditated, feeling more at peace than he had since Nangi had told him about Justine's death. He breathed deeply, in and out, in and out. *Prana.* He knew she didn't mind Celeste being here, would have welcomed the attachment had she still been alive. Where would she have been now, in that event? What would have made her happy? Breathe in and out. That was the saddest part, he thought, that he had lost touch with all the things that made her happy.

Part of him became aware of the *shoji* being slid quietly back, but he paid it no attention. Sashiko came early on holidays, went about her business, and left by noon to be with her family.

A drawer was opened as she got out her cleaning implements. One, two, the tiny steps the small woman took, and Nicholas twisted up and to the left as a voice whispered in his mind, using its own momentum to pull the figure over and down.

It landed flat on its back, the wig coming off, the kimono parting, the blade of the *wakizashi* gleaming wickedly. Recognition was instantaneous. Tomoo Kozo's visage blossomed from the photographs Celeste had shown him in Venice.

He tried a sword-strike, but he was at a disadvantage, sitting with his legs crossed, and Kozo was suddenly inside his defense, the point of the long knife just inches from his throat, and by the fixed glare of hatred in the *oyabun*'s eyes he knew he had no choice at all.

He drove the stiffened tips of his fingers in a killing blow, into the soft spot just below Kozo's sternum, tearing through skin, flesh and viscera, to the hot, beating heart.

He stared into Tomoo Kozo's face as the life left it, listening intently for foreign sounds within the house. Then he searched for the voice in his mind, but he knew that Justine – if it had been Justine – had spoken for the last time.

He relaxed his vigilance. But not for long, he knew. So it had already begun. The Kaisho's inner council was moving against him. But he was

457

still alive. And somewhere, too, Mikio Okami – his charge, his quarry –
was alive, pulling the strings in a still unknown shadow dance.

Nicholas breathed, in, out, feeling the excess adrenalin bubbling in his
veins as it drained away.

Once again, he was so close to death he could taste its peculiar taint
in his mouth. Covered in another man's blood, he steeped himself in the
silence of the snow, bowed his head, greeting New Year's Day with a prayer.

Nicholas Linnear pursues his extraordinary quest
in Eric Lustbader's magnificent new novel *Floating City*,
to be published by HarperCollins in 1994

Shan Plateau, Burma

AUTUMN 1983

It was said that they called him Wild Boy because he had seen every Tarzan film, knew every Tarzan's name from Elmo Lincoln onward. He had his favorites, of course, but he claimed to love them all.

They – that is, the mountain tribes of the Shan – had no reason to disbelieve him, since Tarzan films were the rage in the towns below, in the foothills, lucky enough to have a projector, and able to rent films flown in from Bangkok.

Truth to tell, the Shan who knew Rock – which is to say all of them who were involved in the growing, harvesting, refining, selling and shipping of the tears of the poppy – called him Wild Boy because they had seen him screw together his custom-made rocket launcher, slap it over his right shoulder, and blow the enemy into kingdom come.

Over the years, one opium warlord after the other had tried to kill Rock, but Wild Boy had been, in his own words, born and raised on rock 'n' roll and war. He was a veteran of Vietnam, in charge, at the war's height, of recruiting CIDGs – Civilian Irregular Defense Groups – from the Wa, the Lu, the Lisu, the mountain tribes of Burma, and from the Mekong Delta-born Cambodians to fight the Viet Cong.

He was one of those rare blood-soaked demons who found that he could not do without the proximity of death. He loved everything about it: the smell of it, the cessation of hearts and spirits it caused, the noise of it, and the stealth required to achieve it. But he loved, most of all, the contentment it brought him, the softening of the hard edges of his mind which, like diamond blades, sought to chop his reality into incomprehensible pieces.

He was not one of the casualties of the war who returned home, their

1

heads filled with ARVNs and helicopters and a tide of burst bodies and running blood so high they could never climb out the Pit. The Pit was Asia, and they had been in it up to their eyeballs.

So had Rock, but the difference was he revelled in it. Because he emerged from the war, for the first time in his life, with a purpose. And that purpose had led him here, to the Shan Plateau, the metaphorical apex of the Golden Triangle, the area where China, Burma and Thailand came together, where the altitude, the weather and the soil were ideal for the growing of poppies.

Rock not only accepted the attempts on his life, he welcomed them. He rightly saw in them not merely a macho test of his skills, but a path to his own acceptance up here in the rarefied air of the Shan Plateau. And he knew these people well enough to understand that without acceptance he would be forever adrift, a kind of jungle wraith, no better than a beggar really, making his living going from warlord to warlord, selling his own particular brand of death. Besides, in their eyes, he was a Western barbarian.

Without accepting him, the Shan would never trust him. And without their trust, Rock knew, he would never get rich. Rock wanted very badly to be rich. It was the only thing that mattered to him, save the manufacture, subtle or swift, of death.

In the end, he defeated everything they sent at him, defying General Vinh's public threat that 'Your agony will live forever'.

It was General Vinh, opium warlord of the Shan Plateau, who, over the past five years, had systematically murdered his rival warlords – all Chinese – and who now had a monopoly on the richest and most productive poppy fields in the world. As a Vietnamese, General Diep Nim Vinh was better supplied – officially, chiefly from Saigon – than his rivals, who were obliged to barter inferior arms from itinerant Soviet black marketeers.

A goddamn Vietnamese, Rock had thought, that's who I've got to deal with here. Who said the war was over?

Rock was on his way down the mountainside. He had been waiting for the money that had been promised him, but it had never come. Now he was on his way to Rangoon to telex his partner. He had to know how long the delay was going to be.

He had stumbled across Mai, who was lying along a path with a wooden cart overturned on her leg. It was the animal pulling the cart, however, whose leg was broken.

Even Rock, with his acute sense of paranoia, had to admit that Mai was irresistible, with her golden, glowing skin, her long, lithe legs, her huge eyes and her firm, hard-nippled breasts.

2

Rock had shot the animal to put it out of its misery, and then, after righting the cart and seeing to Mai, he had expertly skinned it, quartered its flesh, scraped down the bones.

Wild Boy had become like every Asian – he never let anything go to waste. In fact, it was safe to say that he thought of himself as Asian. He might once have been American, but now nationality had ceased to mean anything to him. Every so often he would finger the metal dog-tags that still hung around his neck, as if, like jade to the Chinese, they were a powerful talisman. But he never looked at them. He was Rock, the Wild Boy, a state, a country, a law unto himself.

He loaded everything – the meat, the skin, the bones (for soup), the girl – into the cart. When he lifted her up, her long nails gently scratched his skin. The sapphire in the lobe of her left ear sparked in the sunlight.

Rock pulled the loaded cart himself seven miles to his temporary camp. Though he had been on the Plateau for three years, he did not yet have a permanent home; that luxury would only come in time, a perquisite of acceptance and trust. For the present, however, he needed to make it difficult for the assassins to find him; it was part of the game, yet another demonstration of his skill.

Mai told him that she came from a farming village high in the mountains, 'at the top of the world', as she put it. By which she meant amid the poppy fields.

He could see that look in her eyes. He recognized it because he had seen it many times before throughout Southeast Asia, and because he was so attuned to the Asian mind. It was his size. He was six-foot-two. In the States that was medium tall; here in Asia it was gigantic. Rock laughed to himself. He could see right into her mind. She was wondering if all of him was that big. Soon she would find out.

While she tended to the deep purple bruise on her leg, Rock made dinner – a stew utilizing the fresh meat he had brought back. When the pot was simmering, he set about scraping the inside of the hide to prepare it for tanning. While he worked, he wondered about her long nails, something one would never see on a farm girl. His sixth sense – what the Japanese, under whom he had studied hand-to-hand combat, called *haragei*, the divine energy – began to flood his mind with the clarity of insight.

When he looked up, he saw Mai standing naked just outside the flap of his tent. He stared at her, thinking, This one is special. His hands and forearms were covered with blood. He could feel himself getting hard. It had been some time since he had been with a woman, but, seeing Mai, he knew that it wouldn't have mattered if he had had sex an hour ago – he would still be hard.

3

He dropped his enormous Marine combat knife onto the red underside of the skin, and stood up. He saw Mai's gaze lower from his face to the place between his legs. He stood out a country mile. Then she turned, and went inside the tent. Rock followed her, bent over slightly from the fierceness of his erection.

Inside, she was kneeling in the dimness. She beckoned him on, then held her cupped palms in front of her breasts. Rock unbuckled his belt, and she did the rest. She held him tenderly in both hands.

Her head bent, the cascade of her lustrous hair fanned his naked thighs, the flutter of a night bird's wing. She touched him first with the tip of her tongue, then laved him with the flat of it. At length, she used her lips.

When she engulfed him, as he watched with slitted eyes her cheeks hollow, Rock had that flash of insight that the Shan call the Ruby. He knew by her skill and her expertise who she must be. He knew where she had come from, and who had sent her. He knew what he must do.

She sucked slavishly at him. One hand gently squeezed his scrotum, the other snaked between his thighs to probe his other opening.

Rock bent over and, encircling Mai's tiny waist, slowly inverted her until her breasts pressed against his lower belly, her thighs resting on his shoulders. He felt as vibration her moan as he plunged his face into her humid mount.

She tasted of mango and spice. He tongued her while her loins tensed expectantly, then all through the spasms caused by her contracting muscles. And again.

She sucked all the harder, moaning for him to come. Rock put her on the floor of the tent, and entered her. It was not easy. He was very big, and she was not. But, gradually, she accustomed her engorged flesh to his.

Rock began to stroke long and hard, feeling her thrusting up on him with what seemed genuine desire. Even as his eyes began to glaze, he was in touch with *haragei*, connected with the treachery and deceit spun like a web around him.

He was about to come, and he let her know it, grunting and thrusting even harder. Felt her lifting her right hand from his shoulder where it had been gripping him with sweaty abandon. Saw, out of the corner of his eye, a bright gleam, like a darning needle, the metal jacket fitted over one long nail, its tip dark and lustrous with poison.

He grabbed for her hand, but he misjudged her quickness, or his willpower was not quite strong enough, and he began to ejaculate into her. He lost his hold on her wrist, saw the nail, curved like a scorpion's tail, blurring in toward the side of his neck and his carotid, knew he'd be dead within seconds.

4

Devoid of conscious thought, afloat in the void of *haragei*, he smashed his elbow into her face, feeling with some satisfaction the crack of bone, feeling the heat of her inner tissue, the smell of her blood like a rose bursting open.

Then he had her right wrist and, taking hold of her forefinger, he plunged the poisoned nail into her solar plexus.

The next morning, he made the steep, grueling ascent into General Vinh's territory. It had rained during the night, and the day was hot, unusual at this high elevation. Rock was sweating by the time he sighted the first of General Vinh's patrols.

He put down his bundles, set himself against the bole of a tree, and ate a piece of dried fish in the cool shade. He took some water from his canteen. When he was finished, he set about making a fire, hanging up his stew pot. He poured the contents of one of his bundles into the pot.

By that time, General Vinh's patrol had spotted the smoke from his fire. They were coming, AK-47s at the ready. There were five of them, he saw. Perfect. He began to whistle the Doors' 'Light My Fire'.

Wild Boy got out his rocket launcher, fitted the pieces together. When the patrol was in range, he loaded, fired, taking three of them out in a brilliant blaze.

'Get me General Vinh!' he yelled in their peculiar dialect. 'Tell him Wild Boy wants to see him.'

The remaining two soldiers scrambled away, and Rock settled down to wait. An hour later, they were back with someone of some rank. The two Shan kept their distance.

'Who are you,' the commander said, 'to demand General Vinh leave his compound?'

It was a matter of face, Rock knew. In Asia, it was always a matter of face. The man who forgot that, or thought he could circumvent it, would never survive in this part of the world.

'I am Wild Boy,' Rock said, hefting his rocket launcher. 'I demand nothing. I requested an audience with General Vinh. I am a courteous man. To demand is to act the barbarian.'

The commander, who had heard of Wild Boy, was, nevertheless, impressed by this speech. He grunted. 'The General may grant you an audience,' he said, 'if some concessions are made. For instance, recompense must be made for the three men you killed.'

'An unfortunate mistake,' Rock said. 'I was merely attempting to defend myself.'

5

'General Vinh will not accept this explanation. There are now three families who will go hungry.'

'I will pay so that they will not go hungry,' Rock said, knowing the drill.

'Do you have gifts for General Vinh?'

'Certainly,' Rock said. 'Only a barbarian or a witless man would come empty-handed to an audience with the emperor of the Shan.'

Thus mollified, the commander waved Rock upward. Rock packed his gear with great care. He made a show of breaking down his rocket launcher, stowing it away, to further allay whatever fears the commander might still harbor.

The commander led the way, the two soldiers flanking Rock on either side. He had no fear of them at all. He was now under the benevolent protection of General Vinh. If the patrol were attacked at this moment, the men were bound to safeguard him at the expense of their own lives.

General Vinh's compound was bristling with armed men when the patrol arrived. It seemed as if every available man had been ordered to be in attendance at Rock's arrival. This rather primitive display of territorial superiority impressed Rock. It meant that he was being taken seriously. That boded well for the interview.

General Vinh had been dispatched to Shan five years ago to begin to funnel the fabulously rich vein of illegal commerce to be had here in the direction of his terribly impoverished country. He knew he had more to fear from the Chinese opium warlord then in control of the Shan Plateau than he did from the pitiful attempts by the ragtag Burmese army to clean up an area essentially impossible to police.

He was not to be seen when the commander ushered Rock into the main building. Rock was left alone, with not even a young girl to serve him tea. This was quite deliberate on the General's part, since it further displayed his superior position.

An hour later, a young woman did enter. She was quite beautiful. She averted her gaze from Rock's, and knelt before a blackened hole in the floor across which was an iron post, and, gathering dry twigs into a cone, started a fire. Carefully, she placed three hardwood logs across the flames. Then she rose and left.

Another half-hour passed, during which time Rock heard nothing but the dogs barking outside, and orders being shouted by the commander who had left him here or, possibly, other commanders.

General Vinh arrived in a flourish. He wore tanned leather breeches, and a rough muslin shirt over which he sported a goatskin American military

6

flight jacket with a Fourteenth Air Force patch on the right sleeve. Unlike the other Shan warlords Rock had met, he wore no jewelry save a necklace of rubies and sapphires, the largesse of the Burmese lowlands. He was attended by two Shan bodyguards armed with machine pistols.

The young woman re-entered with an iron kettle and a pair of earthenware cups on a lacquer tray. She hung the kettle on the iron post over the fire. Tea was served – hot, thick and sweet, in the Thai tradition. It was quite bracing. Rock hadn't had decent tea in months, and he took his time, savoring it.

At length, he said, 'I have agreed to make recompense for the disagreeable incident this morning. Of course I was at fault, and I wish to make amends to the families of those unfortunately dead.'

General Vinh considered this. His commander had already reported as much to him, of course, but he was gratified to see that this Wild Boy had decent manners, after all. Not that his civilized comportment would stop General Vinh from having this foreign devil killed. He had become far too dangerous to be allowed to remain in the Shan States.

General Vinh could see the greed in the foreign devil's eyes as easily as he could feel the slime on a slug. Wild Boy wanted a piece of the tears of the poppy – what else would bring a foreign devil all the way up here, an interdicted area as far as the Burmese Government was concerned?

Huh, his *wa* is not so strong as the stories tell, General Vinh thought as he eyed the giant from over the rim of his teacup. Now that I have him here, I will humiliate him for the loss of face he has caused me among my men. Then I will bury him up to his thick neck, and let the ants and the sun take care of him.

The only possible cloud on his horizon was Mai. Where was she? And why had she not killed this foreign devil, as she had been ordered to do? Perhaps, the General mused, she had not yet devised a clever way of meeting him. Then, unbidden, the thought arose, as black and ugly as dung, that something had befallen Mai. Perhaps she had been hurt in the jungle, or again kidnapped by one of General Vinh's many enemies. His scrotum contracted painfully at the thought. What would he do without his precious Mai? She was his talisman; everything good that had happened to him occurred while she was with him.

General Vinh smiled at Rock. 'More tea, perhaps?'

Rock nodded. 'Thank you for your hospitality,' he said, bowing. 'I am unworthy of such munificence.' As he watched the beautiful young woman pour, he wondered whether this one might be Mai's sister. For as sure as he was sitting here now, Rock knew that Mai belonged to General Vinh.

From his longtime contacts among the Wa, the Lu and the Lisu, he had heard the jungle rumors about her prowess in effecting, as the Chinese termed it, the clouds and the rain, eliciting spectacular orgasms from her lover. But he had treated them as just that – rumors that picked up embellishments from each mouth that passed them on. Until Mai had taken him between her lips. Then he knew – the Ruby had told him with a certainty impossible to ignore.

When they had finished their second cup of tea, Rock said, 'In addition to the recompense for the grieving families, I have brought the General a special present.' He began to unpack his stew pot and sacks. General Vinh's men reacted by lowering the muzzles of their machine pistols.

'Food!' Rock cried, laughing, as he ladled the stew into the pot, hung it over the fire. 'Food fit for the gods themselves!'

The General watched the proceedings with a jaundiced eye. 'I have been paid in rubies, sapphires, jade and gold,' he said. 'But never with a meal.' He was not displeased, however. Good food was one of his passions, as Rock had heard from his contacts.

Wild Boy ladled out the stew, placing it before General Vinh who, leaning over the steaming bowl, inhaled deeply. 'It smells delicious,' he said.

He signaled to one of his bodyguards, who slung his machine pistol across his back, picked up the bowl and, dipping two fingers into the stew, ate several mouthfuls. General Vinh watched him expectantly.

At length the bodyguard belched, gave a curt nod, and handed the bowl back to his leader. General Vinh made no apologies for this seeming lack of manners and Rock did not ask for one.

General Vinh took up a pair of golden chopsticks encrusted with rubies and sapphires, settled the bowl in the palm of his hand and, holding it just under his chin, began to shovel the food into his mouth. He was like a mammoth machine; even Wild Boy was impressed by this engine of consumption. The General paused only once, and that was to gasp, 'It tastes even more delicious than it smells.'

'You are most kind.' Rock bowed again. He held out his hand. 'Please. Allow me to refill the General's bowl.' He stirred the bottom of the pot with his ladle, then loaded up the bowl General Vinh handed back.

While he watched the General continue his shoveling act, Rock said, 'I had heard that the General enjoys his women fully as much as he does his food.' He turned his head in the young woman's direction. 'Now I know the truth to those stories.'

The General's small eyes were almost closed with the pleasure of gorging himself on Rock's magnificent stew.

'I have also heard,' Rock said, 'that the jewel among the General's

8

women is one named Mai. Is she here, General? Might I see her?'

'Uh.' There was only a momentary lapse in the shoveling act.

'No?' Rock said. 'Oh, what a pity.' He smiled. 'Well, I'm not surprised, I suppose. Such a rare treasure is not so easily on display, even for favored guests, *neh*?'

'Uh.'

Rock shrugged. 'But then, who knows, perhaps Mai is not so far away from us at this moment.'

General Vinh was almost finished with his second bowl of stew. His face was glistening with a combination of sweat and grease. He glared at Rock. 'What nonsense are you speaking?'

'Have you reached the bottom yet?' Rock asked. 'Of the bowl, that is?'

General Vinh probed through the remnants of the thick sauce. 'One more piece of delicious meat.' He picked it up with the tips of his chopsticks, was about to pop it in his mouth, when something caught his eye. He held the piece of meat out so that he could see it better. He shook off the excess gravy.

What he saw was the unmistakable glint of a magnificent Burmese sapphire, and he thought, Ah, the foreign devil is very clever – here is my real gift.

But then his eyes opened wide, his mouth gaped open, and everything he had just eaten came spewing out, along with the General's long, low wail.

The sapphire was embedded in a whole, human ear. His beloved Mai's ear.